I0763474

AUNTIE CLEM'S BAKERY

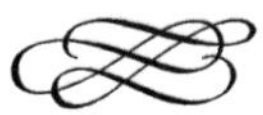

AUNTIE CLEM'S BAKERY

BOOKS # 13 - 15

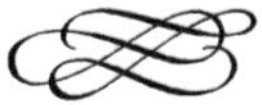

P.D. WORKMAN

ISBN: 9781774681701 (KDP Paperback)

ISBN: 9781774681718 (Ingram Paperback)

ISBN: 9781774681725 (Ingram Hardcover)

ISBN: 9781774681688 (Kindle)

ISBN: 9781774681695 (ePub)

pdworkman

ALSO BY P.D. WORKMAN

Auntie Clem's Bakery

Gluten-Free Murder

Dairy-Free Death

Allergen-Free Assignation

Witch-Free Halloween (Halloween Short)

Dog-Free Dinner (Christmas Short)

Stirring Up Murder

Brewing Death

Coup de Glace

Sour Cherry Turnover

Apple-achian Treasure

Vegan Baked Alaska

Muffins Masks Murder

Tai Chi and Chai Tea

Santa Shortbread

Cold as Ice Cream

Changing Fortune Cookies

Hot on the Trail Mix

Recipes from Auntie Clem's Bakery

Reg Rawlins, Psychic Detective

What the Cat Knew

A Psychic with Catitude

A Catastrophic Theft

Night of Nine Tails

Telepathy of Gardens

Delusions of the Past

Fairy Blade Unmade

Web of Nightmares

A Whisker's Breadth

Skunk Man Swamp

Magic Ain't A Game

Without Foresight (Coming Soon)

Careful of Thy Wishes (Coming Soon)

Time to Your Elf (Coming Soon)

Undiscovered Tomb (Coming Soon)

Zachary Goldman Mysteries

She Wore Mourning

His Hands Were Quiet

She Was Dying Anyway

He Was Walking Alone

They Thought He was Safe

He Was Not There

Her Work Was Everything

She Told a Lie

He Never Forgot

She Was At Risk

Parks Pat Mysteries

Out with the Sunset

Long Climb to the Top (Coming Soon)

Dark Water Under the Bridge (Coming Soon)

AND MORE AT PDWORKMAN.COM

COLD AS ICE CREAM

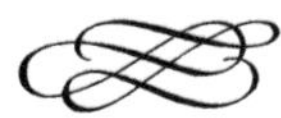

AUNTIE CLEM'S BAKERY #13

To friends who don't judge

CHAPTER 1

As soon as Erin got home from work, Orange Blossom was underfoot, meowing and yowling in greeting, winding around her legs, telling her all about his busy (or not so busy) day at home. Erin put down her purse and took off her jacket and picked him up.

"Hey. Quiet down. Relax. This is the time I get home every day, I'm not late."

He started purring, a loud rumble that filled the room. Erin pressed her face into the short velvety hair at the top of his head and scratched under his chin.

"There. You like that, huh?"

Marshmallow hopped out from behind the couch and nuzzled Erin's toes while waiting patiently for Erin to scratch his long ears.

Terry looked out from the kitchen. His jaw was dark with five o'clock shadow. He'd had an early shift and clearly hadn't shaved afterward.

"Whatever he is telling you about me, it isn't true."

Erin stroked Blossom's back, smoothing down his ruffled fur. "I think he's telling me about K9."

"You'd think he would be used to K9. Most other cats would have resigned themselves to a dog being around here by now."

Erin nodded. She could see K9 lying on the kitchen floor behind Terry, bored or tired after his patrol with Terry. Terry still wasn't back to working full-time at the police department since he had been attacked during an investigation. He was getting gradually better, but was still suffering from headaches, insomnia, and problems with concentration. Not something you wanted to worry about with your police force. K9 had been his partner for a long time and was used to patrolling all day.

"Maybe it's because K9 chased him when he was a kitten," Erin said, "back when we first met. K9 really scared Blossom, so maybe he was traumatized… instead of it being like a normal situation."

Terry raised an eyebrow. "I'd forgotten all about that," he said. "Funny. That seems like a long time ago."

"Maybe she has some kitty PTSD," Erin said, cuddling Orange Blossom up to her face again. "And here we are, just trying to get him to be friends with the person—animal—who traumatized him."

Terry rolled his eyes. "Well, something to think about. Are you hungry?" He segued to food, which Erin assumed was to avoid discussing PTSD any further. Neither of them was particularly good at discussing their feelings or their own symptoms. Terry had been mandated to undergo counseling through the police department following his attack; he probably wouldn't have chosen to do it himself. Erin had been to enough head-shrinkers in the past that she really didn't want to have to deal with another. She would do the best she could to deal with the nightmares and other issues that she had. At least after going through his own ordeal, Terry had stopped suggesting she get therapy. It seemed like a pat, easy answer, but it wasn't as simple as it sounded. It wasn't a matter of going to see a doctor, getting a prescription, and being okay. Even with intense, ongoing therapy, it could last for years and, while pills could help with the depression and some of the symptoms, they didn't fix the underlying problem with the brain.

"Yes. I don't know what you made, but it smells wonderful." Erin put Orange Blossom down and entered the kitchen. Marshmallow hopped along beside her, still waiting for attention. Erin looked at the red sauce bubbling in the pot and the various other pots and bowls on the stove and counter and smiled. "Wow, you went all out. This looks great." She bent down and petted Marshmallow. Terry wasn't an experienced cook, so she wasn't sure how any of the dishes had turned out, but he had obviously been pretty busy since he'd gotten off of his shift.

"I wanted to buckle down and make you a real meal for once. Not just a sandwich or warming up a can of soup. I keep promising to make you something, so…" He gestured along the length of the cluttered counters. "There you go. That's what I did. If you don't like it… well…"

"You must have been talking to Vic and Willie," Erin suggested. She remembered Vic getting after Willie and telling him that opening a can of soup did not constitute making her dinner. Not for a date night, anyway. Maybe other nights of the week it would be acceptable.

"Well, to Willie," Terry admitted. "We're going to do another fishing trip soon. He says it's a good time of year for…" Terry trailed off. "Hmm. I don't remember. But something is good this time of year. I don't think it really matters, as long as we have something to do while we sit around and relax. So no one calls us lazy. If you fish all day, then even if you don't come home with food, people still think that you've spent your day being productive. Not quite the same as if you just sit on the couch all day."

Erin nodded. She went to the cupboard to get out the dishes they would need. She cleared various items off of the table, which he had apparently used as a preparation area when he ran out of counter space, and set out the plates and cups. She cleared various open containers of ingredients as Terry started to fill serving dishes and take them to the table. That way, when they were done, there wouldn't be so much to clean up. Erin always felt more tired after she'd had a chance to sit down and eat. Best to get it done before the lethargy overtook her.

There were some odds and ends of vegetables left over from Terry making a salad, and she fed a few pieces to Marshmallow. Orange Blossom started to yowl and complain about how she was feeding Marshmallow and hadn't yet given him a treat.

"Okay, okay. Your treat is coming." Erin let herself into the pantry, but pushed him back and wouldn't allow him to follow her in there. A few weeks ago, she wouldn't have bothered, but since he had gotten sick, apparently after having eaten something he shouldn't have, she was far more careful about keeping him away from people food, whether it was something she thought would be okay for cats or not. He was only allowed to eat food that came in a package with a picture of a cat on the side.

And the crumbs that K9 left behind. Once Erin had slid a few treats across the floor for Orange Blossom to chase, she got a gluten-free doggie biscuit out of the cookie jar and gave it to K9. He lay with it between his paws, munching on it. Blossom saw that his adversary had also been given a treat and, after gobbling down his own, he slunk closer to K9 to see if he could snatch a few crumbs. It was the only time he would get close to the shepherd without hissing and puffing his fur out.

With the food preparation areas mostly cleared, Erin sat down to eat with Terry, looking over the variety of dishes that he had put together.

"This looks great," she told him.

Terry beamed.

CHAPTER 2

She was happy that Terry was feeling well enough after an early shift to cook a meal for her. A few weeks before, that wouldn't have been possible. He had barely been able to get through his half-shifts, let alone do anything productive afterward.

They sat on the couch after eating, sharing details about their days.

Nothing exciting had happened, and that was perfectly fine. They didn't need any more crime or mysteries. Just routine, everyday baking and policing work. Muffins and parking tickets.

There was a knock at the back door, then the sound of the door opening and Vic's voice. "Y'all decent?"

Erin straightened slightly and smiled at her young employee. "What would you do if we weren't?"

"Well, I guess I'd go all the way back to the loft and entertain myself there," Vic drawled in her slowest backwoods Tennessee accent. "But it isn't like the two of you are ever doing anything… sensitive… out in the open." She chuckled. "Y'all know you could have drop-in visitors any time."

The blond young woman sat down on one of the easy chairs, smiling at her boss.

"Long time no see," Erin said. Vic had driven her home in Willie's truck after they had closed Auntie Clem's bakery for the day. Erin's car had been wrecked before Christmas and she hadn't yet replaced it. Vic didn't have a car of her own, but frequently borrowed Willie's. And it wasn't like they couldn't walk to and from Auntie Clem's if they needed to. It was only a few minutes away. Though neither of the menfolk liked them walking in the predawn hours when they had to start baking to have fresh bread and muffins in the case by the time they opened up to the early-morning customers. Bakers began the workday very early.

"Where's Willie?"

"He took the truck out to one of his claims." Vic shrugged. "I didn't get any details. Something important in the world of mines and minerals."

While Vic sometimes went spelunking with Willie on days off, she wasn't involved in his mining operations. Willie always had a dozen different jobs on the go and he sometimes kept strange hours, especially if Vic used his truck during the bakery hours.

"How is the mining life?" Erin asked. "Things… going well?"

"I have no idea. He doesn't tell me about it. He keeps his head above water, so I guess it's going well. Or his other ventures are going well. I don't get into any of the business details."

Erin nodded. She rolled her shoulders and rubbed her neck, trying to work out a few knots. Terry pushed her hands away and turned her so that her back was to him, so he could rub her muscles. Erin closed her eyes and rolled her neck, trying to relax into it. His fingers were hard, digging down into the muscles and trying to massage away the tightness.

"How's that?" he murmured close to her ear.

Erin nodded. "That's good." She was sore but, even though it hurt, she knew it would help later. "I'll do some tai chi before bed. And then I'll be nice and relaxed to sleep."

Terry's fingers paused for a moment, but he didn't disagree. Both of them had difficulty getting to sleep, but discussing how difficult it was and the likelihood that either of them would be able to get to sleep when they wanted to would not be productive. And neither of them wanted to talk about it in front of Vic, either. She always noticed when Erin had a difficult night anyway.

"There was some mail for you," Erin told Vic, nodding to the side table. Even though they had a separate mailbox for the loft over the garage where Vic lived, the mailman didn't always get the mail sorted properly between the two boxes. Erin and Vic just passed mail back and forth as necessary and weren't really bothered by it.

Vic stretched out one of her long, slender arms and managed to snag the pile of envelopes. She sorted through it, pulling out the couple of mail pieces that were hers. One of them was just a bill, Erin had noticed, but the other looked like a personal letter. It was rare to get actual personal postal mail, so she couldn't help but notice. Everybody used email and social media.

Although that wasn't entirely true. Erin remembered that Vic had also gotten postal mail from an old girlfriend, crazy Theresa, someone that they all wanted to avoid running into again. Ever. There were warrants out for Theresa's arrest after the murder of Bo Biggles and her attack on Terry and Jack Ward when they had gone over to talk to her about it. But so far, she was in the wind and no one had been able to bring her to justice.

Erin eyed the envelope nervously. She didn't remember enough about Theresa's handwriting to know if it were the same writing or not. Theresa had known about Vic's gender transition but had thought that Vic would still be interested in renewing their relationship. Even though Vic was already in a committed relationship with Willie.

Vic examined the letter in the green envelope. She glanced over it at Erin. "What's wrong?"

"Nothing."

"You look like you're in pain. Terry, I think you're massaging too hard."

Terry stopped. He leaned forward, trying to see Erin's face. "Are you okay? You need to tell me if I'm hurting you."

"No." Erin gently rubbed the sore muscles that he had been working on. "It wasn't that. I was just…" She shook her head. "Nothing. I just wondered who the letter was from. Not that it's any of my business. Just curious."

Vic's brows came down for a moment, and then she understood. "Oh! No, it's nothing to be worried about." She worked her finger into the corner of the envelope and slit it across. "It's not from… her."

"Oh." Erin swallowed and nodded. "That's good. I was just wondering. I know there's nothing to worry about, she's not going to show up here or start anything… she would risk getting caught and sent to prison for a few decades. She wouldn't do that."

"Crazy Theresa," Vic intoned, shaking her head. "You can never be sure what that one is going to do."

Erin's stomach clenched. Vic must have seen a change in her expression because she hurried to change her words.

"She wouldn't come here, though, you're right. She'll stay far away from Bald Eagle Falls and anyone who knows that there are warrants out for her. Maybe she'll go north to Canada."

Erin rolled her eyes and gave a little laugh. "To Canada? She'd freeze."

"Good. Maybe a little chill would be good for her."

Vic herself hadn't been too impressed with the northern weather when they had taken a cruise to Alaska. Born and bred in Tennessee, her blood was too thin to appreciate the cooler weather. She'd been chilled the whole time she'd been north of the forty-ninth parallel.

Vic pulled the paper out of the envelope and unfolded it. Her eyes scanned over the page. "Oh, it's Clayton." She raised her eyes to Erin and Terry. "He was one of the group on the cruise," she said. "One of the people I met onboard."

"Oh." Erin nodded and tried to look happy about this. She *was* happy that it wasn't from Theresa. But she couldn't help feeling a little twinge of disappointment that one of the LGBT group that Vic had made friends with on the cruise was sending Vic letters. Vic was already with Willie and she already had a best friend in Erin. She could have however many friends she liked, but Erin couldn't help feeling like the men and women that Vic had become friends with on the ship were somehow trying to wedge themselves between Vic and Erin.

That was ridiculous, of course. It didn't affect her friendship with Erin at all. But Erin had grown up without many friends and felt possessive. Vic shared experiences with the LGBT group that Erin would never have. Erin knew about the challenges that Vic went through living among the cis men and women in small-town, Bible-belt Tennessee, but she would never understand it with the same depth and nuance of people who had lived through it. Erin could never fully be a part of that side of Vic's life.

She would have to settle for being Vic's friend and working side-by-side with her.

"So, how is Clayton?" Erin asked, trying to inject warmth that she did not feel into the question.

Vic's eyes moved over the page. She didn't look up to answer Erin. "Good..."

Erin leaned back against Terry, resting into his warm body. She waited for more information from Vic. Vic's voice was far away, not really engaged with the conversation as she read Clayton's letter.

Terry resumed rubbing Erin's neck and shoulders, but with gentle hands this time, soothing the sore muscles. Maybe he understood how disconnected Erin felt from Vic at times like that. She felt like the little girl left at home when the others went out to play. Erin scratched at a drop of bread batter that had dried on her slacks. She wasn't sure how it had managed to get past her apron. She always seemed to have a few spatters that made it to her street clothes.

"He's coming to Bald Eagle Falls," Vic said.

"Coming here? Why would he be coming here?" Erin answered too quickly before she thought through her answer.

Vic looked over the letter at her again, eyebrows quirked, shaking her head. "Why not? There's no reason he *couldn't* come here."

"No, I didn't mean that. I just meant I was surprised. It's sort of out of anyone's way. Is he coming just to see you, or is he on his way to something else...?"

"There's some kind of contest. He knows that you and I got the tickets to the cruise as part of a prize package, so he says maybe we can give him some pointers on how to win..."

"We?"

"You and me. We did win it together."

"Did he say me? Or just you?"

Vic's eyes went back to the letter. "Does it matter?"

"No. Of course not. Just curious. I don't think he really wants my input, does he?"

"I don't know. I doubt if he really wants anyone's advice. It's just something to say. Small talk."

Erin nodded. "Yeah, I guess. What contest is it? I hadn't heard anything about a contest. Is it in the city?"

"I don't know. I haven't heard of it before. Not one of the big ones like the Pillsbury Bake-Off or something. There are little ones running all the time."

"I guess."

"Especially in the rural areas around here. It's entertainment. A good way to get people together. Have some fun, raise some money. Make people remember your name for the next time that they're buying groceries at the store."

The Fall Fair was the first baking contest that Erin had ever entered, but she had noticed since then little contests that popped up here and there.

"I think we just got lucky with our entry. It wasn't like I really knew what I was doing."

"It wasn't just luck," Vic disagreed. "We worked hard on that cake. It was the perfect selection for the Fall Fair."

Erin's cheeks warmed a little. Vic had been instrumental in picking out their entry and teaching Erin about the traditional way to make it, but it had been Erin's recipe and execution. They had both contributed. But she was glad that Vic didn't think it was just luck that had gotten them the prize.

"When is he coming?"

Vic looked at her phone face. "Uh… in just a couple of weeks. I'll have to give him a call and make sure he has everything he needs while he is down for the contest and make sure that he is going to come by for a visit."

CHAPTER 3

Erin had her massage and did her tai chi and got to bed in good time but, as she lay there cuddling with Terry, she couldn't seem to get her brain under control. She kept thinking about Vic and Theresa. And Vic and Clayton. Clayton was coming to Bald Eagle Falls. Erin's own territory. It was one thing to have to watch Vic making friends with other people and spend her time with them on an Alaskan cruise, but it was quite another to have to deal with it on her own turf.

"Are you okay?" Terry asked, running his hand over her back gently.

"Fine." Erin turned over and tried to find a more comfortable position.

"Do you need a painkiller? How are you feeling?"

Erin relaxed her muscles and tried to decide how her body felt. It was taking a lot longer to recover from the car accident than she had expected. She hadn't had any broken bones or permanent injuries. She hadn't stayed at the hospital overnight. But the doctor and everyone else involved had been amazed that she had gotten through the accident so unscathed. The doctor had warned her that she probably had soft tissue injuries and would have to be careful and give herself lots of time to heal and recover.

Still, Erin had thought that it would only be a few days, and then she would be able to go back to normal. But it had been several weeks and, even though the bruises had faded, she still found herself tiring easily. She had a lot of aches and pains she hadn't had before.

Her joints were hurting. Erin wondered if it meant that a cold front were coming in. Could she now predict the weather by her aches and pains like some of the older people? Maybe she was coming down with a flu bug.

Or maybe it just meant that she hadn't fully recovered from her injuries yet. Erin sighed. How long was it going to take?

"I'm sore," she admitted, "but I don't know if I want to take anything."

"You don't have to… but if it would make you feel better, help you to get to sleep…"

She sighed. "Yeah. I suppose I should probably try. I thought I would be over this by now."

"I know." His experience had been the same, Erin knew. He had thought that he would be able to recover quickly from his head injury and get back on the job and everything would be back to normal. But they were both struggling, waiting for their bodies and minds to heal.

Terry slid out of bed and she listened to him as he padded down the hall to the bathroom and got her a painkiller and a cup of water. He was good to her. It was nice to have someone around, checking to make sure she was okay and looking after her needs.

Erin eventually managed to get the sleep that she needed and wasn't too tired when she got up in the morning. Terry had eventually retired to the couch so that he wouldn't wake her up with his restless tossing and turning and had fallen asleep in front of the TV, as he had too many times since the attack. But it was the only way that he could distract his mind and eventually fall asleep. He didn't have to be awake as early as Erin, so his body wasn't ready for sleep as early as Erin was.

She quietly moved around the house, getting her morning tea and toast and taking care of each of the animals. She knew that Terry had the day off, so it didn't really matter if she woke him up. He could sleep later if he needed to. But just because he had the opportunity, that didn't mean that he would be able to, so she did her best not to wake him. She heard him murmur or move a few times, but he just readjusted and didn't fully awaken.

She texted with Vic to coordinate their departure for the bakery, and met her around the back of the house once they were both ready to go.

"Mornin' sunshine," Vic greeted. She yawned. "How did you sleep?"

"Pretty good."

"Another day, another dollar."

"Let's go make some bread," Erin said, smiling. "We're taking the truck again?"

"Yeah. Willie is going to walk over and pick it up later."

"We could just walk to Auntie Clem's."

"You know how he feels about that."

Erin shrugged and shook her head. "Yes."

They climbed up into the truck and Vic revved the engine. Erin winced, worried that it was too loud in the early morning. She didn't want Mrs. Peach complaining about them waking her up before dawn. But she'd already had that discussion with Vic more than once, so she kept her mouth shut and just started to mentally prepare her list of tasks for the day.

They were through all of the holidays, and Erin felt like it was time to add a few new offerings to the regular cycle of baked goods at Auntie Clem's. Adding fresh new experiences to the menu was a way of keeping people coming back for more. If she wanted to attract the people who didn't have to eat gluten-free or allergen-free and could pick up their baked goods from the bread aisle at the grocery store or at a bakery in the city, then she had to have something to offer them. Something more interesting than what they would find at the grocery store.

"How about lemon poppyseed loaf?" she asked Vic.

"That would be nice," Vic approved. Erin didn't need to tell her she was thinking about what else to add to the menu. Vic understood that part without being told. "A nice fresh taste. Good for breakfast."

"Yeah. We've been doing lots of earthier flavors, pumpkin and sweet potato and savory spices. Something a little lighter. And pretty. I love the color of a good lemon loaf."

"Good idea. I like it."

The early-morning hours zipped quickly past as they discussed other flavors and foods to try while they mixed batters and filled the ovens and then the display case before the earliest customers got there.

Erin loved the rhythm of getting everything ready in the morning. She had a number of employees who worked part-time to help them cover the busiest times and to make sure that she and Vic both got some time off to have personal lives, but Erin liked it best when it was just her and Vic working side-by-side, familiar and anticipating each other's actions.

Erin turned the sign over to "open" and unlocked the door for the customers who were already outside her door waiting. Cooler air blew into the bakery, and the sweet and spicy fragrances of the fresh breads escaped the shop to attract foot traffic as people headed to their work or school but just couldn't resist popping into the bakery for something delicious to start their day.

"Mmm," Mrs. Snell sniffed at the air and closed her eyes. "This is the closest thing to heaven I can think of. Fresh bread, cinnamon—I could just drink it all in."

"It's pleasant," Lottie Sturm agreed, scowling, "but heaven? That's a bit sacrilegious, don't you think?"

"Oh, I don't mean it that way," Mrs. Snell said, her cheeks flushing. "I just meant… it's such a lovely way to start the day. Of course… it's not heaven. I don't even know if people eat in heaven, do they?"

"Of course they don't," Lottie said authoritatively. "How could we eat as spirits? We won't have bodies and have to sustain them like we do here. That's just one of the things we have to put up with during mortality."

Mrs. Snell didn't look encouraged by this. "But I enjoy eating so much. Don't you think that we might still eat our favorite foods, even if we don't have to? And never gain weight however much we eat…?"

"Gluttony is one of the seven deadly sins," Lottie reminded her.

Mrs. Snell nodded sadly. Erin was worried that she would be discouraged by this and wouldn't want to buy the food that she normally did, concerned about the sin of being greedy.

But Mrs. Snell bought more than she usually did. Maybe Lottie had achieved the opposite, instead convincing Mrs. Snell that she would need to get in all of her earthly pleasures while she still had the opportunity. Erin handed her the bag, giving her a warm smile and wink.

"You enjoy that now, Mrs. Snell."

"Oh, I will, dear. I will."

Lottie herself didn't seem to be discouraged from pursuing her earthly pleasures either, getting more than just her daily bread, ensuring that she had a good amount of chocolate on the menu as well. Vic rang everything up at the register.

"Those double-chocolate chocolate chip cookies really are sinfully delicious," she told Lottie, making change for her.

Lottie gave her a baleful look, maybe not sure whether Vic was teasing her or had just picked her words poorly. "We all need to sustain ourselves," she said obliquely.

Vic gave a little laugh after Lottie left. "Some people wear their religion on their sleeve," she observed, "but then they don't seem to follow their own counsel."

Erin glanced around the bakery, not wanting to say anything about it in front of the rest of the customers. An atheist herself, she was acutely aware that many of the church-going people in Bald Eagle Falls said they believed one thing while living another way altogether. Erin never had understood how they could divorce their religious beliefs from their behavior.

CHAPTER 4

The morning rush had ended. Erin moved back into the kitchen to put some cookies into the oven. Once done, she rejoined Vic at the front of the shop. "What do you think about—"

Erin's gaze shifted to the door as the bells announced the arrival of another customer.

A middle-aged man, not particularly striking in appearance. A little on the short and heavy side, dark hair, a bulldog mouth. Small fans of upward wrinkles around his eyes.

Erin's jaw dropped open. It was Chef Kirschoff from the Alaskan cruise.

Vic looked up to see if Erin were going to finish her sentence and, seeing Erin's expression, followed her gaze to the door. It took her a moment longer to recognize Chef Kirschoff than it had taken Erin. He wasn't wearing his whites and tall chef's hat, but just regular street clothes. And Erin had spent more time with him.

"Chef Kirschoff!" Erin exclaimed, excited to see him.

"Hans," he corrected. "We are not in my kitchen this time! I'm just Hans here."

"It's so good to see you! Why didn't you tell me you were coming? I can't believe this!"

Vic was laughing at Erin's star-struck reaction. "I think you have an admirer!" she told Kirschoff.

Erin didn't consider herself a demonstrative person, but she hurried around the counter to shake Chef Kirschoff's hand and, when he reached out to give her a friendly hug, she accepted, squeezing him back and then releasing him to step back and look at his face.

"What are you doing here?" she demanded. "Why didn't you tell me you were coming?"

"I wanted to surprise you. I was afraid that someone would tip you off ahead of time, but it looks like I was successful."

"Yes. Who would tip me off?" Erin turned and looked at Vic. "Did you know?"

"That Chef Kirschoff was coming? No, I didn't know that part."

Erin blinked and tried to process this. "That part?"

Vic laughed again. She and Chef Kirschoff exchanged looks. Kirschoff made a gesture for Vic to explain.

"Well, I told you that Clayton was coming here for a cooking competition."

"Right. You told me that." Erin looked back at Kirschoff. "Are you judging the competition? Or competing in it?"

"I am one of the organizers. I am not judging or participating."

"And you decided to have it in Tennessee?" Erin shook her head. "Why?"

"I found several willing sponsors." He shrugged. "I thought that since you came to me in Alaska, I would come to you this time."

"You picked Tennessee because I'm here? Really?" Erin shook her head at the thought. It didn't make sense that he would choose Tennessee to hold a cooking competition just because he wanted to see her again. He could email her. Video conference with her. Call her on the phone. He didn't have to have a cooking competition as an excuse to see her again.

Kirschoff beamed at her. "Are you interested?"

"Interested… in competing? I don't know. What kind of food is it? When is it? I haven't had a chance to prepare anything."

"I want you and Vic to be judges. You wouldn't have to prepare anything ahead, just make sure that you could take some time off to attend and judge the entries."

Erin looked at Vic. "Judges. I don't know… do you want to?"

"We don't have to both agree," Vic pointed out. "We can each decide individually."

"Yes, of course," Erin agreed. Maybe Vic didn't want to be a judge, but she didn't want to prevent Erin from going. Vic might not want to be in the spotlight. "If you don't want to, that's okay."

"Oh, I'm going to be a judge," Vic said as if it were a foregone conclusion. "But you don't have to if you don't want to. It's up to you."

Chef Kirschoff laughed heartily. "Welcome aboard!" he told Vic. He looked at Erin. "And you, Erin? Can I convince you to be a judge as well?"

Erin shrugged. "Well… it sounds like fun. But what kind of food is it? What's the theme? Because if it's haggis or something like that, I might change my mind."

"The theme is CO2."

"CO2?"

"Carbon dioxide." Kirschoff grinned rakishly.

Erin still didn't understand how the theme of a cooking contest could be carbon dioxide. "How exactly…? I have no idea how you cook with CO2. Are there CO2 burners? Like cooking with natural gas?"

"The opposite. You can freeze with CO2—dry ice—or you can use it to carbonate drinks."

"So, ice cream and coke?" Vic asked.

"Ice cream and soda," Kirschoff agreed.

"Oooh," Erin breathed. "That could be dangerous."

Kirschoff quirked an expressive eyebrow at her. "Dangerous?"

"I could put on twenty pounds. You'd have to roll me back in here."

"You only have to taste the products," Vic pointed out, "you don't have to eat a whole bowl of each one."

"Maybe you don't. I'm not sure I would be able to stop myself."

"Well then, you're right… this could be dangerous."

Word of the cooking contest (or chilling contest, to be more accurate) spread quickly through Bald Eagle Falls and the surrounding areas. Everyone was talking about the generous prizes and the fact that some of the judges would be local celebrities. Erin wasn't sure how she felt about being called a celebrity. People knew her by business and because she had won the grand prize at the Fall Fair. But also because of her involvement in solving some of the local crimes that had occurred over the previous months. She didn't exactly like being known for the way she had stumbled into those cases.

But it was good to get her face and name in front of people to get free publicity for Auntie Clem's bakery, so she couldn't shun the spotlight. She just wasn't sure she was a celeb.

Everyone had family recipes that they thought would win the grand prize for sure. They all wanted to know what the rules for the contest were. Sales increased at Auntie Clem's as people came by to gossip and to get on the judges' good sides.

Erin and Vic wanted to treat Chef Kirschoff to dinner, so both called their partners to see if they would come along. Erin's heart sank as Terry's phone rang and rang without him answering. He was normally good about answering his phone even if he was on duty, though Erin tried not to call him if he was on shift. It was only when he was asleep or not feeling well that he didn't answer right away.

Or if he was in the middle of an investigation or an arrest, of course. But he wasn't on duty. Erin watched Vic talking on the phone with Willie while she waited for Terry to answer. Vic wasn't exactly frowning, but Erin didn't think she was getting very far. Willie often had other plans. He and Vic were independent and didn't necessarily see each other every night.

Erin started to pull her phone away from her ear to hang up the call when she heard Terry's faraway voice. She put it back to her face.

"Terry? Are you there?"

"Erin. What's wrong?"

He sounded groggy. She had awakened him. "I'm sorry. Nothing is wrong. I just wondered if you wanted to go out to supper tonight. Chef Kirschoff is in town. Vic and I are going to take him out."

"No." His voice cracked and faded, and she didn't think it was just the cell service. "I'm not up for that tonight."

"You don't sound good. Is it your head?"

He cleared his throat and took a few extra seconds to answer. "Yes," he agreed finally. "My head. It's really bothering tonight."

It was still mid-afternoon. "Did you take something for it? Do you need me to come home?"

"I can look after myself, Erin. I took a pill… I just need to sleep now. That's all. Go out with Vic. Have a nice time."

"Are you sure? You'll need something to eat and you won't be in any shape to fix yourself anything."

"I'm sure it will be better later. Just go ahead without me, okay?"

"If you're sure. I just want to make sure… that you're going to be okay. Will you call me when you get up later and let me know how it's going?"

"Sure," he agreed, and hung up.

Erin kept her phone at her ear for a few moments, even though she knew he was already gone. He didn't sound good. She wasn't sure she should go out anywhere without him. He wouldn't remember to call her back, and he wouldn't call her if he needed something. He was stubborn and macho that way. He was perfectly fine with insisting that Erin needed to take care of herself, but he would be at death's door before asking for her help.

Erin lowered the phone. Her eyes met Vic's across the room.

"Is it just us girls tonight?" Vic asked, reading her body language.

"Yes. Us and Chef Kirschoff. But I wonder… maybe we should pick another night. He's going to be here for a few weeks, we don't need to run out and do it tonight."

"You sound worried. Was Terry upset?"

"No. I woke him up. He sounds like he's feeling pretty rough. He said to just go ahead without him, but maybe I should stay home with him tonight. We can go out another night."

"If you want. Do you want to call Hans and let him know?"

Erin didn't know if she'd ever be able to think of Chef Kirschoff as just Hans. His chef persona was so much a part of how she perceived him. He wasn't just a normal, everyday Hans.

"I don't know what to do."

"Well, why don't we leave it for now. You can touch base with Terry later on and see if he's any better. If you think you need to be home with him, then go. We'll let Hans know then. He can still eat out tonight. Any of the restaurants are good."

There weren't many dining choices in Bald Eagle Falls, but they put on a pretty good spread. And even a chef didn't need to have gourmet food every night. Kirschoff wouldn't mind if they were forced to reschedule.

"Okay… or you could go on your own if I need to stay with Terry…"

Vic rolled her eyes. "Probably not a good idea. Me and Chef Kirschoff out to eat together… the rumors would fly like feathers in a twister. I might not care what the gossips say… but there's no need to feed them." She looked uncomfortable, her cheeks pinking up.

She might say she didn't care what the gossips said, and she was good at just moving on, but Erin knew that the things people said about her did bother her.

"Right. I wasn't thinking. You're right. That wouldn't be a good idea."

"We'll go home after we close," Vic told Erin. "You can pop in and see how Terry is. If you think he's okay on his own, we'll go out with Hans. If he needs you, we'll just reschedule for another night."

"Okay. That sounds good," Erin agreed. She slid her phone back away and went to the front of the display case to wipe down the fingerprints and tidy up before the after school/before dinner rush. Vic retreated to the kitchen to make sure that everything was in order there.

CHAPTER 5

When Erin stopped at home, Terry was in front of the TV and startled slightly at Erin's entrance.

"I thought you and Vic were going out." He frowned, a crease appearing between his brows. "Didn't you call me earlier to say that the two of you had to do something together? Or was that another day? It's easy to get confused when..."

"Yes, we were going to go out with Chef Kirschoff. But I wanted to check in with you and make sure you're okay first. You sound like you're doing better, do you want to come?"

"Chef Kirschoff?"

"Yes."

He rubbed his forehead. "Isn't that the name of the chef on the cruise?"

"Yes. You're not going crazy. The chef from the cruise. He's here in town. He's running a cooking contest and he's asked Vic and me to be judges."

"What's he doing here?"

"I guess he decided Tennessee was a good place for this contest."

"Bald Eagle Falls?"

"It's actually going to be in Whitewater Junction, but he's asked us if we'll judge. The entries will be from all over the area. Like with the Fall Fair. Anyone can enter."

"Are you entering?"

"No. I'm not going to enter anything. I'm going to help with the judging." Erin studied his face, trying to decide if he was getting it, or if she should just give up and try again when he was feeling better.

"Oh. Okay. That's kind of weird."

"It gets stranger—the contest isn't actually a cooking contest, it's for preparing food with CO2."

"Carbon dioxide? How do you cook food with carbon dioxide?"

"That's what I asked too. But they don't. They freeze it with dry ice, or they carbonate beverages with it."

"Oh." He nodded. "Sweet."

Erin giggled. "Did you just make a pun when you've got a migraine?"

"I guess I did."

"Can I get you anything? Bring you a pill or the cold pack?"

"No. I just put it back in the freezer and I'm at full dose." He gave her a warning look. "Don't think that means it's worse than usual. I just decided to be a big boy and take my prescription instead of complaining that the pills don't work."

"Okay." Erin held up her hands. "I'm not saying anything."

Orange Blossom was sleeping on the top of the couch behind Terry. He stretched and yawned, looking at Erin. He gave a long yowl.

"I'll give the beasties their treats. Do you want anything from the kitchen?"

"No. I'll eat later… before I take another pill."

He was doing everything he was supposed to in order to take care of himself—taking a nap, using the ice pack, taking the pills he was supposed to with food so that they wouldn't upset his stomach. Erin couldn't think of anything else she could do for him.

"Do you want me to pick you up something at the restaurant?"

"Which one are you going to?"

"I don't know yet. Chinese, maybe."

"Well, you know what I like… if there are leftovers, bring them home with you."

"Okay. I will." Erin leaned down and kissed him, then went into the kitchen to take care of the animals.

~

Vic was still sitting in the truck waiting to see if Erin was going to need to stay home with Terry or not. She pushed the door open when she saw Erin coming back out.

"Does this mean he's doing better?"

"Little better. Up from his nap. Took his pills. Told me to just go ahead with the dinner, so…" Erin shrugged. "We might as well."

"Glad to hear it! Climb on in."

A few minutes later, they were at the Chinese restaurant and met Hans. He had on a coat and was flapping his hands near his face. "I dressed way too warm for this weather. I knew it was nice here, but it was winter when I left home!"

"It's winter here too," Vic pointed out. "Where is it you live?"

Erin had only pictured him on the cruise ship. It seemed bizarre that he might actually have a house and live in one place like a normal person, only going on cruises when he was hired for those jobs.

"Colorado," Kirschoff explained, flapping his coat to cool off his body. "We get *real* winter there. Not whatever this is." He gestured toward the door.

Vic opened her mouth to argue the point. Erin raised her brows. "Do you remember how cold you were on the cruise?"

"Well… yes."

"You're always saying that I complain about the heat when it's mild. Well, the same goes for you when you went to a colder climate. You thought it was really cold when someone from there would think it was just pleasant autumn weather."

Sally, one of the waitresses, ushered them to a booth and handed out menus. "Just give me a shout when you've decided what you want."

Hans removed his coat and tugged his collar away from his throat. "I'm glad that we're doing this in the winter. I'd hate to see your weather in the summer."

Erin nodded sagely. "It gets a mite warm," she told him, imitating Vic's accent.

They both laughed.

~

Once the table was spread with food and everyone had exclaimed over and discussed the dishes, Erin turned the conversation to the competition.

"We need to know what the contest rules are going to be," she told Kirschoff.

"You will have plenty of time to read through the rules closer to the time," he told her, making a brushing-away gesture. "Tonight is just relaxing and fun."

"A lot of people are talking about entering the contest. I need to know whether people qualify or not."

"Anyone qualifies. Anyone who wants to try to make something for the contest is welcome to do it. They just have to fill out an entry form."

"But not everybody can take part, can they?" Erin said. "What about friends and family of the judges? What about employees at Auntie Clem's? Or employees of any of the sponsors? Are they allowed?"

"We are going to be very open." Kirschoff drew his hands apart to indicate something large. "We don't want to be cutting a lot of people out because of their relationships. To be honest..." he went on delicately, "I don't think that you are going to find anyone on the mountain not related to one of the judges, one way or another."

Vic laughed merrily. "That's one way to put it."

Erin remembered Mary Lou telling her that if she was related to Clementine, she was kin to half the mountain. After reading through some of Clementine's genealogical research, Erin realized that this was not an overstatement. The families living in Bald Eagle Falls had, for the most part, lived there and intermarried for many generations. Erin saw names that were repeated over and over again in the family tree charts, and they were names that she knew from her neighborhood and the customers at the bakery. Erin would never have gone so far as to call them inbred, but many families had lived in or around Bald Eagle falls for hundreds of years. They came, they saw, they stayed.

"So, no, I don't think we are going to have rules saying that the entrants are not allowed to be friends, families, or employees of the judges or the sponsors," Kirschoff reassured her. "Everybody is going to be. We have multiple judges to help fend off any accusations of impropriety."

"I think you're going to get a lot of entries," Vic said. "A lot of people were talking about it today. If even half of them follow through and make something for the competition, it's going to be big."

"I hope so," Kirschoff agreed, with a firm nod. "It should be the talk of the mountain for months to come. We are going to put on a competition like no one has ever seen here before."

"How are you going to do that when you only have a few weeks to prepare?" Erin challenged. "You have to get the word out, and venues booked, get the press there… is it going to be bigger than the Fall Fair? Bigger than the 4H rodeo? We may be small, but there are a lot of fun events going on around Bald Eagle Falls. People draw together and everyone contributes."

"There is a lot to do, but we've got the money and the staff to do it. Most of that is already planned, it's just a matter of starting the ball rolling."

"Did you hear that a bunch of the group from the cruise are going to come watch?" Vic asked Erin. "Not just Clayton, but a lot of them."

Kirschoff raised his brows with interest.

"No, I hadn't heard." Erin smiled encouragingly. She was sure that Vic would be happy to see all of her friends again. And Erin didn't need to feel like they were going to take Vic away from her, because she and Vic were judging the competition together. Vic would have to be careful not to show them any favoritism.

But Erin couldn't help feeling just a little twinge of jealousy at hearing that Vic's new friends from the cruise were going to be invading Bald Eagle Falls.

Bald Eagle Falls was her territory.

She felt just the tiniest twinge of jealousy. That was all.

CHAPTER 6

Erin kept an eye on the clock to make sure she was home in plenty of time to get to bed and get enough sleep before going back to the bakery the next morning. She always had to be careful to give herself enough time to settle in and get to sleep. Her sleep had been poor ever since finding Mr. Ingersoll's body. And worse yet since Terry had been attacked. Characters on TV might be able to roll with punches finding a newly dead body every week, but Erin found that her exposures to violent crime made it harder to deal with, not more used to it.

Of course, they had ordered a lot of dishes to sample and there were plenty of leftovers. She and Vic split them up to take home to their men. Chef Kirschoff didn't want any to take back to the motel with him.

"No midnight snacks for me," he told Erin, patting his stomach ruefully. "I will not be the chef who indulges too much and ends up weighing three hundred pounds."

Erin nodded her understanding. At her height, she had to watch what she ate very carefully. Every extra pound looked like two. Or more. Vic's height and faster metabolism were far more forgiving. "Your feet will thank you," she told Kirschoff. "I don't know how some of those cooks manage to stay on their feet all day."

"Yes, you're right," Kirschoff agreed. "The more you weigh, the harder it is to prepare food and supervise in the kitchen. You can't do everything sitting on a stool. Working in a kitchen involves lots of movement, going from the cold room to the kitchen, the sink, the different stations, and the restaurant. You are constantly moving from one place to another, and I don't know how anyone carrying an extra hundred pounds or more can do it."

So Erin had plenty of leftover Chinese food for Terry when she got home.

She found him on the couch again—or still—but no longer watching TV. He had fallen asleep sitting up and was listing to one side. Erin knew that she wouldn't be able to shift his position without waking him up; she had tried before. He was going to have a crick in his neck when he eventually did wake up. And that could potentially make his headache that much worse again.

She tiptoed past him to the kitchen but, as soon as she crossed the threshold into the tiled area, Orange Blossom hurried in, meowing loudly, as if he hadn't been fed all day. Of course, Erin knew better. He often tried to tell Terry that Erin had forgotten to feed him, and Terry had fallen for it a few times before he realized that the cat lied. Erin had fed Blossom before she went to work and when she had returned home. She would give him just a little more dry food before she went to bed and, hopefully, that would keep him quiet for the night and he wouldn't be complaining and asking for more if she had to get up to the commode or if Terry were back and forth.

"You be quiet," she whispered to Orange Blossom, quickly putting the Chinese food container in the fridge, hoping to get to the pantry to freshen Orange Blossom's dish before he woke Terry up.

"Erin?" Terry called out sleepily. "Are you home?"

"Yes, in the kitchen." Erin poked her head out the doorway to wave to him. "Sorry, I tried to keep him quiet."

"He works better than a burglar alarm."

"Oh. Speaking of which, I haven't armed it yet. If you're getting up, would you mind…?"

"Do I smell ginger chicken?"

"You sure do."

"Then I'm getting up."

Erin smiled. She went back and retrieved the Chinese food from the fridge. She heard Terry groan as he pushed himself up from the couch. He went to the front door and armed the burglar alarm and then joined her in the kitchen.

"How was your dinner?" He was rubbing his forehead slowly. His head was obviously still bothering him.

"It was good. So nice to see Chef Kirschoff again."

"Aren't you two on a first-name basis?"

"Yes… but I can't help thinking of him as Chef Kirschoff, even if I manage to call him Hans to his face."

He nodded and sat down at the table. Erin handed him the box of Chinese food and a fork. He opened it up and started picking out the pieces of ginger chicken.

"Mmm. I'm glad you didn't eat all of this."

Erin sat down with him, sighing. It felt good to sit down with him at the end of the day. She didn't realize how much she worried about him while they were apart until she could be with him and know that he was okay. She wondered if he felt the same way about her when they were apart. Though she had mostly healed from her physical injuries after the car rollover, he knew she still struggled with emotional issues.

"You look tired," he observed. He rubbed his eyes and yawned.

"You look a little tired yourself."

"I don't know if I'll be able to go back to sleep, or if that's it for the day."

"You should try, though. You obviously needed the extra sleep."

He nodded. "I will… but I don't know if my body will let me sleep any more. It seems like it wants to sleep when I should be awake and won't sleep when I want to."

"I know. The doctor said sometimes that happens with head injuries. It's just your brain's way of trying to heal."

He picked out a few more pieces of chicken. "I wonder if that's just something they say to any symptoms a patient is having. 'Oh yes, that's normal, it will probably go away eventually.' I'm not sure they really know anything. They certainly aren't doing anything to treat it."

"You have sleeping pills."

"Yes… and you know how you feel about taking the sleeping pills they prescribed for you."

Erin shrugged. She hated the way they made her feel. Even if they worked, she still felt so groggy and muddled in the morning that it wasn't worth it. She would rather feel tired in the morning than have that gross, hungover feeling.

Terry didn't react the same way to the pills as she did, but he had his own reasons for not wanting to take them.

CHAPTER 7

After work the next day, Erin went with Terry in his truck to pick up some supplies from the grocery store. She was working from a list, but she stopped when she saw a familiar slim, neatly-dressed woman with a helmet of gray hair.

Mary Lou Cox was in the dairy aisle and Erin didn't know whether to avoid her, greet her, or pretend that she hadn't seen her. She stopped and Terry bumped into her.

He looked up from his phone and glanced around. "What is it? Did you forget something?"

"Uh… no. I just…" Erin motioned at Mary Lou.

Terry raised his brows, not understanding her reluctance at first. He hadn't been around when Mary Lou had reamed Erin out for mentioning her son Joshua to Officer Terry Piper during his investigation of a rash of burglaries before Christmas.

Erin hadn't meant to implicate Joshua. She had just been worrying over something someone else had said to her but, as a result, Terry had invited Joshua to the police department to ask him what he might know about the burglaries.

She had told Terry that Mary Lou was upset about it, but she hadn't given him any details. Mary Lou had stopped coming to the bakery and had not had a civil discussion with Erin since then.

Mary Lou had been a friend, and Erin didn't know what to do or say that would help the situation. She had done her best to support Mary Lou through her difficult times; her husband having to be committed to an institution, Campbell being arrested on drug charges, and then… the problems with Joshua.

Erin looked around, trying to decide what else she could get while Mary Lou was in the dairy aisle. She could come back for her dairy ingredients later. She started to turn the buggy around. Terry put his hand on it to prevent her from going back. He looked at her steadily.

"Don't run away."

"I don't want a scene. I don't want to cause any trouble."

"You're not causing a scene or making trouble. You're here to buy groceries, just like everyone else. Don't let someone else push you around."

Erin looked down at her buggy, swallowing. She knew it was cowardly to keep avoiding Mary Lou. But she didn't like conflict. She had come to hate all kinds of conflict when she was in foster care. Raised voices or threatening body language sent her running for the hills. Growing up hadn't changed the way she felt, even if she didn't physically run away anymore.

She did not want to be in conflict with Mary Lou. Or anyone.

"Come on," Terry said gently. He tugged the cart forward, stepping ahead of her to guide her along. Erin didn't have to listen to him. She could pull back. She could let him take the cart and she could turn around and go to another part of the store. Or out to the truck. Or home.

But she knew he was right. She shouldn't let Mary Lou's anger keep her from completing her tasks. Sooner or later, she had to face the other woman. It wouldn't be at the bakery or at the First Baptist Church, but they were bound to run into each other sooner or later in a small town like Bald Eagle Falls.

She reluctantly let Terry guide her forward. Erin picked up the butter and cream cheese that she needed. They continued down the aisle to the cream and milk. Mary Lou saw their approach.

"Evening, Mrs. Cox," Terry greeted.

Mary Lou's nostrils flared. She smoothed her tunic-shirt over her hips, looking the two of them over. "Officer Piper," she said crisply.

Erin looked intently at the refrigerated shelves.

"Nice night," Terry offered.

"Lovely."

Erin swallowed. She just wanted to get out of there. She grabbed a carton of cream, even though it wasn't the brand she usually got, and reached for a gallon of milk.

Terry and Mary Lou both looked toward her, not saying anything to her. Erin avoided looking at their faces. Her eyes were hot with tears and she was finding it hard to catch her breath. She put the supplies in her basket and pushed it forward, pulling it out of Terry's grasp. She rounded the end of the aisle and hurried down the next one, even though she didn't need anything there.

"Erin."

She ignored Terry's call and kept going. On the next aisle, she stopped and looked at the packages of sugar, but tears blurred her vision, keeping her from seeing anything more than the product names in big, bold type.

Terry touched her back, taking care not to startle her. "Erin. It's okay. Everything is fine."

"Mary Lou was a friend. I know she's always been a little cool; she doesn't share her feelings easily. But I was there for her when Campbell was arrested. I was there when Roger…"

"I know. You've been a loyal friend to her. And time will heal this rift. So she's upset about Joshua being questioned. Most of the children in town ended up being interviewed, even the young ones like Peter. She'll get past it sooner or later."

"But that doesn't mean she'll get over being mad at me. She was really angry about me talking to you about Joshua. And I… just don't know what to do about that. I don't know how to fix it."

"It's not your responsibility to make her get over it. If she's holding on to that anger, it's going to hurt her, not you. She's the one who will suffer from those negative feelings."

Erin swiped at a couple of tears that leaked out onto her cheeks. "And she's the only one suffering?"

Terry took her head between both of his hands and kissed her forehead. He used his thumbs to wipe the tears away. "You have a tender heart. It will work itself out eventually. Let it go and don't stress about it. I promise it will all be worked out eventually."

Erin sniffled. She put her hands over his for a moment. Then she nodded, took a deep breath, and pressed onward.

~

She had mostly gotten herself together by the time she reached the cashier at the front of the store. Sue Anne scanned her items through, smiling and chattering about the weather and inconsequential things. She paused as she ran through the last few items and leaned forward, closer to Erin.

"It was so nice to see you at the candlelight service at First Baptist on Christmas Eve," she told Erin. "I was hoping that we might see more of you…"

"Uh… no." Erin shook her head. She glanced at Terry. "I was just… I wanted to join Officer Piper there, share it with him. But I'm not going to start going regularly." She paused, weighing her words. It wasn't the first time since Christmas she had faced these questions. The citizens of Bald Eagle Falls, even the ones she barely knew, were remarkably persistent in their expectation that she would convert to Christianity and start going to services at First Baptist like all of the respectable women. "I'm still an atheist," she told Sue Anne. "That hasn't changed."

Sue Anne sighed and shook her head. "You'd make a great Baptist," she said, as if she might be able to tempt Erin into it. "Maybe someday…"

Erin and Terry picked up the packed grocery bags from the counter.

"Don't hold your breath," Erin advised.

CHAPTER 8

Notices had been published and, if everyone hadn't already been talking about the contest, they were now.

In addition to the actual food preparation and judging, there were a number of community events being held for the children: science experiments, a family dance, an eating competition, and a traditional Tennessean BBQ.

"I'm going to make wild raspberry ice cream," Bella Prost told Erin excitedly. She was one of Erin's employees. Erin had been worried she wouldn't be allowed to enter the competition because of their relationship. But Chef Kirschoff and the official rules had assured her that there was no problem with any of her employees joining the competition, so Bella was excited to work out what she was going to do. "You can make the ice cream a few different ways—you can use the dry ice to freeze the ingredients by chilling them from the outside of the bowl, or you can actually stir dry ice into the ingredients and freeze them that way. Then it kind of bubbles and carbonates and makes the ice cream light and foamy."

"I don't know if I would want to eat it if dry ice was stirred in," Erin said uncertainly. "If a piece didn't dissolve, you could burn your mouth, couldn't you?"

"Well, yes, you have to make sure that it all dissolves. But it's not that hard to do. And it's not against the rules. If it was really dangerous, it would be against the rules."

Erin nodded. "I didn't say it was. I just haven't heard of people making it that way before. It always makes me nervous when they put it in drinks to make them fog."

Bella nodded. "No one is going to get hurt in this competition," she promised.

~

All day, people were coming through the bakery, talking about who was entering and what they were going to make. Erin was asked her opinion constantly, which she wasn't sure was proper. They really shouldn't be asking her about her preferences, thinking that they could get ahead of the other contestants by knowing what she liked or didn't like.

As it was, Erin would eat pretty much anything, having learned as a child to eat whatever was served to her, and then as an adult experimenting with different cuisines and cooking methods. She'd made her share of disasters. And when she was poor, barely making ends meet, she had to eat what she made, good or not. She didn't have the option of just throwing it out. So she'd learned to eat anything that wasn't absolutely inedible.

"I think everyone in town is joining the contest," Vic told Erin during a lull when they were both in the kitchen, taking baking out of the oven. "Or if they're not entering something, then they're helping out with the other activities. It's like a circus!"

"It sure is."

The bells over the door tinkled, and Erin looked through the doorway to see who had come in. She looked for a moment at the new faces, trying to place them. Not anyone she knew from Bald Eagle Falls, yet she thought that they were vaguely familiar, as if she had seen them somewhere else.

Then it came back to her, and she realized that she had seen them before. On the Alaskan cruise.

"I think your friends are here," she told Vic.

Vic left the cookies that she had been arranging on the cooling rack and went out to the front. Erin heard her squeal as she saw the friends she had made on the cruise.

"Wow! You're here!" Another squeal. "All of you!"

There were hugs and back slapping and a few kissed cheeks as Vic made her way around the group, greeting everyone. Erin waited until the excited reunion cooled a little, then went out to say her hellos. She poked her head out tentatively, not wanting to interrupt anything. Vic saw her.

"Oh, and you guys remember Erin, right? Erin, all the gang from the cruise..."

"You're going to have to remind me of your names," Erin said. "I don't remember them all, and with everything that happened back then..." There were a lot of reasons she hadn't memorized everyone's names.

"Okay, I'll go through them," Vic said, "but everyone should remind you the next few times they talk to you. Because getting all of the names at once is a bit overwhelming."

Erin nodded gratefully. She knew she wasn't going to remember them all without a few reminders, no matter how many memory tricks she tried to use.

"This is Clayton," Vic said, putting her arm around a boy with a red knit cap and a pale, angular face. He was a couple of inches taller than Vic was, and she was tall for a girl. "He's the one who wrote and said he was coming. He's going to enter something into the contest, right Clayton?"

He nodded seriously. "Yeah, you bet. It's gonna be cool."

All of the treats were going to be pretty cool. Some of them frozen. Erin nodded and shook hands with him. He had long, spidery fingers and a firm grip. "Nice to see you again."

"This is Melanie," Vic motioned to the girl standing next to Clayton in the group. She was a black woman in a flared plaid skirt and a green blazer, with no jacket. Very chic.

Erin vaguely remembered her from the cruise. She nodded again. "Melanie."

"And Jack," Vic introduced the heavier man next in line. He had some scraggly whiskers on his chin like he was trying to grow a beard, but it wasn't coming in very well.

Jack smiled a greeting. "They/them."

Erin blinked. "What?"

"My preferred pronouns. I'm nonbinary."

Erin had only a vague idea of what Jack meant by this, but nodded as if it were clear. "Okay…"

"I love cooking. Can't say I'm much good at it, but I'm going to take a run at the contest too."

"Great. I look forward to tasting what you come up with."

Jack grinned as if she'd given them the best compliment ever. She smiled back and looked at the next person in the circle.

"Norman." The imposing-looking man thrust his hand forward with such force and suddenness that Erin jumped, flinching back.

"Oh. Sorry. Hi, Norman."

He took her hand in his, and then sandwiched it with his other hand, giving her a hearty two-handed shake. "It's so good to see you again, Erin. How have you been since the cruise? I know you weren't feeling really well at the end there. Everything back to normal now?"

Erin nodded. She didn't know how normal she could claim to be now, but she was definitely feeling better than she had been while she was on the cruise. Things had gotten pretty dicey toward the end.

"Yeah. Good. I'm good."

Vic introduced the last few people in the group, but Erin had already reached saturation point. If she tried to remember all of the names, she was going to forget the first few that she had learned.

"Well, it's so cool that you all got back together here. It's neat to see relationships that started somewhere like on a cruise continue afterward. People get so busy and go their different directions, but you guys have all kept in touch and are doing something else together again. That's amazing."

Everybody was smiling and chatting with each other; they had an easygoing, casual manner that Erin envied. She always felt like she had to try so hard at relationships or they wouldn't work out. But there didn't seem to be tension between members of Vic's group of friends.

"I'm glad that you're all here for the contest," she offered. "I hope you have a good time and do really well."

~

Vic promised her friends that she would meet them after closing for drinks and dinner, and they set out to explore the town. As Vic and Erin prepared for the afternoon rush, Charley came in through the front door, at a hurried pace, perpetually late. Erin hadn't been expecting her, so she didn't know what Charley thought she was late for. Maybe it was just habit.

"Hey, partner," Charley greeted. "How is my favorite half-sister?"

Erin shrugged. "Same as usual," she said cautiously. It wasn't like Charley had any other half-sister. Not living. At least, not that they knew of. With all of the family secrets Erin had unraveled, nothing would surprise her anymore.

Charley pushed back her hair, longer than Erin's but the same dark brown color. "How are things coming along with the contest? Everybody is talking about it."

"They are," Erin agreed. "You'd think these parts had never seen a cooking contest before."

"Well, it is a big one," Charley pointed out. "You can't sneeze at a two hundred and fifty thousand dollar grand prize."

Erin felt her jaw drop. "Is that what it is? I heard that the prizes were going to be good, but I didn't know they had been announced yet."

"I don't know if they have been officially announced," Charley said loftily, "but I have it on good authority that the top prize in each category is two fifty G's. That's not anything to sneeze at."

"No. It's not."

Charley leaned on the display case, getting closer to Erin. And she couldn't exactly tell Charley not to lean on it when she was Erin's partner in the business. Charley had been there for Erin when Erin had thought she was going to lose Auntie Clem's. Erin couldn't let herself forget that. Not that Charley would have let her.

"I'm going to enter," Charley confided.

"In the contest?" Erin looked at Vic, wondering if she could object. But Chef Kirschoff had already told her that anyone could enter the contest. Even Erin's half-sister and partner in the business. So there wasn't anything Erin could say about it. "That's great."

"Yeah. I figure I've already got one of the judges in my pocket," Charley said with a laugh.

"Which one?" Vic asked dryly.

Charley laughed loudly. Erin couldn't help smiling at Vic's comment.

"Don't you go repeating that to anyone," Erin warned Charley. "I don't want people accusing me of favoritism. Even if you're technically allowed to enter the contest… I might have to recuse myself from casting a vote on your entry."

Charley sobered up. "All entries are blind, so you won't even know which one it is."

"That's probably a good thing," Erin admitted.

"I may just surprise you. I'm a good cook, you know."

Erin had always assumed that she got her culinary skills from her father's side of the family—she had inherited Clementine's storefront from her father's side after all. As a little girl, she had 'worked' with Clementine in her tea room, but neither of her parents had shown any interest in baking or cooking. But Charley was her mother's daughter, and she did seem to have a knack. Even though she had known nothing about gluten-free baking before partnering with Erin, she had quickly caught on and was proficient when she put in a shift. She was a night owl, so Erin and Vic had quickly learned not to put her on a morning shift. But as long as they didn't schedule her before noon, she would usually get there.

"You are a good cook," Erin agreed. "But you're going to have some pretty heavy competition."

"As long as I don't have to compete against you or the chef, I think I've got a pretty good chance."

CHAPTER 9

There wasn't a lot of time to prepare for the competition. Erin didn't know much about carbon dioxide or making carbonated beverages before the competition was announced, but she was learning a lot.

"There are a few ways to carbonate drinks," she told Terry as they relaxed on the couch. He wasn't anywhere near as interested as she hoped he would be in all of the details, but she needed to talk through the processes to firmly entrench the details in her brain, and he was, at least, being a good sport about it. "Of course, the traditional way of making them didn't involve pumping CO2 through flavored water."

"I don't imagine so," Terry agreed with a serious nod. "So what did they do?"

"Fermentation. Just like with wine or beer. Yeast converts the sugars, creating carbon dioxide, and that produces the fizz."

"I see. I prefer the higher-proof stuff."

Erin chuckled. "So do a lot of people. But you can't exactly give that to children. Or drink it while you're on the job. So the new way of producing soft drinks is to inject carbon dioxide right into it, rather than relying on a chemical reaction. It's faster and there is no danger of producing something that's going to make granny drunk."

"Too bad."

She favored him with a glare. "You're not taking this seriously."

"Sorry." He wiped the smile from his face and gave her a flat, blank stare. "Continue with your story, ma'am."

"Those are the first two ways that you can make a carbonated beverage for the contest."

"And the third way?"

"Putting solid carbon dioxide directly into a drink."

He considered that for a moment. "Putting dry ice in."

"Exactly. It reacts with the water and bubbles and makes fog and is very dramatic. So some people entering the contest will do that."

"Very dramatic. Too bad they didn't do it for Halloween."

"That would have been a lot of fun," Erin agreed. She had thought of that herself. "We could have had all kinds of witchy drinks. Although, maybe the Christians wouldn't like that. They can be pretty uptight around here about anything witch-related."

It wasn't the first time they had discussed the fact, particularly since Adele, Erin's groundskeeper, happened to be a practicing Wiccan, something those in the know kept from becoming public knowledge. They didn't want Adele run out of town, as she had been from other towns.

"True. Might not have been able to spin that. Too bad, because it would have been a cool Halloween activity."

Erin pushed a stray lock of hair back over her ear. She looked at the notes she had made as she had taken her crash course on carbonation.

"So, they're allowed to use any of the three methods for the competition?" Terry asked.

"Yes. That means that the people who are doing fermentation get a head start. They need a couple of weeks longer than the rest of the contestants to get their brews going."

"Are they all in different classes, or do the fermented drinks get judged against the carbonated ones?"

"They are all together, to get the grand prize."

"Two hundred and fifty thousand dollars."

"Yeah."

"That will be a nice little injection of cash into Bald Eagle Falls. So many people have had such a difficult time lately."

"If someone from Bald Eagle Falls wins. It could be someone from one of the other towns or outlying areas."

"Well, with two of the judges coming from Bald Eagle Falls, hopefully the Bald Eagle Falls entries will have a *bit* of an advantage over the others."

"We won't know which entries are from Bald Eagle Falls. It's all supposed to be judged blind."

"And you haven't heard what anyone around town is going to enter."

"Uh… well, yes, I guess I have."

"There you go."

"But that doesn't mean that they'll be the only entries. If someone is making a raspberry ice cream, that doesn't mean they'll be the only raspberry ice cream entry."

"I suppose," Terry agreed. He shifted his feet, forcing K9 to move. "Come on, buddy, you don't need to lie right on top of my feet."

K9 groaned and moved away slightly but, after Terry settled again, K9 readjusted, and Terry's feet were soon nestled snugly under K9's body again.

~

The official kick-off ceremonies for the contest wouldn't be held until the week that everyone would be submitting their entries but, since the fermented drinks had to be started early, Erin and Vic had a dinner with the other judges and officials in Whitewater Junction where the contest would be held.

Erin hadn't been to Whitewater before, even though it wasn't far from Bald Eagle Falls. She always drove the opposite direction, into the city for supplies.

It was a nice little town, similar to Bald Eagle Falls in many respects. Though, of course, it didn't have a gluten-free bakery. Sam Litwin, the mayor of Whitewater, was curious about the bakery, and how Erin had managed to keep a specialty bakery like Auntie Clem's making a profit.

"We sell a lot of stuff to people who do not have to eat a special diet," Erin explained to him. "The majority of our clientele don't have any dietary restrictions."

"Ah." Sam nodded. He pushed up the sleeves of his dress shirt and tugged at his collar, looking uncomfortable. "So you sell regular baking too. I wondered."

"No. Everything we sell is gluten-free. And most of it is free of the top ten allergens as well. And we have some that are vegan, or low carb, or that are appropriate for people with diabetes or other special requirements."

"But if you only offer gluten-free baking…" Sam trailed off, frown lines between his brows. "That means that everybody has to buy gluten-free, or go somewhere else."

"Yeah. And it's easier for people to just buy at the bakery anyway, even if they don't follow a special diet, because otherwise, they have to go into the city. Or just buy factory-made stuff from the grocery store."

"And that doesn't bother people?"

"There was some resistance at first," Vic contributed. "But people get used to it. Like everything else in a small town. You can either buy locally or spend extra time and money to buy things in the city. Some people will buy up baking when they go into the city and store it in the freezer until they need it, but…"

"That's not as nice as buying freshly-baked bread," Sam finished. "Although… I don't know what the gluten-free stuff is like. Maybe people prefer frozen stuff from the city to having to eat the gluten-free baking. I've heard…" His cheeks flushed noticeably. "I've heard that it isn't the best stuff. It can be gritty or tough. Or falls apart the minute you touch it."

"Depends on the recipe and who is making it," Vic told him. "We've got some really great recipes. You wouldn't even guess that they are gluten-free. And if you can't tell the difference, why would you drive into the city to get wheat bread?"

"Hmm." Sam nodded. He picked up his glass and had a drink. "I suppose. I think it's amazing that you've been able to keep that bakery open—let alone make a profit from it. That really is extraordinary. Especially in today's economy."

Erin nodded, her face warm. "Thank you."

"Economy?" Chef Kirschoff's voice was raised over the buzz of conversation at the long table. "Who's talking shop? We're supposed to be getting to know each other, not talking business."

Erin's face got hot. She looked away, embarrassed at being called out. Chef Kirschoff looked down the table and saw her. "I know it's hard for business people to get together and not discuss such enthralling things as the economy, but you're here to have a good time and get to know each other on a personal level. You're not here interviewing for a loan. Let's talk about food!"

"We were," Vic protested. "You just heard one word out of the whole conversation."

"Try to keep that boss of yours in line. I know it's impossible to tell Erin Price what to do, but do your best..."

Erin put her hands over her flaming cheeks. "I was just answering the mayor's questions..."

"She's right," Sam said, lifting his hand in acknowledgment. "It was my fault. I'll stop talking about business."

Kirschoff gave them a broad grin and nodded. He turned his head to talk to someone down the table in the opposite direction. Erin rubbed her cheeks, even though she knew that wouldn't remove the flush of embarrassment.

"Don't worry about Hans," Vic laughed. "He's just teasing."

"I know, I know!"

"What's even more impressive about your business is that it was already burned to the ground once," Sam contributed, clearly not worried about following Kirschoff's instructions. "Most businesses would have gone under at that point. How did you keep it afloat?"

Erin glanced down the table at Chef Kirschoff to make sure that his attention was still elsewhere and dropped her voice to try to keep him from hearing that they were still discussing business. What else was she supposed to talk about? She worried about Auntie Clem's Bakery almost every waking moment, and Sam asked her a direct question about it. If he wanted to talk about her business instead of the contest or more personal information, that wasn't her fault.

"I would have gone under for sure if it weren't for Charley."

"Who is he?"

"She. Charley is my half-sister, and... well, to make a long story short, she inherited the other bakery in town, the one that would have been my competition. She was going to run it as a competing business... which probably wouldn't have been very good for me. But she doesn't have any business experience and, after Auntie Clem's burned down... she offered to become my partner. She had the space, so we didn't have to buy another property or rebuild. She injected some capital into the business, and I got money from insurance for the fire. So we managed to keep it going. But I couldn't have done it without her, even though Auntie Clem's had been doing pretty well before that. We just wouldn't have survived a rebuild."

Sam nodded. He buttered a roll and tore pieces off of it while they waited for the main course to be served. "Now, you can't eat this, can you?" he indicated the roll in his hand.

Erin smiled. "Actually, I don't follow a gluten-free diet. I can still eat anything I want to. I started the bakery for other people. People who don't have that choice."

"Then why don't you do both? Gluten-free and conventional? If you don't have to eat gluten-free, don't you think it would do better if you had a wider offering?"

"No. You end up with problems if you are cooking both gluten-free and gluten products in the same pans and equipment. Even having wheat flour particles in the air can be a problem for some people. And the amount of gluten in a crumb of wheat bread could be enough to make someone with severe celiac disease sick. If I want to serve the people who are severely affected, not just people who decided to try a gluten-free diet to lose weight or because it is a fad, then I have to keep the kitchen completely gluten-free. No gluten flours of any kind on the premises, nothing with gluten being cooked in your pans or mixed in the bowls."

"That seems pretty extreme. You could just wash them in between."

"It's not worth the risk. People in the area know that my bakery is completely gluten-free, so they can trust it."

Waiters arrived bearing plates and started to place them along the table. Erin sat back and waited for hers.

CHAPTER 10

Erin and Vic had taken several days off from Auntie Clem's, knowing that the dinner and other events that were planned for the judges and other officials would end up running late into the evening. Erin would need several days to get back on track after staying up late just one night.

She was yawning through the welcoming speech and a tall, severe-looking woman reading through the competition rules at long, tedious length. Erin was doing the best she could not to fall asleep in her chair, but she kept catching her eyes closing and her head tipping down, then bobbing up suddenly. Keeping her up late, feeding her, and then reading long, boring rules was a perfect recipe for putting her to sleep—something she needed to remember the nights that she had insomnia.

She got to her feet, blinking hard to try to wake herself up. Vic's eyes, focused off somewhere in the distance, turned to her questioningly. "You okay?"

Erin nodded. "Just need to walk around, or I'm going to fall asleep."

Vic grinned. "Tell me about it."

Erin went to the back of the room and wandered slowly along the back wall. But her eyes were still closing even as she paced back and forth. She left the room and went out to the lobby, then out the hotel's front door.

The air was cool and refreshing. She wasn't wearing a jacket but, having grown up in the north, she had better cold tolerance than Vic. She took a few long breaths of the cold air, waiting for it to wake her up. She yawned and breathed all of the air out in a steady stream. A few minutes in the fresh air, and she should be more awake.

"I don't think I could listen to that hot air balloon blather on for another minute," a voice said at her elbow.

Erin jumped and turned quickly. A woman was leaning against the building, a cigarette between her fingers. She gestured toward Erin with it.

"Out for some fresh air?"

Erin never could understand smokers saying that they were going out for fresh air when they wanted a smoke. When they would clearly be smoking polluted air.

"I don't smoke."

"I didn't either before this started," the woman joked. "What was that, like twenty years ago?"

"It has been a long night," Erin agreed. She looked at the woman's name badge on her lapel to see if they were both there for the same event, or whether the woman was there for some other lecture.

Beryl Batcombe. It sounded vaguely British. She was part of the CO2 cook-off—or cool-off, as they were now calling it. She had dark hair and eyes, a slightly round face and well-aligned teeth. She was wearing a knitted raspberry-colored hat. She was taller than Erin, heavier, a solid-looking woman who would have been at home doing chores on a farm. Her eyes were narrow and fierce.

"I'm Erin," she introduced herself, holding out her hand. "I'm one of the—"

"One of the judges," Beryl finished for her, blowing smoke in her face. "Yes, dear, so am I."

Erin backed away from her, turning her head to the side and giving up on the idea of shaking hands. She tried to decide whether she needed to stay there and talk to Beryl because she had started the conversation, or whether she could find somewhere else to stand where she could get some actual fresh air.

"Sorry, I haven't met everyone yet. I know Chef Kirschoff wanted everyone to meet and get acquainted, but it's kind of hard with the long tables they had us at. You can really only talk to the people beside or across from you."

Beryl nodded. "I don't think it's been very well-organized," she said brusquely, "Too fast to get everything done properly. You need people who have done this before, many times, to be on top of all of the details. An event like this should have six to twelve months of run-up. Having only a few weeks… that's just crazy."

Erin had to agree. When she was planning an event with a lot of moving parts, she started well ahead of time. She would have lists written down and reference material in a binder. If she'd been pulling together a big event, she would definitely have started six months or further out, as Beryl had suggested.

"So are you from Whitewater?" she asked Beryl.

"Yes, I'm one of the locals. And you're from Bald Eagle Falls. But you're a transplant."

Erin hesitated. She didn't really feel like explaining, but she didn't want Beryl thinking that she was an outsider. She was as much a part of Bald Eagle Falls as anyone else.

"My family is from here. I lived here as a child. But when my parents died, I was put into foster care and I ended up mostly growing up in the north. I came back here after my aunt died. She left me the storefront where I started Auntie Clem's Bakery." Erin shrugged. "So… I guess I was a transplant for a while, but now I'm not. I left and then came back. I have… roots in these mountains."

"Ah. Well, there's no reason they shouldn't have picked you to help judge the contest. You *have* judged a contest before, haven't you?"

"No… I've entered contests before. But I've never been a judge. This is something that's new for me. Kind of exciting."

"You've never been a judge before." Beryl sighed audibly. "And what about the other judge from Bald Eagle Falls, you work with… *them* don't you? This… Vic person?"

"Yes, I work with Vic. She's a great cook. Good hard worker, and always there to help me out when I need something. We've been able to hire on some more help at Auntie Clem's now but, back in the beginning, it was just me and her…"

"Her," Beryl repeated flatly.

Erin shook her head. "What?"

"Her? Vic is a her?"

"Yes, Victoria. Sorry, I should have said that. It can be confusing if people think Vic is short for Victor."

"She's one of those kids that's all loosy-goosy about her sex, though, isn't she? Born a boy, but now she's decided to play at being a girl?"

Erin ground her teeth. She kept her mouth closed as she counted slowly to ten, giving Beryl what she hoped was a scathing glare. "Vic is transgender," she said. "I'd appreciate it if you'd use that language. It's not something to make fun of or for any of us to make light of. If you knew Vic..."

"Oh, I saw her at the dinner. Very pretty. Very convincing. But that doesn't change anything. That doesn't make her something she isn't."

"If you have a problem with it, maybe you should withdraw from judging the contest. If you feel like you couldn't work with a transgender person. If you can't show Vic respect, it would be best to back out now and give them time to replace you."

"So you're militant too," Beryl observed. "Well, now I know where you're coming from. I'm not going to back out of the contest. I worked hard to get this position, unlike others. If it's going to be a problem for you and *Victoria* to be on the panel with me, then maybe you are the ones who ought to step down."

Erin shook her head. Her anger at the way that Beryl talked about Vic instantly wiped out the drowsiness that she'd been feeling earlier. *No one* had the right to treat her friend that way.

CHAPTER 11

Vic could tell something was wrong when Erin returned to the hall where the presentation was being held. Erin made her way back to her seat, her lips pressed tightly together. Vic raised her brows and mouthed, "What's wrong?"

Erin shook her head and sat down. It wasn't the time and place for that conversation. And if she started to talk about it, she was just going to get angrier. Best if she could get a little distance from it and relax for a few minutes. She listened carefully to the woman who was talking about the contest and their vision behind it. It was still just as dry as it had been before Erin went outside and, no matter how hard she tried to concentrate on it, it was still boring and didn't distract her from her anger at Beryl Batcombe.

It was torture but, eventually, they were released from their imprisonment. A big sigh went up from the assembled audience and everyone bounced quickly to their feet to talk with each other or get out of the stiflingly hot room. Vic put her hand on Erin's arm and, as they walked toward the door to make their escape, leaned in to whisper in Erin's ear.

"What is it? What happened?"

"Nothing. I'll tell you later."

"Tell me now! What was it?"

"At least let's go back to our room. I don't want to talk here in front of everyone else." Erin and Vic both looked around, but no one was hanging around them who appeared to be eavesdropping on their conversation. No one looked like they had the least interest in what Erin had to say.

"I think you're safe," Vic said dryly. "All anyone cares about right now is getting out of here and raiding the minibar in their rooms."

Erin wasn't a drinker, but if she were… She might even have been tempted by the overpriced bottles in the minibar. As it was, maybe if there were some chocolate in there…

Vic led the way back to their hotel room. They nodded to other officials for the contest in the elevator. Erin was too overwhelmed to remember anyone's names or why they were there. Their faces and names all ran together.

A few more elevator stops, and they were on their floor. They were the only ones who got off on the third floor. Vic found their room and swiped the key card.

"Well? Spill! What lit your hair on fire?"

"There is this other judge. Did you meet her? Beryl Batcombe."

"Beryl. No. I saw her, but we didn't talk. She was too far away from us."

Erin nodded. "Well, be glad. Do everything you can to avoid talking to her."

"That bad?"

"Yes."

"What did she say?"

Erin rolled her eyes toward the ceiling. That was the tricky part. Vic knew she was angry and Erin wouldn't get away with not giving her all of the details. But Erin hated to tell her the way that Beryl had been making backward comments about Vic's gender identity.

"She was just talking… being rude."

"What did she say? She sure got you riled up."

Erin sighed. She recounted Beryl's words and insinuations quickly, wanting to get them out of the way. Vic didn't act hurt or offended. She just rolled her eyes.

"People are going to talk," she said. "You know how it is in Bald Eagle Falls too. People are ignorant and uneducated, or they're willfully trying to hurt or irritate me. I don't care. I'm not going to give them the satisfaction. Beryl Batcombe can spin her wheels trying to talk crap about me,

I'm not going to pay any attention. The only person it is going to reflect badly on is herself."

"I don't want her spreading that kind of talk around. I know that it's not exactly a secret, but I don't want people chattering on about it and nothing else. Why should anyone care about your identity, or Clayton's, or anyone else's? What difference does it make to any of them?"

"You know how people feel around here. They don't understand gender identity and they just want to convince me of the error of my ways. Repent and go back to the church. Put aside my foolish, childish ideas and find my way back to the truth."

"How can it be a sin to be who you are? What's wrong with that?"

"You don't have to convince me." Vic laughed. She went over to the minibar fridge to check it out. It was, unfortunately, not well-stocked. Vic poked through the nuts, candy, and tiny bottles, looking for a bedtime snack for the two of them. "You didn't happen to bring any bread and jam, did you?"

Erin sat down on one of the beds, then flopped back on it. Her body was tired, even if her brain was revved up again. "Unfortunately, no. But we could probably order something from room service if you're hungry. A peanut butter sandwich. Toast and jam."

"No. I don't want anyone cooking for me this late."

Erin grabbed the price list for the minibar off of the bedside table. "A sandwich would probably be cheaper than that stuff."

Vic took it from her and shook her head at the prices. "Good grief. Well, we can stay within budget if you have a packet of M&M's and I have a package of nuts. How does that sound?"

"It sounds like we should have brought snacks." Erin chuckled. "But, it's probably best if I avoid anything extra for the next couple of weeks. I want to be able to get through the contest without putting on any weight."

"I think you're too worried about it. You don't have to eat a whole bowl of anything. Just little tastes. You could even be like a wine taster and spit them out again."

"Yuck. I don't think so."

"We could all have spit buckets. You just taste the ice cream, and then spit it into the bucket and go on to the next one."

"Stop. No. No way."

CHAPTER 12

The next morning, they were gathered for a tour of the restaurant that they were going to be using for food preparation and judging. Erin kept a sharp eye out for Beryl Batcombe but didn't see her.

"I don't think she showed up," Vic said, catching Erin's searching gaze. "She must have gotten drunk on her minibar and slept in this morning."

Or maybe she had decided to take Erin's advice and back out of the judging.

But Erin doubted it. She looked around one more time. Whatever the reason, Beryl appeared to have ducked out on the tour. Chef Kirschoff looked at his watch then finally shrugged.

"We're one short, but we're going to need to get this tour done if we're going to stay on schedule. She'll have to catch up on the rest later."

Erin heard him say something under his breath that sounded suspiciously like 'old bat,' but was probably just her name.

"Let's begin then," said the perky brunette who seemed to be some kind of party planner. There was a whole cadre of people taking care of all of the logistics. Erin supposed that the rest had been hired by the contest's chief sponsor, a company that sounded like a law firm, but Erin thought it was actually one of the big food service corporations.

"If everyone will follow me," the perky woman suggested. Everyone fell into place close behind her. She led them from the hotel to the sidewalk in front of the restaurant, Buttermilk Biscuits. They waited for her to tell them why Buttermilk had been picked and how its ambiance and reputation would contribute to the contest.

"My name is Sherry Vail," the woman introduced herself. "I know that you're all eager to get started today to get a full picture of why this contest was set up and how it is going to operate."

People looked around, but no one exactly agreed with her. They were eager to get it over with, anyway.

"Buttermilk Biscuits is one of the oldest restaurants in the Whitewater Junction area. Built in 1939, it is a great example of some of the ethnic cuisines that helped shape the Tennessee culture…"

Erin could barely focus on what Sherry was saying. Who cared how long the restaurant was there or how it had influenced the cuisine? They were going to eat ice cream and drink carbonated soft drinks. That wasn't exactly haute cuisine.

She looked around at the other businesses and buildings on what she assumed was Main Street. It was similar in a lot of ways to Bald Eagle Falls. Small, with the colorful, narrow buildings built right against each other, many of them with awnings to keep the brutal summer sun off of customers on the sidewalk. It might be a little older than Bald Eagle Falls, but not by a lot. Maybe there was a little more history there, or maybe the historical buildings had just been better preserved.

Vic caught her looking around at everything else and grinned, understanding her distraction. "Let's get a move on," she said under her breath. "The woman could talk the spots off a leopard."

"Maybe Beryl has the right idea. Maybe we should have stayed away this morning. It would be a lot easier to just say that we had slept in or got called in to Auntie Clem's."

"Shh," someone nearby hushed them like they were being noisy in a library. "Listen."

Erin and Vic looked at each other, both trying not to make the other laugh. It was such a ridiculous situation. They were adults, after all, not children who didn't know how to behave. They were there to get the details on the contest, not to be lectured on the local color.

Erin shifted her feet back and forth. What would she make for the contest if she were one of the contestants?

That got her brain going, and she was surprised when Vic tapped her arm to get her attention because everyone was going into the restaurant. Erin blew out her breath and followed the group. At last. She hoped that there was something hands-on, so she didn't have to keep listening to people lecturing.

They even made cooking boring. And Erin was never bored with cooking.

~

Her hopes were dashed when Sherry stopped everyone and continued her lecture, indicating the restaurant's decor, talking about the items on the menu, both traditional and new. They could have read about any of that in the papers that they had been given. In fact, most of what Sherry said was in the written materials, but she was intent on boring them to death by repeating every detail.

Erin inched her way toward the kitchen. It wasn't like she was budging into line. She just worked her way around the edge of the group so that she would be the closest to the door when they finally got on their way to the kitchen.

Sherry's voice went up and down, still perky, trying desperately to keep everyone's attention. But she had already lost it long ago. Everyone else seemed to be just as bored as Erin, shifting their feet, wanting to get on with the tour.

"Okay, we'll go into the kitchen now," Sherry directed, motioning to the door Erin was standing close to. "Uh, Miss Price..."

She happily took the lead, pushing open the swinging doors and entering the kitchen's sacred realm. She realized that they weren't going to be in there to taste everything, though they would be allowed to check things out as the entrants were preparing dishes. There were cameras to provide top views, but sometimes there was nothing like getting close to the action.

Sherry began describing the various amenities of the kitchen.

"Is she serious?" Vic murmured. "We all have eyes. We can see how it's set up. It isn't like we've never seen a commercial kitchen before."

"I know," Erin agreed. She didn't want Vic voicing her complaint too loudly and being overheard. Or just getting shushed again. She looked around while Sherry talked, imagining how everything would look when there were multiple contestants preparing food in the kitchen.

There was a large, shiny door close to Erin, which she assumed was a freezer or cold room.

As Sherry told everyone about the ovens and where to find the cutlery, Erin tested the handle on the freezer. It was not locked. She pulled it harder. The mechanism made a noise that was too loud in her own ears. She didn't want everyone to turn around and ask her what she was doing. Erin turned her back to it, smiled, and waited a minute or two to make sure that everyone's attention was back on Sherry and hadn't been distracted by Erin's movements.

Of course, Auntie Clem's Bakery didn't have a freezer or cold room. They baked. The few frozen treats that they made were frozen in the small freezer of the kitchen fridge. It would have been great to be able to go into a cold room during the summer when the kitchen was sweltering hot from the combination of baking, the Tennessee climate, and running back and forth, looking after everything. She could just imagine being able to step into arctic temperatures in the middle of the day to suck all of the heat right out of her. It would be heavenly.

Erin gave the freezer door another twist, but found that she had already turned it as far as she could. She gave it a tug. It didn't come the first time. Erin didn't turn around to face the door, but gave it another pull. The door moved an inch. It wasn't open all the way, but she could feel the cold air starting to fall around her hand. Erin turned around and pulled the door slowly toward her.

The interior of the freezer was white with frost. Erin hadn't been sure whether the temperature would be turned down all the way past freezing, or whether they would be keeping it warmer, just a cold room for produce and food that was prone to spoilage. Definitely sub-freezing. Erin opened the door farther and looked at the shelves lining the cold room walls to see what they already had ready to go.

She wasn't usually that snoopy, but she had a thing about kitchens. And she was there to look around. It was part of her job, after all.

But there was something wrong.

CHAPTER 13

At first, she didn't know what it was. Her eyes skipped past what shouldn't be there, staying focused on the foodstuffs.

It could have been anything. A mannequin that was used during some kind of promotion. A few bits of clothing that someone had left behind by mistake.

Erin forced her eyes to focus. Forced them to stop looking at the rest of the freezer room and to focus on what she didn't want to.

She could still hear Sherry talking, going on as if Erin hadn't opened the door, that nobody had happened to notice her eagerness to get a look at everything that was behind the scenes.

Erin no longer wanted to see what was behind the scenes. She wished that she was standing outside the restaurant, bored while Sherry went on about its importance in Whitewater history and the shaping of the cuisine in that part of Tennessee.

Erin wasn't the first one in the freezer. She wasn't the only one who had apparently wanted to get a sneak peek before anyone else.

Beryl Batcombe wasn't back in her hotel room sleeping off a drunk. She hadn't decided that she wasn't prepared to judge beside Erin and Vic and had backed out and gone home.

She was in the freezer. Just where she would be if she had been with the tour.

Erin could feel Vic behind her, pressing in for a look.

"No," Erin told her. "Don't come in here. Go back."

"I just want to see. We need to move in so that people can get in behind us."

"No." Erin blocked Vic's entrance.

"Erin, we're ready, Sherry said to come and have a look…"

"Vicky. No," Erin said firmly.

Vic frowned. "What's wrong?"

"You need to go out. No one can come in here."

"Sherry said we could now."

"No." Erin swallowed. "You need to go get help."

"Help?" Vic's face paled. "Erin, what is it? What kind of help? Do you need something…?"

"Beryl is in here."

"Beryl?" Vic tried to see around Erin. "What's she doing in there?"

Then the penny dropped. Vic's face became a mask. "Oh, no."

"Yes. See if they have EMS. Or a volunteer fire department. Or just… a doctor."

"Is she okay, Erin?" Vic's voice told Erin that she understood perfectly well that Beryl was not okay, even if her words were several steps behind her brain.

"No. Get the others out. And tell them we need help."

Vic turned, pushing back against the people who were pressing in on her from behind, trying to get in to see the freezer. There were protests. No anger, but certainly confusion. Vic pushed them along, repeating that no one was allowed to go in there and that they needed a doctor.

Erin was the only one in the room. Erin and Beryl. Erin wasn't sure why she didn't leave the freezer with everyone else. It wasn't like there was anything she could do for Beryl. But she felt like she couldn't leave the woman alone, no matter what state she was in.

Vic guarded the door from the other side. Erin knew she was having to put up with a lot more crap than Erin. There was no one to get after Erin but Vic herself, if she had wanted to. Instead, Vic stood in the doorway acting as gatekeeper. She kept the door open a few inches. Erin didn't have to worry that she was going to get trapped inside with Beryl. She would be able to get out again once help arrived.

There were new voices in the kitchen outside the freezer.

And this time, it wasn't going to be Terry or one of the police officers that Erin knew so well from Bald Eagle Falls. It wouldn't even be Stayner, the new cop she was still trying to get to know. Young, inexperienced, and somewhat blundering.

She would have been happy to see even Stayner.

Instead, the men who came into the freezer room were completely unfamiliar to her. She hadn't even met them once.

The first cop was older. Lines of experience creased his face. He was heavy, taller than Erin but shorter than Vic, his uniform wrinkled like he'd been sitting at a desk most of the day.

He shifted his heavy duty belt as he entered the freezer, lifting it up and then settling it down again. He looked around the freezer warily. His eyes went first to Erin and then to Beryl.

"What happened here?" he questioned. He took several steps toward Beryl.

"I don't know," Erin whispered, her throat dry.

"Something happened," contributed the younger cop who came in behind the first. "Looks like we've got a body."

"You're not qualified to declare a death," the first cop reminded him. He looked down at Beryl, frowning. He didn't reach down and touch her. Erin thought he should check her pulse, but he didn't. "Get Dr. Manuel on the phone."

"But she is dead," the second cop pointed out. But that didn't stop him from pulling out his phone and swiping through it to find the number he wanted. He waited for a minute, the phone pasted to his ear, as he waited for the call to connect. "Dr. Manuel…? I need him, please." He listened to the answer, seeming neither surprised nor angry at the answer. "I know he's probably in with a patient. But we have an emergency situation here."

A little more cajoling, and he apparently managed to convince them to interrupt the doctor for him. They all waited, no one talking.

"Dr. Manuel. Sorry to interrupt you like this, but we have a situation. Over at the Biscuit. No, I know no one is supposed to be cooking yet. That's not the problem."

There was the buzz of a response from the phone. Erin couldn't make out the words, just the impatient tone.

"There's a woman in the freezer."

Another pause as he listened to the reply.

"She's dead."

The younger cop grimaced as he listened to whatever the doctor had to say.

"I know she's not officially dead, that's why I'm calling you. We need you to check her out and do whatever needs to be done..."

More waiting, more words.

"I'm sorry. Can you come, though?"

Eventually, he convinced the doctor to make the trip to look at the woman in the freezer.

He arrived a few minutes later, dressed in a white lab coat and stethoscope and carrying a small bag, looking as iconic as if he were dressed up as a doctor for Halloween. He saw Erin first, then apparently decided that she wasn't the one he was there to see to, and looked around the freezer, his eyes eventually landing on Beryl.

"Well, that's something you don't find in your freezer every day."

He walked over to her, took her pulse, and listened to her chest for a heartbeat or breathing. He hung the stethoscope around his neck again.

"There's a saying. They're not really dead until they're warm and dead."

"What kind of sense does that make?" the younger cop demanded. The older one shook his head at his attitude toward the doctor.

"It means that we have to get this woman warmed up before I can declare her dead."

"But she's obviously dead."

"'Obviously dead' doesn't cut it when someone has been frozen to death. There have been cases where a heartbeat has been reestablished after an accident like this. Usually in children, but there have been cases of adults surviving as well. And I'm not going to take the chance or open myself up to a lawsuit. Taking the time to warm her up is not going to hurt anything. So let's get it done."

The first cop looked down at Beryl's body. "What do you want to do? You want us to carry her out of here? Turn off the freezer? Put blankets on her?"

"We need to get her out of here."

"We might be destroying evidence."

"We'll just have to be careful. But we need to get her out of here before we can decide that she's permanently dead."

Erin stood there watching as they navigated around Beryl, looking at her position and the various angles, and came up with a plan to pick her up and move her. The older cop apparently had back issues, so the doctor and the younger cop were nominated for the job. He made his first attempt to pick up Beryl's legs and let go again.

"Ugh. She's definitely dead! I can feel ice crystals crunching. And she's in rigor."

"Are you the doctor now? Frozen stiff is not the same as rigor. Grab her and let's get this done."

The younger cop picked up Beryl's legs a second time, and they moved toward the exit door.

CHAPTER 14

The older cop's name was Coleman, and he was the one who directed Erin to the police station and told her not to talk to anyone on the way. She exchanged looks with Vic, but obeyed, heading to the police station where she would be expected to give a statement.

There was an actual police station in Whitewater, different from Bald Eagle Falls, where the police department had a few offices at the civic center. The Whitewater police station was a small red brick building away from Main Street and the shops. Erin looked around, feeling disconnected from her surroundings. She didn't belong in Whitewater Junction. She didn't know anyone there. She was going into an unfamiliar police department to talk to unfamiliar police officers about the death of a woman she had only just met. She wanted to go back to Bald Eagle Falls and talk to Officer Terry Piper.

She just stood there, looking around, feeling anchorless.

Eventually, she shook off her torpor and forced herself to walk in through the front doors. There was a uniformed female officer at the front desk. Her hair was pulled back, but it was curly and tendrils were sticking out here and there. The uniform was not well-fitted; a large men's shirt rather than one cut for a woman's figure. Her name tag said M Sommers. She gave Erin a smile and raised her brows.

"How can I help you?"

"Uh—Deputy Coleman sent me over here. About the woman… in the restaurant."

"Oh, are you one of the people with the contest? He said some of you would be coming over." Sommers looked at her watch, then turned around and looked at the rooms behind her, as if everything were full and she didn't know how she was going to fit Erin in.

"Did you know the… victim?"

"I met her last night. Just had a short conversation with her."

"And what was it that happened today?"

"I was the one who… was the first one in there, and found her."

"Ah, okay." Sommers nodded her understanding. "You're an eyewitness. We're going to want to keep you on your own until you've had a chance to make your statement to make sure your recollection isn't influenced by someone else. I'm sorry, it's not much fun to sit all by yourself, but I'm sure Deputy Coleman won't be too long. He'll want to question you as soon as possible."

Erin shifted uncomfortably. "I don't know anything. He's going to know just as much as me from looking at the scene. Probably more, because of his training. I don't know anything at all."

"I'm sorry. Come on back here, and I'll get you a hot beverage while you're waiting. You're probably chilled after being in that freezer, and then the weather outside."

She gave a shudder. Erin smiled. Sommers had to be a native Tennessean, or from somewhere even hotter, if she thought it was that cold outside. Sommers directed her to a little gate through the counter, unlocking it with a button. She escorted Erin through.

"You don't have any weapons, do you?"

"No. I don't have anything."

Sommers didn't bother to check. She was very trusting, for a policewoman. She took Erin to a glassed-in office with a table and a couple of chairs and motioned her to take a seat. Erin sat down, her stomach tight with anxiety.

"Would you like coffee or tea?" Sommers asked.

"Tea, please."

"Coming up. You just relax in here and I'm sure Deputy Coleman will be here in no time. You can tell him what you know and be on your way."

"But I really don't know anything."

"Then it will be even quicker, won't it?" Sommers gave her a stern smile, then left the room, pulling the door shut behind her. Erin heard it click into place and had a pretty good idea that she was now locked in.

At first, a glass-walled interrogation room seemed like a pretty bad idea. She could just see a prisoner punching a hole in the glass or picking up a chair and launching it through one of the walls, bringing the whole thing down in a shower of broken shards of glass. But of course they would have made sure that it was some kind of armored glass that a person couldn't put a fist through easily. Erin looked at the chair across from her. Both the chairs and the table were anchored to the floor. So no throwing a chair through it, either.

Sitting in the middle of the glassed-in room, Erin was visible to everyone working in the cubicles of the police department. Everyone walking by could see her. It wasn't like in Bald Eagle Falls, where there was only a narrow window. Anything an interviewee did in the glassed-in room would be visible to everyone else, as would anything anyone did to the interviewee. No one could pretend not to see police brutality. And anyone who should not be there would be noticed immediately.

Erin fidgeted for a while, watching the people outside of her fish tank, waiting for Deputy Coleman to show up. At first, she thought he would only be a few minutes, like Sommers had suggested, but that had clearly been wrong. Sommers brought Erin her tea. Erin sipped it slowly, making it last but, eventually, the tea was all gone and there was still no sign of Coleman.

Erin decided that sitting there doing nothing, just waiting for him, was making the time pass even more slowly. If she occupied herself instead of just sitting there, the time would go by much more quickly, and she wouldn't feel like she had wasted her entire day.

She opened her purse and sifted through the contents. She always had pens and notepads, or at least scraps of paper, with her. She knew she should get more organized. If she wasn't going to use her phone like Vic thought she should, she could at least get a dedicated planner to keep track of things and centralize it all in one location. Maybe when she got back to Bald Eagle Falls, she would do that. Or the next time she was in the city. The stationery store would have a lot more options than the little general store in Bald Eagle Falls. Though she did like to support the local businesses as much as she could.

She pulled out several blank sheets of paper and folded them over and smoothed them so she had a good surface to write on. She started to make notes on the contest and what she had learned so far about the rules and the different events that were being planned, and anything she ought to plan for those events. She wasn't the organizer of the contest, but that didn't mean she shouldn't be organized. And if she could tie some of the events in with promotions at Auntie Clem's Bakery, she would be able to get more visibility and sales.

That worked for a few minutes. But Erin couldn't stop thinking about Beryl and how she had looked when Erin had discovered her in the freezer room. She had looked like a sculpture, pale blue and covered with frost. Not like something real. The room and the body were bloodless, like Beryl had known she needed to keep it hygienic for food preparation. What had happened? Had she been looking for something and gotten confused when she got too cold looking for it? Had she been drunk or tired and thought she would just sit down and take a break for a few minutes? Maybe the door had been stuck. But Erin knew it hadn't been stuck. It hadn't been difficult to open. If someone had been trying to get out, she had only to put her shoulder to the door to push it open if it had been sticky.

Beryl hadn't been very nice, but Erin still felt bad for any friends or family. It was never easy to lose a loved one. And if Beryl hadn't had any family or friends… well, that was even more tragic. Then Erin felt bad for walking away from her the night before and not realizing that Beryl was reaching out desperately for attention and validation, not just being obnoxious. Maybe she couldn't help it.

A lost life was a lost life.

CHAPTER 15

Of course, Erin was assuming that Beryl had passed away. The doctor had said that he couldn't declare her dead until she was warm, but did that really mean there was a chance that she could recover? It seemed highly unlikely to Erin, but then, she wasn't a doctor.

What if they could revive her? Would that event change her life, or would she go on as before? What would it be like to be on the same panel with a judge who had just been frozen to death and then been reanimated? That was a creepy thought.

But maybe it wouldn't be any different from working with anyone who had been through a recent illness. Erin had experience caring for people who were older or had gone through an illness or accident and needed assistance taking care of themselves. Not as fun as baking, but it had been rewarding to know how important her work was to those people and their families.

Maybe the reason that Coleman hadn't yet returned to the police station to interview her was that he was waiting to see if Beryl could be revived.

Erin started another list of things she would need to do when she got back home. Not just the regular everyday things, but looking into whether she had enough life insurance that the bakery could keep running if something happened to her. Erin wasn't sure who would run it if she met with an accident. Charley, she supposed. Charley was the co-owner, so she was the one who would take over if something happened to Erin.

But would Charley keep it running? Did the existing employees know enough about baking gluten-free goods and running a business to keep it going if something happened to her? Or would Charley convert it to a conventional bakery?

Or sell it and start another venture somewhere else?

There was a knock at the door, and Erin looked up, startled. She had finished her tea quite a while ago. She had finally been able to put Beryl's frozen body out of her mind as she had been thinking about the long-term future of Auntie Clem's and what she needed to do to ensure that there were people ready and willing to take over if something happened to her.

But seeing Coleman's face brought it all back in a rush. She pressed her hands to the table to stand up but, in doing so, rocked the unsteady surface and her cup spun across the glossy surface intent on self-destruction. Erin grabbed at it and nearly knocked it over the edge, just managing to save it at the last moment.

She held the cup in her hand, splashed with dribbles of tea, and tried to catch her breath. She looked at Coleman with an embarrassed grin. So much for looking like a mature, graceful woman. He would think she was some nut; some crazy, clumsy nut who had turned up another body and couldn't give him the information he wanted.

"Uh—hi. Sorry about that. I didn't mean to…"

"Miss Price. Please, have a seat." He motioned back to the chair she had just bounced up out of. "Would you like a refill on that?"

Erin put the cup down with an unsteady clink. She wiped her hands on her pants. "No. I'm good. Thanks."

"Great. Thank you for coming in. I'm sorry to keep you waiting for so long."

"Oh, I'm sure you had good reason. How is… I mean… did the doctor… Beryl…"

"He's still working on bringing her core temperature up to where it needs to be to, uh, declare her. I have to say, though, that I am not optimistic, and I am treating this as a death investigation until I hear otherwise."

Erin nodded. That was about what she had expected. She settled herself back into the uncomfortable seat. "I don't really know anything."

"Well, I understand that. But we need to run through this anyway, so if you'll indulge me..."

"Of course. I'll help if I can, but..."

"All right." He pulled out a notepad, licked his finger, and turned to a fresh page. "Why don't we start at the top. How did you know Ms. Batcombe?"

"Well, I didn't, really. I just met her last night for a few minutes, but we talked for maybe five minutes. Not long enough to get to know her."

"Where and how did you meet?"

"We had a dinner and event last night. She was at that. I didn't talk to her at the dinner, but I went out for a bit of fresh air, and she was out there smoking. She introduced herself and we talked for a few minutes. That's all."

"What was your impression of her?"

Erin stalled. "What do you mean?"

Coleman studied her. He creased and smoothed a corner of the notebook page. "Where was she smoking?"

"Out front, against the front of the building. A little ways away from the doors."

"Had she had much to drink?"

"Oh." Erin thought about it. "I don't really know. She wasn't slurring or unsteady. But I don't know what she is normally like, so I can't say if she was more talkative than usual, or if she was... more emotional... or anything..."

It was possible that the way Beryl had been talking about Vic was just due to drink. Some people got mean when they were drunk and said things that they never would have considered saying sober. Erin hoped that it had just been because she'd had a bit much to drink.

"Do you think that she... got stuck in there because she was drunk?" Erin asked Coleman.

"We're just at the beginning of our investigation. We don't know anything yet. Just exploring the possibilities."

"Maybe she was drunk, and that was why she went in there… or why she stayed when she got cold. I was trying to figure it out."

"It is a strange situation. People who have had too much to drink often don't realize when they are getting cold. Or if she had something else to keep her mood up or to help her to stay awake… we will investigate whether there were any substances in her bloodstream that might have altered her perception of her environment or her body's signals."

Erin nodded. Meth, she knew, made people overheat. She didn't think Beryl was a meth user, but you couldn't tell in the earlier stages. The soccer mom down the street might have a meth addiction. Someone who wanted to lose weight. It had initially been designed to help soldiers stay awake and alert.

"When did you get to the restaurant today?" Coleman asked.

"I'm not sure what time it was. The woman giving the tour would have a better idea. We gathered at… eight-thirty. We waited for everyone to get there. Beryl didn't show up, so we waited for a little while for her, then started without her. There was some general stuff, and then walking down the street, stopping outside the restaurant while she talked about…" Erin squinted and sighed. "I don't know. Architecture. Local cuisine trends. It was all a little… um… high-brow."

"Boring?" Coleman suggested, the corner of his mouth curling up.

"Well, yes. Incredibly boring. I was really eager to get inside, to see where the competition would be held, the real nuts and bolts."

"Then y'all went into the restaurant, and you went to the kitchen."

"I stayed with the group. There was a bit of information in the main dining hall, and then we were allowed to go into the kitchen, all together. Not just me."

"But at some point, you became separated from the group."

"Not separated," Erin protested. "I was still right there, listening with everyone else. I just… tried the handle on the cold room door. I wanted to get a peek at it."

"I see." He didn't say anything else, looking at her, waiting for her to fill the silence.

Erin didn't say anything right away, not sure what she should say. Coleman scribbled some notes in his notebook, looking down at the page and then up at her as he considered.

"What did you notice about the door?" he asked eventually.

"Notice about it? It was… big, heavy, had a good seal. What do you mean, what did I notice?"

"What made you decide to open it before the tour guide said to check it out?"

"Just curiosity. I wanted to see everything, get a feel for the place. How the contest was going to be run. What it was going to be like when it was full of contestants and everyone else. I just… was bored and wanted to see something more."

"What did you notice about the locking mechanism on the door?"

"The lock?" Erin cast her mind back, trying to picture it. Imagining the movements of her hands, and the way the door had looked, mapping everything out in her head. "Was there a lock? I don't know if there was one."

"Wouldn't a freezer in a place like that have some security? What about when the contest entries were being stored in there? There must have been a way to keep it safe."

Erin shook her head. "I'm sorry. I just can't think of anything. Maybe there was a lock, but I didn't notice it."

"So how did you open the door?"

"It wasn't locked." Erin shook her head. She could feel the handle in her hand, the smooth, cool metal of the lever. "I didn't have to turn any locks. I just turned the handle. It was a little sticky for a second, but that's all. And I wouldn't even say it was stuck, I just had to give it a bit of a pull, because it was… sealed."

Coleman nodded. He made some more notes to himself.

"A freezer like that, they have to make it so that you can't be locked in, don't they?" Erin asked. "Aren't there laws… that there has to be an override, a release from inside or something. Just like the trunk of a car; they all have emergency releases inside now so that someone can't be accidentally locked inside."

Or on purpose. There weren't very many circumstances in which a person would get accidentally locked in a trunk. A small child, maybe, but not an adult. How many movies showed abductees or murder victims thrown into a trunk?

"There are safety features," Coleman agreed. "We will be looking into that. What was required and what was in place. We're not looking to place blame, but we do want to figure out what happened here. It's a very tragic case, you don't want to see something like that happen again."

"Did she have family around here? I feel so bad for her family and friends. So sudden and unexpected."

"Death often comes when we don't expect it," Coleman opined.

Erin shifted restlessly. "That's everything I know. I didn't know Beryl, and I don't know what could have happened last night. It's very sad."

"Have I heard your name before?" Coleman inquired, lifting one eyebrow. "We'll need your ID, of course, to fill out the official paperwork. But your name sounds familiar. I'm wondering where I might have heard it before."

Erin swallowed. She wasn't about to tell him about the other cases that she had been peripherally involved in. "I don't know. I guess you must have heard about my bakery in Bald Eagle Falls. Auntie Clem's Bakery? Most people have at least heard about it. There aren't a lot of places around here where you can get quality gluten-free baked goods."

Coleman's lips pursed. "I don't think that was it. Well, I'm sure it will come to me. If you could get out your driver's license, I'll take a copy of it, and I'll get Meribel started on the paperwork."

"Oh. Okay." Erin opened her purse and scooped out her wallet. It took her a minute to find her driver's license. It wasn't only her purse that needed to be sorted out, but even the wallet was stuffed too full of things that she didn't need to keep on her all the time. She had to learn to leave things at home if she wasn't going to need them right away. But she preferred to have her things with her. After going so many years with few possessions, she liked to have as many things on her person as possible. She found the edge of her driver's license behind another card and pulled it out. "There it is."

She handed it across the table to Coleman. He picked it up and studied it. Erin's face got warm. She hoped she hadn't let it expire. Coleman smiled and nodded and left the room.

The glass walls allowed her to watch him after he left the room, going out to the front of the police station where Erin had come in and handed her license to M Sommers. Meribel. For a few minutes, he talked with her; much longer, Erin thought, than needed just to give her instructions to copy the driver's license and get a witness statement form for Erin to fill out.

She was going to be there for a long time. She knew it. They were going to want a lengthy formal statement, even though she had done nothing more than to open a door and discover Beryl Batcombe's frozen body. But he wanted to make sure he had all of his bases covered. If Erin didn't tell him everything he wanted to know, it would be harder for him to follow up with her once she had gone back to Bald Eagle Falls. But not impossible. She had a cell phone and email.

CHAPTER 16

It was late afternoon, and Erin was tired and hungry when she finally got out of the police station. Her head was pounding and she wanted to lie down for a nap. But she also needed something to eat. And she couldn't eat and sleep at the same time.

She had seen Vic and some of the others at the police station. They had come and gone relatively quickly, filling in their forms at the front counter and not having to have personal interviews with Coleman. Erin imagined that those who knew Beryl better might have to spend longer with Coleman or his staff, but the people who were from out of town and who hadn't actually seen or discovered the body didn't have anything important to tell him. They just happened to be involved with the contest, there was no other connection.

Erin expected to see Vic in their hotel room. Reading a book or checking email on her phone, or watching daytime television. But it wasn't Vic who was waiting for her when she got back to the hotel, it was Terry.

"Oh!" Erin was surprised. She looked around for Vic. "I wasn't expecting you to be here."

"Are you okay?" He pushed himself up from the bed and stepped in close to enfold her in his arms. "How are you?"

"I'm okay. I mean, I don't feel good right now, but…"

Well, she wasn't dead like Beryl.

"Come here," he walked her over to the bed and lowered her to it. They sat side by side and he looked into her face. "I've been so worried about you. Vic said she'd seen you at the police station, and you looked okay, but I've been worried..."

He didn't say that he was worried she would have a breakdown. That seeing another dead body would be too much for her.

"No, no. I'm fine." She met his gaze. "It wasn't anything like..."

She didn't need to finish the sentence. Anything like Ingersoll's death. Anything like finding Terry bound and unconscious. She would be okay. It wouldn't haunt her dreams.

But how could she know that? She hadn't been as shocked and traumatized as when she had discovered Mr. Ingersoll. But that didn't mean it wouldn't follow her into her dreams. It might be added to the horrors that she dreamt almost every night.

She didn't think it had been that bad.

"There was... no blood," Erin explained to Terry. "It was just... she was there... and you could tell looking at her... she was sort of blue-gray and there was frost..." She stopped before describing the delicate frost sticking to Beryl's eyelashes. Frost was always so pretty and she loved how it clung to the trees in the early morning. She looked away from Terry. "It was different."

Terry rubbed her shoulders and the back of her neck. "Okay. We'll leave it at that. But whenever you want to talk about it... we can. Whatever you want to tell me about it."

Erin nodded. "Yes. Of course."

"What can I get for you? You must be dead on your feet."

"I haven't been on my feet. I've been sitting. Why would that be more exhausting than actually being on my feet all day at Auntie Clem's?"

"I think anything related to being questioned about a sudden death is going to be exhausting. It's an emotional thing. And you've been at the police station for hours. I didn't know if I should go over there and ask after you. I didn't want to throw my weight around, but there was no need for them to keep you for so long."

"You know how it is with police work. Lots of tedious sitting and waiting."

"Followed by bursts of heart-stopping insanity."

"Well, luckily, no insanity today. Just the tedious sitting and waiting. And paperwork."

"You can't uphold the law without plenty of paperwork."

"So I'm finding."

"The police officer's nemesis. Do you want something to eat? A hot shower? A nap?"

"Mmm. All of the above."

"Which do you want the most? Or first?"

"I think I'd better eat."

Terry got up and walked over to the mini-fridge, but his mouth turned down when he took a peek inside. "Whatever happened to actually having quality snacks in a minibar? I'll go down to the restaurant and pick something up for you. What do you want?"

"I don't know what they'll have."

"Anything you would order from the family restaurant at home. Do you want a full-blown dinner? Or something smaller?"

"No, nothing that big. A sandwich, maybe."

"With fries? Do you want grilled cheese or something grown-up?"

"Mmm, you know, grilled cheese sounds really good."

"And the fries?"

"I'd better not have fries."

"You sure?"

Erin nodded.

"I'll go get you a sandwich, then. It will probably take half an hour, you want to have that hot shower while I get it?"

"Yeah, that sounds really good."

He gave her a quick kiss and snapped his fingers to call K9, who had been snoozing next to the bed, to his side. Then he was gone.

Erin headed to the bathroom, filled the tub, and poured some of the hotel shampoo into the water to make bubbles. A bubble bath was even better than a shower. She closed her eyes and soaked in the hot water waiting for Terry's return.

Erin was feeling much better after her grilled cheese sandwich and soak in the tub. She felt human once more. She had changed into her jammies and was cuddling with Terry on the bed while watching some old noir murder mystery on TV. Despite her experience, the dramatic danger of the movie didn't bother her at all.

There was a tap on the door. Erin knew who it was. She'd heard that tap on her back door enough times to recognize it. She slid off of the bed and let Vic in.

"How are you?" Vic asked, giving her a brief hug.

"Better now."

"You're okay? I was so worried about you, but you looked like you were holding it together when I saw you. You looked pretty calm. Just bored."

Erin rolled her eyes. "Yes. So far, this 'vacation' has been pretty tedious."

"It will get better," Vic assured her. She looked past Erin to Terry. "And how about you, Officer Piper? How are you tonight?"

"Fine, Vic. Come on in and visit for a while."

"I don't want to interrupt anything…"

"We're just watching TV."

"Maybe for a few minutes, then," Vic agreed, smiling. She sat down on the chair for a chat with Erin. No matter how much time they spent together, they always found things to talk about.

They'd been talking for a half hour when there was another knock on the door. Erin frowned. She hoped it wasn't the police again. She didn't want to have to deal with them again.

She was much slower to get up and get the door this time. She opened the door and found Chef Kirschoff standing there, with a small white dog in his arms. She blinked at him.

"Oh! Hi, Chef Kirschoff. Hans."

"Erin. I was so sorry to hear about what happened… you finding poor Beryl that way."

Erin stepped back, motioning for Kirschoff to enter, though it was getting a little crowded in the small hotel room.

Vic saw the dog and jumped up. "Oh! You have a puppy! Isn't he the cutest thing!" She reached out and scratched the dog's ears and crooned in a baby voice.

The dog nuzzled her and whined, enjoying the attention. K9's head went up and he stared at the interloper.

"He's not mine," Kirschoff explained.

Vic continued to stroke the dog's ears. "Whose is he, then?"

"He's—he was—Beryl's."

"Oh, no…" Vic leaned forward and kissed the top of the dog's head, covering his ears with both hands to keep him from hearing anything upsetting. "Oh, how sad. What's going to happen to him? Was she married?"

"No. She lived by herself. I don't know if there is any next of kin…" He shifted the dog closer to Vic. "I need someone to look after him. I didn't know who to ask."

He fumbled the white dog into her arms. Vic looked surprised, but she cuddled the puppy close, putting her cheek against him. "Oh, poor thing. I don't know." Vic looked at Erin. "Maybe *you* should…"

"No, I've already got two pets, three animals in the house when K9 is there. I can't take another."

"But…"

"He looks pretty happy right where he is."

Vic looked down at the dog. "I can't take a dog. I can't commit to…"

"It's not forever," Kirschoff said. "Just until they find someone else to take him."

Vic scratched the dog's ears. Erin could tell there was no way Vic was going to say no.

"What's his name?" Vic looked at Kirschoff.

"Nilla." Kirschoff grimaced. "Short for Vanilla Scoop."

CHAPTER 17

There had been more activities planned for the judges, staff, and officials over the weekend, but Erin found that everything had been called off. Or rescheduled, at least, while the contest organizers sorted out the wrinkles that Beryl's death had put into the contest plans.

The entrants who were making fermented drinks for their contest entries mixed up and bottled their creations under the supervision of the contest officials. The drinks would need to sit for a few weeks before the judges could taste them and decide which would go on to the next round. It was all done with a decided lack of ceremony, but Erin didn't hear anyone complain about having the pomp put aside in the wake of Beryl's death.

So in another day, Erin was headed back to Bald Eagle Falls with Terry. Vic had decided to take advantage of the fact that they had the hotel for a couple more nights, and invited Willie to stay with her for a bit of a vacation. And, Erin supposed, to introduce him to Nilla.

Erin was glad to get home.

Melissa heard that Erin was back, probably through the police department, where she worked part time. She showed up on Erin's doorstep with a covered dish. "I thought you probably wouldn't feel like cooking," she offered, reaching out with it until Erin took it from her.

"Thank you, that was very thoughtful. You're right… I don't feel like doing very much of anything but eating and sleeping right now."

Melissa nodded, standing there on the doorstep and waiting to be invited in. Erin finally relented. "Come in and set a while. How are you?"

Erin put the dish in the fridge and returned to the living room to sit down with Melissa.

Melissa leaned forward, eager for the details. "So? Tell me all about it. Was it awful? The police in Whitewater aren't releasing many details. I was hoping that we'd be able to get more, seeing as we're sister cities and you're associated with the police department through Terry. But I couldn't find anything out."

"It wasn't that awful," Erin said. "I mean… not like Mr. Ingersoll or Angela Plaint. It was just… like she'd died naturally. No violence."

"But it's not natural to end up dead in a freezer."

"No. But it wasn't like she was killed and stuffed in a freezer as a hiding place. She just… something happened while she was in there. I don't know what. Maybe she'd had too much to drink, or she didn't realize how tired she was and just closed her eyes…"

"I can't believe you found another body."

"But it wasn't a murder," Erin pointed out. "Just a tragic accidental death."

"Maybe. Maybe *not*."

"It wasn't murder this time." Erin smiled and shook her head at Melissa's thirst for drama. "I'm sorry, this one was just your normal, everyday, froze-to-death-in-a-cold-room."

"Did you know her? What was it like when you found her? You must have been shocked to find her there. Or maybe not anymore… maybe it's old hat now."

"No, it is not old hat," Erin said firmly. "It was still a shock. I couldn't believe it at first… but then I guess… it becomes easier to handle. I knew what to do. To keep everyone else out, to call the police. I didn't go in any farther or touch anything…"

"Of all the bad luck." Melissa shook her head. Erin wasn't sure whether Melissa was lamenting Erin's bad luck in finding a body or that Melissa had never found one herself. She'd missed out on Bo Biggles. That could have been her instead of Clara.

"Yes." Erin looked at the face of her phone. She didn't feel much like visiting and was hoping that Melissa would take the hint and leave. Then Erin could rest her eyes for a bit. Have a sleep.

"Of course, we're still cleaning up the mess after the last discovery you made," Melissa said with a little chuckle.

It took a minute for Erin to realize that she meant the burglaries, not the last body she had stumbled across.

"I guess you are… is it moving along? You know who the ringleader was, and I assume you've gotten information from some of the others. Do you think you have all of the names of the people who were involved?"

"I don't think you ever do in a case like this," Melissa said, tapping a finger on the arm of the chair she was sitting in. "I think that there are always going to be a few names that don't come out, or perps throw red herrings at us; the names of people who don't exist, or of people they knew were not involved. Just to throw us off the trail. Even with people you're sure are involved, you still have to have the proof. A gut feeling and overhearing something someone said just isn't enough to make an arrest. You end up letting some people go even though you know they were involved."

Erin rubbed her knee. She didn't like that. At least one of the people involved in the burglary ring had tried to kill her. What if that were someone who ended up evading the police net?

"It's okay," Melissa assured her. "We'll get all the big players. But whether we'll ever find out the names of all of the students who were involved…"

"What if they come back after me because of my involvement?"

"Kids? I don't think you need to worry about kids."

If Melissa didn't think that teenagers could be killers or cause harm, she was sadly mistaken. Adults, with brains that had matured, were less likely to do her any serious harm. Teenagers could be impulsive and unpredictable. And they could use violence without fully understanding the consequences of their actions.

~

Erin eventually saw Melissa on her way, but not until Melissa had exhausted several other avenues of inquiry and entertainment. Erin felt almost as exhausted as she had after Coleman had questioned her. Melissa had a friendlier manner than Coleman, but she was an expert interrogator. Erin had done her best to deflect Melissa's questions and hoped that she hadn't given anything away with her answers. Not that she knew anything to give away. But she felt like Melissa had gleaned more from their conversation than Erin had meant to give.

After Melissa was gone, Erin decided to turn her attention to her meditation. She had been practicing tai chi for some time now, and it was becoming easier to remember the forms and routines and to lose herself in the practice, letting her mind and body relax. It was still a struggle to keep herself from thinking about what needed to be done at the bakery or what she needed to write down and add to her lists. Still, she focused on each of the movements and managed to stay reasonably focused on relaxation and an open mind.

There was the sound of a key turning in the lock. Erin relaxed her stance and watched Terry enter.

"Hi, honey."

He looked her over. "Are you just starting or finishing?"

"Finishing. Good timing."

He walked in through the door, K9 at his side. "I thought you would be too tired for your tai chi."

"I need something to help me relax. Especially after… Melissa."

"Oh, has she been over here?" He rolled his eyes. He gave Erin a peck on the cheek and sat down on the couch, looking more tired than he ever had after a double shift in the old days.

"She came to pump me for more information on the body in the freezer. I think you guys have done yourselves a disservice by keeping her in an administrative position. She should be in the interrogation room."

"She knows how to get information out of people, that's for sure. And how to use the information and rumors that are swirling around to construct new rumors. I get tired just thinking about how much time and energy she puts into chasing after gossip."

Erin turned her head experimentally, making sure that her neck and shoulders were relaxed.

"Did she bug you more about church?" Terry asked.

"No, that one didn't come up this time, thankfully. I guess stories of dead bodies are good for one thing, anyway. They keep her distracted from my personal life."

"I'm sorry that there's been so much talk about you and your religious views because of that. You did something nice for me, and everybody is reading far too much into it."

"It doesn't seem to matter how much I tell people I'm not converting to Christianity, they think I must be lying."

"Why would you? And wouldn't lying about it sort of run counter to any kind of conversion…?"

"I haven't found Christians—at least the ones around here—to be terribly logical about their beliefs." Erin shrugged. "Maybe they think I don't know about the commandment not to lie."

"Well, as you stick to your guns and they see that you haven't suddenly started going to church, they'll fade out a bit."

"Hope so," Erin agreed. She headed for the kitchen. "Melissa brought a casserole. Do you want some?"

"Sounds good. I was going to see if we could get something delivered. But casserole is fine. Comfort food."

"I don't know what kind it is."

"Doesn't really matter. I grew up on them."

"Okay. I'll put it in the oven and make something to go with it. A salad or some veggies."

"You don't need to do anything. You're off duty. You can just eat the casserole and not worry about anything else."

"I have to watch what I eat, though," Erin touched her belly. "That casserole is going to be all carbs and cream. I need to focus on less calorie-dense foods."

"I'll cut up some vegetables for you, then." He sat forward on the couch to get up.

"No. You've been working. You need a rest. I've just been at home all day. I can manage."

"You're recovering from a trauma."

"I'm over it." Erin said it even though she knew she hadn't yet fully recovered from the shock and disbelief of finding Beryl's frozen body.

Terry gave her a skeptical look, but he shrugged and let it be. She supposed he'd come to the conclusion that if she wanted to cut up some vegetables that badly, she could go ahead.

CHAPTER 18

Erin was glad to get back to Auntie Clem's Bakery where she belonged. There, she could lose herself in her work. She could serve the people who needed a gluten-free or specialty diet and give them the sustenance—and treats—that they needed and deserved. It made her feel good that she could make a contribution to the community that way.

Things had been a little different since Christmas, but she thought that was just her own outlook. She needed to focus on the positive and not be so sensitive to the way that people looked at her or the slight dip in sales since Christmas. Of course people had bought more before Christmas and were now cutting back until their spending was back on track. A lot of people had either had their Christmas presents stolen or had contributed to fundraisers to help make up the losses for those who had.

The community had pulled together to help each other. That proved that people were good at heart. And that was how she should see them.

Erin stacked muffins on a tray to take out to the front and then arranged them in the display case. It was the quiet part of the afternoon. Things would pick up a bit when school let out, both with kids stopping by for a post-school snack and moms grabbing a few things for dinner.

Though she hadn't had as many school kids lately.

Or as many moms.

Erin tried to push the negative thoughts out of her mind as she arranged the baked goods.

She heard the tinkle of the bells at the front door and looked up with a smile on her face to see who it was.

It was Mrs. Foster, the mother of Peter, one of Erin's favorite customers, and his sisters. She was now heavily pregnant. Erin didn't know what her due date was, but she thought it might be the last time she saw Mrs. Foster for a few weeks.

Erin preferred it when Mrs. Foster came with the whole family so the kids could get their free kid's club cookies. But lately, she had been coming in by herself when the older kids were at school and Traci was, Erin assumed, in preschool or Mrs. Foster had swapped babysitting with someone else.

"Hello, Mrs. Foster," Erin greeted, standing up and rubbing her back for a moment.

"Miss Price," Mrs. Foster greeted. When she was with the kids, she usually said 'Miss Erin.' The southern way of being friendly yet respectful. 'Miss Price' was cooler, and Erin felt a little sting at the words.

"You're looking well," Erin said, forcing the plastic smile to stay on her face. "Doesn't look like it will be long now."

Mrs. Foster rested her hand on her bulging belly. "No, I don't think we'll have to wait much longer for this little one." She sighed, then looked at the baked goods in Erin's display case. She listed off the items she needed, and Erin silently gathered them together. Vic was in the kitchen taking care of some other tasks while it was quiet.

"It's been a long time since I've seen Peter," Erin said tentatively. "I hope I see him again soon. Everything okay with him?"

Mrs. Foster looked at her for a moment. She shook her head. "Peter is fine. But I don't think you'll be seeing him anytime soon."

Erin wondered whether she should ask more questions, or if she didn't want to know the answers. If Peter was fine and Mrs. Foster didn't plan to bring the children by any time soon, then it was because she didn't want them to see Erin or vice versa. "He's such a smart kid."

"A little too smart for his own good, maybe. But he is just a child, and I don't want him around people who might do him harm."

Erin blinked. "Harm? I wouldn't ever do anything to hurt Peter."

"You may think that, but your actions don't bear it out. Twice now, he has had to talk to the police because of something that you have said. I don't want him involved with the police. I want him to have a normal childhood and not be brought under suspicion by the police or people wanting to know what he's been saying to them."

Erin was tongue-tied. She tried to think of what to say. She couldn't argue the truth of what Mrs. Foster said. Peter had held key pieces of information in a couple of investigations. He was very observant and, while he didn't always know the significance of what he knew, his keen eye had been relevant to the police department's investigations.

"I never intended…"

She nodded. "Like I said. You might not have thought about what you were doing, but your actions show that you are not putting Peter's safety or well-being first."

Erin stood at the cash register and tried to remember what she had just put into the bag for Mrs. Foster. Her brain had stalled, stuck on the realization that Mrs. Foster thought she had put Peter in harm's way by her actions.

"I'm sorry."

Mrs. Foster nodded. She stood there, one hand on her belly, waiting for Erin to finish ringing her purchase through. Erin looked in the bag and, with numb, clumsy fingers, punched in the numbers for her purchases.

"I… Is there something I can do…?"

"No, I don't think there is. I would just like you to stay out of Peter's life. Stay away from the school. Don't talk to him on the street. Don't talk to him at all if I am not supervising."

"Okay."

"It's my job to protect him. And if there is ever anything you think he can contribute to a police investigation…" Mrs. Foster licked her lips and shook her head. "You come directly to me. But that isn't ever going to happen again, is it?"

"I… I really don't know. I don't know what's going to happen in the future."

"You come to me. Not to the police."

Erin nodded. She took Mrs. Foster's money and handed over the bag of baked goods.

"I'm coming here because not coming here to get food that Peter can eat would be punishing him for your actions, and he didn't do anything wrong. But that's the only reason. If he didn't need this food, if he was able to eat gluten or I was able to get good gluten-free baking somewhere else, I wouldn't be here."

Erin nodded wordlessly. Mrs. Foster took her purchase and walked back out of the bakery. Erin turned toward the kitchen and saw Vic framed in the doorway, her eyes wide.

"First Mary Lou and now Mrs. Foster… I just don't understand people! Exactly what did we do that was so wrong?"

"I don't know… I mean, I understand the words, but I don't know how we could have done anything any differently. What exactly do they think I was supposed to do? *Not* talk to Terry? Not say anything to the police when I might have a lead?"

"I guess so." Vic gave a wide shrug. "People are all eager for you to solve a mystery until it interferes with their lives. How are you supposed to figure it out? Without ever talking to anyone? How are you supposed to solve it without all of the relevant pieces?"

Erin sprayed the display case and started to polish it with a dry cloth without paying any attention to what she was doing. "I know what Terry would say."

"That you're not supposed to be investigating in the first place," Vic admitted. "But what are we supposed to do? Just ignore it when someone says something? If we didn't tell Terry or the sheriff when we heard something relevant to a case, we would be in trouble for withholding information. Telling him that we've heard something isn't investigating. It's just… helping."

Charley stopped by while Erin and Vic were cleaning up and preparing for the next morning. She swept in like a whirlwind and didn't help them, but perched up on one of the stools to present her plans while they did the work.

"I have some ideas for getting Auntie Clem's involved in some of the community and kids' activities," she told Erin. "We should make the most of the cook-off. Get some promotional mileage out of it."

"I agree, but there isn't a lot of time to prepare anything," Erin said.

"If we were going to be in charge of some activity, then we should have started on it already. It's only a couple of weeks away now."

Charley brushed this off with a motion. "There's plenty of time. Kirschoff and his group are taking care of all of the promo already, all we have to do is make sure that we're there when scheduled activities happen. We can hand out water bottles and samples, maybe get some buttons made with the two of you listed as judges, make goodie bags for kids with, like, balloons and small toys and a cookie to go with their ice cream treats. All we have to do is show up and take advantage of the crowds."

Erin sighed. "So you're going to take charge of this? Because I don't have any extra time. We already have to work the staff harder because Vic and I will be involved in the judging and other events. And I can't be doing a bunch of self-promo when I'm supposed to be there as an official. It just won't sit well with people."

"Yeah, that's fine. Not a problem. I've thrown parties before."

"It isn't exactly a party."

"It's not that different," Charley declared. "And it's the same skills. Coordinating everything, getting supplies, getting everything prepped to go. I'm good at that kind of thing."

Erin didn't say anything. Charley had not shown a lot of organization and initiative in their time as partners. But Erin remembered that her apartment in Moose River had been neat and well-organized. And she had been part of the party scene there, so she probably had plenty of experience getting that kind of thing organized. Maybe Erin just hadn't given her a chance to shine.

"Okay. It's going to have to be your baby, though, you understand? Whether it succeeds or fails will depend on you."

"Great." Charley nodded firmly. "I'm not gonna let you down. What's our budget?"

"I'm not sure." Erin considered. "Why don't you work something up and we'll go over it tomorrow?"

"Great," Charley agreed. She twirled on her chair. "It's best if I'm the one doing it anyway since the moms are not so happy with you right now."

Erin put down the batter she had been pouring into loaf pans and looked at her.

"Well…?" Charley looked back and forth between Erin and Vic and shook her head. "It's the truth. Parents are not so happy when their kids get in trouble with the police."

"That's their fault for breaking the law," Vic said. "Not Erin's for figuring out what was going on."

"I didn't say it was Erin's fault. I said that it was better if I was in charge of kids' activities because she's not in the moms' good books. I didn't say she did anything wrong."

Vic shook her head. She gave Erin a look. "It doesn't matter what anyone says. You did what you were supposed to. If people don't like it, they're just twisting the issues around to satisfy their own consciences."

Erin swallowed and nodded. She picked up the bowl and continued her work. She thought nostalgically of the old days, when she wasn't anchored to anything or anyone and, if things went bad, she could just pick up and run, go somewhere else and start over again. She hadn't realized back then how much freedom she'd had. Now that she was a business owner and a homeowner, she couldn't just run away when there was trouble.

Charley seemed to finally realize that she had made a mistake in saying what she had. She fiddled with her purse for a minute, then changed the topic.

"So… Chef Kirschoff. What's the deal with him?"

"What's the deal?" Erin repeated.

"Yeah. Is he married, got a girlfriend? Anything?"

"Uh, not that I know of," Erin said. She looked at Vic. "You?"

"No, I don't think he has any close relationships right now. Why? You know someone who wants to meet him?"

"Me," Charley said as if it should have been obvious.

Erin looked at her in disbelief. "You're interested in Chef Kirschoff." She thought of Charley's last boyfriend. A mobster. The son of one of the clan leaders. Wild, reckless, unruly, and powerful. How did Charley go from that to a chef?

"He's older than you," Vic pointed out.

"You're one to talk. Willie is what, twice your age?"

"Well…" Vic shrugged. "It doesn't bother us. But it bothers some people. I didn't think you were ready to settle down with someone. Especially someone older."

"He's not ancient. He's still got his hair. He makes good money and is internationally recognized. He travels. And he's got a cute accent."

Erin couldn't quite wrap her mind around this. Of course it was perfectly fine if Charley wanted to pursue a friendship or relationship with Chef Kirschoff. She was an adult, and it was totally up to her. And him. She just couldn't comprehend the jump from Bobby Dixon to Hans Kirschoff.

"I don't think you should jump into anything." Vic surprised Erin with her comment. "I think you should spend some time getting to know him while he's here for the contest. See whether the two of you really are compatible at all."

"Well, of course," Charley agreed. "I wasn't planning to jump into the sack with him."

Erin's face heated. She stared down at her loaf pans as if they were the most interesting things in the world. Vic giggled.

"Why Erin, you're as red as two beets."

Erin focused on getting the rest of the preparations done, ignoring the laughter.

"Why would that make you blush?" Charley demanded. "It's not like you and Officer Piper are only holding hands."

"Officer Piper and I have taken the time to get to know each other."

"And I said that's what I was going to do. Why are you acting like such a prude?"

"I'm not. And I can't help it if I blush."

"Maybe now that you're going to church, you've realized that you're living in sin. I've heard talk around town that the two of you are going to get married."

"We are not. We don't have any plans to get married." Erin didn't think that her face could get any hotter. She must already be scarlet. "And I'm not going to church now. I went to one service with Terry on Christmas Eve. For him. To make him happy."

"So he's pressuring you into going to church? I thought Officer Handsome was perfect in every way."

"He's not perfect," Erin snapped. She pressed her lips together when she realized what she had said. "I mean, he's not pressuring me to go to church. He's never even asked me to once. I volunteered to go with him because I knew that if I wasn't around, that's where he would have been.

That's the way he observes Christmas. So I offered to go with him so he wouldn't miss out."

Vic looked at Erin and didn't say anything. Charley shook her head, laughing. "You seem a *little* sensitive about the subject, dear sister." She drew the word little out, exaggerating it.

"I'm not. I'm just answering your question. Terry and I are just fine. And we're not getting married."

Charley tilted her head to one side and shrugged. "*Okay*, if you say so."

"Just leave her alone, Charley," Vic warned. "You've gone far enough."

"Fine."

"You'd better get home and work on that budget," Vic suggested.

"I'll work on it tomorrow. Tonight, I'm going out."

CHAPTER 19

Erin looked at the big sedan with a dented fender that pulled up behind Auntie Clem's. Willie was out of town, and she had been expecting Terry to pick her and Vic up. He had volunteered. But the sedan was not Terry's, Erin instantly recognized it as belonging to Beaver. The first time she had seen Rohilda Beaven was when she had rear-ended a drug dealer's car in the middle of Bald Eagle Falls' Main Street. Beaver had claimed that it was an accident at the time, but Erin was quite sure that she had been intentionally provoking Bo Biggles.

Since then, Beaver had become a part of Bald Eagles Falls life when she wasn't on duty. She spent a lot of time in the city with her job with whatever government agency it was she worked for. Erin thought it was the DEA, but it could have been the FBI or another agency. Beaver had never been forthcoming about it.

Beaver had her secrets.

Erin leaned down to look in the window at Beaver. "I was expecting Terry… is he okay?"

"He was feeling a little under the weather, so I told him I'd buzz by and pick you up. Don't worry—I haven't had any accidents recently." She chewed a mouthful of gum, grinning at Erin and Vic.

Erin shook her head. She opened the door behind Beaver and Vic went around to the other side, sitting down in Beaver's passenger seat. The interior of the car smelled strongly of Beaver's usual brand of gum, her deodorant, and a mixture of other smells that Erin associated with her. She clearly spent a lot of time in her car. Driving to wherever her bosses were based to make reports? Sitting on surveillance for hours on end? Making phone inquiries and tracking suspects through social media? Whatever it was Beaver spent her time doing, clearly a lot of it was spent in the car. Erin pulled her seatbelt across her body.

"Terry said he wasn't feeling well?" He wouldn't usually discuss how he felt with anyone other than Erin, and even she had to pry it out of him sometimes.

"It was pretty obvious that he wasn't feeling well. He didn't say so in as many words," Beaver admitted. "But I told him I wanted to pick you up today, since I haven't seen you for a while, and he agreed. That in itself would have told me he's not himself today."

Erin sighed. Beaver had hit the nail on the head. Terry would normally have insisted that he be the one to pick Erin up. He wouldn't want anyone else to take it over. "I hope he's not too bad."

"Did he work today?" Vic inquired.

"Yeah. Morning shift. I prefer he takes afternoons because he's not as likely to stay on for a full shift instead of a half shift. Did he work the full day?" she asked Beaver.

"I don't think so. I was over there mid-afternoon and he was home."

Erin was quiet for the rest of the drive home. She didn't want to discuss Terry too much. Talking about his health, mental or physical, when he wasn't there seemed like a betrayal of confidence. Beaver and Vic were just concerned about how he felt, the same as Erin. They weren't the type who would gossip about him around town. But she still needed to observe some boundaries.

Beaver pulled in front of Erin's house with a slight squeal of tires and a stop that threw them all forward against their seatbelts. Erin looked up and saw Beaver watching her in the rear-view mirror. Erin shook her head.

"I should tell Officer Piper to keep an eye on you. Reckless driving. You could get a ticket, you know."

Beaver chuckled. "It wouldn't be the first one." She reached over in front of Vic to click open the glovebox, where Erin saw a stack of ragged papers. Were those all traffic tickets, or was Beaver just teasing?

"How are you going to pay all of those?"

"I am not. Any tickets I incur in the course of my job will just disappear." Beaver made a 'vanishing' gesture with her fingers like a magician.

Erin released her seatbelt and got out of the car. "You are a menace."

"Yes, ma'am," Beaver agreed. She got out of the car.

Erin glanced at her as they walked up to the house. She had expected Beaver to drop her at the curb, not to escort her in or stay to visit. Erin didn't want to be rude and tell Beaver that if Terry wasn't feeling well, she shouldn't impose on him. Beaver should have been able to figure that out herself.

The door had been left unlocked. Erin pushed the door open and Beaver followed her into the house.

Terry was leaning his head forward, a cold pack across the back of his head and neck. Erin went to him and touched him on the arm briefly. "Bad today?"

He grunted. "I've had worse."

"Beaver is here."

Terry turned his head to look at their visitor, then returned his head to its previous position and closed his eyes. "What is it, Beaver?"

Beaver sat down on one of the chairs. Erin sat down beside Terry, picking up a noisy Orange Blossom who was trying to get her attention and share all of the details of his day with her. She cuddled him and scratched his ears, but didn't talk to him like she would have if they had been alone. Not because Beaver would have thought that there was anything wrong with it. But it didn't seem very dignified to talk to her cat like a baby in front of a visitor. Other than Vic or Terry, who had heard it plenty of times before.

"I've been hearing some chatter," Beaver began.

"About what?" Erin demanded immediately, the words getting out of her mouth before she'd had a chance to think about them. "Campbell? Theresa?"

Beaver gave Erin a thoughtful look before turning back toward Terry. "I would like to have a better fix on where Theresa Franklin is right now, but that was not what I was talking about."

Terry waited.

"What, then?" Erin prompted. She wanted to get Beaver out of there as quickly as she could to take care of Terry.

"About your latest body."

CHAPTER 20

"My latest body? It's not *my* body!"

"Maybe not, but you have a knack for stumbling across them."

Erin looked for an argument, but couldn't find one. Beaver watched her, chewing her gum slowly. Then she turned her attention back to Terry, though he wasn't looking at her, eyes closed as he iced his neck and head.

"I'm sure lots of people are talking about it," Erin admitted. They came to talk to her at the bakery and they quieted when she walked into a room. They couldn't have been much more obvious. "So that's not news."

"There is no news yet. Not… official news."

"What, then?"

"The initial examination suggests that Ms. Batcombe was dead before she was placed in the freezer."

Erin's eyes went wide and she felt the blood drain out of her face. Terry's arm went around behind her back and pulled her firmly against his side.

"She didn't die in the freezer?" he demanded. "Then, how?"

"A finding hasn't been made yet. I'll hear when it is. But the bottom line is… that body didn't walk into the freezer room on its own."

Erin put her hand down on Terry's leg and squeezed it tightly, trying to anchor herself to him.

"How do they know that? If the postmortem isn't done yet, how would they know she didn't die in there?"

"There are ways of telling when a body has been moved after death. Lividity, for one. You didn't move her, right? According to all of the witness statements, you kept well back after the discovery."

"Yes. I mean, no, I didn't touch her or move her. I stayed back and kept everyone out."

Beaver nodded as if this were what she had expected. Erin had seen enough crime scenes to know to keep back and not touch anything. When she touched things, it just made her interactions with the police during the investigation much more difficult. She wanted to stay below the cops' radar. She didn't want to be treated as a suspect.

Been there, done that.

"How did she die, then?" Terry questioned, not looking up. "No signs of violence?"

"Nothing obvious. But that doesn't mean they won't find anything in the post. Maybe she'd had too much to drink. An allergic reaction. A heart attack. Anything is possible."

"If she had just had an accident or dropped dead… then who would move her?"

"Yeah," Beaver acknowledged. "Exactly. If she didn't die in the freezer, then who moved her into the freezer, and why?"

Erin tried to think of an innocent reason someone might have done that. She couldn't think of anything. If someone had found her dead or had been with her when she died, he should have just called the police or ambulance. There was no innocent reason Erin could think of to move the body.

"Have you heard anything through the grapevine?" Beaver asked Erin. "From the other judges or officials? Anyone who is entering something into the contest?"

"No. We've had our initial orientation—or started it, anyway—but we haven't had much of a chance to talk and exchange opinions. I just know Vic, and she didn't know any more than I did about Beryl."

"Someone else associated with the contest must have known her."

"Yes… whoever picked her as a judge. Anyone who has lived here long enough to know her or her family. The officials must have been given packages on each of us. Biographies or CV's."

"Did the chef know her?"

"I don't think so. I only know him from the cruise, not because he's from these parts. He didn't say that he was here to see anyone else or had picked out the location because he knew someone here."

"Just you."

Erin's face heated again. She looked over at Terry, but he didn't look up, in the grips of his headache.

"Not just me. Vic too. And Terry and Willie."

"But you're the one he came for. You and he became friends on the cruise, cooked together. Isn't that the history?"

"Yes," Erin agreed reluctantly. She didn't want to think that he had come to Tennessee just for her. He'd had other reasons for picking Whitewater as the location for the contest to be held. He hadn't picked Bald Eagle Falls. If he'd been there just for Erin, he would have picked Bald Eagle Falls, wouldn't he? Maybe he had known Beryl. Maybe they had a history and he'd chosen Whitewater because of her. Erin and Vic had just been a bonus. Erin rubbed the bridge of her nose. She was getting a headache too, worried about being in the middle of another murder investigation.

"Maybe Chef Kirschoff knew Beryl. I don't know."

Beaver nodded slowly, chewing her gum all the time. "You gave a statement to the police in Whitewater?"

"Yes. Of course."

"You can expect that they'll be calling you back."

"I already told them everything I know. Which was next to nothing. I can't help it that I was the one who found her. Don't you think that if I had done something to harm her, I would have stayed away from that cold room? I would have been the last person in the room instead of the first one. It was just a freak accident. A random chance."

"A normal person might have avoided being the first one to open the door. Someone who was thinking and acting logically might have been the last one in instead of the first. But a psychopath might have. An adrenaline junkie would have for sure. There are all kinds of aberrant personalities who would have reveled in being the first in the room and telling the police about it."

"You know me. That's not what I'm like."

"I know more about you than you would probably like," Beaver said.

"But what a person appears to be and what they are inside isn't always the same. You have a checkered past. And ever since you moved to Bald Eagle Falls, you've been stumbling into crime scenes." She raised her brows. "*That's* not normal."

Erin's mouth was dry. Her stomach was knotted with anxiety. She counted Beaver as a friend, but the woman had always been an enigma. She liked to make trouble. She liked to cause waves. She was probably just provoking Erin to see if she could get a good reaction. She couldn't *really* think that Erin had anything to do with any of the crime in Bald Eagle Falls or the area. She was just teasing.

"Beaver." Terry lifted the ice pack off of the back of his neck and glared at her. "Leave Erin alone."

Beaver grinned her wide, open-mouthed grin. She was having the time of her life. "I'm just following up on what I heard."

"Leave her be. You know she didn't have anything to do with this."

"Know? No." Beaver stood up slowly. She took a couple of steps toward the door. "I don't think she did. But I'm not one to jump to conclusions. We'll see where the evidence points."

"All of the cases that Erin has had any involvement in have been solved. She hasn't been guilty of anything. Except maybe asking too many questions and not staying out of an investigation when she's told to. Poor judgment, but nothing criminal."

Beaver nodded, then raised a hand in a wave and left.

Erin shook her head. She was actually shaking. "You know I didn't have anything to do with that woman's death."

"Of course I do." Terry put the ice pack back on his neck, then grimaced. "This is too warm to do any good anymore."

Erin got unsteadily to her feet. "Give that one to me and I'll get another one out."

She swapped the warmed-up ice pack with one from the freezer. She handed it to Terry, thinking of Beryl's body in the freezer as she did so.

CHAPTER 21

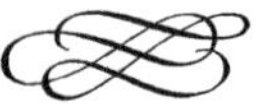

Beaver had not shared her thoughts or the fact that Beryl's body had been moved with anyone else. Erin didn't have to put up with the questions of curious townspeople speculating about who had moved the body and why. If word got out, she was sure she wouldn't have been able to get a moment's peace and quiet.

So she kept her head down and her ears open. Whatever had happened to Beryl, it was bound to leak out sooner or later. People were always gossiping about police reports in Bald Eagle Falls, even if they didn't know the actual contents themselves. Speculating was fair game. And sometimes, someone knew something they shouldn't and ended up giving himself away.

"Erin." Vic tapped her arm.

Erin reined in her attention. She looked around the bakery, feeling like she had been absent for the previous half hour. What had happened? What had she done? Who had she talked to?

Several of Vic's friends were there. Erin had clearly been blanking them out, focused on her own thoughts and worries.

"Um, sorry? What?"

"Jack is really good with cars."

Erin looked at Vic blankly. "Okay…"

"I wondered if you wanted to go car shopping this weekend. It's the last weekend we have before the contest, and you thought it would be good to have your own car to get around in Whitewater and not have to rely on anyone else's."

"Yeah." Erin had forgotten about that conversation. So much else had been going on that it had completely escaped her mind. "We had talked about that. But I don't think there's enough time now. I haven't done any research. I would need to line up a bunch of different possibilities, and then research each of the cars, and its performance and safety ratings. And then there's financing and negotiating..."

"You don't need to finance. You've got the money in the bank. And I was just saying, Jack is really good with cars. They can help you to find one. Something really good. So you don't have to do all of that research. They can just look at the paper this weekend, and pull a few cars that look good, and they can come with us to look and give it a test drive."

Erin looked at Vic's friends, trying to pick out the one called Jack. "That's a really nice offer, but..."

"Happy to help." Jack said with a smile.

"You must have other things you'd rather be doing this weekend. Aren't you entered in the contest? You'll want to be perfecting your recipe..."

"My recipe is all ready to go. No worries there. Don't you want the help?" Jack was beginning to look a little affronted.

"I just wasn't planning on doing anything that fast. I know we talked about doing it before the contest, but I don't want to rush into anything. And I don't have that much time. We need to get ready for the contest ourselves..."

Vic shook her head. "We don't need to do anything to get ready. We've got a couple of events, but we can work around that."

"Charley has been planning all of this other stuff. I really don't think I can spare the time..."

"You told Charley that she had to be in charge of it herself. She's the one who needs to put the time into it. You gave her your guidance. She can call on you with questions, but you told her she has to be the one taking care of things."

"I know. But you know Charley, she's going to need to be bailed out."

"Not literally this time, I hope."

"That's not funny."

Vic peered at Erin, then decided maybe she had pushed it too far. "Okay, sorry. Didn't mean to hurt your feelings. But I mean… the way that you and Charley originally met…"

"We met because I was looking for her. Not because of… all of that."

Jack was looking back and forth between them. "Well? Does that mean we go ahead and do it? Come on. I'd like to help out. And I need to get my hands greasy. I'm going into automobile withdrawal, here."

Erin sighed. She wasn't going to get out of it by being polite. If she really wanted to tell Jack no, she would have to do so bluntly and risk offending.

"Okay, maybe. Take a look at the paper when it comes out and see if there is anything that looks really good. Midrange, I don't want to pay too much. Not an old beater…" She ignored the way Vic rolled her eyes. She already knew how Vic had felt about her previous car. The one that was no more. "But not something luxury, either. Just… a good 'mom' car, easy to drive, good gas mileage…"

Jack smiled. "Excellent. I'll take a look and let you know. I'm sure I can find you something."

"Maybe. I'm not rushing into it, so if it isn't the right time… I'll just work something out with Terry. He'll let me use his while we're in Whitewater."

Erin hadn't heard anything back from Charley about the events and budget that she had approved. She'd expected Charley to be back to her half a dozen times on little things that she wanted Erin's advice or experience on. Not because Charley couldn't be self-sufficient and independent, but because they were partners in the business and Charley wanted to make sure that Erin was fully involved and didn't disapprove of Charley's ideas. It wouldn't look good for them to be on the outs. People would talk and the bakery would lose business.

But Charley had been working away on her own and hadn't gone back to Erin with questions or problems, and that made her nervous, waiting for the other shoe to drop. Sooner or later, Charley would come to Erin with a problem, and the closer it got to the contest date, the more sure Erin was that it would end up derailing everything.

She decided to be proactive and to call Charley and discuss matters with her. If there were any issues, it was best to get them out in the open right away, before they ended up getting blown out of proportion. She tapped Charley's contact picture on the phone and waited for the call to connect.

Charley answered in a couple of rings. "Erin. Hi, how are things coming along?"

"Things are fine on my end, but I don't have a bunch of stuff to plan. How about you? How are your events coming along?"

"Really good. I've been working closely with Chef Kirschoff, and things are really coming together."

"Oh..." That came as a surprise. "Well, that's really good. Chef Kirschoff liked our ideas? He's willing to endorse everything?"

"Yeah. He came up with some really good ways of doing some of them."

"That's great."

"I'm meeting him at lunch today. Why don't you join us, and we can go over anything you're worried about."

Erin felt like she had suddenly been changed from the role of a parent to that of a child. Charley didn't need her to provide any information or advice. Instead, Charley was suggesting that she could bring Erin up to speed and solve any problems she might have. Erin looked around the bakery. Bella was coming on at noon and could help Vic to cover the rush. Erin had left space in her schedule in case she had to rescue Charley, so she had the resources available.

"Yeah, I guess so. That would work fine. Where are you meeting? Chinese?"

"No, the family restaurant. Hans wanted to try it out."

Hans. Charley was calling him by his first name. As if Chef Kirschoff wasn't a world-famous master chef, but just a guy from down the street. Erin gritted her teeth. He had told her to call him Hans. They were friends now. Charley wasn't taking liberties.

"At noon?"

"Yeah. Can you make it?"

Maybe Charley was hoping that Erin wouldn't be able to make it, knowing that they normally had a rush over the lunch hour. "Yes. I can be there."

"Great," Charley responded, sounding surprised. "I'll see you there."

~

Erin still felt a little guilty leaving Bella and Vic to handle the noon-hour rush, but Vic shooed her away, assuring her that they were up to the task. They certainly didn't need three people to handle a shift that was normally covered by two. Erin would just be underfoot if she stayed to try to help. So she gave herself a stern talking to and got on her way.

She didn't have Terry's truck, so she walked over to the family restaurant. It was only a few blocks, not a hardship, especially in the winter, when the weather was pleasant. It wouldn't have been so easy in the sweltering heat of the summer.

Kirschoff and Charley were at the restaurant already. Erin felt like a third wheel joining them, but she had been invited. Hans stood up to greet her exuberantly, shaking her hand with two hands, then hugging her and bussing both cheeks. He sat back down, smiling widely at her. Charley nodded a greeting, not nearly as effusive.

"Hey, Erin. Glad you could make it."

"Yeah. I'm glad you guys are meeting and sorting things out. That's great."

"Your sister has some excellent ideas," Chef Kirschoff offered. "I'm glad that she got involved."

Erin nodded. And she had to admit he was right. Even without any time to organize anything, Charley had been able to come up with half a dozen ideas that piggybacked off of the already-planned events, good ways to get the name and brand of Auntie Clem's Bakery into the event. And of course, Erin's and Vic's biographies would be published in all of the event materials and read at the beginning of the judging. It would be good publicity for the bakery. She was glad that the contest was still going ahead, even if she felt a little guilty about carrying on as if there hadn't been an untimely death marring the event.

"Did you have any questions? Or have you and Charley already sorted everything out?"

"I think we have most of it covered," Kirschoff said. He patted Charley's hand. "Charley has been very helpful."

The look that Charley returned was more than friendly. She clasped

Kirschoff's hand in return, smiling sweetly. "I couldn't have done any of it without Hans."

"And, of course, with the approval of Auntie Clem's Bakery," Kirschoff added, nodding at Erin to include her in all of the accolades.

"Oh, this has all been Charley," Erin said, her face a mask as she tried to keep her smile pinned in place. "Charley was the one who came up with the ideas and has been coordinating everything. All I did was approve the budget and the branding. The broad strokes."

They looked at their menus and discussed Tennessee family cooking, Erin and Charley interpreting anything obscure on the menu for Chef Kirschoff.

"Charming, just charming," he murmured, reading through it. "I'm glad I made time in my schedule to come here."

"You've never been in Tennessee before?" Charley asked. "You fit right in. I never would have guessed."

Kirschoff laughed heartily. "An old European like me? I don't think so. But thank you anyway! It's too bad that it's only soda pop and ice cream. I've been getting as much local color as I could since I arrived, but there could have been so much more if it had been an actual cook-off instead of a 'cool off.'"

"Some of the ice cream and coke flavors will have a Tennessee twist," Charley offered. "I've heard about some of the creations that are being planned, and you'll still get some classic Tennessee flavors."

Kirschoff nodded. They waved the waitress over and placed their orders.

Erin noticed that when Kirschoff and Charley removed their hands from the top of the table where they had been fully visible, they reconnected underneath the table.

Charley had certainly moved in quickly. It would seem that they were well on their way to a relationship.

Erin couldn't object. After all, she had Terry and wasn't looking for someone else. But she couldn't help feeling a little twinge about Charley stealing her friend. Kirschoff wasn't even Charley's type. She should have just left him alone.

CHAPTER 22

The first big event was the science fair. Erin hadn't been sure what to expect from it. She'd never heard of a science fair being held in connection with a cook-off before. But when she walked into the auditorium of the Whitewater school, she realized that it had been an inspired idea.

The carbon dioxide themed cook-off was a great basis for a science fair. Erin started to walk through the exhibits, seeing projects based around respiration, plants, aquariums, pollution, and of course, food preparation.

The science fair covered the whole range of ages. It wasn't just for the school kids, though a number of the exhibits had obviously been created by children. She saw a baking soda and vinegar volcano ready to be demonstrated. She stopped at another with colorful Pop Rocks on display.

The little girl with round glasses and a long pinafore dress gazed up at her.

"What do Pop Rocks have to do with carbon dioxide?" Erin asked.

The little girl pushed up her glasses with one finger. "Pop Rocks are infused with carbon dioxide at high pressure," she explained, "so it gets trapped inside the candy. When you put Pop Rocks in your mouth or water, then that's what the fizzing and popping come from. The candy melts, releasing the pockets of carbon dioxide."

"Really!" Erin was amazed. "Who knew! I thought it was just a chemical reaction." She motioned to the baking soda volcano. "That when something in the Pop Rocks gets wet, there's a chemical reaction that makes it pop. I never realized that there was anything trapped inside!"

The little girl smiled proudly. She motioned to the tiny cups with a few Pop Rocks in the bottom of each. "There are free samples if you would like some."

Erin thought it would be rude to refuse them after stopping to talk, so she picked up a cup of purple rocks and spilled them into her mouth. They popped loudly, making her and the girl both laugh.

Erin went on through the various exhibits. She reached the end of the children's displays and studied the more complex adult exhibits. She stopped at some kind of machine with a pressurized tank and twisting tubes that looked like something out of a steampunk story or mad scientist movie.

"What exactly is this?"

The man at the display moved closer to her. He was tall and thin with dark hair and a small mustache. "This is a DIY carbonator," he explained. "I will be using this to make my entry for the contest."

"You can carbonate drinks with this?"

"Of course."

"It's so big! I've seen the little table-top ones that you can buy at the store to use at home. And the big square ones that restaurants use. But I've never seen anything like this."

"It's basically the same thing as the restaurant ones, if you strip off the outer box, it all comes down to the same thing, a way to add carbon dioxide to your flavored syrup. You need a tank and tubes."

Erin nodded. "I guess. This looks really cool, though. And dangerous."

"It's not dangerous. No more so than your barbecue. You turn it on and off. Make sure everything is properly sealed and that it isn't near any heat sources. Nothing is going to happen."

"So, you're registered for the contest?"

"Yes. You're in for a treat."

Erin was surprised that he recognized her as one of the judges, but she supposed she shouldn't be. Her picture and bio were in the literature and the organizers had been making announcements on the TV and radio. They name-dropped whenever they could.

"Well… I'll look forward to it, Mr.…."

He whipped out a business card and handed it to her. "John Slayer," he offered. "Flavorista extraordinaire!"

Erin smiled, taking the card from him. "Very nice to meet you. That's a really interesting machine."

"Thank you! I look forward to tickling your taste buds!"

Erin was glad that the judging was done blind. She would have a tough time judging which sodas and ice creams she liked best if she knew who had made each one.

Erin reached the end of the aisle and noticed a group of parents and youths standing a few yards away, watching her and talking. She tried to ignore the stares, assuming they were looking at one of the exhibits behind her. She recognized some of them as being from Bald Eagle Falls. Occasional customers or families she had met through the Christmas fundraiser at the school. Erin headed over to the water station to get herself a drink, which brought her closer to the little group.

"Got to watch her with the children," someone murmured, loudly enough for Erin to hear even with the noise of the auditorium. "She acts friendly and then takes advantage of them."

Erin's eyes snapped to the speaker, one of the parents from Bald Eagle Falls. The woman, a tired-looking woman in her late thirties, stared back at Erin, making no attempt at hiding the fact that she had noticed Erin's attention.

"I thought she could be trusted," someone else said. "But it turns out she's just looking out for her own interests. And her friends'."

They had to be talking about someone else. It was only coincidence that the tired woman happened to be looking in Erin's direction. Erin would never have done anything to take advantage of a child. Nor was she in the habit of choosing her own interests over those of others. She always tried to respect and help others, especially the little ones.

They were talking about someone else. Probably someone who wasn't even there. Who Erin didn't even know.

"First she says she's an atheist, then she shows up at church," another mother contributed. "I bet she's been lying this whole time, just because she doesn't want to be called out for being a bad Christian."

Erin blinked at this. They couldn't very well be talking about anyone else. Bald Eagle Falls wasn't exactly overflowing with atheists. Not those who would admit it, anyway. And not people who claimed to be atheists and then went to the candlelight service on Christmas Eve.

They could only be talking about her.

Erin froze where she was, trying to figure out what to do. Pretend she hadn't heard them? Defend herself? Try to find some way to explain and make them understand her actions? Let them know that she had heard them, but then ignore them?

They weren't going to understand, no matter how much she tried to explain. They could only understand their own belief system and didn't think that anyone could fall outside it. Anyone who professed otherwise was simply lying.

Erin continued on her way to the water station, out of earshot of the little huddle of parents and youths, and drank the lukewarm water from a paper cup while she thought about it.

She was used to people not understanding her lack of religious beliefs. She got that. People who believed just didn't understand how anyone could not believe. Her attendance at the church service with Terry confused people. It would pass as real life and genuine concerns took over.

The assertion that she would take advantage of the children she was friends with hurt. She would never do anything to harm them.

Mrs. Foster wouldn't let her see Peter anymore because Erin had reported what he had said to the police. Mary Lou was upset with her for mentioning Joshua to Terry, which had resulted in his falling under suspicion and being questioned as part of their investigation. No harm had come to either child. Their parents didn't like falling under police scrutiny, but she had kept the children safe, not vice versa.

"Hi, Erin!" Melissa broke through Erin's dark thoughts, getting into her personal space and smiling at her, her wild dark curls bouncing. "Everything okay?"

Erin took a small step back, giving herself a little more space. "Yeah. Everything is fine," she said, her voice a little wobbly. She looked over at the knot of parents, still talking to each other. About her? Or had they gone on to something else now?

Melissa followed her gaze. She understood immediately. "People will look for any excuse not to make their kids accountable for what they did," she told Erin. "They'd rather blame anyone else than admit that their kids were involved in something illegal, something that hurt a lot of people in Bald Eagle Falls."

"I was trying to keep people safe. To stop the burglaries."

"And you did. You did the right thing, whether all of those people like it or not," Melissa assured her.

"But how could they be mad at me instead of at the people who were breaking the law and hurting others?"

"Because that would mean that they had to take responsibility for what their own kids did."

Erin shook her head. "I got in plenty of trouble as a kid… none of my foster parents ever had any trouble putting the responsibility squarely on my shoulders." Maybe even a bit too much, blaming her for things that she hadn't done or that they themselves had contributed to.

"Well, good for them. That's what they should do. But some parents…" Melissa scowled at the group, "they're always looking for excuses."

They could see that Erin and Melissa were talking about them, though Erin was sure they couldn't hear what was being said. Melissa wasn't exactly covert with her looks.

"How long is this going to go on?"

Melissa shrugged. "I don't know. Some of those kids will get off with probation and community service, but some of them are going to go to prison. I don't imagine that will make people too happy."

Erin broke out in goosebumps. She sipped at her warm water, her skin crawling. How many parents were going to be watching her, waiting for a chance to get back at her for turning the investigation on their children? If their kids went to prison, they weren't likely to forget Erin's part in the arrests.

On TV, when people solved murders or other crimes, there were never any negative consequences. It was always a "happily ever after," with the bad guys being shipped off to jail and the rest of the town happily going about their business. Erin couldn't think of a single mystery series where the person who had helped solve the mystery was ostracized for her part in the arrests.

But she'd known from the beginning that it wasn't a TV show. TV show sleuths never got PTSD from the violence they witnessed, either.

"Just ignore them, Erin," Melissa advised. "Never let people like that bother you. You know you did the right thing."

Erin nodded slowly. "That doesn't make it feel any better, though." She looked at the group. "Maybe I should pull out of judging the competition. I don't really want… the more I'm at the center of attention, the angrier people are going to be about it. And who knows what they might say or do."

"Don't pull out. Don't let people like that dictate your actions."

Erin sighed and looked away. "Does it ever feel like no matter what you do, people aren't going to like it? That there's always going to be a negative consequence no matter how right the decision seems?"

Melissa patted Erin on the back.

CHAPTER 23

Erin left the school auditorium with a feeling of relief. She breathed in the cool, crisp air and felt like she had just walked out of prison. She was supposed to be meeting Vic and Willie for lunch, and Terry if he felt well enough and was able to make it. There wasn't much opportunity for Erin to go anywhere but the few Bald Eagle Falls restaurants to eat, so it was nice to have a new place to try out. The Whitewater BBQ joint was supposed to be really good and she was looking forward to trying it out, despite feeling depressed about how some of the people of Bald Eagle Falls now hated her.

She looked around the restaurant and spotted Willie. Not hard to pick out his dark face, stained by the mining and processing of minerals from his mines. He got a lot of looks from people who thought he must be some dirty, homeless guy. But he wasn't. He was hardworking and the processing left a stain on his skin that couldn't be washed out by any amount of scrubbing.

Erin sat down with him. "Hi, Willie."

"Erin." He gave a friendly nod. "How are you this fine day?"

"Oh..." Erin tried not to let her mood show too much. "It's been a bit stressful, but I'm fine."

He studied her for a moment. "I'd hope that something like this contest would be fun and exciting, but I'm sure there's a lot of stress that goes with it. So much to be done, being in the spotlight, knowing there are deadlines."

"Yeah. All of that," Erin agreed. She didn't tell him about the parents from Bald Eagle Falls. If anyone knew how judgmental people could be there, it was Willie. He always had people looking down at him, commenting on him being lazy, shiftless, and an outsider. Nothing could be further from the truth.

"And then there's finding bodies," Willie continued. "That always puts a crimp in the festivities."

"One body," Erin said firmly. "Just one. And she was..." Erin wasn't sure what she had started off to say. Beryl wasn't anyone Erin knew? She wasn't murdered, had just wandered in there and died on her own? No one seemed to like her very much anyway? Erin let her words die away. "I don't know. I'm trying not to think about it. To let it bother me."

"That's probably a good plan. You don't want to get yourself into something—" He left the sentence as if it were unfinished. Maybe he'd planned to say 'again'?

Erin eyed him, but he looked innocently back at her as if he didn't know what she was thinking.

"Yeah. I'll just leave it to the police," Erin said flatly.

A woman sitting at a nearby table turned and looked at her, maybe overhearing the phrase and wanting to know what excitement was going on, what it was that the police needed to be called about. She looked at Erin for a moment and then smiled.

"You're Erin Price, aren't you? One of the judges?"

"Yes. I am." Erin studied the slim, attractive redhead with freckles across her nose and cheeks. "Are you a contestant?"

"Yes! I'm really excited about the contest. I would tell you all about what I'm making, but I know we're not supposed to talk about it, especially to the judges. But I have this old family recipe that is really fantastic, it is going to blow you away. Really. It's that good."

Erin smiled and nodded politely. "I'm sure it will," she agreed. "But a lot of people have delicious family recipes. Or new ones. There's a lot of competition."

"Trust me, you'll be seeing this face again." The woman pointed at her own face and drew a circle around it in the air. "I'm Daisy Forsythe."

"It's a pleasure to meet you," Erin told her. She turned her face slightly toward Willie, hoping that Daisy would take the hint and let her continue with her private conversation. Daisy looked at her for another minute, then went back to conversing with the two teen girls at her table.

"You're a celebrity," Willie noted.

Erin glanced around. Vic wasn't there yet, and should have been there ahead of Erin. There was no sign of Terry, but Erin hadn't been sure whether to expect him. She knew that he might not feel like getting into the truck to drive that far, just to have lunch with her. The vibration, noise, and bouncing of the truck tended to aggravate his head. And then there were the crowded conditions and noise of the restaurant. If it were too much for him, he might not be able to make it back home. She slid her phone out to have a look at it and see if either Terry or Vic had texted her. There was a brief message from Vic that she was running late and would be there as soon as she could be.

Erin sighed. "Well, we might as well order. I don't think Terry is going to make it and Vic is running late."

Willie looked at Erin for a moment, then nodded. "All right," he grumbled. "I guess we're on our own."

They motioned for the waitress and placed their orders. Even though Willie hadn't said anything to indicate that he was upset, Erin sensed from his curt manner that he wasn't too happy.

"Sorry neither of the others could make it."

Willie scratched his neck. "At least I've got good company. Officer Piper has a good excuse for not being here. I know he's still having health issues."

"I'm sure Vic has a good reason for being late too."

He shook his head. "She's off with that group of hers. The folks from the boat."

"Still… we don't know what has kept them. There could be a good explanation."

Willie didn't suggest one. Erin had a hard time coming up with one herself. Of course, it was possible that someone's car had broken down. Or someone had fallen ill and had to be taken to the hospital. But other than that, she couldn't really think of a good reason for Vic to be late for their planned lunch. She had known about it ahead of time and should have told her new group of friends that she would need to split at lunchtime.

"She's still coming," Erin pointed out. "She'll be here soon."

Willie raised an eyebrow and didn't argue. Erin knew that like her, Willie didn't particularly like Vic's new friends, or at least the time that she spent with them.

There was no reason Vic couldn't have her own group of friends that she didn't share with either of them, but Erin couldn't help feeling like she had been abandoned when Vic had things to do that didn't involve their little Bald Eagle Falls family.

They had been through so much together, Erin felt unaccountably resentful of Vic having another life.

~

Vic breezed in half an hour later, not by herself, but surrounded by her giggling, chattering friends. She gave a big wave across the restaurant and she and her friends moved in to join Willie and Erin, dragging tables and chairs over to form a big seating group. She had Nilla, the little white dog with her, and Erin braced for an argument from management telling her that she couldn't bring a dog into the restaurant. But Vic got Nilla settled under the table by her feet, and the waitress pretended not to notice him as she got their drink orders.

"He's been kind of cranky today," Vic said, seeing the direction of Erin's gaze. "I don't know if he's missing Beryl or if we just tired him out, but he has been kind of snappish. Maybe he doesn't like large groups."

Erin bit her lip. "Hey, I thought we were going to…"

"Where's Terry?" Vic asked. "He couldn't make it?"

"No. I guess he's not feeling up to it. I thought you were going to ditch us too."

"I wouldn't do that! We just got held up. Things took longer than we expected." Vic looked around at the others. "Do you guys want actual meals? I'm not hungry after everything else we've had. I thought maybe just share some appetizers?"

"Or desserts," Melanie suggested, her white teeth gleaming against her dark complexion. "I wouldn't mind something sweet."

"Mmm, not for me." Vic shook her head. "I've got sugary drinks and desserts coming up in a week." She looked at Erin. "I should probably watch my calories until then."

"And deep-fried appetizers are better?" Melanie countered.

"Well..." Vic opened the menu she had grabbed as they walked in and scanned the appetizers. "There are a few things that wouldn't be too bad. Bruschetta. Veggies with dip. What do you guys want?"

There was some discussion and, eventually, they settled on a couple of appetizers to share. They continued to chatter among themselves, not involving Erin and Willie in the conversation, which centered around the places they had already visited and any other sightseeing that was still on their lists. When their appetizers arrived, they quieted, giving their attention to the food.

"Oh, Erin," Jack touched Erin's arm. "I know we didn't find anything for you before this weekend, but I found some car listings in the city that you might be interested in looking at today or tomorrow. Some pretty good opportunities. Do you want to have a look at them together?"

Erin shook her head. "I have a lot of things to get done this weekend. I don't think I'll have the time."

"You shouldn't let them slide. I think we could put you in a car that you'd be really happy with."

"We?"

Jack laughed. "I sound like a car salesman, don't I? Sorry! I get in the habit of talking that way to clients. I don't mean to presume!"

"I don't think I have the time to do anything until the contest is over. Really. It's going to keep me really busy, and I don't want my attention to be divided with another responsibility."

"Vic can find the time to go out with us, and you both have the same job, don't you?" Jack challenged.

Erin closed her eyes and took a deep breath. She opened them and looked at Vic, signaling for her to deal with it. For a moment, Vic didn't say anything, raising an eyebrow at Erin to see if she would answer herself. When Erin didn't, Vic finally spoke up.

"Erin does have other responsibilities too. She's the owner of the bakery, so even though she's away, there is still work that needs to be done and things that need to be managed. And Terry, her partner, he's still suffering from a head injury. So there's that." She paused, waiting to see if Erin would fill anything else in. Because obviously, those things were not taking up a lot of Erin's time. She just didn't want to go car shopping with Jack.

"I thought that other woman was the owner of the bakery?" Melanie put in.

Erin looked at her. "Who?" Her thoughts went immediately to Beryl. As far as she knew, Beryl Batcombe did not own a bakery. Still, Erin's mind flashed back to the death of Angela Plaint, the former owner of The Bake Shoppe, which would have been Erin's competition, if Angela hadn't been killed or if Charley had decided to go ahead with her plan to run The Bake Shoppe herself. For some reason, Beryl's and Angela's deaths became intertwined in her mind.

But Beryl's death had been an accident and she wasn't a bakery owner.

"We saw Charley earlier," Vic explained, seeing Erin's look of confusion. "That's who she means."

"Oh. Yes, Charley and I are partners in Auntie Clem's Bakery."

"And she's the one getting all cozy with Chef Kirschoff, right?" Melanie persisted. "She's taking care of all of the activities associated with the competition."

Getting cozy with Kirschoff? Erin flashed a look at Vic, who gave a shrug. "They were looking pretty… friendly," she admitted.

"I told Charley not to get involved with him!"

Clayton raised an eyebrow at Erin, interested.

"Why not?" Melanie put in. "What does it matter who he is interested in? As long as it's not a contest entrant, it doesn't make any difference. You have a man, don't you?"

"Who says she can only have one?" Jack challenged.

Erin felt her eyes widen. She shook her head. "Yes, I have a… partner already. And I'm not looking for another one. But the two of them… Chef Kirschoff isn't Charley's type. Charley will just end up getting bored with him, breaking up and hurting his feelings. I don't want her to… upset him. Mess up his life."

"You've got a good opinion of your co-owner." Melanie shook her head. "Everybody gets jammed up sometimes. We'll all end up in relationships that don't work out. If she's happy with him and he's happy with her, then just leave it alone and see what works out. Unless," she gave a nod in Jack's direction, "you already have an understanding with Chef Kirschoff."

"Or unless he has one with someone else," Clayton contributed.

"No. It isn't like that." Erin took a drink, trying to hide her embarrassment. "I just don't think it's a good idea."

Melanie shrugged. "Then let them make their mistakes. That's the way life goes."

CHAPTER 24

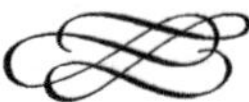

Erin had been planning to spend most of the afternoon relaxing, despite her claim that she was far too busy for car shopping.

And maybe she shouldn't have lied and made out that she couldn't spend any time car shopping that weekend. Maybe it was the universe getting back at her for breaking the rules. Though Erin didn't believe in karma or in universal rules.

She was walking from the restaurant to the hotel to have a nap or spend some time just browsing the web for new recipes or spending some time on social media. She didn't see Deputy Coleman until he was right in front of her. They stopped just a few feet away from each other, Coleman holding his hand up in a tentative signal to stop.

"What? Oh, Deputy Coleman. Sorry, I was off in my own little world. Can I… help you with something?"

She knew better than to ask a cop that. She really did.

"Well, I was actually hoping for the chance to have a further conversation with you. Do you have some time now to come talk to me?"

"Uh… I was just going back to my hotel…"

"I figured I'd probably find you here this weekend, attending to more business with our little contest."

"Yeah. There's lots to be done for a contest like this." Which wasn't quite true, because Erin wasn't actually taking care of any of the organizational details as she implied. She had a few commitments, but mostly the contest organizers and sponsors just wanted her to be seen around town and for her to actually participate in the judging the week after that.

"So is there any chance I could take you away from it for a while? It won't be all afternoon this time."

Erin's mind went back to the tedious questioning in the glass room. She hated being in that fish tank, with everyone looking in at her, watching to see if she would break and admit to… whatever they might think she had done.

"I really don't think I'm up to it. I mean… I could spend a few minutes with you here, at my hotel, but I don't think I have the time to get to the police station."

Coleman studied her with a hint of amusement in his eyes. So maybe he saw right through her attempts to put him off and understood how much she had hated being questioned in the middle of the brightly-lit tank.

"Yes, if you could spare a few minutes, that would be very helpful," he agreed.

Erin wished she hadn't made the offer. She wished that Terry had made it to lunch and was with her. He would be better at turning Coleman down. She wasn't doing a very good job of it.

They walked together the last block and a half to the hotel. They found a table in the bar and grill on the main floor and ordered a round of hot drinks; coffee for Coleman and tea for Erin.

"Never been much of a tea-drinker myself," Coleman confessed when their drinks were brought to the table.

"I really wasn't before I came here. Except I did learn a lot about tea when I stayed here with my aunt."

"Here?"

"In Bald Eagle Falls. My Aunt Clementine owned a tea room, and she looked after me a few times while she was working there, so I learned a lot about the teas she sold."

"How old were you?"

"Just little. I was eight when I… left."

Coleman sipped his coffee. "I have to have my caffeine."

"I'm the opposite. I'm used to getting up very early in the morning to have bread baked before we open. If I had caffeine in the afternoon, I'd never be able to sleep."

He nodded. "So what brought you back to God's country if you left when you were eight?"

"I inherited my aunt's tea shop. Except I reopened it as a bakery. Auntie Clem's."

He nodded. They had talked about her ownership of Auntie Clem's Bakery during their last interview. "That was lucky, then."

"Some luck. Some hard work."

"I don't doubt it," Coleman agreed.

Erin looked around restlessly. "So what did you want to talk to me about? I told you everything I could the first time."

"There have been developments. I was hoping that you might be able to give me a hand with some of the smaller points."

"I can't imagine what I could help you with. I told you everything I know."

"The first thing that came to light was that Ms. Batcombe did not die in that freezer."

Luckily, Erin was already aware of this, so it didn't take her off guard. "So I heard. But you know I wasn't the one who put her there. I have a dozen witnesses who know that I wasn't dragging a dead body when I went into the freezer. People might have noticed that."

Coleman cracked a smile. "I would think that if you had anything to do with it, you would have put her there much earlier."

"And then decided to lead everyone to the body? I can't imagine why I would do something like that."

"We've seen a lot of crazy things. You've heard of criminals returning to the scene of a crime. It's never a smart thing to do, yet people do. They're drawn back there."

"I didn't drag her in there."

"No. I don't imagine you did. What time was it when you saw her the night before?"

"Oh… that's a good question." Erin thought back. "It must have been something like nine o'clock. Really late for me. I was wiped out. No way I could concentrate on all of the speeches. So I went out for a short walk, a bit of fresh air."

"Are you a smoker?"

"No."

"So you went outside for...?"

"Just for the fresh air, like I said. Get out of the stuffy conference room and cool off, clear my head."

"Which door did you use?"

Erin took a moment to orient herself within the hotel and pointed. "Just out the front lobby doors. Other people were coming and going. People must have seen me. Other than Beryl, I mean. There must have been other attendees who saw me go out and end up talking to Beryl." She thought about it. "Though... we were right against the side of the hotel, leaning up against the wall... so nobody inside would have been able to see us. But someone coming up to the hotel, they could have."

"Not a lot of people arriving around that time. The hotel was mostly filled with people there for the orientation meetings. And they were all in the conference room when you went out for your breath of fresh air."

"I suppose."

"So it was around nine o'clock when you spoke to Ms. Batcombe."

"That would be my guess, yes. I don't think I actually looked at the time, so that's not one hundred percent."

"And did you see her after that?"

"No."

"When you separated, did she go her own direction? Back to her car?"

"No. She was still there smoking. I didn't see her after that. Until I found her in the freezer."

"So you were smoking outside."

"No, Beryl was smoking outside. I wasn't. And I didn't enjoy her second-hand smoke, so I didn't spend long out there."

"What did the two of you talk about? The contest?"

"Yeah. It was the only thing we had in common, so that's what we talked about."

"She was another of the judges."

"Right."

"How many of the judges do you know?"

"Just me and Vic. I've seen or met the others now, but I still don't *know* them. Just been introduced."

"Did you and Ms. Batcombe argue?"

"Argue?" Erin knew she was stalling and that he would recognize it, but she needed time to arrange her thoughts. "No, not really. She expressed some opinions… and I didn't agree… so I left. I didn't stay to discuss it with her."

"What opinions?"

"Just opinions about the contest and my friends. I didn't like it, so…"

"What do you know about her history?"

"Nothing. I told you, I don't know her."

"You've read the bios of the other judges. And I'm sure you must have followed the bits that made it to the paper after she died."

"Yes. But that's just… dry facts, really."

"You didn't think she belonged at the conference? That she wasn't qualified to judge?"

"What? I never said that."

"You didn't have a very good opinion of her."

"Well…" Erin felt like she was being backed into a corner. She couldn't afford to get on Coleman's bad side.

There was no reason for him to consider her a suspect. She hadn't known Beryl Batcombe. That was the truth.

"I didn't have any opinion of her before that night. And my opinion that night was just… She was a bad-tempered, close-minded woman, not someone I wanted to get to know."

"And since then?"

"What?"

"Has anything you have learned since then changed your opinion of her?"

Erin hesitated. "Not for the better. No."

"The press coverage of her has not been very complimentary."

Erin had read most of what had been written about Beryl. What was she supposed to do? Ignore it? She took a sip of her tea, shrugging with one shoulder.

"You were not the last one to see Ms. Batcombe," Coleman advised.

Erin was relieved to hear it. She didn't want to be the last one. To be a suspect because not only had she found the body but because no one had seen Beryl between the time that Erin saw her smoking and the time she found the body. That would be a bad situation. She let out her breath. "Good."

He continued to watch her impassively, giving nothing away.

"Someone saw her in her car shortly after that. She was… ill."

"Oh." So maybe it was natural causes. Erin didn't know how that would translate to someone dragging the body into the freezer. Who would find a person who had died of natural causes and decide to put her in the freezer instead of calling the police or ambulance? She looked at Coleman. "Who saw her? How did they know she was sick? They must have talked…?"

"No. She was leaning out of her car door, vomiting."

"Oh."

"They assumed she'd had too much to drink."

"Right… well, maybe… but she wasn't drunk when I saw her. Not that I could tell. She wasn't slurring or unsteady." Erin pictured Beryl in her mind, lighting a cigarette with a steady hand. She had been leaning against the building, so there wasn't any staggering or obviously drunk behavior. "So maybe… she had a drink or two after I saw her? And then she went somewhere… did she have a car accident? Because she had been drinking?"

"No. It doesn't appear the car was in an accident."

"You found it, then? Was it parked near the restaurant?"

He raised an eyebrow. "Why?"

"I don't know… I was just trying to picture it all. She left the hotel, she was sick… If someone thought she'd been drinking, did they stop her? Did she get out at the restaurant and… wander in there? She was sick, and she got disoriented, fell asleep there…"

"I told you she didn't die in the freezer."

"Right… well, did she die in the restaurant, and someone put her in the freezer to… I don't know… hide the evidence that anything had happened there, or to preserve the body, or…"

He watched her, waiting to see what else she came up with. Erin shrugged. "I really don't know. I don't understand why someone would move the body."

"Maybe the reason will come to light when we have gathered more information."

"If she didn't die in a car accident, and didn't die in the freezer, then what happened? Was it natural? Did someone… hurt her?"

"That's under investigation at the moment. And as I'm sure you've been told before, the police don't share what information they have with civilians. I'm investigating this case, not you."

So he had gotten around to checking her background and knew that she had been involved in murder investigations before. But he didn't know that she had done her best to stay out of them.

Usually.

Mostly.

It wasn't her fault that she had been dragged into investigations in the first place.

"I'm not investigating it. I'm in the middle of a cook-off competition. You're the one who tracked me down."

Coleman had the good grace to shrug, admitting that part was true.

"I don't see how much help I can be to you. I really don't know anything. Like I said, I just talked to Beryl for a minute. I don't know her, and I don't know what happened to her after I went back inside. Just because I was the first one to walk into that freezer, that doesn't mean I had anything to do with it."

"No, ma'am," Coleman agreed. "It was important to get your feedback that she didn't seem drunk, though. That tells me that maybe there's something more we need to look for. We still don't have all of the pieces to this puzzle."

Erin was encouraged by this. Maybe he didn't consider her a suspect. She was one of the last people to see Beryl before she died, so her window on what had happened was important.

CHAPTER 25

Erin was finally able to retreat to her room. It had been a frustrating day. Everywhere she went, it seemed like people were criticizing her or being unsupportive. Her mind was spinning with everything she'd had to deal with, and trying to sort out what she had learned from Coleman. Even though she wasn't investigating Beryl's death—she had plenty of other work to do—she wanted to sit down and start writing up some lists. Everything she knew about it, down to the smallest details. The things that Coleman had said that had disturbed her. She also wanted to get down her random thoughts about the bakery and possible ways to deal with the issue of Charley having a relationship with Chef Kirschoff—one option would have to be just minding her own business. But she wanted to do something about it.

She swiped her card to unlock the hotel room door and threw her heavy purse down on the bed. She kicked off her shoes and flopped down. It felt wonderful to just be by herself on the cool bedspread and not have any more obligations.

Her phone vibrated. Erin dug it out of her purse and checked the screen. She didn't want to talk to anyone and hoped that it was just an alarm for an event she had decided not to go to or a message saying that the whole competition had been called off, and not anyone she had to talk to.

It was a text from Terry.

Erin flipped over and straightened out so that she was lying comfortably on her back with the pillow under her head. She tapped the screen and called Terry back.

"Erin, I'm sorry." He apologized without even saying hello. His voice was hoarse. "I wasn't feeling very well and I just now got myself together enough to even send you a message."

"It's okay. Did you take something? Do you need to see someone? You sound pretty bad and I'm worried about not being there to take care of you."

"I don't need anyone to take care of me. I'll just go back to sleep. It will be better tomorrow."

"Have you had anything to eat?"

"No. Too nauseated."

"I thought the headaches were getting better. Aren't they supposed to be going away by now?"

"The doctors said they might last for a few months…" Terry trailed off.

Erin knew that there was also the possibility that the headaches would never go away completely. She had thought that by now, he would be back on his feet, working the same shifts as he had in the old days, getting around town with K9 by his side and taking care of all of the little problems in Bald Eagle Falls. She had not expected that she would still be worrying about him. That he would still be unable to work full time. That the stupid headaches would still be coming almost daily.

"I know." She sighed. "Have you taken a pill?" He still hadn't answered that question.

"They don't help."

"I notice a difference when you take them. It doesn't seem to get quite as bad, and you're able to sleep better and recover faster."

"I think you see what you want to see."

"Then you should talk to the doctor about getting something stronger."

"I don't want something that is going to knock me out or make me too impaired to work." His voice was brittle. It wasn't the first time they'd had this conversation.

"But you can't work if the headaches are bad either. You can recover faster and get back to work sooner if you take them."

"Fine. I'll take one."

She didn't know whether he would or not. He might intend to and then forget by the time they got off the phone. Or he might not have any intention of taking one. Since she wasn't there to see, she wouldn't know the difference.

"Do you want to talk for a bit, or is it too bad?"

She gave him a few moments to consider, not interrupting his thought process. She heard him shift around.

"I can't do anything else. We might as well talk for a bit."

"Okay. Maybe it will distract you."

"Maybe."

Erin fished around for something to discuss with him. Nothing personal. Nothing more about his headaches or how long it was going to take him to recover. And similarly, nothing about her problems, like the dreams that she was still having. She had thought more than once before that she would sleep better alone. If she and Terry weren't both in the house, restless and fighting their demons, then she might be able to get to sleep faster and not be woken up in the night so many times. But sleeping away from him in the hotel in Whitewater had not been restful. She tossed and turned, jumped at every noise she heard in the hotel. The pipes in the walls, footsteps in the halls, the whir of the elevator, people talking or shouting in their own rooms. It was like trying to sleep in a beehive of activity.

"I talked to Deputy Coleman again today."

"Oh? What did he have to say? I don't want you talking to him, Erin. You shouldn't be talking to him without a lawyer or someone else there to protect your interests. Who knows what ideas he might get in his head about you being involved in this woman's death."

"He doesn't—"

"It's not like it hasn't happened before. You can't be too careful. You don't know what he's thinking, even if he's treating you like a confidante instead of a suspect. Some of these guys are really good at getting people to trust them and think that they're best of friends."

"It's not like that. He's not buddy-buddy. He just had some more questions about when I saw Beryl."

"You've already given him a statement. I wouldn't talk to him about anything else. Tell him to talk to your lawyer."

"I don't have a lawyer."

"Get one. I can give you some names. I'm serious, Erin. I don't want to get a call from Vic telling me that you've been thrown in jail."

"I'm not going to get thrown in jail. Everything is fine. I'm done talking with him, I'm back in my room. Just relaxing and talking to you to blow off the stresses of the day."

He was quiet for a minute. "Yeah. Okay. Sorry for being paranoid. It's just… I know how these things can look. Did you find anything out from him? Anything that hasn't been in the news?"

Erin filled him in on what she knew, which wasn't a whole lot. But the fact that Beryl hadn't died of hypothermia in the cold room was important. As was her being sick between her discussion with Erin and her untimely death.

"Do you think she could have been poisoned?" Erin suggested. "The witness thought that maybe she was drunk, but I don't think there was enough time between me talking to her and her… death… for her to get drunk. Maybe someone gave her something… either before I talked to her, and she just hadn't had a chance to react to it yet, or right after we talked?"

"I suppose," Terry said slowly. "You don't know who she might have seen or what she might have had to eat or drink during that time."

"No. Who knows who might have given her something. From what the papers have said… other people didn't like her much better than I did."

"She doesn't sound like a very likable person. And usually, the papers go out of their way to portray a sympathetic victim. You don't want people to jump in and say, 'I would have killed her myself if I'd had the chance.'"

Erin giggled. "I haven't heard anyone say that yet, but they haven't been too complimentary."

"It all reminds me a little bit about when you first came to Bald Eagle Falls."

Erin immediately understood the connection. She'd already been thinking it herself. "Angela Plaint?"

"Yes. While she was alive, people wouldn't say a bad word about her.

But after she was gone, and we were questioning suspects or witnesses… the ugly stuff started to come to light. The Baptist ladies would still defend her, say that she just had rough edges, or had dealt with a lot in her life with her husband and son disappearing and her daughter committing suicide. It wasn't like she had things easy. But other people go through a lot of trials in life and still manage not to act like… Angela Plaint."

Erin shook her head, thinking about all that they had discovered about Angela Plaint and her family's secrets. Most of her problems had been of her own making. Despite being a churchgoing woman her whole life, she had not been the epitome of Christian behavior.

"I wonder what secrets Beryl had. I haven't heard much about her family, have you? I wonder if Coleman has talked to them." She thought about the Plaint boys and the havoc they had caused.

"Haven't really seen anything about any. I don't think she was ever married. Her family has been in Tennessee for generations, so she probably has plenty of cousins and other kin in Whitewater and the surrounding areas. But I don't think there's any immediate family. Her parents have passed."

"She didn't have anything to do with that, did she?"

"Well… I hope not. Maybe something for Coleman to look at." His voice grew firm. "Coleman, not you. Don't you go asking anyone questions about it."

"I'm not. I'm hibernating in my hotel room. I've decided I don't like being around people."

He gave a chuckle. Not quite his old laugh. Weak and cut short. She imagined his wince as he realized that laughing, like everything else, hurt his head. "Sounds like you've had a hard day."

"Between parents from Bald Eagle Falls, and Vic and her friends, Charley and Chef Kirschoff, and being harassed about this woman I don't even know dying, I'm about ready to poison someone myself. Whoever crosses my path next. I'm not going to be picky about it."

"Oh—I was trying not to forget when you were talking about someone poisoning her—Doc dropped off a report from the lab about Orange Blossom."

Erin took in a sharp breath of air. She needed to know everything she could about what had made her cat sick. But on the other hand, she didn't want to hear it. The vet figured that he probably got into some household poison, even though Erin had been unable to find any spills or toothmarks on anything that Orange Blossom shouldn't have been into. She wanted to know what had made him sick, but she was going to be devastated if it were something that she had given to him or let him get into through her own negligence.

She blew out her breath slowly, trying to relax her body. "Okay. Did you look at it? What does it say?"

There was the rattling of paper. Terry didn't say whether he had already looked at it when it had arrived, or whether this was the first time he saw the contents.

"Okay. It says…" Terry sighed. "They found an alkaloid in his system. Probably holly."

"Holly?"

"Yes. You have to be careful of those Christmas plants. A lot of them are poisonous to pets."

"But… I didn't have any holly."

"Then how did he get it?"

"He couldn't have gotten it from the house. Does it grow around here? Could someone have… tracked it in on their boots or something?"

"I'm pretty sure it grows in these parts. Are you sure you didn't have any… in a wreath, or mistletoe decoration or something like that?"

"No. I only had one wreath, and that was from Adele. There was no holly in it. I know what holly looks like. It has these plasticky, spiky leaves and red berries. I didn't have any."

"Maybe there is something else that has that compound in it. Something that we did have around."

"But I didn't. I didn't have anything like that around. I know that Orange Blossom or Marshmallow could get into any plants. I wouldn't have anything in the house without checking first to make sure that it wasn't toxic."

Terry didn't say anything. Erin shook her head, thinking it through.

"But that means… it wasn't an accident. Blossom was intentionally poisoned."

One of the Bald Eagle Falls burglars, one of the Grinches, had poisoned her baby.

CHAPTER 26

Erin had been up for a few hours when there was a light knock on her door. She looked over at it, wondering who would be up already. It was still pretty early in the morning for non-bakers. People who actually slept until after the sun came up. It was too early to be housekeeping. And she wasn't sure she wanted to talk with anyone who was associated with the contest.

She went to the door and looked out the peephole. It was difficult to make anything out. She eventually opened the door, unable to make out who it was through the fisheye lens.

"Oh! Joshua." Erin smiled and took the chain off the door. "What are you doing here?" She opened the door wide and motioned for him to join her.

"I'm covering the competition."

Erin frowned, trying to make sense of what he was saying. "What do you mean, covering it?"

Joshua pulled a notepad out of his pocket and turned to a fresh page. He retrieved a pen from another pocket and held them up, poised to write. "I got an extra credit assignment. To report on the cooking competition. For English Language Arts."

"Oh, I see. Well, good for you." Erin smiled.

Joshua hadn't been doing very well in school. Erin knew that Mary Lou had been worried about him. After Campbell, her older son, had dropped out, she had done everything within her power to make sure that Joshua stayed in school, even though she knew that she couldn't do anything if he decided that he too was done with school. An extra credit assignment would help to bring his marks up. And even more important than that, he was getting out there and making an effort to do something, instead of just hiding at home and not socializing or doing any extra-curricular activities. It was better for his mental health if he got out and did things.

"Have a seat," Erin pointed toward the single chair in the room, pushed in at the table that doubled as a writing table and entertainment center. Erin sat on the bed. "So, tell me about the assignment. What do you need to do?"

"Cover everything. Get as many human interest stories as I can and hand them in to my teacher. She's going to see if she can get some of them published in the paper if they are good enough. Just… being like a real reporter. Looking for the scoop."

"At an ice cream contest, there should be plenty of scoops." Erin laughed.

"Oh, you did not just say that. I'm going to have to put in my article that you tell really bad jokes!"

"You're only supposed to write the truth."

"That would be the truth."

"What have you reported on so far? I guess there's not much you can report on until the actual competition begins."

"No way. There's plenty to report on. The science fair yesterday and today, that's good human interest stuff. Talking to people, reporting on what they are making and what interesting things I can find out about them. And, of course…"

She knew what he was going to say before he said it. Of course.

"Beryl Batcombe."

"Right." Erin looked for a way to avoid the conversation. "What else? You should do a spotlight on Vic, she's really young to be judging a competition like this. And Charley has piggybacked on a bunch of different activities to promote Auntie Clem's. She's really outdone herself. She should get some publicity for that."

Joshua wrote down a couple of notes. "Yeah, those are good ideas. But they're not going to beat out a body showing up in the freezer."

"I'm sure that they'll be able to explain everything before long. It's probably nothing more mysterious than..." Erin cast about for an example. "A heart attack. Or some other preexisting condition. It's probably nothing very interesting at all."

"If it was a heart attack, then who moved the body?" Joshua challenged.

So he already knew that part.

"I don't know. I can show you where the police station is. Maybe they'll give you a statement. A quote you can use in your story."

"Something other than 'no comment'? I doubt it."

"You don't know unless you ask. The policeman in charge over there is Deputy Coleman. Maybe if you took him out for coffee, he'd give you a hand."

Joshua wrote this down, but was not dissuaded from his plan to interview Erin. "You were the one to find the body, Miss Erin. Even if you don't know anything about what happened, just finding the body is interesting. People will want to know what that's like. What you saw and felt. It's perfect."

"No... it's not interesting. It's not a news story. It's... it's somebody's life. Someone who probably had family and friends who cared about her. She's not just a headline in the paper."

"But it wouldn't be very respectful to ignore her death and go on as if nothing had happened," Joshua pointed out. "We should be talking about it, not ignoring it."

He had a point there. Erin kept expecting the contest organizers to make a bigger deal of it. To cancel the contest. To make a statement about how important Beryl had been to the contest and how she would be missed. To name something after her. As it was, they had stayed quiet on the whole subject. Erin knew they were rounding up another judge so that they couldn't end up with a tied vote, but other than that, they had simply gone on as if Beryl had decided not to judge the contest after all. As if she were still at home living out her life.

"You could look at her obituary, track down some of her family, see what they had to say about her. There must be someone who has positive things to say about her."

Joshua raised his brows in a query. Erin realized that she had put her foot right in her mouth. She had vowed not to say anything bad about Beryl to Joshua. And 'everybody hated her' was not the thing that Erin wanted to see on the front page of the paper.

"I mean. There are a lot of people who loved her," Erin amended. "I'm sure there will be a lot of people at her funeral if they hold one… she must have family around here."

Joshua nodded. "Yeah. I don't think I'll have any difficulty finding people to talk about her." He leaned the chair back an inch, making it squeal loudly. "But what I'm interested in right now is hearing about finding her body."

"You said you want to be respectful of her."

"Yes."

"Then writing about her body being discovered isn't really something that—"

"I'll do a sidebar about what a wonderful woman she was and all of her charitable activities," Joshua said dryly. "But what people want to read about is what happened to her. How she was found in the freezer."

"We really don't know what happened, though. That part of the story is still a mystery."

"Mysteries are good. Keep people coming back for more. Keep them talking about it."

Erin shook her head. Joshua cocked his head to the side.

"Do you want me to fail my assignment?"

"No. I just don't think that what your teacher wanted was for you to focus on an accident. That's not the real story. She wanted you to report on the contest. I can give you some literature, talk about what's going on this weekend, and everything that is going to happen as we ramp up to the contest next weekend…"

"I heard," Joshua said slowly, "that they are investigating Ms. Batcombe's death as a murder."

CHAPTER 27

Murder?

Erin's jaw dropped.

She shook her head. "It was an accident," she asserted. "Who would want to kill her?"

But she remembered how she and Terry had compared Beryl's personality with that of Angela Plaint's. And there had been no lack of suspects for Angela Plaint's murder.

"It wasn't what it looked like," Joshua pointed out. "It sounded in the first few reports like she had just wandered into this freezer or got caught in it somehow. But from what I hear, her body was moved there. After she was dead."

Erin didn't know who he had heard it from, but she had already heard it from a couple of different sources. People were clearly talking about it. If Joshua knew about it, then it wasn't just limited to law enforcement anymore.

"Yes… I heard that."

"Then it has to be murder. Who would move the body otherwise?"

"I don't know. I'm still trying to figure it out. Why would someone murder her and move the body? Why not just leave her where she was? That doesn't make any sense, either."

"Maybe they were hoping it would look like an accident. The police would think she was just drunk or disoriented or got stuck."

"I don't know… I suppose it's as good a reason as any. But I don't like to think that… it was deliberate. I was hoping to avoid any more nightmares…"

Joshua nodded sympathetically and wrote something in the notebook. What? That Erin was having nightmares? She didn't exactly want that spread all over Tennessee.

"So why don't you tell me about it?" he urged. "How you happened to be the one to find the body? What you thought when you first saw it. And maybe… any ideas you might have on who the culprit is."

Erin sighed. "I don't really want to be the feature story in the newspaper."

"Then give me another direction to investigate. Point me in the direction of the person you think did it." His eyes sparkled.

"I don't want you getting involved in chasing after a murderer. Nothing that is going to put you in harm's way. Does your mother know that you're here?" Erin hadn't even thought of Mary Lou yet. Mary Lou did not want her to have anything to do with Joshua.

"I told her I was going to talk to you. I told her it was for extra credit, so I can get my English grade up."

"And she said it was okay?"

"She wasn't happy about it. But she wants me to do something other than sitting at home all the time moping around. And she wants me to start paying attention to my academics so that I have somewhere to go with my life."

"I don't want a story to be focused on me and all of my feelings. And… I'm not going to encourage you to investigate it on your own. That's a really bad idea. Remember when you guys wanted to go into the city to help to prove that Campbell wasn't guilty? Just how did that turn out?"

Joshua's expression turned serious. "I'm going to be careful. I'm not going to go chasing after dangerous people. I just want… something to put in my story. A hook that will make it unique."

Erin's thoughts went sideways, from Beryl to Orange Blossom. Had they both been poisoned? If they had, then who had poisoned Beryl? And what about Orange Blossom? Someone would have to have been in her house to give the poison to Blossom. She didn't let him run wild outside. He was an indoor cat. She wanted him to be safe.

"Erin?" Joshua prompted. "It must have been quite a shock to walk into that room and see Batcombe's body there."

"Yes… it was. I certainly wasn't expecting it."

"What did you think? Did you know it was murder right away? Or did you think it was an accident?"

Erin cast her mind back. The shock tended to erase a lot of the other, more logical thoughts. What had she thought?

"I just… I saw her body there… and I guess at first I thought she had just gotten there ahead of us and was waiting for us… or she was asleep… she was supposed to be with our tour group, so I was sort of mad that she had gone on ahead of us."

Joshua nodded encouragingly. "How long did it take you to realize that she was actually dead?"

"It all happens in an instant. It isn't like you're having a conversation with yourself and you can articulate it all… I was mad at her and I realized she was dead all at once, in a split-second."

"Uh-huh." Joshua was scribbling some notes. "Did you scream?"

"No."

"Did anyone?" he persisted hopefully.

"No, I don't think so. Not that I remember." She thought back, but it wasn't all crystal clear. She had kept everyone out of the room, making sure that no one could contaminate the scene, but her mind had been skipping around, trying to avoid looking at Beryl or speculating on what had happened.

An accident. Just an accident.

But it wasn't. Even though she had been shocked when Joshua had said that it was a murder, she had known all along. She had known that Beryl hadn't gone from smoking at the hotel to sitting quietly in the freezer until she died.

She had known that the vitriolic woman must have had enemies. If Erin felt so strongly about her after five minutes, then she could only imagine how much Beryl had alienated the people who had known her for longer.

"Who do you think did it?" Joshua asked. "How did everyone else react?"

Erin thought back. Vic had been behind her, bottlenecked in the doorway so she couldn't get in to see.

No one in the contest group had seen the body except for Erin. Vic had kept everyone else back. There had been protests, but no one was really that intent on getting into the freezer. It was just a freezer, not that exciting. When they realized that there had been a medical emergency, the protests had died away and people had only been curious to catch a glimpse of what had happened.

The police came. The doctor came. Then Coleman.

Vic had been white-faced when she realized what Erin had found. She certainly hadn't known anything ahead of time. Not that Erin would ever have suspected Vic of killing Beryl anyway. If Vic had been in a fight with Beryl, it would have been a knock-down, drag-out, public fight. Vic knew what she was doing and Beryl would not have looked calm and serene, her skin unmarked.

Chef Kirschoff had been on the tour; jolly, making jokes, acting like he was enthralled with Sherry the guide's long and detailed descriptions. He'd probably written most of the patter himself. No one had tried to stop Erin from opening the freezer door. While it was true that their attention should have been on Sherry, at least a few of them were bored and looking for something else to occupy their attention and, if someone had dumped Beryl's body in there, their eyes would surely have been on the door rather than on Sherry.

Had anyone been paying more attention to her than they should have? She didn't think anyone had been watching her, but she hadn't checked to see.

"I don't know who would have a reason to hurt Beryl. I don't remember anyone acting suspiciously when I opened the freezer… if it was someone in that group—" Erin suppressed a shudder, "—then he or she is a good actor."

Joshua nodded. "Who was there?"

Erin shrugged. "Most of the people associated with organizing the contest. Me and Vic, Chef Kirschoff, the guide, other judges, sponsors, people involved in the administrative stuff. So that everyone would know what to do when it was time for the competition."

"The names of the judges are all up on the website. Can you give me the names of anyone else who was there?"

Erin shook her head. "I really don't even know anyone. Contact the organizers. I don't know if they'll give you anything."

"I thought Vic would be here with you. You guys aren't sharing a room?"

"Well, officially we are, but Willie has been in town this weekend, so they have been off on their own and I have the room to myself." Erin thought of the little white dog and wondered how Vic and Willie were handling the new family member. She smiled.

"Do you think she would talk to me?" Joshua asked.

"I don't know. That's up to her."

CHAPTER 28

There was a knock at the door. Erin looked toward it and frowned. She wasn't expecting anyone else, and it was still too early to be housekeeping. Her mind jumped immediately to Vic, since they had just been discussing her.

"Vicky?" she called out without getting up from the bed.

There was no answering call. Erin pushed herself up and went to the door. Maybe a message had been left for her at the front desk. Or there was a plumbing problem.

She looked through the peephole, but there was no one there. Erin waited, but nobody moved into view. She opened the door and looked around. No one was there. She looked back at Joshua.

"Someone did knock on my door, didn't they? It wasn't the next room...?"

"Well, could have been, I guess. It sounded like your door, but it could have just been a loud knock for next door."

Erin looked both directions down the hall, but there was nothing to see. She couldn't hear any conversations going on in the rooms next to hers. And she'd been able to hear voices through the walls the previous night. All night long.

Just as she was closing the door, her eyes caught on a folded note on the carpet. She bent down and picked it up.

"I guess someone left a message for me."

She shut the door and turned back toward Joshua. He looked at his phone. "I guess I should leave you alone. Thanks for everything..."

"Sorry I didn't give you very much. But like I said, I didn't know Beryl. And there wasn't really anything to me finding her... I just saw her there... and told Vic to call for help. I wish everyone wouldn't make such a big deal of it being me."

Joshua nodded as he stood up. "Well, if you didn't have a history, maybe people wouldn't. But this is... an awful lot like what happened to Angela Plaint." He looked apologetic. "Maybe just on the surface, but is anyone looking at whether she had an allergic reaction? And who might have been interested in..." he shrugged, looking uncomfortable, "getting her out of the way?"

"You'll have to ask Deputy Coleman. I'm not getting involved."

Joshua rolled his eyes. Did that mean that he didn't believe her? Or that he thought that she should help? Or that Coleman would never find the culprit or would never talk to him? Joshua said goodbye and she saw him out.

As Erin turned back to her room, her phone started ringing. It was buried in her purse somewhere and it rang a few times before she managed to dig it out. She saw Vic's profile picture on the screen. She picked up.

"Hi, Vic."

"Erin, did you hear?"

"Hear what?"

"Are you in your room?"

"Yes."

"Stay there, I'll come over."

Erin held the phone more tightly. "Is everything okay? What happened?" She thought immediately of Terry. Had something happened to him? Had he done something stupid, harming himself or making a mistake due to the pain and brain fog?

"Just stay there. I'll be right over."

Erin stayed put as she was told. Vic and Willie had taken another room in the hotel, on a different floor because the contest participants had taken a large block of rooms on the floor Erin was on. Erin heard the elevator approaching. She opened her door and stood, waiting for the doors to open. They parted and Vic hurried down the hallway toward her, Willie lagging behind.

"Now, don't get worked up," she warned. "We don't know anything yet."

"You know something!" Erin said. "What's this all about? What happened? It's not Terry?"

"Terry?" Vic looked at her blankly. "No, this isn't anything to do with Terry."

Erin let out a sigh of relief, her legs buckling so that she had to catch herself on the doorframe. Vic took her arm. Willie picked up his pace and took Erin's other arm. They walked her back into her hotel room to where she could sit down on the bed.

"What is it?" Erin demanded, pulling away from them. "What happened?"

"There was an accident. We don't know very many details yet."

Erin was still thinking of Terry, even though Vic had said it wasn't anything to do with him. Had he gotten behind the wheel when he was too medicated to drive? Or was seeing double because of his head? She always worried that he was going to do too much. That he wouldn't be able to accurately judge what he could manage.

"Hans and Charley were unloading some of the supplies and equipment for next week, staging them in preparation for set-up."

"Hans and Charley."

"Yes. And we don't know all of the details, but there was some kind of explosion."

Erin blinked at her. "A bomb?"

"I highly doubt it was a bomb," Willie told her. "They have pressurized canisters of CO2. My guess is that one of them was faulty. A flaw in the canister…"

"Oh." She thought of the big carbonation machine at the science fair. It had looked dangerous. Was it something like that? Erin took in long, slow breaths, trying to sort out what this meant to her. She didn't know whether to be more worried about Charley, her half-sister and partner in the business, or Chef Kirschoff.

Of course, she should be more concerned about Charley. But despite their blood relationship, Erin had a hard time feeling close to Charley.

The two of them had little in common. Charley was hard-headed and wanted to do things her own way.

With Chef Kirschoff, on the other hand, she had an instant connection. Their love of baking and his interest in her specialized knowledge had sparked a deep friendship that had persisted after their chance meeting on the Alaskan cruise.

"I'm sure they're both fine," Vic reassured Erin. "There was an emergency crew, and they were taken to the hospital for treatment. No one has said that they were badly hurt. There is police tape around the area where it happened, so no one can get close, but no one is saying that there were serious injuries."

"They don't take people to the hospital for no reason."

"After an explosion, they would want to take you to the hospital even if you got out of it without a scratch," Willie interjected. "Trust me."

"So, you think that they're both okay."

Vic and Willie nodded. Erin looked around the room. "Who did you hear about it from?"

"Willie went out for coffee."

"*Good* coffee," Willie intoned.

"For good coffee," Vic repeated with a weak laugh. "And he saw the police tape and the emergency vehicles and the crowd gathering."

Willie nodded his agreement.

"But you were there after it happened. You didn't see them."

"That's right. They had already been taken away."

"Has anyone tried to call them?" Erin grabbed her phone and tapped it. She looked for Chef Kirschoff's number.

"We tried both of them. Neither is answering."

"Their phones were probably put somewhere else, with their personal effects." Willie scratched the back of his neck. "They don't like patients trying to call and text in the middle of treatment."

"So you think they were injured. That they're in surgery."

"Not necessarily. They might just be doing a neurological assessment to make sure that there isn't any concussion. Or they could be sitting around bored in a waiting room, but they aren't allowed to have their phones turned on. You know how hospitals are."

Erin shifted around, anxious, wanting to get up and do something.

"We should go see them. Go to the hospital so we can find out how they are."

"We'll hear as soon as there is any news. Some of the other contest people are already on their way." Vic looked at the time on her phone. "Probably there already, just waiting for news."

"They'll shut down the contest," Erin told them with certainty. "We might as well go home because it's not going to happen now. They'll shut it down after this."

"They didn't shut it down when Beryl died."

"But they will now. That's two accidents. People will think that the contest is cursed."

"Accidents…?" Willie raised his brows at Erin. "What makes you think that they were accidents?"

CHAPTER 29

Erin looked at Willie's earnest expression, then at Vic. She dropped her gaze to her hands. She knew that Beryl hadn't walked into that freezer under her own power.

But Charley and Chef Kirschoff? That was an accident. A defective canister, that was what Willie had said.

"Okay… a death and an accident," she amended. "I thought that they would cancel the competition after Beryl's death, but they didn't. But an explosion? That's going to scare people off. They're not going to want to take part in the competition. Not if they think that the equipment is faulty."

Willie nodded. "I suspect so. You can't expect people to want to participate in a contest under those conditions. It's something that's fun to do, but no one wants to risk their life to participate."

"It's too bad. Chef Kirschoff is going to be really disappointed. He put a lot of work into this. He really believes in it."

"He should just be grateful that he's walking away from it alive," Vic drawled. "He could be deader than a lobster in butter sauce."

Erin looked at her, mouth dropping open. She was shocked and amused at the expression at the same time and didn't know whether to laugh or cry. She ended up doing a little of both, trying to catch her breath while Vic gave her a hug and patted her on the back.

"I'm sorry, I'm sorry. I didn't mean to upset you. I've got foot-in-mouth disease. It's okay, Erin. It's going to be okay."

Erin gasped and giggled and tried to wipe at the tears streaming out of her eyes. "I don't—know—why I'm—"

"You're a little bit hysterical," Willie said, stepping back from her a little as if it might be contagious. Or maybe, like many men, he just didn't know what to do when a woman started to cry, and planned to flee the scene. Not that he hadn't seen Erin cry before. "You've had a shock."

Vic rubbed Erin's back. "It's okay. We shouldn't have sprung everything on you so fast, and then me saying something so insensitive…"

"It's okay," Erin gasped. She hiccuped. "Oh—I hate it—when I get—hiccups!" She tried to avoid hiccuping and sniffling at the same time. She looked around for tissues and, not finding any, staggered into the bathroom. She shut the door to give herself some privacy and space to recover without everyone looking at her like she was broken. She blew her nose, washed her face with cold water, and did her best to stop the hiccups. She held her breath while trying to count as high as she could, had a drink, and sat down on the toilet with her head between her knees. The last one might only work for fainting but, by that time, the hiccups were making her head spin, so maybe it would work for both.

Vic knocked on the door. "Are you going to be okay, Erin?"

"I'm good now. Why don't you guys go have breakfast? I just need some time."

"We can wait for you."

"No, go eat. I want to be alone."

"You shouldn't be alone after something like this." Vic's voice was muted as she turned away from the door to talk to Willie. "Should she? You shouldn't leave someone alone when they're hysterical."

"She's quieted down," Willie assured her. "If she says she needs some space, then give her some space."

"Fine. Okay." Vic pressed her face against the door again to talk to Erin. "Do you want us to bring you up some breakfast when we're done? You'll need something to eat too."

"Sure. Just grab me a muffin or something." Erin wasn't hungry, her stomach feeling a bit sick after all of the hiccuping and sniffling. She hated crying and hated the way that it made her feel sick for hours afterward. Some people said they felt better after a good cry, but Erin was always headachy and sick to her stomach. And embarrassed at having been so emotional in front of someone else. She wished Terry were there. He would make her feel better.

"We'll be back after breakfast, then," Vic promised. "I'm sorry, again. I really didn't mean to upset you."

"It's just the news of the accident." Erin blew her nose. "That's all. I'll be okay. I'll be better when I've had a chance to talk to both of them. But it's fine. Really."

By the time Vic and Willie returned from breakfast, Erin had most of her things packed. Vic handed Erin a blueberry muffin and looked around, frowning. She had the dog with her, and Nilla snuffled around the room investigating everything.

"What's going on? You're packing?" Vic asked.

"I'm going home. They're going to cancel the competition, so there's no point in staying around here. I need to see Terry. I'll need to take care of things at the bakery, especially if Charley is… under the weather."

"They haven't announced that they are canceling the competition."

"It doesn't matter. They will. They have to."

"You may be right, Erin," Willie admitted. "But you should probably wait for the announcement. If you just disappear, people are going to be worried."

"I'm not disappearing. I'm going home. I'll leave a message at the front desk. I'll call the organizers and let them know. But I'm not going to stay around."

Erin continued to pack her bags. Vic and Willie stood watching her and Nilla.

"Are you running away because you're afraid?" Willie asked after some time.

Erin turned and looked at him. "I'm not running away. I'm going home. That's completely different."

She had run away enough times to know the difference. She was going home to Terry and her animals. And her bakery. Where people didn't get into accidents or die.

Usually.

Not recently, anyway.

"Are you going to come back if they say the contest is going ahead?" Vic questioned.

"I don't know."

Willie picked up a piece of paper from the multipurpose table. "Is this something important?" He unfolded it with a flick and glanced down at it as he handed it to Erin.

Erin grasped the note, but Willie didn't let it go. Erin tugged harder, frowning. Willie stared at it, then turned his eyes to Erin's face as he finally let go. Erin looked at the paper, trying to remember where it had come from.

"Is someone threatening you? Is that why you're leaving?"

Erin looked at Willie.

Vic gave a laugh of disbelief. "What?"

Erin read the note.

Go home unless you want to be next.

"Oh." Her heart thudded so hard in her chest that it hurt. "I didn't even see that before."

"You didn't see it?" Willie repeated. "It was right here on your table. You're packing your bags. Of course you saw it."

"No, I didn't. I was just… someone left it at my door. I had just picked it up when Vic called, and said to stay put, so I knew something bad had happened. I don't even remember putting it down."

"Who left it at your door?" Vic was beside Erin, looking at the note, her mouth open. "I can't believe someone would…"

"I don't know. When I looked out the peephole, there was no one there. The note was just on the floor. I thought it was going to be you at the door, but when I looked out, there was no one there. Then I saw the note on the floor… I suppose someone might have dropped it there by mistake. It might not have even been intended for me."

"You need to call the police, Erin," Vic told her seriously.

"No. I just want to go home. What does it matter? The note said to go home, I'm going home anyway, so it doesn't make any difference. Whoever left it there will think that I'm doing what they said to do, and everything will be fine."

"You could be in danger."

"Not if I go home."

"There's no guarantee of that."

"It says to go home."

"They might just want to get you away from the hotel or away from the rest of the group. Somewhere you're more isolated."

"In my house? With a burglar alarm and a cop and a police dog?"

"They might not know that part."

"Even if they don't, I'll still be safe."

"Vic is right." Willie put in his bit. "You need to report this to the authorities."

"Can I just tell the hotel or the contest organizers? Does it have to be the police?"

"You already know the answer to that. Why don't you want to go to the police?"

Vic gave Willie a look that said he should have known the answer to that question.

"I've already had to talk to the police twice. They think I had something to do with Beryl's death. I don't want to have to talk to them again. To Deputy Coleman. I just want to go home, and this will all be over."

CHAPTER 30

But she knew she would end up having to go to the police station. No matter how many arguments she had against it, Willie and Vic were right. She needed to let the authorities know what was going on. So she got her whining done and then agreed to let Willie drive her to the station.

"But I don't want you to stay there or go in with me. Just drop me off."

"You'll need a ride when you're done."

"I'll call you. Or I'll walk back here. It's not that far. Nothing in Whitewater is very far."

"I don't mind coming in with you, Erin. I'd like to help."

"No. I'll deal with it myself."

In the end, he agreed to do as Erin asked.

There was a different police officer at the front desk from the one who had been there the last time Erin had been in. So Sommers didn't have to work every shift at reception. It was good that she had someone else to take that duty now and then. Erin imagined it wasn't much fun to be dealing with complaints all day long. Erin sometimes got sick of standing behind the counter at the bakery, and people were much happier to be getting chocolate muffins than citations.

The male officer on the desk this time was Williams. He looked at

Erin for a moment as if trying to place her, then nodded. "Miss… Price, isn't it?"

"Yes."

"How can we serve you today?"

"I need to file a report about a threatening note that I got."

"Oh?"

Erin slid it across the counter to him, under the big window. Williams touched it with a fingertip to reposition it. It didn't take long to read.

"Is that it?"

"Yes. That's it."

"Have you received any other threats?"

"No."

"Do you know who it's from?"

"No."

"How was it sent to you? Mail? In person?"

"It was left on the floor outside my hotel room. Someone knocked on my door, and then left it there for me."

"And you don't have any idea who."

"No."

"Why would someone be threatening you? Why do they want you to go home?"

"I don't know. I guess they don't want the competition to go ahead."

His gaze sharpened. "This is about the competition?"

"Well, that's the only reason I'm in town, so I assume so. I figured that with everything that is going on… Beryl's death and now this explosion today… someone is trying to get the competition shut down."

"How do you know about the explosion?" he asked suspiciously. He had a thin mustache over his lip, and he scratched it now, looking at Erin as if she might be there to attack him.

"Doesn't everybody in town know about the explosion by now?" Erin challenged. "Anyone who didn't hear or see it has at least been told about it by now."

"Did you see it?"

"No. Vic came and told me."

He looked at her for a moment longer, then back down at the note again, weighing what he should do.

"Don't you think you should tell Deputy Coleman?" Erin suggested. "He'll want to know about it, won't he?"

Williams chewed his lip. "Suppose so." But he didn't make any move to call or go find Coleman. Erin looked through the glass guard into the squad room, looking for Coleman. But he didn't appear to be in the cubicles or in the glassed-in interrogation room. He might have been in an office that actually had walls and a door.

"Is he in?"

"He's out on an investigation at the moment."

"Well, I'll just leave that here with you. I'm going back to Bald Eagle Falls."

"You're leaving?" He raised his eyebrows.

"Yes. I decided to leave before I got that. And the note didn't exactly encourage me to stay."

"No, I would guess not."

"So I'll just leave you that."

"You'll need to file a report."

Erin rolled her eyes. "Then please get me the form. I don't want to be standing around waiting all day. I want to go back to my own house and… everyone."

"Does that mean you won't be judging the competition?"

"Do you think the contest is going to go ahead?" she asked.

"Well…" He scratched his mustache again as he considered. "I just don't know about that. Folks are pretty excited about holding it. And the grand prize… that ain't nothing to sneeze at."

"No," Erin agreed. "It isn't. But are people willing to risk their lives for it? I'm not."

She'd had enough 'accidents.' She wasn't about to tempt fate by meeting another head-on. Back in Bald Eagle Falls, she would be safe. She could put the contest behind her and go on with her life. The way it had been before Chef Kirschoff had come to town.

"Do you know how Charley and Chef Kirschoff are? I haven't heard anything and… well, Charley is my sister and Hans is my friend. I'd like to know how they are."

"We will be making an official statement later today."

"Come on. You're not going to tell me whether my sister is alive or dead?"

His eyebrows went way up. "Your sister is alive," he said. "No one ever said otherwise."

"Well, that's something, anyway. Is she okay? Is she badly injured? No one could say how badly either of them was injured. I assume since they were both rushed to the city hospital… that it wasn't just minor scrapes and bruises. Is it… critical? Do you know?"

He shifted uncomfortably. He knew he wasn't supposed to be releasing that information to members of the public. But Erin wasn't the public. She was Charley's sister.

"You don't share the same last name as your sister?"

"No. We had different fathers and she was adopted. That doesn't make her any less my sister."

"I just don't think… maybe when Deputy Coleman gets in, he could give you a call. I'm really not supposed to talk about it."

"So she's okay?" Erin scrutinized Williams's face for any tells. If Charley was in bad shape, she would have expected to see something in his expression that would tell her that. A certain gravitas or blankness. But he didn't seem bothered by her statement that Charley was okay. So she must be.

"And Chef Kirschoff? If he's badly injured, then the contest will be off for sure."

Again, no flicker of worry. And he wanted the contest to go on. Maybe he or a friend or family member was entering something into the contest, hoping to win the grand prize. He showed no sign of being concerned that Chef Kirschoff was too badly injured to continue with the competition.

"Okay." Erin breathed out. "So, where's the form I need to fill out?"

Williams rifled through files under the counter to find the right form for Erin, and indicated the portions she should fill out.

By the afternoon, word of the explosion had spread beyond Whitewater's boundaries, all the way back to Bald Eagle Falls. Several calls had come to Erin's phone, but she looked at the caller ID's and ignored them. Until she saw Terry's number. That one, she wanted to take.

"Terry. Hi!"

"Are you okay, Erin? Is everything all right?"

"I'm fine. Did you hear about the accident? About Chef Kirschoff and Charley?"

"Yes. They hadn't released names, and I couldn't find out… I'm glad it wasn't you or Vic. Is Charley okay?"

"As far as I know. They haven't released an official statement yet. But from what I've been able to discern, I think her injuries were minor."

"You're not at the hospital?"

"No. I don't have a car. Willie said that he would drive me back to Bald Eagle Falls later today; I'm coming home."

"No. I mean, I'm glad that you're coming home. But don't wait for Willie to drive you back here. I'll come pick you up, and we can go to the hospital."

Erin's heart warmed at his offer. "Are you sure? I don't know how you're feeling. That's going to be a long drive and bouncing around bothers your head."

"I'm sure. I will head out right away. If I'm too tired when I pick you up, you can drive."

"I can drive your truck?" He didn't like letting anyone else driving his truck. Erin knew it was a sacrifice.

"If I'm not feeling well," Terry said sternly. "And right now, I'm doing pretty good, so don't count your chickens."

"I won't. Thank you, Terry. I really appreciate it."

"I'm not going to keep you from seeing your sister and making sure everyone is okay. If you were the one who was hurt, do you think anything could stop me from coming to you?"

Her heart swelled again. A lump in Erin's throat that was making it difficult for her to talk. She swallowed hard.

"No," she agreed.

"Nothing," he reiterated.

~

Even though Terry wasn't using his police cruiser, he got there faster than he should have. Erin supposed that if he were pulled over, he could probably still talk himself out of a ticket by virtue of being a policeman. Who would argue with a fellow cop on his way to an emergency, even if he didn't happen to have a light bar?

He called Erin as he approached the hotel, so she was outside waiting for him when he arrived. Erin climbed up into the cab of the truck and greeted Terry with a kiss.

"Thank you again for coming to get me. And for taking me to the hospital."

"You're welcome." He kissed her again, then held her face with his palms cupped over her cheeks, looking into her eyes. "How are you?"

"I'm okay."

K9 stuck his head over the seat from the back and tried to lick Erin's face. She squealed and pulled back.

"What's going on with this competition?" Terry put the truck into gear. Erin pulled her seatbelt on. "I don't understand what's going on. Is it just a coincidence?"

"It could be."

He glanced over at her. "Do you really think that?"

"Well… no. I think… I don't know what to think. I don't want to think about it at all, to tell the truth. Beryl's death looked like it was just an accident… but it wasn't. And this thing with Charley… I want to hear what happened. The police aren't telling anybody anything. I think they'll probably make some kind of release tonight, a statement that they're looking into it and there is no indication of foul play. Something like that."

"Unless there is."

"Right. Although… would they say that there was? Or would they just pretend that there wasn't?"

"The police department won't usually lie to the newspaper. It causes trust issues. So if they thought there was foul play but they didn't want the public to know that yet, they would just say it was still under active investigation. They wouldn't say that there was not foul play, and they wouldn't say that there was."

Erin nodded. Maybe Charley would tell her that they had made a stupid mistake, or that they had recognized that the canister was defective. Maybe it had been dropped or they could see a flaw in the metal. Or Chef Kirschoff would be able to tell them something. He must know something about CO2 canisters. He would have had to learn about how to use and handle them for the contest. He would have had some kind of safety training, wouldn't he?

"You don't think it is too bad, do you? What did you hear?"

"I didn't hear anything official." Terry's tone was apologetic. "They won't be releasing anything until all of the proper authorities have been notified and family notifications made. They don't want families finding out on the news."

"But I am family."

"Yes… but not legally. Her next of kin would be her adoptive parents."

"Next of kin?" Erin echoed. *Why would they need next of kin? Unless…*

"No, don't go there," Terry warned. "I'm not saying that she is dead or dying. Just that when they make family notifications, they will go to the spouse first, and then to parents, and then look more broadly if there is no spouse or parents. They won't be looking for a non-legal half-sister, unless Charley asks them to call you."

"Oh." Erin considered this. "Okay. I know they're probably just fine. Word would have gotten around if they were horribly injured or killed. But I'm just scared that when I get there… I'll find out…"

"I'll be with you. You won't be in this alone. And like you say, I'm sure it will be just fine."

"Yeah. Thanks."

Erin watched out the window as Terry drove, letting the conversation fall away. They didn't need to keep talking. They would just keep going over the same stuff over and over again.

CHAPTER 31

Finally, they were at the hospital. Erin struggled not to appear impatient as Terry found parking and paid for it. Why did hospital parking always have to be so tedious? It should have just been free. And there should have been a lot more of it. People had to go visit their family and friends. It was a necessity, not a luxury. They should have been able to visit without having to deal with all of the problems associated with finding a legitimate spot, dealing with broken or antiquated machines, and having to scrounge for the correct amount of money or make the machines accept credit cards when they were in a grumpy mood.

Then there was the issue of finding someone who could tell them where to find Charley and Kirschoff. Everything was just so overly complicated.

It was going to be more difficult to get in to see Kirschoff, but Erin was finally able to talk a nurse receptionist into believing that she was Charley's sister and was therefore allowed to see her.

Erin breathed a sigh of relief when they entered Charley's room and found her sitting up, playing with the TV remote, a crease between her eyebrows.

"Charley! Are you okay? How are you?"

"Erin! And Terry." Her eyes dropped to K9 at Terry's side. "And… the furry one. I'm okay. Really, everything is fine. I want to go, but they keep saying that I have a *confession* and I can't drive. I said I could get a cab, but they say they want to watch me. To make sure that…" Charley trailed off, unsure how to finish the sentence. She poked at buttons on the remote impatiently. "I can't make this thing work!"

"You probably have to pay extra for TV," Terry suggested. "Did you pay for one?"

"I don't know. They just stuck me in this room and told me that I have to stay here until I confess." She frowned. "Is that right?"

"Pretty close," Terry said smoothly. "Why don't I go ask the nurse about the TV, and you can visit with Erin for now?" He took the remote out of Charley's hand and put it on the side table.

Charley looked again at Erin. "So you finally made it."

"I got here as soon as I could. I needed a ride, and I had to deal with some police stuff, and then getting here and finding out where you were…"

"Oh." Charley nodded her understanding. "Well, that makes sense, I guess. Can you drive me home, then? I want to get out of here."

"We probably can, after we talk to the doctor and make sure. If they want you here under observation…"

"I'm sure it would be fine."

"We'll just check to be sure." Erin sat down on the chair beside Charley's bed. "I'm glad to see that you're okay. I was worried that you might have been hurt a lot worse than you are."

"I'm really okay."

"And Chef Kirschoff—Hans? How is he?"

"Last I saw him, he seemed okay." Charley looked around as if she expected him to be nearby. "Where did he go?"

"I don't know where his room is. I was hoping you'd know, because the hospital doesn't want to give us any information. We're not family, they can't give us private health information and all that. What a pain in the neck it is."

Charley nodded vaguely.

"Can you tell me what happened?" Erin asked. "All that I've heard is that one of the CO2 canisters exploded. That sounds really scary. I was afraid that you'd be… all cut up. I thought of a bomb." She felt like a new parent counting fingers and toes, as she studied Charley to make sure that everything was intact. But Charley seemed to be fine, other than a little confusion. Hopefully, her concussion was mild and wouldn't continue to cause problems like Terry's head injury.

"I was helping Hans with getting everything staged for next week. Everything we can. Because next week, things will be pretty crazy, and we'll have to go from one place to another without any time to fiddle around. There will be lots of volunteers helping out, but most of the work has to be done ahead of time."

Erin nodded. That all made sense.

"There are lots of canisters. They need enough for all of the entries. Hans had a bunch in the truck, and we were taking them into the restaurant to be stored there until the contest started."

"Uh-huh."

"And then… I don't know. Hans put several of them down at a time, and there was a clank, you know, from them banging together, and then… boom! It sounded like a thunderclap. I thought… like you say, a bomb went off. We were both knocked around. I'm not sure, it's kind of patchy, what happened between the explosion and getting here… My ears were ringing. My throat hurt. My head was throbbing. Like I'd been out in the sun for too long."

"And Hans? He didn't look like he was hurt too badly?"

"I don't know. I don't think so. We were both… we could both get up. We walked to the ambulance, they didn't have to bring the gurneys out…"

"Was there a fire? Shrapnel?"

"*Shrapnel*," Charley repeated. "I was trying to remember that word! It just wouldn't come. I kept thinking Sharpie, but that's a kind of dog."

Erin suppressed a smile. "So there wasn't any? You didn't get any shrapnel injuries?"

She hadn't been able to spot any bandages on Charley's body, but she was partially covered by her hospital johnny and a sheet.

"No… I don't think so. There was a big blast…" Charley's eyes were unfocused. "There was… there was a hole in the wall. Like a big, gaping hole, and there were clouds of dust. I think it was dust, from the drywall…" She shook her head. "Half of the kitchen was gone."

There was a tight knot in Erin's stomach as she thought about it. She had been so relieved to see that Charley was all in one piece that she had assumed it had just been a little bang, and that everyone had overreacted.

"But you were okay. And Hans. He was okay."

Charley's eyes were distant for a minute. The silence drew out. She finally shook her head. "They said we were lucky. They said we could have been badly hurt or killed."

The knot in Erin's stomach tightened. Was it just an accident? Chef Kirschoff had dropped one of the canisters or put it down too hard? One of them was defective and being jarred had caused just enough damage for it to break open and the pressurized contents to cause the damage?

"You must have been really scared."

"Not really. I think… I was too shocked to be scared. The ambulance came right away. We didn't have to wait for long."

"That's good. I'm glad someone was there to help you out right away."

Charley nodded. She picked up the remote control from the table next to her and pointed it at the TV. Nothing happened. "I can't figure out what's wrong with this thing."

Erin turned to look at the doorway. She could hear Terry talking to the nurse at the central nursing station. Trying to get more details or to get them to turn on Charley's TV so she could watch something. Charley continued to press buttons on the remote and, eventually, Terry returned.

"They'll turn it on. But it takes time."

"Thanks. That will probably help her to stay calm."

Charley looked up. "Who are you talking about?"

"About you. Getting the TV turned on for you. So you won't be so bored."

"Oh." Charley nodded her head in agreement and pressed a few more buttons on the remote. "I thought maybe you were talking about Batcombe."

Erin looked at Terry.

"What about Beryl Batcombe?" she asked Charley eventually.

"Where is she? Did you hear what happened?"

"Uh… what did you hear?" Erin didn't want Charley to be upset if she didn't remember that Beryl was dead. And she wanted to know if Charley might have some insight that Erin didn't. She had been working closely with Chef Kirschoff. He might have said something to her about Beryl. Being one of the organizers of the event, Kirschoff would have to know more about Beryl than Erin or any of the other people who were only incidental to it.

"She was found in the freezer!" Charley said in a low, secretive tone. She looked around, eyeing Terry.

"He already knows," Erin assured her.

"What was she doing in the freezer?" Charley hissed. "She wasn't supposed to be in there."

"No. I'm not sure why she was put in there. Maybe when we find out why she was put there… we'll have a better idea of who put her there."

"Who put her there," Charley echoed.

"Yeah. She didn't get there herself, you know." Or maybe Charley didn't know that. Or didn't remember it.

"I was asking Hans about her. Did you know that they… knew each other before?"

"Oh. Is that how she got to be a judge for the competition? Because they already knew each other?"

Charley nodded. "They knew each other a loooong time ago." Charley blinked at Erin a couple of times.

"A long time ago. Okay. Well, it was nice of him to remember and to ask her to be a judge, wasn't it?"

"She was… what's the word?" Charley murmured.

"I don't know. I only met her for a few minutes."

"What was she, then? What did you think of her?"

"I don't know what you're looking for. She had… opinions," Erin said delicately.

"Yeah, yeah," Charley nodded seriously. "That's right. Opinions. And recipes."

Erin nodded, suppressing a laugh. "But she wasn't one of the contestants, she was going to be one of the judges. Was she a cook? Is that how Chef Kirschoff knew her?"

"She always had new recipes. Always something new to try. Everybody knew."

"She must have been a good cook."

"That's not the word though." Charley shook her head slowly. "I think… hmm… do you know what it is?"

"No. What word are you looking for? Can you use it in a sentence, and maybe I can think of what word it is."

"Aspirations?" Charley asked, looking up. She searched her concussed memory for the bit of information she was looking for. "Like Caesar. Not the salad."

Erin tried to think of a word that Charley might be mixing up with aspirations. Inspiration? Aspirate? What did any of it have to do with Caesar salad?

"Is it something you put into a Caesar salad? An ingredient?"

"Not that kind of Caesar."

"The drink?"

"No. No, no, no. You're not getting it. Not cooking. Though he was shish kabobbed."

"Who was?"

"Caesar."

It was Terry who spoke up. Of all of them, the one who was having the most serious problems with his brain and proper recall.

"Julius Caesar? He was stabbed," he said as an aside to Erin. "I think that's where the shish kabobbed comes into it. If not… I'm not sure what she means."

"Julius Caesar." Charley nodded. "Stabbed in the back. He was."

"Yes," Terry agreed. "Why are you bringing Julius Caesar up? What does he have to do with anything? He didn't have anything to do with Beryl Batcombe. If there is a connection…. I have no idea what it is."

Had Terry been looking into Beryl Batcombe's background? Had he been investigating quietly, even though he wasn't with her and wasn't on the Whitewater police force?

"Aspirations." Charley sighed. "He had aspirations."

"He sure did."

"And Batcombe. She did too. Hans said."

"Aspirations to do what?"

Charley shook her head, unsure of the answer. She put her hands in the air, lifting them up to one level, and then another level higher. "Aspirations."

Terry looked at Erin and shrugged. Despite Charley's assertion that she was fine, there were clearly still a few issues there. And what about Kirschoff? Would he be able to answer any questions? Would he remember the explosion and what had happened before and after it?

Charley shook her head, letting her breath out hard in exasperation.

"You know how it is when a word is right on the tip of your tongue, and you know everything about it, but you can't quite get it…?"

"Yes, that's really frustrating," Erin agreed.

"I wish I could remember the word. It just… won't come."

"It will probably come back later," Terry offered. "Once you relax and stop trying to think of it. That's how it always is."

"But I don't want to lose it… I want to remember what I'm talking about."

"I'll remind you later," Erin said. "You were talking about Beryl, and you were trying to remember a word that you connect with her. Chef Kirschoff said that she is… that she had…?"

Charley didn't respond to the prompts. She just shook her head in frustration. "I can see it. I know what it means. I just can't remember it."

"I'll remind you later. When you're feeling a bit better. You'll remember."

"I hope so." Charley sank back into her pillow. "You remind me."

CHAPTER 32

They decided that bringing Charley home from the hospital wasn't a good idea. She was still experiencing confusion and lapses of memory and attention, and the doctors wanted to keep an eye on her for a little longer. A day or two. Then they could be more sure that she was completely stable. Or as stable as Charley could be.

"We'll come back and see you again soon," Erin promised. "And we'll try to find out how Chef Kirschoff is."

"I want to go home," Charley repeated.

"I know. I just don't think you're ready yet. We'll listen to the doctors and, hopefully… you'll recover quickly. It's good that you don't have any physical injuries. You'll heal fast."

After leaving Charley's room, they stopped at the nursing station again and tried to get more information on Chef Kirschoff.

"I'm afraid I can't give you any information," the nurse said, shaking her head. "There are privacy issues. Maybe you can get in touch with his family, and they'll fill you in on what you need to know."

"I don't know anything about his family. They're not from around here. They're going to need someone local to deal with the hospital…"

"If you can get in touch with his family, they'll let you know how you can help. They can appoint you his representative. But until that happens…"

"Could you talk to him? Ask him if he wants to see us?"

She looked up and down the hallway. "I'd like to help you. I really would. But we have very strict rules that we're required to follow. Mr. Kirschoff will have to fill out a form with the names of people that he gives us permission to talk to. I can't do anything else."

"We're good friends. He asked me to be one of the judges for his contest. You've heard about the competition that they're running in Whitewater, right? That's his thing. And he asked me…"

"That doesn't mean he wants any medical information shared with you."

"Erin, I'm just going to go for a little walk around the unit," Terry told her.

Erin shook her head in irritation. He could have jumped in, shown his badge, demanded information. Chances were, they still wouldn't have gotten anywhere, but he could have at least tried. He left her to talk to the nurse, K9 heeling close to his side.

"What about Charley? They came in together, she's asking how he is. You could tell her, right?"

"No, ma'am." The nurse's voice was getting more stern and impatient.

Erin couldn't blame her for being irritated. But at the same time, she couldn't let it go. Maybe there was nothing more she could do, but she wasn't going to leave until she was sure she had done everything she could…

When Terry finished looping around the unit, he raised an eyebrow at Erin and jerked his head to the side slightly. Erin stood staring at him for a moment, unsure what he wanted. She gave up on the nurse and walked over to him. Terry put his hand on her arm and, without saying anything, guided her down the hall. Erin wasn't sure what he was up to. He pointed to the name panel beside one of the doors. Erin glanced at it. Kirschoff.

She rolled her eyes and shook her head. "He was here all along? Why couldn't she just tell us that?"

"I suspect they shouldn't even have the names by the door. After you?"

Erin preceded him into the room. There was a man in the bed nearest the door that she didn't know. But when she went past him and around the curtain, she saw Kirschoff.

He was lying in the bed, eyes closed, apparently asleep. Erin wasn't sure if she should try to wake him up or just be satisfied that she had seen him and that, like Charley, he seemed to have been relatively unscathed by the explosion. He had a bandage across part of his forehead and temple, but all body parts seemed to be accounted for. For an explosion that had blown a hole right through the wall, the two people standing close by seemed to have been miraculously preserved.

Terry came up behind Erin and, while she looked at Kirschoff, put an arm around her waist and gave her a little squeeze.

"He looks all right."

"Yeah. He does."

"We should probably let him sleep. We can stop in again tomorrow and see them both."

"Okay."

She spent a few more breaths looking at Kirschoff, then nodded and started for the door. Terry followed her out. They didn't say anything as they passed the nursing station.

As they stood waiting for the elevator, Erin tried to relax all of her muscles. "Thank you for finding him. That really helped."

"Glad it helped. I knew it was important for you to see Kirschoff."

Despite all of his help, his voice held a bit of a bite when he said Kirschoff's name. Erin glanced over at him.

"I just wanted to make sure he was okay."

"Yes."

"If it was one of your friends, you would have wanted to see too."

"Yes."

Erin wished she knew what to say to him. Was he seriously upset about her wanting to see Kirschoff? Was he jealous?

"If it was you, I wouldn't just let you sleep and come back tomorrow."

He looked at her.

"I would stay beside you," Erin said. "I wouldn't leave even if they tried to kick me out. I'd be right beside you."

Maybe he remembered how she had been with him after he had been injured. She'd been there with him until he had been released. Sometimes she would let Vic or Willie sit with him while she went to eat, but mostly, they had to bring her food, because she wouldn't leave him to go down to the hospital cafeteria.

Terry reached around her again to pull her against him. "Yeah."

"I hope they were able to reach his family so they know what happened. I wouldn't want him to be all alone here."

"I'm sure they have. Charley said they were both awake and mobile after the explosion, so he would have been able to tell them who to call for him."

"If he has anyone. I don't even know if he has any family."

"Then he could give them the name of a friend. If he didn't have them call you, then he must have had them call someone."

"I suppose."

CHAPTER 33

It felt to Erin like she had been away from Bald Eagle Falls for a long time. Much as it had felt to return there after the cruise. She was glad to be home, away from the turmoil in Whitewater.

The news out of Whitewater Junction was pretty low-key. The police made a statement that the explosion was under investigation and that the injured parties were in stable condition. Erin waited for a release from the contest organizers saying that they were calling everything off, but it didn't come. She was checking her computer again when the doorbell rang.

She got up to answer it but then heard Terry open the door and speak to the caller. He didn't call her to say that it was someone who wanted her, so Erin sank back down to her seat. She would check her email to see if she had missed anything from the contest, and then she would go see who had come to the door. It clearly wasn't for her, or Terry would have called her.

There it was in her mailbox, finally. An email from the contest to all of the judges, volunteers, and participants. Erin skimmed down the page, then returned to the top, confused.

It wasn't a statement that the contest was being shut down, but an assurance that they were still going ahead. The venue would change slightly, but they had already secured another restaurant and were sourcing replacement materials for anything they had lost in the explosion. The email expressed sympathy for Charley and Chef Kirschoff and said that Kirschoff would still be able to spearhead the contest preparations.

Erin shook her head in disbelief. What would it take for them to actually shut the competition down? Didn't they realize that either the two incidents were related or the contest was cursed? Not that Erin believed in curses.

But it couldn't just be a coincidence. First, one of the judges killed under mysterious circumstances, and then one of the organizers nearly died in an explosion? They had to be related.

The note that Erin had received clinched it.

There was no way that someone was threatening her after two random accidents. There were so many other accidents that could occur if she went back to Whitewater to judge the contest. She had recovered physically from the last attempt on her life, but she didn't much feel like putting it on the line again.

She trashed the email, wishing that she could do something more dramatic, like actually crumpling it up and throwing it in the garbage in real life. And then lighting it on fire. But there was no point in printing it out just so she could throw it away.

She closed the lid to her computer and walked out to the living room.

Beaver sat across from Terry, who was on the couch with K9 at his feet. Beaver had one ankle resting across the other knee, legs wide, taking up lots of space. Beaver always seemed to take up the maximum space possible. Erin wondered whether it was because, as a woman in a profession that was dominated by men, she needed to physically show her coworkers that she deserved just as much attention and respect as anyone else. Or maybe it was just Beaver's nature. She was no shrinking violet.

"Erin!" Beaver cracked her gum. "Good to see you back here. I'm sure Terry's glad to get you back from Whitewater. I wouldn't want *my* partner out there, fending for herself."

Erin shrugged. "I just… couldn't justify staying out there with everything that is going on. I was sure that they would cancel the competition."

"Are they going to?"

"I just got an email. They're going ahead."

Terry frowned. "What are you going to do?"

"I don't know. They have other judges. It's not just me. So maybe if I duck out… They should still be able to go ahead using the other judges. In fact, if I drop out, they've lost two judges, and they're back down to an odd number. So no tied votes."

"What about Vic?"

"I don't know what she'll do. But if enough of us quit, they're going to have to cancel."

"If she stays with it, will you?"

Erin shook her head. "I just don't know. I have a few days… I'll have to make a decision. I just don't know what it will be."

"Fair enough," Beaver allowed. "It's wise not to jump to a snap decision."

Erin shrugged. She sat down with Terry. She didn't know if Beaver had shown up to have a discussion about law enforcement, but she didn't feel like staying by herself in front of the computer. She wanted to be around others. Terry put his arm around her, making no objection.

"How has Mary Lou been toward you?" Beaver asked.

Erin was startled at her bluntness. She shouldn't be surprised by anything Beaver did, especially not being blunt. That was Beaver.

"I haven't seen her. She hasn't come by the bakery. I was hoping that… she would have forgiven me by now. But…"

Beaver nodded. She chewed her gum. "I didn't think she would be quite so stubborn either," she admitted. "I was hoping that once she'd had a chance to cool off, she would see…"

"I can understand her being upset," Erin said. "I mean, I did… mention Joshua's name to the police. That was… I don't know. I guess if I was put in that position again, I would probably do exactly the same thing. I didn't do it to get Joshua in trouble, I just wanted to find out who was behind the burglaries."

Beaver grunted her agreement.

"And as far as the stuff that happened when Campbell was in jail… I didn't… I didn't really have anything to do with that. I was trying to talk the others out of it. I told them what they were doing was dangerous."

"But they went ahead. And so did you."

Erin nodded. "I wanted to keep them out of trouble. But I guess Mary Lou didn't see it that way. She thought I should have done something else. I don't know what. I don't think it would have done any good for me to have called her. Maybe we could have stopped Joshua from going that time, but it wouldn't have stopped him from trying to clear Campbell's name. The next time, it might have been without any backup."

"Teenagers don't always have the best judgment. Joshua's got a pretty good head on his shoulders. But where Cam is concerned…"

"His heart overruled his head."

"Yes. The boys were very close before Cam left home. They looked after each other. At first, I thought that was just Cam looking after Josh, but I think a fair amount was going the other direction. Josh reining big brother in. Keeping track of him. Making sure Cam didn't go off and do something stupid. Cam may have been older, bigger and stronger, but Josh is more careful. He thinks things through."

"I saw him in Whitewater. He is doing a report on the contest for his English class. Or reports. They're hoping to publish something in the paper."

"You saw him…?"

"He came to see me. Wanted to interview me, because I'm one of the judges and because of… well… Beryl. Finding her. You know."

Beaver chewed her gum, considering this. "How much interest does he have in Batcombe's death?"

"I think it interested him more than the contest. I told him I didn't really know anything and didn't want to talk to him about it, but he was pretty persistent. Of course. It makes perfect sense that he would be more interested in a… death than in ice cream and coke."

Beaver nodded vigorously. "Of course. Far more interesting reporting on a human popsicle."

"Eww."

They all laughed.

Erin leaned her head on Terry's shoulder, thinking about Mary Lou and Beaver. "I didn't think you cared what anyone thinks of you. You just do what's right for you."

"Well…" Beaver chewed thoughtfully, shifting her wad of gum from one side to the other. "I don't let it affect the choices I make. I'll do what I need to do. Or what I want to. But that doesn't mean that I'm not disappointed if I get cross-threaded with someone. A good decent person, like Mary Lou or you."

"Me?"

"I can't guarantee I'm not going to do anything that will upset you. Something that would threaten our friendship." Beaver sighed and stared up at the ceiling. "I hope that day doesn't come, but I can't guarantee it. I do tend to… rub people the wrong way."

"Oh." Erin shrugged. "I was pretty ticked when you and Terry didn't tell me about the safe house and forced me to be a part of all *that.* But I got over it."

"Yeah. Some people, like Mary Lou, it's not that easy. She doesn't like to let it go."

"But she wouldn't do anything about it," Erin hastened to put in. "She might tell you off and avoid you, but she would never… poison your cornflakes or anything like that."

Beaver laughed loudly. "I can just see Mary Lou doing that."

"It's funny because she would never do anything like that. She's the person that Angela Plaint probably hurt the most, other than her own family, but Mary Lou didn't do anything to hurt her. And when Roger… did what he did, Mary Lou was horrified. She would never say that was okay. She holds herself to certain standards."

Beaver's eyes were far away. She chewed and tapped rhythmically on her knee, deep in thought.

CHAPTER 34

Erin went into Auntie Clem's Bakery even though she had arranged for her other employees to cover all of the shifts while she and Vic were involved in the competition. Erin hadn't gone as far as to cancel those arrangements, even though she didn't plan to go back to Whitewater, but she needed to lose herself in some baking. There was nothing like working batters and doughs and pulling something delicious out of the ovens. It was therapeutic, and she missed it on the days she didn't go in, no matter how tired she got when she was working. Often enough, if she didn't have to go to Auntie Clem's, she could be found baking something in her own kitchen. It had become such a part of who she was.

"Hi, Erin!" Bella greeted enthusiastically. "I wasn't expecting to see you today! You just couldn't stay away, could you?"

Erin shook her head. "You know me!"

"Everything is on track, but if you wanted to get started on some banana muffins, I wouldn't argue."

"Sounds good," Erin agreed. She put on her hat and apron and started to pull out the bowls and ingredients she would need.

Gwen, one of the girls that Bella went to school with, was also on shift. Bella took a peek out front to make sure that things were not too busy for Gwen, then started on washing up the pans in the sink.

"So, what are you doing back in Bald Eagle Falls?" Bella asked. "I thought you were going to stay in Whitewater until the competition was over."

"I was, but I'm concerned about everything that's happening. I thought… I expected them to cancel the contest after the explosion. For them to just go ahead like nothing had happened…"

"I thought it was a little strange too," Bella agreed. "But I guess they've already sunk a lot of time and money into the contest, and they would lose out if it didn't go ahead now."

"I suppose so," Erin agreed. "I figured that with Chef Kirschoff being put out of commission, they wouldn't be able to do anything."

"He's a big part of it, isn't he?" Bella asked.

"Yes. Definitely. When he first came and asked Vic and me if we would be judges, I thought it was just some small contest, and that he got involved because someone wanted to use his name. This famous chef, you know. Good publicity. I didn't realize that he pretty much floated the whole thing. His idea, he drummed up the sponsors, picked the judges personally, all of that."

"Really? I didn't know that. So is he directing it all from his hospital bed or what?"

"He called me this morning. And yes… he's been driving the doctors and nurses crazy trying to run a three-ring circus over the phone while he's supposed to be resting and recovering." Erin smiled. She'd been able to hear the complaints in the background, with Kirschoff's ebullient voice booming over everyone else.

Bella giggled. "Well, good for him, I guess. He's really lucky that he wasn't killed in that explosion."

Erin carefully measured flour into the bowl. "He says they have to completely replace the CO2 bottles. Send them all back and have them replaced with new ones. So that they can be sure that there aren't any more defective ones. Big expense."

"Yeah, I got an email about that. I'm glad. I didn't know if I wanted to go ahead with my contest entry. I didn't want to have to worry about whether the canister I was using was okay or not."

"I thought you were making ice cream." Erin was pretty sure that Bella would be using dry ice for that, not a CO2 bottle.

Bella looked at her sideways. "I might have changed my entry."

"Oh, okay. Well, that's good, actually, because I won't know which entry is yours."

"Exactly. I don't want you giving me the grand prize just because you think I'm a great employee."

Erin laughed. "That could happen."

"See? I don't want to put you in that position."

Erin thought about going back to Whitewater to judge the contest. She didn't want to, but she also didn't want to let down the competition officials. And Vic. And all of the contestants like Bella, who had put the work into developing new recipes for the contest.

"Are you okay?" Bella looked at Erin.

"Yes, I'm fine. I'm just worried about the competition. We don't want any more accidents."

"Do you think that's what they are? Just accidents?"

"I don't know how Beryl's death could have been an accident, but the explosion… I don't think someone did that on purpose, do you? Charley and Chef Kirschoff could have been killed. It's amazing that they got out of there without any serious injuries."

Bella didn't say anything, scrubbing the pans thoroughly. Erin watched the beaters whirl the batter around and around in the bowl. Bella didn't point out that they'd been confronted with people with murderous intentions in the past. It wasn't as far-fetched as it might sound. And that was exactly why Erin didn't want to be put in that situation again.

"What did Chef Kirschoff say when you told him you don't want to go back?"

"Well… I didn't tell him. I let the other organizers know, but I didn't want to upset Chef Kirschoff while he was recovering… he could have a heart attack or a stroke."

Erin peeled bananas and worked on mashing them into a chunky slop. "He said that they are tightening up security measures. Maybe he doesn't think that anyone is trying to kill him or to sabotage the competition, but he's taking precautions."

"That's good. So you don't need to worry about keeping safe. He'll make sure that everyone is protected."

Erin nodded in agreement. Chef Kirschoff was taking the situation seriously. She wished he had canceled the contest, but the next best thing was that there would be security guards and a police presence. There would be ambulances and paramedics in the parking lot.

What could go wrong?

CHAPTER 35

Happily, both Chef Kirschoff and Charley had been released from the hospital, cleared to return to their regular activities. Both had minor after-effects from the explosion, but they were expected to recover quickly and were allowed to do whatever they felt up to.

Erin invited them both over for dinner. That way, they didn't have to worry about getting up the energy to make their own meal or go out, and could still have a nourishing home-cooked meal. Erin was feeling a little at a loss without having to go to the bakery every day. Cooking gave her something to do.

The animals had all been given their treats and were out from underfoot. Erin, Terry, Charley, and Chef Kirschoff sat around the table to partake.

"This looks great, Erin." Charley looked over the dishes on the table. It wasn't anything fancy, just some noodle casserole, garlic bread, and salad, but it was good food. "The stuff that they serve you at the hospital…" She shook her head. "It shouldn't really be called food. I'm sure it passes all of the nutritional requirements, but so do vitamin pills."

Chef Kirschoff nodded vigorously. Erin had been a little nervous about feeding him. Charley was young and she was Erin's sister. Erin didn't feel like she had to impress Charley with her cooking skills. That wasn't going to change if she didn't think Erin's cooking was up to snuff. But serving a world-famous chef was another story. Terry had told her to just make what she normally would; Kirschoff wouldn't be expecting a gourmet meal. Erin knew Terry was right, but she was still anxious about it.

"It smells delicious," Kirschoff agreed. "This is just what we need. Good, home-cooked comfort food."

Erin nodded, relieved. "I hope you like it."

"Your casserole is fine," Terry assured her. "They would be crazy not to like it."

She shrugged and started passing dishes around for everyone to dish up. They ate a few bites, made the appropriate noises, and the conversation turned to the topic on everyone's mind—the contest.

"Are you sure you should still run it?" Erin asked. "You're not worried about any more trouble? And you can get everything done, even though you had to take a couple of days off in the hospital?"

"Yes. I'm sure it will be just fine," Kirschoff assured her. "We are taking all of the necessary precautions. And I can't afford to lose a judge, Erin. You have to be there."

Terry gave Erin a stern look that told her to stand her ground and not let Kirschoff push her into participating. She gave him a brief nod.

"I'm just worried that... I don't know. That this was all targeted. Someone wants to shut the contest down."

"No one wants to shut the contest down. This is the best thing that's happened to this region in years. It's bringing in a capital injection that the area is badly in need of. It's giving people something to do, to be happy about, to draw closer together and bond as neighbors. It isn't just a cooking contest," he said gravely. "It's so much more than that."

Erin shrugged and nodded. She knew it was all of those things, but she was afraid that it was going to crater and all of the people Kirschoff was trying to help were going to end up getting hurt and being angry and bitter about it.

"It's just ice cream and cola," Terry pointed out. "Let's not forget that. It's great to have all of those lofty goals, but we need to stay realistic about it. It's a fun time, good entertainment, sugary food, not the United Nations."

"Not the United Nations," Kirschoff repeated, laughing. Erin had been afraid that he would be offended by Terry's words, but he took them with good grace. "Ah. It's too bad that Beryl will not get a chance to see it. She had the vision."

There was a moment of silence while everyone considered this. Erin ate a couple of bites of casserole.

"Did you know her well?"

"Yes, yes, she was a good friend." Kirschoff used a crust of bread to soak up some of the sauce from the casserole.

"You'd known her for a long time? I wondered how she had been picked as a judge."

"Well, you are right. It was my choice. A perk of being in charge is that you can give all the good positions to your friends. Repay people for supporting you through the years."

"Where did you know Beryl from?"

She couldn't imagine that they had known each other through school or work. And Kirschoff had said that he hadn't been to Tennessee before.

Kirschoff cleared his throat a couple of times. "Years ago, she was very interested in food and cooking, had some old family recipes that she wanted to make into a book. Thought about opening a restaurant. Some mutual connections put us in touch with each other. Beryl was a very... persistent woman. She generally got what she wanted, sooner or later."

"Ambitious!" Charley said suddenly.

Everyone looked at her. Kirschoff pursed his lips. "Well... yes."

"That's the word I was trying to think of! Oh, it's been stuck in my brain for two days! I'm so glad to finally shake it loose!"

"Ambitious." Erin remembered how Charley had been struggling to find the word when they had visited. "What's the connection to Caesar?"

Kirschoff cleared his throat and quoted:

"The noble Brutus
Hath told you Caesar was ambitious:
If it were so, it was a grievous fault,
And grievously hath Caesar answer'd it.
Here, under leave of Brutus and the rest–
For Brutus is an honorable man;
So are they all, all honorable men–"

"Wow." It sounded vaguely familiar to Erin, but she certainly didn't have any long passages of Shakespeare memorized as Kirschoff did.

"Yes! That's it. That's what I was trying to remember." Charley slapped the table. "That's why Brutus said he murdered Caesar, who was supposed to be his best friend, almost a father to him. But he did it because Caesar was too ambitious."

And Charley had said that Beryl was ambitious. Kirschoff had verified it with the little that he had said. Had Beryl's ambition led to her death as well? Had she stepped on too many toes in her quest to get what she wanted?

And what was it she wanted? To judge the contest? To publish her recipes? Open a restaurant?

They were all quiet for a while.

"So did she ever open a restaurant?" Terry asked. "Did she ever do any of those things she wanted to?"

"She published her recipes through a small local printer. Sold a few copies in tourist shops, but it didn't make the big hit she hoped it would. And no… she never opened that restaurant. But if she'd lived, I wouldn't doubt that she would have, sooner or later."

"Ambitious," Charley repeated, savoring the word. Now that she remembered it, she wasn't going to let herself forget.

Kirschoff's pocket started to trill. He jumped and clutched at it. He pulled his phone out and fumbled to silence it. "I'm so sorry. How rude of me. I thought it was on silent."

Looking at the screen, he frowned.

"I hate to do this, but I need to take this. It will only be a minute."

"Sure," Erin said. "Grab one of the bedrooms if you need some privacy."

He only walked out into the living room and took the call there. The normally effusive Chef Kirschoff was unusually quiet, his voice pitched low and his back turned to them. Erin attempted to carry on a conversation while he was on the phone so that they wouldn't be eavesdropping on his conversation. It was only natural to be curious and listen in on what he was saying.

Kirschoff was longer than one minute but, eventually, he returned to the kitchen and sat down. He wasn't smiling. His brows were drawn down thoughtfully, so that he was almost scowling. Erin touched his arm as he sat back down.

"Is everything okay?"

His eyes flicked over each of them. He scratched his chin, mouth turned down in a frown.

"I have a contact who promised to get me any new information from the medical examiner's office."

Terry raised his brows. He would want to know who the contact was, but he kept quiet for the moment and waited to see what Kirschoff would volunteer.

"About Beryl?" Charley asked, leaning toward Kirschoff. She put her hand on Kirschoff's other arm. Erin withdrew her own hand, slightly embarrassed. It looked strange if they were both pawing at Kirschoff's arm, trying to comfort him. Charley was the one who was interested in a relationship with him, he was her territory more than Erin's.

No one else seemed to notice Erin's embarrassment. Terry and Charley were both watching Kirschoff's face intently. Erin too was interested in hearing what his friend in the medical examiner's office had passed on about Beryl's autopsy. It was a little grim for dinner conversation, but she couldn't exactly tell him to wait until they were finished eating to bring up postmortem results.

Kirschoff picked at the food on his plate, but no longer looked interested in it. He looked troubled. "The cause of death was apparently carbon dioxide toxicity."

"Carbon dioxide? That can kill you?" Charley shook her head. "There's carbon dioxide in the air we breathe all the time, isn't there? That's what we exhale."

"Apparently, it can kill you if you get too much of it," Kirschoff said slowly. "It is not common, and it is very hard to find in an autopsy, but I guess when it was suggested that Beryl might have been poisoned—the police said something about her acting intoxicated—the medical examiner connected our cook-off theme with some of the indications in the postmortem, and… he was able to confirm that the air in her lungs was much too high in CO2." Kirschoff looked at them. "How could that be?"

"Didn't he have any suggestions?"

"I know people sometimes use compressed gasses to get high, or to change their voices, like helium… but how would… why would she be breathing CO2?"

"It must have gotten into her car from her exhaust system," Charley suggested. "I've heard of that before. If there is a leak in the system and it is feeding carbon dioxide into the car, that can kill you."

"That's carbon monoxide," Terry corrected. "Fires, exhaust, things like that can cause carbon monoxide poisoning. But carbon dioxide? Have you ever heard of that before?" he asked Kirschoff.

"Yes. Yes, all of the training that we needed to take for this project. Carbon dioxide is toxic, so we have to get instruction about how you could get it… signs and symptoms… what to do…"

Erin nodded. "So what did they say? People must get it accidentally if you had to have safety training. So maybe it was just an accident."

"There have been cases where theaters or other venues have had carbon dioxide leaks in the tubing for their carbonation machines. People start getting dizzy or faint… throwing up… you have to be aware of the danger. Get them inspected regularly. Recognize the symptoms when you see them." Talking about it seemed to have galvanized him. He spoke more fluidly, remembering what he had learned. "There are guidelines for transporting dry ice, because that's another time when you can end up with too much in the air. If you have a bunch of dry ice in an enclosed area."

"You probably have to cover it tightly," Erin suggested.

"No. If you seal it, the container could explode." He touched the bandage on his temple, then lowered his hand again. "And then there are cases when someone has done something stupid like dump a load of dry ice into a swimming pool, asphyxiating a bunch of people at once."

Erin tried to reconcile any of these methods of poisoning with what had happened with Beryl. Coleman had said that she had been in her car. She had leaned out of it, throwing up, and the witness had thought that she was drunk. Maybe she wasn't drunk, but was being poisoned by carbon dioxide in her car.

"Would Beryl have been transporting dry ice?"

"No. We won't be using dry ice until the weekend. It would have been too early to be transporting and storing it. It would all be gone by the time we were ready to use it."

"But she could have been doing it for some other reason… maybe she had a recipe she wanted to try out. Or some kind of… experiment for the science fair. Anything…?"

"She was a judge. She couldn't participate in the contest or the science fair."

"You said she had a bunch of family recipes, though. Maybe she was experimenting just for her own entertainment. She wanted to prove to herself that she could make… better ice cream than the people who were entering the contest." Erin floundered for a more reasonable explanation. Did Beryl seem like the kind of person who would be experimenting with dry ice for fun? She hadn't seemed to Erin to be the fun-loving kind.

Kirschoff was shaking his head. "None of that sounds plausible. I can't imagine how she would have gotten exposed to that much carbon dioxide."

"Well then, it's simple, isn't it?" Charley asked, looking at Terry. "It was deliberate. She was poisoned."

"Murder?" Kirschoff protested. He pushed his plate away from himself firmly. "No. It couldn't be. No."

"Why else would someone move her body and put it in the freezer?" Terry asked. "They were trying to cover up the cause of death. They figured if she was found in the freezer, we would just assume that she froze to death."

"That's what I thought when I saw her," Erin agreed. "I just assumed… until they said that she'd been moved."

"And clearly, whoever did it didn't think that the police would be able to tell that she had been moved. Or that the medical examiner would be able to tell that she had been exposed to that concentration of carbon dioxide."

They all sat in silence, thinking about what that meant.

"So she was murdered," Charley said.

Erin looked for a way that Beryl could have been accidentally poisoned, but the methods that Kirschoff suggested didn't seem to fit. Beryl wouldn't have been transporting a large amount of dry ice. She hadn't been sitting in a theater or restaurant with a carbon dioxide leak. And if it had been an accident in a restaurant, they would have called for the paramedics to see if she could be revived. It would have been all over the news.

It had to be murder. And the murderer had next moved to an exploding gas canister, something that could have killed multiple people. Whoever wanted to stop the contest was desperate. They were willing to see a lot of people die.

CHAPTER 36

Despite Erin's resolution not to judge the contest, Kirschoff was able to wear her down and convince her that notwithstanding all that had happened so far, she and the others involved with the contest would be perfectly safe. He expounded upon all of the security measures they would have in place.

Once Erin broke down and agreed to go back to Whitewater and follow through on the contract she had signed, she got one more security measure. Terry would not let her go back on her own. He would return with her and stay with her at all times. She kept the hotel room and Vic had already booked another room with Willie and Nilla. If Willie were not staying over for the full time, Terry would pay Vic's hotel bill for the remainder of the time. She could have a room all to herself. But Erin suspected that once Willie caught wind of the possible danger to the judges, he too would decide to stick around and make sure Vic was safe.

In a couple more days, they were back in Whitewater, ramping up for the actual contest.

Vic came up to Erin's room with Nilla and they introduced the dogs. Erin expected that the little dog would be cowering behind Vic's legs upon being faced with the much larger German shepherd, but instead, Nilla appeared to be the aggressor, barreling in to sniff K9 thoroughly, circling around him. K9 stood there, shoulders rounded a little as he looked down at the little white dog, shifting his feet as Nilla poked his nose in awkward places. He sniffed Nilla curiously and looked at Terry.

"Sorry, bud," Terry chuckled. "Good boy. You're being very patient."

K9's big tail swept back and forth slowly. Eventually, he lay down, tired of the little dog's antics. Nilla investigated the rest of the hotel room, then returned to K9 and snuggled close to him.

Terry supervised the dogs while they talked. Erin told Vic about how Terry would be staying with her, and that maybe Willie should stick around to provide extra security for Vic as well.

"I don't need anyone guarding me," Vic protested. "I'm perfectly capable of looking after myself!" She patted her concealed holster, eyes blazing. "Willie can go back to Bald Eagle Falls if he wants. I don't need him to look after me."

Erin looked over at Terry, but he was watching K9, carefully avoiding their discussion.

The last time they had gone in somewhere expecting Vic to be able to protect herself with her gun—the last couple of times, in fact—Erin and Vic had ended up being held at gunpoint. Vic's gun hadn't even come out until it was too late. There had been no shoot-outs; someone had gotten the drop on them and they had been unable to do anything about it.

"It never hurts to have one more person on your side," Erin said tactfully.

Vic glared at her, but finally nodded. "Yeah. As long as you don't think I'm some helpless woman that needs a man to protect her."

"I never said that."

"I can take care of myself."

"I know. It's just that this time, we have some psycho out there who could be targeting us because we're involved with the contest. And that's… not a position we want to be in. We don't want… this person… to be able to get to us easily."

Terry looked over at them suddenly, his face full of tension. His quick movement made Erin jump and the anxiety in his face was so pronounced it actually made her look back toward the door to see if someone had snuck in behind them.

"Terry….?"

Terry looked at Erin, apparently not seeing her panic, and his gaze slid past her to Vic. "What about… Theresa?"

Vic rolled her eyes. "What about Theresa? She got the drop on you too, if you remember. I wasn't exactly helpless. We rescued you, not the other way around."

He shook this off with a toss of his head like a dog. "That's not what I mean. I mean… she's still out there." He blinked at them. "What if this is Theresa?"

"What?"

"What if the person who is sabotaging the contest, trying to get it shut down, is Theresa."

The color drained from Vic's face. "No. It couldn't be. It's too dangerous for her to show her face around here. She wouldn't come back looking for trouble when she might get caught. She's too wily."

"If she heard that you were judging it, you and Erin, she could decide to do something about it. Figure she could get at you if she was careful."

"But she hasn't been careful. Whoever it is hasn't been careful. If it was Theresa trying to get at me, then why would she kill off Beryl? Why would she cause the explosion that could have killed Charley and Hans? That wouldn't make any sense. She would stay under cover until she could target me."

They all sat there, looking at each other and trying to calculate just how crazy Theresa was. She had attacked them all before. She'd had all of them under her control. She'd nearly killed Terry and Detective Jack Ward. She'd killed Bo Biggles. The police figured she was responsible for the death of her parents and a number of hits for the Jackson clan. She wasn't called Crazy Theresa for nothing.

She might go after Vic or Erin, or even Terry or Willie, but there was no motive for her to kill Beryl. It wasn't like Theresa could have mistaken Beryl for Erin or Vic. There would be no reason for her to kill Kirschoff or Charley or to shut down the contest.

Erin was pretty sure that there was no way it could be Theresa.

Pretty sure.

~

Erin was jumpy being back in Whitewater.

Everything would be fine. She now had plenty of security. And Vic was armed, though Erin wasn't sure how much good Vic's gun would be if someone managed to make it past the rest of the layers of security. It would probably mean that someone had managed to sneak through the security and got the drop on them. Or that it was someone close to them that they would never have suspected. Or maybe that the security had been faced with overwhelming force. In the first two cases, Vic probably wouldn't even get her gun out until it was too late and, in the last, a single handgun wasn't going to do much good against such power.

They just had to hope that whoever was behind the incidents was finished or would be too cautious to attack again because of the increased security.

During the opening ceremonies for the contest, Erin was all eyes, continually checking the wings of the stage to make sure that no one was sneaking up on them, searching the crowd for anyone menacing or any sign of weapons, unable to concentrate on what Chef Kirschoff and the sponsors had to say. Vic had to nudge her when they were expected to get up and acknowledge the applause as their names were called.

More speeches. No apparent threats. Everything went as smoothly as if they had been planning for this for two years instead of just a few weeks.

More applause.

Unexpected fireworks. Erin nearly jumped out of her seat. She clutched at Vic's arm and looked around, thinking they were being attacked from all sides. Vic put her hand over Erin's, trying to calm her. Lots of *oohing* and *aahing* and thrilled gasps from the crowd as, for the next twenty minutes, the fireworks kept going on in a dazzling display overhead.

The fireworks were followed by a social event with sponsors and contestants. Not a full dinner, but drinks and hors d'oeuvres. Erin was glad to get away from the open-air amphitheater. It felt safer inside the ballroom at the hotel.

"You okay?" Vic asked, patting Erin on the shoulder as they were able to rejoin the men.

"Yeah. Just a little jumpy."

"Well, Terry's here." Vic looked around and pointed at the doors. "And there's plenty of security. Nothing is going to happen in here."

Erin nodded her agreement. If she could just make her body believe that too. Terry gave her a hug, holding her close.

"You want to dance?" he suggested, nodding to the dance floor. Erin hadn't been planning to, but she hadn't been able to do much that could be considered romantic with Terry lately, so she agreed.

"Sure. Sounds good."

Terry had K9 *stay* close by. He sat watching them, ears pricked up curiously. It was a slow song, so she didn't have to worry about Terry bouncing around too much and aggravating his head. It felt good, holding each other close and pretending that everything was normal again. That nothing had ever happened to put their lives or relationship at risk—just a normal couple in love, enjoying time together slow-dancing.

When the song ended and they left the dance floor, however, Terry seemed a little unsteady. It was hard for Erin to put her finger on anything. It just seemed like he was moving more slowly than he should, his reactions just a bit off. The lights started to flash as a faster number started. Terry's hand went up to his forehead.

"You're not feeling well," Erin guessed.

He tried to shrug it off. "I'm fine."

"I don't think you are. Is the music bothering you?"

He sighed. "The music. The lights. The fireworks. I have to admit… they made me a bit jumpy too. Nothing like loud bangs and the smell of gunpowder to get a policeman's adrenaline going."

"Do you want to knock off for the night? Head back to the hotel room?"

"You still need to circulate and make nice."

"I can circulate for a little while and then come up. I'm safe while I'm here, and Willie can walk me up."

Terry shook his head. "No, really… I said that I would stay here and look after you."

"I was mostly worried about being outside or going around town by myself. But here, it's all secure. I'll be all right." Even though Erin was still nervous and jumpy, she didn't want Terry staying there if his head was bothering him. If he didn't take care of himself, he would be out of commission for several days. Which wasn't what either of them wanted.

"I don't know. Are you sure?"

"Why don't you go over and talk with Willie, see what he thinks."

Even though Terry had never fully trusted Willie, he did trust Willie's opinion on security matters. Whatever his personal opinion, Willie was the first one Terry would go to for things like search and rescue or Willie's other areas of expertise.

"Okay. You stay here. Don't get into any trouble."

Erin wasn't sure what trouble she was going to get into at the event. She wasn't going to leave the ballroom or even have any alcohol. Terry called K9 to heel and left her to talk to Willie.

Erin smiled at people, shook hands, and tried to remember names to go with all of the faces. Crowds were not her thing, but she had signed up for it when she had agreed to help Chef Kirschoff out with the judging. The judges were expected to schmooze with the contestants, town council members, sponsors, and anyone else who might bring in more business and good publicity.

Everything was pretty much a blur. Smile, shake hands, say nice things about the contest and looking forward to trying out all of the great entries. Move on to the next person and repeat.

"Hey, Erin," a large hand clapped over Erin's arm, nearly sending her through the roof. She yelped and pulled back, but the offender didn't even seem to notice. "Hey, how's it going? Good party!"

"Yes." She pulled back from him, trying to get perspective.

Norman. She remembered the name, but where did she know him from? Was he one of the sponsors or the competitors? She smiled politely, waiting for him to fill her in on the details.

"I'm really glad that they decided to go ahead with the competition," Norman said. "I'll bet you are too."

"Well… I wasn't too sure about that."

"But all of the exposure that you're getting, and the honorarium. You wouldn't want to miss out on that."

"I don't want to get in the middle of something that might be dangerous, either."

"Oh, come on…" He gave her a knowing look. "You say that you don't want to be involved, but I remember what happened on the ship." He tapped the side of his nose.

He was one of Vic's friends. That's how she knew him. He was one of the contestants.

"I didn't want to get in the middle of that either… it just happened. I never… I don't want to put myself or anyone around me at risk."

"But you don't think there really is any risk, do you? I mean, what's going to happen? It's a cooking contest!"

"You know what happened to Beryl."

He made a *pfff* noise and waved her comment away. "Beryl? That was just an accident. And if it wasn't... well, I can think of a lot of people who wanted her out of the contest."

"It wasn't just an accident." She didn't tell him it was CO2 poisoning or murder, but if it wasn't an accident, then he had to know that it had been intentional and targeted.

"I think it was. The police here, this podunk little town, they're just making up drama. Probably the first death they've had to investigate in twenty years. They're making the best of it."

Erin shook her head. Not only was she irritated at him for arguing, but she didn't like him talking about Whitewater that way and, by association, any little town in the area, like Bald Eagle Falls. "Sorry, I have to go see someone..." she told Norman, and headed across the floor to a knot of people.

He followed her, talking the whole time as if she wanted to hear him instead of leaving him behind.

"Beryl. Everyone wanted her out. The only reason she was selected as a judge was that she was Kirschoff's old flame. So he gave in to her badgering and let her be a judge."

Erin stopped and stared at him. Was that how people thought of her too? Because she was friends with Kirschoff, he had been persuaded to put her on the judges' panel? She hadn't approached him, he had approached her and asked her to be on it. And they had never been lovers, just cooking friends, enjoying the exchange of recipes and tips and whipping up a couple of creations together.

"You didn't know that?" Norman laughed loudly. "I suppose he told you that you were the only one. You didn't know that he was involved with Beryl?"

"I don't know anything about it," Erin said icily. "His affairs are his own business. It doesn't have anything to do with me."

"I bet you would have liked to have stabbed her! Am I right? Acting like she owns Kirschoff, when he's out dogging around with everyone else?"

"I don't know what you're talking about. I haven't seen him since we were on the cruise. We didn't have any kind of relationship then or now. I don't know anything about who is… friendly with him."

"Yeah. Did he tell you he's married, too?" His braying laughter rang out again. People turned to stare.

Erin swallowed. Had Chef Kirschoff ever mentioned that he had a wife? Or even implied it? Charley had her sights set on him, and that didn't seem to matter at all to Kirschoff. He was happy to play along.

She could bet that Charley had no idea he had a wife.

"I wouldn't know anything about that."

"Well, he is," Norman asserted. "You just ask him."

Vic appeared at Norman's side, looking at him like she wasn't sure what was up with him. "Norman? What's going on?"

"I was just telling your friend here about Beryl Batcombe and Chef Kirschoff." He raised and lowered thick eyebrows in a Groucho Marx leer.

"Beryl and Hans?" Vic shook her head and took a step back. "No way. Who told you that?"

"I saw the two of them together myself, heard them arguing."

"How much have you had to drink tonight?" Vic arched her eyebrows.

"I'm not drunk. Okay, maybe I'm a little bit buzzed, but that's all. Hardly had anything yet."

"Well, maybe you'd better cut it off there. I wouldn't want you to put your foot in your mouth and say something that you can't take back later."

"It's true. I haven't told you anything that isn't true."

"But maybe you'd better call it a night. You get buzzed like this, and your judgment is off."

He rolled his eyes at Vic and stalked away. Not out of the ballroom, but toward the bar and more people he could share his theories with.

"Thanks," Erin told Vic. "I was having problems getting away from him."

"He should not be spreading rumors like that around. He should know better. And maybe he does when he's sober."

"Did Terry talk to Willie?"

Vic nodded and looked around. She spotted her boyfriend across the ballroom and gave him a little wave. "Yeah. They talked. I think he convinced Terry that he could manage to keep us both safe and sent him up to his room to sleep. I don't want his head getting too bad."

"Yeah. Me either. It seemed like it could be the beginning of a big one. I'll just stay down here for a few more minutes, then I'll go up and make sure he's taken his medication and gone to bed."

Vic nodded. She took another look at Norman. "Sorry about him. I don't know what he's going on about."

"He says… that Beryl and Chef Kirschoff were—uh—together. And that Kirschoff is married…?"

"Yeah, I think I heard that."

"He's married? But he and Charley…"

Vic shrugged uncomfortably. "I don't know. Maybe he told her. Maybe they have an open relationship. Or they're separated."

Somehow, Erin couldn't picture that. "She certainly doesn't sound like a very nice woman."

"His wife?"

"Beryl."

"Yeah, well, that's exactly what you told me, isn't it? You said that she was bad news before she died. She really wound you up that night."

Erin gave her a sideways look. "Just don't go spreading that around. I don't want Coleman hearing that I had a motive to murder her."

"I know you didn't. I won't say anything." Vic patted Erin on the arm. "Every time I hear something about her, it seems like there's someone else who would have liked to have gotten her out of the way."

"That's what Norman was just saying. But he… put Chef Kirschoff at the top of his list. Hans would never do anything like that! He's not a violent man."

"We don't really know him well enough to know what kind of a man he is," Vic pointed out. "So we've had dinner together a couple of times and had a few meetings and conversations. That doesn't mean that we know him. Not like you would need to know someone in order to say that."

"Can you see him hurting anyone? Getting violent?"

"Whether I can or not, that doesn't mean anything. Getting violent…? I've seen some videos of him blowing his top in the kitchen. Believe me, he was not a meek and mild-mannered little chef."

"A commercial kitchen can be high-stress." Erin knew that wasn't an excuse. She just didn't want to hear what Vic had to say. She sighed. "Don't tell me that he could actually be a suspect."

"We don't know," Vic said. "You know how hard it can be to tell whether someone could actually kill someone else or not."

Erin, unfortunately, had learned this. It was one of the reasons she hadn't wanted to go back to the competition.

CHAPTER 37

Erin had already been in the ballroom for longer than she had wanted to. Each time she approached a competitor, Beryl and the explosion were the topic of conversation. All kinds of speculations were tossed around about who or what kind of person could have killed her. Erin really didn't want to hear any more guesses.

"Would you mind walking me upstairs now?" she asked Willie. "It's not a big deal. I could just go up on my own. But… I did tell Terry that I wouldn't walk around on my own."

"Of course," Willie agreed. "He asked me and I said I would walk you up."

Vic tagged along so that she wouldn't be on her own either.

"I'm sorry about this," Erin apologized. "Acting as security guard probably wasn't the way you planned on spending your weekend."

"I'm happy to do it," Willie assured her. "Other work can wait. I'd rather know the two of you are safe."

"There probably isn't any real danger. But…"

"One person is dead and two others ended up in the hospital. In my books, that's enough reason to be cautious."

"I suppose. I just feel a little silly about it."

Willie shook his head. "No worries."

He walked Erin to her door. Erin swiped the key card and let herself in. The lights were on, so she suspected Terry hadn't gone to sleep like he had said he would. She rolled her eyes and prepared herself to patiently coax him into doing what he needed to do for his health.

"He's not sleeping?" Willie asked.

"I don't think so."

"Do you want me to stick around?"

"No, we're good for the night."

Erin took a step into the hotel room, then heard Terry in the bathroom being sick. She stopped where she was.

It was possible that a migraine had made him sick to his stomach. Sometimes that happened, but it was rare for him. But she again heard Coleman telling her about Beryl throwing up before she had died. One of the symptoms of carbon dioxide poisoning.

She looked over her shoulder at Willie. He had also heard and hadn't turned around to leave. "Hang on…"

"Yeah."

K9 lay outside the bathroom, looking concerned. Erin tapped on the door. "Terry?" She opened it and peeked in.

"Sick," Terry muttered. "Be out in a few minutes."

"Terry, is it your head? Is it because of a migraine?"

He shook his head uncertainly. "Really wobbly on my feet. Room is spinning. And then my stomach…"

Erin looked at him, hunched over the toilet, her stomach in a tight, sick knot. She looked at Willie once more, and Vic behind him, straining to see past and find out what was going on.

"Do you have a headache too?"

"Some… not like usual."

Erin sniffed the air. But she knew that CO2 was odorless. There would be no way for her to sniff it out if there were a higher-than-normal concentration of CO2 in the room. All she could smell was vomit and sweat.

"I think we should take you to the hospital."

"No. I'll be fine."

"I'm worried, Terry. Beryl was poisoned with CO2. She was throwing up. If someone is trying to kill the judges or the contest, they could have poisoned the air in the room…"

"I wasn't feeling well before I came up here. That's why I came up," he reminded her.

That was true. Was it something else, then? Could someone have poisoned food or drink that was being served in the ballroom? If so, they could have dozens of sick people on their hands before long.

"I really think... we need to make sure this isn't another 'accident' related to the competition."

"I'll just go to bed once... I'm done."

Erin looked at Willie. "What do you think?"

"I think there have already been too many accidents in the course of this competition. He's probably fine." Willie pressed his lips together in a thin, straight line. "But I wouldn't want to bet anyone's life on it."

"Willie agrees," Erin told Terry. "Grab the garbage can and let's get you out of here in case there is carbon dioxide."

Terry rested his head on his arm, leaning on the edge of the toilet. "Erin... I'm not up to it."

"We'll help you. You can't stay here."

He was ready to argue, but Erin dug in her heels.

"I'm not letting you tell me no. So you can waste your time arguing, or you can come," she told him as firmly as she could. She hated arguments and really hoped that he wouldn't fight her on it. It would just make him sicker and weaker.

"Okay," Terry agreed. "Give me a minute to get my strength..."

Erin pulled her phone out and took a look at the time. "One minute. I don't know how long it takes someone to be poisoned by breathing too much CO2, so I'm not leaving it any longer than that."

"Mmm. A little less literal...?"

"No." Erin kept her eyes on the clock.

After another pause, Terry reached for the garbage can and tried to push himself to his feet. It took a couple of tries. He was much more unsteady than he had been down in the ballroom. There was a pain in Erin's chest and she tried to keep herself from panicking. It wouldn't help anyone for her to flip out. She pushed the door open the rest of the way and slid an arm around Terry, trying to stabilize him and help to support his weight.

Once she got him out of the bathroom, Willie inserted himself on the other side and helped to steady the garbage can Terry was carrying. "There you go. Let's go."

"I don't want to go to the hospital," Terry said. "Can we just… get another room?"

"No. I want to be close to the hospital in case you get any worse."

K9 followed. They let the hotel room door shut behind them. It was slow going to get Terry down to Willie's truck and to get him settled into a seat.

"Thanks. I'm going to be fine now," Terry assured them. "Really. I'm feeling better in the fresh air."

The rest of them piled into the truck. Erin sat next to Terry and tried not to stare at him. They only made it a couple of blocks before Terry started throwing up again. The pungent acid smell made Erin gag. It was a good thing she was sitting the closest to the garbage can, because she might end up needing it as well. She'd always been super sensitive to smells.

"Uh oh." Vic buzzed down her window and motioned for Willie to do the same. "We'll try to get you lots of fresh air."

Erin inched her face closer to the open window, gulping the chilly, sweet air as if she were drinking it.

"I'd be fine in another hotel room," Terry muttered.

And maybe he would have been. Or if they went home or booked a hotel in one of the nearby towns where nobody knew where they were to follow them and poison them again.

But she didn't know how much CO2 he might have in his system already, and if they had to do something special to clear it out, or if he just needed to replace it with clean air. She couldn't stop thinking about Beryl dying so quickly after throwing up. She hadn't had anyone to take care of her. But Terry did, and Erin was not going to let anything happen to him on her watch.

CHAPTER 38

"Do you remember when you were poisoned and I had to rush you to the hospital?" Willie asked Erin. She suspected he was trying to distract her and get her thinking about something other than whether Terry was going to die from how much CO2 he'd inhaled already.

"I don't remember much about it," she said. "You went really fast. I was kind of confused as to what was going on."

"Yes, you were," he agreed.

"And you were singing, weren't you?" Erin shook her head. "Did I ever thank you for how quickly you got me to the hospital for treatment?"

"You did. I'm glad I managed to get you there in time."

"Me too," Terry agreed, still hanging his head in the garbage can, breathing shallowly. "But I don't think this is CO2 poisoning. Just… a bug, maybe. I could just sleep it off…"

"Then you can sleep it off at the hospital," Erin advised. "I just need to know that you'll have medical care if… something goes wrong."

"Just a bug," Terry repeated.

"If is it carbon dioxide, then how did it get in the room?" Vic asked. "How does that work? I know you could get it from a malfunctioning furnace."

"That's carbon monoxide," Terry said into the can.

"Chef Kirschoff says it happens with carbonation machines with bad tubes, or from dry ice," Erin told Vic.

"But there wasn't any carbonation machine or dry ice in the hotel room."

"No. But… someone could have leaked it there earlier in the day when we weren't around… maybe just opened up the valve on one of those canisters. That would work, wouldn't it?"

"Sure," Willie nodded. "I don't know how fast after that it would dissipate."

"I guess maybe we should have looked around for anything weird before we left the hotel room. I didn't think about finding a CO2 source, just getting him out of there."

"I'm sure that was the right thing to do," Willie assured her. "You have to worry about safety first, investigating later. If there is a CO2 canister in the room, it will be there when we get back."

"No, it won't. Whoever put it there will take it back out. If they could get in without being detected once, they can get in a second time when they realize they've failed."

"True."

"Maybe we should call that policeman," Vic suggested. "He could investigate before they have a chance to remove the evidence. Don't you think?"

"No…I really don't want to talk to him again. He's going to have questions…"

"That's his job. You wouldn't be a suspect, just a witness."

"That's what they told me the first time. But I sure felt like a suspect."

"What did he say about the threatening note?"

Erin breathed out in a hiss. "Oh, boy."

Terry raised his head slightly to look at her. His face shone with a layer of sweat. His hair was gathering into little peaks from the moisture. "Threatening note?"

Vic's eyes widened. She mouthed, "You didn't tell him?"

Erin just closed her eyes.

"What threatening note?" Terry demanded.

None of them said anything at first. Willie finally spoke up. "Erin received a threatening note before she went back to Bald Eagle Falls. Telling her to get out of the contest. Or else."

"Why didn't you tell me this?"

"I… meant to. It didn't come up. There was so much else going on, with Charley and Chef Kirschoff. And… everything."

"You should have told me. You don't hide something like that, Erin. If we're a partnership, a team, then…" he trailed off.

She didn't want him thinking that they weren't.

"It isn't that. It's just like I said. Too much going on. I didn't really… take it that seriously. And… I didn't want to worry you. You have enough to worry about these days."

"You still tell me. I want to know. It's a lot more stressful thinking that you're trying to do everything alone and not sharing with me."

"I suppose."

"You didn't take it seriously?"

"No… Yes and no… I was planning to go back to Bald Eagle Falls anyway, so it didn't really make any difference."

"And *did* you report it?"

"Yes. I went in and reported it. But I don't think they took it too seriously either."

"With one person already dead and two injured? They certainly should have."

"But it could have just been a hoax. Someone unrelated to Beryl's death. I don't know. I didn't want to take it seriously either. I just wanted… to get home to you."

They were quiet.

Terry wasn't able to continue the discussion. He was soon retching again, though there wasn't anything but stringy yellow acid left in his stomach. Erin looked away, trying to ignore it and keep her own stomach under control.

They reached the hospital without any mishaps. Erin helped get Terry checked in and his garbage can was swapped for a basin. He sat in the waiting area for a doctor to be freed up to deal with him. When a nurse finally called him to a curtained area to hear his story and give him a preliminary check, she noted he was dehydrated and started an IV.

"We'll take good care of you," she promised. "Probably just a stomach bug."

"That's what I said," Terry agreed.

And they were all happy to believe that, until the other cases started to roll in.

Erin had been kicked out of Terry's curtained cubicle while the doctor examined him. It was Vic who first saw Melanie come in, hunched over, carrying a bowl. Her lips were dry and cracked. She looked miserable. Vic looked at Erin and then hurried over to Melanie.

"Hey, Mel, are you okay?"

"Sick," Melanie groaned. "I don't know, maybe just the flu, but it feels too..."

"Do you think it could be something else?"

"Maybe." Melanie positioned herself in the line for the triage nurse. "Food poisoning, maybe?"

Vic patted her on the back and murmured some encouraging words, then returned to Erin's side. "I think you should place that call to the policeman."

It *was* weird that the two of them both got sick at about the same time. Erin tried to find an explanation. It could be something completely innocent. Someone carrying a virus had been in contact with both of them. Something that they had eaten in the ballroom. The flashing lights and pounding beat of the music. Different things could affect people.

But they had to be careful in case it was poisoning. Erin couldn't just ignore that because of her own reluctance to talk to the police.

"Okay. I will." They weren't supposed to have phones turned on in the emergency room, so she went out the doors to sit in the patio area that everyone used for smoking, even though there were signs with big lettering warning people that it was against the by-laws to smoke there. Erin shivered. She found Coleman's contact information and tapped it.

She was hoping that Coleman wouldn't answer. He'd be busy with something else. But even if he were busy, she still needed to report her suspicions to someone official. Maybe, like with the written threat, they would brush it off.

CHAPTER 39

By the time Coleman was convinced that there was something for him to look into, there were three more people from the contest in the emergency room. And they just kept coming.

A policeman showed up, not Coleman himself, and confirmed that they were looking into it. They had shut down the event in the ballroom and taped off all of the food serving and preparation areas. The hotel was doing a room-to-room check and checking participants off a checklist to ensure that no one was non-responsive in their hotel room or unaccounted for.

"Must be food poisoning," Deputy Wake said with authority. "Shrimp or something that was being served at the event. Seafood and egg dishes can wreak havoc if they're not properly prepared and stored."

Erin nodded and scratched K9's ears. He was restless sitting with her when he was used to always being with Terry.

As a baker, she didn't have to worry as much about food poisoning, but she did have breakfast muffins with bacon in them and used eggs and milk in the kitchen. Surfaces had to be kept clean and everything washed thoroughly so that uncooked egg didn't come into contact with prepared food. But a catering business should have been knowledgeable about all of the necessary precautions and should have been able to prevent the spread of any pathogen.

"This is pretty crazy. I've had what might have been food poisoning before, but I've never seen anything like this."

"Probably negligence," Wake said with a vigorous nod. "I bet the catering company gets their butts sued. And probably the event coordinators too."

"It's not their fault."

"They're cooks, they should know well enough what precautions need to be followed."

Erin hadn't considered that. She could see his point, but Chef Kirschoff couldn't have been involved in every little detail. Surely no one expected that he would be inspecting kitchens and taking the holding temperature of the dishes the catering company had prepared. He would be relying on them to know what they were doing.

"How is Chef Kirschoff? I haven't seen him here." Erin looked around, in case he had shown up since she had been talking to Wake.

"Sounds like he's got it, but not badly enough to be hospitalized yet. They'll be keeping an eye on everyone to make sure they are okay."

Erin looked at the time on her phone. Terry was finally sleeping peacefully. She wanted to be by his side when he woke up again, but with the amount of time he'd spent throwing up, she figured that wouldn't be for a few more hours. In the meantime, she wanted to know what was going on with the competition and whether they were going to cancel it or not.

"Are you shutting down the contest?"

He barked out a laugh. "I don't have the authority to do that."

"I mean… the police department. Or the Town Council. Is anyone going to say that there have been enough problems with it, it needs to be closed down?"

"I don't think anyone but the organizers or sponsors can do that. It isn't really up to the PD or Town Council."

"The Town Council could withdraw their permits."

"You'd have to talk to someone there. I don't know. But I get the feeling that people are more interested in going ahead than in shutting it down. They've worked so hard to get this far, they're not going to let some psycho with an agenda get it shut down."

"Who would want to shut it down so badly?" Erin mused. "I mean, it's not like it's political, supporting some kind of controversial charity. It's just a fun contest. A chance at a prize."

"Maybe someone trying to eliminate their competitors. Make them too sick to enter anything."

"But the first victim was a judge, not an entrant. And Charley is a competitor, but Chef Kirschoff is an organizer. I can't figure out who would have a motive to harm all three. And then… everyone who's sick now."

"Maybe it's a smokescreen. Not everyone was being targeted. Some of them were to throw us off. Especially the food poisoning." Wake made a motion to include all the victims in the waiting room. "That could just be intended to throw us off the trail. Or only one person was actually being targeted, and the rest are collateral damage."

If that were true, then the mind behind all of the incidents was very disturbed—someone who didn't care who got in his way.

When Terry was released from the hospital, they all went back to the hotel. Willie dropped them off to gas up the truck. Terry was still looking tired and drawn, so Erin had him sit on one of the cushy lobby chairs with K9 and she and Vic went to the front desk to inquire about whether their rooms were available or whether the police had sealed them off for their investigation. Vic put down a couple of bags of groceries she had picked up while they had been waiting for Terry to be released.

"Everything is just as it was, Miss Price," the young woman at the desk assured Erin. "The police did ask to have a look at it, but they didn't find anything wrong. Of course, there were many more people who were affected by then, so we knew it wasn't was localized to your room."

"Right, of course," Erin agreed. She leaned forward, keeping her voice low. "Have they made any progress on figuring out what happened? Was the food contaminated? Was it food poisoning? Was it tampered with?"

The woman looked back and forth. "We're not supposed to say anything about it, I'm sorry."

"I think the hotel owes it to their guests to let them know what they have found out and what they are going to do to keep it from happening in the future. We still have other events scheduled. No one wants to get sick from going to them."

"I'm sure there will not be a repeat at any of the other events. We have identified the problems and they have been taken care of."

"What was it, then?"

"I don't know all of the details."

"I'm one of the judges and I'm a cook. I want to know if it is going to be safe for me to go forward. I want to know where the problem was."

The hotel worker hesitated. "I don't know..."

"Was food not prepared properly? Stored properly? Was something put into it?"

"It was the storage," she said finally. "There was something wrong with the thermostats or the temperature sensors. I don't know all of the details, but I guess it means that they were not kept cold enough."

Erin nodded. "Who had access to the fridges?"

"The police are investigating. I'm sure the cooks have given them all of the information they need to investigate it. We won't be using our own fridges for the remainder of the activities. We will be outsourcing, and there will be monitoring and extra security." The woman shook her head. "It's a nightmare, I'll tell you that. They're worried we're going to end up with a loss from this competition instead of a profit. When the hotel is hosting all of the guests! It should have been a great money-maker."

Erin nodded sympathetically. "Well, who knows, maybe it will still turn out all right."

CHAPTER 40

Erin beckoned to Terry. He got up and joined them. Erin watched as Vic picked up her groceries once again.

"Do you want some help with that?"

"Oh, I'm okay. You go ahead and get Terry settled."

"Terry will be fine." Erin looked at him, and he nodded. "This looks like a two-person job."

"I can manage."

They all walked to the elevator. "Where's your keycard?" Erin asked Vic. "You're going to have to put everything down to find it and get it out."

"Uh… in my wallet…" Vic bounced her handbag with her hip. "In there."

Erin hit the buttons for her floor and Vic's and unzipped Vic's little bag. She pulled out Vic's wallet and managed to find the room key. When the elevator stopped, she got out on Vic's floor and nodded to Terry. "I'll see you in a minute."

"Sure."

Erin followed Vic to her hotel room and slid the card key into the reader. The indicator light turned green, and she turned the handle and pushed it open for Vic. She followed Vic in.

"There you are. I'll just put the key—" Erin cut herself off.

Vic looked around the room in dismay. "What happened? Someone broke into my room!"

Everything was in disarray. Pillows and blankets strewn on the floor, clothes everywhere, the lamp knocked over, clock hanging off of the bedside table by its electrical cord.

"What were they looking for?" Erin breathed. She tried to imagine what someone might think Vic had. Valuables? Some evidence that was related to Beryl's death? Did they confuse Vic's room with Erin's and think that they were tossing her room?

There was a growling and yipping sound from the bathroom. They both turned toward it at once.

"Nilla!" Vic opened the door and saw that the bathroom was in a similar state, with a yellow puddle in the corner. She smacked her forehead. "Oh no!"

"You left him here by himself?" Erin asked.

"I thought he'd be okay for a couple of hours. And then… when everything happened with Terry, I didn't even think about him being locked up here by himself…"

"Well…" Erin started picking up the clothes strewn across the floor. "At least he found things to do to keep himself entertained!"

Back in their room, Erin brought up the competition once more time. They had discussed it at length at the hospital, but Erin could see just by looking at him that Terry was still feeling pretty rough.

"Are you sure you still want to go ahead with this? I feel bad that I'm causing all of this trouble and that you got sick because of my thing. You don't want to just go back to Bald Eagle Falls?"

"I already told you no. I'm not going back without you."

"And I could quit and go back with you."

"This is supposed to be good publicity for your bakery. It's going to be negative publicity if you back out now, right before the contest. You've worked hard to make this happen. I'm not going to back down because some psycho is trying to sabotage the thing." He gave her a hard stare. "Tennesseans are tough. You just try pushing us and see what happens. We just push back harder. People might have been willing to close down the contest after Batcombe's death. But after everything that's happened? Hell, no. We're not letting someone push us around."

Erin chuckled and shook her head. "That's crazy."

But she'd seen the same reaction from others. Fold in the face of danger? Run from the threat? No way. Each misfortune just seemed to make people more determined to keep the contest going. There was no way people were going to back out after the food poisoning incident. They would stand strong and show everyone the stuff they were made of.

"It may be crazy," Terry agreed. "I know I should be telling you to just stay out of it and be safe. How many times have I told you that? But this guy—whoever he is—has my blood up now. I want to see this thing through."

"Okay. So I guess as long as the contest goes ahead, so do we."

He nodded firmly. "That's right."

Terry was still short on sleep. He soon drifted off as Erin did some work on her computer.

Well, *some* work.

Some mindless entertainment, reading social media, and following rabbit trails. The internet offered unlimited possibilities for letting her mind wander.

Erin read through each of the social media posts that she came across about the contest. And of course, about the bad luck that had plagued it since Beryl was found dead in a commercial freezer.

But Beryl hadn't died there. The news stories didn't follow up on that detail. They made it sound like an accident. Erin read through the articles, comparing them to see who had the most recent details and who was just reposting what had happened days before.

One of the local sites had more details on Beryl than the rest. Not about her being dead before she was put in the freezer, but her biographical information. Most of the sites just copied what was written in the contest promotional bio, or some of the later stories used phrases from her obituary. But the Tattler did not.

Beryl Batcombe, author of the controversial book, *Recipes from Mawmaw's Kitchen, Traditional Tennessean Cookery...*

Erin frowned. She recalled that Chef Kirschoff had told her that Beryl's cookbook had not done as well as she had expected it to. But how could a cookbook be controversial? She couldn't think of what could be less controversial than a collection of recipes.

She tapped the name of the book into her search bar. The article that Erin had been reading did not pop up, but several older articles did. Written, Erin assumed, soon after it had been published. She clicked on the first one and scanned the page.

Beryl had been accused of stealing other people's recipes and then passing them off as her own (or her mawmaw's.) Always a difficult allegation to prove, since many different people could have similar recipes. Sometimes basic recipes that had been passed down for generations and may have originated from the back of a tub of Crisco. She knew from her own business research that lists of ingredients could not be copyrighted, only the narrative instructions.

But it would seem that Beryl hadn't bothered to put the directions in her own words, and more than one person had spoken up to say that she had stolen their family recipes and was pretending that they were from her fictional grandma.

Well, Erin supposed she did have a grandma—two of them, plus more in each previous generation—but it would appear that none of them had passed down her collection of recipes to her.

She got out her notepad and made a few notes. Had Beryl been planning to open her dream restaurant on the back of the contest? It seemed just like her to use the competition as the publicity and leverage she needed to get a leg up with her new restaurant.

She was ambitious.

Maybe that was why she had been in the freezer. Maybe she had been hoping to get the Buttermilk Biscuits restaurant shut down and to take over the location for herself, and had ended up getting stuck there.

But that wasn't what had happened, because she hadn't died in the restaurant.

Not in the freezer, anyway. Had the police figured out where she had been killed? Had she died inside the restaurant and her killer had dragged her into the freezer to get her out of sight? Or had she died in her car? Had it been parked in the restaurant parking lot?

Erin stared thoughtfully at her notes.

CHAPTER 41

Terry was still asleep when Erin decided to call Chef Kirschoff. She didn't want to wake Terry up but, after waiting for a while, she decided she couldn't wait. She would have to take the chance. If he were deeply asleep, her call wouldn't wake him, and if he were only in a light sleep cycle, he would probably want her to wake him up anyway.

She dialed Kirschoff's number. He might not be up yet either. The police officer she had talked to had said that he only ended up with a mild case of food poisoning, but it could have gotten worse over time. He might be trying to catch up on his sleep, just like Terry.

The phone rang a few times and then it was answered. "Hans here."

"Uh, Hans. Chef Kirschoff. It's Erin."

"Erin," his voice was warm. "How are you? Don't tell me that you got this beastly food poisoning, please!"

"No. I managed not to get it, but Terry got a pretty good case. One of the first ones. We spent the night at the hospital."

"Oh, how awful. Tell him how sorry I am. It seems like we can't catch a break for this contest. Every time we think we have put all of the bad luck behind us, something else comes up."

"It's not just bad luck."

"I know that… but you don't think that the food poisoning is related, do you? That wasn't intentional. Just an equipment malfunction."

"Have the police identified whether it was a malfunction or tampering?"

"Tampering? Who would tamper with the fridges? Why would anyone *want* to give people food poisoning?"

"Why would anyone want to kill Beryl? Or you or Charley?"

"No one tried to kill us," Kirschoff grumbled. "That was just… there's no proof that anyone tampered with the canister that blew up. That was just a coincidence. There's nothing to tie it to Beryl's death."

"Except that she was killed with carbon dioxide, and it was a carbon dioxide canister that exploded."

"That was just… coincidence. Everything is connected with carbon dioxide right now. That's the whole theme of the cook-off. Wherever you go, you're going to run into something to do with carbon dioxide."

Erin had to admit that was true.

The only incident that they knew for sure was not an accident was Beryl's death. And not knowing exactly how she had been poisoned, they couldn't prove that it was murder and not just some bizarre happenstance, like the people who had dumped dry ice into their swimming pool and ended up poisoning their party guests. Her death could have been accidental and the moving of her body… Erin couldn't think of an explanation for that.

"Anyway, that isn't exactly why I was calling you."

"Oh, I am sorry. I have distracted you."

"No, that's okay. I was actually wondering whether you know where I could get a copy of Beryl's cookbook."

"Her cookbook? I don't know if it is in any of the stores anymore. It didn't sell, so they've probably all been returned to the publisher."

"But somebody in town must have bought it. Did you? The library or Chamber of Commerce? Or maybe she has family members that have a copy?"

She thought about the revelation that Kirschoff had a family. But it was not the right time to bring it up. He would not want to talk to her about that and she wouldn't get a lead on the cookbook.

"No, no family. I don't know if the library would have a copy. Maybe they pick up publications by local authors," Kirschoff said doubtfully.

"How about you? Do you have a copy? I only need to borrow it, I would give it back to you."

"I don't think I have a copy… certainly not here. It would be at home, if I do."

"Oh, okay. I'll check around town. Someone must have a copy or two."

"Yes, I would think someone would."

"So… you knew, Beryl, right?"

"Yes. We already talked about that. At your house."

"Right. I just wondered… I guess she must have contacted you and told you that she wanted to be one of the judges. You said that she was persistent. That she would get what she wanted."

"Yes…?"

"She reached out to you, then? It wasn't like with me and Vic where you just dropped in on us and asked us if we would be judges?"

He cleared his throat. "I don't know who started the conversation…"

That sounded like an evasion. He didn't know whether she had brought it up or whether he had? Did they talk to each other all the time? Or had it been a call out of the blue? Beryl looking for a way to advance.

"Anyway… it doesn't matter who started the conversation. I just wondered if she had told you why she wanted to be one of the judges. Did you guys talk about that?"

There was silence from Kirschoff. Maybe he thought she was trying to trap him somehow. But if he were just interested in promoting the contest, and she had just wanted to be a judge, then what was there to hide?

Nothing, right?

"I mean, Vic and I agreed that it would be good publicity for Auntie Clem's. A good way for us to get the bakery out there in the public eyes. And because I like ice cream."

Kirschoff laughed. "It was the same for Beryl, I'm sure. She wanted the publicity. And she liked ice cream." He chuckled to himself.

"She wanted the publicity? Because of her book?"

"Well… maybe it would have helped her book sales…"

"Why did she want publicity then? Was she…"

She hoped that he would fill in the blanks. It was hard for her to guess what Beryl might have been thinking. Some people just liked to be in the limelight.

"Was she what?" Kirschoff prompted unhelpfully.

"I just thought maybe… she was trying to get publicity for the restaurant she wanted to open. Maybe she was doing a financing and figured if people saw her judging the contest… they would have more trust in her…?"

"Maybe."

She hadn't expected him to spill all of Beryl's plans, but it would be nice if he'd at least jump in with a few of the details.

"Was she going to open her restaurant?"

"I don't know… it was in the early stages. She needed a location, the financing, all of the beginning steps. She needed a plan."

"So was it just a dream? Or did she figure that with the contest, she could make it a reality?"

"I don't know, Erin. Maybe a bit of both."

Erin gave an exasperated sigh. "So you guys were just talking… and she said she would like to be a judge, and you said 'okay, sure,' and that was it? That seems… unlikely. How did she even know you were going to be running a contest? And why did you decide on Whitewater as the location, if not because of Beryl?"

"I really don't think you need to pry into it, Erin. It's just one of those things. We don't know what happened to Beryl. We'll probably never know. It will be one of those cold cases on TV."

"You know a lot more than you are saying."

"Beryl was an old friend."

"A lover."

There were a few seconds of dead silence. "Who told you that?" Kirschoff eventually asked.

"A lot of people talking about Beryl. More than one person must know that the two of you were in a relationship."

"You make it sound sordid. It was nothing like that. Just… two friends… enjoying each other's company."

"Even though you were married to someone else."

"I travel a lot. I am away from my family for long periods of time."

"So you do have a family. And you're carrying on with Beryl and with Charley and who else?"

"I told you, you don't understand. It wasn't like that."

Erin was silent in response this time. She waited. Chef Kirschoff didn't say anything for a long time.

He had been such a nice man. She had enjoyed cooking with him. He had been so warm and real, so comforting to work with. Someone who understood what it was like to adapt his food to different diets so that everyone could enjoy it.

It was like Vic with her LGBT friends from the cruise. They shared certain experiences with each other that Erin would never have. Erin had enjoyed experiences with Chef Kirschoff that were different from what she had with her other friends. A shared base of experiences that made her feel like she really knew him.

When, in fact, she had not even known that he was married.

"Erin. When I am home with my wife… I am with her. She has all of my attention. Everything that I can give. We are good friends and very close. But when I am traveling, it is different. She isn't there. I can talk to her on the phone, but I can't… reach out and touch her. And I am a person who needs… I need the physical presence."

"That's a cop-out for cheating."

"You can't judge someone else's relationship by your own standards. Every relationship is different. The relationship I have with my wife works… and it has enough room in it for me to… have other friends."

Erin snorted in disgust. "Okay. Whatever works for you. But you'd better make sure that Charley knows you have a family. Or I'll tell her. And she won't like it coming from me."

Kirschoff's long sigh carried down the phone line. "Fine. Yes, Erin. I will tell her. You leave it to me to do it my own way."

"I'm not waiting for long. So don't wait until the contest is over. Give her a chance to make an informed decision."

"When I leave here, she will be staying and I will be going away. Why does anything have to change? There is a natural breaking point."

"No. I'm not letting you play around until it's time to leave town, and then just disappear without explaining."

That wouldn't be fair to Charley. She deserved to know before she went any further in the relationship just exactly what the parameters were. Maybe she wouldn't care that he already had a commitment with someone else.

But Erin would have. So she felt it was her responsibility to let Charley know.

~

When she got off the phone, Terry rolled over and looked at her. Erin's face got warm.

"How long have you been awake?"

"Long enough." He smiled and didn't say anything about her being a good or bad sister. Or about investigating something that was none of her business. Maybe he knew it was pointless to try to rein her in. It had never worked before, so what was the point in trying?

"How are you feeling? You look a lot better."

"Yeah." He stretched. "I'm feeling pretty decent right now. I don't know whether it is the IV from the hospital or something else, but I actually feel human again."

He didn't say that he felt better than he had in months, but there was something about him. The way he was holding himself. The warm smile. The little hint of a dimple in one cheek. He seemed like the old Terry for once.

CHAPTER 42

The day that Erin had been waiting for and dreading had finally arrived. Lots of fanfare and flags. Crowds of people who had come to watch the competition and to hopefully get some tasty samples themselves.

The day dawned bright and clear. The first day was the contest for the carbonated drinks. The second day would be ice cream. And then things would go back to normal again. Or settle at a new normal. Maybe things would be better than they had been, with some new customers for Auntie Clem's Bakery. Maybe things had been permanently changed and Erin would lose Chef Kirschoff as a friend. She hated to think they would never see each other or cook together after the contest. But if he was the kind of guy who traveled all over the world with a girl in every port… was that really the sort of person she wanted to be associated with?

But the anticipation was finally over.

During the morning, they had watched both live and recorded video of contestants working in various commercial kitchens that the contest had rented. They were not allowed to know who had made what beverages, since the judging was a blind taste-test rather than contestants being judged on their skill or professional demeanor in the kitchen. The audience was told the background stories of a number of the contestants, but the judges were not privy to that information.

Viewers might have their favorites, but the judges would not hear any of the inspiring or gut-wrenching back stories until after the judging was complete.

The judging was to take place in the high school auditorium. There were tiered benches along one wall, and the judge's table was on a stage that also functioned as a separate, smaller gym. Erin felt nervous having to sit in front of the crowd of people and cameras. It was even more nerve-racking than she had anticipated.

She looked for the people she knew. Vic was at the judging table with her. Terry stood near the front of the gym with K9 at his side. She could see Willie out in the hallway through one of the gym doors. He had Nilla with him, and Erin assumed that he wasn't allowed to enter as long as he had the dog with him. K9 was different, being a police dog.

Vic hadn't managed to find anyone else who would look after the dog during the judging, and she wasn't going to leave him alone in the hotel room again. Erin smiled, remembering the chaos the little whirlwind had wreaked in the small room.

Erin sat down at the long table with the other judges. Each beverage was brought to them in a tiny glass flute. They could drink it down, or taste it and spit, or some combination. In the first round, each judge would give each of the entries a numeric score out of ten. The scores would all be added together, and entries with the top twelve scores would go on to the second round, where they would have a series of "face offs" where each drink would be paired with another. The judges would vote on which of the two drinks would go on to the next round, and so on until they had a first, second, and third place.

That was the portion for which they had to have an odd number of judges so that they could not be deadlocked as to which of the pairs would move into the next round. Erin looked at the newest recruited judge with curiosity.

Lara Gross looked more polished than the rest of the judges. Erin felt like a country bumpkin next to her, though she wasn't even sure what it was that made Lara seem that much more distinguished. She wore a chef's jacket with black accents. Her hair was gathered in a neat bun, like it would be for working in a kitchen. She worked in a steakhouse in the city, and looked cool enough to juggle knives without breaking a sweat. Because she was brought into the judging panel late, her bio wasn't included in any of the contest promotional material. Erin would need to look her up online to find out anything else about her.

She pulled her attention away from the new judge as the first round of drinks were distributed for tasting. She had a job to do, and that didn't include investigating the other judges.

Erin was surprised to find that she could tell the drinks that had been fermented for carbonation from those that had been carbonated with a CO2 canister, which she could tell from those carbonated with dry ice. There was something about the dry ice beverages. It wasn't a scent exactly, Erin knew that dry ice didn't leave taste or smell behind, but the drinks just had a different quality from those that had been carbonated with machines or fermentation.

She savored each drink carefully, letting it sit in her mouth and bubble for a moment before swishing it around and eventually spitting it into the bucket next to her. There were a couple that she swallowed. They were just so inviting that she had to test the 'finish' that she wouldn't get except by swallowing.

There were ninety-seven beverage entries. They seemed endless. It took a couple of hours to get through them all. Erin carefully scored each one, although she knew she wasn't taking the same care on the later entries as she had on the earlier ones. After having tasted so many different offerings, some of them just didn't make the cut, no matter how generous she tried to be. And it took more to impress her. That unevenness in scoring would be evened out in the head-to-head comparisons. Any inferior entries that had squeaked in because they were among the first the judges had tasted would soon be compared to the handful of late entries that had stood out over everything else.

When they scored their final cards, there was a round of applause and they were allowed to leave the judging table and mingle with the audience for a time.

If any of the contestants revealed which of the entries was theirs at that point in an effort to curry favor and get a judge to endorse their entry, they would get an automatic expulsion. Erin hoped that no one tried to talk to her about their entry. She would hate to have to rat someone out and have their entry canceled.

As soon as she left the judges' table on the raised stage, Terry was at her side, taking her arm. He and K9 guided her through the crowd.

Despite all of the security measures that the contest had in place, neither she nor Terry had the confidence that Erin would be completely safe. A weapon could be missed by metal detectors and x-rays. Or someone could have already visited the room and planted a weapon to be used later. Or they might use an improvised weapon or their bare hands.

Erin felt better with Terry and K9 at her side. Their eyes all sharp and bodies held alert for any sign of trouble.

Nothing would happen during the contest. The organizers promised. But Erin was sure they would have promised that no one would be harmed right from the beginning, and yet Beryl still had been, and so had Charley and Kirschoff.

As Erin greeted the various people who came forward to smile and shake hands and introduce themselves, her mind wandered again to Chef Kirschoff.

He was the one who had dropped the CO2 canister in the restaurant, resulting in the explosion. What if it hadn't been an accident or a canister that had been tampered with, but something intentional on Kirschoff's part? Neither of them had been seriously injured, but either of them could have been. Everyone kept saying that they had been so lucky.

So he couldn't have detonated it on purpose.

CHAPTER 43

When she could sneak away from the festivities, Erin went to the Whitewater Junction Public Library and looked for Beryl's book. She had already checked their online catalog to confirm that they had a copy, and it didn't look like it was out on loan. She wandered the aisles, reading the Dewey Decimal designations on the ends until she found the section the recipe books were in.

She had jotted down the call number for Beryl's book and hunted down the shelf for it. When she arrived at the right shelf, she ran her finger along the spine labels, looking for the BAT designating Beryl Batcombe's book.

It wasn't there.

Erin double-checked the call number and looked for it again. She tilted her head and read the titles and authors. Maybe it had been mislabeled. It should be there if it wasn't out on loan.

But it was missing from the shelf. Erin took a step back and let her eyes wander over the rest of the shelves. She loved cookbooks, and she recognized a number of the titles, though there were still many that were new to her. She resolved to go to the library in Bald Eagle Falls and be sure that she read every cookbook they had there. Then she could ask for the ones at Whitewater on an interlibrary loan. Who knew what recipe gems she might find.

Her eyes rested on a thin volume with the title *Recipes from Mawmaw's Kitchen*. Erin bent down and snatched it up. Beryl's book was there! It had just been mis-shelved. That happened all the time. People pulled a book off the shelf and put it back in the wrong place. Librarians were forever trying to identify books that were out of place and to put them back, but it was a losing battle; there was always another one just down the row.

Erin wandered over to the nearest soft chairs and sat down. She opened the book and started to browse through the recipes.

There wasn't much there that was interesting or unique. They were mostly recipes she had seen before. Some weird sixties and seventies stuff, but the really traditional stuff was pretty straightforward. Basic recipes that could be found in any grandma's recipe collection.

There were some interesting recipes for home-brewed sarsaparilla, rubdown, meatloaf, sausage patties, fried green tomatoes, moon pies, even a stack cake, which was what she had entered into the Country Fair to win the Alaskan cruise. Hers, of course, had been gluten-free.

Erin took a few more minutes to look at the dessert recipes in the back. Desserts were her specialty, after all. There were a few that had interesting local twists. There were even a couple of ice cream recipes, which she stopped to look at in light of the contest. But traditionally, ice cream had been vanilla, so Mawmaw didn't have any inspiring ideas.

She looked up from the book and saw Charley walking toward her.

"Someone said they'd seen you coming in here," Charley said. "Are you hiding from your responsibilities? Aren't you supposed to be schmoozing?"

"I schmoozed. Now I'm taking a break before I have to get back to the judging."

"Yeah, 'cause the judging looks so hard. All of that sipping must get tiring." Charley grinned to show that she was joking.

Erin rolled her eyes. "You try sitting up there with hundreds of people watching you take a drink and write down scores a hundred times. It's actually pretty nerve-racking. What if there was something stuck in between my teeth?"

Charley made a show of examining Erin. "Nope. You look perfect, like usual."

"Like usual?" Erin couldn't help wondering what Charley was

buttering her up for. Like a kid getting ready to ask a parent for money. "Usually, I'm a hot mess, hair coming out from under my cap, spills and fingerprints all over my apron, flour on the end of my nose…"

"Like I said, perfect. That's just how a baker should look. Would you buy treats from a baker who looked absolutely polished, without a hair out of place? You'd think they must be fake. A baker can't make all of those different things without spilling something."

"Nice save." Erin took one last look at Beryl Batcombe's book, then put it down on the little table next to her chair. "So, what's up, Charley?"

"I've just been talking to Hans," Charley said, the laughter leaving her eyes. She spoke carefully. Not exactly like she was upset, but as if she needed to make a plan to form every sound.

"Yeah? How's he doing?" Erin couldn't make herself feel the same level of warmth and concern for him as she'd previously had.

She straightened suddenly, remembering.

"Oh. So, uh… what were you talking about?"

"About Beryl," Charley confirmed.

Erin let out a sigh of relief. "So he told you?"

"Not like I didn't guess as much before," Charley said with a shrug. "I couldn't see any other reason he would have made her a judge. Or picked Whitewater as a location. But he wasn't with her anymore. Just doing a favor for an old flame."

Erin pursed her lips. Kirschoff had put a good spin on it. "I'm not sure she was an old flame. I think they were still involved."

"Doesn't matter. She's out of the way now. I don't need to worry that she's going to come back into his life."

No, that much was a certainty. "Did he… tell you anything else?" Erin was fishing for confirmation that Kirschoff had also told her about his wife and family back home. That no matter what they had shared, he would leave her behind and go home to his family when everything was done.

Charley sat down in the chair next to Erin. She readjusted its position so that she and Erin could see each other's faces and body language. Charley leaned forward in her seat, lowering her voice even more than she had out of respect for the library.

"Yeah, I guess he did. He didn't just give Beryl the position because they used to be together."

"Oh…?" The conversation was going in a different direction from what Erin had anticipated, but she rolled with it.

"He didn't come out and say it in so many words, but I think… she was blackmailing him."

CHAPTER 44

Erin's surprise must have shown in her face. Charley gave a little laugh and settled back.

"Yeah. Can you believe it? Everything I hear about this woman… everybody who talks about her has something different to hate about her. You know how they tell you not to speak ill of the dead? I don't think that applies to Beryl Batcombe. Lots of people around to talk about what a jerk she was, sticking her nose into things that weren't her business, saying rude or racist crap, and now this! Blackmail!"

"So she told him that if he didn't appoint her as one of the judges, then…?" Erin trailed off, waiting for Charley to pick up the narrative.

"I'm not sure exactly what she threatened him with. Like I said, he didn't tell me in so many words, but I guessed."

"She threatened to do something that he wouldn't like. Reveal something about him that he didn't want other people to know."

Charley nodded and waved her hand at this. "Lots of people have things that they'd rather not have spread around. Everybody's left fingerprints somehow. You can't hide things in today's world."

"You didn't ask him what it was?"

"No. I don't need to know what it was."

So Kirschoff had only done the job halfway. He had told Charley that he and Beryl had been together, but not that he was going home to his wife when the competition was over.

Erin chewed on her lip, looking at Charley's open, comfortable expression. Was Erin really going to break the spell and tell Charley Kirschoff's secret? Charley wouldn't be looking quite so comfortable and smug then.

"Charley…"

"You're going to tell me anyway, aren't you?" Charley scowled. "Why do you gotta rain on my parade?"

"I'm sorry. But I think you should know…"

"Look. We're not that serious. I know that when he leaves here, he probably never calls me again. He travels. He doesn't live anywhere near Tennessee. It's the first and probably the last time that he's stopped here. So what does it really matter?"

"I just think… he should be honest with you. He's only telling you half the story."

"And is it really important for me to know the rest?"

Erin nodded. "I would want to know."

"Yeah, you probably would. But you live a different kind of life than I do. We're not the same."

"Then maybe you won't care. Maybe you'll be happy to just take him as he is. But he really should have told you."

Charley growled. "You'd better not be telling me that he's dying."

"No!" Erin puffed out a breath of laughter. "No. I think the closest he's come to that is the explosion of the CO2 canister."

"Me too. And I don't plan to come any closer in the next few years."

"I thought you were the one who likes to live dangerously. Go ahead and try risky things. Live a full life. Live fast, die young…"

"No. I've never said that." Charley rolled her eyes.

Erin couldn't imagine being as wild and carefree as Charley and, maybe subconsciously, she was looking for a way to knock her down. She needed to just take Charley as she was.

"So tell me whatever it is about Hans," Charley said, clicking the button on her phone to see what time it was. "You have to be back in your seat in ten minutes, so we should be heading back."

Erin looked down at her purse as she got ready to return to her judge duties. "Well… it's just that he's married."

"What?"

Erin had been half-expecting Charley to say that she already knew that, and to object to Erin being so dramatic about it all. But Charley's voice was shocked.

"Chef Kirschoff. Hans. He has a wife and children."

Charley shook her head and swallowed. "A wife and children? Estranged?"

"No. He just likes company while he's on the road."

"So he's going back to them after this is over? All of this is just… a little fling while he's away from home?"

Erin nodded silently. She felt terrible to be the one to break it to Charley, especially since Charley seemed to be upset about it. She didn't just take it in stride.

"Yeah. I'm sorry."

Charley swore.

"That's probably what Beryl was holding over him," Erin said. "Make me a judge, or I'll tell your family about us."

"Yeah. Sheesh. He seemed like a nice guy, didn't he?" Charley looked earnestly into Erin's face. "Tell me you thought so too. Maybe you weren't interested in him romantically, but you liked him and thought he was a good guy. Right?"

Erin nodded. "Yeah. I really enjoyed working with him and I thought he was a nice guy. I never thought… that he had another side like this."

"Okay… well…" Charley stood up and took the first few steps toward the door. Erin followed quickly behind her. "Okay, so that's the news about Hans. We still have the rest of the competition to get through. It isn't like I didn't know we only had until the end of the contest together. I knew it would all be over soon and he would be pulling out again."

Erin nodded, knowing that it didn't make Charley feel any better. They made it to the library doors before Charley made the second connection. She turned and looked at Erin.

"You don't think he had anything to do with Beryl's death, do you? You don't think that he got tired of her making demands and threatening to expose him and decided to… get rid of the problem permanently?"

"No, I'm sure it couldn't have been him." Erin tried to recall the details of the night that Beryl had died. "He would have to have been in the conference room when Beryl was poisoned. He's the big name. People would have noticed if he had just walked out. Especially when they found out later that Beryl had died. Wouldn't they?"

"The police haven't released any details of how and when she was killed, though. And most people wouldn't know that… there were issues between the two of them."

Erin bit her lip. It was getting sore and swollen from her anxiety. "I don't think he left the conference room before the conference let out. So he couldn't have had anything to do with her death."

Charley raised her eyebrows. "You'd have to talk to the cops. Until they release what her time of death was… you don't know if he had time to meet with her and kill her after the conference let out. You don't know where he went after that, do you?"

"No." Erin felt like there was a lead weight in her stomach. It was a good thing she hadn't swallowed all ninety-seven different samples of soda. She might have brought them all back up. "I don't know where he went. But I'm sure he couldn't have had anything to do with it. He isn't that kind of person."

"Before this, I would have said he wasn't the kind of person to marry and have kids. I would have told you he was a permanent bachelor. Maybe a bit of a player, but not a cheater."

Erin sighed. Charley patted her on the arm.

"Don't think about it right now. You have a job to do."

CHAPTER 45

It was difficult to concentrate during the second stage of the competition. Erin tried to focus on the two drinks that were placed in front of her, ignoring the spectators, the war going on inside of her head, and everything else. Just two drinks. Taste them both, decide which she liked better, and wait for the next head-to-head.

After a few minutes, she fell into a rhythm. She was sure she was right. There was no way that Kirschoff had killed Beryl. There was no need for her to agonize over it. The drinks were pleasant. She could just focus on one sense, and put everything else out of her mind. It was a sort of dissociation, but it was the only way she could continue to judge the contest and not be derailed by Beryl's death and the latest revelations.

She focused on the taste of a pleasant, fermented root beer. It had made it past the first round of head-to-head tastings and was back in the second round. Erin sampled the drink it was up against, a surprisingly refreshing watermelon soda. Mixing memories of eating watermelon on a hot summer day with the Snapples they consumed in large quantities. She had a hard time deciding which drink should go on to the next round.

Lara muttered something next to her. Erin looked at her.

"What?"

"That root beer. Reminds me of something, but I can't put my finger on it."

Erin considered. She tried to identify each of the flavors. If she were trying to recreate it, what ingredients would she use? As a young child, Erin had shown off her excellent senses of smell and taste in identifying the teas that Clementine sold in her tea shop. She could tell most teas simply by scent, picking out the different herbs and spices or recognizing the full bouquet as one of the commercial blends.

"Judges?" Kirschoff prompted, voice booming over his lapel microphone. "Place your votes as to which of the drinks will be in the final round."

"Most root beers used to be made from sassafras root," Erin told Lara. "But there are health risks, so they switched to using artificial flavoring or other roots or barks."

Lara looked over at her. "What do you think of this one?"

"Doesn't taste like artificial flavoring to me. It's been brewed and fermented." She closed her eyes, taking another tiny sip and swishing it around her mouth. She smelled the glass. "It's a blend. There's birch in there. Ginger. Sarsaparilla. All blended together."

"So can you call it root beer if it has all of those things in it?"

Erin hadn't thought much about the names of the contest entries. Some of them had fanciful names, others were quite generic.

"Ginger and sarsaparilla are both roots. So if it is a fermented concoction of ginger and sarsaparilla, then by definition, it is a root beer."

Lara nodded. "Even if it doesn't contain the ingredients that commercial root beer is made with."

"Right."

Lara marked her choice on her ballot. Everyone else had passed in their ballots and were waiting for Erin's vote. She marked her choice and dropped it into the ballot box. There was applause. One of the scrutineers moved forward to open the ballot box and count the votes.

Erin was happy for a break while they waited for the votes to be counted and for the three drinks that had made it to the final round to be announced. She shut out the crowds, closing her eyes for a few moments of peace before the pressure of the final round. The audience was chattering excitedly.

"You from around here?"

Erin didn't want to be pulled out of her thoughts, but it was too late. Once she had processed the question, she couldn't return to floating behind her eyelids in a state of suspended animation. She opened her eyes.

It was Lara, of course, sitting beside her and making small talk while they waited for the next round. Their mikes were shut off, so they were able to talk to each other without it being broadcast to all of the spectators.

"Well… yes and no," Erin admitted.

"How can it be yes and no?"

"I have kin on the mountain…" That was enough for most of those in the area to accept that she was 'one of them' even though she hadn't spent her whole life there. She went on, giving Lara a little more detail. "I lived here as a young child, spent some of my time in Bald Eagle Falls. But after my parents died, I migrated north. Eventually ended up in Maine before coming back here. It's been a long journey."

"Ah, that makes sense," Lara acknowledged. "Someone said that you were native Tennessean, but you don't have the accent and I don't remember hearing about your family before."

"Yeah. There were Prices here, but it's been a long time since there were very many of them. End of the line."

"You could always have a passel of kids and bring the name back," Lara laughed.

"I don't think that's going to happen," Erin said with a tolerant smile. She didn't even know if she were going to have kids. "And even if I did, they'd have their father's name, not Price."

"Of course. I didn't mean it seriously."

"I don't think we've met before," Erin said. She put her hand out to shake. "You were a last-minute addition, and I don't remember hearing your name before either."

"Gross? There are still some around. But I'm more of a transplant too, like you. My grandparents came from the area, but my dad grew up in South Carolina, and my mom was French. I didn't settle here until a couple of years ago."

"Where did you grow up?"

Lara's eyes were on the crowd rather than on Erin. "Can't believe the amount of publicity this little contest has gotten."

"A quarter of a million bucks. That's not chicken feed around here."

"No. Lots of poor folks that would make a real difference to."

"So where did they find you? Are you associated with someone in the contest?"

"I used to work for one of the sponsors. Someone gave the organizers my name with a bunch of others. I don't know how they made the decision, but they decided to invite me to be a judge. I figured I have the time and wouldn't mind the honorarium, so I said yes."

Erin chuckled. "Well, I hope you're enjoying it."

"I am, actually. Which three do you think make it to the final judging?"

"The last one was a toss-up. I don't know which way it will go. The others… the vanilla cola was nice. Really smooth, lots of depth." Vanilla always made Erin feel warm and cozy. It would be a good scent for a candle to light close to bedtime. "And… let's see… the cherry."

Lara nodded. "Could be. And out of those three, which would you choose as the winner."

"Really hard to decide. They're all delicious, with just the right amount of fizz."

"If you could have a case of one of them in your basement, which would it be?"

Erin thought of the finalists she had suggested. "To be honest, I think… the sarsaparilla."

"Ah. The root beer."

Something jiggled in the back of Erin's mind. Something about sarsaparilla. She closed her eyes, trying to picture it. Another of the drinks? Something someone had said to her? Something she had read?

She pictured Beryl's book in her hand. There had been a sarsaparilla recipe in the book. That must have been what made Erin feel like she'd already been talking about sarsaparilla. She had flipped past it pretty quickly. What had the ingredients been?

Erin touched Lara on the arm like she needed to stop Lara from talking, even though she hadn't been saying anything. She waved for the attention of one of the organizers, standing nearby, waiting for the results. The tall man stepped closer and bent over.

"Miss Price? What can I help you with?"

"We need a recess. Can we break for a few minutes? Just make it an extra-long commercial break?"

"We're just about ready to announce the finalists." He looked at Erin, waiting for her to say that she didn't need a break. She could hold on until the winner was announced. But Erin couldn't go on, she needed to talk to someone.

"I just need five minutes."

He looked at his watch. "This has all been carefully timed. We really can't step off of the schedule."

Erin looked at the spectators. She couldn't see anyone familiar.

Vic was sitting on the other side of Lara. She reached behind Lara to touch Erin on the shoulder. "What is it, Erin? What's wrong?"

"I need to talk to someone."

"Who?"

Erin looked at the wings of the raised stage and spotted Terry. He was looking concerned, standing just at the edge of the stairs, leaning forward, K9 at his side.

"Erin?" Vic prompted.

Erin motioned for Terry to come to her. He was up the stairs and past the hired security in an instant. He stood at her shoulder, looking around tensely for any threat.

"What's up, Erin?"

"We need a break. I need to talk to…" Erin tried to think of the best solution. "Umm, Chef Kirschoff and Deputy Coleman. I guess that would be the best…"

The tall man was shaking his head. "That's not possible. We are ready to proceed with the final judging. We can't put that off. You can talk to whoever you need to after."

"It needs to be before."

CHAPTER 46

There was a buzz of activity. The spectators clearly wanted to know what was going on, but Erin was careful to keep her voice down. Her mike was turned off so that her words wouldn't be broadcast over the whole crowd. Erin wouldn't back down. The staff were forced to bring Chef Kirschoff over. Terry was standing behind Erin on his phone, and she could hear him over everything else, calling for Deputy Coleman to join them on the stage.

Chef Kirschoff wasn't nearly as jolly as usual. His face was red, and he hovered over Erin, trying to talk her into just proceeding as planned. Erin covered her mike even though she knew it was turned off.

"I know the recipe for the sarsaparilla."

Kirschoff rolled his eyes. "We don't require that entries are unique recipes created by the entrant. There are probably a number of them that were made from exactly the same recipe."

"But this is one from Beryl's book."

He looked at her, brows pulled down. "I guess you found a copy. But it doesn't matter where it's from."

Erin looked around. Deputy Coleman was mounting the stairs and joined the scrum around Erin.

"Beryl published a cookbook," Erin said quickly, trying to get everyone up to speed. "It was supposed to be her family recipes. But after it was published, there were allegations that she had stolen recipes from other people. They weren't her family recipes. She had taken other people's recipes and not even bothered to reword the directions. Straight up plagiarism."

"We already know about that," Coleman said. "After the accusations, her sales fell off completely, they were pulled from stores, and she couldn't sell the books as firewood. No one would buy them. No stores would sell them. Eventually, none of the people who claimed she had stolen their recipes bothered to prosecute. If the books were no longer being sold, that was enough. And a sight cheaper than trying to sue her."

Erin wasn't really concerned with why there had been no consequences to Beryl. She looked at Lara and then around the others gathered close.

"The root beer. I don't know whether it is going to the final round or not. But if Beryl was up here judging, she would have known that was a recipe from her book."

"Why does that matter?" Coleman demanded.

"Because Beryl wouldn't have wanted it to make it to the final round. She would have blocked it before it could make it there and get any publicity."

"One judge couldn't keep an entry from advancing."

"If she gave it low scores in all categories, she could. There's no way it could make a high score overall if she didn't grade it fairly. Or she could say that there was something that should disqualify it. We're allowed to talk among ourselves and decide if an entry violates the rules."

"Like what?" Kirschoff asked. "She could not have disqualified it."

"Lara and I were just discussing whether it qualified as a root beer when it used sarsaparilla for flavoring. Because traditionally, root beer and sarsaparilla are two different things. If it uses sarsaparilla root, it is sarsaparilla, not root beer."

"Are you saying you want it disqualified?" Kirschoff ran his fingers through his hair worriedly.

"No. We would have said so. It also uses ginger root, not just sarsaparilla, so it can technically be called root beer. But if Beryl had been here, and it got through the first round, she could have had it disqualified for misrepresentation."

"And she would do that so that someone else would not win with her recipe?" Terry asked. He shook his head, a very slight side to side gesture. "Why wouldn't she want it to win? Wouldn't that be good publicity for her?"

"It would bring up the whole plagiarism issue all over again. Whoever entered it would make it known that she had stolen it from them, and all of that stuff would be out in the public again. This time with a much bigger audience." Erin nodded toward the crowds in the audience waiting for them to finish their discussion, and to the TV cameras that were broadcasting to the even larger virtual audience.

"So, you think that whoever entered this sarsaparilla is Beryl Batcombe's killer," Coleman said slowly.

"Yes."

"Thinking you've got the killer is all well and good… but there's no proof. It's completely circumstantial. Having a motive doesn't mean that the contestant was the one who killed her. Lots of other people had motives too."

"And then there's Chef Kirschoff."

Kirschoff's eyes widened. He held his hands up in protest. "I didn't have anything to do with killing anyone."

"No!" Erin nearly laughed. "I didn't mean that. I mean, you were the next one who was targeted. Because you had picked Beryl as a judge. The contestant thought that you were being unfair. That you were showing favoritism toward Beryl just because… the two of you were close."

He shifted uncomfortably. "I can pick whoever I want as judges."

"Yes. But you picked someone who has a reputation for being a cheat, plagiarizing other people's hard work. Someone with a background like Beryl's should never have been picked as a judge."

He was uncomfortable, making a face and looking down at the table as if he were fascinated with something there.

"Why did you pick her?" Coleman asked.

No one answered at first. Erin tried to catch Chef Kirschoff's eye and raised her eyebrows questioningly. Did he want her to tell Coleman, or was he going to step up and admit the truth? Hans sighed, shaking his head.

"I picked her because she was blackmailing me."

There were no gasps of shock. Terry and Coleman were cops, used to people doing underhanded and illegal things. And Lara hadn't been around for long enough to be shocked by anything. Maybe she had already sensed some of the undertones and knew that there had been something strange going on with Kirschoff and Beryl.

"The fact that Beryl was getting publicity for an opportunity that never should have been given to her and that Chef Kirschoff was unfair in his selections and put her in that position give motives for both Beryl's murder and the explosion when Chef Kirschoff was handling the CO2 canisters," Erin reiterated. "And as soon as Beryl tasted that sarsaparilla, she would have known it was the recipe she had stolen, and she would have known who had entered it. Maybe she wouldn't have eliminated it, but the contestant couldn't count on that."

"It all fits together neatly," Coleman admitted. "And the food poisoning on opening night? Who was your contestant trying to get even with—or rid of—with that little caper?"

"I don't know," Erin admitted. "Maybe it *was* just an equipment malfunction and we jumped to conclusions. Or maybe it was to distract us from the killer, to make us think that they just wanted to get the contest shut down, not that Beryl and Chef Kirschoff had been targeted."

"But it's still all circumstantial. We need actual evidence. Chef Kirschoff, can you check the entries and let me know who submitted the drink in question?"

"They're supposed to be blind. I can't reveal it now, before the final judging."

"But if it wins…" Erin protested. "It can't win if the contestant killed Beryl to keep it in the running. And if it doesn't win, then what's to stop him from killing again in order to disqualify the winner?"

"I need the name," Coleman said firmly. "This isn't about the contest, this is about solving a possible murder."

Kirschoff scowled, thinking about it. "You can wait a few more minutes. It won't make any difference to whether or not he is convicted."

"Are you obstructing an investigation?"

"If you wait, you may get the evidence you need… the contestant's reaction to the results of the judging may give you what you need to arrest him."

Coleman shook his head. "Get me the information now. Then I can have eyes on him. I won't reveal it to the judges, so that it won't affect the contest results."

How was Erin supposed to ignore the fact the contestant who had entered the sarsaparilla might be a killer and judge the drink on its merits?

Eventually, Kirschoff and Coleman went off to look at the entry details. Terry stayed with Erin, though she started to feel a little self-conscious with him standing protectively over her.

None of the other judges had bodyguards.

"It will be over soon," he promised.

"Yeah." Erin breathed out slowly. "And then I can really enjoy the ice cream tomorrow and not worry that someone will try to poison me. Or that something else dreadful will happen. I know lots of people here, and I don't want anything bad to happen to any of them."

"Of course not. Think about the ice cream tomorrow. And about going home to Orange Blossom and Marshmallow."

Erin looked down at K9, nodding and trying to keep from tearing up. Soon everything would be back to normal.

CHAPTER 47

Finally, everything was settled and they were ready to move on. Terry moved to the wings again, K9 at his side, both of them ready to run to her aid if needed. Erin waited, stomach tense, for the big reveal as to which drinks were the final three.

Kirschoff rambled about the sponsors, how great the contest had been, and the talent represented, before finally getting to the entries.

"The finalists for the beverages competition are…"

Erin held her breath. A strawberry cream soda that she had really liked. A carbonated mint tea that was remarkably refreshing.

And the sarsaparilla root beer.

Erin tried to keep her expression pleasant and not show any reaction to the news. She looked around at the audience, looking for someone who was too happy about the advancement. Someone with a much deeper reaction than seemed normal. But everyone was clapping and whooping, encouraging the three finalists on. Some disappointed faces, but Erin wasn't worried about them. If the sarsaparilla maker was the killer, he was going to be happy at this news. The anger would come later when it didn't make it to first place and win a huge windfall. Or maybe it wasn't even the money, but just the fact that they hadn't recognized the brilliance of the recipe.

Three glasses were placed in front of Erin this time instead of just two. She looked at them, preparing herself.

Should she go with her conscience, picking the one she felt was the best even if it might trigger a reaction from the killer? Should she intentionally advance or block the sarsaparilla?

"I've never faced a decision like this," she murmured to Lara. "What do we do?"

"Taste them," Lara said simply. "And then you will know."

Erin looked sideways at her. Lara was an unknown entity. Picked at the last minute. Chef Kirschoff was the only one who knew her background. And so far, his track record was not great. What if *Lara* were the culprit? She could easily have entered the sarsaparilla under a different name. No one was checking people's ID against the entries. Her challenge to Erin to just try the drinks felt wrong. How would Erin know when she tasted them? She was still going to be in exactly the same dilemma.

Unless the sarsaparilla was poisoned.

She'd already drunk it twice, so she didn't think that was possible. Lara hadn't moved from her seat or tampered with Erin's glasses. An accomplice? A volunteer working the contest?

It didn't make any sense. But she was suddenly paranoid. The killer was still out there, watching her and the other judges. Maybe planning to take Kirschoff out. Or to harm one of the rest of them. There was no reason for anyone to target Erin, except that she was a friend of Kirschoff's. Maybe the killer didn't care about collateral damage.

Lara picked up the first of her glasses and tasted the entry. She set the glass down again, and nodded at Erin.

Go ahead.

Erin cleared her throat and looked at the drinks. She picked up the strawberry cream soda. She admired it in the glass for a moment, the delicate pink color and tiny bubbles. She had already tasted it twice and knew that she liked it. She took a tiny sip. Hardly enough to wet her lips.

She put the glass down. She looked over the crowd. Nothing looked wrong. Everybody was doing exactly what she would have expected them to. Smiling, waiting with interest for the final results. A few tears from people who had probably just been ousted in the last round. There were a few familiar faces. Charley. Terry. Bella. Vic's friends.

Erin picked up the next glass. She and Lara both took a sip of the carbonated mint tea at the same time. Erin forced a smile and nodded. It was not a beverage she would have tried outside of the contest, but it came together very nicely.

Lara picked up her root beer. She tipped it in Erin's direction, toasting her. Then she took a mouthful and let it sit in her mouth before swallowing.

Erin licked her dry lips and looked at the root beer. She'd already had it twice. She knew it was fine. She liked it, and it hadn't caused her any ill effects. It was just someone's old family recipe, left over from the days when there weren't commercial sodas around and it was brewed as a health tonic.

She lifted the glass to her lips, mimed taking a drink, and put it back down.

Erin picked up her scorecard. She had only to assign a one, two, and three in the order of her preference. She set it in front of her and picked up her pencil.

She saw a sharp movement out the corner of her eye and turned her head quickly. It was just Vic's friend, Clayton. Erin was jumping at everything.

Clayton called something out to her. Erin couldn't hear him over the chatter of the crowd. She leaned forward, shaking her head and frowning. Clayton shouted again, repeating himself a few times before Erin could see his lips and hear enough of his voice over the crowd to understand what he was saying.

"You didn't drink it!"

Erin looked down the table toward Vic to see if she had heard. Vic looked back at her, eyebrows raised. Her facial expression clearly asking whether Clayton was right.

Erin's face warmed. She wanted to hide it, knowing she was turning bright red. She looked down at her score sheet, ignoring both of them. She had tasted all three entries twice before. She knew exactly what each of them tasted like. She would rate the strawberry cream soda first, then the mint tea, and last the root beer. She liked it, but it really was sarsaparilla, and there was no special twist to make it the entrant's own. It was nice, but it didn't take a risk like the mint tea. And the strawberry cream soda was just so perfect in every way, making her think of warm summer afternoons spent picking wild berries as a child.

And if the person who had entered the root beer in the contest really was Beryl's killer, then there was no way Erin was going to play right into his hands.

CHAPTER 48

Erin put her ballot in the box. Lara also put hers in through the slot. She looked at Erin. "Are you okay?"

"Yeah. Fine."

"You're just looking a little… I don't know. Anxious. Frazzled."

"It's been a long day. That's all."

"And a bit stressful," Lara contributed with a smile.

"Yes. But that's it for today. Then we can relax until the ice cream tomorrow."

Lara nodded cheerfully.

But Erin knew there was still more drama coming before she could relax. They weren't just going to announce the winner and all retire to their hotel rooms.

Each of the judges had put their ballots in the box. The scrutineer went through each of them, entering the scores on a clipboard and making a show of tallying them up and then of double-checking his results. There were shouts from the crowd, pushing him to announce the results. Finally, the scrutineer handed the clipboard to Chef Kirschoff.

He cleared his throat, made a little speech about the importance of the results, and thanked the various sponsors by name, making everyone groan with impatience.

"And the runner up is… entry sixty-eight, Summer Strawberry Cream Soda!"

Bella squealed and made her way up to the stage. She was presented with her runner-up ribbon, pictures were taken, and then the spotlight turned back to Chef Kirschoff. Erin couldn't help grinning like a proud parent. Her Bella had made it to runner-up! And the cream soda had been really good.

But everyone was waiting for the news of the grand prize winner. They clapped politely for Bella, but were waiting for the real news.

"And the winner of the beverage portion of the Great Tennessee CO2 Cool-off contest and winner of $250,000 is…"

Everyone held their breaths.

"Entry thirty-four, Mint Tea Fizz!"

A cheer went up. Erin didn't know the man who walked up to the stage to receive his recognition. His name was announced as Eugene Bath. More posing, handshakes, and pictures.

"And that means that third prize goes to entry fifty-seven, Traditionally Brewed Meemaw's Root Beer," Kirschoff announced genially, looking out at the crowd.

Erin watched as Clayton pushed his way toward the stage. For a moment, she thought that he was approaching to talk to Vic, believing that everything was over and he would be allowed up onto the stage. Her hand made an involuntary movement to shoo him off.

Vic rose partway out of her seat, face pale. Chef Kirschoff studied Clayton, maybe wondering where he had seen the young man before.

But pretty much everyone's eyes were still on Eugene. He was smiling and bowing and posing for pictures as people held their phones out at arm's length to try to avoid getting all of the other phones in the picture.

Clayton broke into a run and vaulted up onto the stage, avoiding the guarded stairs completely, and with a yell of rage, charged directly at Kirschoff, bowling him over. They both fell to the ground in a tangle of arms and legs, Kirschoff letting out a yelp of surprise.

Erin was on her feet, not sure when she had actually stood up. Everyone was pressing forward, trying to see what was going on. Erin tried to see everything that was happening in slow motion rather than the quick and violent blows exchanged between the two.

Was there a weapon? A knife or a gun? She couldn't spot anything. No blood blossomed from Chef Kirschoff's snow white chef's apron.

Clayton was screaming and yelling something incomprehensible, Kirschoff's words sharp and cutting like a knife, guttural German she couldn't understand.

She was holding her breath as the policemen and hired security men rushed in to separate the fighters. She leaned over the table watching, her whole body tense.

They hauled Clayton back and he yelled in protest.

"You both deserve to die!" Clayton bellowed, spittle flying everywhere as he tried to pull himself free of half of the Whitewater Junction police force. "You're like two snakes breeding in the grass! You're both as bad as each other, pretending to be honest, upright citizens when you're really rotten to the core! Stealing people's property, manipulating the results of this contest, thinking you can just ride into town and take over everything and shape this town to do your will!"

"Clayton!" Vic said faintly from her place at the judge's table.

He couldn't have heard her over his own shouts, but he turned and looked at her. "*You* were supposed to be one of us! How could you turn your back on us and consort with the likes of him? Both of you! Pretending that you care about other people, and then letting Kirschoff and Beryl Batcombe walk all over us, grinding us into the mud! Just because he has money. And we don't, we're just no-account hillbillies. He thinks we're not even human!"

Vic shook her head in protest, as white as a sheet.

"I couldn't believe that you accepted the judgeship from him. You should have known how corrupt he is! How could you look at someone like him and not know that he was corrupt all the way through?"

Vic didn't say anything. The police continued to wrestle Clayton around to secure him in handcuffs, search him, and eventually get him back to his feet. He continued to spout more accusations and bile in the direction of Kirschoff and the judges as they hauled him away.

When they got him out into the corridor, Erin heard yapping and growling and a howl of protest from Clayton, and caught a glimpse of Willie working to detach Nilla from Clayton's leg.

Then he was gone. Things seemed suddenly too quiet, a black void of silence in the landscape.

Others who were closer to Kirschoff helped him to get to his feet and brush himself off. He made a few weak, laughing comments into the mike that no one understood. He turned the mike over to one of the other organizers. In a clear, concise voice, she apologized for the disruption and gave everyone directions to the next event, where they could taste samples of some of the entries and fill their stomachs with hot dogs.

CHAPTER 49

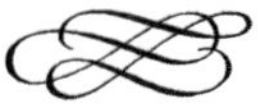

Terry waited until people were on their way, then climbed the stage stairs to smile at Erin, pat her on the back, and nudge her to her feet.

"What do you want to do? I assume you probably don't want…" he gestured to the crowds headed to a hot dog orgy. "All of that."

"No. I don't think I can look at food right now."

She knew that there was going to be an eating contest. One of those competitions where the entrants tried to gobble as many hot dogs as they could in the space of three minutes. She didn't feel like eating, and she certainly didn't feel like watching anyone else gorge like that.

Terry nodded. "Why don't we go somewhere quiet, then. You don't want to eat?"

"No. If you want, we can go somewhere. I just don't think…"

"It's fine. I don't need to be social right now."

"They have a nice library here."

"You want to go to the library? Not to the hotel room?"

"Yeah. Unless… if you've got a headache and want to go back and lie down."

"No. The library is fine with me."

They walked for a few minutes in silence. Erin's arms were wrapped around her body, as if she were cold or trying to hold herself together. She wasn't sure which. Just that she didn't want to let go.

"Do you think they'll have enough to charge him? Like Coleman said, it's all circumstantial."

"They've got him dead to rights on assault. That will hold him while they gather more evidence. They'll get his fingerprints, search warrants issued… we don't know what they'll find until they look."

"I always thought… you know, you watch TV crime shows and murder mystery movies… and you think that once you've identified the killer, that's enough. Everything is neatly tied up in a bow and you can put him away for the rest of his life. But that's… I'm finding out that's not really true."

Terry held the library door open for Erin. She went in and wandered toward the recipe books.

"I can't believe that it was one of Vic's friends. They were always so… friendly and welcoming. They seemed open. But…"

"Just like anyone else… people wear masks. A public face that keeps other people from knowing who they really are and protects them from judgment."

Erin nodded. "I guess. You do things to protect yourself, and forget that other people do too. You think that you're seeing the other person as they really are when, in reality, we're all wearing masks."

Terry looked at the shelves that Erin was standing in front of. "Hmm. I wonder what you're in the mood to read today."

Erin grinned at him and grabbed a handful of books on traditional Tennessean cooking.

~

Vic poked her head through Erin's back door. "Yoo-hoo. Everyone decent?"

"Come on in," Erin invited.

Vic let herself in. Orange Blossom got up from the warm little nest he was curled up in on the couch and marched over to see her, stopping once on the way to stretch out his front and back legs and to arch his back.

"Morning, Blossom! Are you glad to have your mommy home?" Vic crooned, picking him up. He sniffed at her suspiciously, probably smelling Nilla on her. So far, no one had come forward to claim the dog, and Erin suspected he'd already found his long-term home.

"At least he didn't give me the cold shoulder like last time."

"Well, last time you were away for weeks, not just a few days. And maybe he's realized that you still come back even when you've been away for a long time. That has to be stressful to an animal. You can't explain your plans to them."

"Yeah. I'm glad Adele could look after him. I know that witches aren't actually anything mystical, but... she does seem to have a certain understanding with animals that I can't explain."

"She's gentle," Vic said. "She doesn't move suddenly or make loud noises."

"Yeah. Maybe that's it."

Vic cuddled Orange Blossom against her face. "Terry's working?"

"Yes." Erin smiled. "He's been feeling pretty good. I hope it lasts."

"Oh, me too. It's been long enough. He deserves to be able to get back and feel good about himself again."

"Yeah."

"Have you heard anything from Detective Coleman? About Clayton?" Vic grimaced. "It's so weird wanting to catch a killer, but not wanting my friend to be punished."

"It's a strange position to be put in," Erin agreed, thinking of how she had felt about Roger Cox's arrest. "I guess Clayton was pretty eager to talk about Beryl and Kirschoff and everything they had done to hurt him and his family, at least to begin with. I was right, that recipe in Beryl's book was from him. Passed down from his grandma. That's the name that he wrote on the entry form, so when Kirschoff and Coleman looked at it, they didn't know whose it was."

"Isn't it weird that he would end up on a cruise where Kirschoff was the chef? What a bizarre coincidence."

"I don't think it was a coincidence." Erin shook her head. "I think that's why he was on that cruise to start with. He knew about Kirschoff and Beryl. Wanted to get a look at him. Maybe he even intended to attack Kirschoff while he was on the cruise."

"But with everything else going on he got spooked?" Vic filled in. "Huh. I wonder. It just seems so strange to think of him that way... I just thought he was a fun guy to hang out with. Kind of… carefree. Someone who knew how to have a good time."

Erin remembered what Terry had said about people wearing masks. Everyone trying not to let their own mask slip…

The doorbell rang.

"I wonder if that's Adele," Erin guessed, looking at the kitchen clock. It was a little late in the morning for Adele.

But it wasn't Adele.

Mary Lou stood on Erin's doorstep, looking uncomfortable.

Erin was surprised but tried to act as if she weren't. If Mary Lou were ready to make up, Erin was happy to do her part. She hated the rift that had developed between them.

Mary Lou looked past Erin to see who else was there. "Erin. Victoria."

"Hi, Mary Lou." Erin opened the door farther and motioned her in. "Would you like to come in?"

"No."

They stood looking at one another.

Mary Lou held out a folded newspaper. Thin, like all of the editions of the Bald Eagle Falls weekly. Erin had seen more substantial school papers.

"I wanted to see Joshua's article," Mary Lou said. "You know he wrote an article for the paper?"

"Yes!" Erin thought about how Joshua had approached her against his mother's wishes. She knew that Mary Lou would not be happy about it. "I haven't had a chance to look at it yet. Is it good?"

Mary Lou unfolded the paper and opened it up to the appropriate page. She passed it to Erin.

There was an upside-down-L-shaped hole where an article had been cut out of the newspaper. In its place was a sticky note with something scribbled on it. Erin brought it closer to her face. The handwriting was jagged and difficult to decipher.

If you want to know where your son is, maybe you should ask Erin Price.

CHANGING FORTUNE COOKIES

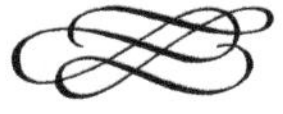

AUNTIE CLEM'S BAKERY #14

To those who are willing to help
and those who are waiting for it

CHAPTER 1

Erin invited Mary Lou into the house and, at first, it looked like the older woman was going to refuse. She hadn't been happy with Erin recently. This latest development wasn't going to make her more likely to forgive Erin for past mistakes. But then Mary Lou nodded her head, patted her gray bob, and entered. Erin motioned toward the couch, her brain spinning, trying to sort things out.

Vic stood in the kitchen doorway, her long blond hair tied back in a ponytail, her mouth open slightly. She knew how Mary Lou felt about them lately, so she was surprised by Mary Lou coming into the house. Vic looked at Erin, her brows coming down.

"Erin? What's wrong? Is everything okay?"

"No." Erin shook her head. She couldn't explain it. She pointed at Mary Lou for her to explain to Vic. "Tea? I'm going to put on the kettle." She passed Vic in the doorway and started to get the tea things ready. She turned on the electric kettle and gathered teacups, an assortment of tea bags, and the other items she needed.

"What is it?" she heard Vic ask Mary Lou, her tone anxious and uncertain. "Did something happen? Is it Roger?"

But it was not about Mary Lou's husband. As far as Erin knew, he was still safe in the facility where he had been held since he'd been arrested for murder and assault. Not jail, but somewhere they would, hopefully, be a little more compassionate and be able to handle his brain injury.

Nor was it about Campbell, Mary Lou's older son, who had been in some trouble in the past.

Erin listened for Mary Lou's answer, but she didn't explain to Vic. She probably handed Vic the same paper that she had shown to Erin. The Bald Eagle Falls weekly newspaper, which had included a news article written by Mary Lou's younger teenage son, Joshua. But the article had been cut out and there was a sticky note in its place.

If you want to know where your son is, maybe you should ask Erin Price.

The kettle started to whistle. Feeling numb and distant, as if she were enclosed in a bubble, Erin poured the steaming water into the teapot and then took the tea service out to the living room. She set it on the coffee table and sat on the couch beside Mary Lou. Not too close—she didn't want to impinge on Mary Lou's personal space—but close enough that they could talk and Mary Lou would know that Erin was there to help and support her. Vic sat in one of the easy chairs across from her, looking as pale and horrified as Erin felt. Mary Lou herself, appearing composed as she always did, smoothed wrinkles in her pantsuit and didn't immediately help herself to a teacup. The newspaper lay folded on the table in front of her.

"Can I pour for you?" Vic offered. "What kind would you like?"

Mary Lou seemed far away. It took her a few extra seconds to process Vic's question and focus on the tea bags in the basket.

"Earl Gray," she said eventually. "Thank you."

Vic busied herself with preparing a cup for Mary Lou, then passed it across to her. She poured for herself and Erin, and let Erin choose and add her own teabag. They sat there, looking at each other. They looked like three friends gathered for a gossip session. But that wasn't how it felt.

"I don't know anything about where Josh is," Erin told Mary Lou. "I hope you know that. I don't know what this note means, but… I don't know anything about where Josh is or what he is doing. I haven't seen him since he came to Whitewater Junction to interview me."

That had been days before. She remembered his coming to her hotel room, notepad in hand, eager to act the part of a mature reporter. Erin assumed that Joshua had gone home after that interview, had carried on his life as usual through the remainder of the cooking contest. And he had, of course, handed in his report to his English teacher and submitted it to the newspaper.

And then…? What had happened? And why did the note say that Mary Lou should ask Erin, when she knew nothing of Joshua's whereabouts?

"He isn't home?" Vic asked the obvious.

Of course Josh wasn't at home, or his mother would not be concerned about a note that implied something had happened to him.

"No. He was home yesterday… everything was normal. I thought… everything was even better than normal. But something happened. This morning… he didn't come down for breakfast. When I looked in his room to wake him up… he wasn't there." Mary Lou's gaze sought out Erin's. "His bed hadn't been slept in."

Erin's stomach clenched into a tight ball. She felt like she was being strangled. What could have happened to Joshua? If his bed hadn't been slept in, he hadn't just gone for a walk or to visit a friend or pick up a cup of coffee that morning. Something had happened to him the night before. He had left the house without Mary Lou being aware of it and he had not returned.

"Have you called the police?"

"No." Mary Lou shook her head. "I haven't talked to anyone. I just… I called him on his phone, but there was no answer. The newspaper was on the table and when I saw the note… I was going to call you, but… I just came over."

"Yeah. This is really crazy. But I… I don't know where he is…" Erin trailed off. She didn't know how to explain the note. Someone was trying to throw suspicion on her, but she hadn't had anything to do with Joshua's absence.

"But maybe if you thought about it, you would have some idea," Mary Lou said. "Even if you haven't seen him or heard from him, you must know something about what is going on. Why would the note say that if it wasn't anything to do with you?"

"But it isn't. I don't know anything."

"Where would he go? You two have been involved in everything going on around here. You must have some idea."

Erin felt lost.

"What about Cam?" Vic suggested. "Maybe he went to visit his brother. And this note is just… I don't know. Some kind of cruel joke."

Mary Lou had her phone in her hand. She stared at it as if it were something foreign to her. Or might blow up any minute.

"Have you called Campbell?" Erin asked. It was probably the first thing Mary Lou had done.

"No. He won't be up yet. He stays out late. Sleeps half the day. He wouldn't wake up."

"But if Joshua is with him… they must know you'd be looking for him. Or if he's not, won't Campbell want to help look for him? He would want to know right away."

Mary Lou shook her head. "There's no point, Erin. I said he won't wake up. I can't ask him or tell him anything if he is asleep and doesn't answer his phone."

Erin understood this, but still felt like Mary Lou should at least try.

"If he really is missing, we should call the police," Vic said.

"Yes," Erin agreed. "The earlier they can start looking for him, the better the results."

"I don't think they'll look if it hasn't been forty-eight hours, will they?"

"No, they'll look sooner than that," Erin assured her. "If you think something has happened to him, you should tell them right away. The first few hours can be critical. We don't want to lose them."

"I don't *know* that anything has happened to him. This could just be… a joke. Someone being silly. He's a teenager. They do stupid things without realizing what the consequences could be."

"But if he was just out with friends, wouldn't you be able to get him on the phone?" Erin pointed out.

"Maybe. Maybe not. There are a lot of places in these mountains where you can't get a signal. If he's out of range of a cell tower, or in a canyon, or spelunking, I wouldn't be able to get him."

"Spelunking," Erin repeated. Just thinking about being underground in a cave was enough to take her breath away. Still. "He wouldn't go into a cave without friends, would he? And without letting someone know where he was?"

"N-no..." Mary Lou drew the word out and, even though she said he wouldn't do it, she immediately contradicted herself. "Like I said... he's a teenager. And teen boys do all kinds of crazy things without understanding the dangers. As you well know." She gave each of them a hard stare. Erin looked down at her cup, her face hot with embarrassment. "You try to tell them something they need to be careful of, a decision that could bring them to harm, and you just get 'I'll be fine, Mom. I promise.' As if they can control the consequences." Mary Lou took a sip of her cooling tea. "I don't know how many times I've told them you can't choose the consequences. You can only choose your actions."

Erin looked at Vic. "Well... we can look around town. See if he's at the school or any of the regular hangouts. We can't check out all of the caves in the area, of course, but maybe Willie could drive by a couple of the more popular ones. See if there are cars parked outside."

Vic nodded. "If you aren't sure yet if there's really a problem and want to look for him first, we can help with that."

Erin remembered the search party for Roger when he had wandered off on his own. It was different for Roger because of his brain injury. He wasn't just a teenager off having a good time. He was easily confused and could have hurt himself. The whole town had shown up to help look for him and to comfort Mary Lou. Should they send out the call for help with Joshua?

But Erin could see that would not go over well. If Mary Lou made a big fuss about his being missing and it turned out that he'd just taken a day off to mess around, the police and everyone else would be irritated, Mary Lou and Joshua would be embarrassed. Tensions between them would increase instead of decreasing.

"Do you want us to help look?" Erin asked Mary Lou.

Mary Lou sipped her tea and looked around, a small crease between her eyebrows. Then she finally nodded. "Yes. I suppose so. We can at least do that."

Erin and Vic nodded their agreement. Auntie Clem's Bakery was covered for the day, so they were free to spend the day as they wished. Erin had been planning to do some business planning and later to run some errands, but those things could be put off. If Joshua was missing, it was an emergency. She needed to be flexible and concentrate on what was most important.

"With this mention of you," Mary Lou said, motioning to the newspaper lying on the coffee table, the sticky note incongruous in the sea of black print, "do you think… that he's back in Whitewater?"

Erin looked at Vic. She didn't feel like driving back to Whitewater and, once she got there, where specifically would she look? But the notes said to ask Erin where he was. That implied that something Erin had done had resulted in Joshua's disappearance. And lately, all she had done was to be a judge at the cooking contest and to help solve Beryl Batcombe's murder.

A murder that Joshua had been asking questions about.

In Whitewater.

"I guess," she said reluctantly. "If it has something to do with me… that's really the only thing unusual that I have done lately. And Joshua interviewed me about it."

Vic nodded her agreement.

"I don't have a vehicle, though," Erin realized. "Willie took his truck and Terry took his."

"You should have gone with Jack to look at cars when they were here," Vic pointed out. "They had their eye on a few good deals."

"I know. But there was so much going on with the contest and everything else." And Erin hadn't wanted to go with Jack. She'd felt pressured before even getting near a car lot. She didn't want to be pushed into anything. She would buy a new car when she was ready. On her own. Without someone else pushing her into it and spouting facts and figures at her.

"Is Terry actually using the truck?" Vic asked. "Could we borrow it?"

"I'll check." He was often on foot patrol around the town, his truck just parked in the lot at the Town Hall, where the police department was housed. It was only a short walk to get there from Erin's house.

CHAPTER 2

Mary Lou raised her hand to stop Erin as she slid out her phone and looked down at it to dial Terry.

"What are you going to tell him?"

"That I need the car to go to Whitewater and..." Erin trailed off. She could see the warning in Mary Lou's eyes even before she said anything. "And... you don't want me to say anything to him about Joshua?"

"I've told you before that you need to watch what you say to him. If I wanted the police involved, I would call them myself."

"Okay." Erin looked at Vic. "Then I guess... tell him that I decided that my errands might take longer than I had originally planned, so I want to get started. And after we check out Whitewater, we'll have to run into the city to take care of them, so it doesn't look suspicious."

Mary Lou gave a brusque nod.

Erin swallowed. "Okay." She didn't like the subterfuge, but it was really just a lie of omission. She really would do her errands as she told him.

"Should we split up?" Vic asked. "I suppose I should stay here and look around; we can cover more area if we split up."

It was a sensible plan of action, but Erin bit her lip and shook her head. "I'm not sure... I don't want to go by myself."

Vic cocked her head. She raised her eyebrows in query. "It's just for a few hours. You wouldn't be staying there alone."

"I know. But since the accident, I don't really want to drive the highway by myself. I can, but... I just would feel better if I had someone with me. So that if anything happens..."

Nothing would happen, of course. Just because she had been followed and forced off the road once, that didn't mean that it would ever happen again. It was a once-in-a-lifetime occurrence.

Not something that was going to happen to her again.

"Oh, hon," Vic leaned across the coffee table and touched Erin's arm. "I didn't realize."

Erin squirmed. She wasn't looking for pity or even just attention. She wasn't doing it to be the poor, damaged little girl. She'd filled that role too many times in the past, the only survivor of the rollover that had killed her parents when she was just a child.

"I *can* go by myself," she asserted, looking at Mary Lou. "It's just... safer with two people in the car."

Mary Lou nodded. "If you could see if there's any sign of him in Whitewater Junction, that would help," she said, without comment on Erin's weakness and the inconvenience it caused. "I think I should stay here, in case he comes home, or in case... I don't know. The police call me with news."

Erin was about to ask why the police would call Mary Lou if she didn't report Joshua missing, but then bit back her response.

If they found Josh's body, Mary Lou meant. If they found him injured or dead, Mary Lou would be the one they called and she would want to be close at hand. Erin tried to blink back tears and not let the lump in her throat change her voice.

"Yeah. If he's in Whitewater, we'll find him."

If he were in Whitewater.

If he were alive.

If someone hadn't kidnapped him and hidden him away somewhere.

~

Erin managed to borrow Officer Terry Piper's truck without giving away that she was running over to Whitewater to see if she could find a missing teenager. There had been a couple of awkward pauses during the call. Like he knew that Erin was keeping something from him. Like he was trying to figure out how to ask her what was really going on but was afraid to ask.

Or maybe she just imagined it.

"He said it's fine," Erin told Vic. "He and K9 are just out on foot patrol, and he'll either walk home or get Stayner to drop him, depending on how he's feeling at the end of his shift."

"He's been doing better lately," Vic contributed. "It's nice to see him looking bright-eyed again."

It had been a difficult few months, a hard recovery after Terry had been attacked, hit over the head, and choked out. The damage went a lot deeper than she had expected. Nothing like TV cop shows where people got knocked out all the time and seemed to go on with barely even a headache or moment of vertigo. Things had been much worse for Terry.

But he had seemed to be doing better the last few days. She could only hope that he would continue to feel good and not relapse back into migraines, insomnia, and nightmares. And the irritability and mood issues.

"We'd better head out pretty quickly," Erin suggested. "If we're going to look for Josh and try to get our most urgent errands done, we can't waste any time."

"Yep," Vic agreed. "We'll be quick as two winks. Do you want me to make some sandwiches so we don't have to stop for lunch later?"

"Good idea. I'll check the animals' bowls"—she had two pets at home, Orange Blossom the cat and Marshmallow the rabbit—"Then, why don't I walk over and get the truck while you make the sandwiches. I'll make sure it's gassed up, and then we'll head out."

"Sounds like a plan," Vic agreed. She shook her head and *tsked.* "Poor Mary Lou. If we end up finding Joshua and this was just some kind of joke or ill-conceived teen prank, I'll whup that boy myself."

Erin had seen Vic's father try to beat her. He did not approve of her being transgender or getting together with a man from a rival clan—and she knew that Vic was only blowing hot air. There was no way she could do the same to another teen, no matter what he had done.

"I don't think it is a prank," Erin said. "I can't see Joshua doing something like this. He loves his mom and he knows all the stuff that she's been through. He wouldn't do something that might hurt her more just as a prank."

"No. I don't think so," Vic agreed. "Okay. I'll see you in twenty minutes or so."

After checking the food and water dishes, Erin grabbed her purse and headed over to the police department at a brisk walk.

Erin didn't run into anyone who slowed her down on her way to the Town Hall, so she was able to get Terry's truck and top off the gas tank in the allotted time. She picked Vic up at the house, and they were on their way to Whitewater.

Erin didn't want to keep going over the same ground when they hadn't found out anything yet. They could speculate all day long on where Joshua had gone or why he had disappeared, but they wouldn't know until they'd had some time to turn up some clues. Erin looked around for other things to talk about as she drove the highway. She didn't want to admit how anxious she was about being followed again, and she wouldn't be calmed just by listening to the radio. She needed something that took enough of her attention that she wouldn't constantly be thinking about the cars and trucks on the highway behind her.

It was a busy highway, not like the secondary road she'd been on the day that she'd been forced into the ditch. Nothing was going to happen to her out in the open where everybody could see.

"I did a few trials of recipes for the fortune cookies," she told Vic. "A few other people have done gluten-free fortune cookies. Mostly based around tapioca starch or cornstarch. They are pretty simple, actually. Just a matter of rolling or pressing them, cutting them into a circle, and then folding them while they're still warm. Then they get crispy when they cool."

"I always wondered how they baked them with paper inside," Vic laughed. "Because you would either have to bake them at a really low temperature, or the paper would light on fire. And I'd never even seen a scorched fortune."

Erin smiled and nodded. "I always wondered too. It's a bit of a letdown to realize that they insert the fortune and fold the cookie after they are baked. Removes some of the mystique."

"Won't it be great for the Chinese restaurant to offer gluten-free fortune cookies for their clientele? It's such a nice touch. I can't wait to see Peter Foster try his first gluten-free fortune cookie."

Erin was determined to keep her smile from fading, so she kept it firmly in place even though it made her sad that Mrs. Foster had decided Peter would not be visiting the bakery in person any time soon. Like Mary Lou, she was upset with Erin for mentioning Peter's name during a police investigation, resulting in Peter being interviewed by the police. Not just once, but twice.

It wasn't Erin's fault that he'd been a witness in both cases. He'd told her key clues that had led to her figuring out what had happened, but which also led to his being questioned.

It wasn't like he'd been a suspect, like Joshua. It was understood right from the start that the little boy had only been a witness, and one who didn't even realize what it was he had seen.

"I thought we should do some kind of care basket for Mrs. Foster," Erin said, changing the subject. "She'll be having that baby any day now, and it would be nice if she didn't have to be on her feet coming around to the bakery for a couple of weeks. We could take or deliver her the things that she normally comes around for... bread, muffins, after-school snacks..."

"What a great idea," Vic enthused. "You're always coming up with such creative plans."

"You don't think she would be offended, do you? Thinking that I was saying she wasn't capable of looking after her own family, or that I was just trying to get closer and interfere with things..."

"Of course not. It's a lovely thing to do. No one could find fault with you for helping a customer out during a challenging time."

"Okay." Erin wasn't always sure. People did seem to find fault with her for the littlest things. Even when she was doing something she thought people would approve of, doing something nice for someone just to be nice, they would criticize or put some kind of negative spin on things.

"Don't worry about the old gossips," Vic said, reading her mind. "Some people are negative no matter what. You're not going to change that. You have to just ignore them and live your life."

Erin nodded. “Yeah. I will. I just feel sometimes like I missed out on a bunch of etiquette lessons because of the way I was raised. There are all of these little rules that I never picked up on.”

“That’s just the south for you. And small-town living. There *are* a bunch of special rules. But you can never do them all, so you have to just develop a thick skin about the rest of them.”

CHAPTER 3

Welcome to Whitewater Junction.

Erin slowed as she approached the town limits sign. She had not expected to be returning to Whitewater any time soon. She had thought that when the contest was over and she had returned to Bald Eagle Falls, it would be the last time she'd be there for a few years. It wasn't exactly the center of civilization. It was the opposite way from the city, so she would always be traveling away from it. There were no tourist sites and, with everything that had happened during the contest, she had been glad to see it in her rearview mirror.

But now they were back again.

"Where should we go?" Erin asked. "The hotel?"

"I suppose… if Joshua intended to stay here, he would have to book a room, right?"

"I don't know… it just seems like such a bizarre idea, him coming back here on his own and staying by himself. Would they let a minor book a room by himself? Wouldn't they want an adult's signature on the register and some kind of guarantee that he wasn't going to have wild parties and mess things up?"

"If he had his own credit card, I don't know if they would ask how old he is."

"You had to show your driver's license, didn't you?"

Erin thought back. "I don't even remember. There was so much going on. I think that with the contest having booked all of the rooms, I didn't have to do anything but claim one."

Vic considered. "Yeah, maybe. I know when I first left home… there weren't a lot of places that I could have stayed. But I didn't have a credit card or any money, really."

"Most of these places don't let you stay for free," Erin agreed, smiling slightly.

"No, for some reason, they don't."

Erin pulled the truck carefully into the parking lot of the hotel away from the other vehicles so that no one would open their doors into it and mess up the paintwork. It wasn't like it was pristine anymore. Terry had driven over plenty of gravel roads and got other chips and scuffs on it. But Erin didn't want to contribute any damage. They walked into the lobby.

There were promotional signs up from the cooking contest. Actually, it had been a 'cooling' contest, using carbon dioxide to make fizzy drinks and ice cream treats—a very unique idea.

There were two big boards on easels displaying the three winners' faces in each of the classifications and the large cash prizes they had received. Eugene Bath, the man who had won the grand prize in the beverages section, Bella Proust, one of Erin's part-time employees below him, followed by a woman named Louisa David, who had received Clayton's third-place position when he had been arrested. And on the board for the ice cream winners, Doc Edmunds in first place, followed by two people Erin didn't know, Deidre Robinson and Hannah Clark.

Erin recognized the girl at the registration desk. They had spoken to each other several times during the cooking contest.

"Anita, hi." Erin smiled at her. "Long time, no see!"

"Erin Price. What are you doing back here so soon? Do you need a room?"

"No, I'm just here to see Joshua Cox. What floor is he on?"

"I didn't think there was anyone from the contest still here," Anita mused, tapping on her keyboard and squinting at the computer screen. "Joshua Cox… hmm… how is that spelled?"

"C-O-X." Erin had a sinking feeling. Of course it wasn't going to be that easy, but she had hoped.

"No, I don't see anyone by that name still registered here…" Anita tapped something else into her search parameters. "In fact, I don't see any registrations in that name at all. Would it have been under the name of one of the sponsors or someone else?"

"No, I don't think so," Erin admitted. "Is there somewhere else he might have stayed? This is the only hotel, right?"

"Yeah, unfortunately. There are a couple of B&B's or holiday rental places. I don't know, did he tell you he was going to be staying here?"

"Maybe I misunderstood," Erin said. She brandished her phone. "I'll give him a call."

"Okay. Let me know if you need anything else." Anita went back to answering phones and doing other work. Erin grimaced at Vic and they headed back toward the truck.

"Where else?" Vic asked. "Should we just drive around? It doesn't seem like we're very likely to turn him up that way."

"We might as well check B&B's. We're here anyway. And maybe… I don't know. The tourist center. Chamber of Commerce. The library. Anywhere else he might have gone if he was doing more research here."

"But why would he stay here? He'd already turned in his article for the paper."

"But he could have been researching something further. Maybe… he ran across something he thought was suspicious or interesting and wanted to do some more research."

"Like what? I think we pretty much got everything the first time around. Theft, murder, corruption. Do you think there was something else?"

"Well… no… I don't know what else he would be investigating. Maybe just more background, a more in-depth article on Beryl and what she had done. Or something about Clayton and his family."

"Yeah… Clayton's family." Vic thought about that. "I didn't really think about the fact that he must have family around here."

"If the reason he did what he did was because of the way his family had been taken advantage of, then he must have someone around here."

"He could be the last of the line, and that's why he thought it was all up to him to do something about it."

"But if he's a member of one of the old mountain families here, then he's related to everyone else. Not closely, maybe, but cousins, second cousins…"

"Yeah. How about the library, then? Josh might have gone there. They must have some genealogical records, histories of the local families."

That sounded like a good idea to Erin. She had not spent a lot of time in the library when she had been there, just stopping in to look at a few recipe books and get away from the crowds. The librarian had seemed friendly enough.

~

The library was quiet, just a couple of people reading or browsing through shelves. Nothing like the bustle that Erin had seen at big-city libraries. It was a cozy little place. That had attracted her when she had been trying to get away from the contest for a few minutes and to sort things out in her mind.

The librarian working at the computer at the circulation desk looked up when they walked in and smiled an invitation. Vic and Erin approached.

"We're looking for a friend," Erin said when they got close. "I think he might have stopped in here to do some research. A teen boy from Bald Eagle Falls…?"

"Oh… what was his name? James?"

"Joshua."

"Joshua." She nodded. "Yes, he was here a couple of weeks ago. While the contest was on. A budding young reporter."

"Yeah." Erin was relieved. It hadn't occurred to her until she walked in that she didn't have a picture to show the woman. How were they supposed to find Joshua without a picture of him? "Is he around today? Or yesterday?"

"With everything shutting down, it's been mighty quiet. He hasn't been around. I assume he went back to Bald Eagle Falls." She raised her brows. Obviously, Joshua would go back home after the contest was over. Why would he stay?

"Well, he's not back, that's why we're looking for him. Do you know… where else he might have been going? Did he say that he had some other research he needed to do…?"

"I haven't seen him lately, I'm sorry. I think everyone is done with that now. All of the excitement… it turned out to be kind of an embarrassment. The contest was supposed to generate so many tourism dollars for the town, lots of positive publicity that would last even after it was over… but all of the negative press has not been good for us. I don't see it being much benefit, to tell the truth. You can bet the town council will think twice before approving something like that again."

Erin rubbed the back of her neck. She wasn't sure why she felt guilty. Her role in the contest had been completely innocent. Chef Kirschoff was a friend, he'd asked her to be a judge, and she'd agreed. Everything had happened so quickly after that.

Erin hadn't been responsible for anything that had happened, of course. She had helped identify Beryl's killer. But she felt like she'd been the cause of the problems in Whitewater instead of just an innocent bystander.

"Yeah, it's too bad the way everything blew up—turned out," she corrected quickly. Her face heated. She avoided looking at Vic, who she knew would be trying not to laugh. "We just thought… Joshua was going to do a follow-up story. Or maybe some background on Beryl or on… you know, Clayton… and I figured he would come back here."

The librarian shook her head. "No, sorry. I can't help you there."

"Can you think of where else he might have gone? If he wanted to get some background on Beryl's or Clayton's families?"

"We have a section on histories of the old Whitewater families." The librarian looked toward the shelves where they were situated. "I would expect him to come here. Aside from that… maybe an amateur genealogist in town. Or if he knew one of the older people, who might remember some of the history that wouldn't be in the books."

"Can you think of who he might go to?"

She shook her head.

"Does Clayton have any kinfolk around here?" Vic suggested.

"Some distant cousins, maybe. The Hinchey line has pretty much died out. Times are difficult. People move their families into urban centers where they can get jobs and get into good schools. And the kids don't come back here."

"He doesn't have any grandparents? Great aunts?"

"No." The librarian shook her head slowly. "No one who comes to mind."

Perhaps that was the reason that Beryl had thought she could get away with stealing from the old families. She figured there would be no one left to complain.

"Well... thank you for your time," Erin told the librarian, disappointed.

The woman gave a sympathetic smile and went back to her work. Vic and Erin walked slowly back to the truck.

"One more down," Vic said bracingly. "It's only one place. We can still check with the Chamber of Commerce, pop into the coffee shops with Wi-Fi, maybe check with the paper. They must have a weekly."

"Yeah, that sounds good," Erin agreed, trying to be cheerful about it.

After all, they hadn't found out anything negative—no hint of any violence. Joshua just hadn't been to the library. There were plenty of other places he could be.

If he were even in Whitewater.

And he probably wasn't.

CHAPTER 4

Their search petered out after a couple of hours. Neither could think of anywhere else to go, and no one they had talked to had seen or heard from Joshua. Some of them knew him from when he had been doing the research for his school project. Vic downloaded a picture of Joshua from Facebook to show people who didn't recognize him from their description. But no one had seen him recently. It would appear that Joshua hadn't gone back to Whitewater Junction after all.

They even drove around for a while, methodically covering all of the streets that crisscrossed the town. As if they might see Joshua walking down the road or be inspired by a storefront. But there was still no sign of him.

On their drive into the city, they focused on lists of what they needed and how they would tackle the various stores. They worked out an efficient plan of attack to get done as quickly as possible and return home to Bald Eagle Falls.

They were, Erin knew, avoiding the real issue.

They hadn't gotten a call from Mary Lou saying that she had found him or that he had called.

He wasn't in Whitewater. He wasn't anywhere obvious in Bald Eagle Falls.

It would be a lot more challenging to find him in the city. They couldn't just drive all of the streets there. It was a small city, but it was still too big for two people to search in one vehicle.

They shopped like they were on a mission. Like that was the more important thing. As if everything would magically fall together if they could get everything done, like the pieces of a puzzle fitting together.

When they were finished their errands and eating the second round of sandwiches, they avoided looking each other in the eye and admitting their failure.

"Should we see Campbell while we're here?" Vic suggested. "He might know something. Joshua might have gone to him."

"I'm sure Mary Lou must have called him by now," Erin pointed out. "He'll be out of bed and able to answer his phone. If she wanted us to go see him, she would have let us know."

Besides, Erin remembered the last time they had gone on a search in the city. Not looking for Campbell, but for his girlfriend Brianna. That had turned out to be a dangerous proposition. Erin had no desire to go back to any of the flophouses they had searched for Brianna. Or to run into anyone from the Russian mob. That was off the table.

"I suppose," Vic agreed with a sigh. She wadded up her sandwich wrappers to throw them out. "I'm worn slap out. I don't think we could manage much more today anyway."

Erin nodded. She needed to get back home. She needed to see Terry and to make sure that she was prepared for the next day at Auntie Clem's Bakery. She would only have a little while to relax, and then it would be time for bed. Bakers had to rise before the rest of the world to get the daily bread in the oven.

~

Erin wasn't quite sure how to handle their report to Mary Lou. They could make a call to her on the way back to Bald Eagle Falls. Or they could go back to Erin's and ask Mary Lou over. But calling her seemed way too impersonal, and making her come to them after she had spent the whole day stressed out and waiting for Joshua seemed cruel. They had exchanged a few quick texts during the day to report. Still, Erin thought it was important to see Mary Lou face-to-face and go over everything they had done, in case something turned out to be important. She didn't think they had discovered anything of consequence, but Erin knew that the outcome of an investigation could hinge on the tiniest of details. Sometimes just a gut feeling about how it all fit together.

"Do you think it's okay to go by her house?" Erin asked Vic tentatively. "I know that she might not want us there… but I don't want to drag her out somewhere else."

"We can go by. If she doesn't want us there… she can tell us so."

That didn't make Erin feel much more confident about going to Mary Lou's house. But it seemed like the only reasonable solution, so once they arrived at Bald Eagle Falls, she pulled to the curb in front of Mary Lou's house. They walked up to the front door and knocked.

Hospitality in Bald Eagle Falls dictated that if someone was expecting you or had opened up their home to you, it was fine to simply knock on the door or 'yoo-hoo' and walk in. But while Mary Lou had previously welcomed them, she had not been keen on them lately, so Erin didn't think it would be a good idea. Vic apparently agreed, because she didn't push the door open and walk in ahead of Erin. She stood to the side and slightly behind Erin. Erin hoped that was just reticence and not concern that Mary Lou might welcome them with a shotgun blast.

It was a few minutes and a few more knocks and a doorbell later that Mary Lou finally came to the door. She looked Erin and Vic over, her face pale and drawn, looking like she had been sitting up for days waiting for Joshua to come home. Erin's heart hurt. She wanted to take her former friend in her arms and give her a comforting hug. But she refrained, waiting to see whether Mary Lou would even allow them in or be interested in hearing what they had to say.

"Nothing?" Mary Lou asked dully.

"No," Erin confirmed. She was prepared to leave. That was really all Mary Lou needed to know. Erin's search had not come to fruition, Joshua had obviously not returned on his own. It was up to Mary Lou to take the next step.

Mary Lou sighed, rubbed her hand over her face, then turned slightly and motioned the other women in. Erin led the way, Vic trailing behind her. Erin had a strong feeling of deja vu on entering the front room. She remembered arriving there on Thanksgiving, seeing the cops outside taking Campbell away, walking in to find Joshua there comforting Mary Lou.

Joshua should have been there with Mary Lou. But he wasn't.

They sat down and looked at each other, silently working out who would speak first.

"We went everywhere we could think of in Whitewater," Erin offered. "And when we couldn't think of anywhere else to look, we just drove up and down the streets. *All* of the streets."

"Was there any sign he had been there? Any hint at all?" Mary Lou asked.

"No. No one had seen him since he did the research for his report on the contest. People remembered him. The librarian. Other people he had talked to when he was tracking information down. But they hadn't seen him for the last day or two. Nothing since he wrote the article, I guess."

"He's been at home since then. He didn't say anything about going back to Whitewater or doing a follow-up story. He's been at home… going to school and doing homework…" Mary Lou shook her head. "He's been here. Everything was normal. And then, just… gone. How could he be gone?"

"I don't know." Erin looked at Vic, raising her brows. "He never said anything to you either?" They were, at least, closer in age than Erin and Joshua. Both still teenagers, even if Vic was legally an adult.

"No. I haven't seen him at all. We weren't close friends." Vic wasn't even from Bald Eagle Falls. She had probably seen less of Joshua than Erin had. But Erin didn't want to reveal to Mary Lou that Joshua had been by to talk to her more than once since Erin had been told to stay away from him and not involve him in any more police investigations.

That wasn't Erin's fault. She had never contacted him or encouraged him to talk to her against his mother's wishes. He had just shown up, and would not be dissuaded by any of her arguments.

"Well, that's it, then," Mary Lou sighed. "I was hoping it would be something simple… that you were right and he just wanted to get some more research done. Off being an intrepid reporter." Her eyes moved to the newspaper that she had previously brought to Erin's house, which now resided on her dining room table. "Except for that."

"It could still be something innocent. Maybe he just… lost track of time."

"For an entire day?" Mary Lou snapped. "No. He didn't just wander off in the middle of the night and forget to come home."

"No." Erin looked down, her eyes suddenly swimming.

"Are you going to call the police?" Vic asked.

"It looks like I don't have any other choice now," Mary Lou said. She squeezed her lips together tightly, trying to keep her own emotions under control. "I guess I'll do that now. The two of you can see yourselves out."

"Don't you want us to stay with you?" Erin protested. "At least until the sheriff gets here?"

"No." Mary Lou's words were clipped. "I will be fine by myself. You have had a long, unproductive day. You'll want to get some rest tonight. I know I won't."

Erin forced herself to her feet. Her legs were shaking and she hated to leave Mary Lou like that. She must have been screaming inside. Erin couldn't imagine how terrified she must be about what had happened to Joshua. If Erin could feel so worried for someone who was nearly a stranger to her, she couldn't imagine how badly Mary Lou must be taking it.

But Mary Lou didn't crack. She watched Erin and Vic head back toward the front door, looking down at her phone to make the call she had been dreading making all day. The call that would mean she could no longer deny being worried that something had happened to Joshua.

Something terrible.

CHAPTER 5

Josh awoke groggily. He lay still for a long time while waiting for his brain to start working and to join the real world again. After a while, he wondered what time it was and if his alarm was going to go off soon. It seemed like he always hit that floaty, unreal feeling just a few minutes before his alarm went off. If he looked at his clock, then he would be awake, but if he could just maintain that floatiness, he could get a little more sleep. Or at least a little more rest.

Then he started wondering what day it was. Maybe it wasn't even a day that he had to get up early. He still had to get himself out of bed on Saturday and Sunday, but he was allowed to sleep in for a couple of hours. His mother said that she understood that teenagers needed more sleep, but he had to do his part and go to bed in good time. He couldn't just stay up all night and then sleep all day just because it was the weekend.

He liked it when he woke up early on a Saturday morning and realized he could go back to sleep for a couple more hours. It was a great feeling.

But he wasn't feeling great.

He couldn't remember what day it was.

Maybe that in itself told him that it was a weekend. He wasn't a big drinker, but he had gone to a couple of parties where alcohol had been snuck in. Or he had dipped into Campbell's stash when Campbell was still living at home. He didn't particularly like alcohol and was just as happy to leave it alone. Especially if it left him feeling so rocky in the morning. Who needed that?

It was still longer before he started to wonder *where* he was.

He was still so close to sleep that he couldn't be sure, but nothing in his environment felt familiar. He wasn't in his bed. There was a bad smell. There were strange noises that were both close and far away at the same time.

It wasn't his house.

CHAPTER 6

Erin and Vic drove back home in silence. What else was there to say? They had done their best to help Mary Lou, but they had failed. Neither had any idea where Joshua was, or why Erin had been named in the cryptic note left in Mary Lou's paper.

A day that should have been a calm, relaxing, regenerating day had ended up being dark and depressing.

And she wasn't allowed to tell Terry about it. Mary Lou had made it abundantly clear that Erin was never to bring Joshua or Campbell up with Officer Terry Piper. Not ever. Not a casual comment in passing. Not pillow talk. Not saying she was worried about him.

Not telling anyone that he was missing.

That wasn't Erin's place. She needed to just stay out of it and mind her own business.

She pulled Terry's truck in front of the house, and she and Vic got out slowly.

"I'll see you in the morning," Vic offered.

"Sure. It will be good to have a normal day at the bakery tomorrow."

Except Erin didn't feel good about it. She felt horrible. She would be working, baking, pretending that there was nothing wrong, knowing that Joshua was missing and that Mary Lou's heart was breaking.

While Erin walked up to the front door, Vic took the sidewalk around to the back, where she had a loft apartment over Erin's garage. Erin hadn't even thought to ask whether Willie would be home. Or would Vic be sitting over there all by herself stewing about what had happened to Joshua and if he was okay?

Just like Erin would be stewing, even if Terry were home.

She raised her hand to unlock the door, but it opened in front of her. Terry smiled and took a couple of bags from her.

"You must have had a successful time in the city," he observed. "You were later than I expected you to be."

"Um… sorry about that," Erin apologized, without answering his comment. She carried the rest of her bags into the house and put them down. Orange Blossom meowed loudly, rubbed against her legs, and then started thrusting his head into the various bags, checking to see if she had bought him any treats. Or just because he liked to stick his head in bags.

"Nothing for you, sir," Erin told Blossom, scooping him up and cradling him in the crook of her arm. "How is my furry baby today?"

He meowed, objecting to being treated that way. Still, when she didn't release him, he chirped and yowled and huffed at her like he was telling her all about his day. Erin encouraged him with little noises and questions, as was her usual routine. She stood on her tiptoes to kiss Terry in greeting without letting Orange Blossom go, squashing him between their bodies. He complained loudly and squirmed away. Erin let him go, putting her arms around Terry to give him a squeeze.

"Thanks. I needed that," she said, putting her head on his chest and relaxing in his arms.

It was nice to see him on his feet at the end of the day. So many times recently, he had been knocked down by a migraine by the end of the day, unable to enjoy himself or the time they had to spend together.

"How was your day?" she asked him.

Terry released her from his grip. Erin stooped to pet Marshmallow, the brown and white rabbit patiently nibbling at her toes.

"And hello to you too."

She and Terry made their way over to the couch to cuddle.

"Do you need anything?" he asked. "A drink? A cookie?"

K9 was sleeping beside the couch, and Erin saw his head jerk up at the suggestion of a cookie. He looked hopefully in Erin's direction.

"Oh, you said one of those words. Now you're going to have to get everyone a cookie."

"Fine with me. I want one too."

Erin sat down and let him do the honors. Terry gave K9 one of Erin's gluten-free doggie biscuits, fished treats out of Orange Blossom's treat can and slid them across the floor for him to chase, and got a couple of small carrots out of the crisper for Marshmallow. He opened the freezer to check out the supply.

"Chocolate chip or ginger snap?"

"Chocolate chip. Today has definitely been a chocolate chip day."

Terry got a couple of chocolate chip cookies from the freezer and put them on a plate to be microwaved.

"Been a long day?"

Erin nodded. "Yeah. Kind of."

"Well, you did it to yourself with all of that shopping."

"Uh-huh."

Half a minute later, the microwave beeped and Terry brought the melty-chocolate-chip cookies out to the living room. They each took one and tried to eat them over the same plate so that no crumbs or drips of chocolate would get into the couch and carpet.

"Sorry," Terry said through a mouthful of cookie. "I should have brought two plates."

Erin just laughed.

She should have known that the idyllic moment wouldn't last. She wasn't going to be able to forget about the rest of her day that quickly. Terry sat back as his phone started to buzz and pulled it out of his pocket. He thumbed the fingerprint unlock button and his eyes moved quickly over the words on the screen.

"Uh-oh."

Erin's stomach clenched again, and she regretted having just topped it off with chocolate and sugar. "Is everything okay?"

He looked at her, thinking about what he could tell her, and decided that he wasn't free to give her any information yet. "No… I'm going to be needed."

"Will it take long?" Erin asked, pretending she didn't know exactly what it was. "You already put in a shift today; you don't want to push it with your health."

"I put in a half shift," he corrected. "And I'm feeling okay. I can put in a few more hours."

"Not too long, though, right? You can't pull an all-nighter. You need to make sure you get enough sleep."

He evaded her concerns. "I don't know how long it will be tonight. I won't stay any longer than necessary, but I am needed." Terry stood up, licking chocolate off his fingers. "I'll put this in the sink."

Erin didn't say anything as she watched him get ready to go. K9 was on his feet and prepared to follow, recognizing Terry's body language and eager to work.

She carefully avoided saying anything that would indicate she knew he was going to Mary Lou's house and that Joshua was missing.

It wasn't a lie.

She just wasn't allowed to tell him that she already knew what was going on. As soon as it became public knowledge—and gossip spread quickly through Bald Eagle Falls—then she wouldn't have to pretend she didn't know anything about it.

But even then, Mary Lou wouldn't want her talking to Terry about Joshua.

Erin didn't see how she was going to be able to avoid it.

CHAPTER 7

Terry hadn't returned before it was time for Erin to go to bed. She hadn't expected him to. She didn't know how long to expect him to be, but she assumed he would need a few hours to start the preliminaries of the investigation. Talk to Mary Lou, ask her everything he could think of about Josh. Maybe drive around town to talk to his closest friends or to check out places where they might hang out.

When she got up in the morning, he wasn't in bed beside her and he wasn't asleep on the couch. Erin glanced at the door and could see that his shoes were still gone, as was his truck.

She was going to need to have a word with Sheriff Wilmot about letting Terry work that long. If he crashed and couldn't work again for a week, it would be their fault for exceeding the number of hours that the doctor had said he should work during the transition period.

She did her best to put her anger and worry aside and get ready for the day. She loved her job and needed to be in a good mood for her customers.

She talked to the animals, made herself tea and toast, and checked her lists for the day, adding an item here and there. Terry was obviously not there to drop them at the bakery. Looking out the back, she could see Willie's truck on the gravel pad beside the garage. She texted Vic to see whether they had a ride. They would need to leave a few minutes earlier if they were going to walk, and she would leave her shopping bags at home and only take the necessities that they needed for that day.

Vic texted back that Willie would drop them off. Erin took a few more minutes to load up the dishwasher, change the water bowls, and check one more time to make sure she had everything ready to start the day at Auntie Clem's.

~

Josh was a little less groggy when he awoke again. He tried to move around but found that his arms wouldn't move. His shoulders hurt. A lot of things ached, but his shoulders and his head were the worst. Whatever he had drunk, it had really bothered him. He'd had way too much.

He tried to move again. If he wasn't at home, then he needed to wake himself up and get home. Before his mother awoke and discovered him gone.

He didn't know what he had done. Had it been Campbell? Had they gone out together? He'd been calling Cam, trying to set something up. But Cam hadn't been eager to get back to Bald Eagle Falls and Josh didn't want to get in trouble for driving into the city. Mary Lou was already irritated about his going to Whitewater to do interviews on his own. She said he shouldn't have gone without a responsible adult to make sure he didn't get himself in trouble.

But what was going to happen? He was doing news interviews. On a public contest. It wasn't like he was doing anything dangerous.

He groaned, trying to get his arms into a more comfortable position, but he couldn't move.

He knew in his heart that Mary Lou had a point. There *had* been a murder in Whitewater associated with the contest. And he had previously shown that he didn't have the best of judgment as far as the criminal element was concerned. So she was right; he could have gotten himself in the crosshairs of the murderer by approaching the wrong person or saying the wrong thing.

But the culprit had been found. And Joshua had never even met Clayton.

It was kind of disappointing, actually. He had hoped to be able to break a story that would be picked up by syndicates across the country. Or at least to provide the background, the story behind the story. He had been conditioned by Disney movies and Marvel comics to think that a teenager could make a difference. Could break the big story.

But of course, the world didn't work that way. He had known that all along, but he had held on to the fantasy. Nothing else in his life had gone like a Disney movie, so why did he think that his investigative reporting would?

~

At the bakery, everything proceeded as usual for the first few hours of the day. They got the initial morning baking done and opened up the shop. People drifted in with their coffees to go and picked up muffins or pastries. Moms stopped in either on the way to school or after dropping their kids off. Then there was a lull, and Erin and Vic took a break for their early lunch. There was a tap at the back door.

Erin unlocked and opened the door, and found Terry there. He looked tired, but he didn't have the heavy-lidded, haggard look he got when he had a migraine.

"Hey." Erin gave him a peck. "How are you doing? You just getting off now?"

Terry nodded. "Yeah, I just thought I'd let you know. In case you try to reach me and I'm too far gone to wake up for the phone."

"Thanks. I can't believe you worked this long. You must be wiped."

"I am. But I'll sleep until you get home. It will be okay."

"You need to be more careful. You know you're not supposed to be working those hours."

"It was an emergency. I really did have to be there." He hesitated. "Have you heard…?"

"Not yet," Erin admitted, though she was dying to talk to him about it. News of Joshua's disappearance hadn't yet reached Auntie Clem's, and she couldn't talk about it with Terry until it did.

Terry sighed. He cupped the side of her face with his strong hand for a minute and ran his thumb along an escaped tendril of hair. "Okay." He gave her no clues. He wouldn't tell her anything about his investigation that wasn't already public knowledge, so they would both just keep dancing around the topic and saying nothing. "I'll see you tonight." He looked past her and sketched a wave at Vic. "Hello and goodbye, Vic."

Vic smiled and waved. Terry gave Erin one more kiss and then left, K9 following close at his heel.

CHAPTER 8

"Here it comes," Vic said in a warning tone.

Erin looked at her to see what she was talking about and followed Vic's gaze through the front door. Melissa was coming down the sidewalk at a quick clip. In a moment, she was through the door, the bells ringing wildly and her brown curls dancing and swinging around her face.

"My, what a day!" she exclaimed, placing a hand dramatically over her heart.

Erin and Vic both put on innocent expressions, waiting for her to break the news.

"What's going on?" Vic prompted.

"As if she hadn't had to put up with enough already," Melissa said, shaking her head in pity.

"Who?"

"Mary Lou."

"What happened?" Erin asked. "Did something happen to Roger?"

"No, not Roger. As far as I know, he's still doing just fine. No, the latest news is that Joshua is now missing."

"Josh?" Vic repeated innocently. "What happened to Josh?"

"No one knows. And believe me, we have been investigating intensively ever since the call came in." Melissa was only a part-time admin at the police department, but one would never guess it by the way she talked. To hear her tell it, Erin would have thought that she was a high-ranking detective, not a typist and file clerk.

Vic leaned closer to Melissa, and Melissa drew in so that their heads were close together. "Nobody knows anything?" Vic asked. "What happened? He just took off?"

"There was a note," Melissa said ominously. She straightened her posture and nodded solemnly.

"A ransom note?" Erin asked. Even though she knew there had been no ransom note, her heart still beat faster at the thought.

"No, not a ransom note. A note saying that…" Melissa looked around dramatically as if she were afraid someone would hear her. When in reality, she was probably making sure that everyone was paying close attention. "A note saying that if she wanted to know where Joshua was, you know something about it." She looked pointedly at Erin.

Erin had known that it was coming, but she couldn't stop her body's automatic reaction, her face getting hot. She dabbed at her cheek with the back of her hand, wishing she could hide her flush. How many people would take blushing as an admission of guilt?

"I didn't have anything to do with Joshua disappearing," she said. "I don't know anything about it!"

"Well, you can expect a visit from the police today, I'll tell you that. I'm surprised they haven't been here already."

Erin cleared her throat. "They know what time I work and where they can find me."

"They certainly do," Melissa laughed. "I'm sure they'll keep in close contact." She waggled her eyebrows suggestively. Erin's face heated even more.

"I need to check some cookies," she advised, turning her back on Melissa to hide in the kitchen.

"I don't think this is something to kid about," she heard Vic say as she left.

"Oh, I don't think there's really anything to worry about," Melissa said breezily. "Just teenagers pulling a prank. You know how they are. Well, you still *are* a teenager. Maybe you're in on the whole thing."

"I may be a teenager, but I'm not a kid," Vic retorted. "I wouldn't do something like that. And Josh and I barely know each other."

"I don't really think you have anything to do with it," Melissa assured her, still not adopting a more serious tone. "And neither do the police. But they're not convinced that it is a real disappearance."

"A *real* disappearance? What would make it not real? If they found him in his bedroom?"

"No, I just mean, there isn't necessarily anything sinister or criminal about it. Not if it's just kids fooling around."

"What would make them think it was just a joke?" Vic asked.

Erin fanned her face, but she didn't want to miss too much of the conversation or observing Melissa's face and body language, so she returned to the front of the shop as if she'd finished checking on the fictional cookies.

Melissa's eyes closed slightly, looking like a contented cat. She stepped closer and peered into the display case. "The writing on the note. It looks like a teenager's writing." She again paused for dramatic effect. "It looks like Joshua's writing."

Erin caught her breath. Joshua's writing? What kind of sense did that make? Why would Joshua have written a note like that? And then disappeared? What reason would he have for making his mother worry about him or pointing the finger at Erin? He had apologized to Erin several times for the way that Mary Lou treated her. He didn't want Mary Lou to be mad at Erin, so why would he do something that would make Mary Lou even more upset? And after all that his mother had been through, he wouldn't want to make her suffer more.

"Joshua didn't write that note," Vic said firmly.

Erin nodded.

"Mary Lou said it looked like his writing," Melissa persisted.

Erin looked at Vic. She ran the previous day's events through her head. Had Mary Lou known that Joshua was up to something? Had she thought that it was just some big prank? She shook her head. Mary Lou had been concerned. She was worried that something had happened to Joshua. She had worried about staying close to home in case the police found his body. That wasn't a parent who thought her son was just off on a jaunt enjoying himself.

"No," Vic agreed. "No way."

Melissa raised her brows. "I'm just telling you what they have found out. It's the truth. How you interpret it..."

"Someone might have a similar handwriting style to Joshua's," Erin said. She bit her tongue before adding that the writing had been messy. It could have been any teenager's. It wasn't like they were being taught penmanship in school anymore. She didn't know how a forensic expert would have been able to tell anything from looking at that little square sticky note.

Someone might have been attempting to mimic his handwriting style. Or Josh could have been forced to write the note himself.

"Just because it looks like his handwriting, that doesn't mean that it is," she told Melissa. "Or that it means it's a prank."

Melissa shrugged. "I guess we'll find out."

"Yes."

Melissa picked out a brownie for her snack and a loaf of rosemary bread to take home for supper.

"You and Mary Lou have been pretty close lately," she said to Erin. "I'm surprised she didn't call you as soon as this happened."

Melissa, on the other hand, had not been as supportive of Mary Lou as she could have been following Roger's incarceration and Campbell's arrest. Many of the friends that Mary Lou had thought she would have been able to depend on had been silent over the past year. They had stopped going to her house, defending her, or inviting her out with them. Erin knew that she'd felt isolated, betrayed by the people she had thought were loyal friends.

"Matter of fact," Melissa went on, not waiting for Erin to respond. "She didn't even call the police right away. You would think that if your child disappeared and you were concerned about what might have happened to him, you would at least call the police to make a report."

"I'm sure she was concerned," Erin said coolly. "But maybe she was concerned about gossip. Or that the police department wouldn't take her concerns seriously. It sounds like not *everybody* who works at the police department thinks this is something to be concerned about."

Melissa either didn't feel or else intentionally ignored the barbs. "Maybe she thinks he's old enough that she doesn't have to worry about him anymore. Or maybe he's gone to stay with Campbell, and she didn't want to admit both have wandered from the fold."

"I don't think Cam has wandered from the fold," Vic objected. Erin was an atheist, so she let the younger woman take that one. "Just because

Cam has moved out on his own, that doesn't mean that he's turned away from God."

"Drinking, drugs, immorality… who knows what he's been doing." Melissa tapped her card against the reader to pay her bill and took the proffered bag from Erin.

"You don't know anything about what Campbell has been doing. And if you're listening to gossip and making judgments based on that, how Christian is that?" Vic demanded. "Didn't Jesus say not to judge people? To welcome them and love them—"

"He was arrested for dealing drugs!"

"He was framed! You know that."

"But if it wasn't credible, if people didn't think that he could have been doing it, because he *was* involved in drugs, then they never would have charged him. They would have known it was planted and that Campbell didn't have anything to do with it."

"That's ridiculous."

Melissa raised her eyebrows. She turned back toward the door, her expression saying that she had done exactly what she'd come to do. Not to tell them that there was a child in danger and to get the town's assistance in starting a search and rescue for him. To revel in the fact that she once again had firsthand knowledge of a crime that had taken place in Bald Eagle Falls. To incite drama and speculation. To be in the spotlight and have other women in Bald Eagle Falls envying her position.

Erin didn't say anything as Melissa smiled goodbye and left the bakery.

CHAPTER 9

Vic cussed under her breath, something she was usually far too ladylike to do.

Erin looked at her. There were a couple of other customers waiting to be served, so they couldn't talk about it yet. Erin wouldn't stoop to gossiping about the situation with the other customers.

One of the waiting customers was Mrs. Peach, Erin's next-door neighbor. She hobbled forward to the counter and checked the goods on display.

"You don't think there's anything to all of this, do you?" she questioned. "I would hate for anything else to happen to Mary Lou Cox and her family. They've already been through so much."

"I know," Erin agreed. "It's more than one person should have to go through." If she'd believed in God, she would have had a word with him about it.

"Could I get the raisin bread?" Mrs. Peach pointed. "No, not that one, Miss Victoria, the one to the left. My left. It has far more raisins than the others."

Vic picked up the loaf that Mrs. Peach wanted with her gloved hands and put it into a bag.

"Anything else?" Erin asked.

"I don't know about all of this nonsense about a note. Does that sound right to you? I wonder if there even was a note. That girl has been known to exaggerate at times," she took a look in the direction Melissa had gone, back toward Town Hall.

"It really isn't any of my business," Erin pointed out.

"You ask that handsome policeman of yours," Mrs. Peach advised sagely. She pointed at the blueberry muffins. "Are those fresh today, or are they from a couple of days ago?"

"They're fresh today, Mrs. Peach." Erin tried to ignore the comment about her handsome policeman. He wasn't going to share anything about the investigation with her, and Erin was going to have to take care not to reveal to him how much she had known before he even started.

"I'll have… six of those. If you can put them in a box for me so that they don't get crushed."

"Can you carry all of that?" Erin asked as she packaged Mrs. Peach's purchases. "I've told you before that if you want to just tell me what you want ahead of time, I'll set it aside for you and take it home. You don't have to come all the way here and carry it home."

Mrs. Peach smiled and shook her head. "I'm not that infirm, dear. I can carry my own bags. If you had a furniture store instead of a bakeshop, things might be different. But I can carry my own bread and muffins."

"Well, you know you can change your mind and ask any time. If it's ever more convenient for you to just have me bring something home for you."

"I like to be able to come in and see what I'm buying. And to make sure that it is all fresh."

Erin shook her head. "Everything is fresh, Mrs. Peach. I don't sell day-olds unless it's labeled that way."

"You never know," Mrs. Peach advised. She paid for her purchases with cash money and left, wobbling a little, but perfectly capable of carrying her own bags.

In a few minutes, the bakery was empty of customers. It was the lull between lunch and school letting out, so it would likely stay just a trickle until parents started to arrive to pick up their children from school.

"Can you believe Melissa?" Vic whispered. "I can't believe that she would be so… blatant about spreading her speculations around. And she and Mary Lou used to be best of friends. I can't believe she's spreading that garbage around about Joshua not really being missing and that Campbell is… some kind of drug lord now. Why don't they fire her?"

Terry had complained more than once about how Melissa gossiped and spread around the information she learned while working at the police department.

"I don't know why they don't do anything about it," she admitted. "It isn't like they don't know. There must be other people they could hire in her place."

"They have a duty to keep things confidential," Vic said, shaking her head. "What if Mary Lou sued them for spreading stuff around?"

Erin nodded. She liked Melissa. But the police department really should do something about her. It was getting more and more blatant.

"I'm going to put together a basket for Mrs. Foster. You can handle things out here?"

Vic looked around pointedly at the lack of customers. "I don't know, Erin. You really want me to just jump into the deep end like this?"

Erin grinned at her and went into the kitchen.

The Foster family was growing. The new baby would be number five. That was a lot of work for a mom. She would be tired and sore after the baby came—she was undoubtedly tired and sore waiting for the event—and it would be nice if Erin could help her out a little bit. A few care baskets for those initial weeks, so that Mrs. Foster didn't have to spend as much time on her feet and running around town.

And Erin secretly hoped—maybe not so secretly—that she would be able to repair the rift between herself and Mrs. Foster. And she would start bringing Peter and the other children to the bakery again. Erin loved little Peter especially. He was very mature and well-spoken, advocating for himself and his celiac disease. Maybe arguing a bit too much with his mother, who was doing the best she could to ensure that he was both safe and polite and respectful. It wasn't an easy thing for anyone raising kids in the present state of the world. Erin didn't know if it were something she would ever take on herself.

She packed bread and muffins, bagels, cookies, and some of the granola bars that Peter particularly liked for school. It was hard for a kid who was so sensitive to gluten. Before Erin had opened Auntie Clem's Bakery, he had been limited to less-than-stellar loaves of commercial gluten-free bread from the grocer and boxes of stale gluten-free cookies. If the grocery store didn't get anything in, Mrs. Foster would have to drive into the city to pick up what she needed. Or make something from scratch. Not easy for a mom of four. But otherwise, Peter had to avoid baked products altogether.

Since the opening of Auntie Clem's Bakery, Peter had been able to explore a whole new world of gluten-free baked goods. Erin was his new best friend.

But Mrs. Foster was understandably wary of her son getting so close to a stranger. She taught him about boundaries, but Peter was inclined, like any other little boy, to break the rules when he was out of his mother's sight and hearing. An observant little fellow, he had provided key clues to a couple of important police investigations lately. Something that would have been commendable in an adult, but Peter's being interviewed by the police had produced considerable anxiety for his parents.

And Mrs. Foster blamed Erin for that anxiety. If she hadn't said anything to the police…

Erin sighed as she wrapped everything carefully. It was depressing to have so many of the Bald Eagle Falls parents upset with her.

Unlike Peter, many of the other children had not just been witnesses.

Erin breathed slowly in and out as she looked at the Foster house. She hadn't been there before. She wasn't surprised to find the lawn littered with children's ride 'em toys, the paint peeling from the siding and porch railings, and the gardens somewhat overgrown. People in Bald Eagle Falls were not wealthy, and having that many young children was enough to overwhelm any mother.

Willie looked over the seat into the back of the king cab, raising his brows at Erin. "We're here."

His face was reassuring. She remembered how leery she had been of him when she had first arrived in Bald Eagle Falls and he had offered to help her with her groceries. She had taken him for a dirty homeless man. She hadn't known back then that his skin was perhaps permanently stained by the mining and processing he did on his own. Now that she knew him, she didn't even notice. It was only brought to her attention when other people saw him for the first time and treated him like a second-class citizen.

"Yeah. I'll just be a minute."

Erin still didn't move. She knew what she needed to do, but she was nervous of the reception she would get. Mrs. Foster wasn't expecting her and might not be happy to see her, even if she was there bearing gifts.

Vic gave Erin a reassuring smile. "Just this one thing, and then you can go home to Terry and relax for the evening."

Erin nodded. She took one more deep breath, pushed the anxiety away as best she could, and climbed down out of the truck. She rang the doorbell, listening for the sound of the bell on the other side of the door so that she would know it worked and she didn't have to knock or press it again. She heard children playing, a dog barking, and footsteps approaching the door.

There was a scuffle and some yelling, Peter's voice over the girls', insisting that he was in charge and they had to let him answer the door. Then the doorknob turned and Peter peeked cautiously around the door.

His face broke into a grin. "Miss Erin!" He pulled the door open the rest of the way. The little girls stood back and looked out at Erin, uncharacteristically quiet.

Erin smiled back at Peter. It was good to see him again. But she knew she wasn't supposed to be visiting with him. "Is your mom available?"

"She's having a nap," Peter informed her.

If she had slept through the sound of the doorbell and the children fighting to see who got to answer the door. Erin was surprised that Mrs. Foster hadn't been right behind the children.

She was surprised that the children were allowed to answer the door while Mrs. Foster was lying down. Or maybe they weren't supposed to.

"I brought some things from the bakery." Erin handed the basket to Peter. "You put that in the kitchen and none of you open it. It's for your mom."

Peter took the basket and peered at the goodies through the plastic wrap. "But this isn't all for Mom," he protested. "It's for me."

"I don't want you eating cookies or anything else before dinner and ruining your appetite. You aren't to open it until your mother says so."

Peter opened his mouth to argue with her. He could negotiate like a lawyer. Erin raised her finger at him, trying to look stern.

"Peter. You listen, or I'm not going to bring any more. You aren't to open it. Your mom will open it when she wants to."

Peter rolled his eyes and shook his head a little, giving Erin attitude. "I wouldn't ruin my appetite. Mom says I have a hollow leg. I'm always hungry."

"No arguments. You aren't allowed to open it."

"But if Mom says. Then I can."

She could just see him sneaking into her darkened bedroom and whispering to her as she was in a state between sleeping and waking, trying to get her to say yes to him so that he could open the basket of goodies.

"When she's up from her nap and wide awake. Then if she says you can. Until she's up, you're not allowed."

Peter huffed, but he couldn't hide a little smirk from her, acknowledging that she was on to him. "Okay," he said with a note of exasperation. "Fine."

CHAPTER 10

She felt much lighter with the job out of the way. Now, as Vic had said, she could go home and relax for the rest of the evening.

She opened the front door quietly, not wanting to wake Terry up. She walked in and closed it behind her, punching the security code into the burglar alarm so it wouldn't start shrieking. Terry was not sleeping on the couch in front of the TV. That was a good sign. If he'd been restless or had a migraine, that was usually where she would find him.

Orange Blossom jumped down from the back of the couch, yowling at her. Erin picked him up and cuddled him and asked him about his day. He was eager to tell her all about it. She had been astonished when she had first rescued him, at how loud he was. She was used to it now, and he wasn't quite as noisy now that he was no longer a kitten but a more mature, settled adult. But she still winced at how loud he was when Terry was sleeping.

"Let's get you a treat and put something in the oven," she whispered to Orange Blossom. "Then maybe you'll be quiet so that Terry can sleep."

But as she got Orange Blossom's can of treats out of the pantry and grabbed a couple of cans of food to make them some supper, Erin could hear Terry moving around and K9's dog tags jingling in the bedroom in the far corner of the house.

In a few minutes, he wandered into the kitchen, rubbing his eyes.

"Hey," Erin greeted. She kissed him when he got close enough and searched his face for signs of how he was feeling. Had she woken him up too early? Had he gotten in a few solid hours of sleep before she had arrived home? "How was your sleep?"

Terry nodded. "Not bad. How was your day at work?"

"Fine. The usual. Except, of course..." she trailed off.

Terry waited, not contributing his own details.

"We heard about Joshua's disappearance," Erin told him.

Terry nodded. His arms were still around her body, resting and holding her casually close to him. "I figured you would by the end of the day."

"It's so terrible for Mary Lou," Erin said. "I wish that everything would just go right for her. Joshua would get on track, Campbell would come back home or at least get himself straightened out, and they would find something that would work for Roger. For her to have to deal with all of this stuff, one thing on top of another, it's just not fair."

"Tell that to Joshua," Terry said, shaking his head.

"You don't really think that it's just a prank, do you? When Mel—when I heard that—I just couldn't believe it. Joshua wouldn't do something like that to his mother. He loves her. He's good to her. He tries to help her out and to do the things she wants him to. He wouldn't do something like this."

"We don't know yet. There isn't a lot of evidence one way or another."

"You don't think he wrote that note himself."

Terry grimaced. He sat down at the table. "I can't really say what I think or discuss any details about the evidence. Let's just say... we have yet to establish that a crime has been committed."

"But you are looking for Josh, right? You're not just blowing it off."

"Anything that involves minor children needs to be taken very seriously. Yes, we do end up having to deal with pranks, especially with kids Joshua's age. We're not just blowing it off... you know I was investigating all night and most of the morning today. I wasn't just going through the motions."

Erin nodded. She busied herself with opening cans and trying to pull together something that would be both tasty and good for them. Baking was her forte; she was not as good with the main course, especially when it was just the two of them at the end of a long day at the bakery.

"I know. I didn't mean that you're not doing what you're supposed to. I'm just saying that... if you start with the wrong assumption, you might go the wrong direction."

"Investigative bias," Terry agreed. "I know. We try to be careful of that."

Erin didn't say anything for a few minutes. She wanted to know all of the details of the investigation, but she had to be just as careful about what she asked as he did about what he revealed to her.

"Do the police really think that he might have written the note himself?"

"It's a possibility."

"He wouldn't do that."

"I have to look at all the possibilities. It is possible he wrote it himself. It's also possible that someone else wrote it, either trying to imitate his writing or just someone with similar writing. It's not a very big sample. Not a lot of points to compare. And kids these days... they don't handwrite anything. It's all on the computer. So there aren't a lot of samples of Joshua's handwriting to make a comparison."

"You haven't asked me if I know where he is." Erin turned from her pots and leaned against the counter, looking at him.

"Come sit down."

She joined him at the table. Terry took her hand.

"Do you know where Joshua Cox is?"

Erin shook her head. "No."

"How did you know what the note said? Melissa?"

"I don't reveal my sources," Erin said with a smile. He could interpret that as he liked. He would probably assume that she was trying to protect Melissa. Not that she was trying to avoid telling him anything that was Mary Lou's business. Mary Lou had apparently not told him that she had talked to Erin and Vic about it a full day before talking to the police. And if Mary Lou didn't tell them that, Erin couldn't very well reveal it. That would make Terry suspicious of Mary Lou. They didn't need to investigate Mary Lou. They needed to spend their time tracking down the real culprit, whoever that was.

"I don't know why someone left that note," Terry said slowly. "I don't think that anyone seriously believed it would throw suspicion on you. No one thinks that you snuck off in the middle of the night and met Joshua or did something to make him disappear."

"Good. Because I didn't." Erin pulled her hand out of Terry's grasp. She was too anxious to sit still. She got up and checked the pots on the stove, giving everything a quick stir. She opened the fridge and started to pull out the makings of a salad. She was trying really hard to eat salad at every meal. Or at least, at every dinner. Marshmallow hopped over and started to nibble at her pant leg. He knew the rustle of vegetables in plastic just as well as Orange Blossom knew the sound of his can of kitty treats.

"Hello, bun. How are you doing?" Erin murmured to Marshmallow. She cut off a few vegetable ends for him. She bent down and scratched his ears after giving them to him. She washed her hands and continued assembling the salad.

"I think that something really did happen to Joshua," she told Terry. "I don't think it's just a joke."

"It seems like it's been going on a bit long if it was just intended to be a joke," Terry agreed. "Any sensible person would understand there is a big difference between pretending someone has been kidnapped for a couple of hours and making them disappear for a couple of days."

"Yeah. And Josh wouldn't participate in something like that. Maybe someone else would cover and say that it was just a joke because they didn't want Mary Lou to know what really happened, but... Joshua wouldn't do that. He knows how much Mary Lou worries about him."

"Sometimes that's exactly the reason kids rebel. They find it suffocating, parents always worrying and trying to make sure that nothing happens to them."

"Well... yes. I think Campbell is more like that. He needed to get out of there... to find a way he could make his own decisions."

Terry nodded.

"Did Mary Lou—or you—did anyone get ahold of Campbell? To see if Josh was with him, or if he knows what Josh's plans were?"

"Mary Lou spoke with him on the phone. Stayner was going to drive into the city to have a chat with him this afternoon." Terry worked his phone out of his pocket and tapped through a few screens. "No messages. I guess I'll find out later what the results of that trip were. But if Josh had been found, there definitely would be a message on my phone."

And word would have quickly spread through Bald Eagle Falls too.

"I'm really worried about him. What do you think happened?"

"We don't have enough information to make an educated guess at this point. Maybe nothing."

"But he might have been kidnapped. Or hurt. You don't have any evidence that he *wasn't* either."

"There are no indications that anything violent occurred."

"No?"

"No."

That was a little reassuring. If someone had come into the house and kidnapped Josh, then there would surely have been some sign of that. Someone couldn't just grab a teenager and cart him off without knocking a few things down.

"So you think... he just walked away, under his own power."

"That is the most logical explanation. But why? And what happened next? Where did he go?"

"Maybe he met someone..." Erin tried to visualize it. It wasn't that long since she'd been a teenager herself. And she had been around a lot of other teenagers, kids who had very different personalities from hers. Who had grown up with different rules and had different experiences from hers. "A girlfriend. A party that he knew Mary Lou wouldn't let him go to. Even just... feeling restless and going out for a walk..."

"Exactly. There are lots of different possibilities, and not all of them would suggest that something happened to him."

"He could have planned to drive into the city with someone. Or Campbell might have been coming over for a visit."

Terry's lips pressed together.

If Joshua had gone somewhere to meet with Campbell, then they should know that by now. Campbell would have told Mary Lou when she called him, or Stayner would have found out when he went into the city to talk to Campbell.

But Joshua had apparently not gone to see his brother. Or if he had, then things had fallen apart and something had happened.

"Do you really think that it's just something innocent? That he'll show up again and everything will be okay?"

Terry considered, scratching his stubbly jaw. "We don't have enough information yet to make that kind of judgment. If it was just a prank, then it is surprising that he hasn't shown up again yet. It's been two days. But if he ran away for another reason, it could still be voluntary."

"But why would he?"

"You never know all of the reasons someone might choose to run away." He gave her a half-smile. "I'm sure you've seen that, living in foster homes. You must have known a few runners."

"Kids that run away chronically, sure. But that's not Joshua. He isn't a troubled kid who has grown up in half a dozen different homes or has had to fend for himself or defend himself against an abuser. He's a kid living with his mom, who he's always lived with. She has a good job and looks after him. He goes to school and was trying to get his grades up again. He's not involved with a gang or drugs."

"But you are a casual outside observer. How much of that do you *know* to be true?"

CHAPTER 11

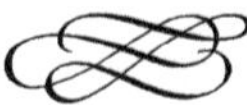

Even though she didn't want it to grow from a discussion to an argument, Erin wanted to defend her position. She knew Joshua. She knew Mary Lou. She knew that Mary Lou gave Joshua a good home.

But what did she really know? The way a family looked from the outside was not necessarily an accurate representation of what was really going on. Abusers could act sweet and caring in public. Molesters could be upright citizens, making good money and acting like responsible parents. They could be women as easily as men.

Mary Lou was tough, Erin knew that. She wanted Joshua to shape up in school and to get back on track. Campbell had come from the same home, and he had dropped out and moved to the city, essentially running away from home, before turning eighteen. He was possibly into the drug culture and was close enough to street life and organized crime that Beaver—Federal Agent Rohilda Beaven—used him as a confidential informant.

Erin didn't know how bad things had been when Roger was still living at home, but she didn't imagine living with a confused, increasingly violent parent had been fun for either of the boys. They had worked hard to help support the family and take care of their father, a lot to expect from a couple of teenage boys.

"Well, you don't know what goes on behind closed doors," Erin admitted. "I don't think that Mary Lou was too strict with him, but… she's not an easy woman to get along with. But we at least know that he wasn't running with a bad crowd or involved with drugs."

Terry raised an eyebrow. Of course, he might know details that Erin did not. He wouldn't be in a position to tell her if he knew that Joshua had been caught with drugs or was suspected of being an addict or dealer. He had dropped out of his sports teams and extracurricular activities. His marks had plummeted. He'd spent a lot of time at home alone. All classic signs of a kid involved in drugs. Or human trafficking. Or both.

"I'm sure he wasn't," Erin protested. She had seen his honest reactions when they had gone looking for Brianna. Joshua had been shocked at what he saw in the city, at the state of the girls they had talked to. If he were taking drugs, it was still at a recreational level. He hadn't seen addiction like that before. "And he was working on bringing his marks up. He was in Whitewater to do interviews for the paper. It wasn't drugs, it was just everything else that had happened in their family lately. All of the disruption. The stuff with Roger and Campbell."

Terry got up from the table to grab some dishes and set the table. He took a jug of water from the fridge, stood staring into the open fridge for a few long seconds, then closed it, returned to the table, and arranged things the way Erin liked them.

"I heard from Mary Lou about him going to Whitewater. You saw him while he was there?"

"Yes. He came to talk to me. To 'interview' me for background on the contest and… on Beryl. He was more interested in what happened to Beryl than in the cooking contest."

"Of course," Terry nodded. "I would be too. Cooking is interesting," he allowed, "but not nearly as compelling as someone showing up dead in a freezer."

Erin shrugged.

"But why do you say 'interview,' like that." Terry used his fingers to put air quotes around the word.

Erin hadn't meant to use that inflection. It had just come out that way. "Well… because I didn't really want to be interviewed for his article. If he wanted to know things about the contest, that was great, it would be good publicity for the contest and for us. But he wanted to ask me about finding Beryl and what I thought… and I really didn't want to talk to him about it."

"Ah." Terry nodded. "Makes sense. How much did he manage to worm out of you?"

"He was good," Erin admitted. She smiled at Terry. "Not as good an interrogator as a policeman, of course…"

"I wouldn't expect so. Though some reporters would give the police a run for their money. Have you read Joshua's article?"

"No. How was it?"

"Good. He did a nice job on it. Didn't come off as a kid's school essay. Good clear language, well thought out. He's not an investigative journalist, but he made a good start."

"I'll have to read it." Erin usually flipped through the copy of the Bald Eagle Falls weekly paper that was delivered to her, but with everything that had been happening, she hadn't yet had the chance.

Josh really needed to get home. He needed to wake up, get himself out of bed or off of whoever's couch he was sleeping on, and get home. If his mother had already woken up and discovered him missing, he would be in big trouble. There would be a lot of explaining to do.

Or not very much explaining, since he couldn't remember for sure what had happened or where he was. But he would have to come up with something.

Josh opened his eyes. They were gritty and blurry, and he couldn't really see anything around him except darkness and darker shapes in the darkness. It was still night. So maybe he still had time.

But his body told him that it wasn't night. There was a part of his consciousness that was growing increasingly alarmed each time he woke up. It had been too long. It couldn't still be night. He had known several wakenings ago that dawn was coming.

He groaned and tried to move. As before, he couldn't seem to move anywhere. His arms and legs did not respond the way that they should. He'd really gotten messed up on whatever he had indulged in. Had it been a party? He was beginning to think that someone had roofied him. That would explain why his memory was so patchy.

The thought both relieved him—because it meant that he hadn't chosen to get so screwed up—and made him more anxious. He felt violated and anxious. It made him angry. Who would do something like that to him? One of his friends, thinking it was a good prank? Someone else who had wanted to steal from him or get something out of him? The joke was on them, since he was dirt poor and didn't even have a dime in his pockets.

He didn't think that it was to take advantage of him physically. That didn't happen to guys.

Did it?

He tried to sort out the sensations of his body, worried. But he couldn't sort out all of the sensory inputs. It was dark, that he knew for sure. He couldn't move his hands to take out his phone and look at the time or at his camera roll in case he had recorded something.

He kicked his feet, trying to turn his body over and look around. Nothing would move the right way. He thrashed around in the blankets, unable to control his position or to right himself.

"Stop that," a hoarse whisper came out of the darkness.

Josh froze. He scanned the layers of darkness for a human figure, but could not see anyone and could not turn over to check the rest of the room. "Who's there? Who are you?"

"The person who's in charge here. The person you need to listen to."

He couldn't build a picture of the owner of the whisper. It wasn't a voice he recognized, but he wasn't sure that meant anything, because it was just a whisper, with no tone or pitch. He couldn't tell whether it was male or female, old or young. He didn't detect any particular accent.

"Where am I? What time is it?"

"None of that matters."

Joshua tried to clear his throat. His mouth was dry as a bone. He needed a drink. Not alcohol, just water. He was dehydrated. Maybe that was why his head hurt so much. He tried to move again.

"I can't… I'm tangled up here," he told the voice, embarrassed. He tried to get free of the blankets once more. "I'm just trying to get up…"

"You're not tangled. You're tied."

Josh stopped moving. He tried again to find the dark figure in the shadows. "What?"

"You are restrained."

Joshua tried to move his hands, and finally figured out why they were not moving the way they were supposed to. They were bound together. Any time he tried to move one of them, the other was dragged along with it. He moved his feet slowly, and found that his left foot followed his right when he tried to move it to the side.

He fought the restraints. Tried to bring his wrists up to eye level so he could look at them. He couldn't get them up to his face or see the restraints that held him. He couldn't feel what they were, but didn't hear any jangling, so assumed it wasn't handcuffs. Maybe zip ties or duct tape. Who would do that? Was it a joke?

"What's going on? Why am I tied up?"

"So that you can't leave."

Joshua couldn't help himself. He fought the restraints, trying to rip his hands away from each other, to kick out with his feet to hit something. He tried to squirm around to turn over but couldn't.

"Quit fighting."

"Let me go! What are you doing? This is kidnapping! You can't tie someone up! This isn't funny."

"Nobody's laughing." There was a strange noise, and Joshua wondered if his captor was, in fact, laughing in a whisper. "This isn't meant to be funny."

"You can't go around kidnapping people. Where am I?" Joshua blinked, trying to bring his surroundings into focus, but still all he could see was darkness and shadows. It wasn't home. He had known that for a while. But he couldn't figure out where he was.

"Stop thrashing around."

Joshua kept kicking and trying to turn over. What was the whisperer going to do? He couldn't stop Joshua from trying to escape his bonds. Josh wasn't going to be quiet and compliant and do whatever his captor told him to.

There was movement nearby. Behind him. He couldn't turn his head all the way around to see. He tried anyway, straining. The noise moved closer.

"Who are you? Tell me what's going on!"

A cloth fell over his eyes. Josh tried to pull away from it, but it was tied tightly around his head, snagging bits of hair and pulling them tightly into the knot of the blindfold.

"No! No, I'll listen to you. You don't need to blindfold—"

He shouldn't have opened his mouth. The gag went in next. A round ball of cloth that felt and tasted like rolled-up socks, and then a rope of something that went into his mouth, pulled tight around his head so that it pulled his lips taut and his jaw slightly open. But it kept the packing material in his mouth and prevented him from opening and closing his mouth to speak. Josh tried to protest this treatment, but he couldn't get anything coherent out.

"Next time, maybe you'll stop when I tell you to," his captor whispered.

There was a pain in his thigh.

He felt dizzy and lightheaded.

And that was all.

CHAPTER 12

Their dinner was a quiet affair. Both were thinking about Joshua Cox and what might have happened to him. Erin hoped that it wasn't something awful. She hoped that the note had just been left by his friends to cover for his absence when he had gone off to see a girl or on a road trip or one of the many other things that a stressed-out teenager might do to escape his life for a few days. Maybe Joshua didn't even know about the note left behind. He wouldn't have caused Erin extra grief, but the same would not necessarily be true of his friends at school. Who knew how many of them had been affected by Erin's investigation at Christmas. There might be several who resented the attention she had drawn to them and the school even if they hadn't been implicated in the police investigation.

"I should call Mary Lou," she said, as she scraped her fork along the bottom of her plate. She licked off the last of the gravy. "Did she have anyone over there with her, when you were there?"

"Women were coming and going." Terry rolled his eyes. "Do you know how hard it is to run a police investigation when women are coming in with casseroles every few minutes? It's not the forensics I'm talking about. We kept things sealed up until the techs were done looking for evidence, but the constant interruptions. Trying to ask all of the important questions while people keep knocking on the door, ringing the bell, or yoo-hooing, and walking in on the interview."

Erin shook her head, suppressing her smile as much as she could. She was surprised that Terry hadn't taken Mary Lou to the police department where he could question her without interruption. Only maybe she hadn't wanted to go there. He couldn't force her to leave the house and she probably didn't want to leave in case Joshua showed up or one of his friends stopped in with news.

"Well… I'm glad that people are trying to look after her, but I'm not sure casseroles are what she needs."

The last Erin had seen, at Thanksgiving, Mary Lou already had a freezer full of food contributions. And with it just being her and Joshua, they probably hadn't made much of a dent in it.

And now it was just Mary Lou, and she didn't eat very much, trying to watch her weight. One casserole would last a couple of weeks.

"You can give her a call. She'll probably go to bed early; she was pretty tired last I saw her. Not that you stay up late anyway."

"She probably sat up waiting for him all night."

Terry nodded. "She had police there all night, so even if she had wanted to go to bed, it would have been difficult."

Erin licked off her fork once more, sighed, and put it down on her plate. "I'll call her once I've cleared everything away, then."

"Leave the dishes. I can do that. Go call now, then it's done and you won't spend the rest of the evening worrying about her."

Erin left Terry in the kitchen and went to her bedroom to make the call. She shut the bedroom door and sat down on the bed. She wished she were more eager to make the call. She wished that she knew ahead of time how it would go over. The dinner sat like a lump of lead in her stomach.

But procrastinating wasn't going to make it any easier. Erin forced herself to unlock her phone and pull up the contact entry for Mary Lou. She tapped it and listened to the ringing. Mary Lou might already be asleep. If she hadn't slept for two days, she might have fallen asleep in front of the TV or while trying to do something else. Or she might have talked with enough well-meaning people that she really didn't want to deal with anyone else.

Erin wasn't sure whether to leave a voicemail. As the phone continued to ring, she tried to script a message in her head. *I was just calling to see how you are… let me know if you need anything…* Everything sounded so lame. The woman's son was missing. What was the appropriate response to a disaster like that?

There was a soft click and Mary Lou's well-measured tones. "Erin. Hello."

"I'm sorry. I hope you weren't sleeping."

"No."

"Do you want me to come over and sit with you? I can tidy up if the police left anything in a mess, or figure out what to do with all of the casseroles."

"No. I don't want anyone else here tonight. It's been like Grand Central Station."

"I could come tomorrow and help with whatever you need."

"I only need one thing, and that is to have my son back."

Erin swallowed. "I wish I knew where he was. I wish I could help with that."

"The note says to ask you."

"I know… I don't know why it says that, because I have no idea. If I did, I would tell you. I swear."

"I don't think it literally means to ask you where he is," Mary Lou said in a studied tone. "I think it means that this has happened because of something you did."

"I didn't—" Erin broke off. How could she be sure that it hadn't happened because of something she had done? Actions had consequences. Not always things that could be foreseen or controlled. Every action sent out little ripples over a growing area. And Erin had thrown some pretty big rocks into the pond. "I don't know what I could have done that would have had any impact on Joshua. I really don't."

"Well, we know that's not true. You had him hauled into the police station."

Erin cleared her throat. Mary Lou knew that what she was saying was an exaggeration. It wasn't Erin who had interrogated Joshua. It wasn't her fault. Not really. It was Harold who had mentioned Joshua and his friends to Erin.

Do you know about them?

He hadn't asked if she knew Josh, but if she knew about him. And Erin had been left to wonder what Josh and his friends were doing that she should know about. She had mentioned it to Terry, and Terry had been the one who had invited Josh in for questioning. That wasn't her fault.

Rocks thrown into the pond.

"And you were the one who went with him into the city. I still don't know what happened there, but I have a pretty good idea that it wasn't the innocent little trip that you and Vic would have me believe."

"I didn't go with him. We ran into him in the city…"

"But you took him to those places. Looking for Brianna."

"I went with him," Erin corrected. She was in the right on this one. She had tried to talk Joshua out of it, and when she hadn't been able to dissuade him, she had gone along to help keep him safe and out of trouble.

"You have shown a shocking lack of awareness of what is appropriate behavior and what could have serious consequences. You should never have let Joshua search for Campbell."

Erin's temper rose at the unfairness of Mary Lou's comment. "I'm not his mother. I couldn't stop him from doing anything. I went along to try to keep him safe and that's the best I could do. What would he have done if I told him he couldn't go look for her? He would have laughed in my face."

"Then you call me. You let me know what's going on. You don't just let him rush headlong into something dangerous."

"Okay, fine. I didn't do that. I guess I should have. But that doesn't have anything to do with him being missing. That was months ago."

"I told you I didn't want you to have anything more to do with him."

Erin rubbed her face tiredly. "I know. And I didn't."

"You didn't talk to him in Whitewater?"

"Well… yes, I did. He came to my hotel. I didn't seek him out. And when I asked if you knew where he was, he said you did."

"I don't know what's going on with Joshua. I don't know where he is or what he's doing. I don't know why he's disappeared. But if it had anything to do with you..."

"It's nothing to do with me. I didn't have anything to do with him disappearing. The last time I saw him was when he was working on the article for the paper. I never saw him or talked to him again after that."

There was silence for a few moments. "Very well," Mary Lou said finally. "If you hear anything... I expect you to tell me. Not Officer Piper; me. His mother. And if you do anything to interfere, anything that puts him in further danger..."

"I wouldn't do anything. I won't. And I hope... I hope he turns up again soon, and that everything is okay."

"So do I."

Mary Lou hung up. Erin put her phone down, put her arm over her eyes, and tried to resist the urge to burst into tears.

CHAPTER 13

Erin was getting ready for bed when she heard Terry answer the door. She hovered near the bathroom doorway, listening to identify the visitor. It didn't take her long to figure out that it was Stayner, the newest member of the Bald Eagle Falls police department. He had been contracted when Terry was unable to work, and they had managed to make room in the budget for him to stay on for an extended period. He was young and didn't have a lot of experience. Erin hoped that he was a quick learner. She found him abrasive and too quick to jump to judgment. He was opinionated and, she thought, sexist, though he had never come right out and told her that her place was in the kitchen. Or the bakery. It was just a feeling she got from him.

But Terry and the sheriff said that he did good work. Yes, he was rough around the edges, but that would improve with experience and a good teacher.

"Ten to one, he's on a binge," Stayner told Terry in the living room. "It's a waste of our time and resources. He'll show up again when he sobers up. Mom is overreacting."

Terry's response was softer, and Erin hoped it was something along the lines of 'Mary Lou is not overreacting. She waited a full day before reporting him missing, and he's now been gone for two days. No one knows where he went.'

"His friends know where he is," Stayner said. "Mark my words. Probably his brother too. He acted all shocked and concerned, but I know the way these kids act. He knows exactly where Joshua Cox is."

Erin moved out into the bathroom, closer to the living room. She didn't want them to see her, didn't want to have to deal with Stayner's 'I know better' bluster, but she wanted to learn what she could.

"What did Cam have to say?" Terry asked.

Erin heard the squeak of springs as Stayner sat down to continue the conversation. "He said he hasn't talked to Josh for a few days. And when they did talk, Joshua didn't give any hint that he was planning to go anywhere. Everything was normal, according to big brother. But I highly doubt Joshua left without telling Cam where he was going."

"No sign of him in Cam's apartment? No hint that someone else has been staying there?"

"He doesn't have an apartment of his own. From what I can tell, he couch surfs between a few different friends. So, yes, there are plenty of signs that someone else has been around, because it's not Cam's own place. And there are others who live or crash there, too. It would be impossible to sort out whether Joshua was ever there."

"So he couldn't ask Josh to come live with him. Or even just sleep over."

"I don't think the fact that it wasn't his apartment would stop him. They all seem pretty casual about it. *I* probably could have stayed there, as long as I promised to look the other way on any drug charges."

"What kind of a mood was he in the last time that Cam talked to him?"

"Fine, according to Cam. Good spirits. Happy with his bonus English assignment. Ready to kick back and relax for a while."

"Uh-huh." In her mind's eye, Erin saw Terry rubbing his chin as he often did when pondering. "And nothing from his school friends?"

Erin had thought that Terry would have been the one to interview Joshua's school friends, but she supposed that since he'd been up most of the night and then would have had a ton of reports to fill out, he probably hadn't been able to get over to the school between the time that school started and he finally clocked out.

"I talked to his loser friends," Stayner agreed.

Erin clenched her teeth at his characterization. Joshua and his friends were not losers. Joshua had been through a lot, that was all.

"Loser friends?" Terry repeated. "Is that what went into your report?"

"No, of course not. But they are. His friends are the lowest class at the school. Nowhere kids. They don't belong to any of the teams or clubs, get rock bottom marks, have no motivation to do anything but go home and game or surf porn on their computers."

"Josh used to be on the sports teams. He got out of them because of the difficult time that he's been having. You have to remember what happened with his dad, and then with Campbell. The kid is lost."

Stayner snorted. "Yeah," he agreed. "They're all lost boys. They're going nowhere and will amount to nothing. Look for them soon begging on a street corner near you."

"And none of them had any idea where Josh might have gone?"

"No idea. I don't know if any of them even noticed that he was missing. It was like, 'Oh, Josh? Yeah, where is he, man?'" Stayner used his best stoner voice. It would have been funny if Erin wasn't so angry at him for his insensitivity.

But he didn't know she was there listening. He thought he was just talking to a fellow cop, and Erin knew that they frequently dealt with the stress of the job with gallows humor and sarcastic or inappropriate comments. He would probably have guarded his tongue if he had known that Erin was there listening. Which was why she hadn't made herself known. She wanted to hear everything he had to say.

"Today was a waste of time," Stayner's tone was annoyed. "The whole day was a write-off. We didn't get any farther ahead on anything." There was a pause in which neither of them spoke. "No one had any motive to kidnap the kid, Piper. He'll show up again when he feels like it."

"You think that he wrote the note," Terry said.

"Him or one of his equally illiterate buddies, yeah."

Erin just about shouted at him despite not wanting them to know she was eavesdropping on the conversation.

Joshua was not illiterate! He had just finished having an article published by the paper. Not the school paper, the Bald Eagle Falls weekly. It might have been small, but it was a real paper and he'd managed to get his article published by them. His marks had fallen not because he wasn't smart enough, but because he'd been through a series of horrible family tragedies and couldn't deal with schoolwork on top of it.

"Well, only time and further investigation will tell. We have to put in the footwork, even if you don't think there was any foul play. We need to do all of the right things, just in case. Don't allow investigative bias to creep in. What would you do if there were signs of violence? A ransom note? What if it was a ten-year-old girl instead of a teenage boy?"

Stayner was silent.

"We'll have a team meeting tomorrow," Terry told him. "We'll go over everything that we've found so far, and we'll talk about what to do next. But think about it. Come up with some ideas and suggestions to bring to the meeting. Show that you can think critically and conduct a thorough investigation."

"Yeah, okay," Stayner agreed, his voice quiet for once instead of blustering. He'd just gotten some good advice from his senior officer, and if he wanted to be respected within the police department, he would follow up on it.

CHAPTER 14

Erin took the first tray of flat cookie disks out of the oven and put them on a cooling tray.

"So the cookies need to be folded while they're still warm. Once they cool, they get crispy, and then it is too late to fix any mistakes. This is how you do it."

Her assistant bakers watched closely. Erin hoped that the cookies held together like they were supposed to. She had tested the recipe out already and practiced folding the fortune cookies, but that didn't mean that a batch couldn't go wrong. Too much moisture or not enough, left in the oven a minute or two too long, or something else that she couldn't foresee or control. There were no guarantees.

"The fortune goes inside," Erin placed one of the slips of paper on the flat disk. "Then, you fold the cookie into a half-circle." Erin demonstrated. "And then bring the ends together into the classic fortune-cookie shape. You can rest it on the rim of a glass to cool, or just place it carefully on the cooling rack."

"That's so cool," Bella said. "But I'm a little sad to know the secret of how the fortune gets inside the cookie."

Everybody nodded and laughed, agreeing.

"One of life's mysteries solved," Erin said. "You'll have to move on to how they get the caramel into a Caramilk bar."

She stepped back from the counter. "I'd like to make sure everyone makes two or three, so you get a feel for it." She moved to the next oven and pulled out another tray as the timer chimed. She put it down on another counter across the kitchen from the first. The group split into two. The kitchen was crowded with so many people there. Still, it had seemed like the best idea to show everyone how to make the fortune cookies at the same time, instead of having to demonstrate several times or have everyone showing everyone else, possibly losing something in translation.

She watched as each of the employees tried several fortune cookies. There were some misfolds and some breakage. That was all to be expected. They would just eat the mistakes instead of sending them on to the Chinese restaurant.

After everyone had a go at it, Erin dismissed them. "Great, thanks for coming by for this. I've had Matt print a bunch of fortunes for us, we'll get the rest of the cookies done over the next week, as per the schedule."

~

Erin had been thinking all day about Terry's advice to Stayner. Imagine that they had proof that Josh had not disappeared voluntarily, and work from there. She put the possibility that Joshua had left of his own accord out of her head and focused on what they knew.

He had come back from Whitewater and written his article. He hadn't been back to Whitewater since then, as far as anyone knew. He had talked to his mother, his friends, and his brother in the days before his disappearance. He hadn't said anything about plans to go away, being stressed out, or anything else that would explain his disappearance.

Had he received any threats? Anything to indicate that he might be in danger? If he had mentioned any threats to his family or friends, she assumed they would have reported it to the police after his disappearance. So he must not have.

How could he disappear in the middle of the night? He'd been there when Mary Lou had gone to bed but wasn't there when she got up. Had he gone somewhere voluntarily, to a party or to see Campbell or a girl, and then something had happened to prevent him from getting home again? Had someone come into his bedroom and taken him away? If so, why wasn't there any sign of a struggle? He could have been drugged or knocked out. He could have been taken at gunpoint or under some other threat. He was a slim teenager, stronger than a ten-year-old girl, but still not man-grown, and not someone who did bodybuilding or martial arts. He had dropped out of all of his sports teams. If someone had threatened him with a weapon or threatened to do something to Mary Lou, he wouldn't have had any choice but to go with them.

If someone had come for him, was it someone he knew? A stranger? Would he have let a stranger into the house?

Was it someone that Joshua connected with Erin and that was why he had written the note?

But if he had been taken from his room under threat, when would he have had the time to leave a note? What kidnapper would have let him do that?

Or had the kidnapper forced him to write that note to throw suspicion onto Erin? As Mary Lou had said, she assumed that Erin's past actions had something to do with Joshua's disappearance. She didn't think that Erin had taken Josh, but she believed it was, in some way, Erin's fault.

"Who would take Joshua?"

Vic looked over at Erin, chewing a bite of sandwich. "What?"

Erin hadn't meant to speak the question aloud. But now that she had, she might as well see what Vic thought.

"Who would take Joshua? If he was taken from his room—or somewhere else in town—who would do that? And why? Mary Lou thinks it was because of me."

"No, she's just worried."

"She said so. She thinks it's because of something that I did."

"Well…" Vic chewed slowly. "I don't know what Joshua would have to do with anything from *your* past. That doesn't make much sense."

Erin nodded. "Right? I mean, I know Josh, but not well. We've talked a few times. But we haven't really had anything to do with each other. So why…?"

Vic wiped a bit of mayonnaise from her lip. "You and Josh. The only time you ever really did anything together was when we were all in the city. Is that what you're talking about?"

Erin thought about it. "You think it's someone who saw us together when we were looking for Brianna? I still don't…" She trailed off, shaking her head. What was the connection? Why would someone kidnap Josh because he and Erin had been in the city together?

"It's not a very long list," Vic said. She licked her finger off and held it up in a 'number one' sign. "There was the girl at the first apartment we went to. The girl with the black eye. The second one, there wasn't anyone there, right? Someone still might have seen us there. Then…" She cleared her throat. "The mob guy. Mickey. But he's in prison, so it wasn't him."

"But there was a girl there, too."

"What reason would any of them have to take Josh?" Vic shook her head. "Nothing I can think of. I mean, he's a white boy living at home; maybe they figured they could get some kind of ransom for him…" "But there hasn't been a ransom demand."

They both thought about that. Someone could have taken him intending to ask for a ransom. But Erin didn't like where that led. That would mean that something had happened to Josh to prevent them from making the demand. She didn't even want to entertain that possibility.

"Maybe one of them liked him," Vic suggested. "They started to see each other quietly, and she eventually talked him into running away with her?"

"Okay, maybe," Erin agreed. She searched in her purse for a piece of paper to write it down. One of the girls they had seen that day. And the note was just to throw Mary Lou off of their trail. So that she thought it was something to do with Erin instead of Joshua running off with a girl. That could be true of any of the girls in town, too. They didn't need to know that Erin and Josh had been in the city together, just that Josh knew her and that Mary Lou had not been happy with Erin.

Mary Lou hadn't exactly kept it a secret.

CHAPTER 15

When he woke up again, the room was a little lighter. Josh tried to crane his neck around to look all the way around it and, while he couldn't make out what most of the dark shapes around him were, he saw a high window above him with some light leaking in around the edges. Not enough to make the room bright. Just enough to lift a few of the shadows.

He remembered the whispered voice. Someone had been in the room with him the last time he had awoken. That person had blindfolded and gagged him and knocked him out with some drug. The blindfold and gag had been removed again, but his hands and feet were apparently still bound. Josh lay still, trying to learn as much as he could about his environment without moving. It was a large room. He couldn't see all the way around it. It was filled with a lot of shadowy objects, but they didn't seem to be arranged in any particular order, like shelves or furniture. More like a storage room where everything had just been shoved in together.

His mouth was so dry he couldn't work up the spit to irrigate it. His tongue felt like it belonged to someone else, clumsy and swollen. There were cracks in the corners of his mouth. His nose also felt dried up, more cracks running from the outside corners of his nostrils down toward his mouth.

There was a noise.

Joshua strained toward it, trying to see if it were a rat or a person or some other random noise from the building itself shifting. He couldn't see well in the dark, but the furtive sound continued and, in a few minutes, he could see the shape moving toward him. Human-sized, not a rat. He didn't dare hope it was someone there to save him. He was grateful for the removal of the gag and didn't want to earn it back by addressing his captor or making any attempt to attract attention.

Eventually, the figure stood over him. He couldn't estimate his captor's height or weight, lying down as he was. His captor wore a dark, shapeless hoodie, and Josh could see a greenish glint of glasses or goggles under the hood. Night vision? A disguise? Just some weird costume or affectation?

It was a struggle to keep from saying anything. Eventually, he heard the hoarse whisper again. It sent a shiver of terror down his spine.

"You're quiet and still this time. That's good. Maybe you're learning."

Joshua's head quirked slightly in a nod, even though he hadn't intended to make any acknowledgment or response. He didn't want the blindfold and gag again.

He wanted to earn his captor's appreciation.

He wanted to live.

"Good," the shadow repeated.

There was a scrape of metal somewhere close. Joshua didn't turn his head to look at it. The figure reached toward him, and Josh turned his head away slightly, worried about being gagged again. Something hard banged against his lips and teeth, drawing an unintentional yelp of pain. Warm fluid flooded over his lip and chin.

"Drink. Open your mouth."

He obediently opened his mouth. Whatever sedative he'd been given was messing with his depth perception. He didn't realize the water flask was right in front of his mouth until it touched his lip again. He tried to purse his lips to drink from it, but his lips were so dry and swollen that he couldn't mold his mouth against the bottle. The shadowy figure spilled water into his mouth anyway. Joshua choked trying to get it down, but he persisted, and managed to get a few swallows down. The bottle was withdrawn.

"More," Joshua croaked. "Please."

"That's enough for now."

"So dry."

"Well, I don't want to clean you up any more than I have to."

Joshua's face burned. It wasn't his fault that he couldn't tend to his own bodily functions. But it still embarrassed him to think of someone else doing it. He swallowed a few times and tried to speak.

"Who are you? Why am I here?" The words came out in a croak, but his captor could apparently still understand him.

"Some people just can't mind their own business," the whisperer hissed sharply. "Some people just have to keep digging into stuff that doesn't have anything to do with them."

Joshua swallowed. He wanted to protest that he hadn't done anything wrong, that if he'd happened to step over the line and breach someone's privacy by accident, he was sorry. He wouldn't let it happen again. But what could he say when he didn't even know what the problem was?

"Can I… are you ever going to let me go?"

"Haven't really learned your lesson, have you?"

"I… don't know. I'll try to do better."

"A little late for that now."

The hooded figure looked around, light glinting off the goggles. Then, he withdrew again, leaving Josh there to stew and wonder what he had done to deserve such a punishment.

CHAPTER 16

They didn't get anywhere. Not really. Erin made a few notes about who might want to kidnap Joshua or might have been able to entice him away, but she didn't really believe any of them. None of them felt right. The motives were thin and, even if she was right, there was no way they could prove anything. They didn't have any evidence to show to the police to help pinpoint Joshua's location.

She was in a fog as she went through her usual procedures to close the bakery for the day and make sure that everything was set for the next morning.

It was strange how life just kept going on as usual, even after such a tragedy.

She kept making bread and cake and cookies and selling them to people as if nothing had happened.

"I'm meeting Willie at the Chinese restaurant," Vic reminded Erin. "Do you want me to walk home with you first?"

"No, no." Erin waved a hand at her. "I'm perfectly fine walking home."

"I can walk with you, Willie will wait."

"No. Go have dinner. I'm fine."

Vic hesitated for a moment. "If you needed something, you would ask, right? If you want a ride?"

"I'm going to get a car soon," Erin promised, though that wasn't what Vic had asked. "I don't know why it's taken me so long. I'll do it soon."

"You don't need a ride home? We could call Willie."

"No. I need the exercise. Go," Erin insisted.

Vic sighed and shrugged, then did as she was told. Erin chuckled to herself and started to head toward her house. It wasn't like it was a hardship to walk a few blocks from the bakery to the house. Clementine had done it for many years until her health had started to deteriorate. She had only used the yellow Volkswagen for occasional errands. Erin knew she should either get the car fixed up or get rid of it. What good was it doing taking up her garage space?

She needed a car, so she should either start driving the Volkswagen or find something else she could use.

Erin's thoughts were far away. She wasn't paying much attention to anything going on around her. Bald Eagle Falls was a sleepy little place. Despite everything that had happened since Erin had arrived to claim her inheritance, it was still a quiet town. Not the kind of place where you expected to find murder or kidnapping. And certainly not more than once.

"Miss Erin."

Erin looked up to see who was calling her. She saw the figure waving, and her heart skipped a beat. She almost ran to him. Then she realized it wasn't Joshua. His face was too old. It was his brother, Campbell.

They had similar builds and features. Erin often had to look twice before she was sure which of them she was seeing. She took a deep breath to calm herself and then walked toward Campbell, trying to smile.

"Cam, it's good to see you."

He swallowed hard and also managed to dredge up a smile.

"You too, Miss Erin." He hovered there for a moment, trying to think of what to say. "I guess… you heard about Josh."

She put her hand over his, worried. "The last I heard was that he's missing."

Campbell nodded, allaying Erin's fears that something worse had happened.

"Yeah." He sighed. "I wish… I wish I could say that he just decided he'd had enough. Like I did. But Josh isn't that sort. We've always had… different perspectives."

Erin nodded. They walked slowly together, toward Erin's house.

"Have you seen your mother?" she asked him.

"Of course." Campbell nodded firmly. "As soon as I could get here… I did. And stopped by to see her."

"Are you going to stay with her until Josh comes back?"

Campbell chewed on a fingernail. "Uh… I don't know. I didn't really plan on staying."

"She needs someone."

"So you say." He looked up at the sky, avoiding Erin's eyes. "But it seems more like… she's pushing everyone away."

"No, don't think that," Erin protested. "She's had a lot of difficult stuff to get through lately, and not everybody has stood by her…"

"I know. I've been through all that stuff too. I know it's different for Mom, because she's Mom… but people who helped—*You…*"

"I understand why she's upset with me. She felt like I'd put Joshua in danger… or into a bad situation. She already thought that before Joshua disappeared. And then with that note…"

"She knows it's not because of anything you've done."

"Did she tell you that? Because that's not what she said to me."

"Well…" He tilted his head uncomfortably. "No. That's not what she said. But she should trust the people who have stood by her. You helped her when I was in trouble. You were the one who was there."

"And the one who went along with Josh in the city," Erin said, not sure whether Campbell even knew that part. "When… I should have talked him out of it. Or called her. I just… I told them that they shouldn't, but everyone else said it was okay."

"You went with him to the city?" Cam repeated, frowning. "What do you mean?"

"When you were… when you had to be here. And Joshua wanted to help you. He wanted to find Brianna and get the real story. So he could get you off."

Joshua and Mary Lou had apparently not told Campbell anything about it. So many family secrets. Even from each other. Erin took a deep breath, looking up the street toward her house.

"It wasn't a good idea," Erin repeated. "But the others insisted on going, so I went along… to try to keep them out of trouble and keep anything from happening."

Campbell looked down at Erin's compact figure. "How could you keep anything from happening?"

"I thought… I could give them advice and they would listen to me. I was the oldest one, so I thought that maybe they would listen." Erin shook her head. She had been wrong. They hadn't listened when it counted.

"So… what happened?" Cam asked. "You couldn't find Brianna, right? Because she was already…"

Erin nodded. "We, uh… went places that Josh said you'd talked about. A couple of… friends. And then this hotel suite. We met Mikhail."

Cam's face grew pale. "What? Mikhail? Not…?"

Erin shrugged. "Mikhail. Mickey. You… didn't know that? Joshua never said anything?"

"No. He probably knows I woulda beat the crap out of him for something like that. He hasn't got a clue what a guy like Mickey could do to him, or order to be done. He's not someone you play games with!"

"Well, he's off the street now. He can't do anything."

Campbell shook his head. "You really believe that?"

"I know he's in jail."

"But there's no way he's going to stay there for long. And even if he does, he can still order or hire guys on the outside. He's not neutralized just because he's 'off the street.'"

"Well… I don't think any of this is because of him, do you?"

Campbell stared off. "I don't know," he said in a distant voice. "No way to tell. Whoever wrote the note mentioned you. And you met Mikhail. He could have blamed you. Sometimes those guys do. They just obsess over something. It gets under their skin, and they think that it's your fault, even though it's not."

"He was arrested when he came after me. It wasn't exactly… unconnected."

"Sheesh. Has Beaver talked to him? She's got a good relationship with him. He would tell her, I think."

"He would tell her if he put some kind of order out on Joshua?" Erin couldn't keep the incredulity out of her voice. "He wouldn't do that."

"These mobsters follow a different set of rules. He'd probably be proud of the fact. Be glad that she asked." Campbell had picked up his pace. Erin ran behind him, trying to keep up with his long-legged stride.

"Do you know where she is?" Campbell asked. He worked his phone out of his pocket and tapped in a number. "Is she in town? At your house? She hangs out with…" Campbell's anxiety was making him flustered.

"I don't know if she's around. You can try her on the phone."

"She hangs out with…"

"Jeremy," Erin filled in. "Vic's older brother."

Campbell snapped his fingers, nodding. "Yeah. That's right." He shook his head. "I can't imagine her with him. He's so much younger."

"I know." Erin agreed. "But it seems to work."

Vic, Erin knew, was not quite so philosophical about it. She was protective of her brother and didn't like the fact that he was spending so much time with a much-older woman, and a federal agent at that. Erin thought Beaver was good for Jeremy. She seemed to keep him out of trouble. For someone who had previously been working for one of the Tennessee syndicates, that was a pretty big deal.

Campbell tapped his phone with his fingernail for a minute before pressing the wake up button and opening the phone app. "Doesn't she know about Joshua and Mikhail? Why isn't she already on top of this? He could have Josh stashed anywhere. He could be…" Cam broke off and shook his head hard. "If Josh was mixed up with Mikhail, then that should have been the first avenue of investigation!"

"I just didn't think… with him being in jail…" Erin protested.

"Being in jail means nothing," Campbell insisted. "That doesn't mean anything to a guy with connections like Mikhail."

Erin didn't say anything. They continued to walk toward her house. Cam made up his mind and put a call through to Beaver.

Beaver had a naturally loud voice. Erin could hear her over the phone, even though Campbell didn't have her on speakerphone.

"Cam. What's up?"

"I want to see you. Where are you now?"

There was a pause before Beaver responded. "I'm in Bald Eagle Falls. What's up?"

"Can we meet? Maybe at Erin Price's house? I'm not that far away."

"You're already in town?"

"My brother's gone missing, what do you think?"

"I think it took you long enough. Why weren't you here the first night he was gone?"

Campbell's face turned red. He looked over at Erin. She pretended that she wasn't listening in on his call and hadn't heard what Beaver had said.

"I didn't know if Mom would want me around. And I… had things I needed to take care of in the city before I left. I can't just drop everything and go, you know."

"I think that you could have if you had been that worried about your brother."

"Okay… well, maybe the first day I wasn't so worried. I thought maybe he just went out and didn't make it home in time. But… he's not the kind that would just take off and stay away this long."

There was another pause while Beaver considered. "If you want to go to Erin's, I can meet you there. How long until you'll be there?"

"Five minutes."

"I'll be longer than that. But I'll be there within the hour."

"Okay," Campbell said curtly. "I'll see you there."

He tapped the phone to end the call and put it back away. He looked at Erin. "I hope you don't mind, Miss Erin. I don't think meeting her at Mom's would be a good idea."

"No, of course not. I don't mind."

It would allow her to listen in on the conversation. Like with Terry and Stayner, it gave her a way to keep track of the police investigation without being accused of stirring things up herself or asking too many questions.

They walked the rest of the way in silence. It wasn't until they got to the house that Cam appeared to notice the bags that Erin was carrying and offered to help her.

"I'm an idiot. I let you carry everything the whole way by yourself."

"It's fine," Erin said, not passing anything over to him. "It's not that much." She juggled everything, trying to find her keys and to fit them into the lock.

"My mom raised me to be a gentleman. She woulda tore a strip off of me if she saw me treating a lady like that."

He was still holding out his hands to take something from her, but Erin ignored him and opened the door. She hit the digits on the burglar alarm and jerked her head to invite him in.

"Come on. I'll just put these things away. Make yourself at home."

Campbell followed her into the house. "Is Officer Piper at work?" he asked. "Does that mean he's doing better now?"

Erin was surprised to hear that Campbell knew anything about Terry's troubles. "He's just off taking care of some other errands today. He worked too much the night that Mary Lou made the report on Joshua, so he's had to take a few days off." She stepped into the kitchen, trying not to trip over the insistent orange cat underfoot. "But yes, he's starting to feel better."

She hoped that he would be able to get back to one hundred percent, but dreaded that he would not. She didn't tell Campbell that. She wouldn't tell anyone that. And if Terry asked her, she would lie and tell him that he was going to get better and be able to go back to exactly the way he had been before the attack.

CHAPTER 17

Erin unloaded day-old bread and cookies into the freezer while she waited for Beaver to show up to talk to Campbell. She decided to keep a few out in case her guests wanted a snack, and arranged them on plates.

Beaver didn't take long to arrive. She didn't wait for Erin to let her in, but knocked briskly on the door and walked in without an invitation. She looked around the front room, then nodded at Erin in the kitchen and Campbell, sitting uncomfortably on the couch.

"Cam." She looked him over. "You're looking pretty good."

Cam rubbed his clean-shaven jaw. "Got cleaned up for Mom," he admitted. "Didn't want to have to listen to her fussing over me too. She's got enough to worry about."

Beaver nodded. She looked at the easy chairs, then back into the kitchen at Erin.

"There's bread and cookies on the table," Erin invited. She went to the fridge to get out butter and condiments.

Beaver made an appreciative noise and motioned for Cam to join her in the kitchen. They both sat down at the kitchen table. Erin slid the butter dish and jam jars onto the table.

"I'm afraid we're all out of Jam Lady jam," she apologized. "And I haven't found a new supplier yet, so you'll have to make do with store-bought."

Cam looked down at his hands, his mouth tightening. Erin realized her faux pas in mentioning the Jam Lady brand. The Jam Lady had, in fact, been Roger Cox. And his incarceration was the reason that there would be no more Jam Lady. Unless someone in his family decided to take it up.

"I'm sorry…"

Cam gave his head a little shake. "He made a good jam."

"Yeah. He did."

"He was a good dad, you know. Before…"

"He seemed like a good guy," Erin said. "I only knew him after the accident, but… I know he was trying to make things work and he loved his family."

"Yeah." Cam's mouth twisted into a grimace. "And we all know where that led."

They were quiet for a minute. Beaver hadn't met Roger, but Erin assumed that Cam had probably told her details of what had happened to his father. And Beaver probably had access to some of his records through her job.

Beaver buttered a slice of bread and slathered it with the grocery store jam. After a few minutes of silence, Cam seemed to have managed to compartmentalize his feelings about his father.

"I want to know about Mickey," he said to Beaver, his tone already accusatory. "Haven't you looked into him with Josh's disappearance? To see if he has something to do with it?"

Beaver took a large bite of bread and chewed slowly. "You think I don't know how to do my job?"

"I want to find Josh. I don't care whether you think it's part of your job or not. Mickey can rot in jail for the rest of his life, but if he had something to do with Josh, I want to know about it."

"What makes you think there was anyone else involved in Josh's disappearance? Other than Josh himself?"

"I know he wouldn't leave my mom like that." Campbell scowled. "He's more responsible than I am. He's the baby of the family, so he's closer to her. And I know he wouldn't leave. We've talked about it."

"He told you he would never leave home?"

"No. We talked about whether he wanted to join me in the city. About getting away from school and life here in Bald Eagle Falls." Campbell's eyes went to Erin. "No offense, but it's smothering. I couldn't deal with living here anymore. And it wasn't much easier for Joshua."

Erin shrugged. She hadn't lived there for that long. She liked Bald Eagle Falls, but she knew that it wasn't for everyone. And she knew there were plenty of negatives. It wasn't all rainbows and roses.

"He could still have changed his mind," Beaver observed.

"He didn't write that note."

"It looks like his handwriting. It's not a big enough sample to be absolutely sure, but it's been sent to the experts for their opinion."

"It might look like his writing, but it's not. Josh didn't talk like that. He wouldn't say that. He wouldn't leave Mom. If he left, he would leave her a long letter, apologizing and explaining everything. That's the kind of guy he is. He wouldn't just leave that little sticky note, accusing Miss Erin…"

Beaver cocked her head like a bird. "What?"

"He likes to write. And he worries about other people's feelings. He wouldn't have scribbled that little note. He would have composed a two or three-page letter. Then I would believe it."

"What did you call Erin?"

Campbell looked confused. He looked over at Erin, not understanding. "Erin?" he echoed.

"Miss Erin," Erin corrected.

"Is that what you always call her?" Beaver asked.

Campbell considered. "I don't know. Most of the time. I think."

Beaver thought about this. "That's considered polite in these parts. You're still a kid, and she's an adult. So even if she's a family friend, you still refer to her as Miss."

Campbell nodded.

Erin watched Beaver, wondering where she was going with this. Beaver half-turned in her seat to look at Erin. "Did Joshua call you Miss Erin too?"

"Yes… I think so. Most of the time."

Beaver turned back to the table and took another bite of her bread. "That's not what the note said."

~

Erin looked at Beaver. She tried to picture the note in her mind—the spiky, messy writing.

"What did it say?"

"It said Erin Price."

"Well… that's still right."

"Calling you Miss Erin suggests that you're closer to him. Not a formal relationship or stranger. More of a family relationship. Not as close as auntie, but…"

Erin nodded. "Yes… that's right. I'm friends with Mary Lou, and even though I didn't know the boys well, I still consider them… close."

Campbell's eyes were intent on Beaver. "So, you believe that Josh didn't write the note?"

"I'm not there yet," Beaver warned. She took a couple more bites of her bread, polishing it off, and leaned her chair back on two legs. "Using Erin Price is quite formal. It suggests a distance between the writer and the subject. And perhaps between the writer and who is being addressed. Is there another Erin? Someone else that would require a last name to differentiate them?"

They both shook their heads. Erin couldn't think of any other Erins in Bald Eagle Falls. Maybe there was a younger child by that name, but not someone else that Joshua would have called Miss Erin. There was no reason for him to call her Erin Price instead of Miss Erin, unless he were angry at her for something. That was still a possibility. Had she made some misstep that had upset him? Not wanting to be interviewed about Beryl's murder?

"Cam… he wasn't mad at me, was he? I thought we were still on pretty good terms."

"Mad at you? For what?" Cam shook his head definitively. "No, he wasn't mad at you for something. He was irritated that Mom was still…" He shrugged, not finishing the sentence.

They were all silent for a few minutes. Erin watched Beaver, waiting to see what conclusion she came to.

"One would think that if he had just left of his own accord, that we might have friends coming forward by now to say that he is fine, even if he didn't want to announce where he is," Beaver said eventually.

Campbell nodded vigorously. "I've tried to talk to some of his friends from school. I get it that if he doesn't want to come forward, they would cover for him and not tell where he was. But they'd probably say to just leave him alone and not look for him. But this… they say they don't know. That he never said he was thinking of leaving. He's not the kind to just disappear for a few days at a time like some kids. It's not the kind of thing Joshua would do."

Beaver sighed. She snagged a couple of cookies and spoke through a mouthful. "It's not my case. I'm not involved in any way. But because it's Joshua… I have an interest in it. I'll talk to the PD about it. Float some ideas."

Campbell looked relieved. "Yes. Thank you."

"Doesn't mean anyone will listen to me. They have their own ideas. But I can at least give them some thoughts."

CHAPTER 18

Terry was not on duty, but Beaver stuck around until he arrived home from his errands to talk with him.

Erin was worried he looked tired. She knew she was fussing over him, which he hated, especially in front of a fellow law enforcement officer, but she couldn't help herself. He came into the kitchen while she finished making him a sandwich for supper and spoke in a low voice she hoped Beaver wouldn't overhear from the living room.

"You need to give yourself a chance to recover after that night you were up with Mary Lou," she told him. "If you keep spending all of your days working and running around doing other things, you're not going to be able to get caught up, and…" she trailed off. He knew what would happen. He'd finally been able to kick his migraines, and didn't want to trigger another cluster. She didn't want to suggest that he was weak or frail, but they both knew it was a danger. If he could just take care of himself and make sure that he got enough sleep and didn't work too hard, he might be able to stay in good health and not have to take days off due to migraines or other symptoms.

"I'm tired," he told Erin evenly, "but that's all. Just normal tired after a normal day of kicking around and running a few errands. I'm okay, Erin."

"I just don't want you to get sick…"

"I know. And I can take care of myself. I'm telling you, I'm okay. Relax."

They both looked toward the doorway. Erin couldn't see Beaver from where she was standing. She looked down at the sandwich as she handed it to him.

"Thank you." He took it from her.

"Don't stay up too late with Beaver."

"Beaver is not going to stay long." Terry's voice was firm. "I want to spend time with you, not her. I can talk to her tomorrow if we need more time."

Erin's face got warm. "Oh. Okay."

"I'll see what she needs and send her on her way."

Erin nodded. "Okay. I'll just tidy up in here."

She didn't really have much to do in the kitchen, but wanted to be able to listen in on the conversation. Terry gave her a sidelong look.

"Don't you spend too much time working either. You need a chance to rest just as much as I do."

"I don't have much to do."

He nodded and exited the kitchen. He took his sandwich to the coffee table and sat down on the couch.

"Beaver. What's up?"

"Been talking to Erin and Campbell about Joshua," Beaver said succinctly.

"Not your case."

"No. Not my case. But Campbell is my concern and he was upset about it. He wants me to look into the possibility that Mikhail might have had something to do with Josh's disappearance."

"Mikhail?" Terry's voice was clearly disbelieving. "What would he have to do with someone like Joshua? He's not exactly a high-value target."

"It's always possible that he blamed Joshua and Erin for his arrest, and this was one way of getting back at them."

"You don't think that."

"No," Beaver agreed.

"The police department thinks that Joshua is probably voluntarily missing. If that's the case… there's no point in us investing a lot of resources into it."

"What are your reasons for believing he's voluntary?"

Terry took a moment to reply. Erin tidied a few dishes into the dishwasher, waiting for his explanation.

"He's a high risk after everything his family has been through, especially with Campbell dropping out and taking off like he did. Makes it far more likely that Joshua would be tempted to do exactly the same thing. He's been having problems with school."

"But he's been working on extra credit work to bring his marks up."

"Yeah. But he might have just found that to be too much. Campbell burned out trying to do everything—working and keeping up with his marks at school, sports teams, home, and family responsibilities. It's not a stretch that Joshua hoped to do what Campbell couldn't, but in the end, he decided he just wanted to get out."

"You've interviewed his friends? What do they say?"

"They don't know where he would have gone. But that doesn't mean anything. Just that he didn't tell them what his plans were."

"What else?"

"What else?" Terry's breath whistled out. "There's no indication of break and enter. There's no sign of violence. No ransom note. The note that was left for Mary Lou wasn't looking for ransom and appears to be written in Joshua's own hand. None of that points to abduction."

"Was there anything about the note that struck you as being off?"

Terry cleared his throat. "Well… I did find it a little surprising."

"In what way?"

"The fact that he would mention or try to throw suspicion on Erin. Josh is a decent kid. Not the kind I think would try to cause his mother extra worry. And he was on good terms with Erin. There is no reason I can find for him to want to smear her reputation and make Mary Lou angry at her."

"From what Campbell says, Josh was upset that Mary Lou was angry with Erin."

"I wouldn't be surprised. Mary Lou is someone who doesn't usually get riled up… I was a little surprised myself that it has lasted this long."

"Josh didn't discuss that with you?"

"No. But he was by to see Erin more than once. If he agreed with his mother and thought that she was responsible for the police department's investigation of him back in December, why would he visit her?

As far as I know, he was expressly forbidden from seeing Erin, but did it anyway."

"So why would he put her back into the crosshairs by implicating her in a note?"

Terry grunted. "Exactly."

"Did it surprise you that he referred to her as Erin Price in the note?"

"No… why?"

"Was that how he usually referred to her? Addressed her?"

"No, but it is her name."

"You don't think it would have been more natural for him to refer to her as Miss Erin or just Erin?"

"I guess so. But if he was trying to make it sound like a third party had written the note, then it would be normal to refer to her as Erin Price. A stranger wouldn't refer to her familiarly."

Beaver readjusted her position. Erin could see her through the doorway. She had put her feet up against the edge of the coffee table. "So, what would your instinct be? Written by Joshua to sound like it was a third party, or written by an actual third party?"

"It is similar to his handwriting."

"Similar doesn't establish that it's the same writer. Even with expert analysis, which you don't have yet. Could it be someone trying to imitate his handwriting, or who just happened to have similar handwriting?"

"Of course," Terry admitted. "In fact, I wondered whether the brothers had similar writing styles."

Beaver made a sucking noise, considering this. She pulled a package of gum out of her pocket and folded several pieces into her mouth at once. She chomped for a few minutes before responding to this.

"What is your scenario if it was Campbell who wrote the note? He came to rescue his brother? To take him out for a drink? And then what happened? It went sideways. Something happened to Josh and Campbell doesn't want anyone to know? Or Josh truly wanted to disappear to where no one could find him?"

"Hmm. I don't really like any of those."

"Then you still think Joshua wrote the note."

"Yes… I think the simplest solution is the most likely."

"And that Campbell didn't have anything to do with it."

"That no one else had anything to do with it. Just one teen who didn't realize what kind of trouble he was going to cause."

"And who still doesn't know what trouble he's caused? Or who is afraid to come forward and straighten it out?"

"Probably doesn't even know. It's not like it's been in the papers or on TV."

Beaver cracked her gum. "I'm going to talk to the sheriff tomorrow. Ask him to consider the possibility that it was a kidnapping."

"Well… that's your right. Do you really think he was kidnapped? Or you're just letting Campbell talk you into it?"

"There are inconsistencies. I don't like them. The more I hear, the less I like them."

"If it was an abduction… we're in trouble. We're already past the first forty-eight hours."

"Yes," Beaver agreed grimly.

"You think that Mikhail's syndicate was involved?"

"It's not the Russians' style, but I think I need to look into it anyway. It's an open loop that needs to be closed."

"Okay. Well… if I'm going to get called in tomorrow, I'd better get to bed in good time tonight." Erin heard Terry get to his feet.

Beaver pulled her feet back from the coffee table, letting each of them fall to the floor with a thump. "A pleasure as always, Officer Piper."

Erin moved to the doorway of the kitchen as they shook hands, and Beaver headed to the door.

"Thank you for the cookies, Miss Erin."

"Any time."

As Beaver walked out of the house, Terry turned back to Erin. "There are cookies?"

Erin laughed. "There are always cookies."

She went to the freezer to get a couple out for him.

CHAPTER 19

Joshua was growing accustomed to his imprisonment. He didn't wake up expecting to be free. He remembered from one awakening to the next that he needed to be quiet and still and speak respectfully to his captor.

This time there was a smell. Not the rank smell of the room he was being kept in or his own body. Something that smelled warm and enticing. His stomach, previously fallen into a sort of a dormant state, growled and made itself known.

Food. There was food somewhere close by.

He wasn't able to see where his captor came in from, but could sense him getting closer. Josh pressed his lips together, not wanting to make any extra noise because of the smell, but it was so entrancing, it took all of his willpower not to moan out loud.

The shadows of the figure separated from the surrounding darkness. Joshua's world shifted as the figure sat close to him. He tried to grab something to prevent himself from falling, before realizing that he was still bound and unable to grasp anything, even if he could see it. As the world stabilized, he realized that he must be on a bed, and the dark figure had sat down on the bed, making it sink under his weight.

Joshua remained frozen for a few minutes until he was sure that nothing else was going to move and that he was not going to fall.

"Something for you to eat," the familiar whisper informed him.

Joshua blinked, trying to see through the darkness to see what it was. The figure was making small movements. Joshua heard a spoon scrape across the bottom of a bowl. He started salivating in response, even though he'd thought he didn't have any more spit left in him.

The figure brought a spoon up slowly to Joshua's mouth, perhaps remembering how he'd misjudged distance with the water. Joshua opened his mouth early to make sure that none of the precious food would be wasted.

It was soup. Warm, nourishing chicken soup. Joshua couldn't close his lips properly, they were so cracked and swollen. He slurped, trying to get every last drop without any spilling. The spoon returned to the bowl for another spoonful.

He couldn't believe that he was going to get more than one spoonful. It seemed like an embarrassment of riches. He'd never known that food could taste so good and be so satisfying. Just one spoonful had been enough to change everything.

He ate the next bite, and the next. They kept coming.

He didn't ask for water. He didn't ask his captor any questions about where he was or why he was there, or why his hands had been bound. He didn't know what the shadow shape wanted, other than for Joshua to be quiet and compliant. And it didn't matter.

As long as he got soup.

By the time the spoon was scraping across the bottom of the bowl for every spoonful, his stomach hurt. It felt full to bursting. But he was determined not to say that he was full. He would get every drop he could, no matter how big and bloated his belly got from the soup.

"That's it," the whisperer said.

Joshua swallowed once more, grateful for the way that soup had soothed his raw, dry throat. "Thank you."

"You liked it?"

"Yes, it was wonderful."

"It's an old family recipe."

Joshua breathed in and out a few times. "That's the best kind of recipe."

"Yes, you're right." There was silence for a few moments. "Do you cook?"

Joshua cleared his throat, not sure how much he was going to be able to talk. He hadn't used his voice for several wakenings, though he didn't know what kind of period that covered. It seemed like a long time.

"I cook a little. My mom doesn't always have time and we try to help out." He swallowed. His tongue and his tonsils still felt swollen, hard to speak around. "My dad… he was a good cook."

"What happened to him?"

Joshua wondered if it was a test of his honesty. Everyone in Bald Eagle Falls knew what had happened to Roger. "He's… in a place now. For people with… he has a brain injury. He was… a danger to others."

"That must be hard."

"Yeah. It is. But it's easier than when he was at home, and we had to keep track of him, try to make sure that he didn't wander off. And to… try to keep him calm." Another difficult swallow. "He had… moods."

"He hit you," the figure guessed.

"He… he never hurt us on purpose."

A derisive snort from his captor. "Sure."

"He had a brain injury. It changed things."

His captor covered the empty bowl, obviously preparing to get up and leave.

"Can you… stay for a few more minutes?" Joshua asked.

The reflective surface of the goggles turned toward him. "Why?"

"I just… I miss people. I like having someone here for a bit."

The shadowy figure stayed by him, but didn't continue the conversation. Eventually, Josh's eyes started to close. He tried to keep himself alert, looking for something else to talk about or another way to keep himself awake.

But he was too afraid of how the figure would respond if he started asking questions or did something unexpected. Eventually, he lost the battle against his body and drifted off to sleep.

CHAPTER 20

Erin's mind was finally at ease, sure that the police department would now put all of their resources into finding Joshua. Was it just her nature that made her want to fix everything, or was it because her name had been mentioned in the note? Either way, she felt like it was her responsibility to find Josh, or at least to convince the police that he had really been the victim and was not just a runaway.

Maybe it was because when she was a runaway, people had found her and brought her back. Until she was old enough that no one cared to look for her anymore. Right around the time she was Joshua's age. Things had subtly changed at that point. Even though she hadn't yet aged out of foster care, officials were more inclined to shrug their shoulders and say she was old enough to decide where she wanted to be.

Even if she didn't know where she wanted to be, just that she needed to be somewhere else. Somewhere safe.

Terry would find Josh. Or the sheriff or the FBI or one of the other officers would turn up a vital clue that would lead them to Josh. And they would take him home to Mary Lou.

Josh was still wanted.

Erin was more cheerful, mixing her batters and doughs and preparing the sweet and savory treats for Auntie Clem's loyal customers. She felt generous and benevolent toward them, willing to look past their minor failings. She liked Bald Eagle Falls. She loved Auntie Clem's and her employees and her customers. Things were looking up.

She put a couple of items on sale just for the heck of it. She always carefully planned and advertised her promotions, so the spontaneous sale made Vic raise her eyebrows in surprise.

"Okay… that's nice. That will make people happy."

Erin nodded cheerfully. "I hope so. I'm feeling very philanthropic today."

"Philanthropic. Well, there's a five-dollar word."

Erin just smiled.

If Charley came in, Erin might even give her a free muffin for once.

"We should take some treats over to the police department today."

"Sure. Since you're feeling philanthropic," Vic agreed.

Erin grabbed a box and retreated to the kitchen to fill it with cookies set out on the cooling racks. They were still warm from the oven, but cool enough to be handled without falling apart.

"Do you mind if I run these over?" she asked Vic.

"You're in charge! You can do what you like."

"You don't mind handling things for a few minutes."

"Not at all. Go ahead. Things won't pick up for another hour."

Erin nodded her agreement. She set out toward the town hall to take her gift to the police department. They would need a calorie boost to kick their brains into high gear to solve Joshua's case. She would do everything she could to help them do that.

She was happy and feeling good about herself and the bakery when she returned. There were a few more customers than she had expected, so it was a good thing she had arrived back when she did to help Vic out.

There was a knot of women talking among themselves, not standing in line or checking out the products in the display case. Erin approached them, wondering what the excitement was about.

She saw a familiar neat figure with gray hair. Mary Lou hadn't been in the bakery since Christmas. Erin smiled, pleased. Maybe Mary Lou had heard that the police were now investigating Joshua's disappearance as a possible abduction, and so had forgiven Erin for being mentioned in the note.

Mary Lou had the remains of a fortune cookie in her hand. Erin looked down at it, puzzled. Mary Lou's mouth was a slash of scarlet lipstick across her perfectly white complexion. Not smiling.

No forgiveness, then.

Erin glanced over at Vic, hoping for a clue before she stepped right into something. Vic's mouth was open slightly, but she didn't explain. It took a lot for Vic to be at a loss for words. She always knew the right things to say.

Mary Lou looked Erin in the eye, her own eyes blazing.

"Explain *this*."

Erin looked down at the fortune cookie. She wasn't sure what she was supposed to explain. Mary Lou obviously knew what a fortune cookie was, she didn't need to explain that.

Explain the fact that she was now supplying the Chinese restaurant with gluten-free fortune cookies? Erin didn't know why Mary Lou would care about that. Whether the Chinese restaurant had gluten or gluten-free cookies didn't make any difference to her, did it?

Mary Lou held up the printed fortune from the cookie. It took Erin a minute to focus on the small lettering.

You are never going to find him.

CHAPTER 21

Erin gasped in shock. It was a good thing that she had already delivered the cookies to the police department, because she would have dropped anything that she was holding on to the minute she read that fortune and it sank into her brain.

"What? Where did that come from?"

"Where did it come from?" Mary Lou repeated, looking like she had tasted something horrible. "Why don't you explain that to me?"

"I... I don't know." Erin shook her head. "That's not one of ours. That's not one of the fortunes we had printed."

Mary Lou displaced the broken bits of fortune cookie in her hand. "This is one of your cookies. One of your gluten-free fortune cookies."

Erin looked down at it. The texture and color were slightly different from a regular fortune cookie. Not enough that a casual observer would have noticed, but Erin had worked hard on that recipe and had folded dozens of the fortune cookies to be delivered to the Chinese restaurant. If she looked at it really closely, she might be able to tell whether she had folded it or whether one of her employees had.

"Yes," she agreed faintly. "It's one of mine. But that's not one of the fortunes that we put in them."

"Then how do you think it got there?" Mary Lou demanded. "It didn't just crawl in there on its own."

Erin looked for an explanation. Someone had clearly tampered with one of her fortune cookies. How would they do that? Was it possible to remove the fortune that Erin or her staff had inserted and to place another one in its place? It was a possibility, but it wouldn't have been easy. And doing any number of them would have been impossible—one or two, perhaps, but not a dozen.

"Is this… the only one? Where did you get it? Who gave it to you?"

Mary Lou looked surprised at the questions. She pursed her lips to answer, then shook her head. "They're your cookies. You put the fortunes in them. You put a fortune inside this cookie that would get back to me. Saying that I would never find Joshua. I thought you were my friend at one time, Erin. I can't believe you would stoop so low. I can't believe you would want to hurt me like this."

"I didn't. I swear, Mary Lou. I wouldn't do something like that. I don't know what happened, but it wasn't me. I'm just as shocked as you are."

"No, I don't think you could be as shocked as I am. I don't understand why you are doing this. *Did* you have something to do with Josh disappearing? Or are you just taking advantage of what happened to get back at me?"

"No. Get back at you for what? No. I didn't do this."

"Because I accused you of being involved in Joshua's disappearance. You decided to do something that would hurt me. Even worse than him disappearing in the first place. You wanted to rip my heart out."

Tears spilled out of Erin's eyes. "No. No, Mary Lou." She tried to take Mary Lou's hands to reassure her. Somehow, physical contact would communicate to Mary Lou that Erin would never do something like that. "Please, please. No. I wouldn't do anything to hurt you."

Mary Lou jerked back, avoiding her touch. "I'm reporting this to the police. I don't suppose there is anything I can charge you with, but they will have to investigate whether it is actually related to Joshua's disappearance."

Erin nodded. She didn't know what else to say. Who could have replaced the fortune in the fortune cookie? How would they have made sure that Mary Lou got it, and why would they do such a thing?

Whoever had left the note for Mary Lou and had arranged for the fortune to be changed was trying to drive a wedge between Erin and Mary Lou. Looking at Mary Lou's face, Erin doubted they would ever be able to be friends again. Even if they found Joshua. Even if they proved that Erin didn't have anything to do with his abduction or disappearance, she didn't see Mary Lou ever trusting her again.

~

Everything after that moment was a blur. Erin would never be able to forget how Mary Lou looked as she stood there and accused Erin of changing the fortune and trying to rip her heart out. Until the day she died, it would remain clear in her memory.

Mary Lou thought it was telling that Erin had just been over to the police department. She sneered and insinuated that Erin was trying to ingratiate herself with the police or to influence the direction of their investigation.

It was unfair when Erin had been trying all along to get the police to investigate it as an abduction instead of a runaway. She had been Mary Lou's greatest advocate.

Within the hour, Sheriff Wilmot and Stayner arrived at the bakery looking grim.

"We're going to have to shut down Auntie Clem's to investigate, Miss Price," Stayner informed her.

"But… I didn't have anything to do with this. Not with changing the fortunes in the fortune cookies or with Joshua's disappearance. You know that. I've been trying to get the police to investigate, not the other way around."

"On the surface, it would appear that someone at Auntie Clem's Bakery might have been complicit in the kidnapping of a minor. Maybe only after the fact, but you know we have to check it out."

"I'll show you my records."

"That's appreciated," the sheriff said. "But we're going to need more than that. We're going to need to complete our own investigation, unimpaired. I suggest that you close for the rest of the afternoon and give us the run of the place. You should be able to reopen again in the morning. If you're going to insist on a warrant, then it's going to be closed for longer while we get the official paperwork."

One afternoon wasn't that bad. And not even all of one afternoon. Erin wanted to fight it to assert her rights as a citizen and business owner, hoping that they wouldn't be able to get a warrant on such thin evidence. But she would be better off cooperating.

Maybe Mary Lou would see that she was doing everything she could to help. The police would know that she hadn't been involved in the substitution of the fortune in Mary Lou's cookie or in Joshua's kidnapping.

And maybe they would find something that would help in the investigation. Something that would point back to the actual criminal in the case.

Stayner and the sheriff waited for her decision. Erin rubbed her temples.

"Okay. Of course. I'll close the bakery. It's just… yes. Vic, we'll start cleaning up." Erin looked at the small group of women gathered in front of the counter. "I'm sorry, ladies, you're going to have to go. If you come back tomorrow…"

She suspected that they weren't going to buy anything anyway. They had been attracted by the drama. Perhaps they had come from the Chinese restaurant when Mary Lou had opened her cookie to see what was going to happen.

Erin herded the women out the door and flipped the sign over to 'closed.' She walked around the counter to join Vic and get started on the closing procedures.

"We would appreciate it if you would just leave everything as it is," Sheriff Wilmot advised. "It would be better if you didn't touch anything."

Erin stood there at a loss. She stared at the sheriff. "But I need to… we need to cash out, and clean up, and get tomorrow's batters prepared so we're ready to start baking in the morning. Some of these batters need to soak for a few hours for the best texture."

"We'll get done as quickly as we can, and maybe you'll be able to come back tonight and finish up. But right now… we want everything left as is."

Erin looked at Vic. Vic nodded encouragingly. "We'd better go, hon."

Erin moved like a zombie, taking off her apron and hanging it up, grabbing her purse, and thinking through what the police were going to do.

"I can show you the order for the fortune cookies… everyone helped make them…"

When had the rogue fortune been inserted in the cookie? At the Chinese restaurant? When the cookies were originally prepared? Erin had merely glanced at the pile of white paper strips she had received back from the printer. Had someone swapped them at the bakery?

"And there are more fortunes here, we didn't use all of them. You can compare..."

"We can find everything. If you'll just make sure the computer is unlocked. And if I could have a look at your purses before you go, ladies?"

Vic turned to face Sheriff Wilmot, her face white. "Certainly not! I have rights."

"Of course you do," Wilmot agreed. "That's why I'm asking for your permission."

Vic and Erin looked at each other. Erin was ready to hand her purse over to Sheriff Wilmot to check. That was the right thing to do, wasn't it? Vic had encouraged Erin to let them search Auntie Clem's Bakery, but now she was going to balk at having her own property searched?

Finally, Vic gave a little nod. Erin handed her purse over to Wilmot as well. Her face was burning with embarrassment. It was a disorganized mess, as it always was, despite any attempts to keep it tidy and well-organized. And of course, it was well-stocked with feminine items that she didn't want the men pawing through. There were personal notes, makeup, used tissues...

Wilmot handed Erin's purse to Stayner, and held his hand out toward Vic. "Miss Webster?"

Vic reluctantly handed her purse over. "There's a handgun in there," she warned. "I have a permit."

Wilmot nodded.

Erin and Vic stood there watching as Stayner and Wilmot methodically searched their purses. Erin felt almost physical pain as she watched Stayner pull each item out and examine it closely. She had thought that he would just take a quick look, seeing if she had anything related to the fortune cookies inside, making sure that she wasn't walking off with any evidence. But he was very thorough. She hated the violation. She folded her arms across her chest and concentrated on breathing. In and out. Slowly and evenly. Beside her, Vic turned away, unable to watch.

Erin was the opposite. She couldn't tear her eyes away. Like watching an assault and being frozen in place, unable to say or do anything.

It couldn't have been more than a couple of minutes, but it seemed like it went on forever. Stayner took one more look into each of her purse pockets to make sure he hadn't missed anything and handed it to her.

"I'll let you repack. So you can put it back the way you want it."

Erin's face burned. She was sure he must be thinking what a slob she was. And just what had he learned about her as he went through her bag? Her whole life was in there. She didn't store everything on the phone or a planner like some people did. Instead, it was all loose notes and papers in an unruly stack in her purse. Hard to break the bad habits she had established.

Erin started to go through the pile, sorting through miscellaneous papers and throwing out what she didn't need anymore. Getting rid of the tissues and random cough drops or hard candies. Making the rest as neat as possible. Maybe she would start using a planner. She wouldn't have to rewrite as many lists that way.

Wilmot had finished going through Vic's purse. He set it down gently and looked at her. "Do I need to verify whether you have a permit?"

Vic's lips tightened and formed a thin line. "In my wallet."

Vic hadn't been watching, but Erin had, and she knew the sheriff had already gone through Vic's wallet. She tried to give Vic a warning look.

Wilmot picked up the wallet and handed it to Vic. Vic impatiently flicked it open and started going through the card file. She stopped after going through it once and tried again, more slowly. Then a third time, separating cards to look in between. She swallowed.

"It's not here. I do have one! I don't know where it could have gone. I'll have to… get them to send me a replacement, I guess."

"If I do a database search, it will show up?"

"Yeah, of course."

Wilmot nodded. He motioned for Vic to pick up her things. "Please leave the handgun at home until you get your new card."

Vic's face was rosy red. She began packing her things back away without answering.

CHAPTER 22

Terry picked them up from the parking lot behind Auntie Clem's. His expression was serious and he didn't initiate a conversation with them on the way back. When they got back to the house, Erin got out of the truck and looked over at Vic. Vic seemed torn whether to go in with Erin or go around the back to her own loft.

"Can we talk?" she asked.

Erin nodded. "Yes. Sure."

They all went into the house. Terry's eyes moved back and forth between Vic and Erin. "Is this a private discussion?"

Erin raised her brows at Vic inquiringly.

"No." Vic sighed and flopped down into an easy chair. "Neither of us has done anything wrong, and if the police department can get that through their thick skulls, all the better."

"Don't attack Terry," Erin warned. "He wasn't there."

Vic chewed on her lip, a stress behavior Erin hadn't seen in her before. Vic was clearly very upset. "Fine," Vic agreed. "As long as he doesn't give us grief and act like we must have been the ones to mess with Mary Lou's fortune cookie."

Erin rolled her eyes and looked at Terry, giving a small shrug of apology. Terry sat down on the couch and patted the seat next to him for Erin to sit down. She took the seat and Orange Blossom immediately jumped up into her lap. He had been yowling around her feet, but she had ignored him.

"Shh…" She petted the cat and snuggled him close. "The grown-ups are trying to talk."

Terry looked down at Erin and stroked the cat once. "I guess the sheriff made it over to Auntie Clem's."

"Yep."

"Are you okay?"

"I'm fine." Erin looked over at Vic. "We're fine. But… it's embarrassing. Being treated like we're criminals when we didn't do anything. He shut us down right in front of our customers, saying that he was going to get a warrant if we didn't voluntarily let him search Auntie Clem's. And I couldn't supervise or show him anything, just unlock the computer for him and let them do whatever they want."

Vic nodded. "And they searched our handbags! Like we were shoplifters."

"They just needed to be able to say that they didn't miss anything. They made sure that you couldn't walk out of the bakery with any evidence."

"I don't care why. It was… humiliating. So invasive and demeaning! And I have a gun license!"

Terry raised his brows at her angry tone. "Okay."

"I don't know where it could have gone," Vic said in a more thoughtful tone. "It's not like I take it out of my wallet very often. It just stays there unless someone asks for it."

"You don't remember when you had it out last?" Erin asked.

"No. No idea." Vic frowned, trying to remember. "I don't know… when I bought a replacement gun, I guess. After…" Vic glanced over at Terry, swallowing. "You know, after Mickey."

"Maybe you left it at the store? Is that possible?"

"They would have called me, don't you think? If I left it on the counter?"

"I would think so… maybe you dropped it when you thought you put it back and no one saw. Or… it got put in the garbage with the bag or box the gun came in."

Vic shook her head. "It doesn't make sense. I don't see how I could have lost it. Unless someone has been in my purse. But who would go into my purse?"

Erin couldn't think of anyone who would have had access to it. Other than Erin or one of the other employees when it was placed in Erin's office for safekeeping.

"I don't know."

"I'm so steamed. That's just the cherry on top of everything else."

Erin scratched at a splash of batter on her pants. Despite her apron, she could never seem to get through a day at Auntie Clem's without something getting on her clothes. "I'm more worried about Mary Lou. You can get your card reissued. But I can't take back what happened to her. On top of Joshua being missing… she just doesn't need something like this."

Vic deflated. "Yeah. I'm being miserable for no reason. She's the real victim here. So what if I misplaced my license?"

"How could this have happened?" Terry asked. "Can you walk me through how the cookies were prepared and how Mary Lou got this… strange fortune?"

Erin nodded. "Yeah, I guess… I can't understand what happened. We got the order for gluten-free fortune cookies from the Chinese restaurant. I got the fortunes printed at the Quiki. It was a big cookie order. They keep forever. So… we had everyone working on baking and folding small batches over a few days. You have to fold them while they're still warm, so you can't just do a great big batch and fold them over a few hours or days."

"Who is 'everyone'?"

Erin shrugged. "Everyone. All of the employees. Everyone wanted to try their hand because it's such a unique item. Most people never get the chance to make fortune cookies."

"So it could have been done by any of your employees."

"I guess. But… I can't imagine anyone doing that. Sneaking a different fortune into the bunch. And how would they know… how would they make sure that Mary Lou got the wrong one? Or the right one, I mean."

Terry pursed his lips. "Okay. So what do you think happened?"

"I think… someone must have done it at the restaurant."

"How would they do that?"

"I think... just pull out the fortune that was already in the cookie and then... feed a new one in through the crack into the cookie..."

"Would that have been easy?"

Erin shook her head. "I never tried it. I guess if it was a big enough crack. Or you folded the fortune in half. The fortunes aren't supposed to be folded. But you could."

"So for someone to give Mary Lou that particular cookie, they would have to see her at the restaurant, swap out the fortune, and take that one to her."

"Yeah. And if she was eating with other people... she was at the bakery with other women, I don't know if they were all eating together or if they just... gathered because of the spectacle."

"Then how would anyone make sure that she got that particular cookie?"

Erin nodded.

"Maybe it was someone who was eating with her," Vic suggested. "They took one of the cookies, did a little sleight of hand, and gave her the swapped one."

That sounded a little better to Erin. At least if the fortune had been swapped by a restaurant worker or by someone in Mary Lou's dinner party, that took Erin and her employees off the hook.

"That seems a little complex to be doing at the table," Terry said doubtfully.

"Well then..." Vic stared off into space. "They could have taken a fortune cookie home without eating it, and then replaced the fortune at home. Then go out to lunch with Mary Lou, and pass the swapped fortune cookie to her."

"That's possible," Erin agreed. "Someone could do that."

"Possible," Terry agreed. "You are avoiding the possibility that it could be one of your employees, though. Who had a motive to replace the fortune?"

"It couldn't have been someone at the bakery," Erin insisted. "There would be no way to get the replaced fortune to Mary Lou. Someone had to give it to her at the restaurant."

"What if it wasn't targeted," Vic mused. "What if it's only coincidence that it got to Mary Lou?"

Erin didn't need that kind of help. She glared at Vic, mentally urging her to move to another possibility.

"It had to be targeted to Mary Lou," Terry objected. "It wouldn't mean anything to anyone else."

"Sure it would," Vic argued. "This is Bald Eagles Falls. Everybody knows that Joshua is missing. Anyone who got that fortune would wonder if it was about him and take it to the police."

"That's too big of a coincidence to be believed," Terry objected. "I can write off a small coincidence. But that one fortune was swapped and Mary Lou just happened to get it? I don't believe that."

"She likes Chinese." Vic leaned forward in her seat, trying to explain it away. "She eats at the Chinese restaurant, so she would have a better chance at getting that fortune cookie."

Even Erin couldn't believe that. "The switch can't have been made at Auntie Clem's," she insisted. "It had to be at the restaurant."

CHAPTER 23

Joshua wasn't sure how long he had been trying to wake up. He'd been having dreams of waking up. Every time, something bad happened. He couldn't open his eyes. He walked into traffic. He was forced to do something to hurt someone else. He couldn't find the bathroom.

He was pretty sure his brain had been trying to wake him up for some time, but his body wasn't ready to get up.

He shifted back and forth restlessly. He was hot and clammy, sweat standing out on his forehead and temples and running down his back in the occasional cold drip.

He tried to raise his arms enough to wipe his face, and managed to wipe part of his head along his sleeve, mopping up the sweat. But it wasn't long before his face was coated with sweat again.

Eventually, he opened his eyes.

Things weren't much different with his eyes open instead of closed. He still couldn't see anything, just shadows in the darkness.

"Is anyone there?" he asked in a soft voice, reaching out mentally into the darkness, trying to feel someone there. Or not there. He should be able to tell whether the figure was watching him or not. But the air seemed empty and still. How long had he been lying there?

He held his wrists in the best lighting he could find and moved his head down to study the bonds.

Just zip ties. Nothing fancy or recognizable about them. They were crusted with blood and his fingers were swollen like sausages. Joshua opened and closed his hands a few times, looking at them. They were numb. He felt like they belonged to someone else. How long had they been tied? Were the zip ties cutting off his circulation? If they were, how long before he would be in danger of losing his hands?

And his feet. Joshua rolled onto his side and pulled his feet up, trying to get a peek at them. But his pant legs were gathered around the bond and it was impossible to see how they were tied or what kind of condition they were in. Like his hands, his feet were numb. And his legs too, for that matter.

He wasn't sure he wanted to live if he were going to lose his hands and his legs. That would be too much.

He looked around him, trying to make sense of the slightly lighter shadows around him. How long had he been in the dark? There was too little light for his eyes to adjust. He would need to be a cat to make out anything around him. Or be wearing night-vision goggles. Maybe when his captor came around for a visit, Joshua could ask to borrow the goggles for a few minutes. Just so he could see what it was like to wear them. Then he would give them back.

He thought he heard a far-off click. Joshua strained to hear anything else. He was lucky that the place he was being held seemed to be free of rats.

Or if they were biting his fingers or toes, he was lucky he couldn't feel them. He studied his hands an inch from his face again. He didn't see any marks that would suggest rats had been anywhere near them. That was a relief. At least if he were found, his family wouldn't have to see anything gruesome.

There was another rustle of sound, and Joshua watched the shadows for any shifts in density.

"Are you there?" he whispered.

His captor didn't answer but, in a minute, stood before him. Joshua didn't say anything, waiting. More food? Water?

"They're never going to find you," the dark figure said.

Joshua's stomach tightened. He had already suspected this. Whoever had taken him away had hidden Joshua too well for anyone to find him. He had no idea whether he was in a warehouse or some other kind of storage unit. No idea whether he was close to home or far away, in the town, the country, or the city. Even if someone from his family had been able to contact him, he wouldn't be able to tell them where to go. Not even a clue, like they often gave on TV. A train going over the railway tracks. Chapel bells. Traffic sounds. He couldn't hear anything outside the room.

"Why did you do this?" Joshua asked.

It wasn't a demand this time. Not something he shouted at the top of his lungs or hurled out as an accusation. He just wanted to know. What was the point of it all? Was it because of something he had done? Some fatal misstep in the past? A girl he hadn't paid attention to or a boy he had beaten in grades or some sport? It wasn't like Josh had even done that well in school. Not lately.

"I needed to put a stop to it," the shadow whispered. "I couldn't think of any other way to stop it."

"Stop what? What did I do?"

"I needed some time. Some space. People were getting too close."

Too close. Josh closed his eyes, thinking. Too close to what? Physically too close to the hooded figure, infringing on his personal space? Town development getting too close to his farm? Or something else?

Too close to what?

"You don't know what it's like," the shadow hissed at him. "You live in a whole different world."

Josh tried to puzzle through this. But the half-clues were not helping him. He didn't want to die without even knowing why.

"I'm not feeling well."

The hooded figure didn't answer for a few minutes.

"Don't feel well how?" he asked after a few minutes.

"I just… I'm so tired and sore. And…" He used his arm to wipe his face again. "I'm hot. I don't know… if it's a fever."

The figure reached out and touched him, but the hands wore medical gloves, so he didn't know how that would help him figure out whether Joshua really was sick.

The hand touched his forehead, then his cheek. The hand grasped one of Joshua's numb hands and raised them to study the ties and wrists as Joshua had done.

He released Joshua's hand and moved down to his feet, checking them out as well.

"Does everything look okay?" Josh asked. He didn't want to be surprised. If he were seriously ill, he wanted to be prepared.

"Looks fine to me," the shadow told him without emotion.

Did that really mean he was okay? Or did the shadow just not care?

"What do you want? Is there… some way I can get you to let me go?"

"No. There's nothing you could do."

"I want to do something. Isn't there anything?" Josh didn't want to suggest anything specific, but he worried that it was something to do with Campbell. Had Campbell cheated Josh's captor out of money or product? If Joshua could just do something to make up for it, to pay the captor back, he would. He would do almost anything. He didn't care if it were illegal or unethical. People would understand that it was a matter of pleasing his captor or dying. They would understand.

"You've already done enough."

That made it sound like it wasn't Campbell's fault that Joshua was there, but his own. Something that he had done. But what could he have done? He was a kid. And he wasn't involved in anything he shouldn't be. He went to school and tried to get his schoolwork done. He tried to do chores at home and to work part time to contribute to the household income. And when Mary Lou was not going to be home to make dinner, Joshua tried to help out. Too often, he didn't have anything on the table by the time Mary Lou got home. But he tried.

"What did I do?" he begged. "What can I do to make up for it? Isn't there anything I can do to… get out of here?" He swallowed. "I promise I won't turn on you. I won't tell anyone anything I know. I'll help you. And then I'll say I escaped. That I don't know anything. No one will ever know anything."

"It's time for me to go." The figure made a looking-at-his-watch gesture, though Joshua couldn't see anything on his wrist. But maybe there was and his captor could see it with the goggles.

"Is there… did you bring anything to eat?"

The shadow patted pockets in various locations on his body. He had obviously not come prepared to feed Josh. Maybe hoping that Joshua would have fainted with hunger by now.

There was a crinkle in one pocket, and the figure pulled it out. "A cookie," he whispered. "But it's broken up in pieces." He made to put it back in his pocket.

"No. I'll eat it. Please."

His captor considered it for a few moments, then shrugged. He wrestled with the plastic wrapper and managed to get it open. Josh's hands were out of commission, so it was the figure's job to get the pieces of cookie into Josh's mouth.

One at a time, the shadow put little bits of the crispy, bland cookie into Josh's mouth. He didn't have much saliva to moisten it and get it down, but he did his best. He had to do everything he could to get some sustenance into his system.

"That's all." The whisperer crumpled the plastic wrapper and shoved it back into his pocket.

"That soup was so good. Do you think you could bring me some more?"

"No."

Josh tried to swallow the lump in his throat. He had expected a 'maybe' or 'if I can,' not a flat-out no. Didn't his captor think it worthwhile even to string Joshua along? Make him at least think he was going to get fed again?

His eyes stung. He didn't cry. He probably couldn't spare any of his body's moisture for tears. But he was crushed by the denial. The figure intended to let him die. That much was pretty clear.

"Can I… can I write a note to my mom? Or make a recording? Anything?"

"Why would I let you do that?" The whisper was an angry hiss.

"Because… I never got to say goodbye. I'd like to say goodbye."

"People don't get to say goodbye. Lots of people leave or die without ever saying goodbye first. You should know what that is like."

CHAPTER 24

Erin stared out at the night. It was late. She should have been asleep already. She would be tired at the bakery the next day if she didn't get the sleep she needed.

But how could she go to sleep when Joshua was still out there somewhere? It had been too long. The longer it took them to track him down, the less likely it would be that they would find him alive and unharmed. She hated to think of him out there, alone and scared.

The police were now intent on finding out who had swapped the fortunes. But it seemed like a mistake to Erin for them to be so concerned about the fortune. It could have been a prank. It could be completely unrelated to Joshua's disappearance. Maybe, as Vic had said, it was never the intention of the fortune-swapper to send the swapped fortune to Mary Lou. If it were just a coincidence, they were wasting their time trying to catch someone who had not even committed a crime.

Erin needed more. There had to be a reason for kidnapping Joshua. It wasn't just random. Not when they had either gone into his house or somehow lured him out in the middle of the night. Someone had gone there intending to take him. And that person had to have a motive.

What?

If they had something against Erin, as implied by the note, why had they taken Josh? Why hadn't they taken Erin herself? Or done something to hurt her—either physically or by hurting someone close to her. Terry or Vic or one of the animals. Joshua was a friend, but they hadn't been that close. She knew him to talk to, but they hadn't shared a lot. Not like with her closest friends. If the kidnapper's motive was to upset Erin or make things difficult for her, there were much more direct ways to do so.

Terry cracked open the door to look at her, then pushed the door open the rest of the way. "What are you still doing up? You're not waiting for me, are you?"

"No… just thinking."

"Do you need anything? You should be getting to sleep so you can get up in the morning."

Erin sighed. "I know. I just can't stop worrying."

"About Joshua?"

"Of course."

"There isn't anything you can do. I know you would like to, but there are only so many avenues to investigate. The police department is looking into them. Beaver and the sheriff are getting the FBI involved as well, in case it was something to do with Mickey, so there will be more manpower on the case. Everyone is doing everything they can. It isn't up to you."

"But I can't *not* be worried about it. Joshua is my friend. My friend's son. And Mary Lou thinks that I had something to do with his disappearance. Or that I'm making it worse. Those fortune cookies… if someone wanted to implicate me in all of this…"

"They couldn't have done much better than to swap the fortunes," Terry finished. He looked at her thoughtfully. "Mary Lou knew that you were supplying the fortune cookies to the Chinese restaurant?"

"I don't know if she knew anything about it. But when she got one, she would have known. There's a note on the menu now that gluten-free fortune cookies are supplied by Auntie Clem's Bakery. And when they bring you the bill in the little tray with the cookies on the tray, there's a little tray liner that says…"

"Compliments of Auntie Clem's Bakery," Terry suggested.

"Something like that, yeah. So… she would have known when she got it that it came from the bakery."

"And then she opens it and sees a message that seems like it was intended just for her."

"Yeah. She was… not very happy."

"No," Terry agreed. "I got that."

Erin was up early as usual the next morning, assuming that the police would be done with the bakery and she would be able to reopen at the regular time. She looked at her phone and found that she had received a text during the night from Sheriff Wilmot.

Have finished with processing the bakery. All yours.

That was considerate of him. Erin didn't have to wonder about whether she would be able to open or not.

But they would have extra cleanup and prep to do since they hadn't been able to run through their usual closing procedure the day before. Erin was going to have to make some adjustments to have the display case filled in the morning and everything ready to go. Less variety than usual. Bigger batches. Maybe some promotional price would attract people's attention and distract them from the fact that the display was plainer than usual. She hadn't had a chance to cash out, so she would have to go with the running totals from the day before and hope that there wouldn't be any large discrepancies. And cleanup. There would be a lot of cleanup, with pans and bowls sitting out for hours with the remnants of batters and doughs drying to them. Ugh.

There was nothing she could do about that.

When Erin got to her kitchen, she was surprised to see that Vic's light was already on. Vic didn't usually get up until some time after Erin, savoring those last few minutes of sleep.

Erin started the kettle and put a couple of slices of bread in the toaster. Before the kettle started whistling, Vic let herself in the back door.

"Morning," she greeted, and smothered a yawn. She was dressed for work, not still in her pajamas as Erin had expected.

"Hi. I'm surprised to see you up so early!"

"I knew you would be worrying," Vic said with a shrug. "You're going to be trying to figure out how to get everything done before opening this morning when we didn't get a chance to close properly last night."

Erin laughed. "Yup. Exactly right."

"So I figured I'd be ready for work as soon as you were, so we can get in a few minutes earlier than usual if we have to."

"You're the best, Vic."

Vic shrugged modestly. "I know."

They both laughed. They moved around each other in the kitchen, used to the routines and anticipating each other's movements. Orange Blossom wound around Erin's legs, seeming like he was trying to trip her up. Even after she fed him, he still wanted attention. Marshmallow was more sedate, watching the morning preparations. K9 hadn't yet put in an appearance. Though he still slept in his crate, Terry usually left it open now. There had been too many close calls. They both wanted K9 to be free in case someone tried to break in.

"How's Nilla?" Erin asked, thinking of the new fluffy white dog that Vic had ended up taking in after Beryl's death.

"Well, you know. Still acting out a little. He hasn't totally destroyed the apartment, but he's not as well-behaved as K9."

"I figured Willie would have him whipped into shape in no time."

"Willie..." Vic's voice was amused, "...is a pushover!"

Erin gasped dramatically. "No! Willie?"

"He spoils Nilla. Feeds him at the table. Tells me not to get after him. Lets him sleep on the bed."

"On the bed?" Erin repeated. She shook her head. "Here I always thought Willie was tough. Disciplined."

"Willie is a puffball. With that dog, anyway."

"Well. I'll have to have a talk with him about how to properly train an animal," Erin said loftily.

Then she yipped as Orange Blossom dug his claws into her leg, trying to get her attention.

"Ouch! Stop that, Blossom. You're supposed to be demonstrating how well-behaved you are."

CHAPTER 25

Erin walked into the kitchen, expecting to find it in a complete mess. She knew that the police weren't required to put things to rights after a search, and she knew how much work there normally was to do at the end of the day. Even with a plan in place and arriving earlier than usual, she was still not looking forward to all of the extra work they would have to do.

At first, she thought they must have taken a bunch of her pans and equipment with them as evidence because the counters were clear. She and Vic looked at each other and then started to explore the kitchen to see what was missing. If they had seized her pans, it would make it even harder to reopen in one day. They'd need to go into the city to get all of the replacements she needed.

But a closer inspection revealed that most items were put away in their appropriate slots or drawers. There were a few muffin or loaf pans in the sinks, soaking in water that was now cold, but most of the cleanup they'd been unable to do the evening before had been done.

"Who did this?" Vic demanded, looking around. "Did any of the employees come in last night after they were gone to fix everything up?"

"I don't know." Erin pulled out her phone to look for text messages or emails that she might have missed. "No one said anything!"

She ducked into her office and looked around. There were no papers scattered around, no drawers left standing open. Even the mug was gone from beside her computer and had apparently been washed and put away.

Erin put in her earbuds as she and Vic started with their morning preparations, so she could place calls with her hands free. She called Sheriff Wilmot's number, planning to leave a voicemail message on his office phone. But it clicked through, and she heard him live on the other end, voice tired and a little clipped.

"Sheriff's."

"Sheriff Wilmot? It's Erin Price."

"Oh, is it that time already?" A pause as he looked at his computer or phone to verify. "I guess it is. I'm just finishing off here and then I'm going to knock off for a few hours. Everything in order there?"

"Yes!" Erin looked around the kitchen, shaking her head. "Did you do all of this? I was so shocked to find everything put away!"

"I helped. Mostly it was Stayner."

"Stayner?" Erin couldn't keep the disbelief out of her voice. She'd always butted heads with Stayner, right from the start. She found him impatient and overbearing. Someone who made assumptions too quickly, was egotistical and didn't have the discernment that he needed to be a really good cop. "He was the one who cleaned up?"

She could see him tearing the place apart, pulling every dish and bowl and mixing spoon out to see if she had anything hidden, but she couldn't see him taking the time to wash all of the dirty bowls and pans and to find their proper places.

"His momma must have raised him right," Wilmot said. "No way he was going to leave your kitchen in a mess."

"Well, please tell him thank you for me. And I'll bake him something nice."

"Will do," the sheriff agreed. "But before you go, Miss Price..."

"Oh." Erin had been about to hang up. She stopped herself. "Yes...?"

"We seized the remainder of the package of fortunes for examination."

"Oh. Well, okay. That's fine." Erin supposed it made sense for him to take some kind of evidence. The fortunes didn't prove anything, except that the fortune Mary Lou had received was not one of the ones Erin had printed. So that was a good thing. It would help convince the police department that Erin hadn't had anything to do with the fortune in Mary Lou's cookie. Even if Mary Lou herself wouldn't believe it.

"What can you tell me about the fortunes you had printed? Where did they come from?"

"We looked for some online. We presented them to the employees, and had everyone vote on them and make suggestions of their own. Eventually, we pared it down to twenty that we liked, and we had the Quiki print them on little slips of paper."

It had been a fun exercise. Erin and Vic had enjoyed going through the suggestions and tallying everything up. In the end, she thought they had ended up with a really good pool of fortunes. They would last for a long time, but when they ran out, they could refresh them, adding some new ones in. People who ate at the Chinese restaurant wouldn't always get the same ones but would see some new fortunes every now and then and stay interested.

"Did you make any changes to the order after you put it in initially?"

Erin frowned to herself as she mixed the batter. Why would she do that? She shook her head. "No. I didn't make any changes. I just gave them the instructions and they let me know when they were ready to be picked up."

"Did you check the order when you picked it up?"

"Yeah."

"How did you check it?"

"Well… I just looked through a few of the fortunes. Made sure that they had printed clearly and weren't cut off."

"How many is a few?"

"A few?"

"You said you checked a few. How many? Two? A dozen? More?"

"I'm not sure. Maybe…three to five. I just pulled a few out, looked at them, and put them back in the bag for later, when we would put them into the cookies."

"And did you check them as you were making the cookies? For quality control?"

"No. I probably looked at a few of them, I don't remember. But not… I wasn't checking each one to make sure that it was perfect." Erin dumped some frozen blueberries into the batter and stirred them gently before starting to scoop batter into cupcake wrappers. "Sheriff… it wasn't really that technical. Everything looked fine. We made the cookies. We delivered them to the restaurant. It wasn't a big thing. I mean, it was a big order, but it wasn't like… it was the moon landing."

"The problem is… Mary Lou's wasn't the only fortune that was… odd."

"Oh." Erin leaned against the counter to steady herself. She pulled her stool closer and sat down. She left the muffins alone for a moment, giving her full attention to the phone. "There were others? Who got them?"

"We opened a number of the cookies at the restaurant and found a few that were strange. Fortunes that could have been referring to Joshua Cox's disappearance. We went through the fortunes remaining in the bag, and a number of them were also… wrong."

CHAPTER 26

Erin's head spun "That doesn't make any sense. It had to be someone at the restaurant. No one here would have swapped them."

"Apparently, someone did."

She thought about her employees. Who could have done such a thing? She couldn't think of how anyone would have had the nerve to go into Auntie Clem's and tamper with the fortunes. Had Erin been there while it had happened? How long would something like that take? Had she been out at the front, serving customers while one of her employees excused herself to the kitchen and added the wrong fortunes to the bag Erin had printed?

"No one here would have any reason to do something like that. It must be some kind of mistake."

"We are still investigating."

"I can't understand it. No one here had anything against Joshua." Erin turned and looked at Vic, who was trying to look as though she wasn't listening in on the conversation, and was just putting bread dough into loaf pans as usual. "Vic, no one had any reason to do anything that would hurt Joshua. Or Mary Lou. Right?"

Vic shook her head. "Not that I can think of. But if that's what happened…"

"I don't think that could be what happened. I just can't even picture it. The fortunes were stored in my office. No one went in there."

"Someone could have," Sheriff Wilmot countered, his voice sounding far away. Erin put the phone back up to her ear.

"I would have noticed if someone had been in there."

"Would you? If Miss Victoria had been in there, for example?"

Erin glanced over at Vic. "Well… no."

"And you've never sent an employee in there to get something for you? Or had them stow their valuables in there?"

It was the regular landing pad for purses or backpacks. Out of the kitchen, behind closed doors. Not that it was particularly secure. If people had started to notice things disappearing from their bags, Erin would have locked the door or found a better way to secure them. As it was, everyone just dumped their bags there and pulled the door closed. It kept personal items out of the kitchen. The only people who had access to them were other employees, so it had never been an issue.

"Well… yeah, it's where we put our purses."

"So any employee could have been in there and it wouldn't have seemed out of place."

"At the beginning or end of her shift, yes. But not in the middle of the day."

"An employee would never access her purse in the middle of the day to check her phone or get out... sanitary items?"

"Well..." Of course they would have.

"We don't know what time this substitution took place. I'd like you to think about whether you can narrow the timeframe down. And whether everybody in your shop had access during that time."

"Just the employees."

"Right. I didn't mean the customers. I just want to know if we can eliminate anyone."

Erin sighed unhappily. "Okay. I'll think it over. Thanks."

Erin hung up her phone and looked at Vic. "It couldn't be any of our employees. They've all been just fine… there haven't been any other problems."

"Maybe when they investigate further, they'll find out something that eliminates them. But until then… we're going to have to be more careful."

Erin started making a list in her head of each employee and whether they had a motive to hurt Joshua.

Or Mary Lou.

Or Erin.

~

Most of the part-time workers at Auntie Clem's Bakery were students. They were fine with just working when they could and not earning a living wage. Most of them were still at home, so their major expenses were covered. They earned what they could to pay for clothes or classes and were happy for the experience. They had stepped up when Erin and Vic had gone on a cruise to Alaska. And when they had judged the cooking contest in Whitewater.

Certainly, none of them had any reason to want to hurt Erin. She paid them. It was because of her that they had been able to find work in Bald Eagle Falls. She and Vic couldn't think of any problem they might have with Joshua, but they didn't know the school politics, so they asked Bella in to pick her brain. Bella was the one who had referred the majority of them in the first place, so she knew them better.

She arrived during the quiet period in the afternoon, when they would be able to talk without being overheard. Bella put on her apron and helped tidy up and put in the afternoon baking so that it wouldn't be obvious that she was only there to talk about the case. And because Bella always helped out. That's what the employees at Auntie Clem's were like. They were like family.

Bella had already heard the basics about the fortune that Mary Lou had found in her fortune cookie, as had everyone else in town. Erin and Vic filled her in on the sheriff's suggestion that the fortunes had not been swapped at the restaurant, but in Erin's office.

Bella shook her head, her big blonde curls bouncing around her face. Her eyes were big and round. "Somebody who worked here? No one would do that!"

"That's what I thought too," Erin agreed. "But… if it was someone who worked here, we need to figure out who it was, or eliminate them, so that the police department doesn't spend all of their time looking into who had access here. That would be a waste and… we don't know how much time Joshua might have."

Bella's blue eyes brimmed with tears. "I can't believe this is happening. I feel so bad for Joshua. I want to find him and bring him home safe. So badly."

"Yeah. We all do. Right now… this is all we can do. Try to help the police out so that they can put their resources into the right places. Not tracking down who at Auntie Clem's could have tampered with those fortunes."

"We don't even know if the fortunes had anything to do with Joshua," Vic pointed out. "It sounds like they're talking about Joshua, but what if they're not? Or what if it is just someone who wants attention, and they're just pretending that it has something to do with Josh? Anybody could have added a few extra fortunes in there, just to see what would happen."

"A prank," Erin said.

"Yes. It could be."

"That's what they said about the note that was left for Mary Lou too. But we know it wasn't a prank. This is serious. We have to assume that the fortunes are serious too. That they are a real clue to… something."

"What did Mary Lou's say?" Bella asked. "I've heard a lot of different stories." She wrinkled her nose. "Some of them pretty nasty."

"It said… that she was never going to find him."

Bella's face was pale. "Man. Talk about cruel. I can't imagine anyone doing that. Especially anyone at Auntie Clem's."

"Everybody has been so good here," Erin said. "I feel guilty in even looking at anyone and asking the question. Is there anyone who… might have had a problem with Joshua at school?"

Bella shrugged. "I always liked the Cox boys, Josh especially. Even Campbell was nice to me, though."

"Even Campbell?" Vic repeated.

"Well, he was kind of a jock, you know? Involved in all of the teams? But I never got any grief from him." Bella ducked her head. "He was never one of the ones who would… make fun of me for my weight or anything like that. And Josh wasn't so big on sports, he was more… bookish. More my speed, I guess. We were never that close, but I knew who he was, and he was always nice."

"Maybe he wasn't nice to everyone?" Erin suggested. "Was there anyone he didn't get along with? Or maybe… an ex-girlfriend who might have a beef with him. Anything like that. Maybe a rival. Someone trying to get higher marks than him in school. I know it sounds stupid, but sometimes people do get upset about the littlest things."

Bella pressed her lips together, thinking. She sighed. "We weren't in many classes together. He did good, but I don't remember him competing for top marks."

"And no girlfriend?" Vic prompted.

"No. I don't know if he went out with anyone. There's kind of a core group of kids at the school who date… but Joshua wasn't one of them. Might have taken a girl out for ice cream one day, but… no serious relationships that I know about."

"Someone who wanted to be a girlfriend?" Erin suggested.

"Like a stalker?" Bella asked.

Vic gave Erin a sharp look.

"No. None that I know about," Bella admitted. "I guess I'm not much help here. But Joshua was really pretty quiet. I think he got along good with everyone. I can't think of what anyone would have against him."

"Then maybe he's not the one," Erin said. "Maybe it's Mary Lou." She looked at Vic and Bella, seeking their input.

"Mary Lou." Bella rubbed her face, looking uncomfortable. "I gotta say… I've always been a little bit scared of her."

Erin laughed. "Yeah, I can see that."

"Whenever I talk to her, I feel like she's remembering back when I was four or five and wet my pants at a town picnic. Like she still can't believe that I would have the nerve…"

Vic giggled. Bella glared at her.

"It wasn't supposed to be funny."

"No… but it kind of is. I know exactly the expression you're talking about."

"What does she have on you? I bet you never peed your pants at the picnic."

"Uh… there's the whole transgender thing," Vic pointed out. "I don't suppose you've ever heard her lecture on how being trans is an offense to God."

"Oh, yeah." Bella's face flushed pink. "I didn't even think of that. I'm sorry—I forget sometimes."

Vic grinned. "That suits me just fine. I don't need to be the transgender girl who works at the bakery. I'd rather just be a girl who works at the bakery."

Bella nodded shyly.

"So, Mary Lou," Erin said, trying to bring them back on point. "Do you think it's someone she's hurt or offended? I hate to say it, but I can see her making somebody mad more than Joshua. You don't think that someone is doing this to get back at her, do you?"

"I don't know," Bella said. "I don't think anyone would go from Mary Lou giving her that look to deciding to kidnap Joshua. Especially not anyone at Auntie Clem's."

Erin had to admit that was true. She had seen a lot of things since she had come to Bald Eagle Falls, but as a motive for kidnapping, that sounded pretty weak. Especially someone who had kept Joshua for several days now. Kidnapping was something that needed lots of planning, energy, and follow up. Unless the kidnapper had already gone further than kidnapping and no longer had anyone to look after. Erin didn't want to think about that. Whoever had taken Joshua had to be taking care of him, looking after his daily needs.

"If someone took Joshua… then where is he?" Erin mused. "He would have to be somewhere close by, or someone would notice the kidnapper following a different routine. Right? Everyone knows now about Joshua being missing, and wouldn't someone notice if they were going out of town every day or disappearing for long periods…?"

Vic considered this, nodding. "I guess… but there are lots of places close by that you could keep someone. Old farms, moonshine shacks, caves, mines…"

Erin tried to focus on Bella's face rather than thinking of her own experiences. Bella had been kidnapped and held in a mine, so she knew what that was like, even if it had only been for less than a day. Bella gave a little nod, her expression not changing, but Erin thought she looked a little green.

"Yeah. I guess. Maybe we should ask, though. Whether anyone has gone on vacation or been taking time off work that they normally wouldn't…"

Vic looked in Erin's direction, and she knew that Vic would also be going over their staff list in her head. Was there anyone who had stopped taking shifts recently? Or changed which shifts she was taking. Erin didn't come up with anyone, and Vic must not have either, because she didn't offer anyone.

"I guess we can't exactly ask Mary Lou if she had a problem with anyone in town," Bella said.

"I'm sure the police will have asked her whether she has any enemies. Or whether Joshua does." Erin's chest hurt as she said it. If Mary Lou had given a list of enemies to the police, had Erin headed the list?

CHAPTER 27

It had been a long day. Erin had hoped to get somewhere in her discussion with Vic and Bella. She had hoped that they could identify the kidnapper's motive and point the police department in the right direction, not just to tell them that they were looking in the wrong direction. Erin was sure it could not have been any of her employees, even though the changed fortunes had been found in the bag that she had there. There had to be some other explanation.

As far as they could tell, none of the part-time employees would have any reason to do something to hurt Joshua. And it wasn't for gain since there had been no ransom note. Erin didn't want to believe that something had happened to Joshua to prevent the kidnapper from making a ransom demand.

There was, of course, still Charley. She was Erin's partner in the bakery, and she put in her time too. She had worked several shifts around the right time. It would have been perfectly natural for her to put her purse and other personal items in Erin's office, just like any of the other employees. And if she had been caught going through the fortunes or files or computer in Erin's office, she might be accused of being snoopy, but she had the right to look at any of the financial or electronic records for Auntie Clem's.

But Erin couldn't think of any reason Charley would have for wanting to hurt Joshua or Mary Lou. Or Erin. They were sisters and partners in Auntie Clem's Bakery. It would make no sense for Charley to do anything to jeopardize their relationship. Charley might not get along with Mary Lou. They were both a little prickly and hard to get close to. But Erin hadn't noticed any major issues between the two of them. And Erin couldn't think of whether Charley and Joshua had even met.

She had some fresh, warm cookies that she had made for Stayner. Despite all that she'd had to do that day, she had still held back one tray of cookies and had put it in the oven just before closing so that they would be cooled just enough to transport when she was finished. Willie was picking Vic up, but Erin declined a ride.

"I'm just going to walk over to the police department. I'll give these to Officer Stayner and see whether they've made any progress today."

"We can wait for you," Vic offered.

"No. I don't know how long I'll be. I'll just walk home after."

"Not if it's dark. If it's dark, you call me, okay?"

Erin nodded. It wouldn't be dark for a couple more hours, and she wouldn't be that long. "Sure. Thanks."

"We can drop you at the police department on the way home."

"I'm just going to walk," Erin insisted.

Vic shrugged, giving in. "Guess it won't hurt you to walk a couple of blocks."

Erin waved goodbye and headed out. She was glad for the fresh air and exercise after being at the bakery all day. She didn't get enough exercise, even though she was on her feet all day at the bakery, back and forth between the kitchen and the front counter. It felt good to stretch her legs and feel the sun on her skin.

The police department was tucked away into a suite of offices at the town hall; it didn't have its own building like they did in Whitewater Junction. Erin had not liked the police station at Whitewater, with its glass walls that made her feel like she was in an aquarium.

Clara Jones was still on reception at the front desk. She would be going home before too long. She gave Erin a measuring look over the top of her rectangular glasses. She pushed back a few strands of reddish, thinning hair. Clara had allowed Erin too many liberties in the office previously and had been reprimanded, so she wasn't about to let Erin just waltz in because she had a box of cookies.

"How may I help you, Miss Price?" she asked crisply.

"I wondered if Officer Stayner is in." Erin displayed the cookie box. "I have something for him."

Clara looked at Erin for a minute before moving. Then she pressed a few keys on her phone and picked up the receiver. "Erin Price here to see you."

Erin took a half-step toward the office. Previously Terry's dedicated office, it was now shared between the two of them. She raised her brows at Clara.

"Just wait here until he's ready for you," Clara said as she firmly placed the receiver back in the cradle.

Erin stayed where she was, looking around the reception area. It wasn't like a doctor's office with inspirational posters or artwork, and magazines to read. There were a couple of hard plastic chairs for visitors, but they were stacked with paper files. Erin didn't want to stare at Clara, but there wasn't really anything else for her to do while she was waiting.

It wasn't long before Stayner came out to see Erin. A young officer, well-built, intimidating when he wanted to be.

"Miss Price. If you'll follow me."

Erin had been expecting to just hand over the cookies and thank him, but she obediently followed him back to the office. He sat at his desk—Terry's desk—and motioned her into the visitor chair.

Erin sat down. She held up the box of cookies. "I brought you some cookies. I wanted to thank you for everything. For the way that you cleaned everything up at Auntie Clem's. That was so considerate of you."

He looked at the box. "I'm sure you know that law enforcement officers can't take anything that might be perceived as a bribe."

"A bribe?" Erin looked down at it. "It's just cookies. I'm not asking you to do something, I'm thanking you for what you've already done."

"You can understand how it looks."

"It's not a bribe. I bring muffins and other treats to the police department all the time."

"But that's to the whole department, and not for one particular thing. This is different."

Erin thought it through. "Well, I can just give it to the police department, then. To everyone. Because you guys are always working so hard."

He nodded. He still didn't take the box from her.

"I'll give it to Clara on the way out."

"Yes, that would be good," Stayner agreed stiffly.

"They're still warm. You should grab one while they're still all melty."

He wiped his mouth. "I will." He allowed a tiny smile, making his face suddenly boyish instead of so stiff. He quickly wiped the expression from his face. Erin put her hands on the arms of her chair to push herself to standing.

"I wanted to talk to you about the fortunes," Stayner said, making a motion for her to stay where she was.

"Oh. I already talked to Sheriff Wilmot about them. He told me that they were substituted at the bakery. I've been talking to Vic, but neither of us can figure out why any employee would do that, or who could have a motive to do something to hurt Joshua or Mary Lou. It just doesn't make any sense."

"Actually…"

Erin's blood turned icy in her veins. She didn't want him to tell her that they had a suspect. They thought one of her employees had cold-bloodedly kidnapped Joshua Cox. She couldn't even wrap her brain around the idea. Who would do anything to hurt Joshua?

Stayner leaned forward slightly. His eyes were intense, drilling into her. "Our investigation has shown that the fortunes were substituted even before they reached the bakery."

"What?" Erin stared at him. "How could that be?"

"Because you changed your order at the printer. You asked them to add some additional fortunes."

"*I* did?" Erin felt the blood drain from her face. She was glad she was already sitting down. "I didn't do that."

"That's what Matt Chatman at the Quiki says. You called in with changes after you had sent in the original order."

"No. I didn't do that. Is he sure it was me?"

Erin knew that he couldn't be sure because it hadn't been her.

Someone had called the Quiki and told them that she wanted different fortunes? She should have checked them when she got the order. She should have checked all of the fortunes, not just a few of them and made sure that they all said what they were supposed to. But that would have been a huge job. How was she to know that they had been changed to something other than what she had ordered?

"He *thought* it was," Stayner admitted. "He said it sounded like you. More or less."

"Well, he's mistaken. It wasn't me. I don't know who would have done that. Aren't there phone records? Can't you look back to see who it was?"

"We will make a request for your phone records and for his. If you could make them available without a warrant, things would go faster."

And time was of the essence in finding Joshua. She didn't know how long he had left.

If he were still okay.

Joshua didn't want to wake up. His mother was shaking his arm hard, but he didn't want to get up for school. He had been up too late, or he had drunk too much. There was no way he would be able to get out of bed and attend to his work.

"Joshua."

"Mmm. No."

"Wake up. Come on, get up!"

"Can't."

The whisper was harsh in his ear. "Wake up now. Or you're not going to be happy with the consequences."

Joshua shifted. It was not his mom. She might warn him about consequences, but that whisper was from somewhere else. Mary Lou would use her voice. She wouldn't care if anyone overheard her. If she had to correct the boys and someone overheard her getting after one of them, it was an embarrassment for them, not for her.

The whisper sent an icicle snaking up his spine. He tried to rub his eyes and open them, but he couldn't move his hands. His eyes were sticky and gritty and didn't want to open. He really needed to sleep more. But the back of his brain told him he was in danger. He needed to wake up and be aware of his surroundings.

Something was wrong.

He rubbed his right eye against his shoulder, and then his left, and blinked hard, trying to clear both of them. But he still couldn't see anything. Just darkness around him, blurry and amorphous. He couldn't identify anything.

"Mom?"

"I'm not your mother."

Josh blinked and tried to moisten his lips, but his mouth was too dry. He looked around for a glass of water, but he couldn't see one. He couldn't see anything.

"What happened?"

"No more questions."

It started to seep back. The long periods spent in the dark, the world looking the same whether he had his eyes open or closed. The dark, whispering figure. The hopelessness of his situation. If someone were going to pay a ransom or find him, they would have done so by now. It had been too long. He and his chances of survival were fading away.

"Do you have food?" he asked finally. It was a question but, hopefully, the shadow wouldn't put it in the same category as questions about what had happened to him or what was going to happen.

The shadow didn't move for a while. Then there was a sigh. "I will get you something. What do you want?"

For a moment, Joshua couldn't speak. He could ask for whatever he wanted? His head filled with all the wonderful foods he missed, his favorite foods as a child, the specials at the restaurants in Bald Eagle Falls and in the city. Even the little packaged cakes and cookies sold at the convenience store that Mary Lou complained had probably been sitting on the shelf for twenty years.

If he asked for something too difficult, his captor would say no, and maybe he wouldn't get anything. If he just said 'anything,' he might get popcorn or chips, something salty that would make him even more dehydrated than he already was and would burn the raw sores on his lips and mouth.

"That soup," he said in a hoarse voice that sounded too quiet to be his own. "That was really good."

"The soup? You want more soup?"

"Yes."

He didn't know if he dared to ask for water too, or if that would just push his captor over the edge. He couldn't risk it. The soup had a lot of water in it, and that would have to do. He could live with that.

At least, he hoped so.

CHAPTER 28

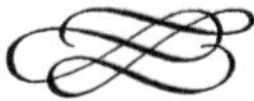

Erin wondered how long it would take Mary Lou to get word that it was Erin who had, allegedly, made the call to the Quiki to get the fortunes for the cookies changed.

She kind of wished that crimes could be solved as quickly as gossip was spread. But if anyone knew who had taken Joshua, they weren't talking. Not to the police. This time, there was no Peter to innocently spread clues to Erin to allow her to solve the case.

Thinking about Peter, she realized that it had been a few days since she had dropped the baking off for Mrs. Foster and she hadn't heard anything back. Not a thank you from Mrs. Foster. No word that she'd had the baby. Nothing at all.

She'd expected at least a thank you, even if Mrs. Foster still wasn't happy with her. It was the Tennessee way. Erin would have to go by there later to check in and make sure everything was all right. She knew how fast Peter would eat through the baking; it wouldn't hurt to take over another loaf of bread and some of the cheese pretzels he liked.

Terry was at home when she got there, awake and watching through the window for her. He opened the door as she walked up the steps to let her in. She was greeted by an enthusiastic caterwauling and Marshmallow frisking around the house like he'd been into the ginseng. Terry shook his head at the animals. K9 was, as usual, sitting politely beside Terry, though Erin thought that from the way he was watching the other animals, he might have been wishing that he could run and play a little too. Maybe he needed to have a little more off-duty time than he had had recently. With their concerns about intruders, he was on guard even when Erin and Terry were both home.

"You shouldn't have walked alone," Terry admonished, taking her in his arms and kissing her on top of the head.

"It's still light out. There hasn't been any trouble. I do need to walk now and then or my legs will shrivel up and fall off."

Terry rolled his eyes at this. "You say there hasn't been any trouble like we didn't just have a resident disappear. Or have you decided now that Joshua is a runaway after all?"

"No, I haven't," Erin snapped. "You know very well that he's not a runaway. He wouldn't be doing this to Mary Lou. He would have come forward when he realized how upset she was, even if he didn't want to come home."

"How would he know how upset she was?" Terry asked.

"I don't know. His friends would tell him. Campbell would. He'd see the paper or hear his name in the news. Something."

So far, it hadn't been in anything but the local weekly paper, and that hadn't even been a very good article, since the police had still been saying that there was no foul play involved at that point. There were no quotes from Mary Lou or long descriptions about how overwrought she was. It hadn't made it to the city news, let alone national. Kids disappeared every day. If there was nothing to set Joshua's disappearance apart, it wasn't news.

"Next time, call me and I'll pick you up. Or I can come over and we can walk home together. I don't know why you didn't just have Willie wait for you. He would have."

"I don't feel unsafe walking around Bald Eagle Falls," Erin said. She frowned. Should she? There had been enough trouble since she had moved there. Maybe a reasonable person would be afraid to walk through the town's streets alone. Maybe Erin had faced so many shocks that she no longer knew what was normal and reasonable.

Terry's lips pressed together.

Erin petted Orange Blossom and squeezed him, kissing his head and scratching his chin until he settled down. She reached for Marshmallow to scratch his ears, but he jumped up surprisingly high, switching directions mid-air, and took off, so graceful he made her think of a ballet dancer. Erin laughed at him.

"Well. Everyone else seems to be in fine fettle tonight." She put her purse down and stretched. "Shall we get dinner on?"

"We? Does that mean it's my night?"

Erin shrugged. "I thought we would come up with something together."

Terry seemed to cheer a little at that. Erin was surprised. She didn't think he usually liked to be roped in for the chores, especially in her special domain. Maybe they hadn't been spending enough time together lately. There had been a lot of distractions and outside concerns. And their individual health problems had caused extra stress and friction. They were both feeling somewhat better now; maybe it was time to mend fences.

"What do you feel like?" she asked, walking into the kitchen and considering what was in the cupboards and the fridge. "Soup and sandwiches? Salad? Something more substantial? How hungry are you?"

"Maybe soup, if it's something hearty."

Erin nodded. She opened the big pantry cupboard and looked at the larger cans of soup. There were some chunky soups, some chili, and of course, they could always use one of the lighter soups as a base and add some potatoes, meat, or vegetables to it.

"Mmm… chicken and dumpling?" she suggested.

"Yes!"

She seemed to have hit on a winner the first attempt. Erin smiled and pulled the can off the shelf. "You can get started on that. But if we're going to have chicken and dumplings, we're going to need biscuits."

Terry nodded in agreement. He went to get the can opener while Erin scanned the shelves for the biscuit mix. She turned on the oven and checked the instructions on the side of the box while Terry got out a pot for the soup.

"I can't believe that you use biscuit mix." Terry chuckled.

"I should make gluten-free biscuits from scratch?"

"Of course."

"I've been baking all day. For supper, we get a boxed mix."

"It's fine with me. Just don't let any of your customers see you."

"I think most of them know that I'm not gluten-free at home. And I've never said that I don't use mixes. At the bakery, no. But at home..." She shrugged. "I want to relax at the end of the day."

"We could just defrost some rolls from the freezer. That would be simpler."

"No. For chicken and dumplings, we have to have baking powder biscuits."

Terry was smiling. "Okay, then," he agreed. He dumped the contents of the big can into a pot and set it on the stove. "What else do you want me to do?"

"Maybe some salad," Erin suggested. She knew she needed to watch her weight, and chicken and dumplings with baking powder biscuits weren't exactly low-cal. She'd better be an adult and eat her veggies too.

"Did you hear from the police department about the fortunes?" Erin started to form the biscuits and set them on the pan. "The latest, I mean?" She felt a knot settle in her stomach, taking away the feeling of lightness and well-being that she'd been feeling since they started making dinner together.

Terry looked at her as he ripped up lettuce at the table. "The latest? Was there something today?"

"Yeah. I found out from Stayner when I dropped the cookies off. No one tampered with the fortune cookies at the restaurant or with the bag of fortunes at Auntie Clem's bakery."

"Well, that's good news." He paused, then looked up at her. "What does that leave?"

"They think I called the Quiki and changed the order."

He frowned, brows drawing close together. "They think that you ordered different fortunes than you did?"

"Yeah."

"Why would you do that?"

"I guess I'm an evil genius. Or just evil. Decided Mary Lou wasn't suffering enough and wanted to give the knife an extra twist."

"Maybe if someone didn't know you. No one who knows you would ever think that."

"Thanks. I hope not."

He reached for a tomato and started to dice it. The knife was sharp and his movements were slow. She could tell that he was thinking through all of the implications and figuring out what this new information told them.

"You just got those fortunes. When did you start putting them into the cookies?"

"Just on Wednesday."

"After Josh went missing."

"Right."

"But when did you get the fortunes printed?"

"Saturday. When I—" Erin cut herself off. "Before Joshua disappeared," she realized.

"So you supposedly had fortunes printed before Josh disappeared saying that he would never be found."

Erin put the biscuits in the oven and turned on the element under the soup. She gave it a stir.

"So it wasn't just a spur of the moment thing," she said quietly. "It was planned ahead. Taking Josh, putting new fortunes into the cookies. Implicating me. It was all thought out ahead of time. There wasn't anything spontaneous or off-the-cuff about it."

"No. Couldn't have been."

"But why? Why would anyone do this?"

"The typical motive for kidnapping, if not for the kidnapper's own… recreation… is greed or coercion… but the kidnapper hasn't asked for anything."

"Revenge?" Erin asked, the knot in her stomach tightening even more. How was she even going to eat her chicken and dumplings? "It isn't like the kidnapper hasn't communicated at all. He hasn't asked for anything, but… he left the note for Mary Lou, pointing the finger at me. And he arranged for the fortunes to be printed saying that we would never find Joshua. That's more like… he's trying to get back at Mary Lou or me… turn us against each other, make us feel worse."

Terry sighed. "I need to talk to the sheriff."

"Wait until after dinner?"

Terry nodded. "Yes. Of course. There's plenty of time after dinner to discuss it."

"I was really happy at first, realizing that the fortunes weren't tampered with by someone at the bakery. But… all of this just makes me feel worse. I'm still glad it wasn't someone that works for me. But it's personal. I just don't know which of us it is aimed against."

CHAPTER 29

Erin had arranged to take the day off at Auntie Clem's so she could get some other things done. She stopped in anyway at the quiet part of the morning, arriving through the front door like a customer and checking to make sure everything was going smoothly.

"No problems," Bella offered cheerfully, "other than the occasional misshapen loaf. Business has been brisk today."

Probably because of the rumors about Erin being involved with Joshua's disappearance. The findings about the fortunes being printed wrong probably just ramped up speculation more. Business always improved at Auntie Clem's when a major crime was committed. She could almost count on it as a marketing technique if things ever slowed down too much. Commit a crime, or start gossip about a crime being committed, and everybody would start coming around to find out the details.

"What can we get for you today?" Gwen asked cheekily. "There's a sale on banana bread."

Erin smiled. "I want to grab a few things for the Fosters, actually." She indicated the various baked goods that she thought she should take, and Vic put them into a box, which would be easier for her to take to the door than multiple bags, which might end up crushing the goodies.

"Thank you. Give me a call if anything comes up," Erin advised.

They agreed, but Erin wasn't expecting there to be any trouble. It wasn't like Mary Lou would be coming in with another fortune cookie.

But that made Erin think about the Chinese restaurant. They still had a large supply of cookies, and there was no way to know how many of them contained fortunes designed to upset people. They would have to completely redo the order. Get new fortunes printed, mix up new batches of dough, and start baking and folding all over again. It had been a big job the first time. It would go faster the second time, but she still wasn't looking forward to it. They would all be thinking about Joshua and whether he were going to be okay.

With every day that passed, it became less and less likely that they would find him well and safe.

But miracles happened. There had been that girl in Utah. And there had been other cases. Sometimes girls escaped after years of being held prisoner in basements or back yards.

Girls, Erin realized, not boys. It was never boys.

"Are you okay, Erin?" Bella asked.

"Oh. Yes, I'm fine. I was just thinking…" Erin didn't finish her thought, but Bella could apparently read it in her face and voice anyway.

"Yes," she said soberly. "I'm worried too."

When Erin arrived at the Fosters' house, Peter and his sisters were playing in the yard. They were noisy, and Peter directed and bossed the girls mercilessly, taking his role as big brother very seriously.

When he saw Erin pull to the curb in front of the house, he ran over. "Miss Erin!"

"Hi, Peter. How are you?"

"Good!" He looked at the box as she picked it up to take to the door. "When do I get to come to Auntie Clem's Bakery again?"

"I don't know, sweetie. You'll have to ask your mother."

"Dad says it's nice that you're bringing food to the house so he or Mom don't have to go out to get it."

"I hope it helps. I know your mom probably isn't having a very easy time getting around these days."

"She has to rest a lot," Peter agreed. "That means she has to lay down and we're supposed to be quiet and not disturb her." He rolled his eyes and looked around at the little girls. "They are not very good at being quiet," he informed her. "It's best if we come outside."

"Yes, better to be where you can make some noise," Erin agreed. It would be difficult for them to all be inside, playing or looking for something to do that wouldn't make any noise. She remembered being in homes where one of the parents worked on shift, and how hard it was not to raise her voice or do anything that might involve banging or other noises for hours on end. It had been so easy to forget and get involved in something either by herself or with foster siblings that would end up getting out of hand. Then the foster mom would be thundering in, shouting at them to be quiet. Erin could remember that feeling of horror when she would suddenly realize what she had done and have to face the fury of an angry parent.

At least Mrs. Foster wouldn't be that way. She had always seemed like a very nice woman, patient even when Peter was in his argumentative 'lawyer mode.'

At least, Erin hoped she was as patient when she was out of the public eye.

"Is she on bed rest?" Erin asked Peter.

He looked at her, scrunching up his brows, uncertain. "She's resting."

"Is she sick? Did the doctor tell her she has to stay in bed or it will hurt the baby?"

Peter shook his head. "I don't know."

"Would you take these things into the house? Or should I ring the doorbell?"

"I'll take them in. Do you want to watch the girls for a minute…? I'm not supposed to leave them alone."

"I'll watch them," Erin agreed. She smiled at the little girls and chatted with them while Peter took the box into the house.

Peter was back again a few minutes later and, by the working of his jaw, she guessed he had helped himself to a cookie as payment for his labor.

"Is there anything your mom needs? Does she need me to pick something up or need people to help with meals…?"

"Nnno…" Peter was hesitant with his answer. "She doesn't want people doing things for her."

"It's hard to accept help sometimes. Would you tell her that if she needs anything, she should give me a call? She knows how to reach me at the bakery and, if I'm not there, my employees can give her my cell number or shoot me a text. Okay?"

Peter nodded. "Okay."

"Are you looking forward to the new baby coming?"

"Yeah. She says maybe this one will be a boy. I'd like it if she had another boy."

"That would be nice, wouldn't it? But he won't be big enough to play with you for quite a while."

"I know." Peter looked at the girls he was watching over, and toddler Traci in particular. "But I could still share boy things with him. Like trucks and Spiderman stuff that I've outgrown."

"Yes, that's right. That would be nice."

"How is your kitty?" Peter asked. "Is he okay now?"

Orange Blossom had recovered from his poisoning and didn't seem to have suffered any long-term effects. Peter had mentioned it more than once.

"Yes, he's okay now," Erin told him. "Back to yowling at me, demanding his dinner."

Peter giggled. "Is he really noisy?"

"Yes. Just ask my neighbors. They can hear him all the time."

"People complain about dogs barking."

"Yes. But not usually about cats meowing, unless they're outside cats that are… really noisy. Not inside cats!"

"I'm glad he's okay."

Erin nodded. "You don't know who made him sick, do you?" she asked tentatively. She knew that she shouldn't be. Mrs. Foster had made it clear that she didn't want Erin involving Peter in any of her investigations, even if he offered something. She should just say goodbye to Peter and continue on with her other errands.

"I don't know…" Peter trailed off. "Maybe one of the guys that was being the Grinch."

"One of the boys involved in the burglaries?"

He nodded.

"But you don't know for sure. You don't know who it would have been."

"No. I don't talk to the big boys."

"And no one at school ever said who it was."

Peter shrugged. "They say lots of different things. You can't tell which ones are true, though."

"So is there someone… that you think might have been involved in making Orange Blossom sick?"

"No. I just think… it must have been one of them because they're the ones who wanted you to stop. So if you were taking care of your cat, maybe you wouldn't keep looking for them." He shrugged. "But I don't know who it was."

Erin suppressed a shudder. She hated to think of someone getting into her house or getting some contaminated food into her house that Orange Blossom had eaten. She had a burglar alarm, and a policeman and K9 unit living with her. It should not have been easy to poison her cat.

She remembered the man who had walked up to her at one of the fundraising activities. A Santa beard and suit had obscured his identity, so she still didn't know who it had been. Someone she would have allowed into her home? Was he a friend, an acquaintance, or a complete stranger? Could *he* have anything to do with Joshua's disappearance?

She couldn't imagine that anyone she knew would have had anything to do with kidnapping Josh. Still, she would have said the same about the burglaries. Was it one of the boys she had served after-school snacks to at the bakery? A teacher or administrator at the school? Someone from out of town? She wasn't even sure he had been an adult. Some of the kids at the school were as tall as adults and had deep voices. There was no way to know who had been lurking behind that beard.

The motive for the burglaries had been obvious—greed. But the motive behind Joshua's disappearance and the swap of the fortunes was not anything to do with money. Not that she could tell. The kidnapping and notes seemed to be aimed to hurt.

That didn't eliminate those who had been accused or arrested in connection with the burglaries, though. They might very well have wanted to hurt Erin.

"Peter," Karen whined as she rode closer to him on her tricycle. "You're not supposed to talk to strangers."

"Miss Erin isn't a stranger," Peter said. But he shrugged at Erin. "I need to watch them."

"Of course. I'll see you later, okay?"

He looked as if he would say something else, then nodded. "Sometime," he sighed.

CHAPTER 30

Matt, the owner of the Quiki Print outlet down the street from Auntie Clem's Bakery, didn't look happy when he saw her approaching.

"Miss Price," the words burst out of him in a rush. "I am so sorry about all of this. I didn't tell the police that it was you that changed the order. I told them that I thought it was you when you called—when I got the call—but I don't know you well enough to know for sure yes or no. I told them I don't really know you, just from you coming in the day you put in the order. I never thought when you called after to say that you wanted some other fortunes added, that it might not be you. You see?"

He wiped his mouth with the back of his hand, his eyes round and worried.

"It's fine, Matt. I don't know what happened or who it was that called, but it isn't your fault. You thought it was me, and you did what you thought I wanted done."

"Yes." He nodded vigorously. "I would never have done something like that on purpose. If I wasn't sure that it was you when you called, I would have called back or emailed you to verify. It just never occurred to me."

"I understand."

"And the police…" He looked sick at the thought of her being tangled up in the police investigation. Apparently, he didn't know how many other times she had gotten cross-threaded with an investigation. "I did not mean for them to think that it was you, just that it sounded like it could have been you and I never thought to ask."

"Yes. Matt. It's okay."

"They are pulling my phone logs, to try to figure out who it was that called. I know about the time you called—that the call came in—so they should be able to figure it out, right?"

"Right. That will help. Because that call didn't come from my phone." Erin stopped for a moment and considered whether she had lain her phone down where someone else might have picked it up and used it for a minute to make a call to the Quiki. But she couldn't think of any time that day it would have been out of her sight or off of her person.

Matt nodded, looking only slightly reassured.

"Was there anything about the person who called in?" Erin asked. "Anything that might tell us who it was? Like… if they had an accent, or a cold, or their voice was different than mine in some other way?"

"I'm sure the police will believe that it was not you," Matt rushed to reassure her.

"I know. But I'd still like to know who it was. We need to find out who is doing this, not just to convince the police that it wasn't me."

"Oh." Matt thought about it. "Well… no, I can't think of anything special about the voice. It was just for a minute, you know—very short conversation. I didn't notice… that it was any different than yours." He considered it further. "Maybe… maybe the accent was different, I don't know."

He was clearly not a native English speaker, so Erin wasn't sure how good he would be at identifying different American accents.

"Different how?"

"I don't know," Matt muttered. He bit his lip and rolled his eyes to the ceiling, trying to come up with something. "You sound like… you didn't grow up here. The Bald Eagles Falls families, they all sound the same. More or less."

Erin nodded. "A Tennessee accent. And I pretty much lost mine, because I was raised up north."

"Yes. But some people, it comes and goes. It depends who they are talking to and what they are saying. If they are talking to me, less accent. If they are talking to an old friend from high school here, very strong."

"So you didn't think anything of it when I called back and talked with more of a Tennessee accent."

"Yes. I thought it was you, still."

Erin thought about that. Someone around her age and timbre. But who had grown up in Bald Eagle Falls or the surrounding area. Unfortunately, there were a lot of people who fell into that group.

"Was there anything else? Any background noise? Where did you think I was calling from?"

Matt scratched his nose. "I thought… you were maybe in your garage or in a storage unit. I just thought you had ideas of more things to add to the fortunes you asked for. And you were busy with something else, so you called instead of coming in or emailing me."

"Right."

"I am so sorry that my mistake caused anybody pain."

"I know. Me too. I'm sorry that this ended up being such a mess. I just wanted people who can't eat gluten to be able to have fortune cookies. To put some fun sayings in them so that people would enjoy them."

"What can I do? Do you think the police will be able to find who did this? Is there anything else I can do?"

"Well…" Erin shrugged. "The reason I came in here was to see if you could reprint the fortunes for me. Just the original ones this time. Because we have to remake a whole bunch more cookies."

Matt's face lit up. "That is a wonderful thing to do. Very good. And this time, free of charge. I will replace them at my cost."

"You don't need to do that. You're still putting time and materials into it."

"But I should have gotten verification the first time. I should have gotten it right. So this time, I will get it right."

Erin protested once more but, in the end, she let him do the reprint at his own cost. She had to cover her costs to replace the cookies, and that was not insignificant when she had to eat the cost of both of the ingredients and her employees' time to bake and fold the replacement cookies. The Chinese restaurant was going to get their cookies. Erin would make sure that they were right this time.

CHAPTER 31

"A woman," Erin mused as she went through her tai chi forms. "I don't know why I assumed it would be a man."

Vic was sitting on the steps up to her loft apartment. "What?"

"Oh. Just being a crazy lady and talking to myself."

"Yeah; what about?"

"The person who called in the change order to the Quiki was a woman. Someone pretending to be me. So the kidnapper is a woman. Or the kidnapper has an accomplice who is a woman. I don't know why..." She paused as she worked through a form that made her turn her back on Vic. "But I always assumed that it was a man."

"It's probably two people," Vic said. "Sometimes it's couples that do this kind of thing. Working together. The woman is emotionally abused or thinks that she has to."

"Or in some cases, she's the leader," Erin said. She remembered a couple of cases. It wasn't necessarily the men who were always the planners.

"Well, but *usually*," Vic reiterated.

"I don't know. Maybe. I pictured a man, anyway. I know Joshua isn't big, but I thought it would take a man to kidnap him. Someone big enough and strong enough."

Vic nodded.

"Not that women aren't strong," Erin said. "Or can't be big. But..."

"You assume," Vic agreed. "I thought a man too. I don't know why, after what happened with Theresa. And not just her, but some of the others we've run into since Aunt Angela died. We've both had firsthand knowledge of women committing violent crimes."

Erin paused in her tai chi, thinking about that. She turned her head and looked at Vic. "It couldn't be Theresa, right?"

They had never captured Crazy Theresa. Erin kept waiting for the news that someone had been able to track her down, or that she had been pulled over for a traffic stop. Somehow, someone had to find her and arrest her. She couldn't keep running for the rest of her life.

"No. She wouldn't come back here, it would be too dangerous."

"But she's crazy. Would she care?"

"She doesn't want to get caught. And why would she do it? Take Joshua? There's no reason to."

"Just because she's crazy." Erin shrugged.

"She still doesn't do things without a motive."

"But it doesn't have to be one that we would understand."

"Maybe she... thinks that I like Joshua. I don't know. You know she gets ideas into her head, and that she might do something that didn't make any sense to us, if it meant that she could hurt one of us or... get one of us close to her. I don't know the reason."

"She likes you." Erin pondered. "So is there any way that taking Joshua would get her closer to you?"

"He's not a rival. She wouldn't know that he was any kind of friend. The only time I've done anything with Joshua is when we went into the city looking for Campbell, and Theresa wasn't around for that. She wouldn't know that me and Josh even knew each other."

"She hates me. And Willie. Because she thinks that we've alienated you from her."

Vic turned her hands palms-up. *So?*

Erin couldn't connect it up. Kidnapping or hurting Joshua would hurt Erin, but only indirectly. And Theresa would have to know that she cared about Joshua or Mary Lou.

"And you don't think she would randomly take Josh and try to make us feel bad with the notes," Erin suggested.

"This wasn't random," Vic reminded her. "She planned this out. She knew about the fortune cookies, and she knew about you and Joshua being friends. Or you and Mary Lou."

"So it has to be someone in Bald Eagle Falls. Nobody outside of town would know about either of those things."

"Well..." Vic wobbled her hand back and forth in a 'maybe' gesture.

"Who else would know?"

"I don't know. Not specifically. But word spreads. Maybe this wasn't anything that anyone was gossiping about, so it didn't go very far. Still, people do leave town, talk to friends out of town, post stuff on social media, all that. You posted on the Auntie Clem's social media accounts about the gluten-free fortune cookies, didn't you?"

Erin's heart sank. "Yes."

"So anyone who follows you or liked those posts, they could have seen that. Or if someone shared it, one of their friends might have seen it."

"I always ask the employees if they would share stuff around when appropriate," Erin sighed. "If they think something is interesting or worth sharing."

Vic nodded. "It's sound business."

"But I didn't post about Joshua," Erin said. "I never posted about him."

"We need to go right back to the beginning."

Erin closed her eyes as she started to go through the final forms of her tai chi. "Let me just think for a few minutes. Finish this up."

Vic fell silent and let Erin finish without any further discussion. When she was done, Erin sat in the grass. It wasn't the most comfortable place to sit, but the weather was warm enough that it wasn't *that* uncomfortable.

"Back to the beginning how?" she prompted.

"We need to go over anybody who had a motive to kidnap Josh, to hurt you or Mary Lou, or to drive the two of you further apart."

Erin wanted to say that the list was pretty short. But, in fact, it wasn't nearly as short as she would like it to be. She had been involved with investigations that had hurt the organized crime clans around Bald Eagle Falls who had tried to establish business there. And the Russian mob. Anyone in those organizations could have something against her. But having fortunes printed? That didn't sound like something a mobster would do.

Then there were the people she had put in prison since arriving in Bald Eagle Falls. None of them could have done anything to Joshua directly, but there were other ways to reach out and influence people from prison. Someone could have been hired to do the job. Or it had been a favor. Or someone had just thought that it would make the person in prison—or still in jail awaiting their trial—grateful, and that was enough. It wasn't a short list. How had she accumulated so many enemies in the short time she had lived in Bald Eagle Falls?

"Are you thinking about the parents?" Vic asked.

Erin hadn't been, but she didn't need to ask who Vic was talking about. Of course it could have been the parent of someone arrested for the Grinch burglaries. That had been Erin's doing as well. Dozens of families had been affected. And most of them probably knew of Erin's friendship with Mary Lou and with Joshua.

"Oh, boy."

Vic nodded slowly. "That was very recent and people are still sore about it. I mean, things will go back to normal eventually, but it's going to take a while."

"I just keep thinking about Mrs. Foster and Mary Lou. If they could both be so angry with me because the police had to *talk* to their sons… not that they were arrested or even suspected… then how much madder are the parents of the kids who were arrested?"

"They shouldn't be." Vic asserted stubbornly. "If their kids got arrested, that's not your fault. They shouldn't have been involved in the burglaries to begin with!"

"I know… but that's not the way they feel. As far as they're concerned… it's almost like I'm the one who coerced them into a life of crime."

"Stupid. If they were my kids, I wouldn't be protecting them and giving them excuses for breaking the law and hurting other people."

Erin shrugged. "You can never tell what you would do in someone else's situation."

"I know I wouldn't condone my family members breaking the law."

Erin looked at her for a minute. Vic's brows grew closer together.

"What?"

"I was just thinking about Jeremy. And about the rest of your family being involved with the Jackson clan."

Vic's face flushed. "I wasn't talking about that."

"I know. But is it that different?"

"I don't know what Jeremy might or might not have done. If he was mixed up in something when he first came here... well, I don't know exactly what it was. And I don't want to know. He's clean now, right? He's an honest, law-abiding citizen here in Bald Eagle Falls. He's left whatever clan stuff behind."

"As far as you know."

"Yes."

"And if he's still involved in some illegal activity? Would you go to the police if you suspected something?"

"I don't know. I guess I would... probably talk to him first, find out what was going on. See if there was a way to get him back on the right track..."

Erin nodded. "And the rest of your family? What have your dad and other brothers been involved in?"

"I don't know, and I don't—"

"And you don't want to know," Erin finished. "You mean, kind of like those families whose kids were involved in the burglaries? You want them to stop, but not to have to go to prison for it."

"The school kids aren't going to get sent to prison."

"Some of them will. The ones who were old enough. Or violent enough."

Vic stared off into space. "I can see them being upset about what happened and wanting to get back at you somehow."

"Yeah. But by kidnapping Joshua? Why wouldn't they do something to hurt or scare me directly? Joshua wasn't the one who got them arrested."

CHAPTER 32

It seemed like a long time had passed. Joshua didn't know how long he had been asleep or passed out. He didn't like being awake. It was tedious and painful, and he ended up lying there for hours just waiting for something to happen. It was better if he could escape to unconsciousness as quickly as possible. He didn't have to worry about the pain and the fever. He didn't have to worry about the long periods of boredom.

"Joshua. I brought food."

Even before his captor said the magic words, Joshua's senses were coming alive, telling him that there was food in the area. Making him start to salivate like a wild animal. *Food, food, food!*

Josh sat up as well as he could and blinked his eyes, rubbing them on his shoulders, trying to wake up as quickly as possible.

The shadowy figure sat again on the edge of the bed and worked the lid off of a plastic container. As soon as the seal was broken, Joshua's stomach hurt with the smell of the chicken soup. He wanted and needed it so badly.

"Thank you," he breathed. "That smells wonderful. Thank you so much."

He tried to wipe the unsightly drool away from his mouth. But despite how dehydrated he was, the saliva continued to gush.

The shadowy figure pulled out a spoon and dipped it into the warm, fragrant broth. He brought it up to Joshua's lips. Joshua greedily slurped it. He had a hundred things he wanted to tell his captor at once. How wonderful it was, how he never needed to eat anything else, if he would just keep bringing the chicken soup. How it tasted like what his grandmother used to make with homemade noodles in it. Josh was transported back to her kitchen, always full of delightful simmering soups, baking bread, jams and preserves and pickles.

But he didn't say anything to start with, slurping the soup off of the spoon as quickly as it could be lifted to his mouth.

Eventually, the spoon started to slow. Joshua could hear it scraping the bottom of the bowl. His captor scraped up as much of the remaining liquid as he could and offered it to Joshua.

"It's so good," Joshua said. "Just like my baba used to make."

"It's not your baba's recipe," the figure hissed.

"No. I didn't mean that. I just mean… it reminds me. It's so good. It makes me think of all of those days helping her when I was little. We would go there in the fall. Mom would make Campbell and me help get all of the garden produce put up for the winter. We were good at it. And Dad too. He was always good at cooking."

"But now it's just you. You're the only one who is left of your family."

Joshua bit his scabby, dry lip. He wanted to protest that his dad and Campbell were not dead, they just weren't at home anymore. Joshua wasn't the only one left. He wasn't even the only one left in the house. His mom was there too. He had always loved her, wanted to tell her all of his successes and to hear her praise. He knew that she didn't give praise like some of the other moms did, always telling their kids that they were so smart and talented at everything. No one was talented at everything. Joshua knew that when his mother said he had done a good job of something, he really had. She didn't make stuff up or gush. The slightest word of approval from her meant that he'd done a stellar job.

"Soon, you won't have to be here anymore."

Josh cocked his head and blinked his eyes. Because he was being let go? Or because he was going to die? He was glad that his captivity was coming to an end, no matter which way it was.

He just hoped that his mom would be okay.

CHAPTER 33

The ladies' tea had been a quiet and somber affair. Usually, there was lots of visiting and laughter. The women enjoyed getting together on their day of rest to just sit and relax and have a cup of tea together and talk. They shared what had happened during the week, any gossip that hadn't yet been shared and rehashed, and expectations for the coming week. A nice way to end the week.

But with Joshua still missing, and people now believing that he really might have been kidnapped rather than just running away, people didn't want to smile or laugh too much. Mary Lou wasn't there, and they talked about her in hushed tones. All of the disasters that had befallen her family in recent years. She really didn't deserve to have something else like that.

Charley was assisting Erin. The ladies' tea was a bit early for her, but she made it when she was needed. Vic was, Erin assumed, in the city to run errands, maybe to attend the LGBT-friendly church there, or maybe she had gone to do some spelunking, or visit a mine with Willie. She hadn't said what her exact plans were, but that was generally how she spent Sundays off.

Most of the women had started to wrap it up and say their goodbyes. A couple had left already. Erin collected teacups as they were finished, wiping down the tables as she went.

The bells on the door jingled. Erin looked up to see if someone had forgotten a purse or if Terry had come to help her with clean-up. He sometimes did if he wanted to go somewhere together.

She was surprised to see Mary Lou in the doorway. The low buzz of goodbyes between the ladies who remained in the bakery ceased. Everyone was quiet, looking at Mary Lou.

She nodded and smoothed non-existent wrinkles in her pantsuit self-consciously. She forced a smile and a few hellos.

"Yes, nice to see you…" she murmured to no one in particular. She was looking toward Erin. Not directly at her, eyes kept low, but it was clear that it was Erin she was there to see.

"Hi, Mary Lou," Erin greeted warmly. "It's good to see you."

She waited for the other ladies to vacate the bakery, but they hung around as if they wanted to see what was going to happen next.

"That's it for the day," Charley said loudly. "We need to close up shop. See you on Monday. Sale on blueberry muffins." She made motions to shoo everyone out.

The women renewed their goodbyes and reluctantly left Auntie Clem's.

"Old vultures," Charley muttered as she shut the door behind them and flipped the sign over to 'closed.'

"Thanks," Erin told her.

"Yeah, no trouble. You just need to speak up. Don't be so worried about offending people."

"I have to think about that," Erin protested. "If I want to keep people's business, I need to stay in their good books."

"Not as much as you think you do," Charley said firmly. "You're the only bakery in town. If they don't want to pick up mushy bread at the grocery store or drive into the city, you're the only game in town. So stop acting like people will stop coming if you tell them it's closing time."

Erin shrugged, knowing that Charley was probably right. Erin was too much of a people-pleaser. She had grown up trying to keep her various foster parents happy, trying to read every tiny change of expression and to understand all of the unwritten rules. It hadn't always been easy to make friends at new schools and to fit in with families or cliques that had been formed years before. Charley hadn't had to worry about stuff like that. She didn't understand how precarious relationships could be.

"I'll wash up in back, you can take care of things out here," Charley offered. She grabbed the last of the teacups and trays and took them into the kitchen.

Erin turned to Mary Lou. She wanted to hug her and ask how she was doing, but Mary Lou had always been cool. Even when they were getting along, Erin wouldn't have dared hug her without a clear invitation.

"Hi."

Mary Lou looked around. She'd been in Auntie Clem's many times before. There wasn't exactly anything to comment on. "The tea went well?"

"Pretty quiet today." Erin didn't say that people were worried about Joshua and Mary Lou. She would know that without Erin having to twist the knife.

"I see. And you are doing well? Where is Victoria today?"

"In the city, I think. She goes to church there."

"When she goes to church."

"She goes pretty regularly." Erin didn't want Mary Lou judging Vic to be less of a Christian because she didn't get to church every single week like most of the Baptist ladies. Mary Lou's opinion of Vic was already low enough.

"Does she."

Mary Lou again looked like she was searching for something to talk about. What was Erin supposed to do? Ask her about Joshua? Ask her why she had come? There was no clear path for the conversation to follow.

Erin looked away from Mary Lou, out the front window of the bakery. It was a beautiful day. Clear blue sky. Before long, Terry would probably be coming to pick her up.

"I owe you an apology," Mary Lou said finally. She was a plainspoken woman and she didn't try to weasel out of it. "I shouldn't have blown up at you over the fortune cookie. It wasn't anything to do with you."

Erin shrugged. "Well, they were my cookies. You knew that."

"But you weren't the one who put it in there. I should have gotten more information before assuming that it was your fault."

Erin looked at her curiously, wondering what it was that had made Mary Lou change her mind. "I would never do anything to hurt you. And something like that... it was cruel."

"And I should have known that isn't the kind of person you are. I jumped to conclusions without thinking about what kind of a person you are or whether my conclusion was reasonable. I was hurt and I just lashed out." Mary Lou gave herself no quarter. "That was the wrong thing to do. I know better."

"You're going through a terrible time. It's understandable."

"That does not excuse it."

"Then… I accept your apology." Erin looked at Mary Lou directly. "How are you managing?"

Mary Lou shook her head. "Not well."

"The police are investigating who it was that had my order for the fortunes changed. Maybe that will lead somewhere."

"Officer Stayner told me that. But… it probably won't lead anywhere. Who knows if it was even the same person, or if it was just someone who wanted to… hurt me."

"The order was changed before Joshua disappeared."

Mary Lou's eyes widened. "What?"

"So it had to be the same person, or an accessory."

The older woman nodded slowly.

"Have they told you anything else?" Erin asked. "About their progress, I mean. Whether they have found anything. Actual evidence."

"They won't say very much to me. I don't know whether it is because parents are always suspects in their children's abductions or just because they are playing things close to the vest."

"You're not a suspect."

Mary Lou leveled a stare at her. "Of course I am. How many parents have tried to cover up violence they have done to their children by saying they were abducted?"

"But Josh isn't a two-year-old. If you had done something to him, he would have fought back." But even as Erin said it, she knew it wasn't necessarily true. There were plenty of reasons for teens to stay quiet when they were being abused. Domestic violence victims learned to keep quiet—even adults. There were women and men killed by their partners every day. The police department couldn't overlook those statistics just because they knew the spouse or parent. However reasonable and nice people seemed in public, you never knew what happened behind closed doors.

"Do you have any idea who it was?" Erin asked.

"I wish I did. I'm afraid that I'm not the easiest person to get along with. I'm sure I have offended many people over the years."

"But people who would kidnap your child? That's a pretty severe consequence."

"I suppose it is. But I don't know who it was. I can't think of anybody in my life, in Bald Eagle Falls, who would do such a thing."

Despite her feelings about the gossip and the secrets in Bald Eagle Falls, Erin had to agree. That level of violence seemed extreme. Yes, they had seen more than their fair share of crime since Erin had arrived in Bald Eagle Falls, but that had mostly been related to the Plaints and to organized crime. And those had been cleaned up. There wasn't any reason to suspect that they were still operating in Bald Eagle Falls.

Except that a boy had been kidnapped.

"I wish we could just rewind," Erin said with a sigh. "I wish we could just go back in time and stop this from happening."

"I would do things differently," Mary Lou asserted. "I would keep a better eye on him. I would pay more attention to what he was doing for school, and that he wasn't getting into any trouble. I thought that after he was questioned by the police about the burglaries, when he was released, that he would be safe. But what if one of the kids who were involved thought that he had informed on them?"

"And they did this… to get back at him?" Erin thought about that. "Or to keep him from being able to testify in court?"

"They must have, don't you think?" Mary Lou asked. "People knew that he had been questioned by the police. When they started to make arrests, they thought that he had something to do with it."

"Right. I guess that's possible."

"What else?" Mary Lou demanded. "What else could I have done?"

"I'm not sure there's anything else you could have done. You can't protect someone twenty-four hours a day. Even if you had been awake and someone came into the house, how would you stop them from taking Joshua?"

Mary Lou looked at Erin, frowning.

"What?" Erin asked, disconcerted.

"You really don't think that I had anything to do with it."

"No. Why would I?"

"Because I'm the most likely suspect. Especially with the notes pointing in other directions. Why would anyone want to implicate you? The only person who would want to implicate you would be someone who wanted attention distracted from themselves. And that would be me. Family members. Spouses and parents," Mary Lou said bitterly.

"I don't know why someone would want to misdirect attention to me. I assumed… that was for your benefit. Someone wanted you to think it was me. That I had… done something that had caused harm to Joshua."

"Why?"

Erin sat on one of the chairs that had been vacated by the ladies from First Baptist and motioned Mary Lou to take another. After a hesitation, Mary Lou sat down.

"If that first note hadn't had my name on it, then who would you have suspected?"

"I have no idea. Just like I have no idea now. Maybe the parents of the other kids. Maybe… someone that Campbell was in trouble with."

"But you wouldn't have suspected me of having anything to do with it."

"No. You're not the first person I would have suspected of kidnapping Joshua."

"I didn't know anything about it." Even though Mary Lou said that she didn't suspect Erin, she wanted to be clear that she hadn't known about it or had anything to do with whoever had decided to take Joshua.

"No," Mary Lou agreed. She closed her eyes and massaged the worried creases in between them. "Nothing to do with it. It was a diversion."

Erin nodded. She tried to imagine what Mary Lou's day would have looked like without that note on the paper.

CHAPTER 34

"Did you ever read Joshua's article?"

Mary Lou gave her head a little shake. "Maybe sometime… but I couldn't bear to now. It would just be too hard."

"Did the police look at it?"

"I'm sure they must have. They wanted to know everything Joshua was doing. Where he had been, how he was doing at school. I told them about him going to Whitewater Junction to do interviews, all of that."

"I never read the article either."

"I'm sure you still could. The newspaper will still have copies of it. And the library will have kept an archive copy."

Erin nodded. There wasn't any way for someone to get rid of all of the copies of Joshua's article. But the note had distracted Mary Lou from reading it. And Erin too.

"We should read it. In case there's something in there… the kidnapper didn't want you to read."

Mary Lou shook her head. "I don't know if I can."

"Well, I will." Erin pulled her phone out. "Do they post it online?"

"No, they are old school."

"How late is the paper open?"

Mary Lou looked at her watch. "Everything will be closed now."

"Somebody must have it."

"Everybody has it. You must get it at your house. They deliver to everyone."

Erin couldn't remember seeing it. "Maybe. In the recycling pile, or maybe Vic picked it up."

Mary Lou nodded. "I don't want… to get my hopes up. So I'm going to let you go home and look at it. I won't expect to hear anything from you. Okay?"

"Okay." Erin touched Mary Lou's arm. "Take care, okay?"

Mary Lou sighed. She didn't answer. Erin really hoped that things didn't take a turn for the worse. She couldn't imagine how Mary Lou would get through it if they did.

"Is Campbell still in town?"

"Yes. He's at home. I don't know how long he's going to stay."

Hopefully, until things were resolved.

Erin really hoped that they wouldn't end badly.

Mary Lou left. Erin went to the kitchen to help Charley finish up. Charley raised an eyebrow. "So? How did it go?"

"Okay. She's not mad at me anymore. She doesn't suspect me."

Charley rolled her eyes. "She never should have in the first place. I can't think of anyone less likely to have kidnapped the kid. Really? You?"

"I don't think that she thought I kidnapped him… Maybe that something I did caused him to be kidnapped, and that I wanted to hurt her and get back at her by putting the bad fortunes in the cookies. I don't know. It's all emotion, not logic."

"Yeah. You're right there. It doesn't make any sense that you would have something to do with his disappearance."

"Thanks for cleaning up back here." Erin took a look around, and everything seemed to be more or less in place. "I guess that means it's time to go home."

"Is Terry picking you up?"

"I think I might walk." Erin hadn't heard anything from Terry. But when she said she would walk, she suddenly remembered how upset he'd been about her doing that after visiting the police department. Maybe not a good idea. She hesitated.

"You want a ride?" Charley asked.

"Yeah. Maybe that would be a good idea. If it's not an inconvenience."

"How could it be an inconvenience for me to drive you a few blocks?"

Which Erin took to mean that she didn't mind doing it. They grabbed their purses and went out the back door to Charley's car, taking care to lock the bakery securely. No point in inviting people to mess around in there while she was gone. She'd discovered enough bodies already.

Erin had a sudden flashback to Mr. Inglethorpe, lying in the middle of the floor of Auntie Clem's kitchen, a pool of red pie filling around him.

"Whoa!" Charley grabbed Erin's arm and steadied her. "Are you okay?"

Erin blinked, trying to clear the images from her brain. "Yeah." She breathed hard. "Sorry, just moved too fast, I guess."

Charley walked Erin to the car and opened the door for her, supervising to make sure that Erin got in without any further difficulty.

"You don't need to cover up for me," Charley said flatly when she slid into the driver's seat and put her key in the ignition.

"Cover up?"

"That you're having flashbacks."

"Oh." Erin was a little flustered. "Was it that obvious?"

"I've known for a long time."

"Well… it's not really a secret. But I don't like to talk about it."

"Sure. Understandable. I'm just saying, you don't have to pretend for me. Personally, I don't think you need to pretend for anyone else, either. It shouldn't be a secret. People should be able to talk about what's bothering them, about mental health and trauma and all that stuff."

Erin nodded, the movement very small. Charley might not have even seen it. "What about you? Do you… have that?"

"Flashbacks to when Bobby died?"

Erin didn't say anything. Both of them were quiet almost all the way to Erin's house.

"Yeah. Of course I do. It was a terrible thing. I try not to let it bother me, but sometimes… well, you can't control it, can you? And sometimes it controls you."

"Yeah. Sometimes."

"It's easier for me, I think," Charley said. "I'm the irresponsible sister, so it's okay if I blow off some community event or stay up until the sun rises before going to sleep, or have a bit too much to drink now and then. People just say…" Charley made a careless motion. "That's Charley. What do you expect?"

Erin knew that she herself had written off many of Charley's behaviors as just Charley being irresponsible. Was she being unfair? Was it not Charley being irresponsible, but Charley trying to handle her own PTSD symptoms?

"I didn't know."

"I wouldn't expect you to. Like I said, it's easier for me. People don't pay that much attention to my outrageous behavior because they expect it. I can handle it however I want."

"You could get therapy."

"Like you do?"

Like Erin didn't. She'd had enough therapy in the past that she just didn't want to have to deal with it again. Therapists wanted to know all of her secrets and history, wanted to know all of the intimate details of her life, and then just had generalized recommendations for relaxation exercises or pills that didn't work.

Erin cleared her throat and opened her door. "Thanks for the ride."

"No problem. Have a good rest of your day."

Erin slid out of the car.

"When are you going to get that Volkswagen fixed?" Charley asked.

"What?" Erin bent down to look down into the car at Charley.

"The yellow Volkswagen in your garage. If you're keeping it, you might as well drive it. Why don't you get it fixed up and drive it?"

"It was my Aunt Clementine's."

"Yeah…?"

Erin knew that the car was now hers, and there was no reason she couldn't take it out, get it tuned up, and drive it. Why was she holding on to it? It was like people who saved the good china or silver for a special occasion that never came instead of using them every day. What was she waiting for?

"I don't know," she admitted.

Charley grinned. "See you later, Sis."

Erin shut her door, and Charley squealed the tires as she sped away.

~

Terry was sitting on the couch watching TV. He blinked at Erin, and she wondered if he had fallen asleep. Orange Blossom was snoozing on the couch beside him and, while he looked up at Erin, he looked pretty dopey and just put his head back down to go back to sleep.

Blossom knew that Terry was the owner of the bothersome dog, so he usually wouldn't cuddle with Terry. But he was clearly comfortable where he was and didn't intend to move.

There wasn't anything wrong with Terry occasionally falling asleep in front of the TV. She just didn't want him regressing to the point where all he could do was sit in front of the TV and fall asleep during the day. When he'd been suffering from migraines and other problems following his injury, he hadn't been able to do anything else. It wasn't by choice.

"Hey. Did I wake you up?"

Terry shook his head. "No. No, I was just…"

"Closing your eyes for a minute?"

He cleared his throat. "Uh… exactly. Is it that time already?" He looked at the clock on the wall. "I didn't realize it was so late. Did you walk or did you have someone drop you off?"

"Charley."

"Oh." He gave a laugh. "I should have recognized her driving style."

Erin shook her head. "She's so bad. I tell her to behave, but it doesn't seem to help."

"No, the ones like her, it's worse if you tell them how to behave. They always have to do the opposite of what you say."

Erin recognized her own rebellious feelings in his statement. She was pretty good about not letting that little rebellious gut-reaction dictate her actions as a grown-up. As a child, she hadn't been quite so good at it.

And sometimes, just sometimes, she still did things just because someone told her not to.

"I don't think she's the worst driver in town, though," Erin said.

"No? She has to be pretty close, if you're talking about wanton recklessness." He stopped and reconsidered his statement. "Well… except for Beaver."

"Yeah. Did you know she has a glove box full of tickets?"

"Who do you think gave her most of those tickets?" he countered.

Erin laughed.

"And don't ask me why I keep issuing them," Terry said in a tone of disgust. "Considering that she never pays them. She just gets someone to have them wiped off the record."

"She is a federal agent."

"But she shouldn't be able to do that. She should have to take responsibility for her… creative driving."

Erin chuckled. "Yeah. Good luck with that. I think she'd just laugh at the idea."

Terry nodded his agreement.

"Do you know if we have a copy of the paper?" Erin asked, changing the subject.

"What paper? Oh, the weekly?" Terry looked at the coffee table in front of him, stacked with a number of flyers and other papers. He pulled out a copy of the Bald Eagle Falls weekly. "Here." He held it out to her.

Erin took the paper and looked down at it, frowning. "Oh… not this week's, last week's. The one with Joshua's article…?"

"Mmm. I might have taken it in to work with me."

Erin kept her mouth shut, trying to restrain a sharp question as to why he would have done that. It was her paper, not his. He could have picked up the one that was delivered to his house and taken it in. But of course, it was a lot less complicated just to grab Erin's.

"Did you, or didn't you?"

"I don't know." He closed his eyes to think about it, but shook his head, unsure of the answer. "Why?"

It shouldn't be that hard for him to remember whether he had taken it in to work or not. But he still forgot things more easily. Things he should have been able to remember.

"I want to read Josh's article."

Terry's eyes narrowed. "What are you investigating now?"

"Nothing. I just want to read his article. I didn't, because it came out the same day as he disappeared, and I was more worried about helping find him."

Terry continued to look at her, not believing it. Or maybe remembering that the day Joshua had disappeared, she had pretended to know nothing about it.

Erin ground her teeth. A bad habit and one that she shouldn't let creep back in. She forced herself to yawn and licked her lips. "I need a drink. You want something?"

"It must be late enough for a beer, if you're home."

Erin nodded her agreement and got him a beer and herself a glass of water. Terry popped the top on his can.

"You just want to read Joshua's article. Not because you're conducting your own investigation of his disappearance."

"What's wrong with that? He was pretty proud of the article. I should at least read it."

Erin went back through the kitchen to the back door, where the paper recycling bin was stored. She skimmed off the top couple of layers of flyers and miscellaneous lists, looking for the weekly. But it didn't seem to be there. She dug farther and found the previous week's. So Terry must have taken the issue with Joshua's article in to work.

"Can you go to your house and get me your copy?"

"Erin…"

"I want to read it. If you don't want to go out, just give me your keys and I'll go."

Terry didn't move to do so. He hadn't given her a key to his house. There was no reason she needed her own key, because he had taken to staying with her almost all the time.

Erin shook her head and walked out the door.

CHAPTER 35

Terry didn't chase after her, calling for her to stop, like she half-expected him to do. He didn't get up and offer her his key or to go get the paper at his house. He didn't follow her outside at all.

Erin went to Mrs. Peach's door and rang the doorbell. It took a few minutes for Mrs. Peach to get to the door. She was an older lady and moved slowly, but she still took a daily constitutional around the neighborhood. Erin just had to be patient and wait for her.

"Oh, hello, dear," Mrs. Peach greeted. She looked around Erin as if expecting someone else to be with her. Terry or Orange Blossom, maybe. Or Vic.

"Hi, Mrs. Peach. I was wondering if you could do me a favor. Do you have the weekly paper from last week? The one that had Joshua Cox's article on the front page."

"Oh, yes. I have that around here somewhere."

"Could I borrow it? I'll give it right back, I don't need to keep it, I just want to be able to read it."

"So sad about that boy, isn't it? I wonder what on earth happened to him."

Erin nodded. Her eyes burned and she wasn't sure if she could say anything, with the lump in her throat.

"I'll just see if I can find that," Mrs. Peach said, giving Erin's arm a comforting pat.

Erin wondered if Mrs. Peach knew that she and Josh were friends, or just recognized that she was a little teary-eyed over the comment.

She had to wait for a while as Mrs. Peach walked through her house, probably to the back door where she kept her own paper recycling. Then searched through it for the paper and walked back across the house again to the front door. Erin wondered if she should have offered to go around to the back door so Mrs. Peach didn't have to make the trek all the way back and forth.

"There you are," Mrs. Peach offered, holding it out to Erin. "That one?"

Erin looked down at the front of the paper, half expecting it to be the wrong edition yet again. But it wasn't. Josh's article was right there on top, the lead story.

Of course, Bald Eagle Falls didn't get much real news, and the lead story had been about the cook-off in the next town over. Not anything earth-shattering.

"Thanks so much, Mrs. Peach. Do you want it back?"

"No, you can keep it, dear. Or put it into your paper recycling. Don't throw it in the garbage. It should be recycled, you know."

"Yes," Erin agreed. "I'll do that. Thanks."

Mrs. Peach nodded and closed the door.

Erin walked back into the house. Terry was still sitting on the couch, and pretended to be occupied with the TV. If he didn't want to discuss it, that was fine with Erin. She walked past him into the kitchen and picked her glass of water up. She sipped it as she sat down at the table by herself and spread the paper out, looking for what was wrong.

Josh's assignment had been to write about the cook-off, but of course, he had focused on the murder that had taken place before the kick-off event. Beryl Batcombe. She had been one of the judges, like Erin. They had arrested Clayton for it. Beryl had stolen his family recipes and passed them off as her own family recipes. The plagiarism had incensed Clayton and he had started stalking Beryl and her part-time boyfriend, Chef

Kirschoff. Eventually, he had killed Beryl and had also tried to kill Chef Kirschoff.

Josh didn't know all of the details, but he'd gotten everything he could from Erin and the other witnesses, and had put most of it together, filling in the cracks with guesses and speculation that were pretty close to being on target.

He was a good investigative reporter. Better than Erin had expected him to be. Especially considering that he was still a teenager.

Erin read the entire article and then sat looking at the paper, her eyes unfocused. So what had he discovered that someone didn't want Mary Lou to read? The kidnapper had cut Joshua's article out of Mary Lou's paper and had left the sticky note about Erin there in its place.

What had Joshua discovered that the police didn't already know? They had Clayton in custody. He had been charged with the murder and would go to trial.

Was Clayton involved in the kidnapping? Had he hired someone or imposed on one of his friends to make Joshua disappear? Or was there someone else involved?

She studied the article again.

Who had he interviewed?

Erin. Each of the winners—six of them.

Not Clayton, because Josh was a juvenile and couldn't get into the jail to see him without permission. And of course, Mary Lou would deny him permission.

He had a few quotes from Chef Kirschoff as well.

For a moment, Erin just let sadness wash over her. She had counted Chef Kirschoff as a friend. She had enjoyed working with him and talking about recipes with him. But he had turned out to be amoral. Cheating on his wife with Beryl Batcombe, giving her the judgeship even though he knew she had stolen the recipes she had published as her own family recipes.

The guy probably cheated on his taxes too.

Joshua had focused mostly on Beryl Batcombe's murder, because it was, as he had said, the most interesting part of the contest. Who would really be more interested in the coke and ice cream treats than in the woman found dead in a freezer?

Erin already knew all of the details. Beryl had been gassed with carbon dioxide and dragged into the freezer, most likely hoping that everyone would believe she had died in there. But they hadn't. It had been evident to the medical examiner that she had been moved.

Joshua had been good. He'd asked Erin about how she had felt, what it had been like to find Beryl, and so on. And he'd apparently asked other people involved in the contest about their feelings as well. The responses were emotional and resonant. They pulled the reader in.

She tried to picture each of the winners. She had looked at their pictures on the display boards at the hotel when she and Vic had gone back to Whitewater to look for Joshua. All of the happy faces, people excited about placing top in their class. And about winning the large cash prizes. Who wouldn't be happy about that?

We look forward to hearing more from Joshua Cox.

It was just a little note at the end of the article. Joshua's name and photo were at the top of the article, and his name was included again at the end, indicating that he would be writing again.

Erin frowned.

She picked up her phone and dialed Mary Lou.

"Erin?" Mary Lou sounded frightened. Surely she didn't think that Erin had discovered evidence that something worse than being kidnapped had happened to Joshua? Not that fast. If Erin had found out something serious, it would have been the police calling Mary Lou, not Erin.

Or maybe she was just afraid of what Erin was going to tell her about Joshua's article. Maybe that she had to read it. Or that Erin knew what it was that had inspired the kidnapping.

Or that she didn't.

"It's okay," Erin said. She didn't want Mary Lou to think that it was all over. Not either way. "I just wanted to know… was Joshua going to write more for the paper?"

Mary Lou didn't respond at first. Erin pictured her patting her hair thoughtfully, trying to get herself into the right frame of mind, considering Erin's question.

"He enjoyed writing that article," she said slowly. "He was fascinated with the process of interviewing people and developing the story. And his teacher was hoping that some extra assignments would boost his marks. So… yes, I know he planned to do more than just the one article. But I don't think there were any particular arrangements."

"The news article said they were looking forward to more from him. You don't know if he had started on something else?"

"No."

"Do you have his notepad?"

"What notepad?"

"The one he was using to write notes about the interviews. He had one when he came to talk to me in Whitewater."

"I just assumed he made notes on his phone. You know how kids these days are. Everything goes on the phone."

Erin shook her head, remembering clearly. "No. He was using a real notepad. Pen and paper. Like a reporter."

"What did it look like?"

Erin tried to remember the details. "It was just a little pocket memo pad, you know, they fit in a shirt pocket, spiral-bound on top. It was a dark color cover, but I don't think it was black. Maybe dark green."

"I'll look in his room."

Erin wasn't sure whether Mary Lou would hang up, call her back, or go and check while Erin was still on the line, so she waited. She could hear Mary Lou moving around, and pictured her climbing the stairs at her house to Joshua's room. Erin vividly remembered Josh mounting the stairs to go and prepare the guest bedroom for Brianna after Campbell had been arrested. She assumed that's where all of the bedrooms were. She could be completely wrong. He might have a man cave in the basement.

She wondered whether Mary Lou had to walk past his empty room every day. But if their bedrooms were close to each other, then Mary Lou would have heard something the night that Joshua was taken, wouldn't she? Unless he had gone willingly. Erin still didn't know what had happened, how the kidnapper had managed to get Joshua out of the house. It wasn't necessarily with brute force. Especially not if it was a woman. A woman would have to be pretty athletic to overcome him and remove him by force, especially without waking Mary Lou.

Mary Lou laid the phone down and began opening and closing drawers, dragging them open, shuffling the contents, and banging them shut again. Erin imagined Joshua's drawers as being filled with a combination of stuff from school, electronics, and some old books and toys from when he was younger. The old Joshua and the new Joshua, trying to make sense of his life and what he was going to be.

She couldn't hear Mary Lou anymore, and wondered where she was looking. Under the mattress? In his school backpack? Through the clothes hanging in his closet or scattered on the floor?

Mary Lou returned to the phone, sounding out of breath. "I've got it. Memo pad with a dark green cover. Don't schools do anything to teach kids penmanship these days? I remember when I went to school, we had to practice our printing and writing every day..."

"I'll come over," Erin said.

Mary Lou didn't respond immediately. "I'm going to call the police," she said. "This is their job, not yours. They can look through it and see if there is anything that might relate to his... disappearance."

"I might be able to figure it out," Erin said. "I've read through his newspaper article, and I remember when he interviewed me. I know more of the background for Beryl's murder and the contest. I'll spot something a lot faster than the police."

She was aware that she was venturing into dangerous waters. How many times had she been told to stay out of an investigation? But she wasn't going to stop now. She was the only one who had thought of the notepad. Who knew how much else she would be able to spot that the police wouldn't have any idea of? The murder had taken place in another town and been investigated by another police force. The Bald Eagle Falls police department wouldn't even know where to start.

"I am calling the police," Mary Lou repeated firmly. "I don't know how long it will take them to get here. So if you want to see it before they get here..."

"I'll be right over," Erin promised.

She folded the newspaper and jammed it into her purse. She paused in the living room, looking at Terry.

"Can I borrow the truck?"

He looked at her, frowning. "Where are you going?"

"To talk to Mary Lou."

"Have the two of you made up?" He sounded surprised.

"Yes," Erin said, impatient. "Just today. And I want to go over to her house to have a visit, now that we're on speaking terms again. So can I borrow the truck?"

"First you're reading Joshua's article and now you're going over to his house."

"Yes."

"What did you find out?"

Erin chewed on her lip. "He might have planned to write other articles. I want to look through his notes."

"That's not your job."

"I want to help. What is it going to hurt to look through his papers and see if he has any notes for other articles he wanted to write?"

"You know how it has turned out in the past, these harmless investigations of yours."

"I'm not doing anything dangerous." Erin turned toward the door. "I'll walk, I guess. I'll see you later."

She didn't need the truck. Mary Lou's house was just 'over the way.' Hopefully, the police wouldn't be in a rush to see what Mary Lou had found and Erin could still get there first. It was a Sunday afternoon. The sheriff wouldn't want to be rushing over to Mary Lou's to look at new evidence that probably wouldn't lead anywhere. Stayner wouldn't want to. Terry was home, off duty. Tom was also off.

"Erin!"

Erin turned her head back toward the door when Terry called her. He was standing on the threshold. "Here."

He tossed her the truck keys. Erin wasn't expecting him to throw them. She batted them out of the air and then had to step onto the lawn and fish them out of the flower border.

"Sorry," Terry said with a chuckle.

"Thank you."

Erin climbed up into the truck and started the engine. She waved at Terry and pulled out, careful to start off smoothly and not make the tires squeal. She was in a hurry, but there was no point in aggravating things further.

CHAPTER 36

Erin knocked on the door at Mary Lou's and waited impatiently. She knew that local custom said she could just knock and enter, but she wasn't comfortable with that. Especially not with Mary Lou.

Eventually, the door opened. Mary Lou didn't greet her, just pulled the door open and motioned Erin in. She had the memo pad in her hand. They sat down in the living room. Erin leaned eagerly toward her.

"Can I have a look? Maybe we should be wearing gloves."

"It's not something that whoever took him touched. If it contains something incriminating, they would have taken it with them. If they knew about it. They obviously didn't know anything, or it wouldn't have still been in his room."

Erin swallowed. She had a big lump in her stomach. Would there be anything in the notebook? Chances were, it would just be short notes of his interviews with the various people he had talked to about the contest and Beryl's death. Nothing new and nothing incriminating. Nothing that would point them in the direction of the kidnapper.

"Have you looked at it? Is there anything…?"

"I don't know. You read his article?"

"Yes."

"Hopefully… you'll recognize if something is out of place… something that someone wouldn't have wanted him to know or to follow up on."

Mary Lou handed the notepad over to Erin.

Erin held it in her hand, looking down at it and remembering the moment that Joshua had taken it out of his pocket, looking all professional and proud of himself. Not just a kid doing some boring work for extra credit. Writing was something that he was really interested in. While it may have started out as an assignment to write about a somewhat boring cook-off contest, there was a murder involved. He was excited to dig into the details and to figure out what had happened.

Erin wished she had spent a little more time with him. She didn't think she had said much that had been helpful to him. And then… it was right about that time that Charley and Chef Kirschoff had nearly been blown up with a CO2 canister. Erin had been right in the thick of things as she tried to get to Charley to find out what had happened and if she was okay.

Erin focused on the memo pad and turned the cover. There were a few random facts about the competition and questions to ask in the interviews. Then some more excited notes about Beryl Batcombe's death and questions like "Murder?" and "What was it like to find her?" that Joshua had, in fact, asked her those questions. She had told him as little as possible and sent him off to talk to the police or the contest organizers.

Would it have made a difference if she had spent more time with him? If she had listened to what he had to say as well as what he had asked?

Had he known something that had led to the kidnapping?

Joshua's penmanship wasn't *that* bad. Still, Erin did have to spend some time deciphering a number of the entries and wasn't even sure then if she had interpreted them correctly.

Erin was aware that she was under the microscope. Mary Lou watched her every move and change in expression, trying to analyze whether she was finding anything that would help them solve the case and recover Joshua safely. She hated the pressure and the scrutiny, but what was she going to do? Tell Mary Lou to quit looking at her? Say that she had to go somewhere private to read the notebook?

Instead, she did her best to ignore Mary Lou's stare and just to focus on what was in the book.

The notes got shorter and more excited as Josh proceeded through the interviews, and culminated with the day that the carbonated beverages had been judged and Clayton had blown up about Chef Kirschoff and Beryl Batcombe being corrupt. The day they had caught Beryl's killer.

Then the notes started to run dry. Facts and figures about the contest. Listings of expenses and how much it had cost to run. The hundreds of thousands of dollars of prize money that had been awarded.

Erin kept going. There were a few more notes about the winners of the prizes. Short bio notes and questions he had asked them. And then… nothing more. A few blank pages remaining at the end of the book.

Erin stared at the blank page. "Did he… were there any more notebooks?"

Mary Lou shook her head. "A few from when he was a kid, you know the little cartoon ones you put in birthday loot bags. That one," Mary Lou nodded toward Erin's hands, "came from a package of six." She easily anticipated Erin's next question. "That was the only one taken out of the package. The other five are still there."

Maybe he had switched to using his phone, like Mary Lou had expected. Maybe he found that he wasn't an old-style newspaper reporter, but one who was more comfortable in using modern technology than an old analog system that couldn't even be searched by keyword.

"What about his phone? Did he put anything on it? Was it… missing? Did he have it with him?"

"The police have his phone. It was still here." Mary Lou swallowed. She would know as well as anyone how important a phone was to a teenager. It was his lifeline, his entire world. He wouldn't have voluntarily gone anywhere without it. He wouldn't have left it behind on purpose.

"And there wasn't anything on it about the contest? More interview notes?"

Mary Lou wrapped her arms around herself as if she were cold. "I have no idea. I don't know what they found on it. They don't call me and tell me all of the developments. But I don't get the idea that… they thought it was very important. I don't even know if there is anyone in the department who is qualified to search a phone properly."

"I wouldn't expect it takes a lot of skill."

"There's more to it than just opening each app," Mary Lou countered. "How much stuff is stored in the cloud? What's on his camera roll? How many programs did he use where the information disappears after a few minutes or days? Kids use some pretty sophisticated methods to hide stuff."

Erin thought about the police department. Stayner was young enough that he would know some of the tricks. But the rest of them?

The sheriff was still using a *flip phone*. He claimed it got better reception than any of the newfangled smartphones. Maybe he was right. It was important, as remote as they were, to have coverage that was as reliable as possible.

Erin started going through the notebook a second time. She had to find something of importance before the police came and took it away. If she didn't find anything, what were the chances that they ever would? She was the one who had been in the contest, who knew all of the players.

Mary Lou gazed at Erin with sad eyes. She could tell that Erin wasn't getting anywhere. It had ended up being a dead end, just like every other avenue that had been investigated.

"The contest was already investigated," Erin said. "With Beryl's murder, the police already did background checks on everyone who was involved. They would have checked to make sure that everything was kosher, right? When Clayton accused Beryl and Chef Kirschoff of being corrupt, they would have looked into everything."

Mary Lou made a face. "It isn't like on TV," she pointed out. "You don't get an answer in half an hour. It can take years to root out corruption. All kinds of federal agents looking into every possibility."

Erin shook her head. Would it really take as long as all of that? They already knew that Beryl had plagiarized the recipes in her book and that Chef Kirschoff hadn't been honest about everything he was handling. So they would have known if there were other problems. They already knew who to look at.

"And that's if they got anyone other than the local police department to look into it," Mary Lou continued with the bad news. "Do you really think that the FBI would get involved in a backwoods Tennessee cooking contest?"

Erin held her arms over her stomach. "But there was a murder. They must have taken it seriously."

CHAPTER 37

Mary Lou shrugged helplessly. "I don't know. You would have to talk to the police department in Whitewater Junction and see if they would tell you anything. But I suspect you already know that they aren't going to tell you anything at all. They're not required to tell you about their investigation and what they have found yet, and whether they involved any federal departments."

Erin nodded. Of course they wouldn't tell her anything. She could barely get anything out of the Bald Eagle Falls police, which her boyfriend was a part of. Although she had always suspected that it would have been easier to get information out of the members of the police force other than Terry. He always tried to be extra careful not to tell her anything unless it were already public knowledge.

She had to start at the beginning. Erin paged through the notebook again. If she knew nothing about the cook-off, what information would she have found the most interesting? What would be the best parts to write additional newspaper articles on? Any follow-up news was being published after the contest was ended, so all of the hype was gone.

He could publish the results of the science fair that had been held in coordination with the contest. Or the hot dog eating contest. But those were not really exciting, other than for the people who had won.

He could do a follow-up story on what people were going to spend their prize winnings on, or where the next contest was going to be held. He could do profiles of the winners, or the sponsors, of any of the organizers who had been involved in getting it set up in the first place.

But Joshua didn't have notes on any of those topics. Other than some basic bios. A follow up on the contest winners would be interesting to people. Where the recipes they used had come from, whether they were traditional family recipes or of the winner's own creation. What had drawn them to enter the contest. What they did in their 'normal' life. Maybe a couple of profiles a week. Or the three winners of the beverage contest one week and the three winners of the ice cream contest the next. That would have a nice symmetry.

Erin stared down at the facts and figures in the notebook, her vision blurring.

"Erin?"

Erin closed her eyes, thinking.

"What is it?" Mary Lou asked, her tone more urgent.

"I'm not sure… I don't know where it takes us or if it helps us to find him…"

"What?"

Erin opened her eyes and looked at the page she had open. "He's written down all of the information on the prize monies and the costs of the contest. The sponsors and what they all contributed, stuff like that."

"Yes," Mary Lou nodded. "A reporter would need to know the basics when starting a story."

"Yes… but we knew the prize monies back at the beginning before people entered the contest. That was what attracted so many people. The chance to win a quarter of a million dollars."

"Right."

"Then why isn't that information at the beginning of the notepad?"

Mary Lou cocked her head to the side. "Does that matter? He needs it to write the story, whether it's at the beginning or the end."

"He wrote it after Clayton was arrested."

"I don't understand what your point is."

"All of that stuff was well-established by that point. And with everything that had happened, there was speculation that a lot of the local sponsors were going to lose money. The hotel, the restaurant that got blown up, there were all kinds of losses."

Mary Lou got up and walked across to the kitchen. She turned on an element on the stove and put the tea kettle over it.

"Why is that important?"

"I don't think he was writing an article on how much money was being offered for the prizes."

"No. You're right. It would be a bit late for that. And he must have included that information in his first article. It wasn't published until after the winners were announced, but he must have written how much each one was awarded."

"Yeah. He did," Erin agreed, remembering the little table showing that very information.

"Then what is it you think he was writing about?"

"Did the police say that they were going to send someone today?"

"Yes… but I don't know when. I didn't encourage them to come immediately, because I knew you wanted to look at it before they got here."

"I think… do you think it's possible that Chef Kirschoff's reason for running the contest didn't even have anything to do with food?"

"Well… of course. It could have been the money rather than the food. But he was giving money away, so it wasn't greed, was it?"

"The sponsors must have provided some of that. Otherwise, why were there sponsors?" Erin mused. She watched Mary Lou watch the kettle.

"But the prizes were announced before they recruited any sponsors. So the prize money must have come from Kirschoff. Or he already had it from somewhere."

"He comes here, he offers these great prizes, he says it's all about culture and Tennessee and giving the local communities a well-deserved boost. But he's never even been here before."

"He must have been, to be involved with Beryl," Mary Lou pointed out.

"But he said he'd never been…" Erin trailed off. Of course he had lied to her about it. To avoid any suspicion. He said it was his first time ever in Tennessee. Why would anyone think anything different? Why would anyone suspect him of being involved with one of the judges, who he had apparently never met before? "It wasn't about the food. It wasn't about Tennessee and giving our economy a boost and bringing our communities together. That was all just cover."

"But cover for what?"

The kettle started to whistle.

~

"It's time to get up, Joshua."

Josh didn't want to move. He was too tired to get out of bed. He didn't know why anyone was waking him up in the middle of the night. He kept his eyes closed and tried to drift back off to sleep. It wasn't hard. He didn't seem to have any energy at all anymore, and the best thing for him to do was just to close his eyes and turn off his brain.

He didn't want to think. He didn't want to escape. He just wanted peace.

The hooded figure was there. Hood and goggles. That was overdoing it a little, wasn't it? He had nearly figured out who she was.

At first, he hadn't known. The figure dressed in shapeless clothes, hood, and goggles was sexless. It could have been anyone. And that had been the point, hadn't it? To be anonymous. To keep her identity from Joshua.

But he'd gradually pieced together that his captor wasn't a man. She didn't smell like a man, for one thing. Not that she was wearing a bunch of perfume, but he caught hints of her shampoo and deodorant when she leaned over him, and he knew they weren't men's products.

It was hard to judge her height when he was lying on the bed. But he knew that when she sat on the edge of the bed to feed him that she was shorter than he was. He wasn't huge, but mostly women were shorter than he was and men were taller. Campbell said that he'd shoot up the rest of the way one day and be as tall as any of the other boys in his grade.

The whisper that was intended to hide her sex also masked her accent, but she seemed local. The speech patterns all sounded Tennessean. Her food tasted like his grandma's food. No hints of different origins. No unusual spices or textures. All exactly like his grandma had made in her kitchen those autumns that he and Campbell had gone to help her with her canning and preserving. They didn't come out of a can. She wasn't lying when she said it was one of her grandma's recipes.

And he knew. He knew that taking him had not been chance. He hadn't been held for ransom. She hadn't wanted to harm him. But she had not planned to keep him alive, either. She hadn't brought him regular meals or been concerned about his health. He'd been dehydrated since that first day, and she confirmed that she was intentionally withholding water.

It wouldn't be long. That's what she had said.

He didn't know why she wanted to get him up now, but he didn't see the point. It wouldn't be anything good.

CHAPTER 38

Erin was hoping that she would be able to relax and they could work everything out once the sheriff got there. But when he showed up, he had Terry and K9 with him, which did not help Erin to relax at all. She had just told Terry that she was not going to be investigating Joshua's disappearance. Then they had arrived to find out that she had been reading through the notebook and trying to come up with a theory on the case.

He raised his eyebrows at her and didn't say anything to censure her. But he also didn't sit beside her on the couch. He sat on one of the easy chairs a few feet away. K9 lay down obediently beside Terry's feet as he was trained to do, but he pointed his nose at Erin and whined, clearly confused by the situation.

Welcome to the club, K9.

It just didn't seem like anything could be easy for her.

Mary Lou explained about the notepad, how Erin had known that Joshua had used it when he was conducting his newspaper interviews and had taken note of the fact that the paper said he was going to be contributing further stories. So, one thing had led to another, and there Erin was, full of theories that she hoped to run by the police department. Like she was the detective and they were not the first line of investigation.

Terry paid careful attention to Mary Lou and did not look at Erin, even when it was her turn to talk. Erin turned the notebook over to Sheriff Wilmot, open to the page that began with the listing of the prize monies.

"He was investigating the financial affairs of the contest *after* it was finished," Erin pointed out.

Wilmot looked down at it. "Maybe. Or maybe he kept reference materials in the back and interview questions and notes in the front."

Erin frowned, thinking about that.

"It's an old technique," Wilmot said. "Maybe not something that someone your age would have thought of..."

"But Joshua is younger than I am."

"Yes."

"Where would he learn that?"

"Maybe from a seasoned reporter. Someone mentoring him about how to handle the interviews and writing the article. Why would he use a notepad instead of something electronic? Because he was learning from someone old-school."

Erin cleared her throat and looked down.

Was that all it was? He was keeping reference material in the back of the book?

She didn't believe it.

"I don't think that's why," she said, though all she had was a gut feeling and not proof. "I think... he was investigating the contest itself."

"For what?"

"For something financial. Like... money laundering."

Wilmot considered this. He looked at Terry, who didn't have anything to say about it.

"Why do you think that?"

"I wondered a few times myself, when Chef Kirschoff first came here and said that he was going to run this contest. I wondered why he would choose to do it here, when he said he'd never even been in Tennessee before. If he was going to run a contest like that, why wouldn't he do it in a bigger metropolis?"

"But that's an argument against trying to launder money here. It would make more sense for him to do it somewhere there were a lot of similar contests running and a bigger population, so it wasn't as obvious, wouldn't it?"

"It depends. It was a big deal for us, and everybody knew it was going on, but there aren't many federal agents out here who would ask questions. And all of those 'know your client' rules that banks have for money laundering, they would know exactly who Chef Kirschoff was, and that the money being transferred around was for the contest, right? They wouldn't need to ask for a bunch of details, because they already know, it's all for the contest. They know who Kirschoff is, they know the sponsors and the prize winners, so it's all established."

"I suppose. So what exactly would make you think there is anything like money laundering going on? It all appeared to be aboveboard."

"He didn't have sponsors before he came here. So, where was the money coming from?"

"Maybe he was just confident in his ability to raise money," Terry contributed.

"A million dollars? The prize money itself was three-quarters. Then, you add in all of the expenses, advertising, honorariums for the judges, salaries for employees, and all of that. He knew that he could come into backwater Tennessee and raise a million dollars in a depressed economy?"

"But he did, didn't he?" Sheriff Wilmot turned a couple of pages in the notebook, where Joshua had written down the amounts being contributed by the various sponsors. "He was able to get the money, the venues, cover all expenses…"

Erin nodded. "I'm no expert," she said. "I'm not even great at math. But right from the beginning, it didn't make sense to me. Especially on such a tight timeline. Why rush in and do this contest with only a few weeks' lead-up? Somewhere he said he'd never been before?"

"But he clearly had been here before," Terry said. "Considering he was having some sort of affair with Beryl Batcombe. We don't know how long he was planning the contest and what contacts or sponsors he already had in place when he got here. It seemed like it all fell into place pretty quickly."

Erin nodded.

"Yeah. And there was the part about holding it in the winter. If you're using dry ice, why not hold it at Halloween when you can tie into a spooky theme? Or if you're making ice cream and cold beverages, then why not hold it in the summer when it's hot and people will appreciate it more? Why hold something like that in the winter?"

"Well, we'll look into it," Wilmot said. "I'll review the notebook and maybe we'll get the feds in to see if there was money laundering. But if there was… those investigations can take a long time and I'm not sure it gets us any closer to… figuring out what happened to Joshua."

"If he was investigating money laundering, then he was kidnapped to stop him from figuring it out," Erin pointed out.

"And that makes it… who? Kirschoff himself? Someone in his employ?"

"It could have been Kirschoff, I suppose." Erin thought it over. "But I thought he was out of town by then. He could have come back, or assigned someone else to do it, but pretty much all of the organizers were gone the day after the contest concluded. And… there was a woman involved. We know that."

"How do you know that?" Terry demanded.

Erin looked over at him. "Because whoever called in to the Quiki to change the order impersonated me successfully. I suppose some men can do a convincing woman's voice, but the more obvious solution is that it was a woman."

"Oh." Terry looked taken aback. Obviously, he thought she had been digging more deeply than that, finding things that the police hadn't and not letting them know. "So… a woman. It could have been a girlfriend."

"No." Erin shook her head. "He was dating Charley."

"That doesn't mean that he wasn't dating someone else, from what I understand of the man's morals. And," Terry gave Erin an uncertain sideways look. "You know Charley's history. Would you be able to say with one hundred percent certainty that she wasn't involved? Even if it was only the phone call?"

Erin knew that Charley's history with organized crime was a problem. She could never say that Charley wouldn't be involved with something like a kidnapping. She had turned out to be innocent of Bobby Dixon's murder, but she had still been a soldier in the Dixon clan, until she and they found out that she had Jackson blood. Erin couldn't be one hundred percent sure. She was pretty sure, but not that sure.

"She's your sister," Mary Lou contributed. "Her voice is similar to yours. More Tennessee, but…"

"She wouldn't do something like that," Erin insisted. But her face was warm and she knew that it was only her feeling, not proof of any kind.

"Kirschoff could have been seeing someone else," Wilmot reminded. "Or it could have been an employee. Or someone else who benefited from the money laundering scheme."

"Who benefits?" Erin asked. "I mean, besides Chef Kirschoff, who wouldn't want it to be discovered?"

"Anyone involved in the money laundering."

"The promoters," Terry contributed. "It sullies their reputation to find out they were involved in something like that, even if it was innocently."

"You and Miss Victoria as judges," Mary Lou said.

The thought made Erin sick. If she didn't know what was going on, how could she be thrown in with everyone else? But she knew it was true. If it turned out that the contest was just one big money laundering scheme, it would reflect badly on everyone involved. And everyone knew that she and Vic had been involved, that Auntie Clem's Bakery had gotten as much positive publicity out of it as they could, under Charley's direction. If the contest was tainted, so were they all.

"The winners of the contest," Terry said. "What is going to happen to their prize winnings? Do they lose it? Does it get tied up for ten years while the feds investigate?"

"I have no idea," Wilmot said, shaking his head. "I've never been involved in an investigation like that."

"They participated in good faith," Erin protested, "they didn't know what was going on." She would feel terrible if Bella got bad publicity and lost her winnings. She had been counting on putting her money toward college. She didn't know the other winners very well, but she felt bad for them too.

"Maybe I'm just imagining things. Maybe there's good reason for all of this…"

Sheriff Wilmot raised his brows. "It's not for us to decide whether it's true or not, just to follow the breadcrumbs. No one is going to even know that you suggested it, unless you spread it around town."

"Well…" Erin's face got warm. "Sometimes things *do* leak from the police department."

Wilmot and Terry looked at each other, and the sheriff nodded, conceding the fact. "Sometimes, they do."

"But this isn't about who would suffer if money laundering was exposed," Mary Lou said flatly. "This is about finding my son."

Erin needed to hear that. "Yes. It's about Joshua," she agreed. And she knew Bella would give up all of her money if she knew that it meant Josh could be returned home safely. Bella was just that kind of person. She cared for others. And Josh, even though he wasn't a close friend, was still someone she cared about.

"We'll need to dig down," Wilmot told Terry. "Background on the winners. Anyone that Joshua mentioned having an interview with either in the article in the paper or in that notebook. They are all suspects—" He glanced aside at Erin. "Especially the women. They are the first priority."

"Can you find him?" Mary Lou asked, looking at Wilmot, her eyes as intense as spotlights. "Is this going to find him, or is it just going to… make someone take action if they haven't already?" She looked at her watch. "Or has it been too long to even have hope anymore?"

"We have to have hope," Erin encouraged. "Don't give up."

"But I need to know. I need to know whether to expect to find him again." She stared at the sheriff. "Please."

His mouth thinned and formed a straight line across. "I don't know, ma'am." He gave a little headshake. "At this point… it doesn't look good."

CHAPTER 39

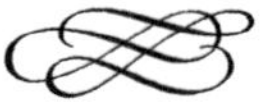

Sheriff Wilmot and Terry got up. They had work to do. It was late in the day, and maybe it was already too late for Joshua, but they had to try what they could.

"Erin, I'll drop you at home," Terry said, reaching a hand toward her to help her up.

Erin stayed where she was. "If you don't need the truck, just leave it here and I'll get home in a bit. If you need it, go ahead. I can walk."

"I don't want you walking by yourself."

"I'll be fine."

"You don't know what kind of people may target you. If people know that you're looking into this… look what happened to Joshua. I don't want you getting snatched or hurt."

"Do you need the truck?"

Terry sighed and looked at the sheriff. "Can I hitch a ride with you?"

"Of course."

"Okay." Terry nodded at Erin. "I'll leave it with you. But still don't leave it too late, please. And maybe… let me know when you're leaving here and have Vic and Willie watching for you to get home."

"Are you really that worried?"

Terry's brows drew down. "Of course I am."

She again felt herself blushing. She stood up and kissed him goodbye.

"I won't stay too long. And you take care of yourself. You can't pull an all-nighter like you used to. I don't want your head getting worse again…"

He nodded. He was probably embarrassed at her saying so in front of the sheriff and Mary Lou. Men wanted to look strong and invulnerable. Especially a police officer like Terry. So much of his self-worth was tied up in being the protector. Not someone who could fall prey to illness or injury. She shrugged an apology and sat back down, letting him go without any more fuss.

She and Mary Lou watched the two men leave. Mary Lou turned back to Erin, eyes narrow. "Was there something else…?"

Erin pulled the folded newspaper out of her purse. "I have the article here. I don't know if it will help, but…" She unfolded it, spreading it across her knees. "Okay. It has the names of the winners in both categories. I guess we start there."

"Who were they?" Mary Lou leaned forward.

Even though Erin didn't know all of them, Mary Lou had lived her whole life in Bald Eagle Falls. She would know not only the people, but their families and their histories. Sheriff Wilmot and Terry could conduct their background checks, but they wouldn't know the mountain's history like she did.

"Okay. Here we go. The first prize in beverages was Eugene Bath. He's the one who made that carbonated mint tea. It was actually really good."

Mary Lou just looked at her.

"Right. And then Bella Prost."

Mary Lou closed her eyes, thinking about Bella.

"I really don't think it could be her," Erin said. "I work with her, and… she's just not that kind of person. She liked Joshua. She wouldn't have done anything to hurt him, even if it did mean losing her prize and people thinking that she participated in something underhanded. She just wouldn't."

"I make it a policy not to assume that children will follow the examples of their parents and make the same good choices—or bad ones—that their parents would make." She met Erin's eyes. "I think you're right about Bella. I don't think the girl has a mean bone in her body."

Erin nodded, relieved. "She said that Campbell and Joshua never bullied her like some of the other kids at school. She thought they were both really nice boys. I've never heard her say anything against them, and I just don't think she would do anything to hurt Joshua."

"Who else?"

"Louisa David. She's the one who got third place after Clayton was disqualified. She made this really good mango fizz. Like a mango lassi, but fizzy..."

Mary Lou nodded.

Erin wasn't sure why she kept babbling. What did Mary Lou care about what kind of drink Louisa had won third prize for? Or even what Bella had said about Campbell and Joshua? Those things didn't matter.

"Louisa is a young woman, like you," Mary Lou said after some consideration. "Her voice would have the same timbre. Again, more of Tennessee in her accent. But that's true of pretty much anyone around here."

"Matt at the Quiki said that she probably did have more of a Tennessee accent than me. So that's okay. Do you know anything else about her?"

"Her people have been around here for a long time. I've never heard much about Louisa. Graduated school, got married, had a few kids. But nothing... exceptional. Not someone who I think had a lot of ambition."

Erin remembered Charley babbling about Beryl's ambition while she had a concussion. Beryl had wanted to be something. She wanted to be famous for her recipe book, for her cooking, she wanted to start up her own restaurant. She had used all of her influence to get the opportunities that she wanted. Louisa sounded about as far from Beryl as she could be. Erin couldn't picture a woman her age with young children making the trek from Whitewater to Bald Eagle Falls in the middle of the night to kidnap a young man. And then what? Where would she stash him? How would she look after him in between all of her other commitments? Or would she?

She could always have an accomplice. Her husband, probably. He could have been the one to kidnap Joshua, and was holding him in a cabin in the woods somewhere that no one knew about.

But it didn't feel right.

"So that's all of the soft drink winners. Then it's the ice cream winners."

Mary Lou fiddled with her teacup, empty or cold by now. She waited for Erin to continue. She must have heard who the winners were at the time, but a thing like having her son abducted could certainly have erased that knowledge from her memory.

"Doc Edmunds won first place."

"I remember hearing that," Mary Lou said, the corner of her mouth lifting in just a hint of a smile. "I imagine he'll be using his money to rebuild the veterinary office. He'll probably add on a full-service animal shelter."

"Probably," Erin agreed. "And if we're only looking at women, we can probably skip over him."

"He has a nurse-receptionist there. And he has a daughter, though she moved away a long time ago. I can't imagine she would come back here to kidnap Joshua because she wants the prize money. She'd have to get rid of her father before she would inherit it."

"Do you think we should look into Sarah, the receptionist?"

Mary Lou rubbed her eyes. How much sleep had she gotten over the past week? Probably not very much.

"No, not yet. She's too many steps removed. Maybe she has a burning desire to work at a fancier vet office or to open an animal shelter, but I doubt it."

Erin went on to the next name on the list. "The last two are both women. Deidre Robinson and Hannah Clark."

Mary Lou sighed. "Does that mean it has to be one of those two, or that we're on the wrong trail? Do we really think that one of the prizewinners took Joshua? Because she didn't want to lose her money?"

"I don't know. But if it was related to the contest, if they really were laundering money, then these are the names we have to work with. I don't know all of the people who worked with Chef Kirschoff or for the sponsors. I met a few people in Whitewater…" Erin let her mind do a quick review of the people who had worked on the contest. "There was a woman who acted as a tour guide, telling us about Whitewater and its storied history… but I don't think she was even from there, I think she was someone with Chef Kirschoff. She wouldn't have known where to find Joshua. She would have had to come back here from… wherever they went to next."

"I haven't noticed anyone strange around town. Any outsiders, I mean," Mary Lou said. "It's all been very quiet since the contest ended. Like everyone was taking a breath."

"I knew a few of the people at the hotel. And the other judge that they brought in, Lara Gross."

"Lara Gross."

Erin waited to see what Mary Lou thought of her. Mary Lou shook her head. She wasn't going to magically come up with the answer.

"Deidre Robinson. Hannah Clark. Lara Gross. Is it one of them?"

Mary Lou covered her face with both hands. She rubbed her face briskly and palmed her eyes and sat there for a minute with them covered.

"Do you know them?" Erin asked.

"Deidre Robinson. Is that the mother or the daughter?"

Erin looked down at the newspaper. They hadn't included pictures of everyone. There had been too much else of interest. Beryl's death, the explosion at the restaurant, Clayton's arrest. Who wanted to see the faces of the prizewinners? But Erin had seen them at the hotel when she and Vic had gone back. There had been posters with pictures of all of the prizewinners. If Erin could just access them in her memory.

"I think… oh, it's hard to be sure. I think that Deidre was an older woman. Grandma type. White hair."

"The mother, then. She wouldn't be able to sound like you on the phone."

"No. Probably not. I should check, though…" Erin pulled out her phone and did a web search to find the pictures of the prizewinners. There had to be promotional pictures of them online. The first couple of searches that she tried didn't bring up any results.

"What is it?" Mary Lou asked.

"I can't get anything…"

"No service? It can be spotty out here."

"No, I mean… my searches aren't producing any results. I'm looking for the contest results, but searching the name of the contest doesn't bring anything up."

Mary Lou shrugged. "That's not surprising, is it?"

"Well… yes, it is. All of the publicity that they did, and none of that got posted online? No summary of events or promotional flyers for the contest?"

"It was all done locally. Not on the internet. People in these parts, they're a close community. Posters go up at the library and town hall. Or in people's shop windows. In the weekly newspaper or the penny saver. We don't go looking for that kind of thing online." She gave a little laugh. "Not us old folks, anyway."

"I knew the newspaper wasn't online, but nothing? They didn't put anything online? I didn't even know that was possible." Erin switched over to one of her social networks and did a search there. People must have posted pictures and tweeted and shared the results on social media. At least the young people, even if the older ones weren't into social media.

But the results were sparse, and she didn't find any pictures of Deidre Robinson. Erin switched over and searched for Hannah Clark. More results for her. Social media profiles. Some pictures of her with a bowl of the ice cream she had made, smiling sunnily at the camera. Erin searched for Lara Gross. She had professional headshots on her company website, her work history on LinkedIn, and all of the other things that Erin would have expected.

"I guess Deidre just doesn't have any social media," she said.

Mary Lou nodded, not surprised.

And Erin shouldn't have been surprised either. There were plenty of white-haired grandma types who didn't have social media accounts. They hadn't grown up on computers. Many had never learned to do anything on the internet but read their mail, if that. Maybe just texts on their phones. If they had smartphones and not an old flip phone like the sheriff.

But no social media? No one else had posted pictures of her on their accounts either? No one in her family had written about granny winning a big cash prize in the cooking contest?

No one?

CHAPTER 40

"This doesn't feel right," Erin said. "You said that she has a daughter?"

"Yes… oh, you're taxing my memory if you expect me to be able to remember that. She would have been my age. But we didn't go to school together."

"And she was in Whitewater, so she wouldn't be in your school yearbook."

"No."

Then Mary Lou raised her hand in a 'wait' gesture. Her brows drew together.

"Yes."

"Yes?"

Mary Lou got up. She spun in a slow circle. "Where did I put those? I don't know if I ever even unpacked them after we moved here."

She hadn't always lived there. Erin had forgotten that the house was just a rental. Mary Lou and her family had lost everything in the financial disaster involving Angela Plaint. Including their house. It was really remarkable that Mary Lou hadn't held a bigger grudge against Angela.

"I think… in the attic," Mary Lou decided. She started toward the stairs.

"Do you need help?" Erin asked, standing, unsure what to do.

"No, no. There are actually stairs. No messing about with ladders."

Erin sat back down. She watched Mary Lou go up the first flight of the stairs and then she disappeared down the hall.

Erin held her breath. Were they going in the right direction? It could be completely wrong. It could be someone who worked for one of the big sponsors. Some of them were huge corporations with thousands of employees. How would they ever find a needle in a haystack like that?

She waited. She had figured it would only take Mary Lou a minute to go up to the attic and find the books she was looking for. But they were packed away. And there were probably a number of other boxes that had never been unpacked either. And maybe none of them labeled clearly.

Erin shifted her position, anxious. She wanted to be there, digging through the boxes, finding the books. Like when Erin had been looking for Clementine's journal, back when she had first come to Bald Eagle Falls.

But Clementine's journal hadn't been in any of the storage boxes. It had been in the hands of Davis and Joelle. They had stolen it from Erin and used it for their own purposes.

What if someone had stolen the yearbooks? Maybe that's what it had all been about. Not about kidnapping Joshua, but about getting into the attic to find the yearbooks.

But who would know that they were there, other than Mary Lou? How would anyone know that she hadn't just thrown them out? Not everyone kept their high school yearbooks. The teenage years were a horrible time. Plenty of people didn't want to remember anything about that time. Erin had never had a yearbook, and she wasn't sure she would have wanted one. What good would it have been for her?

She could hear boxes being moved around up in the attic. So Mary Lou was still at it. She hadn't passed out in the hot, dusty attic.

Erin forced herself to look down at her phone and to work through a few more searches. The time would go faster if she kept herself busy. Before she knew it, Mary Lou would be back down with the yearbooks for the years that she and Deidre's daughter had been in high school.

She almost succeeded in distracting herself from Mary Lou's search.

But not quite.

It was eerie how nothing was showing up on her searches for the contest or for any mentions or pictures of Deidre Robinson.

"Here we go," Mary Lou announced, appearing at the top of the stairs. She held a small stack of hardcover books in her hands. She rejoined Erin, and they sat side-by-side on the couch so that they could look at the books together.

"So I was thinking, we didn't go to the same schools, so there wouldn't be any pictures of her in my yearbook. But I forgot about sports. Our school teams played against each other more than once. And she was on the basketball team."

"Great! Good thinking."

Mary Lou picked up one of the books and started to flip through it. She started at the back, which appeared to be the standard place to put pictures of the various winning teams. Her eyes searched for the girl that she remembered. Or nearly remembered.

"Ah-hah. Here she is." Mary Lou put her face close to the page, taking in the small black and white picture. "Rosalie. Deidre's daughter is Rosalie."

"Rosalie," Erin repeated. "Rosalie Robinson?"

"She probably went by her married name. It was… Brandon." Mary Lou pointed at one of the boys' teams. "She married Marcus Brandon, her high school sweetheart. Of course, they didn't stay together, but she kept his name. Probably the only thing she ever got from him."

"Okay. Rosalie Brandon." Erin tapped it quickly into her phone. There would be hits for Rosalie Brandon. She still wasn't young enough to have a huge social media presence, but it would be more than her white-haired mother. "Let's have a look…"

Erin trailed off. Again, the results were sparse. There were other Rosalie Brandons, of course, but no Rosalie Brandon in Whitewater Junction, or one of the other small towns nearby.

"Why aren't they on here?"

"Not everyone is," Mary Lou said. "The only reason I have an account on any social media is so that my sons can share things with me or message me. But I figure… by the time they have kids, at least I'll know where to find the baby pictures." She laughed weakly.

The laugh quickly turned to a sober expression. She was clearly reconsidering whether either of the boys would ever have children for her to spoil and coo over their baby pictures. Campbell wasn't exactly pursuing the path toward being a responsible father. And Joshua…

Erin tapped in a couple more searches. She tapped one of the results. "There's an obituary." She skimmed through it quickly, checking the names of the mother and ex-husband. "Did you know she had died?"

Mary Lou shook her head. "It's been so long. I didn't remember that, but I'm not surprised. It isn't like we were ever friends or kept in touch. It just would have been one of those cases where you say, 'Oh, I remember her, she was on the Whitewater girls' basketball team the year we won the championship.'"

Erin nodded. "So this is a dead end." Clearly, their kidnapper was not Rosalie Brandon, returned from the grave. That would be a whole other genre of mystery.

"I suppose it is. I thought for a minute that we were on to something. Like maybe somebody had intentionally erased information from the internet. You always hear that once something is uploaded to the internet, it can never be deleted, but that always seemed a little far-fetched to me."

Erin continued to look at the obituary, her eyes unfocused. She blinked a couple of times. She was getting tired, and she knew that Mary Lou was tired too. They both needed to sleep. Maybe she would have a dream that would tell her where to look next. Her subconscious brain could work on the problem while she was sleeping. And then in the morning… they could figure it out. They could find Joshua.

The words in the obituary cleared when she blinked. Erin looked at it again. "Rosalie had a daughter?"

"Oh, did she?" Mary Lou was politely uninterested.

"Kim Brandon." Erin tried one last time, tapping the name into her browser search box.

Nothing.

Kim Brandon had to be the right age. If Rosalie and Mary Lou had gone to school together, then Kim Brandon had to be somewhere between Erin's age and Joshua's. If Rosalie had married her high school sweetheart, then the baby had probably followed quickly. She had taken the Brandon name, so she wasn't likely a child of a later marriage or relationship.

"She has to be here. She has to have a social media account. Something. Who wouldn't have some kind of internet presence?"

But looking harder didn't help. Erin couldn't find anything on the woman. It was, as Mary Lou had said, like she had deleted herself from the internet. She had closed all of her social media accounts. Had every reference to herself that she could find deleted from the record.

And not only that, but had any pictures of her grandma deleted as well. She had wiped out every reference to Deidre Robinson that she could find. Made people take down any pictures they had posted of her receiving her check and showing off her maple ripple ice cream. Kim had probably made up some sad story about her grandma. How she was being stalked online after winning the contest, so they had to take everything down for her protection.

And why? Why had it been so important to take down any online information about Deidre and her granddaughter?

CHAPTER 41

Because Kim had a plan. She had a plan to stop Joshua from finding out about the money laundering. Erin didn't know how Kim had figured out about any financial issues to begin with. Maybe, like Erin, she wondered about the rush to run the contest, the large sums of cash, and the unlikelihood of picking Whitewater Junction, Tennessee for the location of a contest that was supposed to garner attention from sponsors and media.

Maybe she was an accountant or some kind of agent or auditor herself. It was impossible to know, since every trace seemed to have been removed from the internet. Maybe she was a computer genius.

But Kim had discovered financial improprieties in the contest and she didn't want her grandmother's name sullied. Or didn't want her to lose the prize money. If Kim were the only grandchild, then she would be in line to inherit that money. Maybe grandma was sick, or Kim planned on helping her along, or she just wanted the money to be there when she eventually died.

"It's Kim," she told Mary Lou with certainty. "Got to be."

Mary Lou looked at her, unblinking. They were moving things forward, but she didn't seem to be happy or excited to have discovered this news.

"Maybe she is," Mary Lou said. "But where does that get us?"

Erin considered what to do next. They clearly couldn't just go to Whitewater and knock on Kim Brandon's door. That wouldn't help them to find Joshua. Terry would probably throttle her.

"Call the guys, I guess. Let Terry and the sheriff know what we found and let them follow up. I met Deputy Coleman over in Whitewater, he seems like he knows what he's doing. They can call him and have him look into it…"

Mary Lou nodded. But her eyes were empty. There was no guarantee that the police would find any reason to interview Kim Brandon. And if Kim didn't feel like talking to the police, she didn't have to. And they still wouldn't know where to find Joshua.

Terry and Sheriff Wilmot agreed that there was good reason to look more closely at Kim Brandon, but it didn't feel like progress. They would run background, check to see if she had any previous charges or convictions, and talk to Deputy Coleman to see what he thought of her. But they still had to check out the other suspects as well. They couldn't just trust Erin's and Mary Lou's instincts on Bella or any other contestants. They would prioritize the women over the men, but only because the person who had called the Quiki with the changed fortunes was a woman. Or passed as a woman on the phone.

"Maybe we should go back to Whitewater," Erin suggested. "I know it's getting late, but…"

"I'm not going to sleep tonight," Mary Lou said.

"No. We could just look around. Talk to Detective Coleman and answer any questions he might have. It's better to go to him than to make him come to us, or interview us over the phone. He'll want to see us face to face."

"Of course," Mary Lou agreed.

"Yeah. Do you mind if I drive?" Erin didn't want to tell Mary Lou that she looked terrible. Erin was afraid that she wouldn't be able to drive to Whitewater safely. Mary Lou might not be able to fall asleep, but that didn't mean she was alert enough to drive.

Mary Lou nodded. "That's fine. You know the way."

It wasn't hard. There were paved highway and road signs all the way.

Erin shifted to rise. "Do you need to do anything before we go?"

"I should tell Campbell where I'm going."

Mary Lou didn't pick up her phone as Erin expected, but got up and walked toward the back of the house.

Campbell was home, but he hadn't bothered to come out when the police were there to talk to his mother about Joshua? She was surprised that he hadn't at least been there to offer emotional support. But Campbell's experience with the Bald Eagle Falls police had not been positive. Maybe he was afraid he would distract them from the real issue. Or that they would accuse him of having been involved.

Mary Lou came back a moment later, Campbell slouching along behind her. His head was bowed. He looked up at Erin through his lashes, looking remarkably vulnerable and childlike for a young man that she knew had been experimenting with the wild life.

"Do you mind if I come along, Miss Erin?"

Erin considered. Of course she didn't mind him going along, but she needed to make sure that he wasn't going to cause trouble. He couldn't be jumping in to do anything rash. If she said he couldn't come along, he would probably just follow along in his car without permission anyway.

"Yes, you can come. But if you have any weapons, you leave them at home. Same with anything else you might have that you wouldn't want the police to find on you."

"No one is going to search me."

"Those are my conditions."

Campbell looked at his mother, blushing around the neck. "Fine," he said. "I just need to get something from my room."

He went up the stairs, hands in pockets, still hunched over.

Mary Lou looked at Erin. "Thank you."

Erin wasn't sure whether she was saying thank you for allowing Campbell to go with them, or thank you for ensuring that he didn't have any contraband with him. She nodded.

Campbell was back in a couple of minutes, and the three of them went out to the truck.

Erin was barely out onto the highway when her phone started buzzing with a call. She tapped on the Bluetooth button and saw Terry's number come up on the screen.

"Hi." Maybe he had something more to ask or something to report back on Kim. Erin didn't expect them to get anything that fast, but maybe Kim had a record. Maybe she'd done this kind of thing before or made threats that they hadn't known about.

"Where are you going?"

Erin glanced over at Mary Lou, then looked back at the road. "Uh, we're just heading out of town."

"We?"

"Mary Lou and I wanted to…" Erin trailed off, hoping that something would occur to her. Mary Lou would jump in with an explanation, or Terry would interrupt to discuss whatever he had called her about.

"You wanted to what? Where are you going?"

Erin cleared her throat. "We wanted to check something…"

"In Whitewater Junction?"

"Uh, yes."

"We already have Coleman and his team in Whitewater. If we need something checked out, they can do it."

"I know. And I'm sure they'll do a great job. But we just hoped… I don't know… if Deputy Coleman wants to talk to us about what we found out and about stuff that happened at the contest, I can answer his questions. We'll be right on hand. And if he finds out that she has… a storage locker or something that they check tonight… then we'll be close… if he finds anything."

"You need to stay in Bald Eagle Falls."

"We'll be back. By the time you're done…"

"I'm probably going to be on most of the night. Erin, it's getting dark, it's late, you're not going to be able to find anything or talk to anyone tonight. Leave it until morning."

Mary Lou spoke up. "Joshua may not make it until morning, Officer Piper."

"You're not going to find him tonight. You don't know what kind of condition he is in or what kind of situation you could walk into. Trust the process. Going into Whitewater tonight and messing around… you're not going to find anything. You're not going to move the case forward. I'm sorry, Mrs. Cox, but you need to come back. This is dangerous."

"We'll check in with this Deputy Coleman. Surely it's not dangerous to talk to him."

"No, I didn't say that. But I don't think for a minute that the two of you—"

"We will be fine. You're not going to talk me out of it, Officer Piper, so you may as well not even try."

"It's my truck," Terry protested, his voice rising.

"You said I could use it," Erin argued. "It isn't like I'm stealing it."

"I did not say that you could take it out of town and go looking for kidnappers."

"I'll bring it back tonight, just like I said. You did give me permission."

"Not to go out of town."

Erin was watching the road signs, her foot down on the gas, figuring that once she got far enough away from Bald Eagle Falls, she could say that she was close enough to Whitewater that there was no point in turning back. She might as well go on to their destination. She knew it was a bad argument, but it would have to do.

"How did you know I was leaving town?" she asked, thinking about her phone. A lot of couples had apps to share their locations. She had never installed one, but was it possible that Terry had put one on her phone without her realizing it? Or that he had hacked her location some other way?

"GPS tracker in the truck," Terry informed her.

"Oh." Erin eased her foot off of the gas. He could see how fast she was going and where she was on the highway. There wasn't any point in trying to fudge where she was and say she was closer to Whitewater. Though Whitewater was not far, and she would be reaching the halfway point before too long.

"My truck is valuable to me. If anyone takes off with it, I want to be able to track it down."

"Yeah, right. That makes sense," Erin agreed.

"I wasn't planning to use it to track you," Terry said. "But you're important to me too. Come on, Erin. You know this is a bad idea. Don't make me come to Whitewater to get you."

"You've got work to do there. Do the stuff that the sheriff asked you to."

Terry made a growling noise. Then he sighed. Erin knew when she heard it that he wasn't going to follow her. He wasn't going to try to physically coerce her into returning to Bald Eagle Falls. He'd hoped that just telling her to return would be enough.

And normally, it would. She wasn't an unreasonable person. But Joshua was missing and they didn't know how long he had left.

She couldn't look at Mary Lou's fading hope and do nothing. They had a clue. They had a path to follow.

They had to follow it and see where it led.

CHAPTER 42

Erin felt guilty as they pulled into Whitewater. Night was falling quickly. She knew that Terry didn't think it was safe or a good idea for them to be there. But she couldn't sit at home with Mary Lou and do nothing.

"Do you want to have a look around first? Before it gets completely dark?"

"We won't have long."

"No," Erin agreed. She took Mary Lou's response as a 'yes,' and started to work her way through the main streets of Whitewater. A lot of the residents actually lived outside of the town limits in the surrounding farms and acreages. There would be no way to find Kim without directions if she lived outside of town.

But they weren't going to search for Kim. They would leave that for the police. They were just going to take a look around, get the lay of the land, see if anything jumped out at them, and then they would go to the police station and talk to Coleman. If he hadn't already called it a night and gone home for dinner or bed.

Even though it was getting dark, Erin recognized most of the streets. She had walked them while she was getting ready for the contest and while it was on. She had gone back and looked through the streets with Vic, hoping to somehow just find Joshua. As if he had just run away and they might find him walking down the street or sitting on the library steps smoking a cigarette.

But what more were they going to find this time? They weren't even looking for someone who might be out walking around, but for someone who was locked up, behind closed doors.

But Erin felt strongly that they were doing the right thing. Mary Lou and Campbell did not object, so maybe they had the same feeling. That they were close. If they just drove by the place Joshua was imprisoned, they might feel it. They would find him.

They all watched out the windows, studying every building they went by. Some of them, Erin automatically discounted. Stores and businesses that were open to the public. Joshua couldn't be hidden somewhere close to people, where he might make a noise and draw attention. It would have to be an outbuilding. A storage unit. A garage or shed of some kind.

And those were not in short supply.

"Do you think he's here?" Campbell asked his mother.

Her face was a stony mask. She sat in the passenger seat and didn't turn around to look at Campbell, who was sitting with his knees turned to the side because the seats were so close together.

"If it was Kim Brandon who took him… then he must be here somewhere."

"You don't think that she kept him somewhere closer to Bald Eagle Falls? Or out in the woods?"

"Maybe."

"But she couldn't do anything that would draw people's attention," Erin said. "If she suddenly started disappearing for an hour or two every day, people would notice. They would wonder what she was doing, where she was going all of a sudden."

Assuming she was taking care of Joshua. That wasn't guaranteed. It had been so long, what were the chances that she had kept him alive? Why would she? She wanted him to be gone permanently, didn't she?

They drove by a low brick building. Erin had to strain her eyes to see the sign out front, which had one dim spotlight shining on it. Two other spotlights had burned out and not been replaced. It was the Whitewater Junction General Hospital.

"I didn't know they had their own hospital here. When Charley and Chef Kirschoff were hurt, they were taken into the city."

Mary Lou nodded her head. "These little rural hospitals, they aren't good for much more than broken arms or the stomach flu. If you are very ill, or there's an accident, they don't have the kind of trauma care that a city hospital has."

Of course not. It wouldn't make sense for a little hospital to have the personnel or expertise to man a trauma center. Erin drove slowly past it.

"It looks more like an old folks' home or hospice than a hospital."

Erin had worked in hospice care. She'd been in a few places like that. Rooms that tried to imitate the home environment as much as possible, to be comfortable for the patients despite IV stands and other necessary hospital equipment. Quiet places, where the lights were kept dim, the music quiet and comforting, and any PA announcements were kept to a minimum. There was no Code Blue in places like that. No reason to resuscitate patients who slipped gently into the dark.

"Yes," Mary Lou agreed. "They probably have some hospice care here. Or a dementia ward. Places where you just… house people until they're ready to go."

Erin pulled to a stop.

CHAPTER 43

Campbell and Mary Lou looked at her.

"What is it?" Campbell asked.

Erin looked at the little hospital, frowning and thinking. "So Deidre won the cooking competition. And we figure Kim is probably her sole heir."

"Right," Mary Lou agreed.

"And Kim has kidnapped Joshua to keep the whole corruption thing quiet. So that no one can find out about it and take away Deidre's money or smear her reputation, whichever it is."

Campbell was listening attentively. He hadn't heard the whole theory before. He just knew that they were going to Whitewater to look for Joshua and talk to the police about a suspect.

"How long?" Erin asked.

"How long what?" Mary Lou asked in confusion.

"How long was she planning to hold Joshua? Or how long did she figure she was going to have to protect Deidre or wait until she could get the money?"

"Kidnapping someone and planning to hold them for more than a few days is crazy," Campbell contributed. "You can't look after all of someone's needs for that long; it takes you away from everything else. And if they get sick… and you have to worry about if they are going to figure out how to escape, or someone is going to cotton on to what you're doing. The longer you hold someone, the more dangerous it is."

"But she had this whole plan. She must have been planning to hold on to Joshua, because she didn't... do something permanent in Bald Eagle Falls. If she wanted him permanently out of the picture, she could have done that. Nobody would have connected it to Whitewater. However she got into the house or got him out of it, she could have gotten rid of him permanently. If that was what she had wanted. Then she wouldn't have to worry about taking care of him. Or about him escaping or giving her away somehow."

"Then... you don't think she planned to hold Joshua for this long?" Mary Lou asked.

"No. She had it all planned out. We know it wasn't a spur-of-the-moment thing, because she called in the change order to the Quiki before she took him. She had a plan, and she followed through on it. Only... he should have been released by now. Two days, three, you don't plan to kidnap and hold someone for any longer than that, right?"

Cam's words echoed in her ears.

The longer you hold someone, the more dangerous it is.

Campbell looked at the hospital. "So why are we stopped here? You don't think Joshua's in there, do you? That she's a nurse, or that she would bring him here if he got sick? Kidnappers don't do that. If something happened to him... she would just run."

"Without her money?" Erin shook her head. "We thought it wasn't about money, because she didn't ask for a ransom. But she's waiting for the money. She thinks that Deidre is going to die and she's going to inherit."

"You don't get money the day after someone dies," Mary Lou said dryly.

"No. And if you've been through a death in the family like that, you know that. But does Kim know that? Or maybe she's gotten Deidre to put everything in their joint names, so that they don't have to probate. So as soon as Deidre dies, it is automatically Kim's. She can cash out and run, and send us a message about where to find Joshua."

If she was smart enough to figure out that the contest had been laundering money, then she was smart enough to know how to get around waiting for weeks or months while Grandma's estate was probated.

"And you think her grandma is in there?" Campbell finally made the connection. He looked at the lights still on in the hospital. "And Kim is just waiting for her to die?"

"Or maybe trying to help her along," Erin agreed. It happened. People did things to speed up the inheritance process.

"But there wasn't anything wrong with Deidre," Mary Lou dismissed. "If she was dying, then how would she make the ice cream that won one of the prizes?"

"It only took a day. She wouldn't have needed a lot of energy for that. Or maybe she didn't get sick until after she won the prize money. After Kim decided that she wanted it."

They traipsed into the hospital. Erin was sure that visiting hours were probably over. But she had a few tricks up her sleeve. She had worked in hospice before.

She approached the main reception desk and spoke very quietly to the nurse situated there. "We're here to see Deidre Robinson. Is she..." Erin raised her eyebrows and hesitated awkwardly.

The nurse recognized the signals. Rather than objecting that she couldn't give them any information, she tapped the name into her computer and glanced over the records. "Deidre is still with us," she relayed back in a whisper.

"I'm sorry we're so late. We just got the call yesterday that she might not make it... we've been driving for seventeen hours..."

The nurse nodded understandingly. She picked up a slip of paper and a pen and wrote the unit and room number. "You just go down that hallway," she explained. "Take a right and go all the way to the end. There's another desk for the unit nurse there. She'll show you to Deidre's room."

"Thank you so much."

Erin turned to Mary Lou and Campbell and whispered to them. "We got here in time. It isn't too late."

They all hoped that it wasn't too late for Joshua too.

Erin led the way down the corridor. When they reached the Palliative Care unit, the lighting was dim, as Erin had pictured it. There was an air of quiet expectation about the place. A portal between life and death. Erin didn't usually believe in an afterlife. But when she was in a place like that, when she watched a soul transition from life, that was when she really wondered if there was a place for the person's consciousness to go afterward.

Erin flashed the slip of paper with the room number on it at the unit nurse. "We're here to see Deidre. Do we just go in? Is it okay?"

Neither nurse had even bothered to ask if they were related. Anyone who came to say goodbye to a dying patient was family.

"Just over there." The nurse in a pink smock smiled and pointed. "Third door down. She's sleeping comfortably right now."

This time it was Mary Lou who took the lead. Erin and Campbell followed.

CHAPTER 44

Erin could vaguely remember the white-haired woman smiling on the contest poster. She had seemed bright and vibrant. Matronly, friendly, the kind of person that would have made the perfect grandma in a commercial or family movie.

That woman was gone.

Deidre's hair had yellowed and thinned, as had her face. Her wrinkled cheeks were sunken in, and there was no evidence of the warm pink blush she had worn the day of the contest. Her eyes were closed, the sockets around them appearing bruised. No machines were beeping loudly or monitoring her vital signs. Her breathing was shallow and somewhat labored. Stopping and starting again in an irregular rhythm, so that Erin didn't know when to expect the next breath, if at all.

Mary Lou sat down in the chair right next to the bed. She took Deidre's hand and squeezed gently. "Deidre? Mrs. Robinson?"

Deidre stirred. Erin was surprised. She had thought that Deidre was too far gone, that she was in the last sleep of her life and they wouldn't be able to rouse her again. She had seen that state enough times.

"Deidre? It's Mary Lou Hensley, Mrs. Robinson. Do you remember me?"

Deidre's head moved back and forth and her breathing seemed to grow louder and more strained. Erin bit her lip, worrying that waking

Deidre now was going to be too much of a shock to her system and they would only hurry her demise.

"Deidre." Mary Lou gave the older woman's hand a little shake. She patted Deidre's cheek. Not slapping it, just patting it, hopefully enough to arouse her one more time. "Deidre, I need your help. Please."

Finally, Deidre's eyes cracked open. Her irises were dark, it seemed like her eyes were very distant. Erin didn't know if she could see Mary Lou.

"Who is there?" she asked unsteadily.

"My name is Mary Lou. I went to school at the same time as your daughter Rosalie. Except I went to Bald Eagle Falls. We played Whitewater in the girls' basketball playoffs. Do you remember that?"

"We won," Deidre recalled, her mind much sharper than Erin had expected. "Rosalie was on the team that year. She got twelve points in that game."

Mary Lou laughed. "Yes. She did. Well, I wasn't on the Bald Eagle Falls team, but I was watching. I remember Rosalie."

Deidre licked her lips. Her mouth stayed partway open and Erin knew it was dry. She was dehydrated. They hadn't put her on an IV—no lifesaving measures. There was a cup on the side table. Warm water that had probably been sitting there the whole day. Erin reached around Mary Lou to pick it up and gently put the straw to Deidre's mouth. "Do you want water?"

Deidre sucked. Just a little sip of water. Not enough. Deidre nodded her thanks. Erin went into the tiny bathroom and found a washcloth. She got it wet and squeezed it out, then returned to the bed. She sponged Deidre's dry lips gently. Deidre smacked them together a few times.

"Where is Rosalie?" she asked.

"Rosalie isn't here," Mary Lou told her. "Has Kim been in to see you?"

"Oh, yes." A little nod. "Kim has been here. She's a good girl, Kimmy."

"I'm glad she's been visiting you. Does she take care of you?"

"Yes. Yes, Kimmy is a good girl."

"Does she give you your medications?" Erin guessed. "Or bring you food?"

"Sometimes she brings me soup. Like the chicken soup I used to make her when she was a little girl." Deidre's mouth moved, remembering it.

"She's a good cook, but she doesn't get the soup quite right. Not quite right."

Erin wondered what Kimmy was putting in the soup.

"Is she coming back today?"

Deidre's head moved as she looked around the room. Trying to orient herself as to date and time, probably. Or looking to see if Kim were already there.

"No, it's late," she said finally. "She must have gone home to sleep."

"Where?" Mary Lou leaned closer. "Did she go back to the farm?"

"No..." Deidre's voice was soft. Not uncertain, exactly, but trying to remember the details. "We left the farm a few years ago. We needed to be in town. Here."

"What street? Do you know the address? We should go and see her."

"She'll be back in the morning."

"But we should see her tonight. Can you tell me where she is?"

Deidre closed her eyes and snored slightly. Talking required too much energy. She had done well to even wake up and remember those details in the first place. Very well.

She was holding on better than Kim had expected her to.

They went back out to the unit nurse's desk. Erin put down the piece of paper with the unit and room number, and snagged a pen from the nurse's pen cup.

"I'm so glad we got here in time. We should go see Kimmy, see how she's holding up. I wrote down the address when she called me, but everything has been so crazy in the rush to get here." Erin opened her purse and pulled out a stack of notes written on various types of paper. Her purse was always a mess. "It's in here somewhere, but..." she paused, blinking rapidly, leafing through the notes. "I just can't find it. Maybe I threw it out. I honestly don't even know how we made it here..."

The nurse took the pen and paper and handed her a tissue from the box strategically placed on her desk. "There, dear, let me just write it down."

"Thank you. I think right now I would forget my head if it wasn't screwed on tight."

"It's a very difficult time for family members. Don't be so hard on yourself."

"Is she okay?" Erin looked back toward the hospital room where Deidre was once more sleeping peacefully. "She didn't look like she was in a lot of pain."

"No, that's all managed. We don't let them suffer. Our goal here is to make them as comfortable as possible until the end. It's very important for our families."

Erin nodded. She remembered what it was like. Once an elderly person reached a certain point, it was more important to give them painkillers than to extend their lives.

The nurse slid the paper back to Erin. "There you are, now. Bless you for coming to see her. I'm sure she knew you were there, even if she didn't wake up."

Erin didn't tell her that Deidre had woken up, and even talked to them.

"Thank you for taking such good care of her. Nurses are guardian angels without the wings."

The nurse smiled appreciatively. "You take care now. I'll see you tomorrow."

CHAPTER 45

They went back out to the truck and got in. Mary Lou looked at Erin.

"Guardian angels without the wings?"

Erin hesitated. "Do guardian angels not have wings? Did I mess that up?"

Mary Lou chuckled. "Just don't expect to hear something like that from an atheist."

Erin shrugged. She could feel herself blushing and was glad that it was now fully dark so that Mary Lou couldn't see it. "People still like to get compliments. As long as it makes her feel good, I don't see the harm."

"I just wouldn't expect you to use that form of compliment."

Erin glanced back at the hospital. "I've worked in end of life care before. People say lots of religious things, even if they don't believe it. It's kind of expected. I guess being there just brought it back."

Mary Lou nodded and didn't say anything else about it. "So… are we going to Kim's house?"

Erin looked at her and glanced back at Campbell. "It wouldn't hurt to drive by there, would it? Just get the lay of the land? I know Terry wouldn't want us to talk to her, but we can look, can't we?"

Erin remembered visiting Theresa; she, Vic, and Willie going out there to see if she could answer some questions and find out if she had seen Terry and Detective Jack Ward. That had been a mistake.

It had been terrifying and led to their being held at gunpoint and Erin being injured, but they wouldn't have found Terry or been able to save Jack if they hadn't done it. So in the end, that had been more important than what they'd had to go through. She couldn't imagine what life would be like if Terry had disappeared and never been found. Or if they did find his body later.

So she knew she could be wrong about checking out Kim's home. They might be walking right into the barrel of another gun held by another crazy person. But they had to do what they could to find Joshua. Kim may have initially intended to release him once Deidre died and she could claim her inheritance and run, but it was taking much longer than expected. It was dangerous to try to hide someone for long.

Mary Lou and Campbell both agreed that it was perfectly reasonable to go over just to make sure everything looked fine. They wouldn't go in and question Kim. But there wasn't any harm in just driving by.

"Should we call that deputy?" Mary Lou asked.

"We can go over to the police station after. I know where it is. Then we can tell him face-to-face what we've been able to sort out. He'll be much more likely to act if we talk to him directly, right?"

"We may as well wait until we have some more evidence," Campbell agreed. "If we can find anything else. If not… well, he already knows everything we know or have guessed. We don't have anything new to tell him yet."

"Except about Deidre being at death's door," Mary Lou said dryly.

"Except for that," Cam agreed.

Erin decided that they were all on the same page. She tapped the address into the GPS navigator and waited for the highlight line to appear on the map. The town seemed very small when reduced to gridlines on the LCD screen.

After waiting what seemed an excessively long time with so few streets to choose from, the short line appeared, directing them a few blocks away. It was quiet enough that Erin could flip a U-turn in front of the hospital, and they were soon at Kim's house. Erin removed her key from the ignition and took her foot off the brake pedal so the truck's lights would shut off. They all sat there in the dark, staring at the house.

It was a little, old house. Not as big as Clementine's house, where Erin lived. A dollhouse, a real estate agent might call it. She would be surprised if there was more than one bedroom. It was on a fair-sized lot, land being cheap in a small town. Erin could see the shapes of dark trees around it.

"Is there a shed?" Erin asked, "Any garage or outbuildings?"

"I see the roof of a garage," Campbell offered. Erin could see little in the dark. "Let's just… walk around and see."

Even though Erin had told Campbell not to bring anything illegal along with him, he still managed to open the garage door. Erin had already tested the doorknob and found it locked just a moment before. He was obviously pretty quick with the lock picks. It would have taken her several minutes of fiddling to encourage it to open. Erin pretended not to notice. Mary Lou said nothing. Campbell entered first, his tennis shoes silent as he moved in. After a glance around, he took out his phone and thumbed it on, using just the screen's glow to light up the space in front of him.

As with most garages, there was all manner of parts and equipment around the perimeter of the inside, one car instead of two, and very little clear space for walking. It was pretty obvious from the start that Joshua was not being held captive in the garage. But Campbell didn't retreat. He circled the car, looking in the windows and shining his phone screen inside. He used his t-shirt like a hot pad to open the driver's door without getting his fingerprints on it, then pressed the trunk release button inside.

Erin was nervous about looking in the trunk. She didn't think they were going to find anything horrible and gruesome in it, but…

Mary Lou hung back, and Erin and Campbell advanced to have a peek inside. There was no smell of decomposition as they approached, but Erin still took a deep breath before looking into it to brace herself.

Let it be empty.

They looked in at the same time. There was no body in the trunk. Erin breathed back out. Campbell lowered his phone for a better look. When he still couldn't see very well into the shadowy depths, he turned it around and turned on the flashlight LED.

He ran it over the items in the trunk, moving things carefully without touching any surfaces that might take a print. There was some clothing, not recognizable as Joshua's. As Campbell shifted stuff around, Erin saw a large roll of silvery duct tape and an opened plastic pocket of large zip ties. She felt acid rising in her throat and looked away, swallowing. It took her a moment to get her composure back, and she looked again. Campbell disentangled a headband from a dark hoodie, and Erin saw that it was a pair of hefty-looking goggles like would be used to play a VR game. She looked at Campbell, frowning.

"Night vision," Campbell whispered.

Night vision? So that someone could walk through the woods without a flashlight? Hunting? What innocent reason could Kim have for needing night vision goggles, duct tape, and zip ties? Erin tried to puzzle through it, and settled on hunting, though everything in her screamed that it was not. There was no innocent explanation. Kim had to be the kidnapper.

She wished that she had been able to find something about Kim online. What she looked like, so they would recognize her when they saw her. Whether she was big or small. How old she was. If she could have physically overcome Joshua or whether she had an accomplice.

They could be in the house now, Kim, Joshua, and a big, menacing man.

"We have to call the police," Erin told Campbell.

He ignored her, carefully moving the clothing and the items he had looked at to the side to see what was underneath. Erin tried to memorize the positions everything had been in when they opened the trunk. He was messing with everything, and they didn't want Kim to know it when she next came out to the car.

There was a tote bag that was black on the outside with brightly colored stripes on the lining. Campbell opened it up and shone his phone light inside. Some pretty print fabric like pajamas. Some bottles clinking around the bottom. Things for Kim to take to Deidre at the hospital? Clothes that were familiar and comfy and some drinks to tempt her appetite? Campbell teased the clothing out and unfolded one pajama top.

Erin's stomach again took a nosedive. This time, it was Campbell who looked at her for an explanation. Erin pressed one hand to her stomach and the knuckles of one hand to her teeth.

"It's a nurse's smock," Erin told him. She looked across the car at Mary Lou, worried. What if one of the nurses they had seen had been Kim and now knew they were on to her? Erin fought the impulse to pull out her phone and look the woman up on Facebook to see what she looked like, reminding herself firmly that Kim didn't have a Facebook account and there was no point in looking to see if one had somehow magically appeared.

"This stuff wouldn't still be here," Campbell said. "The first thing she would do if she thought we were on to her is get rid of everything incriminating. She wasn't at the hospital. She was at home, watching TV or in bed."

But they hadn't seen the flicker of a TV inside the house, and none of the windows showed lights on inside. For most of the town, it was still too early for bed. Except for bakers who had to be up before dawn.

And maybe Kim, being a nurse, had to go to bed early for a morning shift. Erin tried to slow her breathing and calm herself down. Kim didn't know about them. She didn't know that they were snooping through her trunk. They were perfectly safe.

Campbell had moved on. He roughly refolded the smock and put it in the pile with the rest. He looked at the soft drink bottles that were clinking around in the bottom of the bag.

But of course, they were not soft drink bottles any more than the nursing smocks were pajamas. They were medication bottles. Not the orange plastic prescription bottles like Erin got at the pharmacy, but glass vials of clear liquids to be injected with a needle.

Campbell didn't let her see them long enough to know whether they were something she might have been giving her grandmother, or something used to incapacitate Joshua during the kidnapping. And maybe to keep him sedated since then.

"But where is she keeping him?" Erin asked. She looked into the trunk for some other clue. She didn't think it could be too far away; she wouldn't want people to notice her absence for long periods of time. She was careful.

Unfortunately, there was no map in the trunk with an X marking the spot where Joshua was being held.

"In the house?" Campbell motioned in the direction of Kim's house. Or her grandmother's house. Whoever's it happened to be.

"No… I don't think so. Why would she need the night vision goggles? She could just turn on the light."

"Then he would see her."

"Keep him blindfolded."

Campbell nodded, conceding the point.

Erin racked her mind for anything that the items in the trunk might suggest. The hospital, but of course Kim wouldn't be able to hold him at the hospital. How? In a closet? The morgue? Masquerading as a coma patient? That didn't make any sense or require the use of the goggles.

There were no other clues in the trunk. So forget the trunk.

Erin walked around the car, using her own phone as a flashlight this time. Mud in the treads of the tires? Some kind of leaves or pine needles that would magically lead them to the exact place in the woods Kim had been visiting?

On TV, the detective always found the necessary clues. They were always right there, and the detective had everything needed to examine them and to come to a conclusion of the place where the abductee was being kept.

In real life, lots of missing person cases were never solved. Some abductees were discovered years later. Sometimes, not even their remains came to light. It was too easy to hide someone, especially with all of the caves and wilderness areas near Whitewater.

Still, Erin kept walking around the car, looking for some clue that they had missed. It was muddy, but she was not an analyst who could tell where the mud had come from. It looked like Kim had been off of paved roads at some point, but how long ago? How far away? She walked past Mary Lou without discovering anything else that would show them where Kim had been.

When she got around to the driver's door, Erin slid into the seat.

"Don't touch anything," Campbell warned.

"I know. I'm not," Erin agreed, holding her hands up in front of her. Though she had put her hands down on the seat when she had climbed inside. She wiggled around in the seat to try to smear or obscure any handprint she might have left on it. She looked at the sun visors. No maps. No park membership stickers on the windows or hanging from the rearview mirror. No gas receipts in the center console.

She used her thumbnail to press the release for the glovebox. It was neat and tidy. Owner's manual. Invoices and receipts for car repairs in a plastic pouch. Sunglasses. She pressed it closed again with her knuckle.

Campbell walked to the door and looked down at her. "Anything?"

Erin sat there, looking around the interior of the car. She double-checked the back seat. Fabric bags for shopping. She closed her eyes, thinking.

They needed to call the police. Like Terry had said, it was too dangerous for them to be investigating it themselves. They needed to let Detective Coleman know what they had been able to find so far. He could get a search warrant. He could get Kim's phone, and maybe that would tell them where she had been.

Terry.

Where she had been.

Erin's eyes sought out the small LCD screen mounted above the radio.

CHAPTER 46

Erin ran her finger around the outside, looking for the power button. She pressed and held it in. The LCD screen flashed to life, the brand name splash screen appearing.

"The GPS?" Campbell asked.

"The GPS."

Mary Lou came closer.

"What?"

"What are the chances that she's going to mark the location she has Joshua on her GPS?" Campbell demanded. "You think she's going to label it 'hideout' or 'abandoned cabin'? She knows where it is, she's not going to mark it for anyone else."

Erin waited impatiently for it to finish booting up. It didn't have a lot of battery reserves. Probably it didn't hold a charge very well and Kim just kept it plugged into the cigarette lighter for power and used it while the car was running. But Erin didn't want to turn on the ignition. Kim might be nearby, and she just might recognize the sound of her car starting and wonder what the heck was going on.

The main menu finally appeared. Erin started tapping the menu choices with her fingernail, trying not to leave any fingerprints on the screen.

"She might not mark it in her favorites, but if she has breadcrumbs turned on…"

"What are breadcrumbs?" Mary Lou asked.

Campbell was looking thoughtful. He raised his eyebrows, nodding. "It's like Hansel and Gretel," he told his mother. "When they walked through the forest, they left a trail of breadcrumbs behind them so that they'd be able to find their way home again. Breadcrumbs on a GPS show you where you have been, so you can follow them back again."

Mary Lou watched Erin fiddling with the menu options. "Do all GPS's have that?"

"Most of them do. It's standard. I don't know how many are turned on by default…"

Erin was hoping they were. She finally drilled down through the menus and found 'previous tracks.' She paged through them. The hospital. The grocery store. Out to the city and back running errands. Out of town to the east, following a secondary road that didn't lead anywhere with a label.

She continued to page back, seeing the same routes repeated several times. She was out on that secondary road every day.

"Look at this," she commanded Campbell. "Memorize it for when we get back to the truck."

She zoomed in, and they both watched the screen intently as it took the route turn by turn, and then back to the house again. Erin tried to commit every inch of it to memory.

"Okay. Let's go."

~

"Should we take the night vision goggles with us?" Campbell asked. "We might not be able to see where we're going without them."

"No." Erin shook her head. "We have to leave everything exactly where we found it so that the police can collect it as evidence."

"How are we going to explain how we found the route out to… the cabin or whatever it is?"

"I don't know yet. That's not important. We need to get out there."

They closed everything up, leaving it the way they had found it, and walked back to the truck. Erin looked at the house several times as they passed, trying not to, but looking for any sign that Kim was in there. Sleeping before the next shift. Tucked away safely so that they didn't have to worry about her. Her car was still in the garage, so it wasn't like she was at the cabin waiting for them. The only person waiting for them at the cabin would be Joshua.

Hopefully.

Assuming she had no accomplice.

The lights on Terry's truck came on as soon as they opened the doors. Erin wished it were an older truck or had some kind of stealth mode. She felt like she was naked in the middle of a spotlight and everybody was looking at her.

She oriented the truck in the direction the car would have been traveling once Kim pulled it out of the garage and onto the street. She and Campbell watched for the curves in the road, the intersections, and the turns they needed to take to get out there.

Mary Lou sat in the back, silent, saying nothing to hurry them along or to stop them. Erin tapped the Bluetooth control and gave it the command to call Terry. He answered almost immediately.

"Are you on your way back?"

"No. We're going to another location, where we think Joshua was being held. You can follow your GPS. Have the sheriff drive you out this way. Call Detective Coleman and let him know where we're going."

"You'd better call him."

"I'm driving, trying to remember the way. You can give him our locations better, watching us on your GPS. I can't walk him through it while we're trying to navigate."

Terry grunted. "Fine. Do you want me to stay on the phone with you? Three-way call?"

"No. I need to focus."

"Do you remember what I told you about staying out of trouble and not chasing this person on your own?"

"She's at home in bed. Her car is in the garage. All the lights are off."

"She could have another vehicle. You don't know."

"There was no space for another vehicle in the garage. It was full of junk."

"That doesn't mean she doesn't have another vehicle. Where did you keep your car?"

"Well... on the street, because Clementine's Volkswagen is in the garage. But the car in her garage is her primary vehicle. We know that she —never mind. It's the vehicle she's been using. She's not somewhere else. She's a nurse. She probably has an early shift."

"You know a lot more than you did when you left here. I told you not to poke around."

"I think you should come out here. And I think you should call Detective Coleman."

"I will. You keep out of trouble and stay safe. Don't go into any more buildings. Just stay where you are and let the police department do their job."

"I will when we get there. I'll either wait for you or for him."

"It won't be me. He'll be closer and it's his jurisdiction. At least, I assume it's within his jurisdiction."

"Unless he tells you he won't come out until morning."

"He's not going to say that. Not with civilians about to get themselves into a boatload of trouble."

"Good," Erin acknowledged. "I'll talk to you when I see you."

She clicked the button to end the call.

Campbell smothered a laugh. "I knew you were trouble, Miss Erin, but I didn't realize just how stubborn you are."

"Joshua could be in danger. It isn't like we can sit around waiting. If I get in trouble for... hurrying things along a little... then I guess I get in trouble."

"That's one way to look at it."

They were all quiet, watching the road and trying to remember all of the turns. Erin had been afraid that she wouldn't be able to remember the entire route. The call with Terry had pushed many of the details out of her head altogether. But she remembered the highway number, so she watched for it on the road signs. Then they only had to find the right exit. That could be challenging at night, especially if it were only a trail. And Erin suspected it wasn't a paved road. Not with the mud that had been splashed onto Kim's car.

The miles clicked by. It seemed like it would take forever, but Erin knew that it was pretty close. As she had suspected, Kim couldn't take huge chunks out of her day to travel to and from the place where Joshua was being kept. It would be too inconvenient for her and too likely to be noticed.

Then she started to think that they must have gone too far. She slowed, and they watched for the turnoff or some sign that they had missed it and needed to go back.

"There," Campbell said, pointing. "That one is the right angle."

Even looking at it, Erin nearly missed it. She slowed some more and pulled onto the gravel road. "You're sure this is the one?"

"As sure as I can be." Campbell didn't sound too certain of himself, though. "This has to be it."

Erin went slower down the gravel road. She had to turn on her high beams to see far enough ahead on the road to be sure she wouldn't hit some animal or miss a switchback.

"Do you think she used the night vision here? So that she didn't have to turn on her lights? No one would even know someone was coming down this road, if they didn't have their lights on."

"Maybe," Campbell agreed.

Erin gripped the steering wheel tightly, the truck jouncing around over potholes. She noticed that Campbell was holding tightly to the door handle to keep himself still. "Sorry. Bit rough here."

And she was nervous. She was sure she wouldn't run into anyone out on that road, but what if she did? What if someone were guarding the cabin? What if Kim were out there in a secondary vehicle for some reason? Maybe she banged up the exhaust system on the pockmarked road and had to get a rental until she could afford to fix her car. There were a hundred other reasons she might not be home in bed like Erin had told Terry she would be.

She looked at the truck GPS, trying to discern whether the route on the GPS screen looked the same as what she had seen on the screen of the GPS in Kim's car. It was all muddled in her brain. She couldn't be sure. They could miss the cabin altogether and end up at some other farmhouse or dead end.

Erin remembered their drive out to Theresa's house and was immediately twice as anxious. They had been so confident going out there that it was the right thing to do, and that they would find Terry and Jack Ward out there.

Well, they had.

Eventually.

There had just been the intervening incident with Crazy Theresa and her gun and wildly jealous temper in between.

And Terry and Jack had not been in good condition when they had found them. So why was she repeating the process again? Why run that risk?

Because if they had waited until the next day, when they could have convinced the police to go out there and talk to Theresa, it would have been too late. For Jack Ward for sure. Maybe for Terry too.

She wasn't going to wait one more day to rescue Joshua either.

CHAPTER 47

"I think this is it," Campbell whispered.

Erin slowed still more and tried to make out shapes in the darkness ahead of them. There were ghostly buildings ahead of them. And yes, the end of the gravel road. They had reached their destination. Erin pulled the truck to a position as far to the right of the road and the clearing where the buildings were as possible and shut off the ignition.

They waited for all of the truck lights to turn off, and for their eyes to adjust to the dark. Erin wished that she had agreed to bring the night vision goggles. The pale buildings looked completely deserted. Like they had been deserted for decades. Who knew how old they were.

Was that where Deidre had lived when she had first been married? Had it been the homestead? Or was it just some random abandoned farm that Kim had picked out, something completely unrelated to her family? That would have been safer. Safer to use a place that had no connection with her and her people. Much harder to find that way.

Erin waited.

They didn't know how long it would be until Detective Coleman got there. If Terry had talked him into following Erin right away, he might only be five minutes behind. If Terry had left Bald Eagle Falls with the sheriff or another driver and used their lights and siren, they might only be another fifteen minutes behind.

They wouldn't have to wait for long. Terry would know that Erin had stopped. She had told him that they would wait. They wouldn't go rushing into any abandoned buildings and mess everything up. They wouldn't put themselves in danger.

There was no sign of a guard. If Kim had an accomplice, he must be at home asleep as well. Or heading to bed in the next couple of hours. There wasn't anyone inside, since there were no other vehicles in the clearing.

Though another vehicle could be parked just behind one of the pale old buildings, or even inside one of them.

Erin shifted restlessly. Campbell looked at her. She couldn't see his eyes in the dark, just his face pointed toward her. She imagined that his eyes were begging to be allowed out of the truck, to go start searching the buildings for Joshua. Erin wanted to. She didn't like sitting there waiting for someone else to come in and do the work. She wanted to be the one to discover Joshua and to bring him to safety.

"Should we—" Mary Lou started, and then stopped.

Erin could only imagine how excruciating it must be for Mary Lou. Knowing that her son was in one of those buildings, tied up, maybe hurt. Maybe dying. But she wasn't able to rush in and find him and give him everything he needed.

"Soon." Erin said. "They'll be here soon and we'll find him."

"Thank you for doing this, Erin. I know it has been at risk to yourself. And your relationship with Officer Piper."

Erin's mouth twisted into a grimace. She wondered how upset Terry was going to be with her for going ahead and doing what he had said not to do. Would he be able to forgive her? Or was that it for them?

She didn't know how long he could stay with someone who wouldn't do what she was told. He would be putting his own reputation and job at risk.

"I just want to find Joshua and for him to be okay."

"Me too," Mary Lou agreed.

"Me three," Campbell chimed in.

They waited. Erin stared up at the stars. It was a clear night, and it seemed like she could see every star in the Milky Way. The tiny pinpricks of light were so brilliant out in the middle of nowhere. Amazing to someone who had spent most of her life raised in urban neighborhoods.

~

Finally, lights were coming down the gravel road toward them.

Erin caught her breath and held it. There were no rotating police lights. Were the police arriving without lights, or was it someone else? Kim or an accomplice realizing that they were made or there to check on Joshua to make sure he was settled for the night?

The vehicle got closer and closer. Erin couldn't see any light bar on the top of it. She ducked down, as if the driver might not see the big black truck if Erin were low enough. She saw Campbell mirror the movement beside her. But whoever was driving clearly saw the truck parked there. The headlights came straight at them, swerving off at the last moment as the car pulled up beside them. It was a long, dark sedan, with rust, dents, and scratches around the lower portion—an old car, driven for years through all kinds of weather.

Erin grasped the steering wheel tightly, her body looking for a way to defend herself or to escape. She reached for the key. If it were somebody threatening, she could start the truck and drive away before he could reach them. If she waited until right before he reached the truck, he would be delayed getting back into his own vehicle.

Unless, of course, he rolled down his passenger window and shot them from there. But the sedan was much lower to the ground than the truck; he probably wouldn't be able to get a good angle on them from there.

The door of the car opened, and a dark figure climbed out. Stocky, not moving quickly. Erin blinked her eyes, hoping they would adjust to the dark faster. The light from his headlights left bright afterimages in the center of her vision. He was nearly to the truck before she could make out the figure clearly enough that she started to relax. As he covered the last few feet, she could finally see his face. The creased, leathered visage of Detective Coleman of the Whitewater Junction police department. Erin buzzed her window down.

"Miss Price." Coleman glowered. "Can I ask what the hell you are doing here?"

Erin swallowed. "Did Terry—Officer Piper—tell you about Joshua Cox?"

"I am aware that he is missing, yes. We received those reports when he disappeared. Piper said that he has not yet been found and you are off on some wild goose chase trying to find him, causing no end of trouble."

Erin wondered how much of that was Terry's actual words.

"We think the kidnapper was Kim Brandon," Erin said evenly. "And she has been coming out here every day for the past week. Kind of strange, don't you think?" Erin looked out at the abandoned buildings. "Why would she be out here?"

He shrugged. "I have no way of knowing. There's no law against going for a hike in the woods. She could be prospecting, sketching wildflowers, looking at buying the place. Fishing. She could be distilling moonshine. Lots of reasons other than kidnapping."

"Well… I suppose. But with night vision goggles? Duct tape and zip ties?"

Campbell gave her a warning look. She realized he didn't want her to give away that they had been snooping in Kim's trunk.

"I have only your word for that," Coleman said. "Hypothetically, that would be suspicious, but not conclusive."

"You could look into it."

"What would the evidence on the warrant be?"

Erin searched for words. "I… she has motive. She wants to inherit her grandma's prize money. Joshua was on the verge of showing that the contest had just been a money-laundering scheme. She might have lost everything."

"And your proof of this is…?"

"Officer Piper is putting that together. They're building the case right now."

"As they should be. And when they have it built, they can put in a request for us to get a warrant to search Miss Brandon's property. Until then, I don't have anything to show that she might have been involved in anything criminal. Even though she drives out to an abandoned property regularly."

"So you're just going to wait? When Joshua could be on this property now?"

Coleman patted his pockets and came up with a cigarette and lighter. He turned away from Erin as he lit the cigarette and looked at the abandoned buildings.

"If he's not going to go in, I am," Campbell said.

"Just wait… see what he decides."

After a few minutes of contemplation, Coleman went to his car to retrieve several items. Erin couldn't see what he was doing very well in the darkness. He switched on a powerful flashlight that made her wince and turn away. When she looked back, Coleman was shining it at the ground. He looked down for a long time, walking a step or two and studying the ground. Eventually, he straightened up and shone it around him. The strong flashlight reached all the way past the trees that encroached on the edges of the clearing. He swept it around 360 degrees, methodical. He shone it on the various buildings. A big barn. Other sheds and outbuildings that Erin wasn't sure of. Storage for tools? Maybe a dairy? There was a little cabin, probably one bedroom, a living room, and a kitchen. Tiny, but big enough for a family of a hundred years ago, especially if they'd only had one child. Or one who had survived to adulthood. There was no sign she could see that any of the buildings had been used for decades.

Coleman returned to Erin's window. "You folks stay right here. If I hear someone coming up on me, I'm going to shoot first and ask questions later. If you follow me in there, you're gonna get plugged."

Erin nodded. Coleman looked past her to Campbell. "Is that understood, young man?"

"Yes, sir."

"Good." His eyes went to Mary Lou in the back seat, and he decided he didn't need to repeat the warning.

CHAPTER 48

They all sat there while Coleman walked toward the buildings, his flashlight on the ground. He picked his way along slowly, and Erin wondered if he were following someone else's footprints in the dirt. At least she and the others hadn't rushed in and obscured that evidence. Coleman really couldn't criticize her for sitting in the car, calling it in, and then waiting for him to show up. He and Terry might not like her following up on leads on her own, but she hadn't done anything dangerous. And they hadn't destroyed any evidence. They had left everything just as they had found it.

Erin wanted to go in with him.

And she didn't.

She remembered only too clearly following Willie into the barn that day at Theresa's farm.

Moving restlessly beside her, Campbell was apparently even more eager than she was to get in there. Erin didn't imagine he would stay put, but for Coleman's warning that he would shoot anyone who came up behind him.

Had Coleman called for backup units? Or did he think that she was off her rocker and that there would be nothing to find?

He was at least armed. Erin had seen the gun on his hip when he had approached the truck the second time.

As they watched, Coleman detoured around one of the buildings. In a few seconds, he was out of sight.

"Why did he go around there?" Campbell demanded. "Why didn't he check out any of the buildings? Does he think there is a car back there? Or something else?" His voice was higher than usual, pulled tight like a rubber band.

"He was following a trail. I guess Kim went around another way. Maybe the front doors are booby-trapped."

"Huh." Campbell accepted this, maybe deciding that Coleman knew what he was doing more than Campbell did. Campbell would probably have just run in through the front door. And who knew what would have happened then. Kim had clearly prepared for the abduction. She had managed to capture Joshua without raising any alarms. She had somewhere to transport him to that was out of sight of anyone else. She had not been caught removing medications from the hospital. And hospitals were usually really uptight about that kind of thing, with lots of security protocols in place.

Erin was on the edge of her seat. How long was it going to take for Coleman to find Joshua? How long before he was back out, confirming that they had found Josh?

And that he was safe.

Erin couldn't imagine having to tell Mary Lou that they were too late. Coleman would have made notifications like that before, but it couldn't be easy. Death notifications were bad enough when the person was at the end of their life and expected to die. A kid like Joshua, just starting to come into his own…

She couldn't help the little twitch that her brain responded with. An involuntary shake of her head. She couldn't do it. But she didn't have to.

And hopefully, Coleman wouldn't either.

It seemed like they were sitting there for hours waiting. Erin was starting to get cold. Her butt was sore from sitting for too long. She needed to get out and get some fresh air and the chance to stretch her legs. They were all so twitchy, reacting every time one of them had to shift position or looked in a different direction.

Erin checked the road again for any new arrivals, but couldn't see any more headlights approaching.

When she looked back toward the buildings, she could see a slight halo of light. Coleman was returning.

He kept his flashlight on the ground and made an arc around the clearing to where the vehicles were parked. He made a grim nod to Erin.

"He's in there."

Mary Lou clutched at Erin's arm, holding on for dear life. Erin expected more details from Coleman, but he wasn't wasting his time talking with them. He reached into his car and grabbed the mike of a radio. They couldn't hear his words as he called for backup and described what he would need from them, what they were going to find when they got there.

He spoke for two minutes? Five minutes? Ten? Erin couldn't parse the time period anymore. She couldn't even hold the current time in her head when she looked at her phone. She didn't know how long they had been there or how long Coleman spoke to his people on the radio. Eventually, he replaced the mike in its holder in his car and returned to Erin's window.

"You folks have water?"

Erin looked into the back seat, where Terry normally kept a go bag and emergency rations. She pointed to the black soft-sided cooler. "In there," she told Mary Lou.

Mary Lou tried to unzip it, her hands shaking so badly that it took several tries to pull the tab back, keeping the zipper track straight so it wouldn't jam. She reached inside and felt the water bottles. She handed one forward to Erin, and Erin passed it to Coleman.

"Is he okay?"

Coleman just looked at her and didn't answer.

But he didn't crack the water bottle open and take a swig himself, so Erin had to assume it was for Joshua as he headed back around the buildings, out of their sight.

Mary Lou was sniffling. Campbell put his hand over the seat to hold hers. "It's going to be okay, Mom. They found him."

CHAPTER 49

Erin hoped Cam was right. All of them stayed put in the car, following Coleman's instructions, but it felt like they had been trapped there forever. Erin was like a wild animal pacing back and forth, looking for the opportunity to escape. Her heart hammered in her chest. She wanted the reassurance that Cam was giving Mary Lou. Joshua would recover and return home. Everything would go back to the way it had been before. The Cox family could, once again, start the healing process. And maybe this time, nothing bad would happen to them.

There were flashing lights on the road. Lots of flashing lights.

Even though they hurt Erin's eyes, she watched them eagerly, mentally encouraging them to hurry. Joshua needed the paramedics. Coleman needed the policemen to secure the scene. And somebody had to go back and arrest Kim before she knew that Joshua had been discovered.

Mary Lou was crying more freely as the ambulance pulled off of the road into the clearing. Even Campbell was wiping away tears.

Coleman emerged from the buildings once more. He motioned for the paramedics to stay where they were, and talked to the men in the police cars, gesturing as he spoke. Then he went to the ambulance and spoke with the paramedics. They got out of the ambulance and removed the gurney from the back.

"They're going to take care of him, Mom," Campbell assured her. "They'll get him all fixed up. Everything is going to be fine."

"Can't I go see him?" Mary Lou begged. Though, of course, he was the wrong person to ask. Coleman was the person to ask, and he clearly did not want anyone else contaminating his crime scene. He led the paramedics in, keeping them to the edges of the clearing.

The other policemen got out of their cars and were putting up big lights, marking evidence, and cordoning off the area with tape.

The paramedics appeared around the buildings, carefully navigating the gurney through the gravel and grass toward the ambulance. Erin and the others all leaned forward, straining to see what kind of shape he was in. Coleman appeared behind them, then walked quickly past them and toward the truck.

He pointed at them and then held up one finger. His meaning clear: only one person was allowed out of the truck to see him.

"Cam, do you want to...?" Mary Lou asked.

"Mom, he needs you. You go."

"Are you sure?"

"Go."

She struggled to release her seatbelt and fumbled for the door handle, scrabbling at the door in the dark. She managed to open the door to get out of the car. Erin held her breath, worried that Mary Lou's legs would give out the instant she hit the ground, but Mary Lou was strong. She steadied herself against the truck and waited until Coleman and the paramedics were close enough to talk to, then walked alongside the gurney as it was pushed over the bumpy ground to the ambulance.

She leaned over Joshua, getting very close to his face. She found his hand beside him and held it as she walked with them to the ambulance. Erin watched Mary Lou's face, trying to read everything from it. Was Joshua awake? Was he okay? Or was he gravely injured or ill?

Erin wanted desperately to get out of the car and see for herself, but she stayed where she was, watching and waiting.

Campbell was watching and waiting with her. He wiped at tears and tried not to sniffle in front of her. Erin gave his shoulder a squeeze.

"Quit being such a rock," she told him. "Your mom is with him now. You don't need to be strong for her."

He cleared his throat.

"And I, for one, don't care if you cry. I promise I'll never even mention it."

Campbell looked at her for an instant, uncertain.

Then he put both hands over his face and let go. He was, in the end, an eighteen-year-old boy who had just been through a terrible ordeal. Being the man of the family and supporting his mother through something that few people would ever experience or understand. He was just a boy.

Erin pulled him against her shoulder with a sideways hug. He put his face against her and sobbed.

In a few minutes, it was over. Campbell wiped his face the best he could with his shirt, sniffled a few times, and sat upright again. His throat worked, swallowing hard a few times.

"There's more water back there," Erin said, jerking her head to indicate the back seat. "Get yourself one and hand me one too, would you?"

He reached his long arm into the back and snagged a couple of bottles. They sat in the car, sniffling, watching the paramedics finally loading Joshua into the back of the ambulance and Mary Lou climbing in beside him.

"Erin!"

She hadn't seen Terry and the sheriff arrive, but there had been a lot going on to distract her. Terry hurried up to the truck, and Erin did the best she could to hug him through the window. K9 was beside him, and broke ranks to put his paws on the door, whining. She wasn't sure whether he wanted to get into the truck or was worried about her.

"Get out," Terry told her, "I want to make sure you're okay."

"I'm fine. Coleman told us to stay put, so…"

"Sure, him you'll listen to?"

Erin laughed weakly. "Well, he did threaten to shoot us."

"Is that all it takes?"

They watched the ambulance pull away.

"How is he?" Terry asked soberly.

"I don't know. No one has talked to us. Still alive. That's all I know."

"I'll see what I can find out."

He circulated among the other cops, talking to them and seeking out Detective Coleman, who shot several poisonous glances in Erin's direction as they talked. Eventually, Terry returned.

"He's not in great shape. Dehydrated and weak. Has been bound the whole time. But no serious injuries, so hopefully..."

"He'll get better," Campbell filled in. "He can get over all of that."

Terry nodded. "Hopefully," he agreed cautiously.

Erin wanted to hear a resounding 'yes,' and she imagined that Campbell did too. She looked at Cam, then back at Terry, and changed the subject.

"Does Detective Coleman want us to stay here to talk to him, or can we go?"

Terry rubbed the back of his neck, thinking about it. "He's probably got enough to deal with here tonight and tomorrow morning. I don't know what he'll need from you. I'll talk to him. Suggest that we all stay in Whitewater tonight so that he can have access to you tomorrow."

"I want to go to the hospital," Campbell said immediately. "Are they taking him to the little one here or to the city?"

"To the city."

"Then I want to go there."

"Okay... I'll let him know that you'll be in the city with Joshua and Mary Lou. And Erin and I can stay here at the hotel."

Cam nodded. Terry went back over to Coleman to talk to him again, then spoke with Sheriff Wilmot, who was watching the proceedings with interest. He returned to the truck. "Yeah. That's fine. Let's go back to Whitewater first and check in." His eyes met Erin's. "I'm sure Erin will want to stop at the hospital for a few minutes before we retire."

She nodded her agreement. She couldn't stop herself from yawning, suddenly realizing what a long day it had been.

"You move over," Terry instructed. "I'm driving. Cam, hop in the back."

They all swapped seats, and Terry climbed up into the driver's seat, where he painstakingly adjusted the seat, mirrors, and air vents. Erin melted back into the warm spot Cam had left in the passenger seat and closed her eyes. It wouldn't hurt to rest them while they drove to the hotel to check in.

CHAPTER 50

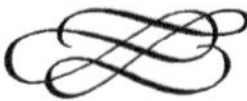

Erin awoke when the car stopped. She rubbed her eyes, opened them, and stretched. She felt remarkably refreshed after the brief nap. Terry looked over at her and smiled.

"Better?"

"Yeah. Much." Erin looked out the window and instead of seeing the hotel, saw the big red brick hospital. She blinked and frowned and turned back to him. "I thought we were going back to Whitewater to check in first."

He grinned. "We did."

"We did?"

"Well, I did. You snored."

Erin giggled, embarrassed. "I don't snore."

"Well, you make a cute little rumbling noise when you sleep. You must have caught Orange Blossom's purr."

Erin looked over the seat at Campbell to say something about how she didn't snore, and found him sprawled on the back seat, limbs in every direction, dead to the world.

"I guess I wasn't the only one who needed a nap."

"He probably hasn't had much sleep since Joshua was taken."

"Yeah. You're right." Erin undid her seatbelt and reached over the seat, having to climb halfway over to reach Campbell and give him a good shake. "Hey, sleepyhead. We're here."

Terry snickered at her calling Cam a sleepyhead. But at least she had woken up when they had stopped. Campbell hadn't.

Cam grunted, flailed, and sat up gasping, like he'd been holding his breath underwater. "What?" he sputtered.

He looked around. Gradually, the wild look left his eyes as everything came back to him. "We found him, right? Tell me that wasn't just a dream."

"We found him," Erin agreed.

"Thank goodness. Let's go in."

He had his seatbelt off and was out the door before Erin, striding toward the hospital's big front doors.

Joshua was in a private room in the ICU. Erin was anxious. She had assumed that since the only things wrong with Josh were that he hadn't had enough to drink or been able to move around, he would just be in a regular hospital room. Once he'd had a couple of glasses of water and the chance to get used to having his feet under him again, he would be fine.

But it was more serious than that. Mary Lou whispered to them while they gathered around his bedside. It was probably a violation of the visitor rules for the ICU for them all to be there, and K9 but, as a police officer, Terry tended to get a little leeway on some of the rules.

"They have him on an IV to rehydrate. The detective gave him some water, but it isn't enough. They have to do IV to get his blood volume back up as quickly as they can safely. That will boost his blood pressure and help his heart to work the right way. But they're worried about his kidneys too because he was so dehydrated. They'll have to watch his fluid output for a few days and make sure his kidneys can both function."

"Poor guy." Erin looked down at Joshua, who appeared to be sleeping peacefully. "Has he been awake? Has he said anything? Can he identify Kim?"

"He hasn't really been able to talk. He recognized me. The doctors said that's good, because being that dehydrated can cause brain damage too. When he starts to get better… He'll be able to talk to Detective

Coleman and hopefully tell him everything he needs to know about Kim Brandon."

Erin looked at Terry. "They have enough to arrest her, don't they? I mean, the stuff that was in the trunk of her car…"

"They have to have enough evidence to get a warrant to search her car," Terry reminded her. "They can't just bust their way in there and look in it. And if she figures out that they've found Joshua, she could destroy everything and run before they get a chance to find anything. That's why you're supposed to wait and let the police do their job, so they can gather the evidence that will be needed to *convict* Kim. They can't just lock her away on your say-so."

"I know. But I thought…"

"Your eyewitness testimony, on breaking into the vehicle, is not enough to get a warrant. Coleman needs corroborating proof."

"But we have that."

"No. You were acting on a theory. One that could just as easily have been wrong."

"But it was right. We found Joshua." Erin looked down at him on the bed. He looked so small and young. So vulnerable. "I'm not sorry we did what we did. How much longer would he have lasted if we hadn't?"

She looked at Mary Lou, hoping that she agreed. She wouldn't be so intent on having Kim locked up forever that she would rather have waited another day or two, would she? She would rather have her son back than justice, if she had to choose between the two.

Mary Lou nodded. She stroked Joshua's hair.

"He didn't have much longer," Terry agreed. He didn't add that he still wasn't sure whether Joshua would recover, but Erin heard it in his voice. She hoped it wasn't true. Joshua would get better. He was young and healthy before the abduction. His kidneys would kick back in. He would do a little physio and be back on his feet again. Everything would go back to the way it was before the kidnapping.

"So… what are the police going to do?" Campbell asked.

With the work that he did with Beaver, he probably knew a good amount about police procedure. He wanted to hear how it was going to go down.

"I don't have all of those details," Terry said. "I'm not part of it, so I haven't been fully briefed. But I gather that they'll fall back tonight and put Kim Brandon under surveillance. They won't tip her off that anyone has been at that farm. They'll clean everything up so that it looks pristine, and wait to see if she goes back for Joshua."

"Assuming that it wasn't her plan to just leave him there to die," Cam said.

"She was going back every day or two," Erin pointed out. "According to the GPS. So she should go out there sometime today."

"As long as it doesn't hit the news," Terry advised. "They're trying to keep it all under wraps, but there was a lot of activity tonight. It's going to be hard to convince all of the neighbors to keep quiet until the police can make the announcement after they have Brandon in custody."

There were a lot of ifs. But Erin was confident that they would be able to catch Kim going back to the farm. It had to work.

"We're going to get her," she promised Cam.

CHAPTER 51

Of course, Erin couldn't be a part of the surveillance team watching Kim's house. And she couldn't be at the abandoned farm to watch the sting go down if Kim went back there.

She didn't even know what Kim looked like.

So after she woke up early the next morning—even when she wasn't working at the bakery and had been up most of the night, her body's internal alarm wouldn't let her sleep late—she moped around the hotel room, looking out the window, hoping to see some part of the takedown in progress.

But all was quiet on the streets of Whitewater, especially so early in the morning. Terry groaned at her a few times to go back to bed, but she wasn't going to be able to sleep and her tossing and turning would only keep him awake.

The only thing that she could see in downtown Whitewater that was open so early was a local coffee shop. Not one of the big chains that dominated the city, but an independent store. Like Auntie Clem's Bakery. She was happy to support a local, independent business, so she decided to go down and get herself a cup of coffee. And she could get Terry a coffee, which would hopefully stay hot enough in its insulated cup, and a danish for when he decided to wake up and join the land of the living.

She grabbed her purse and her card key and scribbled a note on the hotel stationery before leaving so that Terry would know where to find her if he woke up while she was still out. Which she thought was doubtful. She tiptoed around K9, who raised his head to look at her and then put it back down again and closed his eyes.

The air of the coffee shop was thick with the fragrance of fresh coffee and baking. They probably didn't make their own pastries on site, so there must be a bakery open somewhere close by, where bakers like Erin and Vic were following their usual morning routine to get all of their fresh breads, muffins, and pastries baked, making sure that the coffee shop got the first batch so that they would have warm, freshly baked goods ready for their early-morning traffic.

Erin had been planning to order only a cup of coffee. She didn't need any extra calories to pad her waist. She normally would just have a piece of toast and tea for her early breakfast, and then have something more substantial for her lunch. But the baking smelled so inviting that she couldn't resist. She didn't have any work to keep her hands busy and keep her mind off of eating deliciously high-calorie treats like she normally did. It was different being a customer, planning to just sit down and have a leisurely cup of coffee.

So she ordered a nice, healthy, low-calorie bran muffin. Then she canceled the muffin and went for a couple of danishes, one for her and one for Terry. She could go for a walk while waiting for him to wake up and burn off the extra calories.

She watched the other patrons. Most of them were known to the staff, who called them by name and knew their orders before they placed them. People didn't seem stressed out in the before-work rush. They were relaxed and enjoying their coffee rituals.

A couple of nurses in smocks walked in. Coming off of shift rather than going on, Erin thought. They weren't bright-eyed and ready to start their day. They looked ready for bed. They ordered a tea and a soft drink rather than caffeinated drinks, and a couple of muffins to eat as their before-bed snack. The one who had ordered tea turned around while she waited for it, scanning the other customers, maybe looking for another nurse who should be there. Erin smiled pleasantly at her, feeling friendly and full of well-being from the delicious danish pastry. The woman nodded an acknowledgment and continued to look around. She had a heart-shaped face, blond hair that was a little sweaty and tousled from her shift at the hospital, and friendly blue eyes.

Erin thought she had probably seen the woman before. Maybe during the cooking contest. She had met a lot of different people during the competition. It had been chaotic, lots of introductions, hands to shake, personal stories to listen to. Only a few of them stuck with her.

The heart-shaped face turned back to her and the woman's eyes went over Erin again. Maybe also remembering that they had been introduced during the cooking contest.

The barista was holding a cup out toward the nurse. "Kim? Kim? Miss Brandon?"

Kim didn't take it. She remembered who Erin was. And she knew that Erin didn't belong there in Whitewater. She turned and bolted out of the coffee shop, leaving her friend and the barista staring after her, mouths open.

Erin jumped to her feet and ran to the window to watch Kim go. There was no point in trying to chase her. What was she going to do? Put the woman under arrest? Based on evidence that the police still didn't have?

Kim ran down the street and turned, disappearing from sight. Back home, where her car was parked. If she'd been at the hospital on shift, why had she left the vehicle at home?

Maybe someone had picked her up. She had carpooled. Or she liked to walk over when the weather was pleasant. But whatever the reason she hadn't had the car with her at the hospital, she was on her way to get it now. And then she was going to run, and keep on running.

Erin fumbled with her phone. It took her several misplaced taps and swipes before she managed to search for Coleman's phone number. Then, her phone seemed to be taking an inordinate amount of time to filter down to his contact entry and display it on the screen. She tapped and waited for the call to go through. It rang and rang, going through to his voicemail.

Erin hung up and started walking toward the police station. She tapped his number again, hoping that if he saw her number come up twice in a row, he would realize that it was an urgent matter. Did Whitewater have 9-1-1 service? Should she try?

"Detective Coleman." His voice was a snap in her ear.

"It's Erin Price. I just saw Kim Brandon in the coffee shop and—"

"I thought you didn't know what she looked like."

"I didn't. But I heard the barista call her by name, and she was looking at me. She realized who I am and—"

He swore. "Did you talk to her?"

"No. She just saw me across the coffee shop. She ran away. Left her order there and just ran back to her house."

"Stay away from her. Don't follow her, do you understand?"

"Yes, but—"

"But nothing. I've heard how fast and loose you play with the law, and I want to make this clear. If you go after her, if you follow her even at a distance, you will find yourself in a jail cell."

"I didn't. She ran away and I called you. I'm walking toward the police station, in case I couldn't get you on the phone."

"Okay. I'm not there. I'll interview you later in the day. In the meantime, I need you to stay out of the way of my operation."

"I am."

"We have people watching her house and the farm. She's not going to get anywhere, but she might lead us to the evidence that we need."

"What if she destroys the evidence in her car?"

"I told you. We have eyes on her. If she throws something out, we'll see her do it and recover it. If she torches the car or something stupid like that, we'll have officers right there."

"And if she goes to the farm, then that's evidence that she is the one who kidnapped Joshua."

"Or at least, she knew about it. Each piece of evidence is only one part of the story. We need to add them all together before there will be enough to convict her of anything."

"Yeah." Erin took a deep breath. She stopped walking. There was no point in running to the police station when he wasn't there. She would go back to the hotel.

First, she would go back to the coffee shop and grab the food she had left on her table, assuming it hadn't already been cleared away.

"Do you have someone watching her grandma at the hospital too? I don't know if Kim was doing something to make Deidre sick or just waiting for nature to take its course, but… if she thinks that I'm on to her, I wouldn't want her to do anything desperate…"

"Killing her grandma wouldn't accomplish anything if she didn't get her inheritance before leaving town. But yes, I've got someone at the hospital, too. A little more tricky, since she knows the staff there."

"I guess it would be," Erin agreed. She wondered who they had there. Someone pretending to be janitorial staff? A fake patient or a visitor watching from behind a newspaper? "I guess I should let you go. Sorry, I wasn't trying to get in the middle of things… she just walked into the coffee shop and recognized me."

"No problem, Miss Price. And… thank you."

Erin nodded and hung up.

CHAPTER 52

When Coleman came calling, Terry was up, sipping his coffee and eating the danish Erin had managed to recover.

Coleman knocked on the hotel room door. Erin let him in. She looked around. There wasn't really anywhere for a sit-down meeting in the room. She sat on the bed and Terry moved from the one chair at the writing desk and motioned for Coleman to take it. He sat down with Erin on the bed, brushing flaky crumbs off of his face. K9 lay where he was in the middle of the floor, sighing loudly.

"Kim Brandon has been arrested for Joshua's kidnapping," Coleman announced.

Erin let out a breath of relief. "Oh, I'm so glad! Thank you!"

"We're still building the case against her, but we have enough to get the warrants we need to search her house and car, her workplace, and grandmother's hospital room. We've pretty much finished with the farm buildings, but we'll have evidence techs go over it one more time to be sure we've got everything."

"With what was in the car, you should have enough...?"

"We'll see. Nothing is ever one hundred percent, but there isn't much that would explain away a kidnap kit in the trunk. Especially with needles and prescription drugs stolen from the hospital to sedate him or keep him compliant."

"How did she get them?" Erin shook her head. "I thought those things were all inventoried and kept under lock and key."

"Of course they are. We're trying to sort out the details. But I would say that as a nurse, she found ways around the system. She had legitimate access to them, it was just a numbers game."

"So she took more than she was supposed to?"

"Maybe said that a patient needed a higher dosage than they did, and pocketed the extra."

"Devious." Terry shook his head.

"Whatever we can or cannot prove, I think we can agree she is that."

The drive back to Bald Eagle Falls was quiet. Too quiet. Erin could hear K9 panting in the back seat. She knew that Terry was not happy with her for taking the truck and going to Whitewater Junction when he had said not to. She had known that he and the sheriff didn't want her to investigate. She was just supposed to stay out of the way and let them sort everything else.

But Erin couldn't let a friend suffer while she stood back and waited for the police to go through the proper channels. She had risked derailing the investigation and the police not being able to file charges against Kim. But Joshua's life had to come first.

If they argued about it, they would just go around and around in circles. Erin knew that. Terry would be sure that he was right and she would be sure that she had done the right thing. She wouldn't be able to change his mind.

So they were both quiet. She waited for him to start lecturing and criticizing her for using his truck to do something ill-advised and illegal. But he didn't. They both knew that was something that could never be resolved between them. And Erin didn't know where that left them. Was Terry willing to accept that discord in their relationship? Could Erin?

Forever?

CHAPTER 53

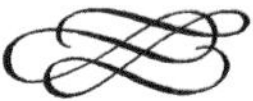

Back in Bald Eagle Falls, life was normal. Everyone was happy to hear that Joshua had been found and were confident that he would recover easily. Kids were resilient. They bounced back faster than you would think. Erin hoped that was the case. She had seen the damage neglect and confinement had done to kids younger than Joshua.

She went by Auntie Clem's Bakery in the afternoon to check in with Charley and Bella and make sure that everything was going all right. She updated her shopping and task lists as she walked around.

"Smooth sailing," Charley assured Erin. "We can hold things together when you have something you need to do."

"I'm so glad you found Josh," Bella said. "I was so scared… when it's been more than a day or two, you know that things don't look good…"

Erin nodded. She felt like she had come through a long, dark, tunnel. She had been very worried. Afraid to even hope that they would be able to find him alive. But she had come out the other end of the tunnel. She could breathe again.

"Were you going to take some more baking over to the Fosters?" Charley asked. "I set some things aside for them."

"Did you? That's a great idea. Yes, I'll take them over now. Have you heard anything? I think she was confined to bed."

Bella nodded. "I think this one has been pretty hard on her. But it's not supposed to be much longer."

"She's a great mom, but having that many young kids must be so hard."

"Some women really love having a full house. I'm not sure I'd be able to manage."

Charley shook her head. "I always wanted siblings growing up, but I think that's too many. She needs to take care of herself. Get Mr. Foster snipped."

Bella's eyes got big and round, shocked. Charley laughed.

"Okay… I'm going to take some bread over to them," Erin decided. Bella would have to fend for herself with Charley.

No children were playing in the yard this time. Erin rang the doorbell, and there wasn't a mad stampede for the door. It was opened a few minutes later by a man Erin didn't know. Mr. Foster, she presumed. He was unshaven, hair tousled, his wrinkled shirt and slightly sweaty odor testifying to the fact that she had probably woken him up. She didn't know if he were a shift worker. He hadn't been there when she had dropped by before.

"Hi," he said tiredly, looking her over.

"Hi, Mr. Foster. I'm Erin Price. I own the bakery?"

"Oh!" His eyes brightened. "You're a really good baker! I wouldn't believe that all of the things my wife brings home are gluten-free, except they don't make Peter sick, so I know they are. It's amazing what you can do."

Erin's face was hot. "Thank you so much! I love to bake for people, and Peter especially. He's such a great little guy."

Mr. Foster nodded his agreement.

Erin made a little motion with the box she was carrying. "I brought some more supplies."

"Sure." He reached for his wallet in his back pocket. "How much do I owe you?"

"Oh, this is just a gift to help your wife while she's indisposed. You don't owe me anything."

He paused, hand on his jeans pocket. "Are you sure?"

"Yes. Please. Don't worry about it."

"Okay." He took the box from her. "Would you like to come in and see the little guy?"

"Oh, she had the baby?"

He nodded, a warm smile spreading across his whiskery face. "Just a few hours ago."

"Wow! Yes, I'd love to see him. Him—it is a boy?"

"Yes."

"Peter must be tickled. Another boy in the family!"

"Believe me, he is. Come on in."

Erin followed him into the house. Everything was quiet. Maybe a neighbor had taken the kids after school, or they had all been up late with the arrival of the new baby and were now napping to catch up. Mr. Foster led Erin into the master bedroom. It was warm and dark and close. Mrs. Foster was propped up in the bed.

"It's Miss Price," Mr. Foster announced. "With another care package."

"You didn't have to do that," Mrs. Foster said softly. "But I can't tell you what a help it has been the last couple of weeks. Peter has been able to make sandwiches for the girls, or to warm up some soup with a roll. I couldn't be up and around at all."

"He told me that. I'm glad it helped."

Mr. Foster went to the bassinet beside the bed. He carefully lifted out a little bundle wrapped tightly in a light blanket. "And here's the new addition to the Foster family."

Erin received him in her arms. He was so small and so perfect. She always said she didn't know if she were ready for children, or if she ever wanted to be a mother but, in a moment like this, when she held a newborn in her arms, it was a totally different story. Her heart yearned for one of her own.

"Oh, he's so precious. Congratulations."

"Thank you," Mrs. Foster said.

Mr. Foster slipped out to put the box of baking in the kitchen. Erin stroked the downy hair on the top of the baby's head.

"Does he have a name yet?"

"We're thinking of Alan. But haven't decided yet. We'll see what fits in the next few days."

Erin swayed back and forth, rocking the baby.

"Come here." Mrs. Foster patted the edge of the bed. Erin sat down, holding the baby so that Mrs. Foster could take him back if she wanted to. Mrs. Foster just stroked his cheek and let Erin hold him.

"I can't imagine how hard it has been for Mary Lou Cox to go through what she has with Joshua. I don't know what I would do if someone took my baby away from me. Or any of my kids, of course. It must be an absolute nightmare. The poor woman."

Erin was happy to be able to report the good news. "We found him last night. The woman who kidnapped him was arrested this morning."

"And he's okay?" Mrs. Foster's eyes filled with tears.

"He's alive. He's in ICU today, and probably for a few days, while they get him back on his feet again."

"Oh." She let out a long breath. "I'm so glad. You said 'we' found him? You?"

"Me and Mary Lou and Campbell. We kind of figured out who it must have been, and we went to Whitewater, and we were lucky in a lot of ways..."

"That's fantastic news." Mrs. Foster shook her head. "I don't know how you do it. It really doesn't make any sense. You're not a policeman or even a private investigator. But you know, just by seeing things and listening to people, like with Peter..."

Erin nodded. "Yeah. I'm sorry about Peter. Sorry that he was involved in those last couple of cases. I know it bothered you."

Mrs. Foster had been quite clear about that fact. And she had stopped letting the children go with her to Auntie Clem's, despite how much they loved picking out their own cookies.

"Let's put it behind us," Mrs. Foster suggested. "I don't want to say don't ever involve him in a case again. I think that you do a lot of good, but I worry about what could happen to him. Especially looking at Joshua. If it's that easy to take a teenage boy, just think about how simple it would be to snatch Peter or one of the girls. But if you think one of them might know something... would you please come to me?"

Erin nodded. She could feel herself flushing and was glad that the room was dim so that Mrs. Foster couldn't see how red she got. "Of course. Yes. I'll try to do that. I don't expect to be investigating any other crimes, though."

Mrs. Foster laughed and shook her head. “Oh, sure. I’m sure that will be the last time.”

CHAPTER 54

Erin knew that Joshua was out of the hospital. She hesitated on the front steps, taking a deep breath before ringing the bell. While things had eventually worked out with Mary Lou, she still wasn't sure whether she would be accepted when a family member's life wasn't on the line. Things might have gone back to the way they were before Joshua had disappeared. Mary Lou might accept that Erin hadn't had anything to do with Joshua's disappearance, and acknowledge that she had helped to find Joshua and bring him home safely, but that didn't necessarily mean that they were friends again.

The door opened. It was Campbell. He smiled and nodded. "Hi, Miss Erin. Come on in."

"Is it okay?" Erin asked, trying to see around him to make sure that it was really okay with Mary Lou.

"Come on," he repeated, stepping back and motioning Erin forward. Erin followed him a little reticently.

Joshua was sitting on the couch. Despite the fact that it was warm out, he was wrapped in a blanket. He pulled it closer to him as he turned to see who had come in. His tense expression relaxed a little when he saw Erin.

"Oh. Hi. Mom just went upstairs for something, but she'll be back in a minute."

Erin sat in one of the chairs. "How are you feeling?"

"Still pretty weak. They said I'll probably recover pretty quickly."

Erin nodded. He looked thin and pale. Who knew what kind of damage there was that they couldn't see? Not just to his organs, but to his mind.

It was hard for her to understand what it must have been like for him. She had been abandoned in a cave, and most of the time she had been unconscious. But to have an experience like that to go on for days… bound in the darkness, not knowing if his captor would come back again, or would ever let him go…

Joshua's eyes hovered on Erin for a few seconds, and then flitted around the room, anxious, looking for danger. Erin put her purse down slowly so that he wouldn't be startled by her movement.

"I'm sorry that it took us so long to find you. I should have been able to figure it all out sooner."

"You did your best. I'm glad that you guys did find me. She said that it wouldn't be much longer. And I didn't think she was going to let me go."

Erin's heart felt like it was being squeezed. She breathed through the pain. "You must have been terrified."

"I wasn't… I figured… it would be better to be dead."

"What an evil woman. I don't know how someone could hurt you like that. You never did anything to harm her."

"I guess… she thought I was going to. That I'd get all of her money taken away—or all of her grandma's money." He stared at the tree outside the window. "I never thought what I was doing might hurt anyone."

"You were just trying to find out the truth."

"But that has consequences." He shook his head. "I never thought of the people. I thought… reporters just *report*. I never thought that what they do actually makes a difference, changes things."

"But that doesn't make it wrong. If they were laundering money through the contest, then that's hurting people. That needs to be stopped."

"But taking the money from the people who thought they were just getting prize money for submitting a recipe to a contest…? That's not really fair to them."

Erin didn't really have an answer to that.

"Are they going to lose their money?"

"I don't know. It's all going to be investigated. I don't know if they freeze everyone's assets while they do that."

Erin thought about the woman lying in the bed in the hospital. She was past caring about whether they froze the assets or not. Kim had been thinking of her own selfish desires, not her grandmother's.

She heard footsteps on the stairs and turned to watch Mary Lou descending.

"Oh, Erin. I thought I heard voices."

Erin rose partway out of her seat to greet Mary Lou, but the woman waved her down. "Make yourself comfortable. You're practically family here."

There was suddenly a big lump in Erin's throat. *Family?*

"You helped us find Joshua. You helped out when Campbell had his trouble. And you were one of the only ones who stood beside us when Roger… had to go away. Even though he had targeted you. I'd say that makes you part of the family."

Mary Lou put her hand on Erin's shoulder and gave it a little squeeze as she walked behind Erin to the other chair. She sat down.

"I need to apologize for the way that I treated you."

"You were worried about Joshua."

"That's no excuse. I let someone manipulate me and thought that you were my enemy instead of my friend. I should have known better from everything you have done in the past. I should have seen what was going on in front of my own eyes."

"It wasn't your fault."

"Oh, Erin. I'm trying to apologize."

Erin pressed her lips together and nodded. "Yeah. Sorry. I accept."

Mary Lou smiled. "Good. I won't ever let that happen again. I know who my friends are."

"What about Vic?"

"Yes, Miss Victoria too. I'm sorry for flying off the handle about that escapade in the city… I wish I had known at the time, but I'm glad I didn't. You were trying to protect Josh and help Cam, but… I wonder if there might have been a better way to go about it."

"I wouldn't doubt it," Erin admitted. "I don't always make the best choice."

"No…" Mary Lou's voice wobbled a little as she decided what to say. "But you always try."

HOT ON THE TRAIL MIX

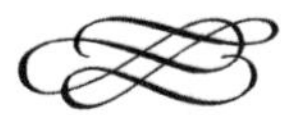

AUNTIE CLEM'S BAKERY #15

To those still searching
for their place in the world

CHAPTER 1

Erin pushed Orange Blossom to the side with her foot, ignoring his meows of protest, so that she could get into the pantry cupboard for the food she had set aside for Vic. In order to keep him from getting into something that would make him sick, Blossom was not allowed in the pantry, even though it had now been determined that he hadn't gotten sick from getting into something he shouldn't have, but had been intentionally poisoned. It was still safest if she only fed him cat food she knew to be safe. Or meat that she prepared for him while making her own meals.

"I made you some sandwiches too, they're in the fridge."

Vic, a slim transgender woman, Erin's best friend and employee at the bakery, opened the fridge. Orange Blossom hurried over to her to see if Vic would be more cooperative about feeding him. Erin grabbed what she needed and shut the pantry.

"I made these granola bars. See what you think. I made some of them with certified gluten-free rolled oats, and some with buckwheat flakes. So the people who can't tolerate oats still have an option as well. If you can't really tell the difference, I'll just make the buckwheat, so I don't have to make two different kinds."

Vic nodded. "They look good. No nuts?" Vic knew that Auntie Clem's didn't sell anything containing nuts. But of course, granola bars frequently had nuts.

"No. I put in some pumpkin seeds and sunflower seeds. And some raisins and goji berries. And I made this trail mix." Erin put a baggie down on the counter. "Sunflower seeds, hemp seed, and chia—loads of protein."

Vic swept her long, blond hair out of her face as she leaned over and packed the goodies into her backpack. "Sounds great. This should be more than enough to get us through the day."

"Make sure you have plenty of water."

"We do." Vic pulled the zipper of the pack closed. "You sure you don't want to come along with us?" she teased.

Erin flashed back to being trapped underground—no light, no water, bound hand and foot with no idea how to get out of the labyrinthine caves. She had been terrified she was going to die there, injured and alone. No one would be able to find her. She wouldn't be able to find her own way out. The oxygen had been thin and she had been dehydrated.

"No," she told Vic firmly. "I am never going into a cave again."

Vic squeezed her arm. "And you never have to," she assured Erin. She gave Erin a mischievous smile. "But I'm going to keep asking. Spelunking is so much fun."

"It's just not for me."

It amazed Erin that Vic was still into spelunking. After having been trapped in a collapsed mine, Vic should have hated dark, enclosed spaces as much as Erin. But she had bounced back quickly and, as soon as she and Willie had their casts off, they were back at it again. Maybe it was because she was so young, just barely an adult, that she had bounced back so fast.

"You can keep asking. As long as you don't think I'm going to change my answer."

Vic nodded. She shouldered the pack. "We're off, then." She looked at the clock. While early, it wasn't nearly as early as when they usually had to get up to bake the day's goods and open up Auntie Clem's. Considering their usual schedule, it was a relaxed morning.

"Say 'hi' to Willie for me."

"Will do."

~

Once Vic and Willie were on their way, Erin sat down to work on her plans for the day and consider the upcoming week. In an effort to get control over the clutter in her purse and on her desk, she had actually purchased a planner. It had been a lengthy process. First, looking over the planners available at the stationery store in the city and considering all of the possibilities of size, layout, and binding type. And, of course, the price point. She didn't want something that would become a craft, with all kinds of stickers and accessories and time required to decorate it. Just somewhere she could keep her lists, plans, and appointments together and organized.

After finally settling on a book that would fit in her purse, she had started to use it. Breaking the habit of years of writing on scrap pieces of paper, napkins, and an assortment of notepads was not easy. She had to train herself to reach for her book instead and write her lists and thoughts in the appropriate place. Where hopefully she would be able to find them again later when she wanted them.

But she was growing to love her little planner. She didn't waste as much time searching for lists and notes that she had written and then 'filed' in her purse, wallet, or pocket for later reference. Her purse, while still full, was a lot less cluttered.

Erin sat on the couch with her feet curled under her. In a few minutes, Orange Blossom jumped up beside her and cuddled up.

She enjoyed the peace and quiet of the morning. Terry was still sleeping and could continue to sleep for however long his body let him. He didn't go on shift until the afternoon. If he got up in good time, they would have some couple's time together and maybe go out for lunch.

Everything was finally calm and peaceful in Erin's life.

CHAPTER 2

When Erin heard Terry stirring in the bedroom, she looked at the time on her phone. She had promised Vic that she would check on her new dog, Nilla, and make sure that he got a break and a bit of exercise. That would hopefully keep him from destroying Vic's loft apartment over the garage.

She went down to the bedroom and poked her head in to look at Terry. "Morning."

Terry stretched and groaned. He scratched the stubble on his cheek and smiled. Not enough to show the dimple in his cheek, but it warmed Erin's heart to see him happy in the morning instead of worn out and miserable because he hadn't been able to get any sleep and had a migraine.

"Mmm. Come here."

Erin obliged, going around to his side of the bed and giving him a good morning hug and kiss. His body was warm, his hair mussed, and he smelled faintly of sweat. Erin buried her face in the hollow of his shoulder, enjoying their closeness and the looseness of his body.

"I'm just popping out for a few minutes to take care of Nilla."

There was a whine from K9 in his kennel.

"Yes, you can come too," Erin agreed. "Come on."

K9 jumped out of his kennel, tail wagging excitedly. He stopped to give Terry a nuzzle and get his ears scratched, then headed out the bedroom door, leading the way for Erin.

"See you in a few minutes," Terry told her.

Erin blew him a kiss and followed K9 to the back door. She disabled the alarm and followed him out.

~

Once in the yard, Erin could hear a frantic yipping coming from the direction of Vic's apartment.

"Uh-oh."

K9 was on his way to his dog run in the corner of the yard. He looked back at Erin with a comical eye roll. Sometimes his expressions seemed very human. Erin left him to his business and went up the stairs to the loft apartment. She unlocked the door, calling out to the little dog.

"Nilla! Come here, boy! What's the matter?"

The apartment was a mess and Erin knew it wasn't because Vic had left it that way. When Nilla got into a mood, he could be a little tornado of destruction. Kind of like the Tasmanian devil in the cartoons.

The yipping continued. Erin tried to home in on him.

"Nilla? Where are you? What are you doing?"

She was afraid at first that he had gotten himself into trouble and was stuck somewhere. But she found him in Vic's bedroom, wrestling with a pair of leggings.

"Nilla! No!"

Nilla turned on her, growling. If he'd been a big dog, Erin might have been concerned, but the little white fluff-ball was not very intimidating. Although he threatened, when the critical point was reached, he would run, not attack.

"No," Erin repeated firmly and bent down to pick up the leggings. She didn't want to start a tug-of-war, which might cause worse damage to the clothes than just leaving them on the floor. "Shoo. Get back." She waved her hands at the dog. Nilla remained, growling fiercely until the last minute, and then he ran away. Erin picked up the leggings and any other clothes that Nilla had pulled to the floor. She folded them and put them into the top drawer where they would be safe. She made sure to shut the drawer tightly so that he wouldn't be able to open it, and pushed the others closed, making sure they were all tight so that hopefully Nilla wouldn't be able to drag any more out.

"Do you want to go for a walk?" She called out to Nilla. "Outside? Walk?"

Nilla growled, but when Erin left the bedroom and headed back toward the front door, he immediately dropped all pretense of being threatening and jumped at the doorknob. It was amazing the height that the little dog could achieve.

There were scratches on the door already from the past few weeks that Nilla had lived there. Erin should probably have told Vic no, no pets allowed, but since Erin had taken in two pets of her own and K9 also spent most of the week there, it was pretty hard to deny Vic the privilege.

It wouldn't have been a problem if Nilla had been better behaved.

She thought about texting Vic to let her know that Nilla was causing problems once more, but decided against it. Vic wasn't likely to have cell coverage where she was. Even if she did, there wasn't anything she could do to fix the problem and Erin didn't want her worrying about it the whole time she was away.

Erin managed to hold Nilla still long enough to get his walking harness on him, then took him outside and down the stairs. She always worried with how hyper and excited Nilla got that he was going to end up getting hung falling down the stairs, or falling off the side through the railing. The dog seemed incapable of moving in a straight line. But using a harness instead of a collar helped allay her worries. He didn't have something around his neck that was going to strangle him.

She managed to get down the stairs without getting tangled up in the leash and gently encouraged him toward the dog run. Unlike K9, Nilla seemed resistant to the idea of training to one area of the yard and always wanted to sniff and pee everywhere.

"Come over here. Come on. This is where you're supposed to go. Watch K9. He knows what to do. Don't you want to be a big dog like K9?"

By the time she got him over to the dog run, she suspected he was empty, but she stayed there with him for a little while, encouraging him to make use of the run.

K9 was sitting watching them patiently, but Erin knew he wanted to go for a walk to stretch his legs. He was a big dog and needed a lot of exercise.

"Okay, you done, Nilla? Let's walk."

Nilla allowed himself to be coaxed toward the gate. He knew that walking was next, and though he was slower than K9 and easily distracted, he was pretty good for his walks.

"Come on, K9," Erin called. K9 bounded after her, quickly falling in at her heel and showing the little dog proper behavior. Nilla gave him a little growl, pretending that he could take K9 on if he had to, and went on with his explorations, ranging out on the leash as far as Erin would let him go.

Even though Nilla was just a little dog, Erin was always tired after walking him. He pulled and moved erratically and she was always worried about what he was going to do next, so the emotional effort took more than the physical. Nilla was also tired, and Erin was able to pick him up and carry him up the steps so that she didn't have to worry about him shooting off the side or between the slats. She took him to his kennel and shunted him inside. She shut the door while she got him some food and water. He was chill enough after his walk that he didn't whine or try to get out. She gave him his bowls and left, locking up behind her.

Terry had already let K9 into the house, and he opened the door for Erin as she approached. "How was it?"

Erin shook her head. "About usual! I'm sure glad that K9 is so well-trained and calm."

"Yeah. Vic really needs to get that dog trained."

"She's trying. And I think he's improved in the time that she's had him. But Beryl obviously didn't know anything about training."

Terry nodded. "Some people shouldn't have pets. Did you put him in his kennel?"

"Yes. But Vic doesn't want him to be kenneled all day."

"Won't hurt him for a while."

"If he was better-behaved, then I would just bring him over here. He gets along with K9. They could hang out together and Nilla wouldn't be lonely."

"After seeing the destruction that little dog can cause, I would not want to see how he would treat a cat or a rabbit."

"They're both bigger than him. He would probably end up with the wrong end of the stick. But I don't want to try it. I don't want any of them to end up hurt."

"No," Terry agreed. "We can try introducing them gradually but, since Orange Blossom still hasn't made friends with K9, I don't know how that would go over."

Erin sighed. "They're as bad as people. I wish that everyone would just get along."

CHAPTER 3

It had been a productive day. Erin had run some errands, gone through her projects and plans for the next week, taken Nilla out for another round of exercise, and made an early supper that involved more than just opening a can of soup or making sandwiches. All in all, she had gotten a good amount done.

Terry was just scraping the last of the pasta sauce from his plate when his phone buzzed with a message. He looked at Erin, raising his brows. She made a motion for him to go ahead and answer it. Supper was over, so he might as well. Besides, it could be a work call, and he should take it. He wasn't on call with the dispatcher yet, but the sheriff could still call him if they needed all hands on deck.

He looked down at his screen and his brows lowered into a scowl. He looked back at Erin.

"Looks like Vic and Willie ran into some trouble."

Erin's heart sank. Her stomach tightened with worry. "What kind of trouble? Are they okay?"

"They are fine. But I've got to go in."

Erin shook her head, wondering what kind of problem might have occurred that would cause that kind of response. Most things could wait until the morning. But Terry wasn't likely to tell her what was going on.

He normally wouldn't even have said that Vic and Willie were involved. He was good about keeping everything quiet, even from her.

"They're not hurt? Sick?" she persisted.

"They're okay," he reassured her. "No cave collapse. They haven't been injured. But I need to go out and help take care of things. I'm sorry. You're going to be on your own tonight."

"Okay. That's fine, of course." They didn't need to be together all the time. In fact, when he had been off work, it had been very stressful to have him home all the time. Of course, a lot of that might have had to do with his irritability and PTSD. *Thanks for that, Theresa Franklin.* "But you won't stay out too long, will you? You'll be careful?"

He wasn't yet putting in full-time hours and Erin was constantly afraid that he would do too much and end up with a week-long migraine or other relapse symptoms. He wasn't yet fully healed. The sheriff needed to understand that.

And Terry himself needed to understand that. He was probably the one who expected the most from himself. It had been too long since he had been injured. He felt that he should have been able to heal in that length of time. And that he should certainly not still be having any PTSD. That should all be behind him.

"I only put in a half shift this afternoon. I'm fresh as a daisy."

"But you won't be if you work all night. Be careful. Tell the sheriff if it's too much and you have to go home."

He scowled at her and didn't answer. Erin knew there was no way that he was going to tell Sheriff Wilmot that he was tired and wanted to go home. Even though the sheriff would send him home. Terry wanted too much to show that he had recovered and was just as tough as ever.

Even though Terry had said that Vic and Willie were unhurt and everything was okay, Erin was still worried. The entire Bald Eagle Falls police department would not be called out there for nothing. It didn't matter that the department consisted only of Terry, the sheriff, young Stayner, and Tom Banks, who was part time. There were few occurrences in Bald Eagle Falls that required all of them to be on site. And if something else happened and they needed to attend to another call, they would all be out at the cave. Or wherever it was that they had gone to take care of Vic's and Willie's problem.

Something had happened. Something serious.

A few hours went by. Erin busied herself in the little attic room reading through Clementine's genealogy files and books, learning more about the history of Bald Eagle Falls and her father's family. It was hard to stay focused and not let her mind wander to the call. But thinking about it wasn't going to solve anything, so she did her best to just dive deep into the pages of history and lose herself in the stories and genealogies.

She saw the flash of headlights out back and looked out the window to see Willie's truck pull into the pad beside the garage. She left all of her papers and books scattered around and hurried down the stairs to see them.

Erin keyed the burglar alarm and stepped out the back door, arriving in the yard as Vic and Willie were climbing down from the cab of the truck.

"Hey, are you guys okay?"

"We're all right!" Vic assured her. "See? All in one piece."

Erin looked them both over. They looked tired, but unharmed. Willie went to the back of the truck to unload Vic's spelunking gear.

"Great granola bars and trail mix," he told Erin. "They came in very handy when we had to stick around longer than expected."

"You liked them?" She allowed herself to be distracted for just a moment. "That's great. Both kinds?"

"Yes, everything. All good. I couldn't tell the difference between the two kinds of granola bars."

"Perfect." Erin turned to Vic. "You too? You liked them?"

"Yes, they were good."

That was one question checked off of her list. Erin raised her brows and spread her hands out in a query. "So...?"

Vic looked over at Willie, but he seemed very intent on the gear. She sighed. "Well... let's just say... Erin Price isn't the only one who can find human remains around here."

CHAPTER 4

Erin felt her eyes go wide. "What? Are you serious?"

Vic nodded. Her eyes were amused and tired, and just a little strained around the corners. She had been acting happy and relaxed for too long and was ready to crash, maybe have a glass of wine, and put it all behind her.

"Tell me about it!"

"Why don't we go inside? I'm about dead on my feet. You'll be okay with the gear?" she asked Willie.

"If it will get me out of the recap," Willie grumbled. "I'll take mine home and unload, I don't want to leave it in the truck overnight. Then I'll be back."

Vic shrugged and rolled her eyes. "Okay, then. I'll leave you to it. Erin and I will go set a spell."

She and Erin walked into the house together. Orange Blossom began yowling as if he'd been left alone all day. With no food, even. Vic laughed at him as he complained noisily and rubbed her legs.

"Really? Has it been that awful? Well, I'll definitely have a word with her." She looked at Erin for permission. "Can I give him a couple of treats?"

"Of course."

Vic knew where everything was. She used the kitchen as much as Erin did, even though she had her own kitchenette in the loft. It was just more natural for her and Erin to cook together or that she would get tea for both of them in Erin's kitchen rather than her own. She got out the can of kitty treats and slid a few across the floor for Orange Blossom to chase and consume. Vic also called Marshmallow in to get a carrot. Then she and Erin made their way to the living room and sat down.

"So spill," Erin commanded. "Tell me all about it."

"Well, what's to tell? You know what it's like…" Vic teased.

"Just tell me. Who? What happened? I can't believe you didn't call me earlier and tell me about it."

"Earlier, we were talking to the police and under strict instructions not to call anyone until we had given full statements and been questioned individually about it. And you know how they have to ask the same question ten different ways to make sure that they got a complete answer and to see if you trip over your own story. It takes forever."

"Yes." Erin nodded sympathetically. She knew all about that. But she wanted to hear about what had happened.

~

"So, it was just a normal day spelunking. Get all of the gear set up, work out your plan, and into the cave you go."

Erin shuddered at that. She was okay with the 'getting ready' part. And with the going home part. It was everything else in between that was the problem.

"Where were you? Or can you even tell me that part?"

"I'll show you on a map later. It's not a popular spot, just one Willie knew about."

Erin nodded. She waited for the punchline. Vic raised her brows as if she didn't know what Erin was waiting for. Then she finally went on.

"We'd been exploring another cave. But Willie wanted to show me this one before we went home, and it was just on the other side of the hill. Well, we got in about fifty feet, where there's an underground spring and pool. Dark as pitch, but we had our lights, so we were okay. I wanted to see what wildlife we could find, so we had on the red lights rather than the big white ones. The white ones would just scare everything away."

Erin thought of bats hanging from the ceiling, dark things scuttling in the dark, and pale blind fish swimming silently in the underground pool. Not her idea of a romantic getaway. She would do her hiking and sight-seeing above ground, thank you very much.

She swallowed, turning her thoughts back toward Vic and Willie and what they had seen. She tried not to envision what they had come across down in that dark, damp cave.

"You okay?" Vic checked.

"Yeah. Go ahead."

"So we had just these dim lights on, and we were scouting around, seeing what we could see before we scared anything away. Some pretty bizarre critters live underground. You just won't see them anywhere else."

"I'm okay with that."

Vic laughed. "I was looking into the pool, and down where it was deeper, I could see something white. Red, in the light, but I still knew it was white. Figured maybe it was a cave fish, so I leaned in for a closer look."

Erin really hoped that she hadn't ended up going into the pool face-first, leaning over too far. She thought about the scene in Harry Potter, where the dead people started coming out of the underground lake, trying to pull them under.

"When I leaned closer, I could see more white things. Maybe a whole school of fish. Or salamanders or something else that might congregate and not disperse very quickly. But then I started to realize that they were *arranged.* And... well, arranged in the shape of a skeleton."

"Ugh."

"And of course, that's exactly what it was. A skeleton in the pool."

"Just bones?" Erin asked. That might not be so bad. It wasn't bloody and gory. Unsettling, of course, but the bones might have been in that pool for hundreds of years. They might even be fossilized.

"That's all I could see with the red light on, because it's very dim, and only white stuff reflected back. I called Willie over, and he had a look, and then we turned on our white headlamps to get a better look at what we had found. It was *mostly* skeletonized. Like, you could see the fingers and the ribs and everything. There was still some..." Vic hesitated, and Erin thought she decided not to say what she had been planning to. "We could see that there was clothing around parts of it. So it was, you know, modern. And besides, Willie has been there before, so he knew it wasn't something that had been there for years."

"That sounds horrible. Are you okay?"

"Yes, I'm fine." Vic rolled her eyes. "It's all been very surreal. We went back outside, called the police, waited for them to get out there, led them to it, and answered all of their questions. It didn't really feel real, if you know what I mean."

Erin nodded. She understood that feeling of unreality. Like maybe it was just a mannequin, or a joke, or some student film project. Her mind always went to other explanations, something to indicate that it wasn't really real.

"So, that's all," Vic said. "I know it sounds like a big, exciting thing, but it really wasn't. There wasn't much to see, and when we saw it, we had to get the police involved and then spend half the night dealing with them."

"Did you see Terry out there?"

"Sure. Officer Terry Piper was on duty. Everyone was on duty. I talked to him. He was very good. Very professional."

Erin knew his professional face and manner. She nodded. "Yeah. He's good at what he does. Did he look okay? Not like he'd been there for too long?"

"He was fine when I saw him. I don't think you need to worry about him."

"I always worry about him."

"I know. And maybe you should ease up a bit on that. He's a big boy. He can take care of himself."

"I just know that he doesn't always do that."

"No one *always* does. We all let ourselves get a bit overtired sometimes, or don't eat right away when we should. Or do things that we know aren't good for us. It's normal. And men are like that. They don't want to look weak. They want to tough it out. Show everybody what a good protector they are."

Erin nodded. She knew that. She'd had plenty of experience with it the last few months. She squeezed Vic's arm. "So, you're okay?"

"I'm okay. Willie's okay. Terry's okay. The only one who isn't okay is the poor guy in the pool."

"And you didn't… recognize him."

"How could I? He had no—" Vic cut herself off. "No, I couldn't tell who it was. It was mostly just bones. And the clothes could have been anyone's. Blue jeans, plaid flannel shirt. Practically a uniform in the wilds around here."

"Yeah. I don't know anyone who has been declared missing lately, do you? I mean… no one since Joshua."

"Nope. No one I know about. He was probably from out of town. Maybe even out of state. Just came here to explore caves…"

"You think so? No one we know?"

"Nah. After what happened to Josh, I think we would have heard if anyone else disappeared. We're kind of a bit paranoid about that right now. If rumors started going around town about someone else being missing, we would have heard about it, I'm sure."

"Yeah. That makes sense. We would have heard about it."

"So he must have been someone from out of town. Another spelunker or a miner. Shouldn't have been exploring by himself. You should always take a partner, at least. File a plan to make sure that people know where you're going to be."

"Yeah. I worry even when it's you and Willie. I know you are together, and he's experienced and good at first aid care, but… like with the mine collapse…"

"At least we were stuck together. If we didn't come back, you'd come looking for us sooner or later. And you and Terry would get us out. Just like before."

Erin hadn't really done anything to get them out when the mine collapsed. She had called it in, and the police department and search and rescue had taken over. All she had done was sit there waiting for someone else to do all of the work.

CHAPTER 5

They only spent a few more minutes visiting. Vic stretched and massaged the back of her neck and excused herself.

"I'm going to need some time to unwind if I'm going to be at Auntie Clem's in the morning."

Erin hadn't even thought about that. "I can call someone else in. Do you want me to do that?"

"No. I'd rather be working. Keep my mind off of things."

"You're not going to be able to do that," Erin warned, thinking about how many people would be at the bakery the next day to gossip and get all of the details.

"Well… no, not most of the time. But work makes it go faster. I'll take a sleeping pill. But I want some time to just decompress first."

Erin nodded. "Sure. Of course. I'll see you in the morning. But if you do have a bad night and want to sleep, just let me know so I can call someone."

"I'll be fine." Vic leaned toward her and gave her a hug goodbye. "See you tomorrow. You should be heading to bed soon."

Erin tried to sleep, but her brain was whirling and she couldn't settle her thoughts. She couldn't help thinking about the bones in the underground pond. She had a feeling they were going to figure into her dreams that night. If she ever got to sleep.

Terry gave her a bear hug in greeting and looked at her face. "I thought you and Vic would still be talking."

"We talked. But we're both on at the bakery tomorrow, so I was hoping to get some sleep."

"She told you all about it?" Since Terry wasn't allowed to tell Erin anything about his investigations, he couldn't really talk to her about anything but what she already knew from other sources.

"Yes. I can't believe it! What a shock it must have been for them."

"I imagine so. That's not one of the things that you expect to discover when you go exploring caves. Although, there have certainly been remains discovered in other caves. Sometimes they were used as natural tombs by the native peoples or early settlers. A lot easier than digging a hole."

"But this one that Vic and Willie found… it's not an Indian or early settler."

"Oh?" He raised his brows.

"Not if it was wearing blue jeans."

"No," he agreed.

"And Vic said that Willie has been in there before and he wasn't there. So it's not even someone in one-hundred-year-old Levis. It's… recent."

"Contemporary, anyway," Terry agreed. "Willie said that he hasn't been there for a couple of months. And even when he was there last, he didn't take a careful look in the pool. It could have been deeper in the mud at that point. Maybe spring rains stirred things up a little to reveal it."

"So, you think it's older?"

"No. There are just other possibilities. It's important not to jump to immediate conclusions."

"Like that it could be someone we know?"

"It's not someone we know," he assured her.

"Does that mean you've already identified the… remains?"

"We have some initial leads to follow up. Probably won't take long, though we'll have to send them to the city to have them make the official identification. Don't want to misidentify them, you know."

Erin thought about her father. "No," she agreed. It would probably take weeks or months before the city had the official identity for them. If the remains were skeletonized. Erin knew it took longer than on TV, when an episode of *Bones* was completed in an hour and things like facial reconstructions or DNA analysis were instantaneous. "And it wasn't… Vic said it probably was someone from out of town, since there hasn't been anyone reported missing in Bald Eagle Falls."

Terry didn't agree or disagree. He shrugged and gave a head wobble that could have been yes or not. Noncommittal.

"You think it *was* someone from Bald Eagle Falls?"

"We'll have to see. But you don't know everybody in Bald Eagle Falls."

"Well, no," Erin agreed. And there were a lot of outlying farms and shacks. Someone could be local and still unknown to her. She'd only lived there for a short time as an adult, though she'd been there as a child before her parents had died.

"Is it someone *you* know?" she pried.

"Can't give you that kind of information."

"No, I guess not." Erin relaxed back into her pillow. "I don't suppose you're ready for bed."

He rubbed his forehead, considering. "I'm tired, but I don't think I'm ready for sleep. If I lay down now, I'm going to be tossing and turning and keeping us both awake."

Erin nodded. They'd been through it enough to know what didn't work.

"I'll need some time to relax and veg out before I'm ready for bed," Terry said.

"Okay… well, come in once you're ready, if you can."

"Sure. I don't want to wake you, though."

"You won't."

Erin wondered if she would wake him. Her brain was still whirling and she had a feeling that she was going to have a night filled with restless nightmares. "Do you want to cuddle for a little while?"

He bent down and kissed her on the forehead. "Better not. I'll just keep you awake. I'll see you tomorrow."

CHAPTER 6

The next day, Erin's mind was not any calmer, but was buzzing with questions about the person who had died in that cave. Who he had been and what had happened. How much did the police know? She knew that she couldn't find out the details from Terry; he was far too careful of what he said to her. There were other ways to find out more information about the investigation. Mostly, she just had to wait, and it would come to her.

Vic was definitely looking worse for wear. She was dressed and ready for work when it was time to go—Terry was still up and said he would drop them off—but Vic was definitely looking a little wilted.

"Are you sure you're okay to work today?"

"I'm fine, boss. Got a few hours in."

"We don't want you chopping any fingers off."

"I'll be sure to stay away from the bread knife. You know how it is; once we get going, I won't be tired anymore."

"Until you get home after the shift and crash. Why don't you see if someone else can come in to cover the afternoon? You can just do the morning and then catch a nap."

"I really am fine," Vic insisted.

Erin shrugged. "Okay," she finally conceded. She'd done everything she could to ensure that Vic had a way out if she needed it. She turned her attention to Terry.

"And you're okay to drop us off? You know all of the warnings about driving tired."

"I can manage to Auntie Clem's and back." It was only a few blocks. "I've driven after much longer shifts."

"That doesn't necessarily mean it was a good idea. Driving tired is driving impaired."

"Are you going to administer a field test?" Terry teased good-naturedly. He closed his eyes and brought both index fingers to his nose. "Okay?"

Erin laughed. "Okay, okay. You pass."

"I'll sleep when I get back," he promised. "I'll get a good long chunk in by the time you're back."

Erin didn't think she would have been able to survive shiftwork, going to sleep during the day like that.

They got their things together and headed out to the bakery.

Erin enjoyed the cool air before the bakery heated up from the baking. It could get pretty hot in the kitchen during the summer, but it was only spring and it didn't get unbearable. Vic and Erin worked together through their well-established routine, getting the morning's goods baked and arranged in the display case.

"You think the body was someone who was from out of town?" Erin asked Vic as they were arranging the display case.

Vic looked at her, brows raised. She nodded. "Yes, I expect so. We would have heard if someone from Bald Eagle Falls was missing."

Erin nodded.

"Why?"

"It's just that Terry… I kind of thought that he thinks it was someone from around here."

"Did he say that?"

"Not exactly. But he said that I don't know everyone in and around Bald Eagle Falls."

"Huh." Vic thought about it. "Well, I mean… it could have been someone I know. He wasn't exactly recognizable in that state. I just figured that since I hadn't heard about a missing person, it must be someone from the city or out of state."

Erin shuddered. "Wouldn't it be awful if it was someone that you knew."

"Yeah." Vic paused in writing the pricing labels, staring in the direction of the front door. Erin doubted she actually saw the door or what was on the other side. "That would be pretty disturbing, actually."

Erin instantly regretted having suggested it. She knew how hard it could be to deal with a scene like that and, instead of reassuring and supporting Vic, she was making it worse by suggesting that maybe it was someone she knew.

"Oh, I'm sorry… that was so stupid."

Vic shrugged. "Well, if it is someone I know, then it would have come up sooner or later anyway. Might as well think about it now and not be so shocked when they identify him."

The Fosters arrived early in the day, before the worst of the gossips came by. Mrs. Foster had been blindsided before by people discussing a murder in front of her children, so Erin was glad that she arrived when it was quiet and the discovery was not yet the main topic of conversation.

"Miss Erin!" The children ran excitedly up to the display case to pick out their kid's club cookies. It had been a long time since they had been there, between Erin falling out with Mrs. Foster and the birth of the latest little Foster.

"It's a boy!" Peter called out to Erin, gesturing to the baby Mrs. Foster wore in a sling. "I can't believe we finally got another boy!"

"I know," Erin agreed. "It's very exciting. Are you helping your mom out with everything? You're a big boy, and taking care of a baby and your sisters is a big job."

He nodded seriously, watching his three sisters crowding around the display case pointing at the day's offerings.

"Yeah, that's what Dad said, too. I try and help."

"Good. Don't leave everything for her to do."

Peter agreed. He took charge of the little girls, asking them what cookies they wanted and trying to talk them into ordering the ones that he wanted them to. Mrs. Foster sighed and listed off for Erin the things that she needed for the week. The baby fussed, and she readjusted the sling, rocking her body back and forth to soothe him. He settled back down. Erin stood on her tiptoes to look over the counter and the edge of the sling to catch a glimpse of his cherubic cheeks.

"Aw. So sweet."

Mrs. Foster nodded, rubbing the dark little curls at the top of his head. "It's always such an amazing experience when they are this new," she said. "Fresh from heaven."

Erin started to collect the bread and other items that the Fosters needed, giving a half-shrug. She didn't believe in heaven or God, and mentions of them always made her feel awkward. She didn't want to challenge people's beliefs, but she didn't want to pretend to agree when she didn't, either. Silence was the best she could come up with.

Vic spoke with the children, using tongs to get each child the cookie he or she wanted. Traci squealed and jumped up and down when she got hers. Peter looked down at his cookie and asked Mrs. Foster if she wanted a bite.

"No, you go ahead and have it," Mrs. Foster told him, giving his arm a pat. "It's yours."

"You didn't get anything."

"I don't need anything, I'm the mom. And I have baby weight to lose."

"You don't need to lose weight."

She smiled and pulled him in close for a hug around his shoulders. "I'm glad you don't think so. But I don't want to have to carry all of these extra pounds around. It's hard enough carrying Allan."

"He's not heavy." Peter stood as tall as he could, grasping the edge of the sling to pull the side down and look at the baby.

"No, but he's going to keep growing. And until he's big enough to walk around, I'll be carrying him."

"You could use a stroller."

"I use a stroller when we go into the city," Mrs. Foster said. "I don't like to use one around town. It just encourages kids to be lazy."

Erin wasn't sure how using a stroller encouraged a child to be lazy but using a sling did not. But she smiled at Mrs. Foster and handed her the order.

CHAPTER 7

Eventually, word started to get around about Vic's discovery in the cave. Erin was happy to see that the most common reaction was the same as hers—horror at what Vic had discovered and shudders at the thought of exploring caves deep underground, dark and damp and full of unearthly critters. There were few women who, like Vic or Gema, a woman who had lived in Bald Eagle Falls when Erin had first arrived there, appreciated the adventure and challenge of spelunking.

"Why on earth would anyone want to crawl into a hole in the ground?" Lottie Sturm demanded. "I can't imagine any good reason for tunneling like a worm inside the earth!"

"I understand your viewpoint," Vic assured her. "There are a lot of people who would agree with you. But I really enjoy exploring. Stepping into a place that… few if any human eyes have ever seen before. And you've seen some of the pictures, right? Some caves can be absolutely beautiful. Full of stalactites and stalagmites, or beautiful underground waterfalls and pools. Even gold or other mineral deposits. You never know what you're going to find."

Lottie made a disgusted noise and shuddered dramatically. "You'd never catch me going into such a place. And this just proves it."

"What…?" Vic asked, her eyebrows coming down.

"Finding a skeleton. Anyplace you find a dead skeleton is a place I don't want to be."

"Oh. Yes, you're right, of course. Dead skeletons," Vic agreed. "I can see how you wouldn't want to come across any of them."

"You're acting like it wasn't any big deal," Cindy Prost, mother of Bella, one of Erin's part-time employees, pointed out. "There's something wrong with you if that doesn't bother you."

Cindy flashed a look at Lottie, which Erin interpreted as a confirmation of what they had long believed—that there was something terribly wrong with Vic. As if being transgender weren't proof enough that she was a deviant.

Erin rolled her eyes, directing a mental apology at Vic. At least the customers knew not to run Vic down in front of her. Anyone who did was not welcomed back into the bakery until they had expressed a sincere apology. Cindy was definitely treading a thin line. Erin wasn't going to put up with much more from her.

"I've got a pretty strong stomach," Vic said. "I wouldn't say that it didn't give me a turn, but as far as it keeping me from spelunking anymore... well, it would take a lot more than a pile of bones to keep me out of the caves."

"It just ain't natural," Cindy affirmed.

"Do they know who it was yet?" Lottie asked.

"It's probably some ancient, prehistoric skeleton," Cindy said. "Been down there for a thousand years."

"Not unless they had blue jeans a thousand years ago." Vic leaned forward slightly to deliver this news and to assess the ladies' reaction to it.

"Blue jeans?"

Vic nodded. "Either that or someone dressed up the cave man later. And with the state he was in, that would have been pretty hard."

"Shocking," Cindy huffed. "I can't believe something like that happening right here in—right outside of Bald Eagle Falls. This isn't the kind of place where that happens."

Who did she think she was kidding? Erin had been stumbling over dead bodies and other criminal enterprises since she had moved to Bald Eagle Falls. Rather than not being the kind of place bodies showed up like that, the universe seemed to be funneling them toward Bald Eagle Falls and the nearby Tennessee towns.

"I'm shore he didn't do it on purpose," Vic drawled. She gave Erin an amused look, clearly in agreement that with all that had happened in the time they had both been in Bald Eagle Falls, it wasn't unlikely that she would discover a skeleton in an underground lake.

"Do you think he had a heart attack?" Lottie mused. "Did he look like he had a heart attack? Or like he drowned?"

"I'm sure the medical examiner will look into that… it's not up to me to say."

The women made shocked noises and placed their orders for baking that they probably didn't actually need.

After they were gone, Vic looked sideways at Erin. The bakery was empty for the moment, and she had something she wanted to say without others overhearing. Erin read all of this in a glance.

"What?"

"I don't think he had a heart attack or drowned."

"Oh." Erin thought about that. She wasn't sure she really wanted to know the details. But Vic wanted to talk to someone about it, and she didn't want to spread rumors all over Bald Eagle Falls. For one thing, Officer Terry Piper would not appreciate that. "You think that… you could tell what it was? From the bones?"

"Yeah." Vic's voice was low and husky. "The skull was pretty smashed up."

Erin mumbled a response, her stomach lurching. She tried again not to picture what Vic had seen, but her imagination was too good. She couldn't help forming a mental image.

"I don't think it was natural," Vic said. "I mean, yeah, maybe he hit his head… on an overhang, or fell into that pool, but I don't think so. And I don't get the feeling that Terry thought so."

"It could have been an accident."

"If it was… then where was his gear? He went into the cave without any? I didn't even see a headlamp. I'm sure they'll drain the pool and look for one, but… no one would go in there without a headlamp. Not on purpose."

"So, you think it's murder."

"The questions that the police were asking us last night… they didn't act like *they* thought it was an accident."

CHAPTER 8

Terry had said that he would go to sleep after dropping Erin off and would probably sleep most of the time that Erin was working. That would get him back on track so that he wasn't in as much of a danger of coming down with a migraine or relapsing in other areas.

When she got home, he was awake. He didn't look like she had woken him up, or like he had just recently gotten himself up and was still groggy. That was good. He must have gotten the sleep that he had needed.

He got up from the couch when she arrived and gave her a hug and a soft kiss. "How was your day?" he murmured.

"Well, you know what it gets like at Auntie Clem's when people are chasing down rumors." Erin bent down to pick up Orange Blossom, who was yowling for her attention. She held him like a baby while she spoke to Terry.

"I suppose there's nothing we can do about it when Vic was one of the witnesses. You can't exactly ground her."

Erin laughed. "No. I don't think that would work very well." She walked into the kitchen with her armful of yowling cat. Marshmallow pricked up his long ears and followed her in to make sure he didn't miss out on any treats. "What do you want today?"

"I can make something. You've been working all day, I've just been sleeping and lazing about."

"You've been sleeping because you were up all night. At least I got a few hours of sleep."

"I've had more than you by this time. How much did you get? Two hours? Three?"

Erin shrugged. She didn't really want to stop to calculate. Less than she needed, that was for sure. But she would sleep better tonight. "We'll make something together, then. Some pasta?"

Terry nodded his agreement. Erin put down the cat and washed her hands. They moved around the kitchen together, coordinating the preparation of pasta, a green salad, and rolls from the bakery with butter. Marshmallow hung around Erin's feet while she chopped vegetables for the salad, so she cut a few chunks for him.

Of course, that set Orange Blossom off again because the bunny was getting a treat and he wasn't. So Erin had to get him something. And she didn't want K9 to feel left out, so she got a doggie biscuit out of the jar for him. She thought about Nilla over in Vic's apartment, but it seemed a little silly to make sure that he got a treat. Vic would see to it that he had what he needed. Hopefully, he hadn't torn things up again while Vic had been at work and he had been in the apartment by himself. At least, Erin assumed that he had been alone, and Willie had been out checking out one of his mines or another venture.

"You didn't hear Nilla during the day, did you?" she asked Terry.

"Nilla? I wouldn't hear him from here, unless he was howling."

Which meant that he hadn't. Erin nodded. "Good. I hope he's settling into the routine."

They worked a little longer in silence.

"Have you heard from the sheriff?" Erin ventured.

"Heard what from the sheriff?"

"Any update on the case. Have they been able to identify the body?"

"Preliminary steps are being taken. Can't really say more than that. There are particular procedures to follow, channels to go through."

"I know. I just wondered if you'd heard an update from him."

Terry nodded, but didn't give any further information to Erin.

"Vic said she thought that it was a murder investigation. Not an accident investigation."

He turned around from the sauce he was stirring and looked at her.

"Well, that was very astute of her," he said. "Or did you hear something from Melissa?"

"She didn't come to the bakery today." Melissa worked part time at the police department with administrative work. And she was a little too eager to spread information on matters that should have remained confidential.

"Well, that's good news. The longer we can keep that woman out of the bakery, the better."

Erin smiled, scooping irregularly-cut vegetables into the salad bowl. "You know that if she didn't come into the bakery, she would just take the news somewhere else, don't you?"

He grunted. "Let's take this one step at a time."

"She didn't come by. So I guess your investigation is still safe."

He nodded and stirred the sauce. He poked a fork into the pot of pasta and teased a piece out to test for doneness.

"So, Vic was right?" Erin asked. "It was murder?"

"That hasn't been determined."

"But you're investigating it as murder? You think it was?"

"We're not making assumptions either way."

"Vic said he wasn't even wearing a headlamp."

"Vic was there. I can't comment on witness testimony."

"If he wasn't wearing a headlamp, or there wasn't one with him, that would mean that there was someone else down there with him. Or he was dragged down there and put in the pond after he was dead."

Terry was silent. He turned off the burner that the pasta was on and picked up the pot of pasta to pour into the colander already positioned in the sink.

"You aren't investigating this, Erin."

"I didn't say I was investigating it. I'm just curious… about what happened. If you think that it was murder like Vic does, or something else."

"We're investigating. A determination has not yet been made."

"Okay." Erin sighed. She placed the salad bowl on the table and circulated through the kitchen, getting out plates, glasses, and cutlery. "And you think… it might be someone local to Bald Eagle Falls?"

"I didn't say that."

"Someone local to Bald Eagle Falls… killed in a cave underground or dragged in there… I guess that means that if it is murder, then the murderer is local too."

"All the more reason to stay out of it. I don't want you to walk into anything."

"Is this cave… who does it belong to? Is it on private land or public land?"

"Why?"

"I can ask Vic… I just wondered if it was on someone's private property. If there was some kind of fight over who the cave belonged to or something like that."

"Leave that to us."

"It wasn't one of Willie's mines?"

Terry finished draining the pasta and transferred it into the saucepan, where he stirred it to coat it with tomato sauce.

"You'd have to ask him that."

"They weren't trespassing on someone else's property, were they?" Erin considered. That could be a problem. She didn't want Willie and Vic to get in trouble for trespassing. They had called the police and cooperated with the questioning, so the police wouldn't lay any charges against them for trespassing, would they?

"Let's eat," Terry diverted. "This smells really good."

Erin got a couple of bottles of salad dressing out of the door of the fridge, thinking through the possibilities.

CHAPTER 9

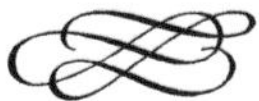

Adele stopped by later in the evening. Usually, she didn't come in when she knew that Officer Piper was there. Not because she had ever run afoul of the law—other than the unfortunate incident when her ex-husband had shown up in town—she just liked to keep things quiet. She lived alone in the summer cottage in the woods on Erin's land, running trespassers off, performing whatever rites and rituals she did late at night where she would not be observed by anyone in town. But she did occasionally come over when Terry was there, or to participate in Thanksgiving or Christmas observances. She was obviously not comfortable doing so and preferred to be by herself.

Erin swung the door open to invite her in. "Adele! How are you doing?"

Adele nodded. "I'm just fine, Erin. And yourself?"

"Can't complain."

"Good."

Adele looked around. She lowered herself into one of the easy chairs. She nodded in Terry's direction but didn't address him. But she didn't ask if she could talk to Erin alone, either.

"I hear there was some excitement," Adele said obliquely.

Erin nodded. She looked at Terry to see if he would contribute anything, but he didn't.

"Yes… I don't know a lot yet. I mean, *I'm* not involved in the investigation, but sometimes I hear things."

Adele smiled wryly and nodded.

"Vic is the one to ask. She's the one who found the body—the remains."

Adele wasn't as comfortable with Vic as with Erin. There was that small matter of a kidnapping that got in the way of things. Vic understood that Adele hadn't known anything about it, but Adele found it difficult to get past.

"I know. But I figured she would have told you all about it. The police can't disclose anything, obviously," Adele looked at Terry, and then back at Erin. "I just wondered… about some of the details. Not that it's any of my business, of course."

"There's not a lot to tell. She found a skeleton in an underground pool. The police are trying to identify the victim and whether it was murder or not."

Adele nodded. "You don't know who it was, then?"

Erin raised an eyebrow at Terry. "I don't know. I guess they have some leads. But they don't release it to the public before they're sure and then they have to talk to the next of kin first. Right, Terry?"

"That's about right."

Adele nodded. She looked out the window into the darkness of the night.

"Do you know something about it?" Terry asked.

"No. Just curious. Like any of the old gossips around here, I suppose."

Erin doubted that. Adele had always been different from the ladies who came to Auntie Clem's. She wasn't just interested in hearing the latest gossip. She had a reason for asking. Erin glanced at Terry briefly and saw that he too was wondering where Adele's inquiry was going.

"It's kind of disturbing," Erin prompted. "You know me, I hate the idea of going underground. I can't imagine what it would be like to go into one of those caves and to find… bones or any other kind of human remains."

"Wouldn't be my first choice," Adele agreed. "I prefer the fresh air aboveground. It may be interesting to search through underground tunnels where so few have visited… but it's not my cup of tea."

"You were just wondering whether the remains had been identified?"

Terry asked.

"I suppose so. I wouldn't want to be wondering about a family member… waiting for them to return home, not knowing they never would…"

"You don't have any family in town, do you?"

"I'm not speaking of myself. Just hypothetically. It would be very difficult, not knowing what had happened and whether you would ever see them again."

"We'll do our best to make sure that doesn't happen. We will inform the next of kin as soon as we are able."

Adele nodded.

They all sat there in silence for a few minutes, thinking about it. Erin wasn't sure why Adele was there. Adele knew that Terry wouldn't tell her anything and that Erin didn't have the scoop on what had happened this time. Erin hadn't been involved in even a minor way. It was all Vic.

"Do you know what they were doing in that cave?" Adele asked eventually.

"I have no idea," Terry said firmly. "I have no way of knowing why he was in the cave or what he might have been doing there. Exploring, prospecting, meeting someone? That may become clearer during the investigation, or it may always remain a mystery. We don't have a time-travel machine."

Adele nodded. She slid her hands to the seat as she prepared to rise. "Well, you folks have a good evening. I'll be on my way."

Erin walked her to the door, said her goodbyes, and returned to sit with Terry once Adele was gone. She looked at him.

"Do you have any idea what that was about?"

He shook his head slowly. "It sounds like she knows something… but I don't know what it is."

Erin tried to put the whole investigation behind her. It would probably be some time before the police had confirmed the identity of the body absolutely. Then they would be talking to the next of kin about it. Maybe they would release a name to the public and maybe they wouldn't. How the man had died might always remain a mystery.

"Do you remember when you were attacked in that mine?" Erin asked Willie as he drove them to Auntie Clem's again later in the week. "When you hit your head and ended up in the hospital?"

Willie looked sideways at her. "No, actually."

He'd had amnesia at the time, of course. But Erin thought he might remember more of it now. And he at least remembered that it had happened, even if he didn't have any recollection of the event.

"I was just thinking about that. I don't know. I was thinking about how you were hit on the head when you were in the mine, and when you came out, you were disoriented and you couldn't remember anything."

"So I've been told."

"And you don't remember any of it happening."

"No. And I doubt I ever will. The doctors figured that it would all start to come back, but they were wrong. I've never been able to remember what happened that day. And maybe that's a good thing, because I'm not sure I really want to."

"So with this guy, it could be the same thing. He might have hit his head—either he hit it himself on an overhang or took a fall, or someone hit him—and then he was disoriented and didn't know what to do. He might not have been able to find his way out again. Or maybe he bent down to take a drink from the pool and then tumbled into it. We don't really know."

"No." Willie shook his head. "I can't imagine anyone drinking from the pool without at least filtering the water first, but people do things without thinking. If he had hurt himself or was disoriented, I could see that happening. But where does that get us?"

"I don't know." Erin sighed. "I just keep trying to construct it in my mind. What happened. How he got there. Why he was in the pool. I guess… trying to figure out how it might just be innocent. An accident."

Willie and Vic exchanged looks. Erin wondered if there was more to it that they had not told her about. Maybe because they were trying to protect her from the extent of what they had seen. Vic had edited herself when she had told Erin about it.

"What is it, then?" she asked. "What aren't you telling me?"

"It just didn't look like an accident, Erin," Vic said eventually. "I don't think it was."

CHAPTER 10

During a lull at Auntie Clem's Bakery, Erin found herself watching a woman through the door and front window. A skinny, tattered looking woman with several children in tow, all looking similarly worn and thin.

"What's up?" Vic asked, noticing her distraction.

"Oh… I was just watching that woman…" Erin nodded toward the window. "Do you know her? I don't think I've seen her before."

Vic squinted toward the window. She nodded. "Yeah, I think I've seen her around. Not in here, but… around town."

"She looks like she needs some help."

"People are proud. She probably wouldn't accept anything."

The woman shouldered a pack and, as she readjusted it, Erin realized she had a baby in her arms as well. A baby, a backpack, and the other children around her feet that she had to keep nudging forward and then grabbing if they got too far off track.

Making a quick decision, Erin bent down to the display case and grabbed several different varieties of granola bars. She hurried across the street toward the little group, Vic calling something after her.

"Hi," Erin greeted brightly. "I'm the owner of the bakery over there, and I thought your children might like some granola bars."

"We're not coming in there," the woman said, her expression pinched.

Her eyes darted in the direction of Auntie Clem's Bakery and then back to Erin.

"No, I brought some with me." Erin displayed them. "We made too many today, so I'm giving out some free samples. Wouldn't you like some?"

The children immediately started to clamor for the granola bars. Erin grimaced, realizing that she might have made a mistake in offering them in front of the children before the woman could make a decision. What woman wanted to tell her children that they couldn't have free treats?

"Maybe I could get you something else instead," she suggested. "Maybe… a loaf of bread? Some sandwich rolls?"

"We don't need your charity."

"No, it's not charity." Erin had never figured out why sometimes charity was good and sometimes it was bad. It seemed to her that if someone had a need and someone else was offering to fill it, that was a good thing. "Won't you take anything?"

Scowling, the woman finally gestured to the children. "Fine. Give them the granola bars, then." As Erin passed them out, the woman spoke to them. "And don't think this is a regular thing. You're not going to get granola bars every time we come into town or see the bakery. Got it? This is the only time."

"Thank you, Mama," one of the oldest of the children said politely. The rest took theirs without any thanks, snatching them out of Erin's hands as if they were afraid she might change her mind and withdraw them.

Erin tried to keep the smile pasted onto her face, to look friendly and non-threatening and not bothered by their behavior.

"They're good kids," the mother said in a tight, clipped tone.

Erin nodded reassuringly. "I'm sure they are. You certainly look like you have your hands full! I'm Erin." She put her hand out, uncertain whether the woman would respond.

The tired-looking woman nodded, but didn't take Erin's hand or respond with her own name.

That, apparently, was all that Erin could do. The encounter was finished. She nodded, wiggled her fingers at the children as a goodbye, and retreated to Auntie Clem's.

A couple of the children said 'bye,' but mostly, their mouths were full.

"What was all that about?" Vic asked when Erin returned. "Did you know them?"

"No. I just thought… they looked like they could use a little pick-me-up."

"But they didn't appreciate it," Vic guessed.

"No. I guess like you said, they're too proud. I thought that just a few granola bars… it would be a way to break the ice. Find out who they were and start a friendship… then maybe I could help her with something else."

"You've got a soft heart," Vic said, smiling. "I remember when you said you were going to help me out. I couldn't believe it. You didn't know me from Adam, but you helped me with the police and gave me a job, and even invited me into your home." Vic shook her head. "That could have turned out very badly, you know. I could have been a serial killer."

"But you weren't."

"How do you know that? Maybe I'm just very good at hiding the bodies."

"Well then, at least you've decided not to kill me."

Vic grinned. "Not yet!"

They got back to work.

~

Sitting in the living room that evening, Erin couldn't help noticing Terry looking through the kitchen at the back window much more frequently than he normally did.

"Is something wrong? Did you see something out there?"

"Uh… no." Terry pulled his attention away from the kitchen window and looked at Erin, focusing on her. Acting like he hadn't been looking out the window to begin with.

"What is it, then?"

Erin's brain started working a mile a minute, thinking about all of the things Terry might be worrying about. Had he heard something about someone he had arrested in the past? Or heard that Crazy Theresa was in town, looking for Erin or Vic? Or was it something else? A danger that she hadn't even thought about yet?

The world could be a dangerous place, and if something was making Terry nervous, then that made Erin nervous.

"Nothing."

"There's something. Why do you keep looking out there?"

"Was I? No. Just thinking about something. Staring off into space."

But she knew that wasn't true. She looked back down at the Bald Eagle Falls newspaper, pretending to be reading again. It was only a few seconds before Terry was looking out the back window again.

This time, though, Erin saw Willie's headlights as his truck pulled onto the gravel pad.

Terry had just been distracted by the lights.

Terry got up. "I need to talk to Willie about something."

Erin wanted to follow. She leaned forward in her seat, trying to decide whether to get up and act like whatever Terry wanted to talk to Willie about was her business. Or to pretend to be getting something from the kitchen and to see if she could overhear them. Or just to stay where she was, with the cat on her lap, and mind her own business.

Eavesdropping won out.

She didn't want to be obvious about it, but she did want to see if it were anything that impacted her or Vic. The men might just be arranging another fishing date. Terry was busy with the investigation of the remains found in the cave, but maybe he had reached the end of the trail of clues and needed to wait until the lab got back to him with the results of some of their forensic testing. Or maybe he'd decided to listen to everyone who told him that he needed to take it easy and not work every day.

But she doubted that.

Erin shifted Orange Blossom to the couch beside her, but Blossom wasn't too happy about this action and yowled in protest. He didn't lie down where she put him and go back to sleep, but blinked owlishly at her, wanting to know why she was disturbing his nap time.

"I just need to get up for a minute," Erin told him. She went to the kitchen and ran water into the tea kettle. Orange Blossom followed her, nudging at his dish and looking at her significantly.

"Are you hungry? It's not time for bed yet."

He meowed loudly a couple of times, expressing his displeasure. First, she woke him up, and then she wasn't even going to feed him?

"Okay, fine," Erin said. "I'll get you a couple of treats, okay?"

At the word 'treats,' the other animals put in an appearance. Marshmallow and K9 were much quieter and better-behaved than Orange Blossom, but they wanted their treats too. Erin got them all their snacks, straining her ears to hear what Terry was discussing with Willie. She couldn't hear anything. She opened the window a crack, which helped, but she was still having a hard time hearing what was going on.

"I've told you everything I know," Willie said gruffly, raising his voice so that Erin could suddenly hear him clearly. "It isn't like there is that much to tell. We found the skeleton. We left the cave and called the police. We weren't involved in anything we shouldn't have been. Just doing some spelunking."

"On land that isn't yours."

"Public land."

"That remains to be seen."

"If a survey shows that it wasn't public land, I'll apologize to the landowner, if there still is an owner. According to my map, it's on public land, and that means I have as much right as anyone to explore there."

"How many times have you been there before?"

"How is that your business?"

"Are you being obstructive?"

"Is this part of your official investigation?" Willie challenged.

Terry didn't say anything for a moment. "I'm just making friendly inquiries at this point."

"Then I'm not required to answer them and I'm not being obstructive. If you have something else you want to know, I can refer you to my lawyer."

"Have you mined in that cave?"

"Talk to my lawyer."

"It's not that hard a question to answer. I'm just trying to get a clear picture."

"I'm not required to answer you, Officer Piper. I'm exercising my civil rights. You can't do anything about that, official investigation or friendly questions."

"And you don't have any idea who the man was."

Willie said nothing.

"Had you ever run into anyone else on that property before?"

Willie still didn't answer, standing there by his truck, waiting for Terry to return to the house.

Eventually, Terry made an exasperated noise and turned back toward the house. Willie nodded and headed up the stairs to Vic's apartment.

The kettle started to sing as Terry returned to the kitchen, so Terry would know that she had been in the kitchen long enough to overhear most of the conversation.

He looked at her for a minute without saying anything. He sat down at the table and snapped his fingers to call K9, who was gnawing on his doggie biscuit, to come to him. K9 looked at Terry's snapping fingers, picked up his biscuit, and walked over to Terry's side, where he lay down and continued to eat the biscuit. Terry scratched his ears.

Erin took a couple of cups over to the table and filled them each with hot water. Terry helped himself to a teabag from the basket on the table and dangled it into his cup.

"You think Willie knows something he's not telling you?" Erin asked tentatively.

"I'm sure Willie knows plenty of things that he's not telling me. Finding out whether any of them are related to this case, that's the tricky thing."

"I suppose." Erin sat down with him and started to prepare her tea. "But he's not a suspect, right?"

Terry stirred his teabag around.

"Willie wouldn't hurt anyone," Erin asserted. "And if he did, why would he put the body in the pool and then take Vic out there to find it? And call you in to investigate? I'm sure he knows plenty of hiding places that are better than that, even in that one cave."

Terry raised his cup to his lips and sipped the too-hot tea. "You're probably right about that."

"It wasn't anything to do with Willie."

"Unfortunately, you're not a police investigator. I can't go by your gut instinct. I need to actually follow the evidence. And you know as well as I do that Willie was in the Dixon clan for five years. He is still involved with them, from what I can tell."

"But just doing things like computer consulting. Not… you know… mob stuff."

"You don't know that. Even if it's true, that's still working for organized crime. It's still a problem. And it means we have a trust problem."

"*You* have a trust problem," Erin corrected, not wanting him to include her in the statement. She did trust Willie. He'd proven to her in the past that he had her welfare and Vic's at heart. Whatever else he might be doing, she was sure that he wouldn't intentionally do anything that might endanger them. And that included taking Vic somewhere he'd disposed of a body or putting her in the middle of a murder investigation.

There was no way that Willie had had anything to do with the death of the man in the cave.

"Yes. I have a trust problem. The police department has a trust problem. Willie Andrews is not someone we can trust to tell the truth or stay on the right side of the law. If he is involved in a case, we have to consider the possibility that he is the perpetrator of a crime. Seriously consider it."

"He hasn't ever been convicted of anything, has he? He's never done prison time."

Terry raised his brows at Erin. She realized that she didn't know that for sure. She knew that he had been part of the Dixon clan because his family had been part of the clan, and that he'd done things that he had come to regret. He had gotten out when he could, but that meant putting in five years of service first. Who knew what he had done during that time. And Erin couldn't state for a certainty that he had never been convicted of a crime or done time. He might well have wanted to keep something like that under wraps.

Willie lived away from Bald Eagle Falls for an extended time, so the gossips in town might not know if he'd had to do prison time. Or maybe they did, and that was why they looked down on him so much and acted like he was lazy and shiftless when Erin knew him to be a very self-motivated, hardworking man.

Terry didn't answer one way or the other. Maybe he didn't want to admit that Willie hadn't ever been convicted or done time. Or maybe he was protecting Willie's right to privacy.

CHAPTER 11

There were a few quiet days. Days when Erin almost forgot about the man in the cave. The image of the skeleton or a decaying corpse started to fade from her dreams. Vic didn't say anything about Willie being questioned by the police and Erin didn't ask or mention the conversation she had overheard in the back yard. Everything was going back to normal and, pretty soon, everyone would forget all about what had happened.

Then on a warm afternoon, Melissa walked into the bakery with a bounce in her step. She pretended to be examining the sale prices on the products in the display case. But Melissa was there often enough to know what she liked and what the regular prices were. Unless she were interested in one of Erin's latest experiments, she really didn't even have to look in the case at all.

Instead, she was there to trade in information. She had something to tell.

"Afternoon, Melissa," Erin greeted. "What can we do for you today?"

"The sheriff wanted me to pick up some sticky buns for the department," Melissa said with a smile. "And he's actually covering the cost this time. He apologized for sending me over to do the legwork, but I actually don't mind that part."

"Sticky buns it is." Erin agreed. "A dozen?"

"That will be more than enough."

"I have some still in the tray in the kitchen. I'll just be a minute."

Erin retreated to the warm kitchen and breathed in the smell of the cinnamon and yeast. It was one of her favorite scents. She could practically taste the particles that hung in the air.

She assembled a box for the cinnamon buns, loosened the buns from the baking tray, and then slid them in. Everything came out without a problem, no ripped buns sticking to the tray. Erin slathered the tops with extra frosting and put a small tub of it into a condiment container so the police officers and staff could add more of their own if they wanted to go into sugar shock.

She closed up the box and carried it out to Melissa. "Still warm from the oven."

"Oh, those smell so good," Melissa enthused.

"They are! They're so good… it's almost criminal."

Melissa groaned at the joke. "Okay, that's enough of that! No bad jokes allowed."

She counted out the money to pay for the buns and passed it across to Vic at the till.

"Did you hear that they have identified the bones you found in the cave?" She asked in a dramatically lowered voice.

Vic raised her brows. "Did they? I'd almost forgotten about that."

Melissa's mouth dropped open and she began to protest, before realizing that Vic was just teasing her.

"Just for that, maybe I won't tell you."

Vic shrugged. "Well, my loss, I suppose."

She knew that Melissa couldn't bear to keep a secret.

"No, no," Melissa protested. She leaned closer to Vic, looking at Erin to make sure that she was included in the conversation. "His name was Darryl Ryder. He was a… a drifter around here."

"A drifter?" Erin repeated. "What exactly is the definition of a drifter? Do you mean he's new in town? Or that he's… some kind of scammer? Or what?"

"I don't know exactly where he lives. You know how it is with these guys. They float around and never do settle down anywhere. No one ever knows where to find them."

"So… he's homeless?" Erin suggested. She hadn't seen a lot of homeless people around Bald Eagle Falls. She saw them when she went into the city. It could be profitable to beg or busk in the city, where there was a large enough audience to make some good money. And there were proper shelters and soup kitchens. It was different in Bald Eagle Falls. There were no shelters, no food pantries, no services to help homeless people to get jobs. Consequently, the homeless people didn't come to Bald Eagle Falls.

At least, not that she had seen.

Their streets were clean of both trash and homeless folks sitting and begging, setting out their caps or holding up their homemade signs. Erin did what she could to help with the situation in the city, donating baked goods that didn't sell quickly enough. She froze them, and once she had as much as she could fit in her freezer, she made a run into the city and donated them to one of the kitchens or shelters. Or to a school breakfast program or whatever else she could find. Erin liked to be part of the solution. She had been on the edge of homelessness enough times herself. She wanted to help others. Make sure that they knew that they were valued and worthwhile people.

"We don't have homeless people here," Melissa argued, wrinkling her nose. "We don't have to deal with problems like that. Big city problems. But… that doesn't mean we don't have our poor people, and people who… would rather get a free ride from a friend or family member than take care of themselves or their own families. What kind of a person won't work and makes other people support his family instead?"

"So you knew him?" Erin asked. "This Darryl? He was out of work?"

"I don't know if you can say out of work, exactly. If you're not looking for a job, are you really out of work?"

"Darryl Ryder," Vic said thoughtfully. Her brows were drawn down like she was trying to think of whether she'd ever heard that name before. "I don't think I've ever run into him."

"Well, except that one time," Melissa pointed out, breaking into giggles at the inappropriate comment.

Vic made a noise of disgust. "Melissa!"

"I'm sorry. I know you meant you never saw him while he was alive."

"Yes."

"Well, I guess we'll see about that. Now that the police have verified his identity, they can investigate the case more deeply. It's pretty hard when you just have a John Doe and you're trying to figure out who might have had motive to kill the guy."

Erin adjusted the positioning of some of the baking in the display case. "Does that mean that it's been determined it was murder? Not an accident?"

Melissa nodded meaningfully. "That's what it looks like," she agreed. "They're still waiting for tests back from the lab and medical examiner, but it looks like the guy was smashed over the head. Not an accident."

"He could have hit it on something in the cave," Erin suggested. "An overhang. He could have slipped and fallen."

"This was no slip and fall," Melissa said. She looked at Vic. "Was it? You know it wasn't."

Vic took a deep breath in and let it out. "No, I don't think it was an accident," she admitted.

~

Melissa was off, headed back to the police department to make everyone fat on sticky buns.

Erin wasn't sure she wanted to know any more about the man in the cave. She preferred to let the nightmares fade away again.

Vic kept looking at her sideways, waiting for Erin to start asking her questions.

Erin didn't ask Vic any more about the condition of the remains.

"You don't know this Darryl Ryder?" she asked Vic eventually. "I don't think I've ever heard the name before."

"No, can't think of it. It sounds familiar, like I might have heard of him before, but I'm pretty sure it isn't someone I ever met. Pretty sure he never came in here as a customer!"

"No. Doesn't sound like the kind of person who usually comes into Auntie Clem's."

How would she have reacted if he had? If he were poor and possibly homeless, Erin hoped that she wouldn't have turned him out, but that she would have found some way to help him. It was difficult to know what to do or say sometimes. She didn't want to enable someone with an addiction or to end up with someone stalking her because she had been nice to him. But people with addictions still had to eat too. If the man were hungry, she hoped that someone would have reached out to feed him. Even if he hadn't gone into Auntie Clem's.

"I'm glad we don't have a big homeless population here," she commented. "That's at least one thing we avoid by living in a small town instead of in the city."

"I think there are a lot of positive things about being in a small town. I wouldn't want to live in the big city." Vic gave a mock shudder. "I'm a country girl at heart. I think I'd waste away to nothing if I had to live in the city, surrounded by nothing but concrete all the time. I need my green spaces. Trees and sky, things that feed the soul."

Erin nodded. "Yes… though you can get some of that in the city, too. Living in the city doesn't mean that you never see the outdoors again. There are parks and sky. Cities are trying to cut down on light pollution so that you can see the stars again."

"Still not for me," Vic asserted, shaking her head.

Terry seemed to be in a good mood when he picked Erin up. He suggested that they go out for a dinner date, which was a nice change from having to make supper. It was still nice to get out sometimes. She liked the idea of letting someone else wait on her for one meal.

"That sounds good," she agreed. "What do you want? Barbecue?"

"Yes," Terry agreed quickly. "Barbecue would be amazing."

Erin smiled at his enthusiasm. "Barbecue it is. I'm surprised that you're hungry."

He raised his brows. "Why?"

"Melissa bought sticky buns today. I figured with one or two of those under your belt…"

"Oh, that." Terry gave a little laugh. "I'd already decided that I wanted to go out tonight, so I didn't overindulge. I didn't even have a full one. Gave the rest to Stayner."

Stayner was a younger man with a faster metabolism, and he probably didn't mind too much having a sticky bun for dinner. He probably went to the restaurant all the time. That, or ate a lot of macaroni and cheese.

She felt a little guilty at assuming he ate like a bachelor. What did she know about his diet? She knew from experience that the man knew how to clean up a kitchen properly. If he knew how to clean up and where to put things away, chances were he'd done a fair amount of cooking himself. He might be a gourmet, she wouldn't have any idea.

They got settled at the restaurant and placed their orders. Erin sipped a soft drink while they waited for their food. "So, I guess you got the identity of the man in the cave confirmed today."

Terry nodded. "The Bald Eagle Falls grapevine is alive and well, I see. Yes. Darryl Ryder. It helps with the investigation. Pretty hard to figure out motives and timelines before you know who you're dealing with."

"That's good, then, I'm glad you have the information you need. So… is he someone known to the police? Melissa said that—the grapevine said —he was a drifter. So does that mean you didn't know him? Or you did?"

"A drifter. Well, that's not the way that I would classify him. I think people around here use the term to describe anyone they see as less desirable. They don't belong in Bald Eagle Falls. So even if they've been here ten years, they're 'drifters.'"

"Had he been here a long time, then?"

"We will need to gather more information about that. But he wasn't just passing through town."

"Did he live in town? Or on a farm?"

"We'll sort that out."

"You don't know?" Erin was surprised.

"With some people, where they live is not as clear."

"He was homeless?"

"We don't have homeless people in Bald Eagle Falls." Terry swirled his drink and reconsidered his answer. "Not permanently homeless, out on the streets."

"Right. But without a legal address?"

He shrugged. "People living with friends or family until they can get on their feet, squatting on land in a shack or an RV, moving from one place to another. I suppose we have a few who are… less adequately homed."

Erin looked at him, her brows drawn down. She shook her head. "Less adequately homed?" she repeated.

Terry looked away, chuckling. "Okay. You got me. I guess we do have our share of homeless. But… it doesn't look the same as it does in the city."

"Even in the city, homeless doesn't always mean begging on the street or living out of your car or a shelter. Sometimes it's couch surfing, or a whole family squeezed into someone's back room, a mom and her kids moving from one relative to another because she doesn't have a place of her own and no one can take her long term."

Terry shrugged. "I suppose. You just don't see those ones. You see the beggars and buskers on the street."

"Yeah. So your Darryl Ryder, did he have a 'less adequate' address?"

"Trying to sort that out. He and his family apparently moved around. They were looking for somewhere more permanent, but hadn't found it yet."

"He had a family?" Erin's heart sank. Those poor people. No home, and now they had lost the head of the family. How were they going to fend for themselves?

"A wife and young children," Terry confirmed, the corners of his mouth turning down. "We are trying to find them."

"You don't know where they are?"

"That's one of the problems with homelessness. It isn't always easy to find people when you are looking for them."

"So where do you go? How do you find out?"

Terry sighed. "Just keep asking questions. Find everybody you can who knows them. Ask if they've heard anything. Ask who else might know. Hopefully, people cooperate enough that you're able to narrow it down over time."

"But people don't exactly trust the police."

"That would seem to be the case," he agreed dryly.

Erin felt herself flush. She knew that she didn't tell him everything. And he knew that too. There were parts of her life that she didn't feel comfortable sharing, even with all that they were to each other.

Their meals arrived, and Erin did her best to forget about poor Darryl Ryder and his young family and to focus on her time with Terry.

CHAPTER 12

Erin worked on her tai chi before bed, enjoying the warm weather outside and the feeling of the grass between her toes. She watched carefully to make sure there were no surprises in the grass. K9 was good about using the dog run, but Nilla wasn't very disciplined in his habits. Even though they tried to monitor him carefully when he was in the yard, he did manage to sneak past them every so often.

Vic was sitting on the steps watching Erin go through her forms. Nilla was calm for once, sitting while Vic slowly fed him kibble one tiny piece at a time.

"So they don't even know where Darryl lived?" Vic asked.

"No. Doesn't sound like it. Terry is asking around, trying to nail it down. They have to inform his wife and talk to her about when she last saw him. If there was anyone he'd had a disagreement with. Stuff like that. They have to sort out all of those things before they can figure out who—how he was killed."

"Yeah. But if he was a drifter, then it wasn't likely anyone in town, right? Maybe he had a business partner who came to see him. Or an estranged family member. Some enemy that followed him here."

Erin let her mind assess these possibilities. She could see that it was possible. Ryder's death might not have anything to do with anyone in

Bald Eagle Falls. And that would be good. She'd be happy if that were what the police determined. She didn't want to think about anyone in her Bald Eagle Falls family being involved with Ryder, even peripherally.

"Maybe. I guess I can't figure out why anyone would want to kill a drifter or homeless person. I mean, it doesn't make sense that it would be for some kind of gain, because he wouldn't have anything. And as far as jealousy, he has a wife and kids. Married men can fool around, but if they weren't from around here, who would he be involved with? Wouldn't he be too busy trying to find a job and get his family settled?"

"Some men are never too busy."

Erin nodded at the truth of this.

"Or maybe he just got in someone's way," Vic suggested. "Started a fight or got in an argument over something stupid."

"In a cave?" Erin paused in her movements to look over her shoulder at Vic.

"Well… maybe."

Erin shook her head. "I still think it must have been an accident. Sometimes an accident scene can look like homicide."

Vic gave her a long look, then went back to feeding Nilla the bits of kibble.

Vic and Erin were working together again the next afternoon. Bella had been scheduled to take the afternoon shift, but something had come up and she called in to cancel with profuse apologies. Vic shrugged and said that she could stay on, so they were covered. Everything was fine until Vic got the call from Willie.

"Hi hon'," Vic greeted, tapping her Bluetooth headphone to answer it. She wouldn't have if she had been out in the customer area, but she and Erin were both in the kitchen while things were quiet, prepping some fresh muffins for the after-school rush.

"I'm heading over to the police department." Erin could hear Willie clearly over the headphone, his voice raised in irritation.

"To the police department. For what?"

"More questions about the Ryder case. I was really hoping this was all out of the way!"

"What else do they want to ask about that? We already told them everything we know. It isn't like we were trying to cover anything up."

"I guess since they identified Ryder, they want to ask me about him."

"You don't know anything about him, do you? Just tell them you never heard of him before and don't have anything to say."

There was no immediate answer from Willie. Maybe he was getting his truck started or was focused on something else.

"Willie? You still there?"

"Sure. I'm here."

"Just tell them you don't know anything about Ryder."

The suggestion was again met with silence. Vic looked at Erin. She probably knew that Erin could hear the whole conversation. And even if she couldn't hear Willie's part of the conversation, she couldn't help but hear Vic's end, which was interesting enough.

"Willie… you don't know Darryl Ryder, do you?"

"Yes. I do. Or did."

"Oh." Vic processed this. She picked up a pan of muffins and started loosening them from the tin. "Well… I guess they figured that out, then. Someone must have told them that you knew him."

"Yeah. I don't think they're just fishing."

"Okay. So you knew him. But that doesn't mean you know anything about what happened to him. Or that you had anything to do with his death. Good grief. You couldn't have."

"I didn't," Willie agreed.

"You couldn't have. You wouldn't have taken me there if you knew his body was there. How stupid would that be? If you'd had something to do with it, you wouldn't have ever gone back there. Let someone else find the body, and they wouldn't ever be able to draw a connection back to you. Do they think you're an idiot?"

"I don't know what they are thinking. I guess I'll find that out. Maybe they think that I did it and then regretted it later. Wanted to find a way to get him off my conscience."

"That's ridiculous."

But was it? Erin could see the police's way of thinking. Willie didn't want Ryder rotting away in that pool, his family thinking that he had abandoned them or forever wondering what had happened to him. So if he could find a way to 'stumble across' the body in a natural way… the police would never suspect that he was involved.

Except that they did.

CHAPTER 13

"Okay, well maybe," Vic conceded. "I think that's a pretty far stretch, though. And why would you kill him in the first place? You'd have to have a reason."

"Yeah," Willie agreed. "You're right about that."

"How did you know him? Just because you saw him around town? Or was he involved in mining too?"

He'd been found in a cave; it wasn't hard to believe that he'd had a reason to be there. Something that connected him to Willie.

"I'm just pulling up now," Willie said. "I guess… I'll talk to you later. Let you know how it went tonight."

"You don't have to go in if you don't want to talk to them," Vic pointed out. "You're not required to unless they arrest you, and they haven't done that."

"Not yet. I'm hoping to avoid that."

"They're not going to arrest you. If they want to keep you half the night, just tell them you're going home. I want to see you."

"I'll get there when I can."

He apparently disconnected, because Vic didn't have to. She worked on getting the muffins out of the tin and onto the cooling rack, her brows drawn down. Eventually, she looked over at Erin.

"How much of that did you get?"

"Well… pretty much everything. Sorry."

"It's okay. Then I don't have to explain anything, right?" Vic shook her head. "I can't believe that they are treating him like a suspect. They say they're not biased. But they are. They think that Willie is a criminal. He's the most likely suspect because he doesn't have a regular job like they think he should. They think he's lazy and dirty. He was involved with the Dixon clan *years* ago, so they think that any time he's faced with a decision, he's going to pick the illegal route. But he's not like that. He isn't a criminal."

Erin remembered what Terry had said and that he had refused to confirm that Willie had never served time. But it didn't seem like a good time to bring it up. Asking Vic whether Willie was a convicted criminal after that tirade was not a good idea.

So she just nodded sympathetically. She wouldn't like it if someone were accusing Terry or Vic of having something to do with Ryder's death either. She liked Willie, and she didn't like the idea of their thinking that he had anything to do with it. Vic was closer to Willie, of course, but he was Erin's friend too, and she didn't like the direction the investigation was going.

"They'll figure it out," she assured Vic. "They'll talk to him this afternoon, and he'll answer whatever questions they have, and then it will all be okay. They'll go on to the next person on the list."

"I don't know." Vic shook her head dubiously. "I doubt that he's going to answer all of their questions. And they'll think that means he's guilty of something. So then they'll have more questions and suspicions. They're not going to go on to the next person or theory unless they feel like he's cleared himself. And I don't think that's going to happen today."

"But if he didn't have anything to do with it, then he shouldn't have any problem answering their questions."

Vic glared at Erin. "And is that how you felt whenever the police wanted to question you about something? That if you just spilled everything to them and told them the truth, they wouldn't suspect you anymore? You wouldn't end up in prison, because they would believe everything you said?"

Erin had to laugh at that. "Well… no. Definitely not. I guess that even after everything that has happened, I still have an idealized view of the police. Blame it on Terry."

"I don't think Terry's given you reason to think that."

"He hasn't arrested anyone without good evidence."

Vic nodded, but didn't look convinced.

Vic was probably right. Erin and Terry rarely saw eye-to-eye on investigations. Erin jumped to conclusions. She jumped into things with both feet without looking first, sometimes getting herself into some pretty dicey situations. How many times had Terry told her to stay out of things and she hadn't listened to him?

If she trusted that the police would eventually arrest the right person, then why was she always putting herself into the middle of police investigations?

When Erin and Vic got home, both Terry and Willie were still at the police department. Probably on opposite sides of the table. Usually, Erin would invite Vic to join her at the house for supper, but Vic was worried about Nilla having already been left alone too long, and wanted to keep him company.

"Why don't you come over to the loft? You never spend any time over there, and you should be as comfortable there as I am in your kitchen."

"Are you sure? I would think you would want your privacy…"

"Some days, yeah. But not all the time. And it isn't like I have a bunch of contraband or questionable literature lying around the place. No secrets."

No secrets?

Beaver had said that Vic had secrets.

Of course, she had said that Erin had secrets too.

Which was true.

Nothing terribly shocking, no dead bodies buried in her wake, but still things that she didn't feel like revealing to her friends and loved ones. Old associations, embarrassing stories, guilty feelings still lingering after years.

One of Vic's secrets had been Theresa. Not because they had been seeing each other behind Willie's back—which would have delighted Theresa—but because Vic was embarrassed about some of her old associations too, and didn't want to have to explain Theresa and their shared past. It was over and done, something best left alone. Until it had flared to life and they had found themselves in a situation that had nearly gotten them killed. Terry and Detective Jack Ward could easily have both died that night if the others hadn't managed to overcome Theresa and to find them when they did.

Odds were Vic still had secrets. But who didn't?

"Okay. I'm just going to feed the animals and shower off, and then I'll be over."

"Perfect. I'll see you soon."

It was funny that after spending almost all of their time together, the two of them were still perfectly willing to spend the evening together too. But they were. It seemed like the most natural thing in the world. Like Erin had always thought that having a sister would be. She and Vic were as close as sisters. Closer than Erin had ever been with any of her foster sisters. And certainly closer than Erin ever expected to be with Charley, who really was her sister.

Nilla appeared to be the perfect gentleman when Erin let herself into Vic's loft apartment. There was no sign that he had torn around the apartment trying to destroy everything he could sink his teeth into. Everything looked remarkably tidy and untouched. She could still see a few areas that he had attacked in earlier days, leaving teeth marks or scratches on various furniture, the wall, and the doors.

Instead, he sat on a dog bed on the couch, regal as a king. Erin sat down on the other end of the couch. Not too close to Nilla, worried that he might get overly excited and either attack her or run away.

Vic came out of the bathroom. "I thought I heard you. Long time, no see!"

"Yes, such a long time," Erin agreed with a smile. She nodded at Nilla. "Isn't he behaving himself well."

Vic gave Nilla a long look, seeing if he would stay still like he was supposed to. Then she stepped closer to him and petted him on the head. "Good boy. You want some treats? Haven't you been good!"

He panted at her happily, waiting for his reward. Vic got out a few pieces of food and fed them to him slowly by hand.

"I think he's finally starting to settle down. I don't know whether he was just really anxious after Beryl died because everything changed, or…"

"I think she just didn't know how to train him. Or hadn't bothered to. It looks like you're doing a really good job with him now."

"I hope so! As long as he doesn't turn into demon dog the minute I start to relax…"

The white, fluffy dog just sat there panting and smiling at her, waiting expectantly for the next piece of food. Like he'd never been anything but an angel. Erin would have believed it if she hadn't seen some of the chaos he had caused.

"What can I help you with? What were you planning for supper?"

"I don't know. Just warm up whatever is around or open a can of something. You sit for a few minutes while I figure out what it's going to be. It won't be anything fancy."

"I don't need fancy. A lot of what Terry and I are doing lately is soup and salad. Better than too many rolls with honey or jam at the end of the day!"

"Well, more nutritious. Maybe not better tasting…"

Erin conceded this point. She wasn't a salad eater. She really didn't appreciate a wide variety of vegetables. She was forcing herself to eat better to stay in shape, but most nights all she could say about her supper was that it was satisfying. Not that she had really enjoyed it.

"Seems like there aren't a lot of things that are both delicious and low calorie," she sighed.

"We'll have to figure a few out. Heaven knows, I don't want to end up all plump and rolls of fat either."

Vic at least had extra height on Erin. She could weigh more without looking heavy.

Vic stuck her head in the fridge to look through the various leftovers and ingredients she had on hand, glanced in the freezer, and opened up a cupboard full of canned goods. "How about tacos?"

"Sure, tacos sound good."

"All right. We'll do them super simple. You can open a can of beans and I'll get some vegetables chopped. We've got salsa, avocado, taco shells, and cheese. That should be all we need."

They got to work. They were only halfway finished eating—and Erin was enjoying the tacos much more than soup and salad—when they heard Willie's truck roar into the parking space beside the garage.

Erin looked down at her plate. She should really go and give Vic and Willie a little privacy, but she couldn't exactly walk out gracefully with her plate still half full of food.

"It's fine," Vic assured her. "We've got all night."

"I'll try not to be too long…"

Willie's heavy boots were clomping up the steps outside the garage and, in a moment, he was opening the door.

"I swear, there are days that I would like to just pick everything up and move—" He saw Erin at the table. "Oh. Hello, Erin."

"Sorry, I'm just finishing up. I'll leave the two of you alone in just a minute…"

"No rush. You'll give yourself indigestion. I'll just save the more choice parts of my conversation until later when I won't burn your ears with my colorful language."

"You can say what you like. I won't be offended. It isn't like I haven't heard bad language before." Erin laughed. "I did grow up in foster care, you know. The language that some of those kids used…"

He chuckled. "I can imagine."

"No… I don't think you could."

Willie sat down on the couch and bent over to unlace and remove his boots. Nilla yipped at him and growled deep in his throat. Willie looked over and stared him down. "You don't growl at me, you little rat."

"Don't tease him," Vic objected. "He's been behaving himself really well, and I don't want him to regress."

"I'm not teasing him. I'm telling him not to push his luck with me."

"He doesn't understand that. Just leave him alone and don't get him excited."

Willie rolled his eyes and continued to take off his boots, ignoring the dog.

"So…?" Vic ventured. "How did things go over at the police department?"

She didn't ask whether everything was all right and cleared up with the police. Erin had a suspicion that things were not all sunshine and rainbows. The interview that must have lasted several hours for Willie to be arriving home so late.

"Well, no blood was shed. There are no more bodies to be cleaned up."

"Oh, well that's good, then." Vic's tone was dry. "I'm certainly glad to hear that. I don't think you would likely be sitting here in my apartment if there had been bloodshed."

"That might depend on who it was."

Erin wouldn't want to hear that anything had happened to Sheriff Wilmot or any of the other regular staff. Officer Stayner, on the other hand…

She tried to push the thought away and think about him charitably. He did have his good points. He was, apparently, a good investigator. He'd gotten good marks and reports in his training. And the man knew how to clean a kitchen. She would try to focus on those things rather than on all of the things that she didn't like about him.

"Did Terry come home too?" she asked Willie. If Willie was finished, then hopefully Terry was too and would be home soon, if he weren't already waiting for her back at the house. She stole a glance at her phone screen to make sure that he hadn't messaged her. The screen was blank.

"He didn't come back with me. I imagine he has a bunch of paperwork to fill out. You know how much red tape and bureaucracy there is in a police department. One reason you would never find me in that job."

Erin expected Vic to make some quip about other reasons Willie wouldn't want to be a cop, but Vic bit into her taco and didn't say anything. It would, perhaps, be a little too close to home after spending hours being interrogated about his relationship with Darryl Ryder.

"So how well did you know Ryder?" Vic asked after a few more bites.

Willie threw his boots toward the door. Nilla yipped and jumped after them, growling and menacing them.

"Nilla!" Vic snapped. "Stop. Leave the shoes alone."

Nilla ignored her, stalking the shoes. Willie didn't get up to retrieve his shoes or to chase the dog away from them. He stretched his legs out in front of him and watched Nilla indifferently.

"Nilla!" Vic put her taco down. She licked her fingers and wiped them on a napkin, then went after the dog, clapping her hands in warning. "Nilla, no! Leave them alone!"

The dog darted out of Vic's way, circling around to the other side of the boots, nose still down, sniffing to investigate how much of a threat they were. Vic picked up the shoes and set them upright, together at the side of the entry mat.

"Leave them," she warned. "They're just Willie's shoes. And if you chew on them, you're going to be in big trouble!"

Nilla sat back on his haunches, considering Vic.

"Go sit back on your bed. Go to bed." Vic pointed at the bed. "Go on. Go to bed."

Nilla didn't go to his bed, but he didn't hunt down the boots, either. Erin considered that progress. Vic approached Nilla slowly, then picked him up and took him back to the dog bed. She put him down gently and murmured to him to stay put. He lay down, putting his chin between his paws, and watched her.

"Good," Vic told him. She went back over to her chair and tried to pick up the taco she had put down without making a big mess. "There's food if you want it," she told Willie. "Come have something. You must be famished."

"No. I grabbed a burger and a beer on the way home."

"Oh." Vic raised her eyebrows.

"I didn't know what you were making, if anything. And I knew you wouldn't want me drinking on an empty stomach." He smiled.

"Well, no, that's true."

"Nothing against your cooking."

Vic shrugged. "Fine. There is beer in the fridge here."

"I needed time to decompress. Didn't want to bring all of my troubles home to you."

Erin thought about the way that Willie had pulled his truck into the parking spot and burst in the door, expressing his displeasure. That was after he had decompressed and had a drink? She would not have wanted to see him immediately after his interview with the police.

And even with a meal and drink, he had still beaten Terry home. She hoped Terry wasn't putting in too many hours.

"So…" Vic returned to the earlier conversation. "Ryder? You knew him?"

Willie considered the question. He rubbed his forehead, just over his eyebrows. A fatigue headache. Tired after so many hours spent in the interrogation.

"I knew him," he agreed.

"I didn't know that. He hasn't lived in Bald Eagle Falls for long?"

"He's been here a while."

"Was he… a friend?" Vic asked tentatively.

Willie grunted. "No. Wouldn't call him that."

"Did you work with him on something? How did you know him?"

"He was… interested in the mines and caves around here. Had it in his head that if he could find a good claim, he could make it rich. Young folk these days," Willie shook his head. "Think that they can get the money without putting the work into it. All they have to do is show up and people will hand it to them on a silver platter."

"He was interested in mining."

Willie nodded.

"And you guys talked about that? Like, over drinks, or…?"

"No. Not over drinks." Willie scratched the back of his neck. "Maybe over the barrel of a shotgun, but not over drinks."

CHAPTER 14

Erin was mid-bite, and had to suppress a gasp and an exclamation of surprise, or she probably would have choked on her taco, or at least inhaled some of the dripping juices.

"Over the barrel of a shotgun?" she repeated.

Willie looked at her as if he had forgotten that there was another witness. Eventually, he decided that what was said was said. He couldn't take it back. He shrugged.

"The guy figured he could squat on my claim. Thought that everything around here was up for grabs, he just had to decide what he wanted."

"So you ran him off," Vic said.

Willie nodded. "I did. What else would I do? Invite him over to tea?"

Vic and Erin both shook their heads. Of course not. But it wouldn't play well with the police. No wonder they had been so insistent about interviewing Willie and had kept him for so long. He threatened a man at gunpoint who later was murdered. Willie looked as guilty as the day was long.

"I didn't kill him," Willie asserted to Vic. "You and the police know that he wasn't killed with a shotgun. Whatever happened to him, it was nothing to do with me. But I can't say I blame whoever did it. If the guy was planning to jump my claim, how many other people did he bother?"

Probably Willie wasn't the only one. Erin didn't know a lot of people who were still mining in the hills. It wasn't like it had been in the early days in Tennessee, when mining was the main industry in the area. The mining was mostly done by big corporations now, and not in the small caves and tunnels around Bald Eagle Falls. Most of the mines around Bald Eagle Falls were abandoned, as far as she knew. And abandoned because they were not producing enough to support a person or a family. Willie was one of the few Erin knew of who still made a living, or part of his living, from mining and processing minerals.

"Melissa said that he had a young family," she said to Willie.

He nodded, scowling. "Yes, he did. Thin, washed-out looking wife and a passel of kids."

"What's going to happen to them?"

"Not my responsibility. Especially since I had nothing to do with the death of her husband. I don't feel responsible for her. She can go back to her own kinfolk and they can look after her. I'm sure she probably has family in these parts. I doubt if either of them ever traveled out of the state in their lives."

Terry had said that a lot of people lived with family or friends. Erin supposed that was probably exactly what Mrs. Ryder would do. She would go to stay with an aunt or a sister until she could find some way to support the family herself. Someone would put a roof over their heads. Although if there were a lot of kids, as Willie suggested, it made it more difficult to find someone who would take them in.

"Have the police been able to inform her that… about what happened to him?"

"Sounds like they're still trying to find them. They asked me a few times where he was living and where they would find his family."

"Where did he live?" Vic asked.

"They live out there." Willie nodded toward the window. "I had to kick them out of a mine they had taken up residence in. Like I said, squatters. They think they can stay wherever they want. If they stay there long enough, it becomes theirs."

"They were living in a mine?"

"Yeah. Had all of their junk stored in there. Kids everywhere. Camp stove in a clearing to cook on. Imagine they were hunting to try to keep food on the table." Willie shifted his position, crossing one leg over the other, stretched out in front of him. He slid his hands into his pockets, considering. "You have to admire them for at least trying to live off the land instead of relying on government or family to feed and shelter them. They were trying to make their own way. I can admire that."

"Those poor people."

"Literally," Willie agreed. "But there's no excuse for trying to take what isn't yours. If he wanted to live off of the land, he should have built a place of his own. Buy or rent a piece of property, put up a house, and live that way. Putting up in a mine or somebody's fishing shack or trailer, that's not making do by yourself. That's theft."

Maybe Willie didn't realize that not everyone would be able to do that. As far as he was concerned, all that was needed was the desire and two good hands. But building a house required materials, tools, and know-how. Not everyone had that. Or the physical ability for the hard work needed to build a shelter.

She couldn't shake the mental picture of the thin woman and her passel of kids, living in some abandoned shack or cave out in the sticks, waiting for her husband to come home. She had thought that kind of thing didn't happen in Bald Eagle Falls. Many people struggled to make ends meet, but she thought that the townspeople took care of each other. That they wouldn't put a family out on the street. There were no beggars on street corners, so she had thought that there weren't any homeless.

"Police will find them and let them know what's going on," Willie told Erin, voice gruff. "They can go back to live with her people."

"Maybe. Not everyone has family or gets along with them. Or if they are abusive, you wouldn't want to take children there. Some people are alone."

"Then some friends can help her out. Or she can go to the city to a shelter or apply for welfare programs. She's on her own now, she'll qualify for help."

She was surprised he would suggest this after saying that he admired them for trying to make it on their own.

"Do you have to deal with that very much?" Vic asked curiously. "Is there a problem with squatters, or was it just a one-time thing?"

"Ryder I've had to deal with more than once. Most people… you confront them once, and they make themselves scarce. They don't want to have to deal with angry owners. They want to stay unnoticed. Invisible."

"I didn't even know that. You never mentioned him."

Willie considered before answering. "I think I did, actually. Rip Ryder."

"Rip? I thought the police said it was Darryl?"

"People go by other names. He took on the name Rip. That's what I knew him by. Didn't even know his last name. Didn't know who the police were talking about until they brought up the picture on his driver's license."

"Rip Ryder. Should have been in Hollywood with a name like that," Vic laughed.

"Yep. Maybe he and his family would have done better out there. There isn't much around here for people looking for the easy way to strike it rich. Not putting his own labor into it, but looking for something that would be a shortcut. The big score."

"You don't know that," Erin said. "He might have been working hard, he just wasn't able to do what you could have."

"I know that some people make it, and some people never do. And he never did. And with another fifty years on this planet, he still wouldn't have. People who are always trying to find the shortcuts never finish what they start. Because it's too hard. If you're not willing to put in the hard work—like you have, Erin—you don't ever make it to the finish line. They'll always have excuses. Why other people could do it but they couldn't."

Erin pressed her lips together and didn't argue. She hadn't, after all, known Rip Ryder. She had never even heard of him until he was dead. But she hadn't lived a sheltered life. She had seen a lot of different people trying a lot of different things. It was true that some of them never made it, and some people never seemed motivated to try hard enough, but she wasn't convinced that it was always their fault. Nor had she been able to start up Auntie Clem's Bakery and make it a success on her own.

She took a couple more bites of her taco and set the rest down. "I'm stuffed. That was really good. I should probably head home, see if Terry is back yet."

Vic took her plate from the table, smiling. "Be sure not to get lost on the way."

"I'll try," Erin agreed.

She said goodbye to them both, gave Nilla a careful pet, and went back to the main house.

CHAPTER 15

It was a while before Terry made it back. Erin had guessed that he wasn't home yet when she had left Vic's, but she thought Willie and Vic needed some time to talk in private, and Willie didn't need her challenging him about Rip Ryder.

She was sitting on the couch with Orange Blossom, reading one of Clementine's journals, and saw Terry's headlights as he pulled up to the house. She didn't get up to open the door for him, which would involve upsetting the cat from her lap. He let himself in and gave a deep sigh as he stepped into the house.

"Long day?"

"Very," he agreed. "I'm fine, mind you. Just fine. But bone tired."

"I don't imagine it's easy to interrogate a friend."

He looked at her for a minute, then shook his head. "An interrogation is never easy. And it is harder when it is an… acquaintance, and they might think they should be given the benefit of the doubt just because you know them."

"Well… I guess I can see that. You expect your friends to believe what you say."

Terry nodded. He stooped to give her a kiss, then went into the kitchen for a beer. He returned and sat on the couch next to her.

"Have you had something to eat?"

"Yes, we ate at the police department. Got some delivery. Everyone was tired and hungry."

Erin nodded and relaxed beside him, happy that she wasn't going to have to jump up and make him a sandwich or warm up something from the fridge.

"So you believe Willie now? About not having had anything to do with Rip Ryder's death?"

"I see you've already gotten his side of the story."

"Not in any detail, but I was over there having dinner with Vic, so we did talk."

"There isn't anything to stop him from telling you whatever he wants to, but I can't respond from the department's viewpoint. I'm not allowed to talk about any of the details of an active investigation."

"I know. I just figured… now that you've heard his side of the story, he's off the hook, and you can go on and investigate other possibilities. There must be other possibilities. Other… suspects."

"There are other avenues for us to investigate, yes. And talking to Willie doesn't stop us from investigating those other avenues. No one is railroading him. We are looking at all of the possibilities."

"And you still think that he's a viable suspect? You know he wouldn't do something like that. It doesn't make sense, any of it."

"People do stupid, impulsive things. That's how they get caught. If everyone was as thoughtful and careful as you think they would be, we would never be able to catch anyone. Someone getting killed in the midst of an argument or altercation—that's not a reasoned decision. It's an instinctual, animal impulse. And even after the deed is done, the perpetrator is not thinking straight. They make mistakes at the scene and they continue to make mistakes."

Erin still couldn't imagine Willie causing someone's death. Or being so stupid as to put the body in a cave where he was later going to go hiking with Vic. Erin knew Willie to be calm under pressure and in an emergency situation.

"I feel very sorry for his family. Did you have to make the notifications?"

"We are… trying to track his wife down."

"Oh. I guess it's harder if they don't live in Bald Eagle Falls." Erin fished for more information.

"People can be very difficult to track down if they aren't living in... traditional situations."

"So they are homeless?"

"I don't know if they are homeless or not... we won't know that until we find them. I am aware that they have been squatting, using land close to the cave, off and on. But whether his wife and kids are still out there somewhere, or if they have moved somewhere else... it's going to take some time to find out."

"What about a phone? Does she have one?"

"Doesn't look like it. Or if she does, it might just be a prepaid phone, which could be in anyone's name. Sometimes family buys phones, so that their loved one will be able to reach them in case of an emergency. It would be helpful if we had Ryder's phone, but we don't."

Erin nodded, thinking about it. "Did he have one? For sure?"

"Nothing in this case is for sure. Circumstances can change from one day to the next. There's really no telling. He did have a phone up until a few days ago. But again, no way to tell who it was registered to. We would have to find out who he'd talked to, so that we could find out what number he was at, and then trace that number to see who else he was talking to and when was the last time and location that the phone was used. All of that takes time. And a starting point. Right now, we don't even have a starting point."

"You can't find his wife or his phone. One would probably give you the other."

"Yes. But neither... gets us anywhere. Just asking more questions from more people, trying to find out where he has been and what he has been doing. It's a lot harder to track people when they operate below the radar like this."

"Maybe if you sleep on it, you'll come up with something."

He took a long swallow of his beer. K9 went out to the kitchen, and Erin could hear him slurping up water from his bowl. He'd had a long day too. Though he probably didn't find his as frustrating as Terry's.

Unless he wanted to go outside and do foot patrol, which was what he liked to do best. If he had been cooped up in an interrogation room all afternoon and evening, then maybe he was just as frustrated.

"I saw a woman in town recently. Thin. With several kids with her. I wonder if it could have been Mrs. Ryder."

Terry raised one eyebrow. "Where did you see this woman?"

"Across the street from the bakery. I just saw them walking along the street… I didn't recognize her or the children, and I thought they looked like they could use some help. I took some granola bars across to the kids. She wouldn't take bread or anything else."

"Could have been her. Fairly young woman? Dark blond?"

Erin tried to picture the woman. "That sounds right, yes. I introduced myself, but she didn't shake hands or tell me her name. She looked tired and… like she'd been living rough for a while. And I'm not sure how many kids she had. Maybe four? Three little ones and a baby?"

"Do you think she was living here in town? Did you see where she came from or where she was going?"

"I didn't watch her for that long. I never thought I would need to know, or I would have. I just thought it would be rude to be watching her and prying into her business. It really wasn't any of my business where she came from or where she was going."

"Did she say anything? About what her situation was or where her husband was? Was she looking for him? Supposed to meet him somewhere?"

"No. There was really no conversation. I felt bad enough for offering the granola bars in front of the kids, because then she didn't really have the opportunity to say no, after they had heard. I just wanted to help out, but she acted offended. You know how people are when they say they don't need any charity."

"Oh, yes." Terry nodded. "I've heard that line enough times."

"Sometimes people do need help. I don't understand why charity is a bad thing. It doesn't mean people are thinking badly about her. Just that they recognize she could use some help."

"I guess you have to be in that position to understand it."

"I have been, though. I mean, not in exactly her situation, not flat out without anywhere to go, but close enough. And I was always grateful when people offered to help. Especially if it was a job. But anything, even a bit of pocket change, at least it was something. I appreciated it."

"Then I guess it is a fundamental difference between you. Maybe the way she was raised. Maybe something happened in her past and she was taken advantage of. Someone made fun of her for accepting charity or thought that she owed them something when she took it. There are plenty of people out there who are not nearly as nice as you are, Erin."

Erin stroked Orange Blossom's head and back and he purred his loud, rumbling purr. "Yeah. There are a lot of people out there who are not very nice. I hate to have them ruining things for those who are good, decent people. There are lot of people who won't help you out without a lecture or religious sermon first." Erin shrugged. "But I figure, what does it hurt? Let them blow off some steam. If it makes them feel like they're doing some good, why not?"

Terry put his arm around Erin's shoulders, squeezing lightly, and rested his head momentarily against hers.

"I don't like to hear about you being that bad off. I didn't know that things had been that rough."

"Not all the time. Usually, it only took me a few days to be back on my feet. I would find work and a place to stay. That's what was so good about being a carer, a lot of times you could get a job and food and place to stay all at once."

"But they didn't always work out."

"No. Someone didn't like you for some reason or another, or the person you were caring for, if they have dementia, they lose things and accuse you of stealing. The family doesn't realize it's just the dementia talking, think you are bleeding them dry or selling off the family heirlooms." Erin rested her head against Terry's shoulder. "Or it would all work out really well, but then the person dies, and… you don't get to stay after that. Doesn't matter if it's the middle of the month and you don't have anywhere to go. The person you are taking care of dies, and you're back out on the street."

"That would be a shock. Didn't they know… that it would mean you were homeless?"

"No." Erin shrugged. "I wouldn't tell them that. I'd do everything I could to make it an easy transition for them. So that I could get a reference at the next place. If I caused trouble, insisted that I needed to stay there until I could find a new place… they'd resent me, and they wouldn't give a good report."

Terry nodded. "It must have been a very precarious existence." He rubbed her back and shoulders with one hand.

"That's one way to put it. Coming here to Bald Eagle Falls and starting the bakery… It was terrifying. But at the same time, I was so excited. I never thought I would have an opportunity like that. My own business. Running things the way I wanted to. Hiring employees of my own." She looked fondly around the living room. "I never had a house of my own before. I never had pets." She snuggled against Terry a bit more, even though her movement made Orange Blossom lift his head to glare at her. "I never had someone to share it with."

CHAPTER 16

Erin's sleep was restless, interrupted with thoughts of the Ryder family. Had it been them she had seen across the street from the bakery? Where were they staying now? What could she do to help with the homeless—or less adequately homed—population in Bald Eagle Falls? The more she learned about their plight, the more she wanted to get involved. She couldn't just ignore them, pretending they didn't exist. Even if that's what everyone else did.

The next morning, she arose a little drowsy, her lids heavy, wishing that she could sleep in for once. But even when she didn't have a shift at Auntie Clem's Bakery, her body was so used to her baker's schedule, she couldn't sleep in. Even without anything that needed to be done urgently, she couldn't sleep for more than half an hour after her usual waking time.

And she didn't have the day off, so she forced herself to swing her feet out of bed and head to the bathroom. Walking, turning on the light, and a duck into the shower for a few minutes woke her up enough to function and get her through the rest of her morning routine.

The houses outside her windows were still all dark. No one else found it necessary to be up so early. Even Vic didn't get up quite as early as Erin did, able to get ready for work in just a few minutes and not be in a state about getting everything done on time.

Vic's light went on in the loft around the time that Erin put on the kettle. She wasn't in Erin's kitchen by the time the kettle started to whistle, but it wasn't much after that.

"I don't know how you get ready so fast." Erin shook her head.

Vic pulled her hair back into a ponytail and wound it into a bun as she took a chair at the table. "I'm just really motivated to get as much sleep as possible. So I get as much ready as possible before bed… just jump into my clothes and head down the stairs."

"You're crazy. And you have to wake Willie up if he's driving us. That must take a few minutes too."

"Nah." Vic shook her head. "As soon as I move, he's awake. He's a very light sleeper."

Erin found that reassuring, somehow. Willie didn't sleep over with Vic every night, but when he did, it was nice to know that she had another watchdog nearby who would be out of bed in an instant if he heard something untoward.

Erin poured hot water into their cups, and they both set about making their morning tea. As soon as Willie was down the steps and in his truck, they would pile in and head over to the bakery for their usual early start.

Erin stared at the blackness of the kitchen window, still hours before sunrise, thinking about the Ryder family. Did they have beds to sleep in? Were they in a safe shelter? Or were they out on the street somewhere? Or in sleeping bags in another cave? All of those little children and the thin woman with her baby. Erin's hips ached just thinking of her sleeping on the ground or on the floor.

"What is it?" Vic inquired.

"Oh. Sorry. Just thinking."

"Long thoughts. About what?"

"Rip Ryder's family. Where they are and if they were sleeping somewhere safe tonight."

"Yeah. I guess. It would be a tough way for a family to live."

"Uh-huh."

Erin sipped her tea. "Did you and Willie talk about it more last night? I mean… don't tell me anything confidential. Just wondering if… he said anything else about the family. Where they might be squatting now. The police are going to be looking for them; they haven't even been able to do the death notification yet. That poor family doesn't even know that he's never going to be coming back."

"They probably have a pretty good idea by now. I mean… just the fact that he left and didn't get back when they expected him to. Wouldn't you figure after a few days that that was it?"

"Not necessarily. We don't know if they even saw each other every day. Sometimes when someone has to go away to work… we don't know whether they would normally see each other once a week, or once a month, or if he was going back to her every day."

"But if they were squatting out in the wilderness…" Vic frowned. "I mean, he wouldn't just leave them all out there to fend for themselves. Would he?"

"If he didn't have any other choice."

Vic shook her head. "Well, I hope they're back here in town by now. I wondered about that family that you fed the other day. That could have been them, couldn't it?"

"Yeah. I told Terry about that. She fits the general description. I'll watch for them while we're working today. If she's still in the area, I might see her again. I can ask if she is Mrs. Ryder, or if she knows where the Ryder family is. The homeless usually have a 'bush telegraph,' ways that they keep informed on what is happening in the neighborhood. So maybe if it isn't Mrs. Ryder, she'll still be able to give us a lead."

"Sounds like a plan." Vic looked toward the other window and saw Willie descending the steps. "That's our cue."

Erin picked up her purse and slung it over her shoulder. She had finished enough tea that she didn't want to be bothered taking it with her, so she dumped the rest in the sink and set the cup down to wash later.

Vic cocked her head as she looked at Erin's purse. Erin touched it protectively. "What?"

"That doesn't look as heavy and deadly as usual. You got your planner?"

Erin squeezed her purse and realized she did not. "Hang on a sec! I was writing in it before bed last night…" She hurried back to the bedroom and tried to retrieve it as silently as possible so that she wouldn't disturb Terry. "Good thing you reminded me! I wouldn't want to be without my lists."

"None of us would want that," Vic agreed with a laugh.

~

There was plenty to do before opening, and if Erin did see Mrs. Ryder, she was sure it wouldn't be until later in the day like the last time, so she tried to put her worries about the little family to the side while she and Vic baked the day's goods and prepared to open the store.

She still found herself inventorying everything that she was working on, weighing whether she should put something aside for the Ryders. A couple of loaves of bread. Some muffins. Maybe some cookies.

But Mrs. Ryder hadn't wanted any charity. So even if Erin put things aside for her, she would probably refuse to take them.

Could she? If she were hungry, if they couldn't afford anything to eat, then they would take the food, wouldn't they? It wasn't like there were soup kitchens and homeless shelters in Bald Eagle Falls. If they weren't able to fend for themselves, they would have to depend on the charity of strangers, like it or not.

"I hate to think of anyone out there on the street," she told Vic.

"You've got a good heart. But you can't help everyone."

"I can try. If there are people who need food here in Bald Eagle Falls, then I should donate to them before taking baking into the city. Don't you think? I'm giving it away either way, but I should serve my own community before going farther afield. Especially since they already have services in the city. They really don't have anything here, do they?"

Vic shook her head. "Maybe someone could go to one of the churches to ask for help. I'm sure they could get taken care of that way. But not everybody is religious or wants to go to a church for help. Would you?"

"I'd go wherever I had to, if I was hungry. I've gone to missions and churches before."

"I guess you can't be choosy."

CHAPTER 17

Erin asked a few of the customers who came into the bakery whether they had heard of the Ryders, or whether they knew who might be willing to help the homeless—or less permanently homed —in Bald Eagle Falls.

Most disclaimed any knowledge of the Ryders or of any homeless in or around Bald Eagle Falls. Erin only asked the women that she thought might be willing to help, yet even some of those she selected gave her a disapproving look for suggesting that there might be people *like that* around Bald Eagle Falls. The townspeople might be poor, but they looked after their own. No one was turned out onto the street.

She watched for the family, but didn't see them again. Apparently, it wasn't a regular routine. They had just happened to be by when Erin had seen them the last time. Maybe they had been in town to buy groceries for the week, which they would cook on their camp stove wherever they were currently squatting.

She was tired at the end of the day, but not ready to go home. Not ready to give up on helping the family or at least some of the people in Bald Eagle Falls who didn't have enough to support themselves. She could be part of the solution instead of the problem. *Seeing* the people who were in trouble. Not letting them be invisible.

It was Terry who picked Erin up, and she was not eager to ask him for help. He had probably been looking for the family for half of his shift anyway.

"Do you mind if we drive around a little? I'd like to see if I could see that family that I gave the granola bars to before. Make sure that they're okay."

Terry looked at her. "Where are you going to look?"

"Well… it isn't like it's the big city. We can check out the most likely places in a few minutes. If we don't see them, then I'll go home. But I'd like to at least try."

"Where?"

"The churches. The library. Maybe check around the grocery store. The dumpsters behind the grocery and the restaurants. Places that they might go for shelter or food."

"We don't have a homeless problem in Bald Eagle Falls. I would know if people were loitering around here, going through dumpsters. That's not legal."

"People need to eat. They need a place to sleep. It's warm enough now that they can sleep outside, but still, somewhere that's sheltered, safer…"

"We can drive around a bit." Terry turned his head to check in with Vic in the back seat. "Do you want to be dropped off or to join Erin on her quest?"

"I'll come along. I'm curious to see what she finds."

Terry nodded. He pulled out into the street. "Library first?"

"Yes."

They cruised over to the library. Some children were playing outside, and a few cars were in the parking lot. Certainly, nothing that looked out of the ordinary. But now that Erin knew what she was looking for, she looked more carefully. Were they children that she knew? Were they dressed like the rest of the kids in the town, or were they wearing dirty or worn clothing? Did any of the cars in the parking lot look like they were being lived in?

"I'm going to pop inside," she told Terry. "You can just wait here."

Terry looked at Vic. "I guess I've been told."

"It might be something to do with the fact that you're a cop. People who are living on the street or have something to do with a murdered man might not want to have any contact with the police."

"True enough," he agreed. He didn't get out of the truck.

"Should I come with you?" Vic asked Erin.

"If you want, but I will probably only be a second."

Vic sat back. "I'll let you have the first run at it. It isn't like you're going to run into anyone dangerous in the library."

Erin went in by herself. She didn't expect to find anything in the first place she looked, but libraries were a good place for homeless people to hang out. They had climate control and a person could stay there for hours without anyone kicking them out for not buying anything. There was built-in entertainment, with both books and computers available for public consumption.

She walked into the tiny library and looked around. It was pretty quiet. At the counter, the librarian was scanning books from a bin of returns and placing them on a cart. She looked at Erin as she came in and smiled. Erin didn't go up to the desk to talk to her. It wasn't like she needed help finding a book. And she suspected that if she asked too many questions, the Ryders and others in the homeless community would avoid her. She had to be more discreet than that.

She wandered over to the children's books but didn't recognize any of the children looking at books or playing on the computers. None of them reminded her of the children she had seen with the thin woman.

Erin made a quick circuit around the library. The woman and her family were not there. There was a man in a baseball cap sitting in one of the chairs with a book open in his lap. He was wearing a baseball cap and watching Erin. She drifted closer to him.

"Hi."

He looked away from her and didn't say anything.

"I'm looking for someone," Erin said, not trying to meet his eyes. She let her gaze wander over the interior of the library and the other people there. "The Ryders. Have you seen Mrs. Ryder and her children around here?"

"What makes you think I know them?"

"Maybe you don't. I was just wondering."

"There isn't any Mrs. Ryder."

"Rip Ryder's wife?" Erin prompted. What did that mean, there was no Mrs. Ryder?

"They ain't married."

"Oh. I'm sorry. What does she go by, then?"

"Dunno her last name. First name is Genevieve."

"Genevieve. Has she been around today? I wanted to get a message to her."

"Nope. Haven't seen her."

He didn't offer any other way to get in touch with Genevieve or the best place to look for her.

"Do you know where she's staying? Where I might be able to track her down?"

"Seems to me you don't really know her. Not if'n you don't even know her name."

"No. I ran into her the other day. I don't really know her. But I wanted to tell her something."

He shrugged.

"Do you know where I might be able to find her? Or how I could get a message to her?"

"Nope."

Erin suspected that he could have given her a lot more. But he didn't know her and might suspect her motives. A stranger poking her nose into a homeless person's business wasn't necessarily helpful or welcome.

Pushing him any harder wasn't going to get her the answers she wanted. So Erin just nodded graciously as if he had told her everything she wanted to know. "Thank you for your time."

He grunted and dropped his gaze to the book in his lap. But his eyes didn't move back and forth like he was reading. He would watch her all the way to the door. Make sure that she wasn't going to cause any kind of trouble.

And maybe if he saw Genevieve, he would tell her that someone was looking for her.

CHAPTER 18

Erin got back into the truck. "No luck there. Apparently, her name is Genevieve and she was not actually married to Rip Ryder."

Terry nodded at this. Something that he had already known, but not been at liberty to share? Or was he mentally filing the information safely away for later?

"Do you know her last name?" she asked Terry.

He shrugged with one shoulder, not looking at her. Erin wasn't sure whether that meant he didn't know, or that he wasn't going to tell her. It came out to the same thing either way.

"Where to next?"

Erin looked out the window. "The grocery, I guess. Just… check around it. Maybe stop in the parking lot and I'll check back behind."

"I don't think you should be wandering down deserted alleys or confronting someone back there that you don't know."

"You don't think the alleys are safe? I thought you said there weren't any homeless people here."

"I don't think you're going to find who you're looking for, but you never know who you might run into back there, out of sight. It isn't like we've been completely crime-free in the time you've lived here."

"You'll just scare anybody hanging around here away. Would you feel better about it if I took Vic with me?"

Terry considered. He looked over his shoulder at Vic, then nodded grudgingly. "Better than you being alone. At least one of you can run for help if the other runs into trouble. Are you carrying, Miss Victoria?"

Vic hesitated, unsure what answer to give him. Which clearly meant that she was, but wasn't willing to tell him so.

"Fine, go," Terry said.

Erin and Vic got out of the truck. Erin glanced over at Vic. "At least he didn't insist on frisking you."

Vic laughed. "I'd give it up before that. But I think he wanted me to be armed."

"I think so. And it wouldn't normally be a problem, except…"

"No, I still don't have my replacement carry permit card. But that doesn't mean I'm not licensed, just that I don't have proof of it on me. Technically, the sheriff did tell me to leave it at home until I had my card."

Erin shrugged. Terry hadn't objected to Vic carrying her handgun. He probably would have preferred it if Erin, too, were armed. So far, she hadn't been able to bring herself to buy a gun, even though she had been in several situations where it might have been helpful. She was more worried about it provoking a violent reaction from someone who would not have hurt her had she been unarmed.

They circled around the grocery store, watching through the big windows in the front for the thin blond woman and her little family. Erin didn't see anyone who wasn't at least familiar to her. They went around the side and then the back. Erin looked up and down the alley. It was deserted. After Terry's anxiety over her safety, it was a bit of a letdown. No one lurking in the shadows.

"Let's just go down there and check the dumpsters." Erin motioned.

Vic walked with her. "Check the dumpsters for what?"

"Just see if there is anyone in there."

"Why would they be *in* the dumpster?"

Erin rolled her eyes. "To get food. Have you ever tried to feed a family with no money?"

Vic seemed to think it unlikely that anyone in Bald Eagle Falls would resort to dumpster diving for food, but she walked with Erin and checked each dumpster. Plenty of cardboard and rotting produce, but no sign of anyone going through them. Erin looked farther down the alley toward the restaurant dumpsters but still couldn't see any sign of life. She hadn't really expected to stumble across Genevieve and her family immediately. Still, she had thought that she would see other people there. She could ask them about Genevieve like she had at the library. But not if there were no one around.

"Okay, let's go back to the truck," Vic suggested.

Erin nodded and they returned. Erin racked her brain for where to look next for the mother and children. If they weren't whiling away their time at the library or foraging for food, where were they? Staying with friends or family? All crammed into someone's guest room or basement?

"Is that it?" Terry asked. "Ready to go home?"

"No… what about the park?"

"What park?"

"The playground over by the school."

Terry nodded. He put the truck back in gear and drove a couple of blocks to the elementary school. Erin could see before they rolled up to it that there were children on the playground equipment. She watched the children. By the time they reached the playground, she could see that it was the family that she had met on the street. She was out of the truck, feet hitting the ground, almost before Terry had pulled to a stop.

She tried to make herself walk slowly. She didn't want to frighten them. They would think she was some predator or crazy lady if she jumped out of a truck and ran at them. She looked around for the mother and found her sitting on a bench nearby, watching the children and nursing her infant. Erin approached her, trying to look casual and non-threatening.

The woman's eyes narrowed as she watched Erin's approach. She looked around for an escape, but there was no way for her to disappear quickly with the children. Erin knew what it was like to try to get children out of a playground. They would complain and negotiate. Even if they had been trained to leave when they were told to, it would still take time for them to finish what they were doing and pull themselves away from the fun.

The woman didn't call them to her. Erin sat down on the bench next to her.

"Why are you here?" the woman demanded. "Just because you gave my children granola bars once, that doesn't make you my best friend. You don't get some special status for that."

"No. I was just… I'm looking for someone, and I thought…" She didn't know whether to say she was looking for the woman herself. Should she pretend she didn't know? That she was just making initial inquiries? "I wondered if you might know where I could find her."

"Who?" The question was clipped.

"Genevieve. Rip Ryder's wife. Or… partner."

"Why do you want her? What business do you have with her?"

"I just wanted to talk to her."

The woman shrugged. "I don't know where she is."

"I thought… you might be her."

"Why? You think we all look alike? Everyone who is… fallen on hard times?"

"No. You match her description. That's all. You have a young family. I didn't know either one of you. I hoped…"

"I'm not Jenny." The woman looked down at her nursing infant, then adjusted her position.

Erin looked down at the baby's face. A tiny thing, probably not more than a couple of weeks old. It was hard to believe that the woman's thin frame could have supported a baby. She must have looked ungainly, with a basketball belly and her stick-thin arms and legs.

The baby rooted around, unsatisfied. His face had been resting peacefully, but he grew agitated. He didn't have the chubby round cheeks that the Foster baby had. Erin wondered whether the woman had enough milk, and whether she was able to supplement if not. Would she have the money to buy formula? Would she be able to qualify for any government benefit programs if she didn't have a fixed address?

"He's cute. What's his name? Or hers?"

"Sarah."

"How old?"

"Three months."

Erin thought Sarah very small for three months. Maybe she had been premature.

"I'm Erin," she introduced herself again.

She knew the baby's name, the woman knew Erin's name, it was only right that the woman would give her own name. It wasn't the first time that they had met. They were sitting together.

The woman looked at her for a long few moments. "Adrienne," she said finally, sighing. "But don't go spreading that around. You don't *know* me."

Erin nodded. "I know. It's just nice to be able to call you something." She watched the children playing on the climbers. Terry and Vic were waiting for her; she couldn't sit there visiting for too long. She had so many questions that she wanted to ask Adrienne. If she were on her own or was married. If she had been in Bald Eagle Falls for long. Where she was living. But none of that was her business, and she didn't want Adrienne to push her away when they had just started to get to know one another.

And what she was really there for was to find Genevieve. Jenny, Adrienne had called her.

"Jenny has a baby too?"

Adrienne hesitated, then nodded. "Younger."

"What about your other kids? Do you both have kids the same age?"

Adrienne looked at her, then away again. She switched Sarah to the other breast and tried to convince her to latch on, but the baby just fussed. Adrienne eventually did her shirt back up and put the baby to her shoulder, patting her back and trying to get her to settle.

"Why do you want Jenny?"

"I have something I need to tell her. I really can't talk to anybody else about it."

"Something about that no-good husband of hers?"

"Someone said they weren't actually married."

"What does it matter? The only difference is a piece of paper. Having to pay a fee to the judge."

Erin shrugged. She didn't know enough about the legal implications to answer the question. She knew that a lot of people had religious compunctions, but that wasn't an issue that bothered Erin.

"It *is* about Rip," she said finally.

"I hope the guy stays away and never comes back."

"Was he… not good to her?"

"Any guy who abandons his wife and children like that doesn't deserve to have them. He's off on a drunk or a gambling binge, and he won't be back until he's blown every last cent. If I was her, I wouldn't be taking him back!"

Erin nodded. But Jenny wouldn't have that choice. "You don't think… he could be off on a job? Something good for the family?"

"If he was, he would be calling her to tell her about it. No man hides his accomplishments. Just his failings."

"Do you know where I could find her?"

"No. I don't know where she went."

Erin sighed. "Okay. Do you think… you could call me if you hear anything about her?"

"I don't have a phone."

"Not even—" Erin bit back her response. If Adrienne said she didn't have a phone, she didn't have a phone. Erin had no idea what kind of life she was leading. If Erin had to choose between buying a phone and feeding her kids, which would she choose? A phone was a luxury, something children could survive without. Or could they?

"Well… you know where to find me if you hear something."

"The bakery."

"Yes. Auntie Clem's Bakery." Erin looked over at Sarah, falling asleep on Adrienne's shoulder. "And look, I always have leftovers at the end of the day. I have to bake enough that we won't run out, and if I do that, it means that there's always something left over at the end. I put stuff into the freezer and then when there's enough, I take it into the city for the shelters there. I'd rather help people in Bald Eagle Falls if I can."

"I told you I'm not taking charity."

"If you're ever trying to pull dinner together at the end of the afternoon and need some bread or rolls, or even something sweet for dessert, then come by and see me. I can't stand to throw it out, and taking it to the city is a waste of gas and time if there are people in Bald Eagle Falls who could use it."

Adrienne was silent, thinking about that.

Erin wanted to say, "It's not charity," but she didn't want to push her luck. It probably was charity. She didn't really know. But she wanted to help the little family and others in Bald Eagle Falls who were in need. She hated to think of them going hungry while she tried to figure out what to do with her overage at the end of the day.

"I guess… I'll be going. You know where to find me if you hear something about Jenny."

Adrienne gave a brief nod. Did that mean she would tell Erin if she heard something? Or just that it was time for Erin to leave and she didn't want to hear about it again?

Erin got up and headed back toward the truck. A couple of the children peeled away from the climbers and ran toward her, laughing and shrieking.

A tousle-haired little girl grabbed her by the arm, hiding half-behind her, like Erin was the 'safe' place in a game of tag. "I know you!" she declared. "You're the lady with the food!"

"Yes, that's right." Erin smiled down at her. "Good memory. But I'm afraid I don't have any today."

"That's okay," the little girl declared cheerfully. "We've had something to eat today."

Erin patted her on the head, choking back an answer. She forced another smile for the little girl and shooed them both back toward the playground.

There was a lump in her throat as she climbed into the truck.

CHAPTER 19

Terry seemed to sense Erin's mood when they got home and didn't engage her in conversation, letting her just work things through on her own.

As much as Erin wanted to help, she couldn't do that unless people were willing to be helped. And if Adrienne was a representative sample, not everyone was going to accept help.

She could invite Adrienne to work at the bakery and help her that way, only what would she do with the children while she was working? Especially Sarah? She wasn't in any position to take on a job.

She must have a husband or some way to make a little money. The children had eaten, so she found some way to feed them. And they were living somewhere, even if it was just a tent or a car. What more could Erin do for them?

"Where are you going to look next?" she asked Terry.

"Me? You're the one who seems to have taken on this search for the Ryders."

"I just thought… if it was the family that I had seen once before in Bald Eagle Falls, I would be able to find them again. But I don't have any idea where to go next."

He nodded as if saying that had been his point in the first place.

"But you have to do the death notification. How are you going to find her to do that?"

"Hopefully, we'll be able to find a way. If she's in the area, she'll turn up sooner or later. Even the people who live in the bush have to come into town at some point, even if it is only every few months. So she'll surface again at some point. With kids depending on her, it's even less likely that she'd be able to stay away from town for any significant amount of time. Kids need food, visits to the doctor, all of that."

"So you're just going to wait? You're not going to look for her?"

"Of course we'll look for her. We'll keep chasing down the leads that we have. But if she's like your Adrienne and doesn't have a phone, or has one but only turns it on in case of an emergency, then we can't use that to track her. And if she has no fixed address and lives out in the bush somewhere, there are too many square miles of land for us to search. Others in the community are probably in touch with her now and then and, hopefully, word will get back to her that we're looking for her. But whether she'll want to contact us or not is another story."

"Yeah."

"She'll know that either she's in trouble for something, or we have bad news for her. There isn't really any other reason that we would be trying to reach her. If she doesn't want to hear the bad news… she just quietly moves away and never comes back again."

"But wouldn't it be better to know? Wouldn't you rather know? And especially if she thinks that he's just taken off on her. Wouldn't it be better to know that something has happened to him than that he just abandoned her?"

"For you, maybe. Not everyone's brain works the same way. Some people would rather not know and be able to make up their own reasons and excuses, and leave open the possibility that one day, maybe he'll return."

"But he won't."

"You and I know that, but if you didn't know he was dead, you could always believe that he might come back someday."

Erin had lived a lot of years fantasizing about her parents returning, even though she had known they were dead. It was sometimes easier to deal with a fantasy world than the stark reality.

"There aren't any homeless encampments? Tent cities? Where everyone bands together so that they are more protected?"

"Not out here. People here are choosing to live somewhere isolated. If they want to live in a large homeless community of some kind, they can find their way to the city. Walk, hitch-hike, get arrested, there are plenty of ways to get to the city, if that's what they want to do."

Erin wasn't sure what Willie had told Terry about his interactions with Rip Ryder, so she asked her next question carefully.

"Do you think Rip got into some kind of argument? About land he was squatting on or something someone thought he had stolen or taken that wasn't his?"

"He clearly upset someone pretty significantly."

"You don't think it could have been an accident?"

"It wasn't an accident, Erin. You can put that out of your head."

"There's no chance?"

He shook his head. "No."

"Has the medical examiner made a determination?"

"Not yet, but I can tell you that it wasn't an accident. After seeing the scene, no. It wasn't an accidental death."

"Sometimes an accident can look like homicide."

He raised his brows. "You're telling me?"

"I just meant… I know you're the professional, but sometimes… you bring your own biases to the scene. You think there is no way someone could have done this to themselves, either intentionally or accidentally, so you see the scene through that lens."

"That can happen," he agreed. "But you're going to have to trust me on this one."

Erin went into the kitchen to get herself a drink. She sipped the cold water from the fridge dispenser. She was teetering between wanting to know more and being afraid that it would be too much for her and give her nightmares or flashbacks. Things were improving and she didn't want to set herself back to where she had been a few months back.

She returned to the living room and set her glass on the coffee table. She moved around the room, tidying up and thinking.

"Can you tell me a bit more?" she asked finally. "Was it… was the murder weapon at the scene?"

"Yes."

"And… was he shot?" Erin vaguely remembered Vic saying something about the state of the skull. She didn't think it was a gunshot.

"No." Terry looked at her. "You know there isn't very much I can tell you. You can read what's in the paper."

"If it's in the paper, then you can tell me. Was he shot?"

"No. He wasn't."

Erin thought about that. She had seen the brutality of stabbings and bludgeoning. She didn't really want to picture either one. But if she just followed the idea to its conclusion… if it wasn't a gunshot, then it was probably a close-quarters killing. Hand to hand. Within reach of each other. If it was something less violent, like poison, Terry probably wouldn't be as sure about it not being an accident. They wouldn't have toxicology reports back yet. An allergic reaction could be an accident.

If the murder weapon was at the scene, then it was something obvious.

Erin tidied away some papers that she had left scattered when she was reading through Clementine's papers the previous day. She liked to have everything put neatly away. If she left papers out, they might get damaged or lost, and she wouldn't be able to put her hands on them when she needed them.

Eventually, she sat down on the couch next to Terry. He looked away from the TV and at her to see if she wanted to talk, his hand raising the remote.

Erin shook her head and bent over to take her planner out of her purse. She had a sip of her cold water and put her planner across her knees to look at the week ahead and what was on her task list.

"You okay?" Terry asked.

Erin nodded. She turned to her project pages to see what she and Charley and Vic had last discussed about themes, promos, and upcoming events. She had almost forgotten about the next book club meeting at the book store across the street from Auntie Clem's. Naomi loved it when they made her a themed treat for the book club meeting. Erin wasn't required to, and sometimes she just sent over a few bites of whatever they had in the display case and freezer. But she liked it when she could match up with a theme. She made a note on her task list.

"I'm really impressed with how you've taken to the planner," Terry commented. "I didn't think we were ever going to wean you off your random bits of paper."

Erin dropped her gaze to her purse. "It makes it so much easier to find things and keep it all tidy."

He nodded. "Of course, if we could get you into the digital world, you could have it all on your phone and you wouldn't need that bulky book."

Erin gripped her planner tightly. They would have to pry it from her cold dead hands.

Terry laughed. "Nobody is going to take your book away from you. I'm just glad it's working out for you. Ingrained habits are hard to change."

Erin smoothed the corner of the page she was reviewing. "We'll see how it goes when my life is really disrupted by something. That's the real test."

He made a noise of agreement. "Do you drop it and go back to random papers or neglect your lists altogether? Or do you use it to pull yourself through the crisis?"

"Yeah. I want to say that I'll use the planner and keep up my good habits, but I know how disrupting stress can be. Who knows how I'll react."

"What are you working on now?"

Erin wrote a few headings on a set of fresh, blank pages. "Uh… nothing… just some planning…"

His eyes were on the TV, and he didn't persist. He was just being polite. It didn't really matter what she was working on. He was making conversation.

Erin wrote down what she knew or had deduced about the murder. She started a column of names, marking them as witnesses, suspects, or persons of interest. She wrote down what she could think of as clues that might point in a particular direction. Of course, she should get the details such as how long Rip had been dead and what the medical examiner had ruled about the cause of death.

She started a list of questions she would ask if it were her investigation. She doodled in the corners of the page, thinking about it, wondering if she knew more than she had noted. Motives. What she knew about Rip's background, which was next to nothing. Was he a native

Tennessean? Or had he brought his family there for some reason? Did he have friends and relatives—or enemies—in the area?

Adrienne said that he was out drinking or gambling, so Erin assumed those were known vices. Willie had fought with him because he figured he could get possession of Willie's property by squatting on it. Willie said they had argued more than once, and Willie had managed to send him on his way, but who knew where he had gone. They might have crossed paths again.

Erin shook her head slowly. She was not going to fall into the trap of suspecting Willie. No matter what anyone said, Erin didn't believe that he could have had anything to do with Rip's murder.

CHAPTER 20

"What's all this?" Mary Lou inquired, looking at the new sign on the display case. Her brows came down, and she shook her head. Her short gray hair stayed perfectly coiffed. She smoothed her tunic shirt over her hips. "Families in need? We already take care of the families in Bald Eagle Falls. You know we had that big collection for needy children at Christmas. And there are other programs in place. There's a hot lunch program at the school for anyone who needs it."

"There may be people who can't access that. And what if the family needs more than children's lunches? What about breakfast and dinner? What about the adults? And weekends and holidays?"

"Bald Eagle families are proud and self-sufficient. You don't want to start giving handouts, people will just come to expect it and get lazy. We don't want to end up with the same problems as they have in the cities."

"Making sure people have enough to eat isn't spoiling them. I just think that we should take care of our own first. I have been taking my extra baking into the city for the shelters or soup kitchens, but if people here in Bald Eagle Falls need it, I would rather get it to them first."

"No one is starving in Bald Eagle Falls."

Erin thought about Adrienne's fussy baby. How her cheeks were narrow instead of round and fat. The children had been happy to get one meal. Had that been from the hot lunch program at school? What was Adrienne eating? She was so thin.

Nobody was hungry in Bald Eagle Falls?

"I have food for people who need it," Erin said. She nodded toward the sign. "Nobody has to show ID or prove their income level, and I won't be sharing their names with anyone else. If they need food, they can come to me and I will make sure they get what they need."

"That's very generous. But I'm not sure it is well-advised. People need to work for their bread. That's what God said to Adam in the Garden of Eden. By the sweat of your brow. That's how he intended things to be in this world."

"So if I feed hungry people, I'm breaking God's law?"

Mary Lou waffled. "I would not say that. But the people who choose not to work, who just take and take, they are not following God's plan for mankind."

Erin avoided rolling her eyes. "I thought that Jesus was the one who said feed the hungry and love thy neighbor and all of that."

"We can still love our neighbor without making them dependent on us. We are supposed to judge wisely, not to just fall for every sob story people give us."

"I don't think anyone is going to ask for free food if they don't need it pretty badly. Like you said, people in Bald Eagle Falls are proud and independent. But if they are in a hard spot and can't feed their families, I think someone should be willing to help."

Mary Lou gave a shrug and spread her hands apart dramatically. "Of course it is up to you. I would just think that you might ask some of us who have been in Bald Eagle Falls for generations what we think about it before rushing in and trying to change the social order all by yourself."

Ignoring the sign, she peered into the display case and pointed out the items she wanted.

"How is Josh?" Erin asked, as she began to put Mary Lou's purchases into bags.

"Well, he's eating, I'll say that for him. He's regained the weight that he lost when he was being held captive. Most of it, anyway. I wonder whether he's going to stop or if he's just going to keep eating! But he's a teenage boy, and you know what their metabolisms are like. They can eat just about anything."

"I'm glad he's getting healthy again. And how about his… outlook? Is he feeling safe? Comfortable with going back out into the world and carrying on with his life?"

Mary Lou didn't say anything. Erin passed the bags over to Bella, who was running the till. Bella quickly entered everything and rang up the total.

"Trust you to ask that question," Mary Lou said, giving a nod of understanding. "I think… that will take longer. He's going to take the rest of the semester off of school. Not what I would have recommended, but he's nearly an adult and I can't make all of his decisions. I could insist that he stay enrolled, but he wouldn't go, and then he would fail. I'm hoping that he'll get bored and feel like he can go back out into the world where it is safe." She looked at Erin. "Because it is safe. Nothing like that is ever going to happen to him again."

"No," Erin agreed. "That would be really unlikely. But I can understand him feeling afraid."

"Certainly. But like the rest of us when we face opposition… he will need to pick himself up, dust himself off, and move forward."

Erin hoped that he could. She made a mental note to visit Joshua soon. She couldn't write it down in her planner right away, so she would have to remember to do it once she was able.

CHAPTER 21

When Erin got home, she found Vic and Terry in the yard talking. From their body language, it wasn't a casual conversation. She hung back, unsure what to say or do, listening to find out what was going on. The smell of barbecue hung in the air, one of her neighbors obviously cooking.

"You can't convict someone based on what family they come from," Vic snapped.

"No one is convicting you of anything. But I would be remiss if I didn't talk to you, considering the fact that you come from the Jackson clan."

"I'm not part of the Jackson clan. You know I don't have anything to do with them anymore. I can't help the fact that I was born into the family. I never worked for the clan. I left home. You've seen my family, you know I'm not welcome there."

"Things change. People change their minds. I don't know if you have reconciled with your family or have contact with anyone else in the clan. You were corresponding with Theresa without anyone knowing about it."

"That wasn't because she was clan. It was because we had a previous relationship. It wasn't anything to do with criminal enterprises."

"But you can't say that you haven't had contact with anyone in the clan. And I don't know how many other people you might have personal relationships with. That's why I would like to talk about it. Go through the details. Make sure there are no connections."

"This wasn't a clan killing."

"It could have been. Ryder may have stepped on some toes. He may have been trying to horn in on someone's business, the same way he was trying to push his way onto claims that were not his. People don't always realize when they are in dangerous territory. If he was trying to make a buck selling drugs or doing something else that the clan felt was interfering with their business..."

"Then you'll have to talk to someone in the clan about that," Vic said icily. "I wouldn't know anything about it, because I'm not in the clan."

"You're refusing an interview?"

"Yes, I am. And Willie should have too. I don't know what made him go ahead with it."

Terry shook his head, his expression darkening at Willie's name. "Willie might not have killed him for the Dixon clan, but I can tell you, there are other reasons to suspect that he is still doing work for the clan. He isn't as pure and innocent as you think."

"You don't know what I think," Vic snapped. "That's none of your business. Willie and I found the body, that's the only involvement we had in it. I didn't kill him. Willie didn't kill him. We didn't have business dealings with him. We don't have any business dealings with either of the clans. Do you think that we could be together if either of us was still part of our clans?"

"People have been known to defect."

"Oh, so now I'm a traitor? Is that it? I didn't like the Jackson clan and I wanted to date Willie, so I decided to join the Dixon clan instead? That way, we wouldn't have any trouble with clashing clans."

"I didn't say that." Terry sighed and rubbed the bridge of his nose. "Look, Vic, I didn't come over here for a confrontation. I wasn't trying to start a fight. I was just hoping that the two of us could talk things through like two adults so that I could come to a conclusion about your involvement. So that I could go back to the sheriff and say that I was pretty sure you weren't involved in any way."

"Pretty sure. Well, thanks for that."

"I'm not sure how I'm supposed to get to more than pretty sure. Do you have an alibi for the period of time in which Ryder was killed?"

"Which is?"

"One to two weeks before you found the body."

Vic stared at him. "How could I give you an alibi for a full week? Unless I was in a coma for that entire time, I don't know how I'm supposed to prove that I never went out to that cave and killed Ryder."

"That's exactly my point. That's why I could never be one hundred percent sure that you could not have killed him. But I can be pretty sure. If you can convince me."

Vic crossed her arms over her chest. "I don't have to convince you."

"No, you don't. But it complicates my investigation if you won't. I don't want to have to spend my time chasing down rabbit trails instead of the actual killer."

"Then lay off of me. Because you already have a pretty good idea I didn't have anything to do with it."

"Now *you're* saying pretty good."

Vic glared and didn't say anything.

"Fine," Terry said. "Be advised that you may be asked to come in for questioning, Miss Victoria. If you refuse an official invitation, we will have reason to believe that it's because you were involved in Ryder's death."

She raised one eyebrow and still didn't say anything.

Terry turned around to go back to the house. He saw Erin standing in the doorway, and his face tightened. He hadn't expected her to witness their conversation. He tried to smile as he approached her.

"Erin. I didn't realize it was that late."

Erin nodded. She stepped back and did not accept a kiss from him as he reached the doorway. He walked past her into the house. Vic was looking across the yard at Erin. She didn't smile or wave, she just turned around and went the other way, up the steps into her apartment. Erin stepped back into her house and shut the door.

"I'm sorry," Terry said immediately. "It's my job. I had to talk to her about it."

"You know Vicky isn't in the clan."

"I know she says she isn't. That's not quite the same thing."

"I don't understand what you could be thinking. She's baking by day and off murdering people by night? That's not happening."

"No, I don't think that. But it doesn't mean she couldn't have had an altercation with someone. And it doesn't mean that Ryder's death didn't have anything to do with the Jackson clan. We have to consider it. Just like in New York they have to consider whether any drug-related killing is cartel related."

"But if Ryder's death was related to the Jackson clan, that doesn't mean it has anything to do with Vic. They're two separate things."

"They are two intertwined things."

"She's estranged from her family."

"She's estranged from her parents. Or her father. And even that could have changed. You and I wouldn't necessarily know anything about it."

"That's semantics."

"She is still in touch with Jeremy, and you don't know what his clan involvement may be. And either one of them might still be in contact with the two older boys. And she could secretly be in touch with her mother or have made up with her father."

"I don't see how somebody getting killed in a cave out in the sticks could have anything to do with the clan."

He opened and closed his mouth a couple of times before answering. "And you know I can't tell you. But I would think you could trust me to the point that you know I wouldn't be asking Vic about the clan if there wasn't a possible connection."

"Do you know there was a connection? Or you just think there could be one?"

"It's a point to check."

"Fine. So you checked, and there's no reason to believe that Vic or the clan are involved. So you can mark that off of your to-do list."

Mentioning a to-do list made Erin suddenly think of her planner and that she needed to add a few items to her lists. And maybe she would look again at the pages she had composed about the murder. Maybe she could make a connection that Terry and the police department hadn't.

She got her planner out of her purse.

"Does that mean the conversation is over?" Terry asked.

"Yes."

He stood there for a moment. Erin headed to the bedroom to change and spend a few minutes with her planner. She looked at Terry, who still hadn't moved.

"But I don't know who won," Terry protested, the dimple appearing in his cheek as he let out a breath and laughed.

"Obviously, I did."

"Okay, then."

CHAPTER 22

Erin and Vic had been texting most of the morning. As soon as Terry headed out for his shift, Erin let Vic know that he was gone, and she came over to the house.

"Sometimes that boyfriend of yours drives me mad," Vic renewed the complaint she had already texted to Erin.

"I know. He's just trying to do his job, though. A man died, leaving a young family behind. He's trying to figure out what happened."

"He should know that Willie and I didn't have anything to do with it. If we had, we wouldn't have bothered to call the police. We would have just left him out there. The bones would have gotten covered over by silt. No one would ever have known he was there."

Erin shrugged. She wasn't going to argue the point. She hadn't appreciated Terry interrogating Vic about it, and she wasn't about to defend him.

"Let's go."

Vic had permission to borrow Willie's truck. "We really should get another car."

"We?"

"Well, I meant you. Just that when you and I go somewhere, it would be nice not to have to borrow one of the men's vehicles."

Erin conceded. "Yes."

"You were talking about getting Clementine's Volkswagen fixed up. Are you going to do that?"

"I don't know. I guess at some point. I don't really want to get something else. I might as well use what's available. No point in locking it up like the good company china."

They climbed up into the truck. Erin did up her buckle. "You know the way? Do you need me to set it up on the GPS?"

"I know where it is."

Erin sat back and tried to be cool and relaxed as Vic drove them out of town and out onto the highway. She watched out the window, wondering how many families and others who did not have the money to cover rent or a mortgage squatted and tried to eke out a living from the land. Getting rid of the one major expense would help, but they would still need to eat. Hunting and gardening would provide some, but not everything. And there were clothes and bedding and other supplies. They would need a way to make some money. Some cash was necessary to survive in the modern world.

Vic turned from the highway onto a secondary road, and from that road to a gravel road. Vic's gaze and posture were alert as she watched for whatever landmarks she knew along the way.

They pulled into a clearing and Vic shut off the engine. Erin looked around. They weren't far from Bald Eagle Falls, and yet they were in the middle of nowhere. She looked at Vic.

"Here?"

Vic nodded. She walked around the clearing, looking down at the ground. She kicked at something in the grass.

"This is where their cookstove would have been. You see where they cleared the grass and put down some rocks?"

Erin nodded. "Okay, yes." They had been careful to avoid setting the grass on fire. They weren't inexperienced in camping.

"There are some clods of dirt that were pulled up by tent stakes." Vic pointed several out. "The underbrush has been cleared here. There is probably a path to their latrine."

"So this was a permanent camp? They intended to stay here?"

"Semi-permanent. They were probably here for a few weeks. But when you squat on someone else's land, you take the risk of getting run off. Especially if you're trying to jump someone's mineral claim."

"Where is the cave? Is it a mine or a cave?"

"A lot of the caves around here are both. If there are mineral deposits visible in the cave, it's worth trying to follow the veins. Get whatever you can that's close to the surface before you put in the effort to dig deeper."

"So... what kind of minerals are there?"

Vic led Erin into the trees. Erin couldn't see any cave. They didn't go too far, though, before encountering a rock face. Erin looked at Vic and then looked around for the entrance to the cave. But it all seemed to be overgrown and the foliage undisturbed.

Vic led her around the rock face and, eventually, they reached a crack. Erin followed it as it widened, and finally she reached what she assumed was the entrance to the cave. She had seen and been inside a few caves, and knew that the entrance was not necessarily an indicator of how big it was inside. A wide hole could lead to a small, shallow cave, and a small cave could open up into a wide cave and multiple branches leading to a whole network of tunnels. She bent down and looked into the hole. It was wide enough to allow a man Willie's size or larger. She couldn't see the inside beyond the entrance.

"Will you go in?" Vic questioned.

"No."

"Just for a second? See what it's like inside?"

"Without a gun to my head—no."

She could see Vic considering this comment, but then deciding that she wasn't going to encourage Erin at gunpoint.

"Do you mind if I go in for a minute?" Vic asked. "Just to refresh my memory."

"Yeah, go ahead. Just don't get lost or hurt in there, because I don't plan to come in after you."

"I won't be long. Do you want to wait here, or back in the clearing?"

"I'll wait here."

Vic nodded. She turned on her phone's flashlight app and disappeared into the cave.

Erin looked around. The cave wasn't easy to find, but it wasn't hard either. If someone knew about its existence, it wouldn't be hard for them to discover. And if someone didn't know about it, they could still find it while scouting for water or a latrine location, hunting, or berry picking.

Erin put her face close to the hole, turned on her own flashlight app, and looked around at the interior. There were a couple of branching tunnels. The walls glittered with water or crystals. But Erin wasn't going to go any farther than that.

Where had the Ryder family gone? Were they still somewhere close? Or had they gone back to Bald Eagle Falls, or to another, more distant point? Maybe to Jenny's parents? Did she have a family? Adrienne hadn't said. Maybe it was just that simple. When she realized her husband wasn't coming back, Jenny just pulled up stakes—literally—and went back to her own people.

CHAPTER 23

Vic was longer than Erin had expected her to be. Erin hung around the entrance to the cave, anxious. She didn't want to entertain the idea that Vic might be hurt or in trouble. She did not want to have to crawl into the cave to check. She didn't want to crawl in there for anything.

When Vic and the others had been caught in a mine collapse, it had been Erin who had heard the rumbling thunder of the explosion and falling rock, and who had called it in so that they could get search and rescue in to do their thing. She remembered standing there just inside the mine entrance, facing a wall of loose rock. She had tried to shift it at first, but it soon became apparent that it was a much bigger job than she could ever hope to accomplish. Even with the number of townspeople who had come out to try to move it, they had not been able to dig the trapped explorers out. Search and rescue had needed to drill into the tunnel from an adjoining tunnel to get them out.

She looked in again and shone her light around. "Vic? Everything okay?"

At first, there was no answer, just her own voice echoing off of the rocky walls. Then Vic answered, sounding very far away. "I'll be out in a minute. Everything is fine."

"Okay," Erin said softly, and sat down in the dirt to wait. It was longer than a minute before Vic came out, and Erin was relieved to hear her approaching footsteps and finally see Vic's face. She let out a sigh of relief.

"I'm fine," Vic assured her. "Nothing happened. Here, I took some pictures. Figured if you won't go into the cave, the cave will come to you."

Erin hesitated. "Is it okay, do you think? There isn't anything… gory?"

"No. The remains were taken out the day that we found them, so it's just an empty pool now. You can see… a little bit of dried blood in some of the pictures. If it's too much for you, just give the word. You don't have to look at anything you don't want to."

"Okay."

Vic met her eyes, not turning her phone around yet. "Okay? You're sure? You want to see?"

Erin nodded.

She and Vic sat down on the ground, leaning against the rock wall, and Vic brought up the pictures on her screen. They were not too bad, the phone's flash doing a pretty good job lighting the scene up well enough to take in the details. Erin saw a large underground cave. Vic had taken several shots to give her a feel for the size of the cave and what it looked like from each side. Then they moved on to the pool where the remains had been found. Even though Vic had said that there was nothing left there, Erin still found herself tensing before examining the pictures more closely.

There were no bones, no body parts; everything looked quite clean. Like it was a man-made fountain built there just for them to look at. Erin could see the silt in the bottom. She didn't know how deep or shallow it was. Maybe there was enough that it could have completely covered the remains, and maybe there was only an inch or two. Erin didn't think that mattered at all.

"If it only happened a week or two ago, then how could he be a skeleton already?" Erin asked. "I thought bodies took a lot longer than that to… skeletonize?"

"It depends on the condition. This may look like a still pool, but there's actually a good amount of water draining through here. So it helps to… wash stuff away as it decomposes."

Erin nodded.

"And there was… you know, there are fish, and they're not picky about the source of food." Vic grimaced apologetically.

"Okay. Yeah. So in those conditions, the process was pretty quick."

"Right. That's what I understand anyway, from what has been released so far."

"What else have they released?" Erin thought about Jenny reading the paper or coming across a story on the internet. She would know that the cave was close to where she had camped with Rip and the children. Would she guess that the remains were her husband's? Or maybe she already knew that from gossip, and that was why she wasn't around for anyone to talk to. If Rip had been a gambler or an addict, Jenny might have lost it, furious with him for losing their hard-earned money once again, leaving her with no way to feed the children. Even though they didn't have much money, that didn't eliminate money as a motive.

She wished she had brought her planner with her to write these new insights down. If she could capture all of her thoughts, she would have everything sorted out all that much faster.

"Okay to look at some more?" Vic offered.

"Yeah."

"So everything has been taken out, but there were a few bits of personal property in the cave." Vic showed her some ground shots with nothing very interesting in them. "Like, a backpack, some water, that kind of thing. Not very much and, like I said, he had no spelunking gear to speak of. No headlamp."

"He could have used his phone like you did. Just for a quick look around."

"He'd have to know where he was going, to know that his phone light wasn't going to die before he turned around again. And… there was no phone recovered there."

"Oh, yeah. They dragged the pool? So they know it wasn't in there, just buried in the muck?"

"I guess so. We didn't get to see that whole process, but they did bring a pump truck down here to drain the pool and run everything through a mesh to catch anything small. I don't know how much they would have been able to go through the silt. It's pretty thick. Maybe they used radar."

"No phone. He must have had a phone. You can't survive in today's world without one, can you?"

"I know I couldn't," Vic agreed fervently. "And I would think that if you were trying to get a job, find land to live on, maybe find a mine that could help to keep you on your feet, you would need a phone for those things. Assuming he didn't have a laptop and Wi-Fi connection."

Erin looked around her. "I think that's a fair bet."

"Wait, let me check," Vic said, minimizing the photo app and switching over to her settings. "See… no Wi-Fi signal, and barely any cell signal. We had to walk out to the road to get a strong enough signal to call the police."

"So, maybe he didn't have a phone because there wasn't any point. He couldn't make it work out here."

"I don't know. I still think you would have to have something, even if it was just an ancient flip or a sat phone. What if… a kid fell and hit his head? Or there was a wildfire? Or someone… had a confrontation and wanted to reach the police?"

"Yeah. I don't think there are too many people these days who don't have a cell phone."

Vic went back to her photo app. "So, this is one that might bother you."

Erin took a deep breath to steel herself. She had seen plenty of scary things. She had seen dead people. Cases that weren't just accidents. And Vic didn't have any remains to show her. Just whatever things were left in the cave.

"Yeah. I'm fine," she said in a strong voice.

"Good. Here." Vic swiped to the next picture and showed it to Erin. There still wasn't very much to see. Just a place on the cave floor that was darker than the rest.

"What is that?"

"That's blood. And they took the murder weapon, but it was right here too."

Erin looked at the bloody cave floor. She tried to measure the distance to the pool with her eyes. Everything was distorted because she didn't have anything to show scale.

"So… that's where he was killed, you think. And how far to the pool?"

"All the way on the other side of the cave. Maybe… twenty feet."

"And he didn't crawl in there himself? Hit his head on an overhang and just got disoriented…"

"No. It wasn't an accident. He didn't crawl over there under his own power. The injury was… very traumatic… if not instantaneous, then close to it."

Erin could see better now why they were so sure it was murder. If the death was close to instantaneous, and he had lost that much blood and hadn't been able to crawl across to the pool where he was found, there was clearly someone else involved. Someone who had, at the very least, dragged the body to the water to hide it there. And at the most… who had stalked Rip Ryder, followed him into the cave, and intentionally killed him. And then dragged him to the pool.

"How big a guy was he?"

Vic raised her eyebrows at the segue. "Hmm. I'd have to ask Willie. I couldn't really tell you from what I saw. Willie knew him before he died and would be better at answering that. If there are no pictures of him online and Terry won't tell you that."

"He might tell me that. What the man looked like can't be confidential."

"Why are you asking?"

"I'm just wondering… how big or strong the person who moved him to the pool would have to be."

"Oh." Vic nodded. "Makes sense."

"Is that all you had to show me?"

Vic looked through additional pictures on her phone and nodded. "Yeah, that's everything that seems like it could be important."

"Let's go back to the clearing."

Vic led the way back through the trees. Erin looked back a couple of times to see the cave entrance or the path leading up to it. Someone wandering around could stumble across it. Someone who had maps, pictures, or even just a description would not have a hard time finding what they were looking for.

Which had it been? Had someone come across Rip in the cave by accident and taken advantage of an opportunity? Or had he been looking for his victim? Or meeting Rip to discuss something or make some kind of deal, and then had turned on him? Had they had an argument and it was done in the heat of the moment or was it an ambush? Could he have planned to meet someone there?

Willie had said that Rip had been trying to jump his claim. He'd been hoping to make it rich off of the minerals he would find in the cave. So where had he heard about it? Had he just happened to find it and didn't realize that someone else had a claim to it? Or had he known about it and went there with the intent of taking what was not his?

They reached the clearing; Erin looked around once more, noting all of the things they had previously spoken of, and then looked for more. She kept her ears pricked for anything out of the ordinary, not wanting to take the chance of anyone sneaking up on them and catching them unaware. Erin had had enough of caves and kidnapping to last her a lifetime.

CHAPTER 24

"Where would they go?" Vic asked. She had been scanning the trees, perhaps as anxious about intruders as Erin was.

"If Rip's family was forced to move away from here, where do you think they went?" Erin prompted.

"I would think… they'd probably move a few miles down the road. Find out where Willie's property ended so that they wouldn't have to deal with him again, and move to the other side of that line."

"Do you think they had another cave or mine in mind already, or would they just… go in a random direction?"

"If they knew about this cave, then I would think they'd know of others in the area."

"Do *you*?"

"Know of any other caves?" Vic considered. "I think I've got some maps in the truck."

They returned to the cab and Vic pulled maps out of the side pocket of the door. She shuffled through them slowly, looking at the labels on them carefully. They were not highway maps, but surveys like Erin had found at Clementine's when she and Vic had first met. Green to show vegetation and blue for water, irregular curves showing slope, close together where it was steep and farther apart where it was gradual. There were various locations marked with codes, some kind of letter and number designation. Vic glanced over at Erin.

"I probably shouldn't even be looking at these. Willie is pretty private about his mines."

"But he takes you to them."

"Mmm. Some of them. Places he doesn't mind showing me. But if it's an active mine, he might have other ideas."

"Oh. Well, I don't want to make trouble, but this is for the greater good… We need to find Rip's family and make sure they're okay, and so the police can make the notification, if they haven't already heard about what happened to Rip."

Vic rolled her eyes and continued to study the maps. "Okay, so I think we're here." Her finger jabbed the page, indicating one string of letters and numbers. "So the road is here." She traced a faint brown line. "The property line seems to be just over here." Vic indicated a straight line on the map, and then gestured to the trees ahead and to their left.

"So they could have camped anywhere over there, and they wouldn't be on this property. Willie couldn't complain."

"Right."

"Let's go over and check. And if… they were not just interested in a place to camp, but in mining particularly, are there any mines or caves close by that they might be interested in?"

Vic stared down at the map. "These hills are like Swiss cheese. There are caves everywhere, and probably a few that haven't been discovered or put on any map, too. There are a few marked locations. Maybe ones that he's interested in investigating or in buying, if the opportunity arises."

Erin nodded.

Vic slid the map onto the seat next to her. "Okay, so let's see if we can find them."

They drove back out to the dirt road. Vic turned carefully, and they traveled along it, watching for any sign of an encampment. People, a vehicle, smoke rising from a fire, anything that might show them that there were people nearby. It was wild. Erin felt like there wasn't anyone around for miles. Maybe all the way back to Bald Eagle Falls. But she knew that wasn't true. There were plenty of little places outside of Bald Eagle Falls. Farms and homesteads. Many people didn't want to live right in town; they wanted space or lived on old family property or farmed.

Way back in her however-many-times-great-grandparents' time, it had been a different world. People moved there with nothing but what they could fit in a wagon, looking for cheap land, full of hope at being able to make a living for their families. Was that the way that it had been for Rip and the other families like his? They were trying to grasp the American dream, to get land of their own and make something of it. Starting with nothing and hoping to end up with comfort or wealth.

"We should be close to the turn-off," Vic said, scanning the trees on the right for a break.

"There… I think it's there…"

"Yeah."

They followed the new path. Trees scraped the top of the truck and Erin found herself ducking, even though she knew they were outside and couldn't reach her.

"Is there enough space?"

"There's no space to turn around," Vic said, keeping the truck rolling slowly forward. "And there has been a vehicle through here."

Sitting up tall to look out the windshield and down at the ground in front of the truck, she could see places where the vegetation was mashed down. She knew that most of it would spring up again quickly, so it must have been driven over more than once to stay crushed down. She settled back down in her seat.

"Maybe we'll find them. Could it be that easy?"

Vic raised her brows. "I'd be surprised. Nothing is that easy."

They both strained to see through the trees. It was a few minutes driving down the long drive before they finally made it through the trees. Erin saw several tents set up. Her heart sped up. Had they found the Ryders?

Vic drove to where there were a couple of vehicles parked rather than right up to the tents. They waited for a moment before getting out of the truck, watching for any dogs or guards with shotguns.

They opened the doors and Erin climbed down. A couple of people came out of the tents to see who was there. A man came out of one, a woman out of another. But she didn't match the description of Jenny Ryder. Or whatever her last name was.

Erin walked toward the woman anyway. She would rather talk to the woman than the man. Vic stayed back, close to the truck. Available if Erin needed her, but out of the way so they weren't intimidating. As if either of them could be intimidating.

"Hi there."

"Who are you?" the woman asked warily.

"My name is Erin. I own the bakery in Bald Eagle Falls."

She scowled. "What are you doing here? What do you want with us?"

"I'm looking for Jenny… Ryder. I don't know her right last name, someone said she wasn't married to Rip. But that's who I'm looking for."

"What do you want with her? You don't think she's got enough problems? If that no-good Rip ripped you off or dumped you, don't go crying to Jenny about it."

"I'm not. I didn't know him. I was just trying to find her. Make sure she's okay."

"Why wouldn't she be okay?"

"I know that Rip disappeared…"

"Good riddance. Best thing that could have happened to her. In fact, if you have any idea of getting them back together again, forget about it. She don't want nothing more to do with him."

Was that what Jenny would say for herself? Or was the brunette just hoping that was what Jenny would say? Some women kept going back to the same abusive or irresponsible men over and over again. Erin couldn't understand why.

"Do you know where Jenny is?"

"It's none of your business. Just leave the woman alone."

"Is she close to here? I know that they were camped just over there," Erin motioned in the direction they had come. "But Willie Andrews ran them off."

"What a jerk. He doesn't live on the property. So what does it matter to him if someone else uses the land? It's better for him if it's occupied, isn't it? Make sure that no one is there to do any harm. It's empty land that brings trouble."

Having Rip and his family squatting outside or inside the cave had not helped Willie. In fact, it had put him right in the middle of a murder investigation.

"I'm not going to cause Jenny any trouble. Could you tell me where she is?"

The brunette's gaze wavered. Not over to Vic or to one of the other tents, but the other direction, farther away from the cave. Then her gaze refocused on Erin's face, the woman trying to correct the 'tell.'

"How about you get off of our property?" The man had come closer to Erin and the woman, and his voice was sudden and harsh in Erin's ear, too close to her.

Erin immediately reacted, stepping backward and turning to face him full on, prepared for an attack. Whether she was expecting a verbal attack or a physical one, she wasn't sure. Her body reacted before her brain had had a chance to process anything.

"Your property?" she repeated. She doubted it was theirs, any more than the land that Jenny had camped on was hers.

"You see our settlement here. We've claimed this land, and you have no right to be here."

"Okay… I'll head out. I guess… you folks don't care much for Jenny, then."

Both of them reared back at this accusation. "Don't care about her?" the man demanded. "What makes you say we don't care about her?"

"I'm trying to help her out, but all you're doing is being obstructive. I guess you only care about yourselves." She looked at the tents. "Your settlement. Jenny is… an outsider and she can take care of herself. Without Rip. Without any help."

"She has help," the woman disagreed. She stepped toward Erin, putting her hands on her hips. "We're a community. We help each other. Whatever we need. We take care of each other."

"She's got a new baby and no husband. And a passel of kids. Every woman's dream."

"It's not our fault what she's got," the man said. "But we do our best to take care of our own. We don't need… whatever it is you think you're going to do to help her. Who exactly are you? Some social worker?"

"She's the baker," the woman told him. "The one from in town. Bald Eagle Falls."

The man looked at her with a frown of consternation. Erin didn't know anything about him, but he looked like he had heard of her. And he knew she was out of place coming to talk to them or to Jenny Ryder. What good reason did she have to talk to any of them?

"The baker." He appeared to be fishing for some memory, eyes screwed up while he tried to retrieve it. "Erin?"

Erin nodded. She put out her hand to shake. "Yes. That's me. And the woman over by the truck, the one who drove me in, that's my assistant, Vic."

What had he heard? That she was a busybody? Always interfering with everyone else's business? She hoped it was something more positive than that.

"Wiseman," he said automatically on taking her hand. "What do you want Jenny for?"

"I just want to talk to her." Erin let out a sigh. "Really. I'm not here to hassle her. I want to help."

"I don't see what you can do to help her."

"I don't either. But I'd like to do what I can. If I can just find Jenny and talk to her, then she can make that decision. I don't see why you should make it for her."

"I'm not making it for her. We're just protective of our own community. No one else is looking out for us, you know."

Erin had to admit that was probably true.

"Is she over there?" Erin nodded in the direction the woman's eyes had betrayed. "If we go over another road or two, we'll find her?"

Wiseman and the brunette just looked at Erin for a moment, not sure how to respond. Erin could hear children playing nearby, their voices carrying through the trees as they laughed and shrieked.

There was a baby or young child's cry from within the nearest tent. "Mama!"

The woman looked toward it. She looked tired, the sun spotlighting the fine wrinkles around her eyes and the deeper ones around her mouth as she frowned. She had lived a hard life, and she wasn't that old.

Her eyes flicked back toward the man, and she shrugged. She gathered herself and turned away from them, going into the tent.

Erin looked at the man to see whether he was going to answer the question. He gave Erin a long, measuring look. She could almost see the gears turning in his head as he thought things through.

"Fine," he said, shrugging. "Yeah, if you go farther east, you'll find her. You would anyway, so it doesn't matter whether I tell you that or not."

Erin nodded her agreement. "Thank you. Is she doing okay?"

He shrugged. "How would you expect her to be doing with a new baby and a bum of a husband who couldn't be bothered to stick around?"

"Not good," Erin agreed. "Well… thank you for your help." She hesitated, not sure whether to say anything further or not. "If you know anyone who is in need of some baking, I'm trying to get rid of the day-old stuff at the bakery. Bread, muffins, whatever. I've been taking it to homeless shelters in the city, but I'd rather help the community around here."

He looked at her, scowling again.

"I know." Erin held up her hands in a 'stop' motion. "Nobody wants to take charity. But it's better than me throwing it in the garbage and little tummies going empty. If you know someone who needs it, send them over. It's confidential. I promise."

His expression softened a bit but still remained stony. He gave a brief nod.

Erin went back to the truck.

CHAPTER 25

She climbed into the cab and melted into the seat, closing her eyes and letting out a long sigh. Vic climbed up into the driver's seat, and Erin could feel Vic looking at her.

"So… you at least had a conversation. How did that go?"

"Try the next road over. We might get lucky."

"We might, or we will?"

"I don't know if it's the next one or not, but we're going in the right direction. We'll get to them sooner or later."

Vic put the truck into gear, turned it around in the little clearing, and headed back out on the road that was too narrow for even the truck by itself. Erin hated to think of what would happen if they encountered a vehicle coming the other direction. There wasn't exactly room for either one to pull off to the side. One of them would have to drive in reverse until they reached a point where one could pull over or pass.

Luckily, they didn't meet any other vehicles coming the other direction. They drove on, found the next access road, and tried it. They came to the end of the road pretty quickly. Erin looked around, searching the trees for any sign of the family or a tent or a vehicle, but didn't see anything. "Not this one, I guess."

Vic turned around and again headed back out to the road. Erin caught her looking at the fuel gauge.

"Just checking," Vic said lightly. "Gotta make sure we have the gas to get back home again."

"Yes. I wouldn't want to break down around here."

"Who knows how long it would take to get a tow truck or someone with a gas can out here. And to direct them to the right place..."

"Maybe we should have brought Terry's truck. At least it has a GPS locator."

Vic laughed. "Yeah. Somehow, I think we might have gotten another call from him..."

Erin had to chuckle too. Terry had not been happy when she had taken his truck out of town previously without his permission. They hadn't gotten a call from Willie complaining about them going out of town, but Vic had probably told him where they would be going. Erin wouldn't put it past him to have a locator on his truck too.

Trucks were expensive. It was an appropriate anti-theft measure. Not to mention, it could help them out if there were ever a day when he didn't come home from checking out a claim.

Erin shuddered, remembering the last time that had happened. It had not been fun for any of them. At least he had recovered.

They got luckier with the next road. It snaked farther through the trees and, with each mile, Erin was sure that they were getting closer to Jenny and her children. But she hated the idea of their being out there, so isolated if something were to happen to any of them. What did a person do when they lived so far out in the sticks and a child got sick or injured? A trip to the hospital in the city would take a couple of hours. That kind of delay could be critical.

"Something up ahead," Vic said, her voice quivering a little with suppressed excitement.

"Is it her?"

Erin didn't even know why she asked. How would Vic know if it were her? Neither of them had ever seen her before.

They reached the next clearing, and Vic pulled in near a beaten-up Ford truck that looked like it had seen better days. In the sixties.

Maybe it was a classic. Maybe fixed up, it would be worth thousands. But with more rust than fenders, Erin suspected not.

Erin was glad to get out again. She hoped that this was the end of her journey. She would find Jenny Ryder. Connect with her and let her know that the police were trying to reach her. Make sure that she and her children were all well and safe. It might not be any of her business, but she couldn't help taking an interest in a woman out in the bush all on her own with a baby and young children.

Of course, it wasn't Rip's fault that he had gotten killed, but Erin was angry with him all the same. Why hadn't he been more careful? Why hadn't he done whatever it took to keep himself safe so that he would be around to see his little family grow up?

Children were playing around the tent, not hidden away in the trees like the children at the last settlement. All blond and skinny. Minimal clothing. By all appearances, having the best time of their lives, wild and free. Erin smiled a little. She couldn't help it. As much as she knew what Jenny and the family must have been going through, seeing the children playing with wild abandon made her smile.

"I guess this is it," she said to Vic.

They walked toward the grouping of tents. Not just one tent for everyone to sleep in. Maybe a few tents for everyone to sleep in, the older children on their own and the little ones with Jenny. One that was set up as a kitchen, not fully covered, with a collapsible table, a cookstove, and a closed cooler, as well as dishes and boxes of tools.

Back in the trees somewhere, there would be a latrine set up. A hole or trench in the ground, a toilet paper roll stuck onto a branch, a shovel to cover up solid waste.

The children shrieked with laughter. Living rough obviously wasn't hurting them.

One of them went into the bigger sleeping tent when the children noticed they had company. The rest continued to play as if they were used to people coming and going. If they were a part of the larger homeless community, then maybe they were used to visitors.

In a few moments, Jenny Ryder pushed her way out of the zippered front of the tent. She turned around and zipped it tightly shut behind her to keep the bugs out. She dusted off her hands and walked toward Erin and Vic.

"This is my property," she asserted. "You don't have any business here."

"Jenny?" Erin said.

Jenny stopped, looking at her with a frown. Obviously, she was caught off-guard by someone knowing her name.

"Who are you?"

"I'm Erin Price. The owner of Auntie Clem's Bakery."

"What are you doing here? And how do you know my name?"

"When I heard that you were on your own, with all of these children, I needed to check and make sure that you are okay. With Rip not having come back…"

"How do you know Rip?" Jenny's voice was suspicious. Jealous, even.

"I don't know him. Just heard about him. I'm sorry to bother you, but I didn't know if anyone was looking out for you, and wanted to make sure…"

"And you can see that we're fine. So you can just go back to Bald Eagle Falls to the bakery and bake your bread. We don't need any of your kind looking out for us."

"I'm glad that you have a community out here where everyone looks after each other. That's great."

Jenny nodded. She stood with her arms crossed over her chest, staring at Erin and Vic. The children stopped and watched, whispering to each other.

"I don't know if you're aware… that the police department in Bald Eagle Falls is trying to reach you."

"Why would they be trying to reach me?"

"They want to talk to you about Rip."

"What kind of trouble has he gotten himself into now? I'm not responsible for the man. I'm not paying bail if he's gotten himself in jail."

"You should call them. Do you have a phone or access to a phone? It's so remote out here."

"I can get a phone," she snapped.

"Then… you should call the police department. They can fill you in."

Jenny shrugged. But Erin could see that she was curious. She wouldn't beg details from Erin, and Erin was just fine with that, because she didn't want to be the one to have to break the news to Jenny that her husband—or partner—was never coming back. Ever.

"So. You've delivered your message. You can get on your way now."

"Okay. We will. Do you need anything? I can bring you out some supplies. I know that you have a new baby, and it can't be easy to take care of... him...? Her...? Out here, with all of the other kids to worry about. I'd be tired with just one..."

"What do you know about raising kids? You got any?" Jenny looked Erin over critically. Erin was embarrassed to think that Jenny was examining her pelvis to see whether she'd borne any children, or her breasts to see if she'd nursed them. But it wasn't like she was giving Jenny advice or critiquing her parenting skills. Just saying that it was a hard job.

"No. I don't have any of my own. But I've lived in big families... and had caregiving jobs. I know it can be exhausting."

"Well, until you have a family of your own, I'll ask you not to be sticking your nose into my business."

"I'm just asking if you need anything." Erin was getting just a bit put out that everyone was making a federal case out of her wanting to look after people who needed help. What was she supposed to do? Ignore them? Then people would be upset about how everyone always ignored them.

"I don't need anyone's help."

"Okay. Good to hear it. I'm glad you're making things work out here."

Erin took a deep breath, and then repeated her spiel about the bakery needing to get rid of its excess product, and wanting to help the local community if there were any need.

"You see any soup kitchens around here?" Jenny demanded. "We take care of our own here, we don't need charity."

"I want to help take care of my community too. I don't think that anyone should have to go hungry while I throw out bread or take it into the city. And I've seen a lot of people in the last few days who look like they spend a lot of time hungry. That's not right. No one should have to go hungry."

The children whispered more. One of them ventured to speak to Jenny.

"I'm hungry, Mama."

"Then go make yourself something in the kitchen," Jenny snapped, motioning toward it. "There's plenty to eat."

The children looked at each other, but none of them stepped toward the kitchen. It was probably against the rules. They were probably not allowed to take anything that their mother hadn't divided up between them. Kids could eat a lot. One child being greedy could throw off the carefully planned meals that a trip to the grocery store was supposed to supply, leaving them without key ingredients. Or calories.

"Are we going to get bread?" one of the little tykes asked.

Jenny clenched her jaw. "We'll get bread when I make bread. Or when I buy it. Not because some do-gooder thinks that I can't provide for my own kids."

The children were silent.

How *could* she provide, now that Rip was gone? How could she make money to support a family with so much responsibility already on her hands? She might not need much, squatting and getting as much as she could from the wilds, but she would still need a little bit of money to buy the supplies they needed. Or medicine if a child fell ill.

Maybe the woman in the other settlement traded off babysitting with Jenny so she could go into the city to work. Or so that she could crochet washcloths or blankets or whatever she did to earn a little bit of money to survive.

"Will you call the police department?" Erin ventured.

"We'll see."

Erin looked at Vic and shrugged. It was time for them to go. She didn't know if she could call what they had done that day progress. They had found Jenny Ryder and her children. But they might be gone again by the time the police department got out there. Erin suspected Jenny had no intention of calling the police department to get news of her no-good husband. She thought that he'd been out cheating or gambling and she wasn't going to help him out.

CHAPTER 26

The ride back to town was quiet. Vic fiddled with the radio, eventually managing to find a station that would keep playing instead of going in and out every time they went down a hill or through the dense trees.

Erin listened to the scratchy songs the station played, sounding like they were records from a bygone era, even though Erin knew them to be modern popular songs. She watched the trees out her window. How many other people were hidden away in the trees, trying to subsist like Jenny and the rest?

Were they ever counted?

Did the government even know they existed?

Erin couldn't imagine that anyone spent much time trying to track them down or count them.

"Well, you did it," Vic said finally. "I didn't know whether we had any hope of finding her, but you did."

Erin nodded. "Yeah."

"Something good will come of it. You care about people, and that's not a bad thing, even if they don't accept any help. At least they know that someone cared. Someone *saw* them."

Erin didn't say anything for a minute, then looked at Vic.

She remembered Vic the first day they had met. Grubby, homeless, spending her nights sleeping in the bakery before Erin had discovered her. She had been one of them. Invisible. Unacknowledged. And she had accepted help. Erin had made a difference to Vic, even if she couldn't help Jenny Ryder.

Erin knew that Terry would be happy to hear that she had found Jenny Ryder and the children. But not happy that it had been Erin who had done it. She and Vic had gone off on their own to do what was really the police department's job. He always told her to stay out of police matters. Erin knew better. And yet, she couldn't seem to keep away from them. There was always something that drew her back.

Solving the puzzle. Keeping friends out of trouble. Righting a wrong.

She could say all she liked that she wasn't an investigator or a 'sleuth.' And yet, what was she doing? Over and over, she got involved in a police investigation or family matter, following a compulsion to find out just a little more. Maybe it was some kind of illness. Something that could have been explained away if they saw the way her brain worked. Some kind of deficit in regulating her curiosity…

"I guess… maybe you should drop me at the police department," she told Vic.

"Why don't you just wait until he comes home?"

"I don't want him to say that I didn't tell him right away. I'm not holding information back, I'm telling them right away."

Vic gave her a sideways glance, then nodded. "If you're sure that's what you want."

Erin didn't exactly *want* it, but she thought it was the right thing to do. So when they reached the town limits, she steeled herself, trying to talk herself into being confident and strong, rather than coming across as tentative or weak. Vic pulled Willie's truck up to the town center. Erin opened the door. "I'll see you later. Be home… whenever I'm done here."

Vic nodded. "See you tonight, then. Or for work tomorrow."

At the police department offices, Erin presented herself to Clara, the receptionist. Clara was wearing big brassy moon earrings that dangled in front of her red hair. She looked disapprovingly at Erin through her narrow-framed glasses.

"What can we do for you today, Miss Price?"

"I need to talk to Terry, if he is around."

Clara considered this. "Is it a personal matter or police business?"

"Police business. Is he in?"

"I'll see whether he is busy. Please have a seat."

Erin sat down in one of the uncomfortable waiting room chairs. Clara picked up the phone handset to make a call. Erin waited. After Clara hung up, she nodded at Erin. "He'll be by in a bit."

So he was out, not just closeted in his office. Erin supposed that was better. He always preferred being out in the fresh air and on patrol to sitting in a stuffy office doing paperwork. He would be in a better mood when he got home at the end of the day. Except that he wouldn't necessarily be in a good mood about her coming by the police department to talk to him. Maybe she should just have waited until he was home to give him her news.

Erin took her planner out of her purse and began to go through it, checking items off that she had completed, adding notes and tasks to her projects and lists. It kept her mind occupied so that it didn't seem like it had been more than a few minutes since Clara had called for Terry.

She heard K9's panting before Terry walked in. Terry looked at Erin, sitting there, and forced a smile. Not the kind that reached his eyes and brought out his dimple.

"Erin. Good to see you. What's up?"

"I have some information for you."

He looked at her for another moment, then nodded. He motioned to his office. Erin closed her planner and tucked it back into her purse. Terry shared an office with Stayner now, but Stayner was apparently out. Maybe not on shift that afternoon. Erin was relieved, because she didn't really want to have the conversation in front of him. Erin sat down in one of the chairs, and Terry sat down behind the desk. K9 lay down behind the desk, out of Erin's sight. But she heard him sigh loudly, something he did when he was bored and wanted to be outside working instead of inside waiting.

"I found Jenny Ryder," Erin explained. "Or… whatever her legal name is. I guess she and Rip weren't actually married, but I didn't ask her what it really is. Genevieve, but I don't know her last name."

"You found her. Where did you find her?"

"Out near where Rip was killed. A few roads over. She's still camping out that way with her children. Squatting. Is it camping when it's a permanent location? Or only when you're on vacation?"

"Where exactly?"

Erin did her best to describe it, beginning at the clearing near the cave and counting off the roads to get to Jenny's encampment.

"So you just thought you would go looking for her."

"I was worried about her. Especially with a new baby. I thought someone should find her."

"Yes, and that someone should be from the police department."

"I didn't know whether you were going to be able to find them. You did have a head start."

"We were trying to track her down through her extended family. But apparently, none of them knew where she was. And she didn't have a cell phone, or we could have used that."

"I told her to call you. I asked if she had access to a phone, and she said she did. But I don't think she meant she had her own, just that she could borrow one from someone else or use a payphone. Are there any payphones in Bald Eagle Falls?"

"There are a couple if you know where to look."

"I guess she would. If that's the only way for them to make contact."

Terry fiddled with a pen on his desk, the corners of his mouth turned down. "So exactly what did you tell her?"

"Just that she should call here. I didn't say what it was about or that Rip was dead. I think she figured he was under arrest. She said she wasn't going to bail him out."

Terry did smile at that. "Well, at least she has some sense. Do you think she had any inclination to call and find out what it was about? Or I guess the more important point… is she going to run, because someone knows where she is camped out now?"

"She could, I guess. But it would take time for her to get everything packed up and ready to go, and I just left. I don't think… she could go somewhere else, but she was all settled there. Everything set up. She's part of a little community. They help each other out. I don't think she'd want to leave all of that behind. But maybe she knows where there are other places she could go… or she could retreat deeper into the woods, hoping you wouldn't look any farther."

"How long ago did you leave her?"

Erin looked at her watch and tried to calculate it out. "An hour and a half, maybe? I really don't think she could pick everything up and be gone in that length of time."

He nodded. "But she also has however long it takes me to get out there to see her. I'm just going to have to cross my fingers that she doesn't run, or doesn't get out of there as fast as she would like to."

CHAPTER 27

Erin knew that she wasn't going to get to see much of Terry that evening. Even if all he did was drive out to Jenny's, inform her that her husband was dead, and drive back, he wouldn't be back until after supper, and Erin had to retire to bed early to be up for the bakery.

And she suspected he would spend more than a few minutes talking to Jenny, unless she chased him off with a shotgun. He would comfort her, question her, try to fill in all of the blanks about who might have had a grudge against Rip and what day he had failed to come home. He would probably ask her about her own movements, and about phones, and what things might be missing from Rip's possessions. It would take a lot of time, so Erin wasn't expecting to see Terry much before bed.

She sat with the newspaper and her planner and thought about upcoming promotional opportunities and themes, what new ingredients were becoming popular in the trendy food shows, and anything else that might dictate the direction of her marketing efforts. If she wanted to keep Auntie Clem's interesting and fresh, she had to keep changing and adapting.

There was a knock at the door. Erin blinked, wondering whether she had drifted off to sleep. She looked toward the window, but it was the wrong angle to see if there were anyone at the door, and she didn't see a vehicle parked on the street in front of the house. Despite the fact that

Bald Eagle Falls was a small town, Erin found that people often drove from place to place. It wasn't very good for the environment. But she was as guilty of doing it as anyone else. Part of that was Terry's fault, since he didn't want her walking to the bakery in the dark. So it wasn't all by choice.

Erin went to the door and looked out the peephole. It was dark out, but she got a good view of the woman's silhouette, and it was one that she recognized. She let Adele in.

"Hi, come on in."

Adele stepped in and took a quick glance at the room. The tall, slim redhead would know from the lack of Terry's truck in front of the house that he was out, but Vic was also a frequent visitor and Adele wouldn't be able to tell if Vic were there unless she saw her through the window or there were some other clue. While Vic didn't harbor any bad feelings toward Adele for what her ex-husband had done in the past, Adele was still uncomfortable spending time with her.

"Just you and me," Erin confirmed.

"We haven't talked for a while, so I thought I would stop in for a visit, since Officer Piper is out."

"Do you want some tea?" Erin didn't wait for an answer. She and Adele always had tea together. She went into the kitchen to start the kettle boiling. Adele followed her, more comfortable in the kitchen than anywhere else in the house. Her own little cottage in the woods behind Erin's house was a tiny one-room affair, where the stove, table, and bed all shared the same space. It was a warm, homey place, and Erin didn't get there as often as she probably should. But she wanted to give Adele her space and a sense of privacy, even though the cottage was part of the property left to Erin by Clementine.

She puttered around in the kitchen. Adele arranged the rest of the tea things and sat down at the table.

"Anything new?" she asked.

Erin wondered how much Adele had heard about Rip. Adele was a solitary person, yet she often knew about things going on in Bald Eagle Falls before Erin did.

"I guess… you know about Rip Ryder…?"

Adele nodded her head once. "Yes. Are you… involved in that case?"

"Well, no…" Erin laughed. "It's nothing to do with me. But…"

"But you like solving puzzles."

"I guess so, yes," Erin admitted.

Erin poured the boiling water into their cups.

"So what is it about this case that interests you so much?" Adele asked. "Just because it was Vic who found him?"

"Partly, yes. I feel like if it's something to do with my family here in Bald Eagle Falls, that… I should do what I can to sort it out, make sure that the wrong people don't get saddled with the blame."

"Why would they blame Vic?"

"Well… with her being the one to find the body, and her family being in the clan, it's just where they go. What if she did it and… I don't know, returned to the scene of the crime. Same with Willie, except it's worse for him, since he had a fight with Mr. Ryder."

Adele look at Erin blankly for a moment. Then she nodded, and amended, "Or two or three."

Erin dipped and lifted her tea bag a few times and looked at Adele. "Two or three? How do you know that?"

"I hear things."

"Who did you hear that from? I didn't think it was common knowledge."

Adele just smiled and didn't answer.

Erin was again left wondering how Adele came by her information. She imagined Skye, Adele's crow, flying back and forth over Bald Eagle Falls and bringing back all of the juicy tidbits he'd heard back to his mistress. She smiled at the thought.

Adele knew people who knew things, that was all. She was quiet and discreet, so Erin didn't know all of the people that she knew or was friends with. But she clearly knew people who heard the gossip around Bald Eagle Falls. Not just the Baptist women who came to the bakery to share the gossip they had heard, but other, less visible people in Bald Eagle Falls as well.

"Well, I guess you're not the only one who knows that Rip and Willie didn't get along together. So the police know and they think, maybe they got into another fight, and it turned physical, and Willie killed him."

Adele raised her brows.

"And put him in that pool and then came back later with Vic to find him," Erin said, pointing out the obvious flaw in this theory.

"Why would he do that?"

"You would have to ask the police department. I don't know the answer. If Willie did kill him by accident or in a moment of anger—and I don't believe he ever would—then why would he do that? Leave the body in the cave there, and then go back later to let Vic find it? Or else bring her in on the secret and 'discover' it together? It doesn't make any sense."

Adele sipped her tea. "People don't always make sense."

"I guess. But that doesn't mean you think Willie did it, do you?"

"I don't suspect Willie Andrews or anyone else. I will leave that to the universe—and our esteemed police department—to sort out."

"I hope they do. And soon. And I'm sure it's not Willie. It couldn't be anything to do with Willie or Vic. It wouldn't make any sense, however much people try to force them into the mold. They don't have any motive."

"Other than Mr. Ryder disagreeing with him about the legitimacy of Willie's mineral claim."

Erin frowned. She stirred her tea, then forced herself to set the spoon aside to stop fiddling. "The legitimacy of Willie's claim? What do you mean by that? It's his claim."

"Is it?"

"Well, yes. He said..."

"He said it was his. But have you seen proof of his ownership? Or did he just lay claim to it and hope to keep everybody else off of it?"

"I don't know. He said it was his. I didn't question..."

"And that's exactly what he intended. He told Rip that it was his claim and he had to take himself and his family somewhere else. He didn't want Rip anywhere near that cave and, even after he moved off of the property, Willie still wasn't satisfied. He was still 'too close.'"

"How could they be too close? Either they were on his claim or not, you can't be *too close*."

Adele nodded her agreement. "You see Rip's argument."

"But it is Willie's, right? He might have been out of line in telling Rip that he was still too close and he wanted him to go farther away, but... it was his claim."

"As far as I know, he never showed any deeds to prove it."

Erin shook her head, finding it hard to believe that the claim might not be Willie's. "So he must have thought that the claim was pretty valuable. Potentially."

"I'm sure he wouldn't tell me if it was. Or anyone else, for that matter. He's worked mines and mineral claims around here long enough to know to keep his mouth shut and not attract attention to any one location. He is very discreet and circulates around from one mine to another. You can't tell by looking at the outsides which one is producing and which is not."

Erin had to admit that was true. "He doesn't even tell Vic. He's taken her caving a few different places, but he doesn't take her to his mines, and he doesn't tell her which one he's going to from one day to the next."

"But he did take her to this one."

Erin sipped her tea as it started to cool. The only way to know what Willie had found inside the cave, and whether he was removing anything from it, would be to go inside.

"Has he allowed anyone else in there?" Adele prompted.

"The police, of course. To remove the remains. He couldn't very well keep them out." Erin shrugged, raising her hands up. "That takes us right back to the beginning again. If he wanted to keep something about the cave a secret, why would he hide a body there and then bring Vic back to find it? And not to help him take it out and bury it, but then they call the police to come take a look and get it out of there."

"That's an interesting suggestion."

Orange Blossom had roused himself from his warm nest on the couch and had just realized that there was someone else in the house. He went over to Adele and started rubbing against her and vocalizing.

"Is he bothering you? He can be such a pest."

"No, I think it's nice having a cat around. I'm still thinking about getting one myself, though…"

Though Erin had told her that she would need to keep the cat inside to keep it safe, and Adele wasn't keen in caging any animal. Skye lived outside and could come and go as he pleased. He just seemed to want to be with Adele sometimes.

Erin bent over to scratch Blossom's ears, then sat up again. "What's an interesting suggestion?"

"The idea that Willie might have taken Vic to the cave in order to relocate and bury the body."

"I didn't say that's what happened. It obviously didn't happen."

"But that doesn't mean it isn't what Willie intended. Maybe he figured Vic would help him to dispose of it. Only she had other ideas and said they had to call the police. Either before or after he explained his plan."

"No, Willie wouldn't do that."

"You have a very… generous view of the world. You realize that, don't you? You think the best of everyone."

"Well… I try to, I guess. I want to believe the best of people."

"And not everyone lives up to your expectations, do they?"

"Most people, if you give them a chance, they'll do the right thing…"

"I'm not sure that's true. I think people's natures tend to be the opposite. They act in their own interests before anyone else's. Unless there is sufficient motivation to pursue another direction."

"You're not like that," Erin pointed out. "You're a good, giving person."

"I have found that to serve me well. It is innately selfish to want to treat others in such a way as to make yourself comfortable. To avoid conflict just because it is an easier path."

"You only make good choices because you want the rewards that come from making good choices? Isn't that sort of… twisted?"

"Perhaps it is. And perhaps it is what the majority of the world does."

Erin massaged her temples. She looked at the clock on the wall. She was getting tired, and the conversation was going in the wrong direction. She didn't want to have to evaluate her own motives, or Adele's, or Willie's. It was too much for her already tired brain.

"I guess everyone has their own reasons for doing things," she deflected. Once she said this, she nodded. It was true. It sounded good. And it meant she didn't have to continue the conversation in that direction.

"Yes," Adele agreed. The corners of her mouth curled up slightly as if at some private joke. She took a couple more swallows of her tea and set her cup down. "Well. I should get back to my wanderings. Take care, Miss Erin."

Erin nodded and stood at the same time as Adele. Orange Blossom went back and forth between them, demanding to know which of them was going to feed him.

"You haven't had any trouble, have you?" Erin asked as she walked Adele to the door. Adele was Erin's groundskeeper and, although Erin had first given her the title on the spur of the moment, looking for a way to help Adele out, Adele did actually keep a good watch on things that happened in the woods. People who walked through there and who might be looking to cause harm.

"No trouble," Adele agreed.

"You haven't had any of the squatters come to our woods? They stay far enough out of town…?"

"Why would they come into our woods?"

"I don't know. It would let them live outside, like they seem to want, but still to be close to the amenities. Be able to go to the library during the day or pick something up from the grocery store easily."

"I'll keep my eyes open," Adele promised.

Erin saw her out. When she shut and locked the door and reset the burglar alarm, she stopped to ponder Adele's responses.

She never had actually said that there were no squatters in Erin's woods.

CHAPTER 28

Erin was restless going to bed, thinking of Adele and how she had deflected Erin's questions and questioned Vic's and Willie's involvement in Rip's death without actually accusing them. She seemed to know a good amount about the arguments that had gone on between Rip and Willie. More than just someone who had heard about it. How would anyone know that Willie might not actually own the claims he said he did? She would have to be pretty close to the situation.

Adrienne had been in town. She and her children were there a couple of days in a row. Where were they staying? With a friend? In a car? Or in the woods back behind Erin's house, pretending that they lived out of town when they were actually right under her nose?

She was irritated with the thought. She had gone out of her way to help Adrienne, offering help to her and all of those who were indigent or homeless. She had been trying to find Jenny, to be sure that she was okay and that the police would be able to find her to make the official notification of Rip's death. Closure. People needed to know what had happened to their loved ones.

Erin had been doing the right thing, so why were people acting as if she was interfering with them or insulting them? She just wanted to help.

~

Erin decided to use her Sunday afternoon to do some visiting, something that she didn't have much time for the rest of the week. There were people she wanted to see that she didn't have as much opportunity for the rest of the week.

So she tried Mary Lou first. She knew Mary Lou generally went to the Baptist services, and then to the ladies tea at Auntie Clem's, but after that, she didn't know if Mary Lou worked or ran errands or relaxed.

"Yes, come over, Erin," Mary Lou agreed. "We're not going too far from home these days. We'll be around."

We was Mary Lou and her younger son, Joshua, who was recovering from being kidnapped and held hostage for a week with practically no food or water. They had all worried after the first couple of days that they would not find him alive. Joshua had believed the same, knowing that his time was drawing to an end. But they had been able to find him and to rescue him.

The physical recovery was one thing. Erin could see that his cheeks had filled in and that he looked stronger and more like himself. But he was also different. He was stiff and he watched Erin and the world around him differently from ever before. It wasn't just hypervigilance, which Erin knew was a common reaction to such a traumatic experience. There was more to it than that. He was wary. Not only of strangers, not just jumping at sudden unexpected noises, but seemingly distrustful of even those he knew. Erin felt him examining her, trying to pick her apart and to predict what she was going to do and say. It wasn't enough to know that she was a friend of his mother's, or that she had been instrumental in finding him and bringing him back home. He wanted to disassemble her and see what made her work so that he didn't have to guess.

"How are you feeling?" she asked Joshua. "You're looking better all the time."

"Yeah. I'm fine. Doing good. It's all… everything will be just the way it was before."

Maybe he was repeating what Mary Lou or someone else had said to him. Because he certainly didn't sound like he believed it himself.

"We're all changing all the time," Erin said. "I'm not the same person as I was a year ago. Or ten years ago. That's why they say you can't go back… you can never be the same person as you were before. We're all growing and changing all the time. And something like this… it can really affect you."

"It hasn't changed me," Josh said flatly.

Erin nodded. "Okay." She turned her attention to Mary Lou, hoping that would give Josh a chance to relax. "How about you? And Campbell? I haven't heard how he is. Staying out of trouble?"

"I'm sure I wouldn't know. He's back in the city now. I wish he had stayed around… but on the other hand, it's kind of tense when he's here. His mother expecting him to follow the house rules and him thinking that he's a full-grown man now and doesn't need to listen to what anyone else has to tell him."

"Yeah. Well, he is an adult."

"So I've heard. Multiple times."

Erin smiled. "He's lucky to have you. He might not realize that right now, but someday… he will."

Mary Lou thought about that for a minute. "Maybe. But it isn't as easy for him to see as you. You've lived on the other side. On your own as soon as you were eighteen, without any family resources. It must have taken a lot of hard work to get to where you are today. To be able to pull yourself up all by yourself…"

"It wasn't exactly all by myself, though. Without Clementine… I wouldn't be where I am today. That was an opportunity that I could never have made for myself. I didn't have the money or resources to take a leap and start up my own business without what she had left me."

"I'm glad… she would have been happy to see what you have done with it. How you have taken her legacy and… made it your own. Built on it. Become a self-sufficient small business owner. She would have been very proud." Mary Lou gave an approving nod.

"Thank you… I hope she would be. I hope that the bakery would be something that she would approve of."

"Yes. I'm sure it is."

Erin tried to think of other things to discuss. Joshua and Campbell seemed to be off the table. They had their own difficulties, and Erin didn't want to pry into family business.

"Have you seen the Fosters lately? I'm going to head over there after this, see if they need anything."

"I don't see much of them," Mary Lou admitted. "I know they're just down the way, but I keep to myself too much. I should go see them, but I don't. With a new baby, I'm not sure they want to have visitors over there all the time." She hastened to reassure Erin. "Not that they won't want to see you. That little boy idolizes you. But for me… I'm just the cranky old lady down the street. The children will have to be on their best behavior and that gets very tiresome."

Erin nodded. "I'm amazed at how Mrs. Foster can handle that little brood. So many young ones to keep in order. And she must be exhausted with a new baby."

"There seems to be a whole new crop of little ones popping up," Mary Lou observed. "Like we're having a mini baby boom in Bald Eagle Falls."

Erin thought about the Fosters, Jenny Ryder, and the two other homeless women who had new babies. She nodded her agreement. "Yes, there do seem to be a lot of them around."

"It seems like just yesterday that I had little ones. It's hard to believe they're already older teenagers." Mary Lou shook her head. "You'll be amazed at how fast the time goes, Erin. I know you've probably heard it before. But it really is true. Time just keeps going faster and faster. I remember when I was a child, it seemed like a summer day lasted forever. And the school break over the summer felt like a year off. Now… it seems like I barely get a chance to sleep, and it's a new month. Don't put things off until you are older, because before you know it, you will be older, and it will be too late."

Erin thought about all of the plans she had been writing down in her new paper planner. Writing down her dreams and plans for the future made them seem that much more real. But Mary Lou was right; she couldn't afford to put them off and act like she had as much time as she would need in the future. She needed to be working on them now.

CHAPTER 29

Erin left Mary Lou and Joshua with some cookies and headed over to the Fosters. She had a box of various baked goods for them, although Mrs. Foster was back on her feet and making occasional trips to the bakery now. Erin wanted her to know that someone was looking out for her and doing what she could do ease her burden. It wasn't really much, but Erin did what she could.

The little girls were playing outside. Erin didn't see Peter, which was odd. He was usually helping to supervise the younger children. Jody ran up to her.

"Miss Erin! You come to visit?"

Erin nodded. "I came to visit. How is everybody doing?"

"I hurt my knee." The little girl bent over to pull up the shorts that reached over her kneecaps to show Erin a skinned knee.

Erin winced at the red, raw patch. "Ow! That must have really hurt. Did you fall down?"

"Yes. I was running, playing," Jody turned around and was gesturing, telling Erin all about what she had been doing when she had taken a spill. She spoke quickly, and with her face turned away from Erin. Erin could no longer make out what she was saying.

Erin made attentive noises and, when Jody got to the part where she had fallen down and hurt herself, Erin shook her head. "Ouch. Well, you try to be careful. We don't want you hurting anything else."

"Yeah!" she agreed with feeling.

Grinning, Erin walked up to the house and reached out to ring the doorbell. The door was opened before she reached it. Mrs. Foster stood inside the door and motioned her in.

"Come in, come in."

Erin entered the house. She took the box of baked goods into the kitchen and put it down on the counter. Mrs. Foster could put things away where she wanted them. Or she could have Peter or one of the others help out.

"I'm trying to keep an eye on them," Mrs. Foster said, nodding to the window as they sat down in the living room.

Erin looked out at them. "They are lucky to have somewhere safe to play outside. Burn off some steam."

"I wouldn't want to keep them cooped up all day. Even on a school day, I try to let them have as much outside time as possible. The skillset they develop when they can move around and experiment and do things for themselves is very different from a kid who just sits in front of screens all day. I want my children to be strong and self-sufficient. Not afraid to try things or tied to a box all day."

"Well, you must be doing something right. They are all such good kids. And I know I can't pick favorites, but… Peter is such a bright little guy. I think you've done very well with all of them."

"He should be home in a few minutes. I asked him to pick up a couple of things for me at the store."

Erin looked out the window anxiously. She had thought he might be doing homework in his bedroom. She didn't like the idea of his going out all by himself to the store. Mrs. Foster followed her eyes.

"He's old enough. He walks to school by himself."

"Oh, of course. It's just that… with Joshua being kidnapped, I guess I'm more nervous…"

"We can't let ourselves be ruled by fear. Joshua didn't get snatched off of the street, and it wasn't some random kidnapper. And they caught the person who did it. If he was taken from his room at night… what good will it do us to keep our children inside all the time? Being inside did not help Josh."

"I guess," Erin admitted. "I'm sorry. I'm not saying you're doing anything wrong. It's just a gut reaction. I think Bald Eagle Falls is a pretty safe place for kids."

Mrs. Foster nodded. "It is," she agreed. "And Peter has been drilled over and over again on what he is and isn't allowed to do."

If he chose to obey. Erin knew that he had stopped to talk and visit with her on the way home from school and told her he wasn't supposed to stop to talk to anyone. But then, all kids were like that. They chose what to obey and what they didn't think was worth obeying.

So did adults, for that matter.

They talked about the weather and things going on around town. Erin did not bring up the remains found in the cave. The baby started to cry in another room, and Mrs. Foster sat there for a moment to see if he would stop on his own before getting up to get him.

"Here is Allan," she told Erin, as she brought the snuggling baby back into the room. She tilted him toward Erin so she could get a good view of him.

"Wow, he's already growing. He's definitely bigger than he was last time I saw him."

"Yes, he is." Mrs. Foster stroked the baby's shock of hair. "And already losing his hair, too. It's funny how sometimes they come out looking like they're wearing a toupee, there's so much of it, and then it all falls out."

She sat back down and unbuttoned a few buttons in order to nurse him.

He looked so much healthier than Adrienne's baby. His cheeks were rosy and round. He nursed contently, rather than moving around and pulling at the nipple as if he weren't getting enough. Erin had a pain in her chest, thinking about Adrienne's baby, and Jenny's, and the baby or child she'd heard crying in the tent in the settlement beside Jenny's. So many hungry mouths to feed.

A few minutes later, Erin spotted Peter walking down the street, swinging a grocery bag at his side. "There he is."

Mrs. Foster smiled. "Safe and sound."

"Of course."

Peter stopped to talk to the girls outside for a few minutes, then entered the house. He smiled and held the bag up for his mother. "I got everything. Hi, Miss Erin!"

Erin smiled at him.

"Good," Mrs. Foster said. "Put it away in the kitchen, please?"

He nodded and did as he was asked. Erin thought she heard him rustling through the box of baked goods while he was in there, and he was definitely chewing something when he exited the kitchen.

"Miss Erin brought pizza shells. Can we have pizza for supper?"

"I suppose so. Do you and the girls want to make your own?"

Peter nodded his head vigorously. "And I get a whole one, not a half."

"Yes, you can have a whole one. The girls are too small to eat a full one, so I'll cut theirs in half and they can each put their own toppings on."

Peter nodded his agreement. He paused. "That will make an extra half, though."

"We can put it in the freezer for next time."

"I could eat the extra half," he offered.

"No. You could not."

Peter shrugged and rolled his eyes at Erin, giving her a roguish grin. He might not be a teenager yet, but he was clearly working on a teenage appetite.

"How have you been, Peter? Helping your mom lots with the younger kids?"

"I always do," he told her earnestly. "I'm a good big brother. I help with a lot of stuff, don't I, Mom?"

"Yes, you do. It's good to have you around here."

Peter sat gingerly down on the edge of a chair, looking as if he weren't sure whether he was allowed to join them. Maybe now that he was home, he was supposed to go outside to play with the girls.

"I saw the sign in the bakery window," Peter confided in Erin. "The one about people going there to get food if they don't have enough to eat? I think that's a really good idea."

"Do you? I'm glad." Erin glanced at Mrs. Foster to make sure it was okay to talk about it with Peter. She'd been criticized before for talking with him about things that she shouldn't and for getting him involved in criminal investigations. Not because she intentionally involved him in her mystery-solving, but because he was observant and she had picked up on things he'd said casually. She didn't want to end up in trouble again. "I don't like to think about people in our neighborhood going hungry."

"I don't think you need to worry about that," Mrs. Foster said. "There's a lunch program at the school, so parents don't even need to feed their children three times a day. We don't have unemployed bums around here who don't contribute. And I think anyone willing to put in an honest day's work can buy their family food."

"A lot of jobs don't pay a living wage, though," Erin said. "And if there is only one parent who can work and take care of the kids, how are they supposed to choose between putting money on the table or looking after their children?"

"We don't have those kinds of problems here. There are enough jobs to go around, even during these times. And if there aren't, you can go into the city and find something there. It's not such a terrible commute. You can still live in Bald Eagle Falls, where housing is cheaper."

Erin bit her lip. She didn't want to argue the point, but she knew it wasn't that simple.

"I've run into some families in pretty desperate situations the last few days," she explained. "Not everyone has cars or the money for gas to commute to the city and, even if they do, unemployment is worse there than it is here. And a mom with young children doesn't always have someone she can leave them with while she goes to work. Especially not if she's making minimum wage, which doesn't give her enough to raise a family on, let alone provide for babysitting."

Mrs. Foster raised her eyebrows. "Some people will use any excuse. Those of us who want to can find a way to make things work. It's never been easy for us, but we manage to get along."

Erin nodded. "That's good. I hate to see anyone on the skids."

Mrs. Foster wasn't sure what to say to that.

"I think it's sad when people don't have enough to eat," Peter said. "I saw some kids at the playground. They don't go to school. I don't know if they're too young or maybe homeschooled." He gave a shrug. "They were all real skinny, and their clothes were…" he searched for the right word. "I guess they were hand-me-downs."

"You're lucky to be the oldest, so you don't have to wear hand-me-downs," Mrs. Foster said. "But there's nothing wrong with it. It just makes economic sense when you have more than one child. Get things that the next one in line can wear. Or the next two or three." She laughed.

Peter nodded seriously. "But even the oldest one was wearing hand-me-downs. That's what it looked like."

"Maybe they were from a cousin or a friend. It's nice when families can help each other out."

"Like Miss Erin is doing with the food," Peter said triumphantly. "She is making sure that the people who are hungry can eat hand-me-down food."

Erin smiled. It sounded better than charity.

"I suppose," Mrs. Foster said grudgingly. "If you have leftovers anyway, you might as well use them instead of throwing them out."

"I always have to make more than I need," Erin explained. "I can't be out of food when people come to pick something up at the end of the day. It's okay if one or two things run out, but I always have to have bread and rolls, and some kind of dessert. So I always have something left over at the end of the day."

"You could just sell it the next day," Peter pointed out.

"I can, but I have to mark it as 'day old,' and not everybody wants to buy day old. And I have to mark it down, put it on sale. And if it's any more than that, I really can't keep putting it out for sale, because it will get dry and stale. Then Auntie Clem's would get a reputation for having stale bread, and people would stop coming."

He nodded thoughtfully. "I guess so. So it's good that you can give it to the poor people, like the kids I saw in the playground."

"That's what I'm hoping. I usually freeze as much as I can and then take it into the city, because they have shelters and soup kitchens there that will take it."

"But then what would the kids here eat?" Peter sounded affronted at the idea. "They can't go all the way into the city."

"You're right," Erin agreed. "They can't."

CHAPTER 30

That night, Erin and Terry ate at the Chinese restaurant with Vic and Willie. It felt a little too decadent to Erin after seeing the homeless people around Bald Eagle Falls and worrying whether they were getting enough to eat. The four of them would probably order enough for three families with young children.

She tried to push these thoughts to the side to enjoy her time with her Bald Eagle Falls family.

"So… how did things go when you went out to give the death notification to Mrs. Ryder?" Vic asked as they sipped their drinks and waited for the food to arrive. "Did you manage to find her?"

"I got her," Terry admitted after a moment, apparently deciding that it was not confidential information. Now that the police had notified the next of kin, the paper would be able to publish Rip's name and details. "Kudos to you guys for tracking her down. Even though… you know I would prefer you would leave the sleuthing to the police."

"Well, yeah." Vic shrugged. "But sometimes pure dumb luck overrules."

"I doubt if it was dumb luck," Willie said. "The two of you are pretty bright. It just so happened that you went about it in a different way than the police did."

That was a good way to praise the women without bashing the police for not finding the Ryders.

"I thought she was the woman here in town," Erin confessed. "But that was Adrienne."

"I wouldn't even have known that we had anyone homeless right in town," Vic said. "I wouldn't have thought it."

"I don't know if they actually live in town," Terry said. "They might have just stopped in for a day or two to pick things up or visit a relative."

"I don't think they were taking any pleasure trips," Erin countered, "They wouldn't be able to afford that. I don't know if she's married, she didn't say. But she has a new baby, so hopefully, that means she isn't trying to take care of her family all on her own."

"Then they're probably staying with family," Willie suggested. "Or they have an RV or van they park somewhere."

"Maybe," Erin agreed.

"You don't think so?" Terry asked, sensing her hesitance.

"It crossed my mind that they might be in the woods. Back behind the house."

"Really?" Terry's brows climbed his forehead.

The waitress arrived with their order, and everyone leaned back while she filled the table with the various dishes. They began to dish up.

"I would think that Adele would let us know if there was any trouble back there," Terry said. "It's her job as your groundskeeper to make sure that people aren't trespassing on your property."

Erin nodded. "Yes… but I just got the feeling… she knows more than she says. She always does. She keeps her own counsel. But I wondered the other night whether she knows that someone is camping out back there. And maybe she doesn't want to tell anyone."

"Why not? If someone is squatting on your property, you need to get them off. You don't want to be liable for anything that happens to them while they're living on your land. If one of the kids has an accident or eats poisonous berries… you don't want to have to deal with that."

"But it wouldn't be my fault."

"You want to get sued and find out?"

Erin frowned and ate her Chinese food slowly. While she didn't want to kick someone who was in need off of her property, she also didn't want to be held responsible for something just because it was done on her property. She tried to balance the two against each other.

"And there's adverse possession, too," Willie put in.

"What's adverse possession?"

"It means that if someone squats on your land, and you allow them to, then they can claim that the land has become theirs."

"They can claim a property just by squatting on it?"

"What do you think all of those people out there are trying to do? They can't afford to buy land, but if they can squat on it for long enough, they can take it over."

"So when you kicked Ryder off, is that why? Because you didn't want them to be able to take it over?"

"I don't like people crowding me or trying to jump my mineral claims. They can start pulling ore out of one of my mines long before they can claim adverse possession." Willie sliced the meat off of a chicken wing with sharp, decisive strokes of his knife. "And no one is taking ore out of my mines but me."

Everyone was quiet for a few minutes, eating their own meals and considering the conversation. Erin caught Terry looking at Willie, his eyes sharp and discerning. Erin was sure that he still considered Willie a suspect. He was happy to sit there listening to Willie talking about adverse possession and his mines, stacking up the motives that Willie had to get Ryder off of his property permanently.

He'd tried telling them to leave once and Ryder had come back. Even when Willie kicked them off again, they had only gone a couple of roads over when they set up camp again. Was it because they still wanted access to Willie's property?

"That cave… were there minerals there?" Erin asked.

"There are minerals in every cave. That's what caves are made from," Willie countered with a smile.

"I know. I mean… precious metals or diamonds or anything like that. Why was Rip interested in the cave? Is there something worth mining there?"

Erin thought back to the way the cave and the property had looked the day that she and Vic went out there. There was no sign that Willie had been mining, as far as she had seen. She hadn't gone inside the cave, but if Willie were taking minerals out of that mine, he had to move them, and Erin hadn't seen any tracks in the dirt. No wagon or cart or truck.

"That's not any of your business," Willie told her matter-of-factly.

Erin nodded her agreement.

CHAPTER 31

"We didn't really talk much about your day," Terry murmured to Erin as they cuddled that night, getting ready for sleep. "How did your visits go?"

"Good. I got in to see Mary Lou and Joshua. They're... coming along, I guess. I wish Josh was doing better, but I guess you can't expect him to recover right away from something so traumatic. Everyone keeps saying, 'kids bounce right back,' so I kind of expected him to be back to his old self again. But... I should know better. I've seen trauma and how it can affect people. Even kids."

Terry nodded, snuggling her close. "That makes sense. We like to think that a negative experience is just that, something that happened that we can just move on from. But it isn't always the case. It still changes us. Maybe a little, maybe a lot."

"Yeah. I want to give Josh a hug and tell him that it is all going to be okay. But he's not my kid. I can't do that. And... I don't know how he's going to be. How hard it is going to be to get over the hump. Some people... don't ever recover."

"Does Mary Lou have him in therapy? She really should."

"I don't know. She didn't bring it up and I would never ask."

"Well... keep an eye on him. You're right, sometimes it's too much for people. If that's the case for Josh, we need to make sure he gets the help he needs before he does something to harm himself."

"Yeah. That would really be terrible."

"It would." Terry rubbed Erin's back and shoulders. She turned a little to give him better access.

"Anyway. So that was Josh. And then there were the Fosters."

"A happier visit. How are they holding up with the new baby?"

"Everything seems to be good. Peter is helping out with the little kids as much as he can. She sent him to the store today to pick up some things for her, and he did a good job at that."

"You don't sound like you approve."

"I hope I didn't sound that way with her, but I think she could see that I was… uncomfortable with it. I guess… I'm just a bit paranoid about things like kidnapping. The things that could happen to him on the way over there. I know Bald Eagle Falls is a safe place, but… nowhere is completely free of bullies and pedophiles…"

"No. Unfortunately not. But walking to the store and back during the day… that should be pretty safe for him."

"As safe as anything," Erin said. She yawned and stretched, tensing and then relaxing all of her muscles. "Safe as houses."

"Just like you're safe here," Terry reminded her. He put his arms around her again, his breathing long and even.

"Yes." Erin closed her eyes. "So many babies this year. Are there always so many babies?"

"Who has babies?"

"The Fosters, the Ryders, Adrienne, that other family out there. Everybody has babies." She sighed. "Except us."

Terry took in a sharp breath. Then he seemed to be holding it, to have stopped breathing altogether. Erin pried her eyes open to look in his direction. She could see his face in the dark, but it was only a pale oval in the darkness. No features.

"What's wrong?"

"You just said that everybody has babies except us."

"Yeah."

"Are you… wanting a baby?"

"No. I don't think so. I don't know. I don't think I'm really mother material. I think all of those years in so many different homes kind of put me off of families. Kids can be such a bother, you know."

"Well… so they can. They can interfere with a lot of plans, tie you down, cause a lot of heartache. But people still choose to have them."

Erin turned over and snuggled into Terry's chest. "You don't have to worry. I'm not making any kind of decision."

"If you're thinking about having kids, I'd like to at least hear about it."

"Not really. Just when I see or hold someone else's baby, I always feel this sort of… tug. Just hormones, I guess. Biology. The drive to perpetuate the species. I start to wonder what it would be like. Think that maybe someday…"

Terry breathed in and out a few times, waiting. "Someday…?"

"Maybe. But not yet."

"Okay. Go to sleep now."

"I am." Erin closed her eyes again and drifted off.

She and Vic had talked off and on a few times over the next day about the various homeless families they had encountered so far, speculating on their plans, how they were going to survive, and if they needed help or would even take it if they did.

After getting home from the bakery, Erin decided that she needed to take the bull by the horns and find out where Adrienne's family was staying. Or at least to make sure that they weren't squatting in her woods.

Terry was working a shift with the police department, so Erin left a note on the kitchen table saying where she was going, and headed out the back, through the gate, into the trees.

It was easier for her to navigate now than it had been when she had first arrived and had explored the woods. It had seemed so vast then, and she didn't know one area of the woods from another. The intersecting footpaths or animal paths had all looked the same to her, as had the trees and other vegetation.

But she knew her way around now. She knew the shapes of the different trees, the clearings, the berry bushes, and the pathways that connected them all. She didn't need a map, she knew where everything was, and no longer got lost if she didn't keep an eye on the sun and the direction she was traveling. It only took her a few minutes to make her way to Adele's cottage. She didn't know for sure that Adele would be there, but she didn't usually head out on her ramblings until the sun started to go down, so there was a good chance she would still be at home or close to the cottage.

She heard a crow cawing overhead and looked up, trying to identify whether it was Skye. Maybe he was the early warning system that someone was approaching the house. When Erin reached the cottage, Adele opened the door.

"Erin, come in. What can I do for you?"

Erin entered but didn't sit down at the table. She looked around at the room, her eyes taking everything in. Were there more possessions there than there usually were? Fewer? Was anything out of place?

Adele followed Erin's gaze, and her lifted eyebrow gave her an amused appearance.

"Well? Can I get you something?"

"No. I'm sorry. I just wondered… The other day when you came by, we talked about people hanging around lately, about the homeless or indigent..."

"Yes…?"

"I wanted to check with you. They're not camped out here, are they? In these woods?"

"There's lots of space," Adele said, not answering the question.

"Yes, I know. And I really don't want to have to search it all myself. I know that everyone needs somewhere to live, but… I could be liable for anything that happens on my land."

"What is going to happen?"

"I don't know. I can't predict. Things go wrong. People have accidents. Hurt each other. I don't want something to happen that I'll be held responsible for."

Adele stared out one of the small windows, considering. Her non-answer had actually been a pretty big giveaway. Yes, of course they were camped out in Erin's woods. Like Erin, Adele did not want to have to kick them out. She wanted a way out of it.

"Do you really think anyone would hold you responsible?"

"I don't know. I guess they could sue me, and then the court would have to decide how much of it had been my fault. How much money I had to pay for what happened. I don't really want to have to pay anything. The bakery is stable financially right now, but if something were to happen and I had to pay thousands of dollars in reparations... I'd go under. Auntie Clem's would be gone. I don't know what I would do. I guess I would have to sell the house and this land."

Erin let Adele think that part out to its final conclusion. If Erin sold the land, then Adele would be out a home as well.

"Or look at what's happened to Willie. Someone gets killed on his claim, and he's the prime suspect."

"No one would hold you responsible just because a murder happened on your land."

"I've been a suspect before. I don't like the way it feels."

Adele snorted and nodded. "Have to agree with you on that one."

They were both silent for a while. Finally, Adele spoke. "I'll get them to move on."

"I'm sorry."

Adele nodded. "That's just the way life works. What is it the Christian scriptures say? He who has the most will get more, and he who has the least, it will be taken from him?" She sighed. "I have always thought that very unfair."

"Me too," Erin agreed.

CHAPTER 32

"Do you think I should talk to them?" Erin asked. "I could explain that it was my decision, not yours, and… I want to do more for them, but I don't know what. I've told everyone I can that they can come to the bakery for food; I need to get rid of day-old baking anyway. But they're all so proud. They say they take care of themselves."

Adele shrugged. "I don't know if it will make any difference whether you or I tell them. It is my job. And as far as finding them somewhere else to live, or feeding them your leftover bread, I can't help you there. I don't know the best way to help people trying to make it on their own. I guess… just offer and then step back. See what happens down the line."

Erin nodded. "I worry about the children especially. It's one thing for the parents to decide that they don't want any help and that they're going to live on land that isn't theirs, but the kids didn't choose that. They don't choose to go hungry and or live like vagrants."

"So, what should happen?" Adele asked gently. "Send them off to foster care to families who will take care of them properly?"

"No." Erin sighed. "I know there aren't any easy answers. I just want to take care of them."

"Like I said, you have a soft heart. That's not a bad thing, but it is uncomfortable. Like having a paper cut on your index finger. It's always brushing against something."

Erin nodded. It was an apt comparison. Would it be better not to have a soft heart, so that it wouldn't be as uncomfortable? She would have to be a different person altogether. She would no longer be herself.

"I think I'd like to talk to them. I want to… be able to explain and let them know that I'll help in other ways if I can. I just can't be worried about what might happen with them on my land."

Adele described to Erin where the family was staying. They were practically in Erin's back yard. Erin laughed ruefully and headed back toward home.

"Thanks, Adele. I appreciate it."

"I know I should have told them right away not to camp on your land. I should have told them it was private property and to leave."

"Maybe you have a soft heart too," Erin teased.

"Not a good thing for a groundskeeper. I need to be tough, not be swayed by every sob story."

"You shouldn't beat yourself up either. You haven't been swayed by every sob story. This is the first one, isn't it?"

Adele nodded. Erin wondered whether it were true. Had there been others that she hadn't known about? Maybe not squatters, but people that Adele had let stay overnight, or to have a quiet campfire together because they weren't bothering anyone? Or inviting her friends over for a midnight pagan ritual? Erin hadn't kept an eye on the property, trusting that Adele was doing her job and keeping everyone else off. Maybe Erin needed to be more aware of what was going on right under her nose.

In a few minutes, she was at the edge of Adrienne's camp. She had neglected to ask Adele if there were a Mr. Adrienne around. Or if she needed to be concerned about sneaking up on people who might be armed. She really should have at least weighed the risks and considered all of the facts before she decided to shoo them out.

For a moment, she considered just returning home and seeing whether Terry was back and could go along with her. Or going back to get Adele or telling her the next day to just go ahead and inform them herself, as Erin had chickened out.

But she didn't want to be a chicken about it. How hard was it to tell a woman that this was private property and she would have to find somewhere else to camp? There was a whole wilderness outside of Bald Eagle falls to choose from.

Erin took a deep breath to center and fortify herself. Then, she moved into the clearing where Adrienne and the children sat around an empty camp stove, warming their hands. The smell of hot dogs hung in the air. The children's eyes went to her immediately. A couple of the kids jumped up, ready to run for it. Adrienne shifted the baby in her sling and looked at Erin with tired, defeated eyes.

"I'm sorry," Erin said. She tried to swallow a lump in her throat.

"We have nowhere else to go tonight," Adrienne said. "It would take more than an hour to break camp, and then it will be dark, and the children should be in bed sleeping."

"In the morning, then," Erin said. "When everyone is up, you can get started… you should have time to find somewhere else."

"You make it sound so easy. You have no idea."

"I haven't had to do anything like that myself," Erin said. "I believe that it's going to be hard. So get a good night's sleep now, worry about it in the morning."

Adrienne wiped at her face with the back of her hand and Erin realized with horror that she was crying. Adrienne had seemed so hard when they had talked earlier that Erin hadn't expected this. She thought that Adrienne would just tough it out and not show Erin how she felt about it.

Or maybe that was planned. Perhaps she was hoping to break Erin down with her tears.

"Mama!" One of the children hurried over to her and threw his arms around her. "Why you crying? It's okay. Don't cry." He used a corner of the baby sling to wipe the tears away.

"I'm just tired," Adrienne told him. "You know how it is when you're so tired that every little thing makes you sad. I'll be fine. You guys need to start getting ready for bed."

"We don't hafta go?"

"Not now."

The little boy looked at Erin. "It's the nice cookie lady," he said. "She's nice."

"Yes. She's trying. Now hop to it. Where's your toothbrush?"

The little boy crawled into one of the tents. Erin noticed that it wasn't a zippered nylon tent, but heavier canvas with snaps. Maybe army surplus. Maybe a hundred years old. Erin hadn't ever seen one quite like it before.

"You heard me," Adrienne told the other children. "It's time to get ready for bed."

One of the girls took a child of indeterminate gender by the hand to take him into the tent and begin their bedtime routine. Another older girl sat there at first, looking across at her mother, not budging.

"You too, Hope," Adrienne said. "No staying up late tonight. You need lots of sleep to give you energy tomorrow."

"We don't have anywhere to go," Hope said seriously.

"We'll work something out."

Hope scratched at a fraying hole in the knee of her pants. She sucked her thin cheeks in, looking worried. "Aunt Ann would take little Jeffey and Samantha. She said she would."

Adrienne said nothing.

"And what about Bell? She said if I could help with chores, maybe I could stay there." Tears started to track down Hope's face. She wiped them away, but couldn't make them stop. "I don't want us to be split up."

Adrienne held out an arm toward her. Hope crawled around the cook-stove into her mother's arms. Adrienne gave her a hug and kissed the top of her head.

"We're not going to split everyone up. We'll figure something out."

"Ike had to go live with his grandma."

"I'm not going to send you to live with anyone else. Okay? You just relax. Get a good sleep tonight so you can help me in the morning. We need to break down the camp and get everything packed. I need help with that. You know how the little ones get underfoot."

Hope sniffled and nodded. "You aren't going to take them to Aunt Ann?"

"No."

"Like Ike?"

"No."

"He was sick, and they had to send him to his grandma to get better."

"That's right," Adrienne agreed. "But you're not sick, are you?"

"No. I'm as healthy as a horse." Hope puffed her chest out. "I never get sick."

"Then I need you right here with me to help me out."

"Okay."

"Now, go get ready." Adrienne looked over at the tent. They could hear giggling and bickering intertwining as the children got themselves and each other ready. "Tell the others to knock it off and get in the beds, or there's gonna be trouble when I get in there!"

Hope laughed and crawled into the tent, where she repeated the threat loudly. There was silence for a moment, then whispers, and, before long, they were all giggling and playing together again.

"Thank you for giving us the night," Adrienne said.

"I'm so sorry that I can't let you stay here."

"I know. I didn't think you would. But it would have been nice if it had worked. The kids could walk to school. It would be so nice to be so close to everything."

"What will you do?"

"Homeschool, like usual. Find somewhere farther out… where people won't be as likely to bother us."

"Out where the others are? Jenny and the other families?"

Adrienne shook her head. "No… maybe for a day or two until we sort something out. But I couldn't live out there. Not where…" She dropped her eyes and swallowed.

Erin understood. Not where Rip had been killed. It didn't feel safe to Adrienne. The others might have decided to overlook the tragedy, but she couldn't.

"We'll find somewhere else," Adrienne said.

"Do you have a husband? Someone to help you?"

"Sometimes," Adrienne said with a shrug. She didn't offer any more. Maybe, like Rip, her husband was not reliable, taking off to gamble or pursue other vices.

Or maybe he was gone looking for work. Or employed in a work camp hours away. Erin shouldn't judge someone she'd never even heard of by the same standards as someone as self-destructive as Rip Ryder.

CHAPTER 33

At home, Erin didn't tell Terry about the family living in the woods or the fact that she had put them on notice that they had to leave. It was her property, and she wasn't required to report trespassers or squatters to the police. She had taken care of it on her own. Without Adele's or Terry's help. Although she felt terrible for having to do it, she was proud of herself for having the strength to just go ahead and do what she knew had to be done.

There was more to Erin Price than met the eye. She wasn't a shrinking violet. Wasn't just a baker or a business owner. She was the type of person who stepped up and did what needed to be done.

But she was glad it was done and out of the way and hoped that Adrienne would just quietly move her family out of the woods without Erin having to do anything more about it. She knew that squatters could be hard to get rid of. Sometimes a person had to get the police or courts involved to get them off of the property. She really hoped that Adrienne would not be like that.

Instead, when she and Terry sat down to relax and visit for a while before bed, she asked him about Jenny. She had inquired before, when they had been at the restaurant with Vic and Willie, but the conversation had not gone in the direction she had hoped.

"How was Jenny Ryder when you told her about her husband?" she asked. "I wonder if I should go out there again… see if there is anything I can help with. I feel bad, her being alone with a new baby and all of those kids. It can't be easy for her."

"I'm sure it isn't. But I'm not sure she would accept any help, even though your intentions are pure. People don't like it when you poke your nose into their business."

"I know. But how was she?"

Terry considered what he could tell her. "She was… not as emotional as I expected. But that doesn't mean anything. Everyone has their own way to deal with grief. Some people weep and wail, and others nod and go on as if you had told them what time it is. Neither one tells you how close they were or how they are really feeling."

Erin nodded. "And you don't know how they are going to act after you're gone… or after a few days when it starts to sink in."

"Exactly. Someone like Jenny Ryder, who has led such a hard life, will be used to dealing with opposition and not showing any sign of weakness. So I wouldn't expect her to bawl her eyes out in front of me. I would have expected more… but that doesn't mean anything."

"What is she going to do?"

"I couldn't tell you."

"How is she going to be able to manage? With those kids and a new baby and no breadwinner? What is she going to do?"

"I am not privy to her life plan. Maybe she has a business we don't know about. Knitting. Reading audiobooks. Writing web content. Just because she doesn't own land or a house, that doesn't mean that she's necessarily destitute. Some people like to live off the land. Not to put all of their hard-earned cash into real estate."

Erin hadn't thought about that. She was only assuming that they were poor because they were homeless and because the children looked skinny and were not well-dressed. But they could just as easily be burning off a lot of energy playing outside, and their clothes reflected that fact. Or Jenny didn't see the need to get expensive new clothing when they were living out in the sticks and just bought whatever she could get cheaply at a thrift store. Or she was given clothing by other members of the community.

"She could be like the millionaire rancher," Erin said. "He walks into a store in blue jeans, with manure on his boots, and everyone assumes he's just some kind of laborer. When he might own half the county and likes working with his hands."

"I doubt if Jenny is a millionaire rancher."

"But she could be anything."

"Yes, exactly."

"Do you think... what did she say to you about the remains? I assume if you're done gathering all of the evidence you need, she has to claim the remains if she wants to bury or cremate him."

"Or she can *not* claim them and leave it to the county to dispose of them."

"Is that what she's going to do?"

"She didn't say specifically. I told her she could contact the funeral home in town and they would help her with the arrangements and request his remains... but she didn't say if she was going to. Just thanked me. There really wasn't much for me to do. She didn't want to talk about Ryder or what might have happened."

"Not at all? She must have said something."

"I had my questions... but she wasn't too inclined to answer. I got only grudging answers as to how long it had been since she saw him last, where she thought he had gone, and so on."

"I gathered from what she and the others said that they figured he was off drinking or gambling. Or maybe off with another woman. They weren't terribly complimentary about him."

Terry nodded. "Yeah. I don't think she had an easy time with him. Some people say that a marriage certificate doesn't make a difference, but I think in a case like that... a marriage certificate would at least say he was committed to the relationship. And the lack of one showed that he wasn't."

Erin nodded. And what about her relationship with Terry? They hadn't ever talked about getting married, rarely even alluded to it. She knew that as far as the Baptist ladies were concerned, she was committing a sin by having a relationship with Terry without being married to him. She had been the temptress who had come into Bald Eagle Falls and led the most eligible bachelor into sin. While Terry was not a regular church-goer, he was a Christian, and therefore a good catch for the young women in the church.

Where would their relationship go? Erin wasn't sure. But if she'd been entertaining the thought of having children with him, she thought she would want to be married first.

"Were all of Jenny's children Rip's? Or was she with somebody else before?"

Terry cleared his throat. "That didn't come up in the conversation. She wasn't very inclined to talk as it was. I think that if I was to start off with questions like that… I might not have gotten any answers to the rest of my questions."

Erin laughed. "I suppose asking a woman who her children were fathered by might not start you off on the best foot."

Terry took a drag from his beer, nodding slightly in agreement.

"She had… how many? Five? Including the baby?"

"I didn't ever get a really good count. They were running around and playing games. And who knows if all the children were even hers. I think the families there kind of watch whoever's kids happen to be over. They're camped close enough together that the kids can mix."

Erin got the inkling of an idea. She frowned, thinking about it for a moment, and then reached for her planner to start jotting down a list.

"Uh-oh," Terry intoned. "What is it now?"

"No, it's nothing. I was just thinking that before when I was trying to give them food, I said that I thought they didn't have enough to eat. That they were too poor to be able to look after themselves."

"Yes…?"

"What if I took over a care package, but it wasn't because they need food, but because they just lost their father and husband. Or almost-husband. People take each other food when they've lost someone. Casseroles, desserts, things for the funeral, food that they can just warm up so they don't have to think ahead or do any work in the beginning, when it is so hard and they might be entertaining guests."

"Ah. So you think you could take food over there and say it was for the funeral."

"Right. And people take food to mothers with new babies too. To cut down on the amount of work they need to do. And Jenny has both. She's lost Rip and she has a new baby. If anyone needs a lighter load, it's her."

"Maybe you've found your way around the pride thing."

"I hope so. And I was thinking—it was because of what you said—that if I can get a load of food to Jenny, that with the other kids coming and going, *they* can get enough to eat too. There will be too much for just the Ryders. If their community really does take care of each other, then they'll distribute the food around the rest of the families, so that everyone gets some, and no one is singled out as being more needy."

"So, what are you writing out?"

"Just… what I think I should take out with me."

"You're not just going to take all of your day old out with you?"

"Well… no. I have some in the freezer, plus whatever is left over tomorrow, but I might want a few extra little things too… just to make it a little easier. And maybe if I pick up a few things from the grocery store…"

"You'll end up crossing the line. From a thoughtful gift to making them feel like it is charity."

"Oh." Erin sighed. "Okay. I'll scale back. Not too much. Do you think… if I mention it to the ladies who come to the bakery, some of them might contribute too?"

Terry considered this, his fingernails scraping across his five o'clock shadow. "I don't think very many of the church ladies feel like the squatters are… part of the flock. But if you mention it to them… maybe make the assumption that they would behave in a properly Christian manner toward the needy whether they are members of the congregation or not… I think that the guilt would probably ensure that you got a few donations."

"Good." Erin nodded. Over the next couple of days, there should be a good number of the ladies coming in to stock up for Sunday dinner. Most of them liked to have soft white rolls to go with their roast beef dinner or whatever their traditional family meal was on Sunday. She could go out to see Jenny after the ladies' tea on Sunday, assured of having a good amount of food for her and the other families in the settlement.

"Don't forget about refrigeration," Terry warned. "If you overdo it on the casseroles, they are just going to spoil. Those families don't have refrigeration."

"Oh. Okay. Yeah. I wouldn't have thought about that. I'll encourage the ladies to donate foods that are shelf-stable, if they can."

"Cream of mushroom soup will be better for the squatters in the can than in a casserole."

"Right. And it's less work for the church ladies." Erin smiled. "Win-win."

~

Erin managed to work the homeless families into casual conversations with her customers over the next couple of days. It was fairly easy to bring them up, with the shocking news of Rip's death. It was still at the top of people's minds, and all Erin had to do was talk sadly about the family Rip had left behind. His destitute widow and fatherless children, including a newborn. So sad, and she hoped that a lot of people would help out, showing a lost sheep that they cared.

"How many children are there?" Lottie Sturm demanded. "We should get their names and ages to put on the prayer list."

"Oh… yes. I can find out," Erin agreed. "I guess… when I'm out there…?"

"We should know before you go out," Lottie disagreed. "We should be praying that the spirit will move them when they receive our gifts. That their hearts will be softened and open to the promptings of the Holy Spirit so that they recommit their lives to him."

Erin swallowed. She nodded her agreement. "Sure. Of course. But, um… how am I going to find that out before I go out to see them? They don't have a phone, I can't reach them that way."

"Talk to the school. You explain what it's for, and they'll give you the names and ages of the children."

"I don't think they go to the school. They're outside the city, and I think they probably homeschool. It would be too far for them to drive in every day."

"Well then, you can still go to the school for their records."

"If they homeschool…"

"They have to register with the school district," Lottie said with a firm nod. "That's the law. If they don't, they risk getting in trouble for the kids being truant. They don't want trouble with the police and the school district."

"Oh. I didn't know they did that. Okay. Do I just… you think the office would give me that kind of information? Isn't it confidential?"

"Not if you ask the right way," Lottie assured her confidently. "You're not asking for anything confidential—just first names and ages. You don't need last names, or marks, or what grades they are registered for, or birthdates, or any of that kind of thing. Just first name and age. Everybody in the community already knows that information, so it can't be confidential. They're just making things easier so that you don't have to go to all of the other families and say, 'Are any of your kids the same age as any of the Ryder kids? And what are their names?' They're just collating the information for you. That's all."

Erin laughed. She had a feeling that the school might see it differently, but she could at least try. If the school couldn't help, then maybe she could talk to the Fosters and to Adrienne. Between the two families, they would probably know the names of all of the Ryder children.

CHAPTER 34

As it turned out, dealing with the school was easier than she had expected. Instead of going into the office, she called up Vice Principal Fitzroy, whom she had coordinated the bake sale with. He had been perfectly happy to help. After alternately cursing and cajoling the computer for a few minutes, he had managed to make it give him first Jenny's full name, and then those of each of her children's.

"They're not all school age yet," he told Erin. "But the district registers them with early childhood learning in situations like this, so that they can evaluate whether any interventions are needed and we know who is coming up before they are in first grade. It's important with families like this who are..." he dropped his voice confidentially, "indigent. Less likely to be seeing doctors or public health nurses. If you have a child in need of early language intervention, and you don't find out about them until they are six, well that just won't do. It's early language intervention. And it isn't so early if you wait until they are six or seven."

Erin made noises of agreement. She was afraid that if she asked anything, Vice Principal Fitzroy would tell her all of the family's confidential issues, and she didn't want to know them.

"So the oldest child's name was..." she prompted, hoping to get him back on track.

Fitzroy read off the name of the oldest child, age eight, and went down the line to the two-year-old. Erin wrote each of them down.

"And then she has a newborn," she added. "I don't know his name."

"Oh, does she have another one?" Fitzroy asked. "We'll need to get his details. I don't suppose you could do me a return favor…?"

"I'll do my best," Erin promised. "Thank you for everything."

Terry offered to go out to see Jenny again with Erin, but she knew that Jenny probably would not take too kindly to her bringing a policeman with her. Terry had done the death notification, so it wasn't like she wouldn't know that he was on the police force.

Instead, she went with Vic in Willie's truck, like they had done the previous time. It was quicker this time, since they knew where Jenny was. At least, Erin hoped that she had stayed in the place and had not run away or gone deeper into the woods with her children. Erin found herself holding her breath as they went down the last road, straining for a view of the children and the tents. When they came into view, she nearly cheered aloud. She let out her breath.

"Good, then. That's good. She's still here."

Vic nodded her agreement. The children stopped playing to watch the truck pull in, and then went back to their games. They had seen this truck and these women before. It wasn't novel enough to end their game.

Jenny was lying on a blanket on the grass with her sleeping baby snuggled up to her, the dappled shadows from the trees overhead swaying back and forth over the baby's bare skin.

Wasn't it bad for him to have sunlight directly on his delicate skin? The UV rays couldn't be good for him. It wasn't direct summer sun, but still… Erin would have thought that you had to be more careful with a baby. Keep him wrapped up to protect his skin.

Jenny opened her eyes and watched them approach, but did not get up or invite them to come any closer.

"Hi," Erin greeted cheerfully. "I don't know if you remember us. We were here the other day and…"

"Of course I remember you," Jenny growled. "I don't get a lot of women coming in from town to harass me."

Erin got closer. She didn't like towering over Jenny, so she set down her bulky box and sat down on the ground close by, watching Jenny and the baby. "We're not trying to harass you. We just want you to… be a part of our community."

"Well, I'm not, am I?" Jenny challenged.

"You are. A bunch of the ladies have sent you some supplies. Because of your—Rip dying, and you having a new baby. One of those things that they do to help out members of the community going through life's challenges. I'm sure you know how these ladies are always making casseroles and desserts when there is a funeral or a new baby born. They know how hard it can be to have to cook on top of everything else."

Erin looked at Vic, hoping for some help, but Vic just nodded that she was doing fine and didn't contribute anything.

Jenny looked at Erin suspiciously. "The church ladies sent casseroles," she said. "Because of Rip dying? They hated Rip."

"I don't think they knew Rip well enough to hate him. Besides, that wouldn't be very Christian." Erin delved into the box and pulled out a can of soup. "I told them that I didn't think you had any way to refrigerate or freeze casseroles, so they should send foods that were easy to prepare and eat that didn't have to be refrigerated."

Jenny's eyes went wide, and the children stopped playing, instantly aware of the food.

"There are a few things in here that will have to be eaten pretty quickly," Erin admitted. "Not everything is shelf-stable. But you can eat those things first…"

"Sometimes we put things in a cold stream to help keep them chilled," Jenny offered. "I mean… not casseroles, but fruit and vegetables… drinks…"

"What a great idea. I would never have thought of that." There were probably a lot of things that Erin wouldn't have thought about. Not until she was actually out in the wilds and had to think up things that would help her to survive.

Jenny nodded slowly. She propped herself up on one elbow. The baby stirred and made little mewling sounds, then settled again and was quiet. Erin gazed at him.

"What's his name?"

"Little Ike. After his granddaddy."

Ike seemed like a strange name for a baby. But they would probably call him by some nickname until he got older. Peanut. Boo. Junior. He'd grow into his own name eventually. The baby was tiny. Erin could hardly believe that he was big enough to be out of the hospital, but she knew that he had to be a couple of weeks old.

"What day was he born?"

Jenny's brows drew down, and a V wrinkle appeared between them.

"How much did he weigh?" Erin went on, trying to demonstrate that she was just asking all of the normal questions that someone would ask about a new baby, not being nosy.

Jenny stroked the top of his downy head with one finger. "The third," she said finally. "And… we didn't weigh him right away. I don't have a scale out here. But we took him to the doctor last week, and they said he was five pounds."

"So he's really small. Was he early?"

The other woman was still frowning at Erin, not liking all of the questions. "Maybe a little. I usually have small ones. Thank goodness," she rolled her eyes, "I don't know how I'd manage to squeeze a bigger one out!"

Erin laughed. "I've heard people say that bigger ones are easier, but I don't know how that could be true."

Jenny put her hand over her lower pelvis. "Ouch. No, I think that's just a story."

"You didn't have him at the hospital, then?" Vic asked. "Just by yourself? Did you have a midwife?"

Erin looked again over the little camp. Had Jenny had the baby out there? In a dusty tent, with no doctor around? What if something had gone wrong? What if she had been in trouble or the baby had not been breathing when he was born?

"I had a friend," Jenny said cautiously. "Women have been taking care of other women having babies for centuries. There's nothing wrong with that."

"That must have been scary," Erin suggested.

"He's not my first baby. Maybe for my first one, I'd want a midwife or to be close to a doctor, but I've had a few before." Jenny looked around at her other children, who had resumed playing.

"I suppose."

Jenny shifted the baby, snuggling him up against her body. "He had a bit of jaundice. They get yellow, you know. The ones that are little are more likely to get it. In the hospital, they put them under special lamps. But the sun is just as good. The doctor said that was just fine, as long as he's not in direct sun for too long. Just getting lots of sunlight on his skin helps break down the yellow stuff."

So it wasn't bad for him to be lying there with the sunlight filtering through the trees onto his bare skin. It was actually good for him. Erin felt a little guilty for assuming that it was bad and that Jenny didn't know how to take care of him properly. She had lots of kids. Lots more experience than Erin did. Of course she knew what she was doing.

Erin studied Jenny's face. She looked tired. What did Erin expect? Jenny had too many responsibilities, all of those children, a newborn, and her husband had just been murdered. Anybody would have been gutted by such an experience.

She tried to identify what else she saw there. Jenny's expression was guarded, not liking these women who came to her home expecting her to answer questions and receive their gifts graciously. They should leave soon, let her rest as much as she could.

But there was more than that. She also looked… haunted. Erin didn't know how else to classify the emotion that lay underneath everything else. Like she had seen too much and wanted to be finished. Maybe it was depression? Postpartum? That could be devastating to someone with as many responsibilities as Jenny.

"Do you have someone to help you out?" she asked. "Maybe someone who could take the kids for a little while to give you a break."

"Who would take all of these?" Jenny scoffed, nodding toward them. "Besides, they help me out. The older ones."

"But maybe someone could take a couple of the little ones for a few days. Or a few families could help…"

"Farming them all out to different homes? They belong here, not anywhere else."

"I didn't mean permanently. Just for a little while, until you have things sorted out."

Jenny lay her head down on the blanket again. "I want my kids close to me. You don't know what it's like…"

She had just lost her husband. Of course she wanted her children to be with her, not taken away. They were a comfort to her. They were the only ones who understood what it was like for her to lose Rip.

One of the small children approached them. She stood on her tiptoes to look down into the box without getting too close to Erin. "Can I put the food away, Mama?"

"Yes. Go ahead. If you don't know where something goes, just leave it in the box."

"Is there food goes in the stream?"

"I don't know what's in there. Stay away from the stream right now."

She nodded and got closer. Grasping the edge of the box, she pulled it, sliding it away from Erin toward the tents. It took a lot of hard work for her to pull it over the bumpy ground to the kitchen tent, but she persisted and got it there. When a couple of the other children approached to see what was in the box, she chased them away.

"Selena is a good little mama," Jenny said distantly. "She's always so good with the others."

"She must be a real help to you."

Erin watched Selena pull items out of the box and stack them onto various shelves or corners in the kitchen. She placed the perishables on the table.

"We should be getting on our way and letting you rest. Will you please let me know if you need anything? The church ladies have added you and the children to their prayers lists. I don't know if you are religious or that means anything to you. But I'll give you my number, in case you need something."

"Really?" Jenny raised her brows. "That's nice of them. I never thought those ladies would care anything about us. Not the way they turn up their noses at my kids. We don't need anything," she shook her head, "so you don't need to come out here again."

Erin pushed herself to her feet. "Okay." She had done all she could. "You take care, then."

CHAPTER 35

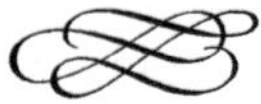

"You've done everything you can," Vic commiserated when they were on the highway again.

Erin let out a long sigh. "I know. I can't think of anything else I could do. I want to help them all out… but what else am I supposed to do?"

"Nothing. You've done everything. You've gone above and beyond."

"Those kids. They deserve better. And Jenny…" Erin shook her head. "She looks so sad. This should be a happy time in her life, just bringing a new baby into the world. But look at what she is facing. Husband murdered. No home. Living out in the middle of nowhere. Six other kids."

"She looked so tired and sad," Vic agreed.

"I just want to hug her. To take all of the kids out for ice cream. To make it all right again. But it's not. Who knows how long it will take for things to turn around for them. If ever."

"I know."

They drove on for a while.

"You know, if you really think that those kids are in danger, or not getting enough to eat, you should call social services," Vic said.

Erin's heart pounded painfully. She couldn't do that to Jenny and her children. Erin knew what it was to be stuck in the system. She wouldn't do that to all of those kids. Unless…

"I don't want to do that. I don't think it's to that level yet… I don't think…"

"Then… you'll just have to let it go. You've done everything else that you could. If you think that Jenny can't take care of the kids, then you need to make a report. But if you think she's doing okay, you'll just have to let her do it her own way."

"There should be lots of berry bushes around there. And other wild foods. There's fresh water. Fish. Birds. Rabbits. Even if Jenny doesn't hunt, they keep saying that the families care for each other, that the community will step up. So they'll all help her when our food runs out."

"There won't be berries for a couple more months," Vic said. "But the rest of that… yeah. Maybe Willie and I will take a couple of hunting weekends and drop some game off for them."

"If they would take it."

"They will if they're hungry enough."

They covered a few more miles before Erin spoke again, so frustrated, her heart feeling like it was being wrung like a wet sponge. "What if one of those kids gets hurt or sick? What are they going to do?"

"Drive them into the city. Go to the hospital there. The same as if a child in Bald Eagle Falls got really sick."

"But they don't even have phones. Or computers to look up symptoms to decide if it is something serious or not. They can't do anything. And what if Jenny is hurt? She injures herself chopping wood or picking up the baby, or scalds herself making breakfast. Who is going to help if she's too badly injured to drive herself?"

"We can't make those decisions for her, Erin. She has to think about it herself, figure out what risks are reasonable. I don't know what else to say. It's true of anyone in town, too. We can't control what people are doing in their own houses. Whether they are cutting something the wrong way, or pouring lighter fluid on a fire, or stepping out into Main Street without making sure there isn't any traffic first."

"Step in front of Beaver, and that could be the end of it," Erin muttered. She laughed bleakly, but there was no joy in it. She didn't snap herself out of her funk with the joke.

"Yes. There's danger everywhere, and we can't do anything about the people who decide to take risks that we wouldn't take. Jenny might think that you're taking stupid risks by living in town, where there are people living practically on top of you. Working in the heat every day. Getting up before the sun just to bake bread for people. Even just making gluten-free products when only a tiny percentage of your customers have celiac disease. She'd think you were stupid, risking your business for such a small segment."

"She'd be wrong."

"Yes. She would. You're running a profitable business and providing an important service. That was the right choice for you."

Erin nodded. "I guess everybody makes different life decisions. But mine don't affect any children. I don't have to worry about whether my kids can eat based on my choice of gluten-free or regular bread. When it's your kids, you have a bigger responsibility. You're not just choosing what you prefer."

"I agree. I'm just saying you can't take it to heart. There's nothing you can do, and she's allowed to make her own choices. If it's not endangering the children, maybe it's time to just let it go."

"Okay. I will."

Erin was not prepared to have Lottie Sturm show up on her front steps. She found the woman difficult enough to deal with when she came to buy bread at the bakery. She was constantly complaining and correcting other people. If Erin was not around or paying attention, she would start preaching at Vic or railing about the evil choices of modern-day youth. She had been warned more than once to mind herself while she was there, but if she thought she could get away with something, she would.

Erin opened the door and didn't know what to say to Lottie. She forced a smile and nodded at her, waiting for her to state her business.

"We've been praying over those poor Ryder children," Lottie explained, fluttering the paper that Erin had given her at the ladies' tea that morning. Had she been praying ever since then? And who was 'we'? Erin knew that Lottie was good friends with Cindy Prost, who was Bella's mother and another difficult-to-manage customer. Were she and Lottie praying together? Or was it a whole covey of the Baptist ladies? It had been a long day, and Erin was sure their knees must be tired and their mouths dry if they had been praying all that time.

"That's so kind of you," Erin said. "I saw Jenny this afternoon, and I told her that you were. She seemed… it seemed like it meant something to her."

"It should," Lottie agreed in a firm voice. "I came by to find out if you had any information on the baby? I understood that you were going to get its name and birthday as well."

Erin nodded. "Yes. Of course. It's a boy. Ike. And he was born on the third."

Lottie fished in her purse for a pen. Erin knew she should invite Lottie in to make it easier for her to juggle things, but she didn't want to have to entertain the woman any longer than was absolutely necessary. She waited while Lottie got the pen out and then lay the paper flat against the door to write the information. She frowned and shook her head.

"No, I've already got an Ike, age five."

"Well… that's what she said. Maybe the school got something wrong."

"You wouldn't have two Ikes in the same family."

Erin had been in foster families where there were two children with the same name. But that was foster care, not a family naming two of their children the same thing.

"Well… it does happen sometimes. People give their children the same name, but they go by a second name or a nickname. Like… George Foreman and Michael Jackson."

Lottie rolled her eyes and shook her head. Erin didn't want to hear her rantings about the people Erin had picked as examples. "Maybe they're both named after a grandfather, or it's a family name. Vice Principal Fitzroy wouldn't necessarily know if the boy who went to school went by… I don't know, Charles instead of Ike. He just gave me the first names of the kids that showed up on his records. That's different than actually knowing the kids and what their preferences were."

"I suppose that's it," Lottie said. She wrote the information down with a scowl. "I don't know how we're supposed to pray for two separate children with the same name. We have to have some way of differentiating them."

"You could say 'Ike who is six and Ike who is a baby,'" Erin suggested.

"But isn't your God all-knowing? So he would know even if you called them both by the same name. He wouldn't even need names."

"You need their names," Lottie argued. "That's how you do a prayer list. You have to have names."

Erin shrugged and shook her head. "Well, now you have the names."

Lottie muttered something under her breath and turned away. Erin waited until Lottie was at the bottom of the steps and quietly closed the door behind her. She let out a whistle and didn't know how else to react. Laugh at Lottie? Call Vic and tell her about the conversation? She felt silly and giddy and knew that she had probably been up for too long and needed to go to bed.

"Holy cow," she said aloud to herself. "I do declare!" She giggled at herself.

Erin was restless knowing that Terry was on night shift. He had been doing mostly afternoons since he had gotten back from his leave, which was good for all of them. She didn't worry much about that. Because of his brain injury and insomnia, the sheriff had promised not to put him on nights. But Terry had since recovered from his constant headaches and insomnia. The sheriff had decided it was time to put him back into the rotation. The others had had to cover all of the night shifts, and Terry said it was time for him to start pulling his weight again.

He'd been doing really well, but she couldn't help worrying that it could set him back again. The doctors had said that he needed to get a good night's sleep if he were going to recover fully. They called for good sleep hygiene habits, which Erin knew meant going to bed and getting up at the same time every day. Not working various different shifts that meant that he had to sleep during the day sometimes and the night others.

Because of their schedules, Terry was just getting home as Erin and Vic were having their morning tea. After kissing him good morning, Erin gestured to the kettle. "Did you want some?"

"No, I'll make my own beverage, thanks." Terry went to the fridge and pulled out a beer. He said that one beer before bed helped him sleep better than any of the other sleep aids the doctors had prescribed. And it wasn't like he was getting drunk. He was very good about keeping it to one drink. Doctors said that was healthy. Erin's experiences with men who did drink too much colored her perception. She tried to remain nonjudgmental and not to let it make her anxious. She knew that Terry was not a drunk and rarely ever had more than one drink in a day.

She smiled at him and turned back to Vic, relating to her the visit from Lottie. Vic nodded, grinning.

"You never know what people are going to name their kids in backwoods Tennessee. I've seen families where all of the brothers and first cousins have the same given name." She giggled. "They're all named after granddaddy and great-granddaddy, of course. So they all have different nicknames, and you have Big Ike and Little Ike and Slim Ike and Red Ike..."

Erin shook her head. "Lottie acted like I must have gotten it wrong. But I wrote everything down right there when Vice Principal Fitzroy was giving it to me, and you heard Jenny say that the baby's name was Ike, right?"

"I did."

Something tickled at the back of Erin's brain. She considered, trying to nail down what it was.

"What?" Vic prompted.

"No, I'm just... trying to remember... something..."

"Don't try too hard, I can see the smoke coming out of your ears..." Vic teased.

"You do not! It's just that I've heard the name Ike before."

"I'm sure you have."

"No. Recently. Just the last few days."

She tried to run through the various different scenarios. One of Jenny's children had mentioned Ike before; she must have been talking about Big Ike. Or was it someone else?

"Oh, no. It wasn't," Erin corrected herself aloud. "It was Adrienne's daughter."

"Adrienne's daughter is named Ike too?"

"What did Willie put in your cornflakes this morning? You're in a silly mood!"

"I don't know. Just trying to keep things light, I guess. I don't want to be sad and solemn all day. Yesterday was too serious."

"Yeah. It was." Erin wanted to move on too. She looked at her watch. "Well, we'd better get going. I guess I'll see you later," she told Terry. "Have a good sleep."

"I will," he agreed. He gave her another kiss, and she and Vic headed out.

CHAPTER 36

Erin continued to puzzle over what she only half-remembered from the visit to Adrienne. She talked it through with Vic in the afternoon lull.

"I'm sure it was Adrienne's little girl that talked about Ike. Something about… Ike had to go with Grandma, something like that."

"So it must be like I said. A bunch of the first cousins are all named after Grandpa Ike."

"Then Adrienne and Jenny must be related." Erin frowned, thinking it through. "Adrienne never said that she was related to Jenny. But if their kids were first cousins, then wouldn't that mean…"

"That Adrienne and Jenny were sisters. Or maybe sisters-in-law."

"They're both blond and slim," Erin said slowly. "But they really don't look like each other."

"Sister don't always look similar. Or like I said, they could be in-laws. Or it could be Great-Grandpa Ike, and Adrienne and Jenny are cousins. Or even further back than that. Sometimes these names get recycled over and over again with every generation."

"Maybe I should talk to Adrienne again. She was a lot easier to talk to than Jenny. Not that either one was easy, but Adrienne was grateful to me for letting her stay on the property for the night, so maybe she'd be more likely to talk to me again. I don't think Jenny is going to."

"But why talk to either of them again? They're living their own lives and it really isn't anything to do with you. Why keep bothering them?"

"I just… want to know." Erin didn't want to put into words what she was thinking, not even to herself. She wanted Adrienne to agree with Vic's suggestion. It would give a nice clear answer to the problem with the names. That would make Erin feel better and then she would be able to go on without worrying any more about it.

"Well… we'll go look for her after work, then," Vic agreed. "Do you know where she moved to? Or if she moved like you asked her to?"

"I didn't check… but I haven't smelled their cooking again, so I don't think they're close by."

"Or maybe they just moved downwind."

"Well… I guess. But Adele knows that I told them to move on, so she wouldn't let them camp on the property again."

"Unless she did."

Erin rolled her eyes. Adele had allowed them to stay there to start with, even though she knew it was her job to make sure that no one trespassed on Erin's private land. It was a possibility.

"I don't think she's still there. I bet she moved back out of town, over where the others are staying. Somewhere close to them, anyway, where they won't be bothered."

"Well, we'll go check," Vic promised.

They closed up as quickly as they could without unbalancing the schedule for the next morning. Some of the batters that they normally mixed the night before and left soaking overnight could be made the next day without too much change in texture. And Erin could hold over a few muffins and loaves from the day before to let the batters soak longer, and make them a little later in the day than usual. Just so they could get out a bit early to go talk to Adrienne. She might be close by, or she might have moved back toward where Jenny and the others were.

Erin went into the house to drop off a couple of things, startling Terry.

"You're home early!" He held his hand over his chest, eyes wide, and laughed at himself.

"Just a few minutes," Erin admitted. "I'm just going to put these things down. Vic and I are going to take Nilla out for a walk."

Terry looked at her, eyes narrowed. Erin kept her face blank. They *were* going to take Nilla out. It wasn't a lie.

Terry nodded. "Sounds good. That will probably be good for him. Work off some of that extra energy."

"Yeah. He hasn't exactly settled down as much as Vic would like!"

"It's a crime that dog was not properly trained while he was a puppy. I realize that there's a big difference between terriers and shepherds," Terry looked at K9, "but a dog has so much more potential when it is properly trained. You add to and encourage its natural abilities. That little dog could be an asset if he was trained, instead of a little whirlwind of destruction whenever there's no one looking after him."

Erin nodded her agreement.

"But Vic's doing her best, and the dog training people said that it's still possible to properly train an older dog. It just takes longer and is more of a challenge."

"Well, I hope it starts paying off soon. Vic shouldn't have her property torn apart just because she did a nice thing and rescued a dog without an owner."

"Yeah." Erin inched toward the back door. She wanted to make use of as much of the daylight as they could.

"And you don't want it destroying the value of that apartment or the yard. Vic won't be here forever and if you want to rent it to someone else after her, you don't want to have to strip the whole thing out and start over."

"She's not leaving any time soon…"

"Maybe not. But you can never be sure. She won't necessarily tell you if she and Willie start looking at a bigger place. Or decide that Vic should move into Willie's house."

Erin frowned. Vic was out in the back yard with Nilla, waiting for Erin. Erin didn't want to think of her ever leaving the loft apartment. It would be so strange living in Bald Eagle Falls without Vic close at hand, coming into the kitchen in the morning, the two of them going into work together…

"I didn't say she was leaving," Terry said apologetically. "Just that you don't know when it could happen."

"You're right. I've got to go. Back in a bit."

CHAPTER 37

Nilla was excited about being outside and being allowed to go into the woods, which were usually off limits. He didn't seem to understand the constraints of the leash and kept getting himself tangled around tree trunks and in the underbrush. Erin was frustrated at their slow progress. It was going to take forever to search anything but the areas closest to the house with him charging around like a Tasmanian devil.

"I'm just going to run ahead and see if she's still at the same site as she was earlier," she told Vic.

If Adrienne had moved farther away but was still in Erin's woods, it would take time to locate her, and Erin wasn't willing to wait for the crazy little powderpuff.

"Okay. Sorry about this. We'll catch up as soon as I can get him untangled. I guess the woods were not such a great idea when he still hasn't gotten the idea of heeling."

"Yeah, it's okay, I just want to check."

Erin picked up her pace and hurried toward the corner Adrienne had been camped in before. Erin had soon left Vic behind and was on her own. She felt a little anxious and uncertain, but she knew the woods and there was no danger. Adele patrolled it for any unsavory characters. Any wild animals would be more afraid of Erin than she was of them. At least, that was what Terry said. Mostly, the big predators didn't come right into the town.

She looked around quickly and kept moving. Keep moving and making noise, and they would run away before she even saw them. Animals were afraid of humans.

Except when they weren't.

As she used the game trails and looked for the place Adrienne had camped, she couldn't help thinking of the squatters' children playing in the trees right out there in the wilds. A predator might never consider taking a grown adult, but a child, small and light, was easy to drag off... what if something was hungry, or wasn't spooked by the sounds of the children playing? What if it went closer for a look, and saw the young prey scampering around completely unprotected? Even worse, what if the children were back and forth between the camps, through the woods on their own, so that no adult knew which children were where? It could be hours before someone realized that a child was missing. Especially if they didn't have phones to connect with each other.

Erin was spooking herself. By the time she reached Adrienne's abandoned campsite, she was jumping at every branch blowing in the wind and the noises of squirrels or rabbits in the bush. She turned a circle, looking around the clearing and waiting for her heart to settle back into a normal rhythm.

"Adrienne? Are you here?" It was obvious that she wasn't, but Erin still wanted to make sure. Willie had said that Ryder, even when told to move on, had only moved a short distance away, believing that he was no longer on Willie's property. Adrienne might have moved her camp and assumed that Erin would not look any farther than the clearing.

Erin looked at her watch. It wasn't getting dark yet, but it was getting closer to sunset, and she knew they would lose the daylight quickly. She hadn't brought her big flashlight with her and had not planned to search in the darkness.

She called a few more times, circled around the outside of the clearing looking for any sign that the little family had just dragged their gear to the next likely spot. But she couldn't see any indication of what direction they had gone.

Vic caught up to her, panting a little and keeping Nilla on a very short leash to keep him from getting tangled again. "No Adrienne?"

"No. I don't see her around here. She must have gone out to where the others are." Erin sighed. "Do you think we could go out there tonight? It's going to be getting dark by the time we get out there."

Vic studied her. "It's not that urgent."

"I know." But to Erin, it was. "But do you think we could anyway? Otherwise, we have to wait until tomorrow, and she could have moved farther away. It's possible that she's already gone."

"And it's just as possible that she's staying with the rest of the families out there. Especially if they are all related. If Jenny is her sister, she's not going to be so quick to take off. They could help each other out trading off babysitting so that they can get work or errands done. And to keep the kids close."

Erin nodded. But she worried there were reasons for Adrienne or Jenny, or both of them, to run away and get out of Tennessee, or at least far away from Bald Eagle Falls. Vic shrugged.

"If you want. Sure. We'd better move it, because like you say, it's going to be dark soon. Not only that, but we're going to want to get some sleep tonight."

Erin breathed a sigh of relief. She supposed she could have gone out there by herself, but she was much happier if Vic went with her.

They retreated to the house as quickly as they could. Nilla started prancing excitedly around the truck, and Vic laughed. "I guess someone likes going for a ride." She opened the driver's side door, and Nilla leaped up into the seat like a cat. Erin wouldn't have guessed that he would be able to jump so high.

"I'll just let Terry know that we're going out."

Vic raised her eyebrows. She had a pretty good idea that Terry was going to ask questions about the necessity for the sudden trip out looking for the family.

Erin went into the house through the back door and retrieved her purse from under a sleepy orange cat. "Vic and I are going to run some errands. Won't be too long."

"Where are you going?" Terry called from the bedroom.

Erin ignored the question and hurried back out. Vic was in the driver's seat, tapping on her phone, and looked surprised to see Erin.

"That was quick."

"Just needed my purse. I don't want to… waste any time."

"Okay. Off we go."

They avoided further discussion about why Erin felt such a burning need to go talk to Adrienne. Erin didn't want to explain what she was thinking, in case speaking it made it true. She knew it was magical thinking and not logical, but she still found herself irrationally superstitious sometimes. She just wanted to be proven wrong. Then no one would know how close she had come to believing the worst of someone.

"Which property do you want to go to first?"

"I guess… Willie's. He hasn't been out there the last day or two, right? So he wouldn't know if she was camped there. We know they've used it before."

"I wouldn't think they'd want to camp there when someone has been kicked off already. And since… Rip died there. People tend not to want to hang around places where relatives died."

"It's the closest property, so we might as well check it out first."

Vic couldn't argue with that. So they went to the property the Ryders had previously camped on.

The clearing that Jenny had used was not occupied but, in looking around, Erin saw that there was a small group of tents on the other side of the fence. She recognized the army surplus tent.

Erin and Vic got out of the truck. Nilla raced around crazily, yipping and running in fast loops.

"That dog is possessed," Erin laughed.

"Just happy not to be cooped up in an apartment," Vic said.

With the noise the dog was making, Adrienne couldn't very well be unaware of their arrival. She walked around from the back of one of the tents with a pot in her hand. She looked from Erin to Vic, angry.

"We're not on your claim. You can't kick us off."

"Whoever owns this land could," Vic pointed out reasonably.

"Nobody owns this land. No one cares that we are here."

Vic shrugged. "Maybe not. We're not here to kick you out anyway." She tilted her head toward Erin. "We just wanted to talk to you."

"Talk to me? Fine, go ahead. Talk to me."

Erin cleared her throat. It was awkward to begin. She hadn't planned on the meeting being so confrontational. She thought she and Adrienne understood each other. Adrienne had known that Erin didn't want to kick them out. That she had been nice to them and given the kids granola bars.

If she'd had a chance to talk to Jenny, she knew that Erin had brought plenty of supplies for the little settlement. But Adrienne wasn't happy to see her, she was defensive and resentful.

"I'm sorry. I didn't mean to upset you. I just want to talk."

"So, talk."

Erin cast about for how to start. "When we were talking before, then one of your kids said something about Ike. Is Ike one of your kids, or…?"

Adrienne's eyes were narrow and suspicious. "No, I don't have an Ike." She shrugged. "Why?"

"It's nothing, I guess. It just seemed like there was more than one Ike around, and it was confusing."

Adrienne stared at her.

"Does Jenny have one named Ike, then?" Erin asked, as if she didn't already know the answer.

"She might."

Erin knew that Adrienne and Jenny were close enough to know the names of each other's children. What did she know that she was hiding?

"Her older boy, his name is Ike, right? He's eight?"

One of the children piped up, a little boy with dark hair peeking out from behind the tent. "No! Ike is five, like me!"

There were giggles from other children, out of sight. Adrienne whipped around to look at him. "Samuel Andrew, do you want a hiding? Quit listening in on other people's conversations and go play. All of you. Go on. This is just boring grown-up stuff. Go find some skipping stones."

There was the sound of little feet running away and more giggles. Samuel stood up taller where he had been hiding so that Erin could see more of him. His bottom lip stuck out. "But it's true. Ike is five."

Adrienne swung the pot that was in her hand. Not to throw it at him, but drenching him with the water that it contained. At least, Erin hoped it was water. Samuel yelped and ran away. Adrienne lowered the pot and looked at Erin, the corner of her mouth twitching. Vic burst into peals of laughter. Erin tried to keep a straight face but was unable to stop a huge grin from splitting her face.

After the tension that had dominated the conversation, it was a huge relief to laugh at little Samuel getting soaked by his mother. The three of them just shook their heads and laughed, relaxing for the first time. Adrienne set her pot down on the ground.

"I declare… when I was a young 'un, I thought my parents knew everything, including how to raise a family. It is *terrifying* to think that they didn't have any better idea than I do now. You're just winging it every day. Right, wrong, you have no clue." She gave a single laugh. "Don't ever have children."

"It looks very… challenging," Vic said, still trying to smother her giggles.

"And it's twice as challenging as it looks. Or a hundred times. Hundreds of little decisions every day, and I don't think more than half of them are right. It's a wonder any of them survive childhood." She sobered suddenly and looked away.

Death wasn't funny. Not when their community had been touched by it so recently. Soaking a pouting child with water was funny. Thinking about their deaths was not.

"Sorry," Erin said, though she wasn't sure what she was actually apologizing for. For reminding Adrienne about what had happened? For coming out and bothering her again, when they just wanted to be left alone?

Sorry for all of the challenges that had brought Adrienne to that place.

Adrienne sighed. "There has been so much going on. Too much, I think. We're all feeling it. I know you've been trying to be kind and helpful. It's just come at a really bad time, and we're not very trusting of outsiders. You want to be nice, but you don't know how disconcerting it is for us to deal with this behavior."

"With what? With being nice?"

Adrienne nodded, then wrinkled her nose and scratched her ear. "When you're not used to it… when all you're used to is people ignoring you, or chasing your kids off, or shouting at you to get a job… then having someone go against all of those conventions and treat you like a real person… I don't know what to do with that. I'm sure it's the same for Jenny. We're just waiting for the other shoe to drop. To find out what's really behind all of this nice behavior."

Erin nodded slowly, understanding. She knew how anxious she would get at a foster home that she'd only been at for a few days, trying to discern where the dangers were. She would be very off balance until she figured out the rules and the personalities of a new place.

"Well, I'm sorry," Erin said, tongue in cheek, "for being so nice."

Adrienne smiled and nodded. She looked in the direction the children had run. "I think I'd better check in and make sure that they're staying together and no one has fallen into the water. You ladies… can get on your way."

Erin and Vic nodded and headed back toward the truck.

CHAPTER 38

As they walked toward the truck, Erin looked back over her shoulder toward Adrienne and the tents. Adrienne was soon out of sight, walking into the trees behind the tents to check on the children—or to escape Erin's and Vic's prying eyes.

Vic called Nilla to her and struggled for a minute to get the leash back on him. "You've had your fun now, it's time to settle down to go home."

Erin looked in Adrienne's direction once more.

"Can we look at the cave again?"

Vic raised her brows in disbelief. "You want to go see a cave?"

"Well… yes. Not to explore it. Just to see it again, and think."

"Why?"

"Why are they camped so close to it? Why do they care about being close to the cave? I mean, Rip wanted to mine it, if Willie is right. But he's gone now. Is Adrienne going to mine it? Her husband, if he shows up again? Why does she care about being close to it?"

"I don't know." Vic shrugged. "I think it's more that she wants to be close to the rest of the settlement, not that she wants to be close to the cave."

Adrienne had said that she would not stay there for long; she didn't want to be close to the place where Rip had been killed.

"But if she and Jenny are such good friends, why isn't she on the other side? Closer to Jenny? It would be farther away from the cave, but that doesn't really matter. Does it?"

Vic shrugged and led the way toward the cave again. The sky was getting dark, and she grabbed a flashlight out of the truck before heading into the bush. Erin tried to ignore the thumping of her heart. She wasn't afraid of the dark. She didn't even have to go into the cave. She just wanted to go over there again, to think about it, and to try to understand what appeal it had other than the possibility of mining minerals.

It seemed like it was farther away than it had been the first time Vic had taken her to it. Maybe the dimness made things appear farther away. Maybe it was her anxiety that made it feel like it was taking longer to get there. She started to worry that Vic had taken her in the wrong direction or walked by it, missing it. But then she saw the rock face, glowing dimly in the falling dark. Vic ran her flashlight along the wall. Nothing appeared to be any different from the last time they had been there. Nothing seemed to be wrong or out of place. Erin followed Vic to the mouth of the cave.

"Come in with me," Vic suggested.

"No, I can't."

"I don't want to go in there myself. If you want to figure out what Adrienne is here for, you need to come in with me. You're the one who wants to see."

"You can just take pictures, like last time."

"Showing you a picture on a little tiny screen isn't going to give you a sense of what it's like in there. And anything smaller than my head isn't even going to be visible on the screen."

"I can't go inside a cave."

"It's been a long time since you were hurt," Vic said reasonably. "Nothing is going to happen to you in here. We go in, we take a look around, and we come out. There isn't anyone else here that's going to bother us. No one knows that we're here, so it isn't like they might have set a trap for us. There isn't going to be a cave-in here."

Any of those things could happen. Erin didn't believe that it was safe to walk into the cave and then back out again. Her experiences had taught her otherwise.

"Vic. Can't you just go have a peek?"

Vic held the flashlight toward her. "Why don't you take the light and go in first, so that you can see everything. You won't be afraid if you can see."

Nilla was scratching around, sniffing at all of the plants and rocks at the cave entrance. He scraped at the dirt with his back feet and then strained toward the cave to go inside and investigate. The furry little beast didn't even have enough sense to be scared.

"Nilla. Let's go back to the truck," Erin called.

Vic shook her head. "Not yet. Come in and see what it is you were looking for. I'll let Nilla in first and then you'll know there's nothing to be afraid of."

"Just because he doesn't have any sense?"

"No. Because if there was anything to be afraid of, he would get eaten first."

Erin laughed.

"Come on." Vic motioned Erin toward the cave, and pressed the flashlight into her hand. "Turn on the light."

Erin did.

"Shine it into the mouth of the cave."

Erin got a little closer and shone the light inside. It was a strong light and lit up the interior well. Just a lot of rock. No one lurking inside. The floor of the cave was sort of sandy. There wasn't a lot of loose rock. The walls were jagged, glistening in the light and throwing odd shadows.

The entrance 'room' was large and, with the light on, it didn't seem that dangerous.

"Send Nilla in," she told Vic.

Vic gave a laugh and did so, letting Nilla off of the leash once more. She didn't have to tell him to go in; he was already straining to explore it. Erin crept in after him.

"I don't know if this is a very good idea."

"You're not going to know until you try it. I don't think it's that bad. Nothing is going to happen."

Vic followed close behind her. Erin felt comforted rather than crowded to have Vic on her heels.

"To the right?" she asked.

"Yes."

Erin followed the curve of the walls, finding her way through open spaces and then smaller crevices. But none of them were too small. She didn't have to crawl on her belly. They were, of course, large enough for a man to get through. Because Rip had gone in there, and the police had gone in there. They would only have to duck or to turn sideways.

There were a couple of places where Vic needed to show her where the passage was but, in a few minutes, Erin could hear the musical tinkling of the underground stream as it flowed over the rocks and then dribbled into a pool. Erin stepped into the larger room, like a dwarfen hall. She shone her flashlight around, looking for anything out of place.

"You see?" Vic said. "Just like my pictures. Only better."

Erin kept shining the light all around them, right up to the farthest corners of the room. She took a couple of steps toward the pool. She was determined not to go too close to the water. She didn't want to see the horror that Vic had seen that day when Willie had taken her there spelunking even in her mind's eye.

"Get closer," Vic urged.

Erin shook her head. "This is close enough."

"There's something in there."

Erin closed her eyes. It was dark. She opened them again. She didn't want to be in the dark. But she didn't want to see what was in the pool, either. Another body? A blind white fish? She didn't want to know what it was. Not at all.

Vic got closer to the pool. "Give me the light, then."

Erin shook her head. The light was hers. No one else was going to get control of it.

"Then shine it over here," Vic insisted.

Erin shone it at the pool without getting any closer, keeping her eyes averted from it. Vic bent over. She laughed. "Well, I don't think it's anything you need to worry about," she said.

Erin looked reluctantly over to Vic. A fish, then? A cave salamander? Something harmless, but undoubtedly slimy and gross.

"What is it?"

"A fridge."

"What?" Erin frowned and squinted toward the pool. There was no big, square, white fridge. She would have noticed something like that.

"They're using it as a fridge." Vic dipped her hand into the flowing water. "It's freezing cold. Must come from snow runoff higher in the mountains."

Erin shuffled closer. There were bottles of juice, some condiment jars, a few items that were weighted down with rocks. Jenny had said that they used the stream to keep things cold. Erin had assumed she meant an outside stream. But the cave would be better. Fewer animals around. Maybe they couldn't smell any food smells once the items were in the water.

"These are some of the things that I gave Jenny."

"Then it looked like your plan worked. She did share it with the others in the community who needed it."

Erin nodded. She was still worried about looking into the pool and imagining Rip's remains there, but she was curious about seeing the crime scene, sterile as it appeared to be. She looked around the cave slowly.

"So… they think that Rip was hit somewhere over there," Erin waved at the opposite side of the cave, "and then dragged into the pool."

"Yeah. The blood they found and the rock were over there."

"The rock?"

"Uh… the murder weapon," Vic said, looking embarrassed. She had been careful before not to say what the weapon had been, not wanting Erin to have to picture it.

"A rock. So… it wasn't a premeditated murder. He wasn't shot or stabbed. Someone picked up what was already here, in the cave." There were a few loose rocks of various sizes around the cave. "It was spur of the moment. Anger or maybe self-defense."

"Yeah, that would fit."

"Two people… who knew and trusted each other."

"Maybe," Vic was less confident in that answer.

"Would you go into a cave with someone you didn't trust?"

Vic considered this. "No," she agreed finally. "I guess I wouldn't."

Erin sat down on a large rock, considering. "The Ryders had already been using the cave. Willie had tried to kick them out a couple of times. Jenny said they used the stream as a fridge."

"Right. They knew about the cave, the stream, and the pool. Rip was going to mine it. Jenny was using it to keep food from spoiling."

"But there wasn't any food in it when you found… him."

Vic shook her head. "No. But they might have run out of perishables.

They wouldn't get too many things at a time that needed to be refrigerated. They might have eaten everything they had purchased. All of the foods that might spoil."

"Is it possible that Jenny didn't know that Rip's body was in here?"

They were both quiet for a long time.

"Maybe… she had the baby and was still too sore to come this far," Vic suggested.

"The baby was born on the third. What day did Rip die?"

"You'd have to ask Terry what they have it narrowed down to now. I know it was around that time, but I don't think they have an exact date."

"So… she had the baby, Rip disappeared and she didn't look for him? And didn't come in here for anything?"

"No. Why would she? If she knew they were out of food, she wouldn't come here for that. If she thought that Rip had taken off on her, then why would she come here? She would assume that he was in town or the city, not that he was lying in a cave somewhere."

Erin got up, walked to the opposite side of the cave and back again. She tried to connect everything up in her head.

"He was too big for one of the women to move him."

Vic agreed immediately. "He wasn't a featherweight. She would be pulling someone almost twice her weight, with lots of friction with the floor to slow her down. And why even do that? Why move him at all?"

Erin went over to the stream and the pool and prodded at the rocks.

"How big was the rock that was used to kill him?"

Vic considered them, measuring them in her mind against what she remembered before the police had taken over the scene. "Maybe… like that one," she said, tapping one with her toe.

Erin handed Vic the flashlight. She bent over and picked the rock up, testing how much it weighed, how easy or hard it would have been for a woman a little bigger than she was, used to outdoor chores and wrangling children, to lift and use as a tool. It was heavy and awkward, but would not be impossible for her to use, especially not if she were angry. If Rip had confessed to infidelity or gambling away their last cent, Jenny could have been very angry.

"But she was pregnant," Vic pointed out. "I don't know if you could do that if you were pregnant."

Erin lowered the rock, then tossed it back in the direction of the tumble of rocks she had taken it from. It landed on a different side, and Erin could see something scratched into it. She got closer, squinting, to make it out.

CHAPTER 39

IKE

It was in large, untidy letters.

Maybe the child himself had scratched it in. Five-year-old Ike. Erin stared down at it, her mind whirling, trying to put everything together in a way that made sense.

"What is it?" Vic asked, bending down and shining the light on it to read it herself. She looked back at Erin, baffled. "What?"

"I don't think he could have scratched that in himself," Erin said, arguing against the first thought that had occurred to her. "These are really hard. It's not like writing with pencil and paper. And he was only five."

Vic picked up a smaller rock from the ground of the cave and tried to imitate the scratchings on the rock that Erin had dropped. Her attempt was not very effective. Her scratchings were fainter than the ones on Erin's rock.

"No… I don't think a five-year-old did that," she agreed.

"What are you doing here?"

Erin shot to her feet, startled by the sharp voice. They both whirled around to face the doorway to the cave, the only direction they could go if they wanted to get out. A man stood blocking the passageway, shoulders broad, a shotgun in his hands. The man from the settlement. Wiseman.

Vic swore under her breath. Erin saw her hand twitch in the direction of her bra holster, but it was going to be too awkward to get at. She wouldn't be able to draw her weapon with the man already holding his shotgun on them.

"We're just looking around," Erin said lightly. "We wanted to see where it was that Rip died. Just… curiosity."

He didn't believe a word she said. "You've already seen it."

"Well… Vic did," Erin admitted. "But I didn't."

He looked back and forth between them. "Why couldn't you just go away and stay away? How many times did we tell you? You weren't invited. You were told to leave. Why couldn't you leave us alone?"

"I wanted to help," Erin said lamely.

"This is helping? Prying into our business? Sticking your nose into something that was none of your business?"

"No… I mean… this wasn't part of it. This was just… trying to understand in my head what had happened. It didn't make sense."

"And now you've gone and screwed things up."

Vic looked down at the rock Erin had dropped, and at her attempt to replicate it. "Is this… a headstone? Is that what it is supposed to be? A grave marker?"

He shrugged one shoulder, not admitting it and not moving the gun an inch away from them.

"Because five-year-old Ike died," Erin said. "Is this…" She looked at the pile of rocks in and around the pool. "Is this where he is buried?" She moved her feet away a little, not liking the idea of standing on or near his grave.

"No, not in here. We couldn't leave him in here. She couldn't."

"Jenny?"

He just gave her a hard stare and didn't answer.

"Then this is where he died," Vic suggested. "That's why the marker is here."

The rocks, the pool, the cold food just out of reach.

It would be a temptation for a hungry child. A child climbing over the rocks, over a slippery wet surface, trying to reach a bottle of juice or a package held down with a large rock. So easy for him to slip and fall and either hurt himself or end up in the water. Maybe a child alone, separated from his siblings, following his daddy. Or sneaking away when Rip was supposed to be watching him. Maybe Rip had been too drunk to understand the danger or the need to watch him closely.

"So Rip… that's what made Jenny so angry? She blamed him for Ike… getting killed?"

"I wasn't part of that conversation," Wiseman growled, "but I can imagine how it went. I didn't get here until it was too late. Too late for either of them to take anything back. And if you think I would ask her to explain exactly what had happened, you're crazy." He stared at the pool, then looked up from it and gazed at the blank wall of the cave as if he could see a movie playing there. "She was in trouble herself. Saving her had to be the priority."

"Saving Jenny?" Vic shook her head. "From what?"

"She went into labor," Erin guessed. "Lifting that heavy rock. Trying to drag Rip's body. Maybe picking up Ike's."

"She was in a bad way." His voice was gravelly. "I had to get her out of here. Away from *him*. But she wouldn't leave her little boy behind. Doubled over with pain, and she still had to carry him." He swallowed, his Adam's apple moving up and down as he tried to keep his voice steady. "She had to save her boy." He saw the questions in their eyes and shook his head. "It was way too late for him."

Vic rubbed at the corners of her eyes. "Poor Jenny. That poor woman."

Wiseman walked toward them. The gun was still pointed loosely toward them. He toed the other rocks with his boot. He turned one over and found what he was looking for. On the reverse side, this one was scratched too.

RIP

Rip? Or was it R.I.P.?

Either way, they were both gone. Jenny's son and her husband. Both killed in that cave.

CHAPTER 40

"Why did you leave Rip in here?" Vic demanded, sounding angry. And maybe she was. Angry that they had just left the body there for her to find. To inhabit her nightmares, maybe for years to come. "If you took Ike out of here to lay him to rest, why couldn't you do the same for Rip? Why leave him here, in this pool?"

Wiseman didn't look at Vic. He was looking at the pool, where he had disposed of the body.

"Have you ever tried to move a man of that size? A dead weight? Do you know how long it would have taken to get him out of here, even with help? I could barely get him over here, pulling and rolling him. I couldn't have gotten him all the way out. And even if I could, why would I? He was stupid and careless and caused his own son's death. Why show him respect? Why give him any dignity in death?"

He circled partway around the pool, like the restless pacing of a bear in a zoo cage, looking down into it and seeing what only he could see.

"So yeah, I dumped him in there. I weighted him down. I cut him. Cut into his flesh so that the fish would be attracted to him faster. After they were finished with him, it would have been easy to move his cleaned bones out of here. To throw them in a trash heap or burn them. Get rid of every last bit of him." His lip curled into a sneer, disgusted with Rip.

Wiseman was no longer between Erin and Vic and the exit. Erin gave

Vic a nudge and started to shuffle toward the passage. It wasn't exactly covert. With the bright flashlight in her hand, every move Erin made was magnified, the light and shadows jumping around the cave walls. She was feeling closed in. Trapped in a cave again. She didn't want to find herself in the bottom of a pit, or injured and blinded by the dark, tied up and trying to find her way around a maze of tunnels. Her heart was in her throat.

No matter how casual and relaxed she tried to appear, Wiseman couldn't help but notice their intention to leave. The shotgun came up, pointing toward them.

"Where do you think you're going?"

"We're going home," Vic said. "Don't you think there has been enough killing here? You don't want two more bodies to dispose of. Especially when one of them is the girlfriend of a Bald Eagle Falls police officer."

"What?" His eyes flicked from Vic to Erin and back again.

"Yeah. You really want Officer Piper looking for you? I don't know how hard they're looking for Rip's killer, and they don't even know about Ike, but if Erin and I disappear, you think Piper won't move heaven and earth to find out what happened to us? And you already know my boyfriend, don't you?"

"I don't know anything about you."

"You didn't recognize the truck outside? Willie kicked Rip out of here twice. He never talked to you? Told you to stay out of this cave?"

Wiseman's finger tightened, starting to squeeze the trigger. Erin's heart was in her throat. Vic's arguments were not helping. They were pushing Wiseman in the wrong direction, making him panic. He would wipe out anyone who knew anything. Anyone who could identify him or knew anything about his role in the cover-up.

"You aren't guilty of murder," Erin told him, her voice squeaking upward so she sounded like a doll playing a recording of a faked child's voice. "You didn't have anything to do with Ike's or Rip's death. Just with disposing of the body. That's all. You don't want our blood on your hands."

The muzzle of the shotgun wavered but didn't move away from them. His finger on the trigger did not relax.

"Go," Vic murmured. "He's not going to be talked down. Just move."

Erin agreed. She jumped to the side, then turned her back on Wiseman and zipped toward the entrance as quickly as she could over the rough ground, trying to ignore the disorienting play of the light and shadows cast by the flashlight. She knew Vic was right behind her. She couldn't look back or she would slow down or freeze up.

Wiseman shouted at them to stop. Of course they didn't. The thunderous blast of the shotgun filled the cave, echoing. Erin couldn't help looking back to see if Vic had been hit. If Wiseman had killed her friend…

Vic was still moving, her face white. "Go, go, go!"

Erin needed no more urging. Wiseman called after them again, swearing. Following them.

Erin heard Nilla yipping wildly.

Nilla. She'd forgotten all about the annoying little white puffball and, apparently, Vic had too. But they couldn't stop with Wiseman in pursuit. Nilla would have to follow them, to find his own way out. At least he was a much smaller, faster target than either Erin or Vic.

Erin couldn't breathe. The walls closed in around her as she left the large cave and had to slide sideways through the passageway, watching the rocky ceiling to make sure she wasn't going to hit her head on some outcropping. She couldn't get any air. She could barely see through a black haze in her vision, even with the flashlight still firmly in her hand.

Wiseman yelled, not in anger but in pain. Erin looked back, but she had left the big room and of course she could no longer see what was going on there. Nilla was barking and growling, a different note in his voice. He must have gone after Wiseman.

Nilla had always been such a coward when threatened by Willie; Erin would never have guessed he would have the courage to attack a man. She sucked in a deep breath and kept going, trying to get out before Wiseman could resume his pursuit. Nilla had given them a bigger head start, but they weren't out of danger.

Erin moved as quickly as she could. In a few minutes that seemed like hours, they were running through the trees, back toward Willie's truck. Erin's lungs burned. She was not a runner and she had put on a couple of pounds in the time she'd been working at Auntie Clem's. She was still slim and had been working on tai chi, but she was not exactly fit.

As they got within sight of the truck, she heard Nilla yipping again, and the dog caught up with them, then burst past, barking excitedly to be let into the truck. By the time they reached it, he was pacing impatiently, wondering what was taking the two-legs so long to get there. Erin and Vic didn't say anything, both puffing and trying to catch their breaths.

They jumped into the truck without a word. Nilla hopped into the back seat of the cab. They slammed their doors shut.

Vic started the truck and shifted into drive, which auto-locked the doors.

As they pulled out, spraying gravel and clumps of grass and weeds, Erin saw Wiseman emerging from the trees, limping after them, shouting, still carrying his shotgun.

She ducked, hoping he wouldn't shoot the truck, and held on to the dashboard as Vic floored it over the washboard surface of the little-used road.

CHAPTER 41

Of course, it wasn't all over. Erin realized as they sped back toward Bald Eagle Falls that she had another firing squad to face. She was going to have to tell Terry what they had found so that the police department could follow up properly. And they had tipped off someone who had been an accomplice after the fact in the murder and who would probably go straight to Jenny to let her know that Erin and Vic had figured it all out.

"Oh, great," Erin muttered.

Vic looked over at her. She opened her mouth to ask what was wrong, then closed it again, nodding her head. "Uh… yeah. Officer Piper."

"He's not going to be happy."

"What did you tell him when you left?"

"Just that I was going out to take care of some things."

Vic considered, staring at the highway stretching out ahead of them. "I think you should call him."

"It would be easier to explain face to face."

"Yeah, but if you call him, then you can explain and not have to be there to take the fallout right away. He can hang up and be mad for a while, but when he sees you, he'll be calmed down."

"Like when we went to Whitewater Falls to find Joshua."

"Right. He was mad at first, but by the time he got out there, he was just happy that everyone was okay. And Terry can get out here faster to deal with *him* if you don't wait."

Erin nodded to herself. Vic had a point. She did a few of her tai chi breathing exercises and took out her phone. She tapped her speed dial for Terry. She wasn't sure whether she wanted him to pick it up right away, or whether to hope he was tired out from working and had fallen asleep so it would go to voicemail. But if he didn't get the message right away, then she'd have to call the sheriff or someone else in the police department and explain to them. She wasn't sure that would be any better. Then Terry would want to know why she hadn't talked to him first.

"Erin? Is everything okay?" he asked as soon as he picked up.

"Why wouldn't everything be okay?" she countered.

"You left here in such a hurry and didn't say what was going on. I didn't know if something was wrong or you just wanted to get to a sale before it closed." His tone was teasing, but had an edge to it as well. Like he hoped it was just something innocent that they could joke about, but was afraid that it wasn't. And of course he was right.

"We're fine," she said to start with. Reassure him of that first. Help reduce the tension. "We—Vic and I—went out to the cave. I wanted to see something."

She left out the part about going to see Adrienne first. That wasn't what had gotten them in trouble, but Terry would think that it was. He would accuse her of sticking her nose where it didn't belong, all that stuff that she'd heard before.

"To see what? You won't even go inside a cave."

"I did!"

"You went inside?"

"Yes. I really did. And it wasn't as bad as I thought it would be. And nothing… there wasn't a collapse and I didn't get hurt."

"No. You see? I told you it would be okay. And next time, it will be easier because you'll know that it is safe. That something bad doesn't happen to you every time you go into a cave."

"I still don't think I'm going to do it again."

"We'll see," he said with good humor. "So… did you see whatever it was you wanted to know about?" The police had already processed the scene, so of course he didn't see what she could have learned from the cleaned-up murder site. He thought they had found everything there was to find, but he had been wrong.

"Well, actually, yes."

"Which was what?"

"The families over there, the Ryders anyway, they were using the cold water in the stream and pool for refrigeration."

"How do you know that? There wasn't anything like that in it when we were there."

"They cleaned it up before anyone found Rip's body."

"I suppose they didn't want to be questioned, so they didn't want there to be any indication that any of them had been in the cave."

"Yeah."

"That's tampering with evidence, but I don't think anyone is going to prosecute them for it."

"There's more than that. That's just how it started."

"How what started? You think that is somehow related to Ryder's death?"

"It was. In a roundabout way."

"You're going to have to explain it to me. Are you on your way back? You can tell me all about it when you get home?"

"We're on the highway right now, on our way home. But I think I should tell you everything right now. You're not going to want to wait."

"Wait for what?"

"Well… you need to go out there…"

"Exactly what did you find out?"

Erin took a couple more deep breaths. "Promise me you won't get mad."

"Erin."

"I just don't want you to blow up."

"Just tell me. The more you say things like that, the more anxious I get."

"It had to do with the baby being named Ike."

There was a pause. "We talked about that. There are a lot of reasons that they might have named the baby Ike."

"But we didn't talk about one of them. That sometimes, a family gives a baby the same name after a previous sibling dies. It happened a lot in Clementine's genealogy that I've been reading. Sometimes a family would have two or three babies named the same thing, because the first few died in infancy."

"Yes, that's true. I don't see it happening very much anymore, but I'm sure it still does happen sometimes."

"Especially with families with long traditions. Like we were talking about, where they want to carry on grandpa's name in every generation…"

"So are you telling me that they had a child named Ike who died, and that was why they named the baby Ike?"

"Yes."

"Only… when did he die? I thought he was registered with the school. Did the school just register him automatically and didn't know that he had passed?"

"He just died recently. Right before Rip."

There was silence on the other end of the phone. Erin pictured Terry grabbing his notebook and pen to start jotting down notes, realizing that Erin had actually discovered something important to the case.

"Tell me what you know," he instructed. "When did the other Ike die?"

"The same day as Rip."

"You think it had something to do with Rip's death?"

"Yes. I think it was the motive for his murder."

Another pause as Terry apparently wrote notes to himself. "What do you think happened?"

"Something happened in the cave. Rip was supposed to be watching Ike, or maybe he was drunk and he did something stupid. Whatever it was, Ike died there in the cave."

"What makes you think that?"

"We found a rock in there with his name carved on it. A makeshift tombstone."

"A rock could be carved with his name for a lot of different reasons. He could have done it himself. Kids like to write or carve their names into everything."

"But he didn't. There's a man in the settlement, his name is Wiseman, and he confirmed it. That Ike died. And Jenny… she's the one who killed Rip. Because he killed their son."

"It would have taken a lot of strength to lift a rock of that size and bring it down with enough force to do the damage that was done."

"And you don't think a woman would be strong enough? You hear about them lifting cars when their children are in trouble. You don't think that a woman used to living and working out there in the wild, chopping wood and stuff like that, couldn't lift a rock?"

"She was very pregnant at the time. That was either right before or right after the baby was born. It isn't that I can't see a woman being able to lift a heavy rock or to kill her husband in a fit of rage or grief. Just… in that condition… wouldn't she be risking harm to the baby? Or to herself, if she'd already had the baby and happened to tear something with the strain?"

"I don't think she was thinking about the consequences. She just acted. She was so upset, she just picked it up and…" Erin didn't finish the sentence. Maybe if she didn't say it out loud, she wouldn't see it in her head. She wouldn't have nightmares about what Jenny had done.

"And this Wiseman, he is a witness? He says this is what happened?"

"Yes."

"We'll need to get someone out there to talk to him, then."

"I think you should get someone out there soon. Or… he won't be out there anymore. And neither will anyone else."

"Because you had to go and put yourself in the middle of it," he sighed.

"We just went to see the cave. We didn't know that anyone saw us and would follow us in."

"You're lucky he didn't do anything to try to shut you up."

Erin didn't say anything.

"He didn't do anything, did he?"

"He had a shotgun. He was threatening us. He fired it, but we're okay."

"Tell me Vic didn't shoot him."

"Vic didn't shoot him."

Beside her, Vic snorted. "He got the drop on us, Officer Piper," she said loudly so that he would be able to hear her. "Or I might have!"

"So… what? He just let you go?"

"Nilla attacked him. Distracted him and slowed him down enough that we could get away."

"Nilla? So that little ball of fur is worth something?"

"You're not allowed to badmouth him anymore. Not after that."

"I guess not. I'm going to have to revise my opinion of him."

"Me too. He was a good dog." Erin looked over the seat at Nilla, who wagged his tail excitedly, tongue lolling out in a wide doggie smile of satisfaction. Erin chuckled. "Yes. Good dog!"

"So…" Terry drew her attention back. "How bad is this? Did he follow you? You figure he'll run, and Jenny with her family?"

"Yeah. That's why I wanted to call you and let you know before we got home. You might want to… rally the troops."

"Yep. Going to have to. I'm still doubtful about whether Jenny Ryder would have been able to do that. We'll need to ask the medical examiner's opinion on height and whether a woman— a heavily pregnant one especially—would have the strength to do it."

"Go ahead. But I think that's what happened. And that's what Wiseman said. Baby Ike was born after that. She went into labor that day, probably because of the exertion, or her mental state, whatever. I think he was probably a bit premature; he's very small and jaundiced."

"It's possible. I can also see, with one child dying and another being born the same day, her being superstitious about naming him the same thing. Sort of a reincarnation thing."

"They're Christian. Christians don't believe in reincarnation, do they?"

"Not officially, no. But that doesn't stop some of them from believing in it, or believing in old superstitions about death and rebirth. I've known a lot of people who have been able to hold competing beliefs. They don't really see the conflict, even if you point it out to them."

"Huh. Well, it kind of makes sense. One child replaces the other. Maybe it brings her a little bit of comfort."

"I'd better go. You guys are on your way straight back here, right? And no one is following you?"

Erin looked behind them, watching for any vehicle that might be in pursuit. She'd been forced off the road once before, and she didn't want to think about it happening again.

Vic shook her head. "I haven't seen anyone following," she said. "I've been watching."

Erin reported this back to Terry.

"Good. I'm going to hang up. You guys stay safe. If you think there is a problem, call me back."

"If Jenny did do it… if she killed Rip in a fit of passion because her son had just died… will she be able to get out of it and not have to serve prison time?"

Terry's voice was gentle as he answered her. "I'm not a lawyer, Erin, but no, I really don't think so. Even with manslaughter, she's still going to have to serve some time. Maybe she has a family member who can help look after the kids while she's in prison."

Erin swallowed, a lump in her throat. "Okay."

"I'm sorry, Erin."

"I know."

CHAPTER 42

It was anticlimactic going back to the house. Everything was quiet and peaceful. Terry was already gone. The animals were there. There were no playing children or men with shotguns. Vic promised to stay with Erin. If Willie got back, he could join them, but Erin didn't have to be alone.

She tried practicing her tai chi, hoping that would help her to unwind and relax. But the sadness pressed down on her. All of those children having to go live with someone else. Maybe being split up. Maybe having to go into foster care if there weren't any relatives around to take care of them. She felt the weight of it on her own shoulders. She had been the one to pursue it, to put the puzzle pieces together and sort out that it had been Jenny.

If she had known when she started where the clues were going to lead, she wouldn't have pursued it. She would rather they just left Jenny alone and let her go on taking care of her children. What justice would be served by putting her in prison? It wouldn't change the fact that Rip was dead and her children fatherless. It wouldn't bring big Ike back. It would leave the children scattered in various homes, with no mommy and daddy and no continuity. They would all be better off if Jenny could just continue taking care of them.

"You were worried about them before," Vic pointed out, reading

Erin's face as she tried to work through her forms and resolve her feelings. "You were afraid of the children not getting enough to eat, getting enough supervision, getting the education they need out there in the woods. So now… maybe they'll go somewhere that they can have those things."

"But if they had to choose between those things and their mama, they would choose to stay with their mama."

"Well… probably. You can't know that for sure, but kids don't always know what's best for them. Just because they want to be with Jenny, that doesn't mean it's the thing that's best for them."

Erin breathed out in time with her movements. "Yes, it is."

Vic looked startled. "It is what?"

"It is the best thing for them. To stay with Jenny. I don't have any doubt."

Vic watched her movements, frowning. "Really? You really think that's the best?"

"Yes. I've seen how being taken away from their parents hurts kids. Especially when it's for something like not being able to provide for them. Not having enough food in the house, or a job, or not having a place to live at all."

"They don't take kids away just because their parents are poor."

Erin stopped and looked at Vic, raising her brows.

"Well, they don't, do they?" Vic insisted.

Erin continued her tai chi movements. "All the time."

Erin couldn't sleep. She lay there awake in the bed, lonely and craving Terry's body next to hers and his comforting arms around her, but knew that he probably wouldn't be home before she got back up for work.

She had told Vic and Willie to go home. She didn't need them to stay up with her. She was safe enough with the burglar alarm and her trusty attack cat. If Wiseman had followed them back, he would have done something right away, while Terry was still away, so Erin wasn't worried about it.

She lay there by herself, worrying, thinking about all of those children being ripped away from Jenny while she was taken off in a police car in handcuffs. It was horrible to think about. All that much worse because it was Erin's fault.

She heard the door open. Terry didn't call out to her, assuming that she would be asleep, but she heard the familiar, comforting sounds of him locking the door and rearming the burglar alarm and of K9 panting and his claws clicking on the kitchen floor. She rolled over on the bed, waiting for Terry to come in, but he didn't check in on her right away, so she eventually put her feet on the floor and went out to him.

"Oh!" Terry startled when he saw the movement out of the corner of his eye. He touched his chest lightly, taking a deep breath. "You're up. I didn't think you would still be awake."

"I couldn't sleep. Not thinking about those children. A newborn, Terry. He won't even remember her."

"Erin."

She waited for the platitudes. For him to reassure her that it would all work out for the best, and that Jenny had to face justice for what she had done. He didn't say anything and, eventually, she looked at his face. "What?"

"She was gone."

Erin swallowed and waited for more information. Jenny was gone? Did that mean she had escaped or that she had killed herself—and maybe taken all of her children with her? She looked up into Terry's face. He put his hands on her shoulders, warm and comforting.

"She and Wiseman and the rest picked up and left. We've got APB's out on them, but I'm not confident that we'll be able to find them again. They got a head start on us, and we don't know by how much or what direction they went in. They could be out of the state already, or they could be deeper into the wilderness. If they've driven out of state, they'll probably have dumped their vehicles or stolen new plates. I think it's pretty certain that we won't be able to find them again. Tracking people who are largely invisible… it's dang near impossible."

Erin hugged herself to him, putting her cheek to his chest. "I know I shouldn't be happy about that. I should want you to catch her. But I don't. I want her to be able to raise her children."

"It will be a hard life. Kids who spend their whole lives on the run don't have it easy. But it isn't like they had it easy up until this point anyway. Or that it would have been easy for them if she had still been there when we got there."

"I'm glad you didn't have to take them away from her."

"To tell the truth, I am too. I don't think any of us were too disappointed."

"Even Stayner?"

Terry chuckled. "Even Stayner. He's not such a bad guy, Erin. Just a little rough around the edges."

Erin snorted. "A little."

CHAPTER 43

Even with Terry in bed with her and knowing that Jenny had managed to escape with her children, Erin still couldn't sleep. She knew that Terry wasn't asleep either. He was still, but she could tell by his breathing pattern and the tension in his body that he was lying awake. She turned around to face him and snuggled up.

"You should take one of your sleeping pills," she told him.

"Nah. I'm fine. If I don't get much tonight, I'll sleep better tomorrow night."

"I don't want you getting sleep-deprived…"

He knew that the lecture was coming. "I won't. I'll take care of myself. I'm just saying that one night won't be the end of the world. Same as for you."

"If I took a pill, I wouldn't be able to get out of bed when it was time. Vic can, but they just knock me for a loop."

They both just breathed for a while, cuddled up together, knowing that they weren't going to be able to get to sleep. They had too much on their minds.

"Erin."

"Mmm-hm?"

"When you talked about how many women were having babies the last few weeks…"

"Yes?"

"You mentioned us. That we weren't."

Erin rubbed her eyes. Her heart started to race. "What about it?"

"Do you want to?"

"Have a baby?"

"Yes," his voice was patient and amused. "Do you want to have a baby? Us together."

She wasn't sure how to answer him. If she said no, he would be hurt and think there was something wrong with them as a couple. If she said yes, then she'd have to deal with the extra pressure, and she wasn't sure whether it was the right thing or the right time.

"I don't know," she said finally. "I thought… maybe someday. But I don't know for sure I want to have a baby. And I'm pretty sure that… now isn't the right time."

He kissed her forehead. "Okay."

"Is it? That doesn't upset you?"

"No. I just wanted to make sure we were on the same page."

"And we are?"

"I'm okay with waiting to see. But when you mentioned it… I didn't want you pining away after a baby or deciding you wanted one but afraid to let me know."

"No, not yet." Erin pressed her face against him. "Sometime, maybe… but not yet."

Did you enjoy this book? Reviews and recommendations are vital to making a book successful.

Please leave a review at your favorite book store or review site and share it with your friends.

Don't miss the following bonus material:
Sign up for mailing list to get a free ebook
Read a sneak preview chapter
Other books by P.D. Workman
Learn more about the author

Sign up for my mailing list at pdworkman.com and get Gluten-Free Murder for free!

JOIN MY MAILING LIST AND

Download a sweet mystery for free

PREVIEW OF WHAT THE CAT KNEW

More Auntie Clem's Bakery to come.

In the meantime, have you checked the spin-off series, Reg Rawlins Private Investigator?

CHAPTER 1

Reg Rawlins climbed out of the car and stretched, her muscles cramped after being in the car all day. According to the dashboard readout, it was a few degrees warmer than it had been in Tennessee. Added to that, it was humid and the air felt muggy. She could smell the ocean. She'd heard that all points in Florida were within sixty miles of the ocean as the crow flies. She was looking forward to spending some time swimming and looking for seashells. She'd always wanted to live near a real beach. A warm, sandy beach.

"Witch!" accused a homeless man sitting on the sidewalk with a cardboard sign. He had long, scraggly hair and a beard, streaked with gray, and he was missing several teeth. His clothes were ragged, and even though he was a few feet away, Reg could smell his unwashed body.

She gave him a scowl, but didn't turn away. His reaction interested her. She was dressed for the part she intended to play—headscarf, heavy jewelry and hoop earrings, a long, flowing peasant dress—so it was not unexpected that he would notice her and comment on her getup. But he had gone with *witch* rather than a fortune-teller or medium, which she thought was an odd choice. She wasn't wearing a pointed hat or black robe.

"What makes you think I'm a witch?" she demanded.

"All redheads are witches!" he informed her.

"Ah." Reg's red hair was all done in cornrow braids, which hung free around her face rather than being wound up under her headscarf. She liked the effect. And she liked the way the braids felt when she turned her head and they all swished back and forth. She ignored the homeless man and looked up and down the boardwalk.

She liked the atmosphere of Florida. Laid back and relaxed, not like in Tennessee where she had visited Erin. There had certainly been some uptight ladies there. She didn't regret leaving, though she was sad things hadn't worked out with Erin. Erin had been a lot more fun when they were kids. She'd grown up too much and become a stuffy old woman instead of the lost child she'd been when they had lived with the Harrises and then again when they had both aged out of foster care and had run a few cons together. Now she was grown up and mature and responsible, no longer interested in Reg's ideas.

"You don't know what you're missing, Erin," Reg murmured, looking around at the blue sky and the green vegetation, the tang of salt hanging in the air. Swimming in Florida was going to be nothing like a dip in the ocean in Maine. Miles of sandy beaches, warm water, and not a care in the world.

She gathered up her braids with both hands and pulled them back behind her shoulders, letting them fall again.

"There somewhere good to eat around here?" she asked the bum.

People looked at her oddly as they passed, and Reg didn't know if it was because of her outfit or the fact that she was talking to a non-person.

"Only if you like seafood!" the man cackled.

Luckily, Reg did.

"You should go to The Crystal Bowl," he told her. "That's where the witches gather."

Reg pursed her lips, considering him. "The Crystal Ball?"

"The Crystal *Bowl.* Get it?"

"Where is The Crystal Bowl?"

He gestured down the boardwalk. "Yonder about two blocks. Big sign. Can't miss it."

~

Reg had been told that Florida, and Black Sands in particular, was *the place* for psychics and mediums but she hadn't expected there to actually be enough of a community to warrant a restaurant of their own. She was glad she'd picked Florida over Massachusetts; she'd had enough of New England to last her a lifetime.

The Crystal Bowl had satisfyingly dramatic decor and furnishings. Blacks, reds, and golds combined into a rich tapestry of mysticism, lit by flickering candles which were actually tiny electric lights. East met West in a sort of a cross between an opium den and a carnival fortune-teller set. They worked together in harmony rather than clashing.

The patrons of the restaurant, however, were disappointingly normal. Shorts with t-shirts or light blouses, sunglasses propped on foreheads, everybody looking at their phones or calling across the room to greet each other. No sense of mystical decorum.

The sign said 'please wait to be seated,' but Reg walked across to the bar counter and selected a stool.

The bartender was spare, his skin too pale for a Floridian. He obviously spent too much time in the restaurant out of the sun. Either that or he was a vampire.

"Afternoon," he greeted, adjusting the spacing between the various bottles on the counter and turning their labels out.

"Hi."

"Don't think I've seen you here before."

"No, just flew in on my broomstick."

He eyed her. "Wrong costume."

Reg grinned. "Good. The old bum down the street said that I was a witch, and I was afraid I'd gotten it wrong."

"It's the red hair."

"So I hear. Mediums can't have red hair?"

"Mediums can have whatever they want. So what will it be?" He gestured to the neat rows of bottles behind the bar and the chalkboard on the wall behind them.

Reg looked over the options. Should she establish herself as someone with exacting and eclectic tastes? A connoisseur? Someone who was obviously unique and memorable?

But she wanted the bar to be somewhere she could let her hair down, not where she had to always be playing a part.

"Just a draft," she sighed. "Whatever is on tap."

He nodded and grabbed a beer stein. He filled it and placed it neatly on a coaster in front of her, pushing a bowl of pretzels closer to her. Something nice and salty to encourage thirst.

"So, Miss Medium, your name is…?"

"Reg Rawlins." She figured she was okay using the name, even though that was what she had used in Bald Eagle Falls. She didn't think any charges would follow her all the way to Florida. It wasn't like she was going to be filing taxes under the name.

He gave a nod. "Bill Johnson."

Reg took a pull on her beer. It had been a long drive and she was glad to be able to relax and recharge her batteries. Thinking of figurative batteries, she decided she'd better check her actual battery. Reg pulled out her phone and checked the charge. Not too bad. It would last her a couple more hours, and maybe by that time, she would have settled somewhere. She launched her browser and tapped in a search for lodgings. There were plenty of hits for short-term rentals. Lots of vacationers. Finding somewhere permanent might take a bit longer, but at least she'd have a place to hang her hat. Or her headscarf. And plug in her phone.

"You need a place to stay?" Bill asked, obviously recognizing the website.

"Looks like there are lots of options."

"Sarah Bishop is looking for a tenant. She's easy to get along with. You two would probably hit it off."

"Oh?"

Bill looked around the room. "She's not here yet. She often shows up for supper. If she doesn't, I can give her a call and let her know you're interested."

Reg raised an eyebrow. "You don't know me from Adam. What makes you think I would hit it off with Sarah Bishop or that you can recommend me to her?"

"Let's just say… I'm good at reading people. And I would know you from Adam, given that Adam was of the male persuasion."

Reg considered pointing out that there were plenty of men who could pass as women or had transitioned from one to the other, but decided that antagonizing him wouldn't be the wisest thing for her to do. So she took a sip of her beer and didn't challenge him.

"Okay. Well, I'd appreciate that. Being able to move in somewhere long-term right away would be a real plus. Thanks."

"No problem." He moved away to help another patron.

Reg continued to browse through the lodging listings to get a sense of what costs to expect for rent and what her options were if she didn't like Sarah Bishop's place. It could be a dump. Sarah Bishop could be Bill's sister or ex and he just wanted her off of his back. He had been pretty quick to offer his help and judge Reg worthy as a tenant for his friend.

Someone took the stool next to Reg's, and she looked up to see who it was. A strikingly handsome man. Thirty-something, short hair slicked back from his face to show off a widow's peak, a stubbly beard that at first glance made it look like he had forgotten to shave for a couple of days, but on a more careful examination was painstakingly trimmed. His eyes were dark but glowed almost red in the dim lighting of the restaurant, reflecting the red furnishings and wall coverings. Add a cape, and he'd be perfect to cast as a vampire.

He gave her an enigmatic look. Almost smiling, but not quite. A smirk. She thought he was going to greet her as Bill had, recognizing her as a stranger and asking who she was. But he merely inclined his head slightly and waited for his drink, which Bill brought over without being asked. Obviously his 'usual.'

"Reg Rawlins, Uriel Hawthorne," Bill said, making a gesture from one to the other by way of introduction.

Great choice of name. Reg was impressed. Still, Uriel said nothing, just threw back his shot and watched her.

"Nice to meet you," Reg said, thrusting her hand out to shake his, forcing him to acknowledge her presence.

He left her hanging for a moment, not moving to take her hand, and then finally responded, taking her hand in his in a soft, caressing gesture that made her immediately want to pull back. But she set her teeth and gave him a warm smile. She gave him one more squeeze before letting go and pulling back again.

"A pleasure to meet you," Uriel returned. "Are you thinking of joining our little community?"

"Well, we'll see how it goes," Reg said with a shrug. "I'm new in town and I've never been part of… this kind of community before. I've always just been on my own."

"There is something to be said for that."

Reg raised her eyebrows in query.

"Setting your own rules, doing your own thing," Uriel said. "No one with preconceptions as to how things should be done."

"Right." Reg nodded. Rules, in her opinion, were made to be broken. She wasn't about to buy into a social construct that tried to control her activities.

~

"Ah, here's Sarah," Bill said, hovering near Reg.

It took her a moment to remember who Sarah was and why she should care. Sarah was the landlord looking for a tenant.

Reg turned, following Bill's gaze. She was looking for a woman of around her age, since Bill had said that he thought she and Sarah would hit it off. But she didn't see anyone who fit her preconception.

Bill gave a little wave, and a woman nodded to him and corrected her course to join him at the bar.

She was an older woman, at least in her sixties, with a round face, bottle blond hair that curved around her face, and wire frame glasses. She looked like a friendly grandmother, lips pink with freshly-applied lipstick, a flowered shirt, pink slacks, and flat white sandals. She smiled at Bill.

"Good evening, Bill. How are you today?"

He nodded and didn't bother to answer the greeting. "Sarah, meet Reg Rawlins. She has just arrived in town and is looking for accommodations."

"Oh!" Sarah's face lit up. "Well, my dear, isn't that wonderful! I just happen to have a cottage that I am trying to rent out! Would you join me for dinner?" She motioned to the tables in the dining area. "I'm afraid I can't manage bar stools these days."

"Sure," Reg agreed, sliding down from hers and taking her drink with her. "That would be nice."

She didn't bother saying goodbye to Uriel, irritated with his distant, disinterested manner. Sarah led her to a table which was probably her regular, as there didn't seem to be any problem with her seating herself instead of waiting to be seated. She smiled and chatted with some of the other patrons as she made her way to her seat.

"Sit down, sit down," she encouraged Reg, as if Reg had somehow been holding her back. "Reg? Is that short for something? Where did you come from?"

"Regina. I've lived all over."

"Well, that's a pretty name. Did you pick it, or was it already yours?"

Reg laughed at the question. "I was saddled with Regina, but I picked Reg."

"Very nice. I like it. And what do you do?" She made a little gesture to indicate Reg's costume. "You read palms? Tarot?"

"A little of everything. Mostly, I talk to the dead."

"Oh." Sarah nodded wisely. "That's a good gig. Have you been doing it for long?"

Reg studied the woman, not sure how honest to be. She wasn't sure whether she should be open about being a medium or a con. Both paths seemed equally treacherous.

"I've always had… certain tendencies… gifts, if you like…" she said obliquely. "I'm just testing the waters now… seeing whether this is something I should pursue…"

Sarah nodded. A waitress came over and handed them menus, introducing herself and showing off a couple of rather long canine teeth when she smiled. Sarah took no note, and barely gave the menu a glance. She'd obviously been there enough times to know what she wanted.

"What's good?" Reg asked, glancing over the offerings.

"The seafood is fresh. Other than that… burger and fries… I wouldn't try anything too adventurous."

"Good to know."

After placing her order, Reg leaned back in her seat, looking Sarah over.

"How about you? Did you retire to Florida, or have you always lived here?"

"I've lived lots of places, dear. Florida is good for my old bones. As for retiring… maybe someday, but not yet."

"What is it you do?"

Sarah raised her brows, as if surprised that Reg didn't know. Was she supposed to have guessed? Did Sarah think that Bill had told her?

"Well, I'm a witch," Sarah said, as if it should have been obvious.

"Oh." Reg sat like a lump, with no idea what to say or how to respond. Sarah had turned the tables on her. Reg was used to provoking a reaction from other people. She liked to dress up and to say extravagant things to see how people reacted to her different personas. This time she was in the hot seat. "Oh. I guess I should have guessed." Reg threw her hands up in what was both a shrug and indicating their surroundings. "After all, we are in the Magic Cauldron."

Sarah blinked. "The Crystal Bowl."

"Whatever. This is a witch hangout, right? So of course that's what you are."

"I thought you knew. You didn't just wander in here of your own accord, did you?"

"There was an old bum down the boardwalk… he called me a witch, and he pointed me this way. So, yes… I knew… It's all just a bit much." Reg looked around the restaurant. "I mean, *everyone* here can't be a witch."

"Of course not," Sarah agreed. "We have people of all different spiritual and paranormal persuasions. Witches, warlocks, wizards, mediums," she gave Reg a nod, "fortune-tellers, healers… people who are gifted and people who are seekers."

"Okay, then." Reg looked around at the patrons and shook her head, having a hard time believing that they were all running the same con. "And there isn't too much competition for the same… customers?"

"Some people think Black Sands has gotten too commercial, and some people complain it has gotten too crowded. But for the most part… people are willing to live and let live. We are peaceful people."

"Uh-huh."

Sarah launched into a lyrical description of the town and its more interesting citizens. Reg tried not to sit with her mouth open as she listened. The waitress eventually came over with their meals. Reg hadn't realized how hungry she was getting, but when the platter was placed in front of her, she suddenly realized she was famished.

"This looks lovely," she told the waitress, not expecting to be getting a beautifully plated fish at the offbeat witches' diner. She dug in immediately, taking several delicious bites before looking at Sarah to ask her if she was enjoying her food.

Sarah's eyes were closed and her hands hovered over her plate as if she were warming them in the steam rising from the food. Reg turned to look at the waitress, but she was already gone. Reg looked uncomfortably at Sarah, wondering if she should follow suit.

Sarah's eyes opened, catching Reg staring at her.

"Uh..." Reg fumbled. "Amen?"

Sarah nodded slightly. Then she started to eat.

"It really is good," Reg said. "Really nice."

"I wouldn't eat here all the time if it wasn't," Sarah agreed. She patted her stomach. "I wouldn't have to worry so much about my waistline if I was cooking for myself!"

She was plump, but in a grandmotherly sort of way. Reg couldn't imagine her skinny; it just wouldn't have fit. Adele, Erin's witch friend back in Tennessee was tall and slender, and that worked for her, but it just wouldn't work for Sarah.

"So why don't you tell me about this cottage of yours?" she asked. "Bill seemed to think that we'd be able to come to terms."

"He's very empathic," Sarah said. "He reads people."

"Ah. Of course." It made sense for a bartender. Reg had known her share of good and bad barkeeps.

"It's just a little two-bedroom," Sarah said, answering Reg's question. "But it's just you...?"

"Yes. No dependents."

"So you could use one room as your bedroom and the other as an office, and still have space for entertaining in the living room."

"Right," Reg agreed. She hadn't thought about seeing clients in her home. She wasn't sure she wanted anyone to know where she lived. If they didn't like what she had to say, they wouldn't know where she lived to confront her. She had thought she would go to them, do readings in their own spaces. She could read a client a lot better if surrounded by their own things. People gave a lot away by the way they lived.

"It's separate from the main house, so we wouldn't be on top of each other. We can each keep our own hours. That can be a problem with night people and day people mixing. The kitchen is small, really just a prep area. You could come use the big kitchen if you needed to do any major baking or entertaining. I really don't use it that much."

"I don't expect I would either. I don't do a lot of my own cooking."

"You see? You'd be perfect. You wouldn't be complaining to me that there's no oven. It really does have everything you really need."

"Well, maybe we could go see it after dinner, and talk business."

"You're going to like it just fine. I can tell."

As Reg wasn't that picky, Sarah was probably right. If Reg didn't like it after a month or two, she'd have a good idea by that point of where to look for somewhere better. It wasn't a long-term commitment.

Which was good, because Reg Rawlins didn't like long commitments.

CHAPTER 2

Cold, clammy fingers traced across Reg's face, awakening her in the wee hours of the morning.

She sat bolt upright, her heart racing. She looked quickly around her, trying to remember where she was and who was there with her. A chaotic childhood had conditioned her to be instantly awake and ready to fight. Strike fast to protect herself and escape to somewhere safe. But there was no one else in the room. Maybe the roof leaked and a drop of cold water had traced its way across her cheek.

She touched it, but it was dry, with only the memory of those icy fingers lingering behind.

Reg listened for a long time, hearing the lap of the waves in the distance. It was a restful, peaceful noise, and gradually the slamming of her heart slowed to its normal rate, though it was still pounding too hard to get back to sleep.

"There's no one here," Reg said aloud, very quietly. "You're perfectly safe, Reg. No one is going to hurt you."

It was comforting to hear those words.

When she was a kid, therapists had told her social worker and foster parents she had PTSD, and that was the reason for much of her unwanted behavior. It was nonsense, of course. Reg had never been in a war or terrorist attack. She'd never been kidnapped. Sure, she'd grown up rough, but a lot of kids had. And Reg was good at adapting. You couldn't call a few nightmares PTSD just because it was the fashion.

She listened to the waves for a long time. It was growing light as she drifted off to sleep again, still not sure what had awakened her in the night.

~

When she got up in the morning, it was with the clear plan to get a cat. She needed a cat. It would be a good prop. Witches had cats or other familiars. People instinctively felt that people who owned pets were kinder and more trustworthy than those who didn't. And it would give her a little company, without having to resort to having another person around the house. Reg liked company, but she liked having her own space.

A cat was the perfect idea.

Reg giggled to herself at the pun. A purrfect idea.

She checked addresses on her phone, thinking about what else she would need to buy in order to settle into her new living space. The fact that it came furnished was a bonus. She packed and traveled light and was used to operating on a shoestring. A fully-furnished cottage was a level of luxury she wasn't used to.

She picked up groceries and the basics she would need to care for a cat before going to the pound, patting herself on the back for thinking ahead and realizing that she wouldn't be able to do the other shopping once she had the cat in the car. She'd have to go straight home, and she wouldn't want to just abandon the poor critter there to go run errands.

At the animal shelter, self-styled as a pet sanctuary, before she was even allowed to look at the animals, Reg had to fill in a bunch of paperwork indicating her willingness to take care of a pet for the rest of its natural life and to follow all of the rules that the shelter set forth, such as not declawing a cat.

The place was noisy and smelly. Every effort had been made to make it a nice place, comfortable and humane for the animals, but it still stank. Reg thought about Erin. She probably would have run out of there puking, she was so sensitive to bad smells. Reg wasn't sure how she even managed to keep pets of her own, what with having to change litter and clean up after any accidents. They hadn't been allowed pets when they had lived with the Harrises, but Reg had seen enough examples of Erin reacting to human smells and accidents that she had no doubt she'd have difficulty cleaning up after animals.

There were old cats and tiny kittens and everything in between. Orange cats and tabbies and calicos. Short hair and long. Unlike the dogs, most of the cats didn't interact with the people walking by their cages, but simply slept, curled up in the corners of the cages. Occasionally, one of them would open its eyes or lift its head for a moment, but mostly they just continued to sleep.

She had thought she would be tempted by the playful younger kitties, but she thought of them keeping her up all night and wasn't sure that was what she wanted.

Maybe getting a cat had just been an impulse. Buying a pet was one of those things you were never supposed to do on impulse.

There were good reasons for getting a cat, but there were reasons not to as well. It might be noisy and wake her up nights. Have hairballs. Scatter litter and shed all over the house. It might jump up on the counter and get into things. Get out of the house and run out into the street.

It was probably a bad idea.

Reg looked into the next cage. The black and white cat raised his head, then climbed out of the nest of blankets in the corner, stretched, and walked up to the front of the enclosure.

"Hey, cat," Reg murmured.

He sat up tall and gazed at her, serious and still. Reg poked her finger through the bars at him, hearing a voice in the back of her head warning her never to poke her finger into an animal's cage. Even a hamster would bite you if you stuck your fingers through the bars. But just like she had ignored the foster mothers who had warned her not to do dangerous things, Reg ignored the voice in her head.

The cat's nose twitched as he caught her scent. For a minute, he just sat there. Then he leaned forward and took a step closer, touching his nose to her finger, and then rubbing his cheek against it. She felt his teeth brush over her finger as he rubbed. She scratched under his chin.

"Hey, you like that? Does that feel good?"

He rubbed against her and started purring a deep, satisfied rumble.

One of the shelter workers walked up.

"Wow, you connected with the tux!"

Reg looked at her. The girl was a teenager, maybe sixteen or seventeen, blond, with round cheeks. "The tux?"

"See, he's black with a white chest. Like he's wearing a black tuxedo and white shirt. So we call him a tuxedo cat."

"Oh, that's cool."

"And he has two different colors of eyes, too. I love that."

Reg looked at him and realized he had one green eye and one blue. "I guess that means he's special."

"I think he is." The girl poked her finger through the bars to try to scratch the tuxedo cat as well, but he only rubbed against Reg's finger. "He's been pretty depressed since he was brought in. His owner died and he hasn't really clicked with anyone. We've tried to play with him and to get him interested in things, but he's been so sad, pretty much all he'll do is sleep. He barely even eats."

In direct contradiction to her words, the cat stopped rubbing against Reg's finger and went over to his food bowl. He sniffed at the food, then began to eat, crunching the kibble.

Reg laughed.

"Well, he wouldn't!" the girl protested. "It must be you. Maybe you remind him of his owner."

Reg watched the cat. "What do you know about her?"

"Her? He's a he. A boy."

"No, I mean his owner. What do you know about her?"

"Oh. Well, he's also a he. A man. Don't really know much about him, just that Tux must have really been attached to him."

If she were going to get a cat, then it was obviously going to have to be that one. None of the other cats had shown Reg any interest at all, and she hadn't been particularly attracted to them. She clicked her tongue, thinking about it, and the noise made the cat turn his head to look at her again. He left his food bowl and again walked to the front of the cage, purring.

"I guess… this is the one," Reg said.

At least he was a short-hair, so he wouldn't get too much fur scattered around the cottage. And he seemed very quiet and sedate, not like a kitten that was going to jump on her face in the middle of the night and keep her awake.

"Oh, good!" the girl exclaimed. "I'll go get Marion, and she can help you with the adoption."

"Okay. Sure."

Reg waited there, scratching and quietly communing with her cat until the older supervisor approached to talk to her about the process.

If Reg had been expecting to just walk in and get a cat and walk out ten minutes later, she was sadly mistaken. Even the intake had taken longer than ten minutes. Apparently she needed counseling, needed to be walked through how to care for a cat, all of the things that could go wrong, budgeting for food and vets, what to do for behavioral issues, and on and on.

Reg had a headache by the time they were done and was ready to just pack it in and go home without a cat. But that would make the hours that she had been there wasted time, and she wasn't going to waste her first full day in Florida. Half of her groceries were already sitting spoiling in the car, and she wasn't going to walk out of there empty-handed.

Marion finally decided that Reg was ready to go and took the tuxedo cat out of his cage and settled him into a cardboard box, transferring the furry blanket he had been sleeping on into the box as well.

"That will help him transition, having something that already smells like home with him. Now you be sure to call if you have any questions about his care. Normally I would recommend that a first-time pet owner start out with a smaller animal, like a hamster, but… that tux needs a home badly, and he seems to like you."

Reg watched Marion close the box securely, and then took it from her. She didn't want to stand there discussing it any further. She wanted her cat home.

~

The *Reg Rawlins, Psychic Investigator* series is a spin-off from the *Auntie Clem's Bakery* series that follows the exploits of Erin's foster sister.

What the Cat Knew, Book #1 of the *Reg Rawlins, Psychic Investigator* series by P.D. Workman can be purchased at pdworkman.com

ABOUT THE AUTHOR

Award-winning and USA Today bestselling author P.D. (Pamela) Workman writes riveting mystery/suspense and young adult books dealing with mental illness, addiction, abuse, and other real-life issues. For as long as she can remember, the blank page has held an incredible allure and from a very young age she was trying to write her own books.

Workman wrote her first complete novel at the age of twelve and continued to write as a hobby for many years. She started publishing in 2013. She has won several literary awards from Library Services for Youth in Custody for her young adult fiction. She currently has over 70 published titles and can be found at pdworkman.com.

Born and raised in Alberta, Workman has been married for over 25 years and has one son.

~

Please visit P.D. Workman at pdworkman.com to see what else she is working on, to join her mailing list, and to link to her social networks.

~

If you enjoyed this book, please take the time to recommend it to other purchasers with a review or star rating and share it with your friends!

facebook.com/pdworkmanauthor
twitter.com/pdworkmanauthor
instagram.com/pdworkmanauthor
amazon.com/author/pdworkman
bookbub.com/authors/p-d-workman
goodreads.com/pdworkman
linkedin.com/in/pdworkman
pinterest.com/pdworkmanauthor
youtube.com/pdworkman

www.ingramcontent.com/pod-product-compliance
Lightning Source LLC
Chambersburg PA
CBHW070824020826
48982CB00014B/453

* 9 7 8 1 7 7 4 6 8 1 7 2 5 *